SPECIAL RELATIONS

'And then as if from a clear blue sky, she heard the question ... "So how are you getting on with President Bradley ... You both went to Oxford, roughly at the same time, I believe. So ...?"

A thin, sharp blade seemed to enter her chest, below the heart.

"So, did you never meet, or have any contact?"

And there it was all plain and simple – the one question she should have expected, and hadn't. The interviewer was staring at her, his mouth slightly open in a half-smile. And you have only a split second, no time for thought on this one, Alison. This is live. And there are two or three million people watching you at this exact moment. *Answer the question.*

"I don't believe we ever did."

She knew it was the wrong answer, even as she said it. She knew – with utmost certainty – that she had made a crucial blunder. "You don't lie," the whips had told her, when she entered parliament. "You feign ignorance, stupidity, you avoid the question, if necessary you throw a fit and roll about on the floor screaming. But you don't tell a lie when there are people around who know the truth."

What have I done? she asked herself.

But she already knew the answer.'

Tim Sebastian was born in London in 1952 and is the author of five previous acclaimed novels. For ten years he reported for the BBC, mainly from Eastern Europe. He now lives in London, where he divides his time between writing and broadcasting.

BY THE SAME AUTHOR

The Spy in Question
Spy Shadow
Saviour's Gate
Exit Berlin
Last Rights

SPECIAL RELATIONS

Tim Sebastian

ORION

An Orion paperback
First published in Great Britain by Orion in 1994
This paperback edition published in 1994 by Orion Books Ltd,
Orion House, 5 Upper St Martin's Lane, London WC2H 9EA

A CIP catalogue record for this book is available from the
British Library.

ISBN: 1 85797 487 5

Printed in England by Clays Ltd, St Ives plc

For Peter

Prologue

June 1966

There's always a last day. But rarely, if ever, do you know when. Like the last day of your life. The last time you'll see a friend. The last day of summer.

Only in this moment does she know it, as the storm passes across the colleges and fields, along the Thames Valley.

She's running now, through the people on the street, no longer seeing or caring.

Each footstep takes her further from the year they spent together, the shared times and spaces, washing away in the rain.

'Stop her,' someone shouts. Because there's danger in her eyes and a wild momentum out of control.

You know it will go badly.

By the roadside little rivers collect, flowing down the main street towards the bridge. A soft night. Darkness at the edges.

Without warning she turns, thinking her name is being called, searching the crowd for his face.

Shaken, she steps off the kerb. Doesn't see the baker's van with the broken headlamps, that doesn't see her either, croaking its way half-blind up the High Street, spinning her body in the air, dumping it in the gutter.

Think on this moment – that a life might go so cheaply.

He can't help any more, for he's far away up the main street, out of sight. Off to a different world. He doesn't hear the sirens of the police cars or the ambulance, or the shouts of the crowd. And nor does she.

The news flashes city-wide that a student has been killed in a road crash. An eighteen-year-old girl. No name until the relatives are told. That's the rule.

He hears it on the taxi radio, riding out to the station, but it means nothing to him. There's no way it could be her.

Not a chance in the world.

* * *

So quietly, so carefully, the university professor of surgery walks down the lino corridor to the parents. Whispers. Says as nicely as he can, that the first reports were wrong, but it's only the prayers of the faithful that are keeping her. The damage, the shock. Would have killed many, if not most.

That's what he tells her mum and dad, in the darkened corridor of the Radcliffe, as they listen to the rain and the words, not understanding.

Dad has come straight from the office. He's so tired inside that shiny blue suit, hasn't shaved since dawn, keeps opening his mouth to say things only no words come out; and Mum is there from the kitchen. She was getting his supper, chops and bacon with mashed potato, way back in time, when things were all right. Before the telephone rang.

At dawn sister Jo arrives. Jo, in her last year at boarding school, still wearing the team tracksuit, a hairband. So much energy she can't stand in one place. Keeps going off to find someone, talk to someone, get something done. She'd been training for the match tomorrow.

The baker's van has hit them all.

Two police officers are there. A man and woman. They want to help, check details. Milky tea comes in plastic cups. The college principal. Also milky. 'Anything I can do?' The little rituals of sympathy. Thank you. Thank you so much. Dad, speaking for the first time.

Later they sleep on the chairs, the three of them, holding each other in a kind of semi-circle, as the light comes up over the city and the girl refuses to die. Refuses.

The professor wakes them at seven, managing to smile, telling them that a twenty-four-hour miracle has happened, the mind is somehow holding the body together. It's rare and extraordinary. But they shouldn't count on it to continue. There are no odds to weigh. No prognosis. They have no medical explanation for why she's here and not there.

He says that – and walks slowly back to his room, doing something he hasn't done since his student days, feeling the tears running down his cheeks, wanting the girl to live, wishing that after all he had chosen another job. Miles away from a hospital. Miles away from the pain.

Mum and Dad begin to measure her life by the mealtimes she lives through. Lunchtime, teatime, suppertime. She survives them all, and at midnight the next night, the professor comes again. They've now identified extensive spinal damage. And he leaves them unintentionally with the question, they never thought to face ... would it be better if she died? Kinder. More humane.

Question for a couple in their late fifties, on a summer night in Oxford.

Jo goes in and talks to her. She talks through the tubes, past the bandages and the pulleys, to the closed eyes of her sister. She reminds her of the times they hurled pillows at each other, how they spied on the teenager next door who always left his curtains open, how well she had done at school, and how jealous Jo had been. In those days, long before.

She reminds her of all the dreadful boyfriends who courted her through the years. The spotty ones, the soupy ones, the ones who dressed up, and the others, whose hair Dad said he could stand on.

Time belongs to the heart machine and the jagged green line.

They are sleeping so soundly on the chairs, when the nurse wakes them. It's four or five, and suddenly she is paler and weaker, moving visibly away into the night. You can see there's no struggle. No pain. She isn't letting go. Someone is taking it from her.

Only they can't allow that. Dad sits them all by the bed. They hold her hand. They talk to her. Surround her. Rapid sentences. Anything they can think of. Like a crossword, fitting parts of her life, one against another. Up, down, across. So little in the way of clues.

They tell her how much they liked her friend – the tall American boy, six foot three from forehead to sneaker. The impulsive one from Kansas, the scholar who always said he could read her mind.

'We'll find him,' Dad strokes her arm. 'It'll be OK ... Can you hear us? Anything?'

Jo whispers ... 'They really loved each other. You know that don't you? Been together for a year now. Talked of marriage, I think. But

3

he was going back to the States. Going into the Army. To Vietnam. Maybe they broke up. I'll try to phone.'

She returns later. 'They think he left already. No one seems to know. It's really awful.'

Two hours go by. The nurse looks in and then the professor but they don't interrupt.

There's a point where you reach the boundaries of medicine, the end of reason's road. And after that anything goes. You can pick any remedy, any hopes, or prayers. Any mystical utterances. Any appeal to the higher order of life.

That is your last right and they know it.

But what they don't know is that she is listening to them. The girl *listens*. She has no sight or power of movement. She has lost the means to communicate. And yet she hears the prayers and the exhortations. The memories of life. The family around her. The casualties she will take with her if she goes.

Outside, the professor removes his glasses and shuts his eyes.

Beside her bed, Mum and Dad are still talking.

If she can live through the night, she tells herself, she'll make it.

Chapter One

thirty years later:

'Let's go eat dinner.'

'Too much trouble.'

'I don't want to eat here.'

David Bradley looked across the table at his mother and recalled the conversation that had preceded their meal. It was odd how the roles had reversed over the years. Now she was the one to demand treats like a petulant child, she was happy to throw tantrums in the most public of places, she had to be bought off and distracted. And tonight of all nights, he would cheerfully have pushed her off a cliff, and laughed as she hit the bottom.

'Come here, Mother, I want to show you the view. There! Little further. That's it. Nothing to worry about.' And then a final heave as she leaned out over the gorge. 'Goodbye, Mother. Ha ha. Goodbye. Enjoy your dinner.'

Wonderful moment.

He looked round the restaurant. A meal for two in the Rio Grande Café in Bethesda, George Bush's old haunt – but that couldn't be helped. Meal for two with marinated steak and guacamole. Some beers, nachos, ice-cream for the old dear.

Total bill, somewhere around three thousand dollars.

That was when you added up the secret service costs, the Maryland police, the communications truck, the counter-assault team, and the medical wagon – all of which had turned out on a Sunday evening, because Mother wanted to eat out with the most expensively protected man in the world. Jesus!

You don't do this when you're president, he thought. Thank God the place had been half empty. Even so the secret service had needed two hours' notice, the kitchen staff and the patrons had all been suitably intimidated, and instead of being able to mix with some normal people instead of mother, he had been quarantined at a special table in the corner.

The only person who dared approach had been two years old

and nearly had her head blown off with a shotgun, because the parents forgot to ask.

One evening they wouldn't forget, thought Bradley.

When it came to the check, Mother's delicious sense of irony shone through. 'Let me pay, dear. It's been such fun. And I do like to buy my son a meal, once in a while, even though he's so big and famous.'

Bradley groaned. 'We have to leave, Mother.'

The old lady made a great play of handing over her credit card to the waitress. 'Such pretty girls,' she murmured. 'I do wish you'd find someone nice again.'

He nodded to the head of the secret service detail, and a handful of men in grey suits rose up from tables along the route to the door. Men of purpose. A customer began clapping and a few people cheered. Bradley grinned at the room in general. He was hard to take in at first sight. Just that bit too tall. Just the wrong side of six foot three. Just beyond what a normal clothes store can provide. Beyond normal range in size and bearing and now a president to prove it. The secret service had codenamed him 'Giraffe' and his mother 'Mouth'.

He knew but she didn't.

Thirteen minutes later the motorcade dropped Mrs Bradley at the Four Seasons Hotel. Thankfully, she refused to stay in the White House, or Blair House or any of the official residences. On her visits to Washington she liked to be 'her own mistress'. Bradley would sometimes wonder who else's she was. But he never made any attempt to find out.

What had happened to Mother, he would ask himself? What had happened to the quick-acting, quick-feeling woman he had grown up with? A mass of hair and ideas, a walking cocktail, fizzy and frothy, and wanted by everyone. Why had she reached an intersection and rolled back down the hill?

'Mrs Bradley, ma'am.' A secret-serviceman helped her through the hotel door and into the lobby. Bradley felt a sudden stab of guilt as he recalled the way he used to run to her to say goodnight, every night, arms around her, holding so tightly, as if they were about to make separate journeys into the darkness and didn't know when they'd meet again.

Tonight she'd be alone in her suite – and he'd be alone in the

White House. And they'd journey a little further apart.

As for the country, he reflected – it was now nine thousand dollars poorer. The cost of a simple meal for two. No wine.

The first snow came in over the Chesapeake Bay sometime after midnight, carpeting wide tracts along the Eastern Seaboard. For just a few hours the city would be a thing of beauty, blind-white, untouched, the way its conscience never could be.

He had lain there for hours, knowing he wouldn't sleep. Pain, he had been told, creates its own calendar. Days and nights that he would grow to fear, because of the memories they induced. Fight it, they had said, on its own ground, in the quiet hours, in the shadows of dawn, whenever it strikes. Otherwise, you too will go under.

At five he got up and stood by the third floor window in his pyjamas. South over the lawn he could see the snow clearers at work along State Street, and in the distance the first of the morning headlights inching towards Capitol Hill.

And then, as he always did, he looked towards the park for the tiny pall of smoke from the ventilation duct. Often there were beggars, crouching beside it for warmth, coated in cardboard and newspaper, frozen against the ground.

Inside the White House, he thought, you could write and re-write history a dozen times a day. And yet a few yards from your window, a man with no home and no money would spend the night, trying not to die from the cold and the country's neglect. A man you felt powerless to help.

'I call it a magic carpet to nowhere,' his predecessor had said, as he packed himself and his tearful family into the limo, before heading out to Andrews Air Force Base and the last free flight home. 'That's what this job is. You turn dreams into speeches, and speeches into television. But don't think it's got anything to do with reality. Good luck! If you need anything, call someone else.'

He lay down on the bed, hearing the slow southern cadences as if it were yesterday. Only he wished it was.

For yesterday was Elizabeth. And today was the day she had gone. Two years past.

They had moved in, full of expectations about the changes they could make.

7

The removal vans, slick and practised, had departed by the time the inauguration was over. Elizabeth returned to find her own sheets on the bed, her own spaniel in her own basket, plenty of warm smiles and fine words. Washington's fickle, over-vaunted honeymoon in full flight, waiting as it always did, for someone to smash it apart.

And yet four months in, when the illness struck her, it seemed they had altered only the wallpaper and the height of the paintings.

He had hurried daily to the Naval Hospital in Bethesda, sat up nights with her in the suite, read out loud to her, because her eyes would no longer focus – and while the country had been with him, and the outpouring of sympathy overwhelming, the government had suffered. Behind his back the wrong decisions had been made, the wrong precedents established.

She had known it, and warned him, her political instincts somehow sharper and more finely tuned than his own. She had trusted none of them. And she had been right.

'When I'm gone,' she had said. 'You'll have to kick them into shape. You've been paying too much attention to me. They've been getting jealous – and going their own way.'

Right again – the way she always had been. 'I'm glad I never had to run against you,' he had told her.

'You did everything else,' she whispered.

It was the last joke they had shared together.

Five-fifteen. The green digits flashed on and off by the bedside light. Outside the apartment the building was still dark and empty. Only the secret service patrols and the duty officer in the Situation Room. Eight hours and he'd be in the air to Europe. Eight hours to the special summit in Berlin and some very urgent mediation. Russia and the Ukraine deadlocked over who controlled their nuclear missiles, who could fire them, who could bargain them away ...

But he put it out of his mind. This morning was for Elizabeth. A few hours for her – and for him. He would shake himself free of the huge entourage, the secret service, the cabinet, the military aide, the whole circus – and head out to Arlington. It would be beautiful in the snow. Just the way Elizabeth had liked it. This was their morning.

He got up and went into the bathroom. It was the first room

Elizabeth had re-designed. And in that, of course, she was no different from any other First Lady. Nixon had ripped out Johnson's bathroom, Ford had ripped out Nixon's. At one time or another every first family had screwed around with the little room, inserting water jets into the floor, the ceiling, the walls. There'd been hard lighting and soft lighting. In the words of the chief usher ... 'there was more time spent on the shower than most of the legislation from Capitol Hill.' And still it wasn't right. The pipes gurgled and spat, the system was overhauled, replaced and overhauled again. But it continued to resist all treatment. Only Elizabeth had liked it. 'Leave it' – she told the usher. 'I like an eccentric bathroom. Tile it white and leave it.'

Now it was a standing joke between Bradley and the usher – Preston Harcourt – a stooping elderly figure from Louisiana, whom Bradley trusted more than the entire cabinet. Harcourt would let the president know when it was 'safe to take a bath', and lament the problems of living in public housing.

When he went away, Bradley would tell him ... 'You're in charge now, Preston. Don't let the animals in.' And Harcourt would grin with pride that the president of the United States would speak to him in such a way, with all the officials and senators around, and would shake his hand before heading out on to the south lawn, past the cameras and the invited flag-wavers, and on to the presidential helicopter.

Bradley fiddled with the shower controls, dried himself and picked up the internal phone. He knew Preston would be there. Preston would always be there. Especially this morning. He wouldn't forget.

'I'll be leaving in a few minutes.'

'Yes, Mr President.' The voice was still and cold.

Bradley was about to put down the phone when he had a thought. 'You're in charge,' he said and smiled into the receiver.

David Bradley had called the head of the secret service detail the night before, so they knew what he wanted. Distance, discretion. The minimum security package.

Just before six a.m. he rode down in the private elevator to the basement, skirting the situation room, through the ante-room where

9

his predecessors had once swam and played pool, and into the tunnel that led to the Treasury.

At the entrance two secret servicemen joined him, already in coats and scarves. A quick 'Good morning, Mr President.' For there was no time for pleasantries. They'd been told to take the commander-in-chief out into the big bad city, enjoying the highest murder rate in the United States. Light and shade on the three faces as they headed down the tunnel. Just the creak of leather on the carpet. Military rhythm – the way Bradley had learned it, then taught it.

This morning there was to be no backup SWAT team, no ambulance, no communications truck – just a White House sedan, warmed up on the east side of the Treasury. From there a fast run past the Lincoln memorial, Memorial Bridge, over the red-brick road to the cemetery at Arlington. Fast as the snow would let them.

As they came to the Treasury door one of the agents went on ahead, the other stood blocking his path. Only when the outside check was complete, did they hustle him to the car, not gently, not slowly either. Their business was his survival. No one said they couldn't bruise him along the way.

He got in behind the driver. But someone else was there as well. Bradley frowned. 'You didn't need to come, Bill.'

'With respect, sir.' The president's military aide, Lieutenant Bill Kemp looked down at the floor of the car. 'I had no choice.'

Bradley slumped into the corner. Kemp was the chain of office that couldn't be broken. Keeper of the keys, keeper of the codes, the man who carried a tiny suitcase around with him, known as the 'football', the president's Doomsday communications, the device by which he could launch America's nuclear weapons on any of their pre-arranged flight plans. It was, Bradley realised, part joke, part tragedy. With Kemp at his side he could sit on a highway and blow up the planet, on the move, they wouldn't even have to stop. You could hold a hotdog in one hand, and the button in the other. Ludicrous. But while America had the weapons, Kemp had the football and Bradley had them both.

The car turned right on to Independence Avenue and skidded slightly.

Unknown to Bradley the downtown area had been swept for the past hour by three separate teams, one posing as snow clearers, the others – local DC police. A special control point had been set up behind Arlington House, the Pentagon was monitoring air space, the vice-president had been alerted and a message sent to the chief of staff.

So while the passenger in the car had the honour to be the forty-third leader of the United States – a widower, a former governor of Kansas, a former US army colonel, a man with history and presence and bearing – he knew nothing of any of this.

He simply enjoyed the facilities of the most powerful country on earth. For the president to dispense with the secret service would be like announcing he was going to live in Takoma Park, or Dupont Circle, or Rockville. It couldn't happen. Wouldn't happen. Wasn't written in the book.

They had promised to give him discretion and distance. But they would give it their way.

Inside the cemetery grounds, he left the car on Sheridan Drive and told Kemp to stay in it. There were crows calling out from the trees as if in warning. But when they stopped the silence was complete. He could hear only the muffled sound of his boots on the snow – the two agents fifty yards behind.

At the top of the hill Bradley moved on to the stone parapet and looked out over the city, still half-dark. The monuments were visible only in miniature, Capitol Hill, the flat sprawl of the Pentagon to the right. And in front of him a great sweep of white, that undulated through the trees, as far as he could see, broken only by the thousands of grey-stone graves in perfect lines. Twenty funerals a day, they had told him. The cemetery would be full in thirty years.

It took him a moment to find Elizabeth's headstone. The wind must have blown the snow against it, for the lettering of her name had been obscured. And he took off his glove, sweeping the surface clean with his bare hand, crouching beside it, making sure it had not been disturbed.

For the first time he looked round to see who was buried beside her. An army lieutenant, a midshipman killed in the second world war, someone else in Korea, someone in the Gulf. It was like crossing through time.

Elizabeth would be at home here, he thought. The army nurse who he had met on her second tour of duty in Vietnam, who had been wounded by shrapnel in the thigh, who had attended the most violent of deaths – and laughed at her own, when it stood before her.

She hadn't wanted to be buried in Arlington, but with her war record she had the right. Bradley had insisted on it. He'd never told her, but he needed her close – still, after all this time. He needed her physical presence.

He got to his feet and thought back to the funeral. Not since Woodrow Wilson had a First Lady died in the White House. And never had it been so public, with hourly bulletins on the networks, with the switchboard inoperable from the weight of calls, with no place to take your tears. Caller after caller, message after message. Politicians from every country, in every language. It seemed as if the whole world had come to lay its sorrow at his door.

He recalled how Elizabeth had foreseen this as well – and reminded him of his duty. 'Tens of thousands of people are dying daily across the country,' she had told him. 'They'll be looking to you to show strength and dignity and encourage them to do the same. You owe them that. It's your role. That's what the country requires from you. Don't go to pieces on me.'

The cold pressed down on him as he stood there. He realised suddenly he had brought no flowers, and then smiled at himself for forgetting that as well.

'Whatever else you do – don't bring me flowers,' she had said, the day before she died. 'You have other more important things to do. And besides,' she had added, 'I'll be watching.'

'You talk as if you're just catching a train,' Bradley had said to her.

'That's all it is, my dear,' she had replied. 'That's all it is.'

Bradley walked on after a few minutes. He always went to the Tomb of the Unknowns. Even in winter they changed the guard every hour. As he arrived to the east of the amphitheatre, he could see the ritual was about to begin.

A soldier of the US Third Infantry was taking his twenty-one paces in front of the tomb, pausing twenty-one seconds, then marching back. The snowflakes had stuck to the back of his greatcoat. Bradley could see the young face, reddened from the wind.

If the guard even noticed him, he didn't show it.

The president watched as the replacement was led out and his rifle inspected.

In the distance he could hear two voices in conversation and assumed they had left open the door to the guard house. And yet he gradually realised that through some freak acoustic inside the amphitheatre, he was listening to a secret service conversation.

'Bradley's lost it. Look at him, he's a broken man.'

'So would you be,' came the response. 'He'll come through.'

'Maybe.'

'He's gonna get the sympathy vote next election. No doubt about it.'

'If he runs. Personally, I don't think he will. The guy's finished.'

For a moment Bradley felt the anger exploding inside him ... those two little bastards ... But then he turned back to the ceremony at the tomb. The inspecting officer had finished the ritual. The rifle was jerked slickly back into the soldier's hands.

He wanted to go now, impatient suddenly, the mood lost. If the secret service thought he'd rolled over – they wouldn't be the only ones. He knew he'd let things slip, failed to concentrate, failed to watch his back.

In Washington a slip could rapidly become a slide. Lies became facts, simply by being repeated. A weak president could be shelved or bypassed, or as some of his predecessors had found out, violently removed. And yet he wasn't weak. Look at the years in the Army, the service in Vietnam. The man who they'd had to promote, because he was better at giving orders than taking them. 'Colonel Impulse', they'd called him, because he could think on his feet, change orders, change tack, throw a whole campaign in the air and conjure a new one.

And now he was commander in chief and the secret service had him finished. If he couldn't impose his own agenda, someone else would impose theirs. It was the wolfpack in suits and ties – same ethics.

Bradley knew he should fear the system, as well as seeking to control it.

He looked back over the cemetery, the gravestones protruding over the snow. Below them were men and women who had fought. Now he'd have to do the same.

Chapter Two

At a quarter to five the White House chief of staff, Harry Deval, looked over to his wife Jane and touched her gently to make sure she was asleep. He always woke at the same time, savouring the pre-dawn light, the stillness. It was the only time he got to think about what he was doing, to ask himself basic questions. The only time he couldn't run away from the answers.

Nearly, so nearly, he had thrown everything away. The family, the house, all those lives and faces that connected with him. You, Harry. You nearly let it go.

He got up and stood looking at Jane. Someone else had pushed her out of his life. For that whole year. A woman who had felt so different in mind and body, who touched him on so many levels, who gave him what seemed to be a second chance, and didn't ask him to choose.

But six months of joy had been followed by six months of guilt and shame, and Harry hadn't been able to live with himself, let alone anyone else. So he'd broken it. He'd walked away. On a night when he'd cried and she'd cried and he thought life would never again be worth living.

Only now, in the first light of morning he thanked God he had.

On the landing he passed his son's room and stopped. Even at that distance he could hear the boy's gentle breathing. Another hour and he'd be up too, charging round the house getting ready, or most likely refusing to get ready, for school.

Sometimes Harry thought he was past coping with an eight-year-old. He remembered the first time he'd been to Jason's class. It was father's day and they had all perched uncomfortably on their sons' school chairs, at their sons' desks, while the teacher had talked about loving and nurturing, the way American schools always did. Harry had looked round to find he was about fifteen years older than the other dads – except the ones on second or third marriages. They all had thick heads of hair, slim waists, bagless eyes. Christ – it had

14

been a shock. Harry was already spending ten minutes each morning deciding where to place which hair. And then in the car he had tried to console himself. He could still stand on the touchlines and yell for the football team. He could still run around at Halloween with flour on his face.

He went into the room and touched the boy's face.

This too, I would have thrown away.

It took him just a few minutes to get ready. Then, without a sound, he tiptoed down the stairs, opened the front door and eased it shut behind him.

The Washington snow was thicker than he'd expected. It would be a day at least before they made any serious impression on it. Snow clearing wasn't DC's strong point, he reflected. Nor were roads, nor was crime, nor drugs – or anything else for that matter.

He had met her in the same kind of snow, just a year ago. She, an administrative assistant in the Old Executive Office building that housed the overspill from the White House.

She too, would walk to work, and had laughed when he'd asked if she needed help with her handbag.

One year ago.

Now Harry wanted her transferred. Didn't want to meet her in the canteen or the corridor. Best if she moved on of her own accord.

At the bottom of Massachusetts Avenue he caught a cab, told the driver to stop on C Street, and walked the rest of the way to the south-west entrance.

Even the chief of staff shows his laminated identity card, and has his name checked against a computer listing. Just in case he isn't chief of staff this morning, in case he's been the victim of a swift and silent coup, in case the president has suddenly taken against him, while having his supper or picking over his breakfast. They were all things that had happened and would happen again. Harry Deval knew that because he'd helped organise them himself.

Holding office in this building was about as safe as cleaning windows on a fifty-floor skyscraper. You were never more than a step away from disaster.

He entered by the west wing and made his way to the office in the south-west corner. Only a small staff room separated him from the president. Inside were a handful of paintings, western scenes loaned out by the National Gallery of Art. But otherwise the room had little colour. It was here that Deval had been sworn in by the deputy executive clerk two years earlier and nothing much had changed. The windows still carried thick, dark blue drapes, edged with ribbon, a large built-in desk spread itself along one wall, and some wing-back chairs, sat upholstered in loud stripes. The effect was cramped and dark – but the position was what mattered – proximity to the president, proximity to power. As they'd said in Carter's era – 'nothing propinks like propinquity.'

At the sideboard he opened a packet of Lavazza coffee and spooned it into the espresso machine.

There were plenty of notes on the desk – the list of people and policies that would have to be traded during the course of the day.

For a moment though, while he waited for the coffee, he took out a small photo of Jane and Jason and stood it on the window sill.

The affair was over. They were all that mattered now. He'd got away with it.

Chapter Three

Bradley was back in the White House long before Washington's alarm clock went off – the seven o'clock shuttle out of National Airport en route for La Guardia.

Due to noise restrictions the plane is prevented from taking off earlier – so, when finally released it climbs hell-bent on vengeance over the pleasant and expensive north-western suburbs, shaking breakfast coffee cups right along the Potomac.

And while it shattered the sleep of tens of thousands of people each morning, it failed once again to wake the president's mother.

Ruth Bradley also missed the eight o'clock shuttle and a few others besides, until sitting bolt upright in her suite at the Four Seasons Hotel, and staring at the telephone beside her bed.

Had it rung or not? Too much dreaming. She looked over towards the dressing table. The bottle of Jack Daniels was no dream. And then as if to answer her question the phone rang again.

'It's Emily, Mrs Bradley.'

'Is it morning again?'

'Afternoon. You said to wake you at twelve.'

'Lord save us, I'm late.'

'The party doesn't begin till seven. We might just make it.'

Mrs Bradley sank back on to her pillow. 'Where would I be without you, Emily, dear?'

'Asleep. I'll be round at six. Bye.'

Emily Laurence put the phone down and shook her head at it. The president's mother was about to live up to her reputation – scatterbrained and extrememly difficult. Unfortunately, when she visited Washington it fell to Emily and the rest of the administrative section to see she was managed, muzzled, and the unavoidable damage contained.

'Mother Wolf' as she was known, was quite capable of doing to the administration, what another wolf had tried to do to little Red Riding Hood.

The result was that Bradley rarely found time to see her – crises would be automatically triggered by her footstep, cracking on to the Tennessee marble floor of the cross halls. She once confided to Emily that the whole place seemed on the verge of total panic. 'Don't they ever plan anything?' she asked. 'Dear God, my poor son seems in a permanent state of nervous exhaustion!'

But Bradley often succeeded in getting her out of Washington. He had sent her to Paris to check on the number of US women employed in international organisations. He sent her to a funeral in Africa, to a party in Egypt. And she had gone to them all with an agenda entirely her own. 'Dig and delve,' she would say. 'That's my role. Find out what's really going on.'

Emily well remembered what she had found out in Egypt – that the US ambassador had been having an affair with a local telephonist. At three o'clock in the morning Mrs Bradley had just happened to be looking out of her window and seen the two of them 'all over each other' in the courtyard below. It had taken two days of blunt talking to stop her blurting it out to the president when she got home. Little wonder that most White House staffers treated her like an elderly Titan missile, that should have been bargained away in the arms talks years ago.

By two o'clock she had bathed and made ready her shortlist for the evening. Three pairs of shoes, three outfits, a few earrings and diamonds, all carefully laid out on chairs, a selection from which the final ensemble would be chosen an hour before departure. That would of course depend on mood. And mood, she reflected uneasily, might well depend on Mr Jack Daniels.

She looked at the bottle, but left it where it was. In the old days before her husband had shut her out, she hadn't needed the alcohol. But that was another life. He hadn't wanted much to do with her after the children, simply hadn't wanted 'to live that way'. No family life, no involvement in the daily household. Gradually there had formed around him something she called 'the exclusion zone' that left the two of them no place to meet. In the end they shared nothing except a roof; and in summer when the sun burned deep into the Kansas plains he would stay out on the farm, and they wouldn't even share that.

Two years earlier he had come to Washington for the inauguration of his only son. He'd come for the funeral of his daughter-in-law, and he had turned away and cried into his handkerchief by the edge of the cemetery. In that moment she had wanted so much to reach him, and yet it was far too late for that. He had long since removed her from his heart and she knew the process was irreversible.

She glanced at her watch. Perhaps a short stroll would be the thing. From her window she could see the Biograph cinema across the street, and Mrs Bradley cringed deep inside. On her last visit she had fancied a lunchtime movie, didn't matter what it was, just somewhere to go for an hour or two, to dilute the loneliness. She had waved away her state trooper and stepped inside the 'dear little place opposite', only to discover she was in the middle of the purest imaginable pornography. What was a normal cinema in the evening, filled its seats by day with titles such as 'Bat Bitch' and 'On Golden Blonde', unadvertised except to the cognoscenti. She had hurried out, her hand over her face, praying most fervently that no one would recognise her.

The memory put her off a walk. Besides, the snow would make the streets so hazardous. She turned and looked again at the bottle of Jack Daniels.

Channel Seven News led that evening with the story of fresh snowfalls and Mrs Bradley had begun to wonder whether the party was a good idea.

'Emily, I've been thinking . . .' she said, as the young White House staffer barged through the door to the suite, nose red, eyes watering.

'We're going,' said Emily, reading the signs correctly. 'Everyone would be mortified if you cancelled now. Besides it'll be fun.'

'I'm not so sure . . .'

'Fun, Mrs Bradley, and of great value to the president. You know what an asset he feels you are on the social circuit.'

Ruth Bradley brightened. 'I suppose we must all do our bit,' she sighed. 'Help me choose what to wear.'

'Which is the warmest?'

'You're so practical Emily. I want to look . . . fun.' She smiled indecently. 'Isn't that what I'm supposed to look?'

Emily ignored her. She wasn't going to walk down manipulation alley – not this early in the evening.

As they rode down in the elevator, Mrs Bradley dabbed at her forehead in the mirror. 'Remind me who's going to be there, my dear?'

'It's a twelfth night party, Mrs Bradley. Each course at a different house. So the guest list is a little unpredictable. I think it's a great idea. All the places are in Georgetown ...'

'Oh God ...'

'What's the matter?'

'If it's Georgetown half the women will tell you they have to leave early because they're ovulating, and the men will be claiming they have to be in the Situation Room at five a.m. They've just managed to squeeze a few hours into their busy schedule. How nice. We'll all be awfully charming. It'll be like swimming in jello. So tasteless somehow ....'

'It's Washington, Mrs Bradley. Everyone talks about everything.'

'Well I don't.'

The hell you don't, thought Emily. That's why I'm here. To keep your trap shut.

The car moved off on to M Street and turned right on Wisconsin Avenue. Emily hoped the food would be worth it. She felt like a guard-dog, looking after an elderly poodle. Still, even guard-dogs got fed.

Washington's north-west ghetto has much to recommend it. It's the one remaining point on the capital's compass where the police do not yet record a daily homicide, stabbing, knifing or other such tiresome distraction. The north-west is for the white minority, with chocolate box mansions and cobbled alleys. To look at some of the houses, Emily reflected, you might wonder if the art galleries of Europe had been plundered by their occupants. Everyone, it seemed, had bought their little piece of genius, a Picasso, a Cezanne, one even sported a Turner, part of the Rouen collection, a pale beacon of distant, unaffordable magic.

Below it sat a Washington lawyer, shrimp in one hand, glass in the other, next to him a middle-aged brunette, puffed up in a dress that reminded Emily of one of those driver-side airbags, another lawyer beyond her, and finally Ruth Bradley. She had chosen the red outfit, she said, because it went with her hair. For the hundredth time Emily listened and said nothing. Mrs Bradley's hair was bottled blonde.

Despite the feigned reticence the president's mother greatly enjoyed her entrances. The moment she appeared in the doorway the other guests would immediately stop talking, stand up and clap – giving her an opportunity to tell them 'not to make such a silly fuss', but to wait around looking touched and tearful while they did.

They all had the same background, fed on cotillions, holidays in Baden-Baden, friends in Hyannisport who knew others in Bar Harbor, who were wintering in Florida, before travelling on.

To Emily their lives were like the lyrics of a song she had once heard – and in her mind she was almost setting them to music. Only then she looked across the table and spotted trouble.

It had arrived in the form of a memorable face. You know the way some faces are like landscapes or moons, wide and open – others sharp and chiselled, pointing forward. Faces that are going somewhere. Well this face was definitely going somewhere. It belonged to a man who blew in late through the door, a mass of nervous apology, a wet stripe on the side of his suit, a trickle of perspiration sliding past the ear. He had fallen down in the snow, he said. Couldn't find a taxi, couldn't find a car, revolting day all round.

Emily saw the hostess wrapping him in the gentle embrace of ownership, her hand lingering an inch above his damp buttocks – and she knew then he was trouble. You learned to look out for such people, you learned to fence them in, rope them off, divert and distract them wherever possible. To her, he had 'Press' written in every ingratiating, sweating pore.

She would have warned Mrs Bradley. On later reflection she should have tugged her screaming into the nearest bathroom and rammed the warning down her pearl-encrusted throat . . . only there wasn't time.

'So how's the president?'

Someone always starts it. Emily had been looking round the faces, knowing full well who would do it first. At every social event from brunch to bar-mitzvah – you gave the president's mum a little space, a little time to strut and preen – and then you stuck it to her. Let's get political. Let's have a bit of dirt on Mr President. She had seen it so many times around the country. Only in Washington it was more finely honed. The knife was sharper, slid in more easily. Sometimes you didn't even notice the primary incision.

The wet stripe on his suit had all but dried. The shrimps were little mounds of crackly carcass on the table. He wouldn't have long before they moved off to another interior-designed banquet – and the process began again.

The president's mother turned her gaze to see who had launched the enquiry.

'Pete Levinson, Mrs Bradley. Good to see you.'

'And what do you do, Mr Levinson?'

'I'm a writer.'

'Anything I might have read?'

'Only some menus.'

Everyone laughed. Relief not humour.

'I worked one summer as a waiter,' he went on. 'Now I'm an assassin – a film critic. I attack all the people who're more talented than I am.'

Mrs Bradley smiled politely and was about to turn her head . . .

'You were going to tell us how the president was?' he raised his eyebrows expectantly.

'Was I? How silly of me. Well . . .' Emily tried to flash a look of warning, but Mrs Bradley wasn't in the receiving mode. 'I sometimes feel so sorry for him,' she said and gave a deep sigh. 'Every time I go round – there seems to be some kind of panic on.'

She looked round the expectant, silent faces, knowing she should shut up. God knows, Emily had monogrammed the rules into her backside. But then you couldn't just be the president's mother and say . . . 'he's fine. Everything's fine.' It wasn't normal and to Mrs Bradley it wasn't very nice. She did so enjoy being liked. She liked the invitations, the company – even the superficiality of being someone. She wasn't going to live any more through her husband – she might as well live through her son.

Emily looked across at her, feeling the danger. 'Goodness,' she said, 'we should really be moving on. Can't miss the main course, can we, Mrs Bradley?'

But Mrs Bradley was sailing under her own steam, careless of the rocks that threatened her passage.

Chapter Four

Preston Harcourt had spent most of the day packing Bradley's suitcases. For the travelling wardrobe is substantial.

As well as everything else, the president has to be a male model. Obviously, the little TV make-up kit is always at hand to enhance nature, but the clothes are highly symbolic. Most people, say the statistics, look for two things – the body language and the coat on your back. You could in theory be a monkey, released from the Washington zoo – but if you spoke clearly enough in eight-second soundbites, and wore a stiff white shirt – hell, the world could be yours.

Preston, of course, didn't think that way. Preston packed for emergency summits or natural disasters – for the tropics or the arctic. Only he had the right to close the lids and send the luggage on its way.

Molly Parks had helped him – the White House seamstress, who spent her days, mending sheets and towels and keeping the inventories up to date.

Just before lunch she had taken away one of Bradley's pullovers to repair the sleeves.

'Can't you get him to throw this thing out?' she asked Preston.

Preston shook his head. 'Only Mrs Bradley could have done that. We used to have a deal. She'd steal the clothes that needed mending from his wardrobe and pass them to me. That's how I used to get them to you. Now I'm the thief.' He put on his glasses and examined the pullover. 'He won't let me get rid of anything any more. Not now she's gone.'

'What time's he leaving?' Molly asked.

'He'll leave when he's ready.' Preston consulted the daily White House schedule, issued to all members of the permanent staff. 'Eight o'clock tonight,' he said. 'That's if he ever gets through with his meetings.'

The door to the Oval Office had been shut for hours. A secret service officer stood guard in the outer vestibule, waiting to be relieved. It looked as though no one was going anywhere.

Sometime mid-afternoon the White House maitre d' had arrived to find out the president's requirements for dinner. But he had been waved away and had returned to the kitchen.

Inside the office Bradley turned back from the window and regarded his cabinet colleagues with some disdain. The meeting had been a mess. Little jabs of interdepartmental blame had been traded back and forth by one secretary after another. Each argument had been countered, each fact disputed. The results – highly inconclusive. Bradley decided to get rid of them. He nodded to Harry Deval.

'Thank you, gentlemen. I'll be in touch later. Clark, would you wait a moment please.' Clark Norton, the secretary of state, basked briefly on the sofa, while the rest of the team filed out. Harry Deval examined the faces. There wasn't a man among them who didn't want to be included in the inner circle. The jealousy was intense. At the White House the only weapon is information – the more you have, the more powerful you become. You can sell it, barter it or use it as a lever. The trick is pretending you have more than you do.

Bradley sat at the desk.

'Why shouldn't I go to Europe, Clark?'

'You don't need to. I can go. Defence can back me up. It hasn't reached the stage where presidential intervention is necessary. It's that simple.'

Bradley smiled inside. The secretary of defence would have blown up like a Cruise missile, at the suggestion he 'back up' Norton.

'The British don't share your view ...'

'The British don't have ...'

'Let me finish, Clark ...' The president stared angrily across the desk. 'We have an escalating conflict between Russia and the Ukraine, over who owns the former Soviet missiles. This dispute has been going on unresolved for well over two years. Now there's a new Ukrainian president who's threatening to back out of negotiations and seize what he can for himself. The Russians want us in, the British want us in. My cabinet is as usual divided. Some say it's day, others think it's night – but you want me to stay here. Why? You signed off on this weeks ago.'

'Situation's changing. Much more fluid. We don't want to expose you to something that could blow up in your face.'

'Go on.'

'We need you in the wings, Mr President . . .'

'If I stay in the wings it may be too late to get in on the game. I have to influence things before it gets that far.'

The president picked up a paperweight and toyed with it. 'I don't need to remind you Clark that there are few things more dangerous at the moment, than the old Soviet missiles. You yourself are aware that many more of them are unaccounted for, than we have ever made public. Something approaching a hundred, I believe, spirited away from the former Soviet Republics and now in China, North Korea, Iraq – and those are only the ones we know about.' He put down the paperweight. 'If we don't act quickly in any and every nuclear dispute, the consequences could be horrendous.'

'I agree.' Norton spread open his palms. 'And that is exactly why we should keep your intervention until it's most needed.'

'Thank you, Clark.'

There was a moment of silence before Norton realised that the conversation had ended.

He stood up, almost painfully thin, a wide academic forehead, thick glasses. 'I take it then that you'll still be going?'

'D'you find it difficult to accept that decision?'

Norton opened his mouth to speak, but thought better of it. Bradley was suddenly very dangerous. The question was like thin ice and he was being invited to skate on it – did he feel strongly enough to resign over this issue? He could hear his own heart beating. Maybe he'd underestimated Bradley. Maybe there was steel left in him after all.

'Of course I accept your position, Mr President.' He attempted a smile. 'I simply felt it my duty to provide you with all sides of the argument.'

'I know you did.'

The meeting was over. Deval opened the door and nodded at Norton as he went through. He turned back to the president.

'You've got an enemy there.'

Sitting by the fire, Harry chose his moment. 'Why are you going to Europe?'

Bradley smiled back. Harry was probably the best friend he could have. It went back nearly ten years to the time he had first run for governor in Kansas. Deval had been one of the powerful State 'interests' he'd needed to win over. By this time he had left State and gone back to the family law firm, trawling in big money. It was money Bradley needed for his election campaign; money and the right introductions. Deval's clients had ranged from the rich to the disgustingly rich. Useful investors, anxious to help build a Republican party that could throw off its cold-war image, and move the economy out of the mud.

Looking back, Bradley realised it had been more than a political partnership. The two men had come to like each other very much. Their wives had become the closest of friends. Since Elizabeth's death Jane Deval would often come over to the White House in the evenings with Harry and Jason and go round the private apartment, turning on lights and televisions and calling out to each other, as if it were a home again. She had even put up new pictures in the central hall on the second floor. Jason had brought a painting from school. They played board games on the living-room rug.

Bradley enjoyed those times. He enjoyed having someone to confide in.

'I need to reassert myself. I need to get out of the past and find a way into the future. Maybe this trip'll do it.'

'Why this trip?'

'I don't know.'

Deval stood up. 'So catch the plane, Mr President.'

'Stay in touch, Harry.'

'Don't I always?'

Chapter Five

'That wasn't a good idea.' Emily sat back in the limousine, scowling. It was lucky the woman couldn't see her face.

Mrs Bradley reddened. 'I only told him David was hurting a little . . .'

'You did what?'

'I told him he was lonely.'

'Jesus, you said that about the president?'

'I'm his mother for God's sake!'

'What else?'

'England. I said I'd been to England.'

Two alarm bells began jangling in Emily's head.

'Any details?'

Mrs Bradley went silent.

'Let me tie this one down. When I went out to the bathroom this guy Levinson started pumping you . . .'

'No! Well, yes . . .'

'All information has to be cleared with the press secretary. We don't just go round blurting everything out. I thought I'd made that clear. Did you say anything else about the president?'

'Of course not.'

There was silence in the car. Emily didn't believe Mrs Bradley. She had a mouth big enough to walk in and sit down. But the instructions were to use mink gloves. God Almighty, you couldn't leave her alone for a second.

'I'm sorry if I spoke harshly, Mrs Bradley.'

There was a few moments' silence while the older woman savoured Emily's apology.

'That's quite all right, dear,' she said. 'But you must remember that if it wasn't for me – there wouldn't be a president Bradley – now would there? Mmm?' She smiled victoriously. 'Well then, where are you taking me for my main course?'

* * *

'Boeuf en croute,' announced the new hostess. There was a ripple of amusement. The lady was from Alabama and despite being the wife of a former assistant secretary of state, she pronounced it 'Bof an Kraut.'

Mrs Bradley stifled her own snigger with a napkin and surveyed the woman's discomfort.

'What a treat, my dear,' she said. 'One of my favourite dishes.'

Emily looked down at the table. Beside her she could see a man tying his shoe lace, contorted with laughter.

This time the guests were more varied. A film actor had flown in from Los Angeles, a fashion model sat mummy-like at the end of the table, picking at a carrot, while her escort finished his plate and began eating from hers.

The talk, though, was standard Washington – high people caught in low places. Emily noticed they didn't tone it down for Mrs Bradley. And she was loving it. As the beef slipped down effortlessly, the knives and forks dissected the well-known names of the capital. There was scandal at Landon School, a male teacher arrested in a drug bust, wearing women's clothes, a senator who'd felt obliged to swear on a pearly-white Bible that he wasn't homosexual – 'As if anyone cared,' said the model, the daughter of a noted anti-abortionist who'd gone to Europe 'to do just that' – a former member of the House armed services committee who confessed he'd once sold secrets to France, 'probably for the food,' said the actor. Each had a tale to tell, except Mrs Bradley, who could really have told a tale, thought Emily. And maybe already had.

They left first, because Emily thought the conversation was taking some wrong turns. The room seemed to be a little full of democrats, fast losing their inhibitions and their tact. She had already picked up some loud whispers about how 'Bradley should sort himself out. Time for weeping was over.' Definitely the moment to go.

'We won't stay too long,' she said as they drove to the last house.

'I always enjoy dessert,' replied Mrs Bradley. 'Sweet tooth, you know.'

If the president's mother had a sweet tooth, it was the only sweet thing she had, Emily reflected. By that time she was tired and the rich food sat uncomfortably in her stomach. She wouldn't be sorry to get back to the town house in Alexandria, where she could shut out the whole evening, put on an old Tom Lehrer record, and think about returning one day to New York.

She was, she told herself, an American. Washington wasn't America. Washington was sleaze and counter-sleaze, big bluff, big pain in the arse. She felt sorry for Bradley, though. That was something else. But Washington sucked.

It was the grandest of the three mansions and absurdly extravagant. The gravel drive was already over-parked with limousines and foreign sports cars. In the powerful arc lights Emily could see that a once beautiful house had been painted primrose yellow. Who the hell would paint a house in Georgetown yellow?

Mrs Bradley was about to ask the same thing, only she remembered exactly who it was.

Larry D'Anna was one of the most flamboyant characters in Washington. During most of Reagan's second term he had been in charge of the Department of Commerce. Or more accurately his wife had been. She would tell him what to do, and then go do it, without him – she it was who decided who to stroke or mug, whose hands were to be held or slammed in the door. Under her care Party funds had never been in better shape – and membership, as the card adverts used to say, had its privileges. For a time Larry was one of the kingmakers in the cabinet. High-profile, loyal but incontrovertibly stupid – in other words a perfect sacrifice for the time, when the administration needed one and the public demanded one.

Of course, in Reagan's final term many lambs were ritually slaughtered on the altar of the latest embarrassment. When Larry's turn came, he was said by the leak machine to have miscalculated badly over the Savings and Loan scandal. He had to go. Most people were aware that Larry possessed no more than the barest understanding of the scandal – and that too was perfect. He couldn't even deny his way out of trouble. In the best White House tradition he duly learned of his dismissal on NBC Nightly News – and was asked to surrender his White House pass as he left that evening.

After that, Larry and Judy covered their pain behind their yellow brick walls and went on much as before – only with one exception. They made a private vow to get even. None of their guests ever knew about it. The parties went on as before and they still turned up, marvelling that the D'Annas had remained so loyal. 'Way to go,' said the faithful. 'Helluva guy.'

In fact Judy and Larry were doing nothing more than waiting for their moment.

But Mrs Bradley had no inkling of this as she swept into the hall. 'Lord,' she whispered to Emily, 'it's like a florist shop.' And so it was. Bouquets and vases, spread around, with everything but taste in mind. Thoughtful little combinations of red and white roses – the kind most people order for funerals. Or were the D'Annas trying to tell them something? Mrs Bradley didn't know and didn't much care.

She was far more interested in piling chocolate profiteroles into her bowl, and moving on down the table to the tiramasu.

Here, of course, the conversation was politically more correct, but that much duller than in the other houses. Entertaining catch-phrases like 'budget deficit' could be heard through smacking lips. As she looked round for diversion, she was surprised to find Pete Levinson standing by the fruit salad, spooning cream over fresh pineapple.

'We're not supposed to meet twice in one night,' she said, conscious that Emily was close by.

'Fate is sometimes generous,' he remarked, smiling.

Mrs Bradley saw a set of good white teeth and approved. In the old days when she'd bought horses for the farm, she had looked at the teeth before anything else.

'I guess it's very presumptuous of me,' he said, 'but I help out at a homeless centre in College Park. Everyone would appreciate it a great deal if you could come by, sometime. Kind of shows the guys that the government hasn't forgotten them.'

'I'm afraid that won't be possible.'

They both turned round. Emily had returned with a red face and a glare that embraced them both.

But Mrs Bradley looked at Mr Levinson and liked what she saw. His suit had dried. His hair had been re-combed, and those teeth really were quite marvellous.

She missed entertaining male company. In fact she'd almost forgotten what it was like.

So she ignored Emily and looked straight at Pete Levinson with the beginnings of a smile in her eyes.

'That would be very nice,' she said firmly. 'I'd like that.'

Across the room Larry D'Anna turned his back and smiled down at the cheesecake.

Chapter Six

David Bradley remembered all the advice about departures. 'Take the steps at a restrained run. Even if you have to sit panting in your seat for the next half hour. The country wants a guy who can get up steps in a hurry, who's fit, goes jogging. No human weakness, OK? Look what happened when Carter flunked the marathon.'

The south lawn was floodlit by the television lights as he made his way swiftly to the microphones.

'Take one question. Give 'em a soundbite and then head for the chopper.' Clifton Till, the large, rotund Press spokesman was beside him all the way.

Bradley smiled into the lights, seeing no faces, hearing the shouted questions, coming at him like missiles.

'How serious is the situation between Russia and the Ukraine?'

He recognised the voice of a network anchor. That was an easy one. But then these guys were hired for looks, not brains.

'As we understand it, Bill,' he frowned as if to signpost the message. 'As we understand it – there's considerable tension between the two States. They've asked us to try to mediate the dispute, and we'll do our best. We don't like quarrels over nuclear weapons. That's why we're going to talk. It's also,' he tried smiling a little reassurance – 'It's also a long overdue opportunity to meet the Ukrainian leader and I'm looking forward to our discussions.'

Anodyne crap, he thought and walked away, saluting the guard at the foot of the helicopter. Everytime you opened your mouth, you risked hanging yourself a thousand times over. If it wasn't serious, why were you going? If it was serious, then Americans would be phoning the White House to ask if it was safe to go to bed. You couldn't win. You just had to hold back the flood, for as long as you could take it.

It's like Beirut, his predecessor had told him. Once you take that oath, there's no safe place to stand. You can go hide in the dog kennel, but the switchboard will find you, because some astronaut decides to call from outer space, or the vice-president wants to know if he's allowed to unzip his pants and take a pee . . .

The helicopter pulled slowly away, turning left of the Washington monument, heading south-west towards Andrews Air Force Base. It was a clear, cold night. No further snowfalls were expected till the weekend. Bradley watched the lights along the Potomac and put his hands into his coat pocket. He knew it was there, even before he touched it – a small thin chocolate bar, which Preston always bought him before a journey. To Bradley it was a little piece of the outside world. True, he could order himself a thousand chocolate bars from all over the world – but this one always came from a tiny vendor on K street that Preston would pass each day on his way to work. And it made Bradley think back to the time when he could walk a public street without bodyguards and without a bullet-proof vest. The restrictions weren't easy.

The day before, he had asked Harry to get him a hotdog.

Deval had smiled. 'You can pick up the phone and order one . . .'

'I want it off the street. Plenty of mustard and onion, wrapped in tin foil. Tastes different.'

And Harry had brought back several and they'd eaten them in the Oval office.

'I told the guy, this one's for the president, so make it good,' Harry laughed. 'He said I should jerk off somewhere else. If the president wanted a hotdog, he'd come and get it himself.'

'Might just do that . . .'

The helicopter was coming into Andrews and he could see everyone in their places. The White House protocol, the military aides, the Press yet again . . .

'They have to film every departure and landing,' Till had explained, 'in case the plane crashes.'

'We wouldn't want them to miss a scoop like that, now would we? I'm lucky they haven't yet found a way to film in my bathroom.'

'They're working on it,' Till replied. 'Believe me, they're working on it.' He had a sense of humour that Bradley enjoyed and counted on.

'OK – let's do it.' The president stepped out on to the runway.

He was about to climb the steps to Air Force One when he glimpsed Preston, standing a little way back among the service personnel who always see off a presidential plane.

He stopped and went over to him. 'Preston,' the voice carried loudly enough for everyone to hear. 'You're in charge till I get back. You hear that?'

Even in the icy wind, the old man's smile shone back at him across the tarmac.

They were well over the Atlantic by the time Bradley found himself alone.

Norton had gone back to his seat. Till was briefing the Press corps, about how the meeting was 'key', but not 'make-or-break.'

'Walk the tightrope again, Cliff,' had been the instruction. 'Lean a little this way and that. Let them have some positive expectations, but don't say we're looking for a breakthrough.'

'That's not a lead. They can put that kind of thing half way down the page. These guys need a lead.'

'Float the idea that we'll use the economic aid as a lever. "Administration weighs tough measures." That should hold them.'

Bradley closed the blind in the little conference room and turned down the light.

With his eyes shut, he could see once again the cemetery at Arlington, the stark simplicity of the gravestones, standing in thick snow.

Why am I going on this trip? The Cabinet's right – I should be dealing with all the domestic problems, getting my act together, getting control.

You have to move on.

Bradley opened his eyes. Air Force One was turning gradually in the Atlantic Jetstream.

He wasn't sure if he'd heard a voice – or said it himself.

Chapter Seven

The duty officer in the Situation Room called well after midnight.

'What is it?'

'Sorry to wake you, sir. The Brits are going to announce a new prime minister – 0600 Eastern Standard.'

Harry looked at his watch. 'What the hell's going on there?'

'Embassy in London says John Gordon'll be resigning on the grounds of ill health. Heart trouble.'

'He only just won an election.'

'Sudden heart trouble.'

Harry raised his eyebrows. The duty officer sounded like a machine.

'Are they saying who'll take over?'

'It's a lady called Alison Lane.'

'A lady!' Harry almost choked. 'You'd think they'd learned their lesson last time round.'

'She was health minister. No one we've dealt with.'

'Has the president seen this?'

'It's been received on Air Force One.'

Harry was well aware that once the White House accessed the communications satellite, transmission would begin in less than two thousandths of a second.

'I asked if the president had seen it.'

'Hold the line, sir, I'll check.

The voice came back in an instant. 'The president's sleeping, sir.'

'OK, then patch me through. He'd better hear this.'

'Go ahead, Harry.'

'How's the flight?'

'It *was* fine. I particularly enjoy sleeping nights.'

'New prime minister in Britain. Thought I'd let you know since you were going to see Gordon in Berlin, and I know how well you got on with him.'

'I love all Labour prime ministers.'

'Anyway this might delay the start of the summit.'

'What happened to Gordon?'

'Probably the stress of the election. But you'll like this one. The replacement is the health minister – lady called Alison Lane.'

'Say again Harry. I think there was some interference.'

'Lane. First name Alison.'

'Jesus Christ!'

'David? Wait a minute! David?'

But the line had gone. The connection with Air Force One had been severed.

In the darkness of the bedroom, Harry replaced the receiver. He could feel Jane moving beside him.

'Did you hear all that?'

'I'm asleep. I never hear anything.'

'He hung up on me.'

'Maybe he was asleep too. You should try it sometime.'

Chapter Eight

The winter day threw itself at the British mainland like a hostile invasion. Gale-force winds, driving rain, bitter temperatures.

Alison Lane switched on the radio at dawn and groaned at the weather forecast. The moment she stepped out her hair would be blown upside down, her dress would fly over her head, and she'd look like a scarecrow, with her knickers on show for all the world to see.

This day of days.

She turned over and faced the bare wall. Some people had wailing walls, great walls, border walls – this was a thinking wall. Plain white and kept that way, a wall on which she projected her friends and enemies.

And now she knew who they were.

There hadn't been much in the way of sleep. Too many powerful images, too many shocks to the nervous system.

At eleven o'clock last night she had learned of her victory. Not a noisy triumph, but a quiet one, bitter and sad. Labour's all-day emergency conference at the Queen Elizabeth Hall had broken up with speeches about unity, and carrying forward the Party's programme, and what a tragedy it was that the new leader, elected a fortnight ago, had been struck by a second heart attack. Much anguish, much wringing of egos, and then a vote. Labour had a new leader. And Her Majesty's government had a new prime minister.

The car had taken her from home, through the darkness to Whitehall, the wheels swishing on the empty wet streets. Inside she was led rapidly through the dimly-lit hall, past the portraits of former prime ministers up the stairs to the private apartments.

His wife had opened the door, dabbing at her eyes, daughter in the background, the moonlight shining in through the little skylight in the hallway. 'He's expecting you, go straight in,' and then the bedroom, the familiar balding head and glasses, the face so white and tired on the pillow.

John Gordon, the first Labour Prime Minister in seventeen years, beaten only by his heart.

'You weren't my choice, I have to tell you.' He pursed his lips. 'But no one listens to you when you're on your way out. Besides, ...' the eyes targeted her forehead, 'you seem to have prepared the path pretty successfully.' Statement of fact. The cool, clipped Edinburgh dialect. No emotion. He'd leave that to his family, thought Alison. It wouldn't come from him.

'You might have waited though. Some of the doctors think I'll make a full recovery, given time.'

'John, we have to push the programme forward. You've been in bed two weeks. Ever since election night. People are getting restless.'

'So much for hero of the hour.'

'There had to be contingency plans ...'

'Contingency be damned. When was I to have been booted out?'

'Not booted out.' She held his gaze. 'Only if you didn't make a quick recovery. And so far you haven't. But you must have known, yourself ...'

'There's a difference between suspecting and knowing. I'd like to have played my hand for myself.'

Mrs Gordon put her head round the door. 'Two more minutes.' She looked hard at Alison. 'That's all you can have.'

Her husband coughed and shifted on the pillow. 'I'm away to a nursing home in the morning. The announcement will be made at eleven, if that's acceptable ...' A single eyebrow rose. 'It's a pity you'll have to jump in at the deep end, but then there is only a deep end in this job. The summit in Berlin, Foreign Secretary's away in India, all the economic measures ... it's always the same – just when you think you've hit the bottom, you hear someone knocking from below.' He sighed, but the expression was blank. 'I shan't miss it,' he said very quietly. 'I wanted you to know that before you celebrate.'

As she got out of bed a sharp pain stabbed at her back. And yet Alison barely registered its presence. The pain was old and familiar – a little like the physiotherapist who came twice a week to treat her. Old Lillian, who looked so gentle and benign, until her fingers stiffened like claws and dug out the pressure points. Old Lillian who would cover up the pain and send it away for the day.

Alison crawled out of bed and went to the wardrobe. Like many women in public life, her clothes were numbered and rotated regularly. The problem was she kept buying the same things – same black and white ensembles, same dark coats and jackets, to the point where one set looked very much like the other.

She surveyed the row of outfits and fished out a hanger. There was little point in trying to please other people. One man's classically-dressed woman was another man's frump. Besides, Labour still contained plenty of the old bags, who hadn't brushed their hair, or put on make-up in fifty years and bitterly distrusted anyone who had.

But today she would see the Queen. The words sounded like a nursery rhyme. They couldn't possibly be true.

In the little kitchen she made toast and coffee and ran through the morning in her mind.

She had already called Mum and Dad, woken them at midnight, listened to the thrill and anxiety coming down the line in equal quantities.

'Be careful,' Dad had said. 'Watch your back.'

'Listen to your father ...' from Mum. And she had laughed because you could never be prime minister in your home. You'd always be the girl who grew up, the girl from Christmases past.

But then the excitement began to wake inside her. God, there was such a hell of a lot to get through ... the packing for Downing Street, the summit in Berlin. She didn't expect the doorbell.

'I'm not dressed, Keith.'

'Best news of the day.'

She opened the door. He was hiding behind a bouquet of roses.

'Been a long time, Alison. Congratulations.'

She laughed. 'Three days, Keith. That's all.'

'Well, it's felt like a long time. To me, anyway ...' He came into the living room, took off his coat and sat down. Alison wasn't sure she liked that. Wasn't sure that, since she was now prime minister, he shouldn't have asked. Or was that being stuck-up? And yet there *was* a difference. Had to be.

'Thanks for the flowers.'

'Are you pleased to see me?'

Alison stood where she was and asked herself the same question.

Keith Harper, Labour's chief whip, was about ten years older, a man coloured wicked grey, MP for Wigan. She had known him since her earliest days in the Party, but it wasn't until three months ago that they'd gone out for dinner.

It was clear even then that Labour was heading for victory, but clear too that Gordon wasn't going to make it. Not for long. The doctors had already made loud noises of protest about his blood pressure. If he went on like that, they said, he'd enter parliament in a hearse.

'We have to think ahead,' Keith had told her, 'and fast. We're looking at options. People options. Are you interested?'

'Christ!'

'I take it that means yes.'

'Christ, yes!'

'Party's in a mess. There's a few too many of my front bench colleagues from North of the Border. Looks like the bloody Scottish National Party. We need someone who's English, not one of the leftists, but plain English, with a lot of charm, and some winning ways ...'

She just kept smiling at him. *This* was what she'd wanted. This and only this.

They had gone to a small Chinese restaurant in Whitechapel, to be certain no other politicians would see them. Just the few remaining yups from the East End, who'd moved out there when it was fashionable, and got stuck when it wasn't.

Keith had been amusing company, talked about all the women MPs as 'perfumed farts', told her there'd been quite a lot of talk in the Members Tea Room about her legs, and a 'good solid bust' and how that wouldn't be at all a disadvantage when the shoving began.

She had looked at him across the table and laughed. God, she'd been excited. He was a good-looking man. Large grey eyes. Bit of a paunch. But she didn't mind that. Strong, dry hands that held hers tight as they walked back to the car. He was a powerful figure in the North, good Union credentials, worked his way through the Party machine. And now he sat on all the committees that mattered. He was mediator, negotiator. He could deliver influential factions, when it counted. A deal-maker. A queen-maker, the way it turned out.

Which was why she took him back to her flat for coffee. Only coffee hadn't been enough for him. He'd wanted to get his hands all over her 'good solid bust', and she hadn't been at all prepared for that. She should have been. God knows there'd been enough amateur gropers in her time to start an Olympic sport. But she hadn't expected it from Keith.

It was bloody awkward. She needed him, needed his friends and his contacts. And yet, even in her excitement, something had told her not to give in. Keep him at bay, don't let him have it, let him work for it. If he gets it now – *you* might not get it at all.

'Listen Keith,' she'd whispered. 'Not while all this is going on. Let's see where we stand. If it goes through then you won't be able to stand the sight of me ... take it slow, love ...'

He had taken it. She wasn't sure how. Dented male egos could sometimes lie down and play dead, only to return with renewed vigour. At any rate, he had made some more coffee, and they'd talked for another half hour, and she had tried to give him a big kiss on the cheek and a friendly squeeze.

Only now he was back. And that ego was alive and well in his eyes.

She answered his gaze. 'Am I pleased to see you, Keith? Was that the question? I'm sorry – bit preoccupied this morning ...'

'I want us to go and celebrate, love. We did it.'

'It's too soon.'

'I meant, you know, when things have quietened down a bit.' The smile contracted.

She shook her head, trying to clear the thoughts. She didn't want to lead him on any more. He might just as well know where he stood. This was the morning for a new start, new decisions.' Listen love, I don't think there *can* be anything between us. You know what I mean?'

'No, I bloody don't know what you mean. You said ...'

'I didn't say anything Keith, and maybe I should have done.'

'Listen you ...' and his index finger was suddenly out there pointing a foot away from her ... 'so what were all the friendly glances about, the holding hands ...'

'Oh, grow up! You think just because you hold a woman's hand you can get her into bed?'

'We had an understanding. I thought ...'

'You thought too much!' There was silence for a moment. She would make one more attempt to do it nicely. 'You know, we're going to be far too busy for anything like that. Don't you see?'

'What I see is you trying to patronise me. Three weeks ago, you held out the possibility that you and I could have some kind of relationship.'

'Did I?'

'You know bloody well you did.'

She looked at him coldly. You didn't speak that way to a prime minister. He would have to learn that.

'Now get this straight, Keith. You are bloody married. OK? Keith Harper. Married, right? So let's just start living in the real world and get on with it.'

'I'll tell you something about the real world, Miss Prime Minister,' and his voice had gone very quiet. 'I'll tell you about all the strings I pulled, going back thirty years, the favours I called in ...'

She looked at her watch. 'This is getting monotonous. I have to go to the Palace, I have a news conference, a meeting of the cabinet. And tomorrow I leave for Berlin. We'll talk when I get back.'

'Couldn't stop you talking three weeks ago – the way you were, dribbling with excitement ...'

She smiled. 'Three weeks is a long time in politics. You know that.'

Chapter Nine

He wasn't going to watch the announcement; wasn't going to watch her swan into the Palace ...

As he walked he could feel the bile rising in his throat, a searing cancer of disappointment, spreading out across his body.

The smell of that woman, the touch of her, the way her index finger would idly caress his palm ... Jesus, fucking ... !'

Two schoolchildren looked round. The street was filling up. Control yourself man. You're chief whip. You're a school prefect. Head of punishments ...

But I wanted that woman ... more than anything, I ...

He couldn't go back to Downing Street. Not with all the cameras and crowds, the whole pissing circus, dancing attendance on her.

There was a meeting all morning of the Policy Committee where he was supposed to sit in. Business as usual. But he couldn't face it. He'd been amazed at the number of committees that had to be attended, with all the bloody civil servants, telling them what they were supposed to do and how to do it.

Keith turned left past the Ministry of Defence, and then up Whitehall towards Trafalgar Square. On the corner was a café. He went inside and sat by the window.

Alison could be a real bitch when she wanted, a real 'Lah-dee' with her university accent, and all that legal training. And yet he couldn't remember a pull like that. Deep down in the gut where it ached. Not since university when girls seemed to grow on trees and you just reached up and plucked them down ....

He'd always watched her, but it was the last three months that hooked him. The phone calls, the private chats.

She wasn't beautiful, but she reeked of it. Sensuality. He played the word a couple of times in his mind, rolling it around.

You would go to bed thinking of her, wake up with her still there, fixed in the mind, mouth slightly ajar, lips wet, the way she did when she was thinking.

'Coffee, love ... ?' the puzzled face of a young waitress in view, looking down at him.

His marriage had faded so fast. Denise. Blimey, I even have to think to remember her name. She'd been fine as the wife of an MP, but when he'd started work in Downing Street, it had become too much for her. She'd begun buying new dresses, talking too much to her friends, wondering why she hadn't been invited to this dinner or that cocktail party. She could be so ... he didn't want to say 'common', not even to himself. Because common had always been good. Common was real and British. *He* was common. But things were different now, and she had stayed the same.

'Got a phone here?'

The waitress pointed to the corner and Keith went over and dialled a local number.

'I haven't got time for this,' the man answered.

'Course you have. It's breakfast, that's all.'

'Only on the worst bloody day of the year! Look Keith, I'm in the bloody radio car in five minutes for the *Today* programme, then I've got to be at Number Ten. So have you.'

'I'm asking as a favour.'

'You've asked a lot of those recently.'

'You took your time.'

'I'm a cabinet minister.'

'Only just!'

'That's neither here nor there.'

Tom Marks, the Trade and Industry Secretary beckoned the waitress over and ordered brown toast, coffee and orange juice.

'Bloody hell. You've changed.' Harper sniggered. 'I remember when it was all bangers and lashings of bacon and fried bread. What happened. You meet a nun?'

'I didn't come here to discuss my diet. What's this all about?'

'Difficult time, this. Party's only been in three weeks and we get a change of leader. People can get over-excited, you know what I mean. Sometimes they think they can jump the queue, get up a rung, curry favour with the new lot. Others, well, others might feel they can throw some weight around.' He shrugged. 'Keep an eye open for me, would you ... ?'

'What?'

'You heard.'

Marks spread a thin layer of butter on the toast. 'You call me out this morning of all mornings, to ask me to keep my eyes open, watch over my colleagues ...'

'One in particular.'

Marks pushed away the plate. 'I don't think I'm hungry any more. I don't think I'm having this conversation.'

'Listen, Mr Industry Secretary, sir, we had to push her in fast. OK? The old boy's heart wasn't dancing the right rhythm, was it? So we pulled a lot of strings and got it through. Compromise candidate. That's how she was sold. And a lot of people's noses are out of joint.'

'What are you saying?'

'I'm saying. Keep an eye on her. If she's not right for the job, then we have to move fast. We've been out of power for seventeen bloody years. If she can't hack it, let's get rid of her at the first opportunity.'

Marks drew in his breath.

'What are people saying about her?'

'They say she's got nice tits. What d'you think? It's too early ...'

'Don't tell me you weren't on the phone half the night, canvassing opinions.'

'All right I'll tell you this. My friends, the people I normally have breakfast with ... we all think the party had to go forward. Instead of people with egg on their ties and slogans, we needed brains, university education, funny accents. Doesn't matter. What matters is we stay in power and try to do something.' Marks summoned the waitress and asked for more coffee. 'What's up then?'

Keith looked away. He hadn't realised how angry he was with Alison. After all the backing he'd given, the days and nights, canvassing up and down the country, the arm-bending and back-scratching. All the broken nights and broken weekends, he wasn't going to take rejection from her. Not now.

Marks sipped his coffee. 'What's the matter, Keith? Don't like her so much now she's got what she wanted? Having second thoughts are we?'

'Hard to tell. Maybe I'm not so sure.'

'We can't start changing bloody leaders like dirty shirts, you know. I called in a lot of favours to get her approved.'

'I know that. I'm just saying keep an eye on her.'

'Christ, you people are odd ...' Marks shook his head. 'Give the woman a chance. She's bright, she's done her time. And the punters like her. When did we last have a Labour leader, anything like as popular out there?' He waved at the rain-spattered window. 'And the other thing. She meets everyone on their own ground. She doesn't have to talk down, and doesn't have to talk up. She's as close as we'll get to classless Britain. Which is more than can be said about the two of us.' He sighed. 'I have work to do – unlike some people.' He went over to the door and was about to step outside when he changed his mind and came back to the table.

'I know what this is about ... You've been trying to pork her. That's it, isn't it? You were coming on to her for months only now she's told you where to stuff it ...'

'Don't be stupid.'

Marks stood looking down at him. 'That's what this is about. This "I'm not so sure" nonsense. Well, let me tell you something, my friend. We've just switched Party leaders, because of a little revolt in which you and I played not inconsiderable parts, mm? Labour has a new prime minister and she's going to be bloody good. And even if she isn't, the public aren't going to know, 'cos we aren't going to tell them. Am I getting through to you?' He leaned down and put his elbows on the table. 'We've got four whole years before a General Election and Alison Lane is going to fight it for us ...'

'Unless ...'

'Unless what?'

'Unless there's a major scandal.'

Marks sat down the same side of the table as Keith. As he did so he moved closer to him, speaking almost directly into his ear.

'There isn't going to be any scandal,' he said quietly. 'Is that clear? Not for your sake. Not for anyone's.'

Chapter Ten

'I hope you enjoy the job.'

It seemed such an odd thing for the Queen to say. Almost as if Alison were taking up the post of cook. She had half expected her to add ... 'We eat at seven. Please be punctual.'

The audience had lasted only twenty minutes. 'I shall look forward to our meetings ...'

And that had been the signal for departure. When Alison thought back, she hadn't really said anything at all. 'What a shame it had been about Mr Gordon ... we do wish him well.' Nothing of substance, not even a comment that the world was in a dreadful state ...

Ah well.

And then it was the cameras and the interviewers. The set pieces for the main news, the impromptu mix and mingle at Number 10. The standard assurances about continuity for the sake of the markets – and meanwhile you set about trying to undo everything the last incumbent had done. 'Mr Gordon was a wonderful leader. It's a very sad day for the Labour Party.' But by late afternoon you forgot he ever existed.

Politics was the sea lapping on the beach. It didn't care whose feet got wet.

A funny little note was delivered. Message about salary, cheques to be signed by the Paymaster General. £4780 per month – the salary of a prime minister, debated and decided each year by the House of Commons.

That would please the bank manager, the grizzled old sod.

She recalled opening the account at a branch in Tufnell Park, soon after moving to London and her first job.

'I get a lot of young people in here,' the manager had said. 'They all want to borrow money, and all of them tell me they're going to be rich and famous. What are you going to do?'

'Probably go on the game,' she told him with a straight face.

'In that case . . .' and there'd been the semblance of a distant smile, 'you'll undoubtedly be a better proposition than most of our other clients.'

Bloody hell, Alison, she thought. Bloody prime minister. You!

But the euphoria didn't last long. From early morning, sackfuls of ministerial baggage (and she included in that, some of the ministers themselves) were dumped at her door for intervention or approval. And three times a day, at one, five and eight, the little green vans would go out again from the Cabinet office, carrying back the prime ministerial responses, the communications of government to its arms and legs and other sensitive parts.

It was, she reflected, a tiny staff, with which to handle the onslaught. About 100 people, from the private secretaries, through to the telephonists and messengers. Just 100 people to keep Britain at bay, and the government from tripping itself up.

As she walked through the door, it had been like a first day at school. All the 'little friends' to be introduced, someone to tell her where the lavatory was, a row of assorted instructors, who'd coached all the others through the course, and finally the head teacher, in the shape of her predecessor's principal private secretary, Dick Foster. He had taken her over to a corner and given her the tightest handshake of the morning.

'Hallo, Prime Minister. There's me and two others you have to see. And then the day's yours. Word of advice. Government is government whether you're Labour, Tory, or the progressive Martian party. Government takes place not on a tennis court or in the tube – but in this building. There are committees, there are permanent secretaries, under-secretaries, sheep and horses – all of whom are there to serve you, according to long-established procedures.' He had coughed, as if to punctuate the little speech. 'Shall we do the tour?'

They had begun at ground level. 'You'll want to meet the garden room girls first . . .'

'The who . . . ?' She had winced visibly.

'I'm sorry. It was Lady Falkender who gave them the name. The secretaries. Their room looks out on to the garden.'

They had stood up when she'd gone in. Three rooms with low ceilings, and the lawn backing on to Horseguard's Parade. Quiet and orderly, with a plaque on the wall, showing that the King had sheltered there during the war.

'Gina, Alice, Susan ...' the private secretary reeled off the names like a waiter reciting dishes of the day. 'Some of them will be travelling with you. So you'll get to know them all in time.'

And then on through the labyrinth. It was a maze of staircases and corridors. 'Plenty of exits if you want to make a dash for it,' the private secretary had smiled. 'Tunnel to the Foreign Office, exit through the Cabinet office into Whitehall. Straight into Number 11, and Number 12 too, if you want.'

She had taken a quick look at the chief whip's meeting room, with the long green drapes, and the green-backed chairs. She noted the credit card sized security permits, and the keypads on the walls.

'By the way, do call me Dick, Prime Minister.'

She had tried hard not to laugh, but then given up the battle. 'I'm sure I won't need to,' she told him.

When they'd recovered they made their way to the prime minister's study on the first floor. A long narrowish room, with three windows looking out over the garden to Mountbatten Green and St James's Park.

She'd been there only once when Gordon had offered her a Cabinet job. She recalled the beige carpet, with the small green flowers, the gold-framed mirror and the fireplace with the pillars. But the cricketing print behind the chair had gone, a left-over from the last Tory incumbent.

She sat on one of the red velvet window seats and stared out.

'I suppose I ought to go over a few mundane details,' Foster said. 'One of the WRAF's normally comes down from Chequers to look after your cleaning and stuff. She'll do the shopping as well if you give her a list. Of course you can go out if you want.' He chuckled. 'I didn't mean it to sound like Pentonville, but you'll probably get mugged by the first crowd that spots you – figuratively, that is.'

'Quite.'

'If you're not having lunch in the House, the steward'll make something in the flat. That's what Gordon did. Alternatively there's a canteen in the Cabinet Office, which isn't bad. But I don't think PM's normally go there.'

'When do I get the boxes?'

Foster sat up straight. 'Immediately, Prime Minister.' He pointed to one of the battered red objects sitting on the desk, with the words 'Prime Minister' embossed on it. 'We fill those up day and night. Please call for them when you want. And of course the duty clerk will bring them up overnight and leave them just inside the hallway of the flat.'

'It's not locked?'

'Never has been in the past.'

'So I shouldn't wander round in the nude.'

'Well, er ...' Foster turned red. 'I really couldn't advise you on that one, Prime Minister ...'

'Depends who has access, I suppose. By the way who does have access?'

'Well, whoever you want, really. Apart from me there's the other private secretary, political secretary, parliamentary secretary, chancellor ...'

There was a knock at the door. Foster moved across to open it.

'Oh yes,' he smiled, 'and of course the Director General of MI5. I'd better leave you.'

'Morning, PM.' The new arrival shut the door behind him. 'I've brought you some reading matter. One or two bits and pieces about the people you might be choosing as ministers.'

'How thoughtful, Sir Henry.'

He allowed himself a broad smile.

She'd seen it first, some twenty-five years earlier. He was just Henry in those days. The 'Sir' had come later.

Alison recalled an invitation to London, a couple of weeks before she'd left university. She was walking slowly and with considerable pain, but she wouldn't use a stick, not that day. Not in front of those people.

It was a long summer afternoon, and she was shown into an office off Birdcage Walk, where the London sun streamed in and turned all their faces into silhouettes and shadows. Typical lunchtime faces, mottled red, drinking steadily into their forties. There was tea and polite, inconsequential chatter about old college days. But it seemed clear that her interlocutors knew plenty about her, knew she was going on to study law, knew she'd become a barrister – but just wanted to put to her 'a little proposition' if she could spare the time.

'I'm here, aren't I?' she told them.

Indeed, they replied. Indeed she was. Cheeky as well.

Odd how the light had stayed in her eyes during the conversation. No one had asked if it was uncomfortable for her, or suggested pulling down the blinds, or moving her chair. She realised later she would be hard put to identify any of them, if ever she had to.

And in the end what had stuck in her mind were the individual words and phrases like 'trust' and 'loyalty' and 'defending democracy'. Not said in a hectoring or unpleasant tone, but almost as an idle conversation, a discourse on the modern world and the duty of the individual.

And when she'd drunk a cup of tea and the shadows had lengthened, they all stood up and thanked her for coming.

Of course the meeting would not be discussed outside that room. Not by her, not by them either. If people say things and other people understand them, they need never be repeated. That was the doctrine. That was the litany. 'We're all grown up. Aren't we?'

'You didn't ask about my accident,' she said as she left the room.

Sir Henry held the door. 'You appear to have made wonderful progress, Miss Lane. I'm sure we all look forward to your complete recovery.'

When he spoke then and in years to come, there always seemed to be a sentence missing. Something he was going to say and then changed his mind. A phrase or a word that would indicate what he really meant. A little key to his mind and his intentions.

As time passed she looked forward to their meetings. Always at his suggestion. Lunch mostly, or a drink in the early evening. A quiet exchange of information. Who was up? Who was getting there? Who were the oddballs, the question marks? They trusted her to see the dangers. Admired her insights. Flattered her when the physical pain became almost unbearable, and she would hold out her hand for reassurance.

Sir Henry could be a comforting figure – when it pleased him.

And when you've established such a relationship, it's hard to break it. For he treated her so gently. A fine lunch in genial surroundings, drink first, three long courses, sometimes a little bunch of yellow roses. Brandy, if she wanted to go all the way.

It was the subtlest of pressures. A secret life within a normal life. A private undertaking. A caring hand to help her up the steps, on which she had experienced the misfortune to fall.

She knew what he was doing – and decided early on to let him do it. She knew he liked her, more than that, would like her a lot if she let him. But that wasn't part of the game.

The game allowed them some fantasy – some flirting, a little challenge, in which both got what they wanted, without ever getting it all.

Soon after entering the Labour Party she had run for the leadership of the Labour council in Islington. Trendy borough – made up of Tories who couldn't be bothered to get into their sports cars and vote – or the good old hard left, who were fighting for London, inch by inch as if it were Stalingrad.

She didn't really stand a chance against their candidate. Not as a Labour moderate. Not until a letter came through her door on a Sunday morning, two weeks before the vote.

It was nothing less than a thorough-going investigation of corruption in the borough, and the officials who had been involved in it. No signatures. No sources. But staggering in its detail and range. Inside the envelope were copies of fake contracts for work never done, fake payments into non-existent accounts, there was money laundering on a scale Alison had never imagined. Many of the names were low-level council officials – some she would have expected. The one at the bottom of the list took her breath away. It was the candidate she was up against. And now she had the knife to gut him.

She remembered sitting on the floor of her bedroom, hearing her heart thumping out a march of triumph. She had no doubt who had done the research. Sir Henry had indicated more than once, that he was watching the local councils, the hard-left cells, the people who might cause trouble if the day ever came, when there was real trouble, and the trouble came to London.

Even then Alison took nothing for granted. She checked several of the cases herself, ran the information through the computers, saw how the links emerged. And on election eve she called a Press conference, climbed out of her trench and slaughtered the enemy. The result was the largest majority in the history of London council elections.

'Lane Walks It,' said the local paper – and so she had.

Three weeks later, after a decent interval, Sir Henry bought her a champagne lunch at the Reform Club. And even though they had never kissed and never would – she was his, and he was hers.

He sat opposite the desk as she leafed through the files. Occasionally she raised an eyebrow. There wasn't much to surprise. Some excesses here, some deficiencies there. If you wanted a Cabinet you had to have a group that reflected society as a whole. Not many angels to be found.

'What do you think?' he asked, after ten minutes of silence.

She smiled. 'Well it varies – either a girl too many, or in one case,' she grimaced, 'a girl too few.'

'Quite.'

She handed him the files.

'I should put them out of your mind for now. It's Berlin tomorrow, isn't it, and President David Bradley,' the name came out very slowly. 'First time in thirty years, I fancy.'

'You don't forget these things do you?'

'How do you feel about it?'

She got up from the desk. 'I've tried not to think about him. Tried to pretend that it never happened, that he and I never happened.'

'And now?'

She surveyed the white telephone on her desk, with the finger pads reading 'White House' and 'NSC ADV'. It had been installed by a US communications team and was a direct line to the National Security adviser and the President. She hadn't dared touch it.

'Now?' she looked up. 'I'm terrified.'

Chapter Eleven

Keith Harper had held the job of chief whip for just under three weeks. But even in that time it had opened a door into the world of rumour, deceit and treachery that he had always suspected lay hidden beneath the solemnity of Westminster.

Not only was there no disappointment. He had found the job a positive delight.

For the whip's office is the prime minister's intelligence corps, the ears and eyes of Downing Street, acquiring knowledge of the most intimate nature, for use when needed. In parliamentary language that is 'persuasion'. Cross the river and most people would call it intimidation.

One of the tasks of the chief whip is to maintain a book of secrets, into which he and his staff enter the personal circumstances of the Party's members of parliament. The pages often detail the records of chance indiscretions, of mistresses, of weekends, clean and dirty, – no everyday story of gentle-folk, but as one member put it ... 'the meat in the scandal sandwich.'

This book of books is kept in the chief whip's office at No. 12 Downing Street, but Keith had taken the precaution of copying a few names and addresses into his pocket diary.

Now as he looked through it, the name of Cindy Tremayne bounced off the page at him – as he recalled the vivacious, black-haired Londoner and the circumstances that had earned her a place in his book.

Cindy was a very bad girl indeed, who had begun keeping some very good company. Long ago she had been the girlfriend of a prominent member of the Shadow Cabinet, a highly qualified nurse, and then later a physiotherapist working at several private hospitals. But the money had not been enough – and when she lost most of her limited investments in the late eighties, it was time to make use of some old political contacts. She was discreet, she was fun. She was caring and soothing.

'You should be in politics,' an MP once told her after she had soothed him on all fours.

'I am,' she replied, untying his wrists. 'Just as much as you are.'

Keith thought back to the time he had met her. Cindy was tall like a tree, shaped like a sculptor's dream. Plenty on which to hang both your hat and your heart. Just the kind of person a tired, front-bench politician far from home, could fall for.

The trouble was that one of them in particular had rapidly become a pest, writing her letters, ringing all hours, threatening to throw himself off balconies and under buses.

And Cindy, being sensible, not wanting scandal or complications, had called the whip's office and told them they had a problem.

Keith was grateful. The Party was grateful. The MP was quietly de-selected some months later by his local constituency. It was all clean and well-handled. Cindy was class. Cindy could be trusted. And among her unusually large and attractive assets they noted her common sense.

Now, as his bitterness towards Alison Lane intensified, Keith realised Cindy might have some additional uses.

He went back to the phone and dialled a number in central London.

'Cindy, you may remember we met a few months ago. Party work. You were most understanding.'

'I do seem to recall something ...' The voice was even, non-committal. Cindy knew all about telephones.

'So we have some work we might be able to offer you on a confidential basis.'

'Perhaps you'd like to come round.' Keith thought she was laughing.

'I'll do that.'

Cindy's apartment was on the eighth floor of a block off Gloucester Place. Not poor, not rich. Too close to the railway line if you were fussy about locations. But then if you were visiting Cindy, location didn't really matter. She opened the door in a plain dark blue suit – to all the world, the head of a major corporation, a lady of means and breeding.

She led him inside. No swing of the hips. No sexual aura. On the contrary, no hint of anything. The sitting room was furnished by

Scandinavians, plenty of pine, the rugs carried geomteric patterns. The atmosphere was clean and cool. This was a place where you brought your own fantasies. A clean slate. No pressure, or influence. The client was king. And Cindy was the queen.

'Won't you sit down?'

'I wanted to thank you for handling that matter a little while back.'

'Thank you for thanking me.' She smiled for a moment and the dark red lips closed soundlessly together. Keith had the distinct impression the clock was now running.

'I came to ask if you were interested in a project I had in mind. It's going to take quite a bit of preparation. But you have the tact and the qualifications.'

'In principle I'm interested in many things. Who is the gentleman concerned?'

'It's a lady.'

The smile returned and after they had talked a while longer, Cindy Tremayne was still smiling – to herself. It wouldn't work, she decided. But she wouldn't tell him that. The whole project would die a death by itself. All the same, it was intriguing the lengths to which politicians would go.

It was close to eight when he got home. Three bars behind him and a day he wanted to forget. She was there in the hall as he fumbled with his keys.

'You've been drinking.'

He looked at his wife and began to laugh. She had such good instincts, such a cutting intellect. Good old Denise. The first person to get an 'O' level in her road. Postman's daughter from Liverpool. Never missed a communication.

'Well done, love.' He started to clap, but she walked away, back into the kitchen and he followed her, more in search of food than anything else.

'You'll have to get it yourself.' She pointed to the fridge. 'I bought some fish today. Fish is good for you.' She was painting her fingers.

'Where you going?'

'Pictures. I'm meeting Iris.'

She went upstairs to change and he stayed at the kitchen table. Bugger Denise. Bugger Alison. It was going to be such a boring, bloody evening. No one to shout at. No row. But then, he reflected, in the last few weeks they'd even stopped arguing with each other. Denise was usually in bed when he left in the morning, she was usually back there, by the time he got home. She had even installed a television on the chest of drawers ... 'liked watching things lying down.'

He took off his jacket and climbed the stairs in search of even a minor argument.

As he entered the bedroom he could see her by the basin, naked from the waist up. Probably going to wear her boob tube. Big girl, our Denise, he thought. Not like Cindy, but two good handfuls there, all right.

She swung round, her mouth turned down at the edges, as if she didn't like what she saw.

'What are you staring at?'

'Nothing.'

'Good. Cos nothing's just what you're going to get. You haven't bloody been near me for months. So don't think you can just stumble up here with your mouth hanging open.'

'At least it's not a permanent state with me.'

She walked purposefully towards him. He couldn't take his eyes off her swinging breasts – so he missed the hand that came out and slapped his face. Hard. Right on the mouth.

He stepped back, intending to swipe her in return. And then all he could feel was the anger. Anger at Denise. Spite for Alison.

Slowly, almost carefully, he took her arm and pulled her on to the bed.

'For God's sake, Keith ...'

But he couldn't hear her, pushing his weight on top of her, grabbing at her underwear, pinning her shoulders on the pillow. All he could think of was that this was for that bitch Alison, who wouldn't let him near her. The only thing he wanted was for her to see him now, in this little bedroom, riding away for all he was worth, with stupid Denise moaning like an old steam train. God, he wished Alison were there.

Eventually he got off and lay on his back, his trousers still round his ankles, underpants half down.

Denise sat up and rolled her tongue around inside her flushed cheeks. After a while she said quietly ... 'I don't have to go to the pictures. We could stay here.'

No we couldn't, he thought. It was bloody awful, the way it always had been.

Chapter Twelve

Sir Henry hadn't dreamt for years. Old men, he told himself, aren't supposed to have dreams, not in their striped pyjamas, with the pills and potions at the bedside, and a body the other side of the mattress, called a wife, snoring into the early hours.

What possible use were dreams?

And yet he had one. The quite discernible merging of fact with fiction. A face and a conversation, and a warm female body that wasn't a wife and didn't snore, and possessed a name he'd known for so many years.

He hadn't wanted it that way. That's what he told himself, as he made his own piece of toast, retrieved the *Daily Telegraph*, and waited for the official car.

But he'd had 'a thing' about her for as long as he could remember.

In the dream, Alison had wanted to show him her new flat, somewhere near Regent's Park – with trees and a lake clearly visible from the front window. As they'd got out of the car she had taken his hand and smiled so warmly that he'd felt himself go weak with pleasure.

'My dear, you look absolutely splendid!'

Her eyes had laughed back at him, the blonde hair falling forward, across them, the mouth glossy with pink lipstick.

As she'd walked up the steps, he couldn't help admiring the shape of her, the 'bloody fine hips', the extra inches here and there that only seemed to offer extra pleasures. This was a woman of plenty. The mouth too generous for politics, the voice too soft, but that word 'plenty' kept revolving in his mind.

The dream must have been late afternoon, for the flat was dark enough for him to hide his excitement. His face had gone red, must have gone red, for all the thoughts it contained.

'Have a look round,' she called out. 'Won't be a minute.'

Hang on, Henry, he told himself. Steady, old boy. Don't do anything stupid.

'Aren't you going to come into the bedroom?'

Oh God. 'Yes, coming.'

She's in the bathroom. Get on the bed, man. Get ready.

And now she's coming out and she's *fully dressed*, all business-like and official.

'What are you doing, Sir Henry?'

'I thought we were going to . . .'

'Of course not. How could you . . . ? No!'

'I don't quite understand.'

'Which part of 'no' don't you understand?'

'Well, all of it really.'

'You *are* a dirty fellow, aren't you . . . ?'

And he had woken there in a hurry, hoping to God it wasn't true, hadn't happened.

He had tried to forget it, wash and dress, think out the day ahead. But it hadn't been the first dream like that. Several times, in fact, over the years they'd known one another. And each time it took a day or so to get over . . .

Of course nothing had ever happened, or would happen. He knew that. Something had always stopped him this side of good taste, of propriety.

But because he could never have Alison Lane, he wanted to be a part of her life, to control it. He wanted very much to use her.

When the car arrived, he sat in the back staring at the newspapers, not reading them.

They bore little relation to the facts that he knew. On every page – 'the prime minister thought this . . . or the prime minister thought that . . .' People wrote about Alison Lane as if they understood her priorities, her motives. But they never even touched the surface.

He could recall their first meeting so well. His colleagues had been horrified by the extent of her injuries. Why was he summoning such a woman for interview? It would be years before she'd be well again . . . one operation after another.

'We need fighters,' he'd told them. 'Think what she'll be like if she recovers.'

And then in the years that followed he had helped to re-build Alison Lane. Not just her politics – the unseen hand in the back-ground – but her confidence, her strength.

The injuries, of course, had done her no harm in parliament. On the contrary they were the political capital that got her noticed in the first place. She was the instant role model, self-made woman, the fighter come back from the dead. She couldn't help but make it.

He recalled the decision to steer her towards the Labour Party. They needed some footholds in there. Real ones. People with prospects. And she hadn't taken much persuasion. Not after the Vietnam war; not when the health service started running down. A home had been suggested to her in Labour – and she had willingly gone to live in it.

To every wing of the Labour party she had appeal – to the sufferers, because she had – to the carers, because she did, to the bright intellectuals because she could argue round corners and out of blind alleys. She was New Labour Party, and in the mid-eighties fitted neatly into the Kinnock re-organisation. She didn't talk in slogans. She either made them up or carried them herself.

It was a march that clinched it. Two thousand people crossing central London to campaign against Health Service cuts – and Alison at the head of them. She shouldn't have gone. She really wasn't up to it – in the cold of a January afternoon. The doctors had all said it was too much for her. Go along at the beginning, was their advice, or make a speech at the end. But don't walk it. Too soon after the latest of so many operations. Too dangerous.

He recalled the photo of her next day across the front pages of the tabloids – a young woman in excruciating pain. A young woman, after major surgery on her spine, and the painfully slow healing of her legs. A woman sitting on a park bench, with tears running down her face, eyes tight shut, a walking stick clasped in her hand like a cross.

Alison Lane, it said. Fighter.

The car took him down a ramp to the underground entrance of MI5. He exchanged it for the lift – and that, in turn, deposited him on the seventh floor. He liked the view – a wide sweep of the Thames at Vauxhall, the trees along the Embankment.

A better view than Downing Street and more power at this desk than at any in Number Ten. More real power.

And yet, as he looked out, he had the uncomfortable feeling that relations with Alison were about to change. In Berlin she'd be meeting the only man in whom she'd ever invested her heart. Inevitably it would upset the quiet, unstated arrangement he'd enjoyed. Had to.

For more than twenty years Sir Henry had played the role of elder companion. A position of trust from where he had watched her mental journey – the way she had put aside David Bradley and the emotions he had woken in her.

But the recovery had been patchy. She hadn't faced it, he decided, hadn't understood it as the natural selection of the sexes. She had simply buried it roughly, haphazardly in a shallow grave.

For a long time he stared out as the boats puttered below and the traffic stood clogged along the bridges. If you could turn back rivers, he thought, maybe you could turn back time.

In the years to come he would always think back to this moment, when the idea first hit him.

Chapter Thirteen

It was seven in the evening before the pile of papers cleared in front of her and Alison knew she had to talk to someone.

If there was to be a meeting with David Bradley she'd have to ensure the past was straight in her mind. Only one person could help her.

She phoned through to the private office. Dick Foster, picked up the receiver.

'What time is the plane tomorrow to Berlin?'

'When you climb on to it,' he said amiably. 'For the rest of us ten o'clock.'

'Is it full?'

'If you mean Press, TV, a couple of ministers in dirty raincoats. Yes, full as can be.'

'Dick, I need to go and see my dad in Brighton – just for half an hour. Can you get me there and back in time?'

Foster was an experienced civil servant and unlike most of his colleagues, he enjoyed exceptions to the rule. After one day he decided he was enjoying Alison Lane.

'Can you leave in fifteen minutes?'

'Dick?'

'Yes, Prime Minister?'

'Don't take this the wrong way. But I think I love you.'

London's like a car park, she thought, as the police cut her a path through the traffic. She stared out at the faces of the ordinary drivers, some curious, others angry. Bloody politicians, servants of the bloody public, forcing us to wait while they swan their way through. She could almost hear the words, watching through the bullet-proof glass as their lips moved and their eyes followed.

Through the East End, through Whitechapel and Bow – and she could pick out the Chinese restaurant beside the cinema, where Keith Harper had taken her, a few weeks back, when they planned and plotted, and never really believed she'd drive past in a Jag, leader of the pack.

You never let yourself believe until it happens. Not any more.

City Airport now and as the car turned on to the tarmac an RAF helicopter landed to the west of the main terminal. The pilot kept the rotor at full speed.

Alison tied a scarf round her head, got out, reached for the arm of her bodyguard.

'Thanks, Jim.'

Just a twinge of pain when you're in and out of cars all day. Good to have a strong arm to hold on to. Now and again. It's not a sign of weakness, they'd said. You can do it, you have nothing to prove. That's what they'd told her at Stoke Mandeville hospital, where she'd forced them to make her walk.

It doesn't hurt to take someone's arm.

'Ready, Prime Minister?'

She loved helicopters, really loved them. Better than all the ferris wheels at all the fairgrounds. The power to land or stand or hover. Power and speed. She gave the pilot a thumb's up, and the Sea-King lifted into the early evening, the sky clear and the freedom to go where she wanted . . .

These were the treats of office, she thought. Maybe she'd get used to them. Maybe she never would.

Thirty minutes later they clattered in high winds along the south coast, swooping down on to a playing field beside a black windmill. The sea was just across the road, the sun already below the horizon. Time, told in a picture.

It was only a ten minute journey, but it was the ten minutes at the edge of daylight when the darkness seeps in from the east. Beyond the cliffs the sea and the sky had somehow merged solid like a curtain, preparing to shut off the day.

They turned off the main coast road, climbed a hill and halted beside a bungalow.

'I'll wait for you here, Prime Minister.' The bodyguard opened the door and helped her out. Instantly she could smell the salty air and hear the waves and the seagulls, out over the channel. The path was slippery and she took it slow, trying to remember the last time, hearing the little sounds domestic – television, kettle, the clatter of dishes. Her mother must have glanced through the window for there was a sudden shriek, the door was flung open and the old lady was in her arms, laughing and crying ...

'Dad, Dad, look who's here.'

She could see him struggling out of the armchair.

'Wait, don't get up ...' hurrying towards him, helping him to his feet. Dad in his old green cardigan, smoothing down his hair, shaking his head in disbelief.

'What do you mean ... don't get up? Wouldn't I get up for my own daughter?'

For a moment the three of them hugged each other in the middle of the sitting room.

'Sit down, girl. Take the weight off your feet. Heavens, you'll stay and have some tea, won't you?'

'It's what I came for.'

'Such a treat,' her mother said. 'We haven't been able to think straight all day. Sitting beside the radio and television. Heavens above!'

'Was I all right?'

'All right? I should say so. Your Dad's like a dog with two tails when he talks to his friends ...'

She laughed. 'But they're all Tories ...'

'Not any more,' said her father. 'Not after I've finished with them.'

She watched him across the tea table. The shaky hands, the face thinner, greyer. And yet the eyes had lost none of their intensity. He would always know her. He would know why she'd come.

As her mum cleared the table, he said quietly ... 'this trip to Berlin ... you'll see David, won't you?'

'I have to talk about it, Dad.'

'Not if it hurts. I don't want you to go through it again.'

'That's just it. I've left it too long. But in the last two years, ever since I've started seeing him in the papers and on television, I knew I'd have to bring it into the open.'

'Why? ... Why do this to yourself?'

'To understand. To understand the reasons he went away ...'

The old man turned and looked out over the garden. 'You know why he went. There was a war. It's not that at all. It's the accident, isn't it?'

She didn't answer.

'You can't blame him for what happened ...'

'I know that ...'

'But you do. Still. You blame him for all the suffering you went through, the operations ...'

'It's easy for you ...' She stopped suddenly. It was as if she'd struck the old man across the face. 'Dad, I'm sorry. I'm so sorry – I didn't mean that. I know how much you suffered, you and Mum. I'm sorry I said that.'

'Doesn't matter,' he patted her arm, the way he had done when she was a child, 'doesn't matter.'

Mum brought the tea. Niceties on a tray. Everything in a bowl or container. Sugar and jam, hot buttered toast, chocolate biscuits. Tea for children.

Alison poured. For a moment, none of them knew what to say.

She looked across to her Dad. It had always been easier to talk to him.

'You know ... I've thought about this for so many years ... the two of us saying goodbye like that. He never knew what happened to me, did he Dad? You never heard from him – letter or anything?'

'No love. I don't think he ever knew.' He shook his head slowly. 'You must have hurt him very badly all those years ago ...'

'But he never wrote.'

'He respected your feelings. The man had his pride.'

'Dad – what could I have done? Turn up at the barracks with a zimmer frame and a stupid smile, saying 'hi, remember me?' I was a wreck. I loved him too much to impose that kind of thing on him.'

'We were all injured. It happened to all of us. Besides, he was a good boy. He'd have wanted to know.' Her father turned away and looked out over the garden. She could see his mouth tighten, the lips like thin lines, the way they always were when he became upset. 'David always made his own decisions,' he said. 'I saw the way he used to look at you ...'

'Your father's right.' Mum was sitting on the edge of the armchair. 'I remember saying so many times ... you ought to call him. But you wouldn't have it. And yet he had a right to know.' She bit into her bottom lip and Alison could see the moisture in her eyes. 'You can't go on blaming him, my love. Not after all these years ...'

The old lady wiped her eyes with a ragged, check handkerchief made from one of Dad's ancient shirts. She could never bear to throw anything away.

The prime minister's VC-10 pointed down the runway towards the rainclouds, north of London. It was loaded and full – the defence secretary, the foreign secretary, the Press spokesman, the Press themselves, all strapped in by RAF stewardesses and given triple measures of alcohol – a ritual designed to keep them enthusiastic and compliant.

They reached cruising altitude over the Thames estuary, heading east towards the Kent coastline.

Alison sat alone in the forward compartment, wondering what she would say to David Bradley, trying to push back a whole crowd of memories that seemed to be clamouring for attention.

An RAF steward appeared round the curtain. 'There's a call for you, Prime Minister. It's from the chief whip's office – Mr Harper, I believe.'

Alison looked up sharply .She didn't want to be interrupted. Least of all by Keith Harper. 'Tell him I've gone out for a walk.' She could see the puzzled face turn red. 'Tell him I won't be back for quite a while.'

Chapter Fourteen

David Bradley hadn't slept since Harry's call to Air Force One.

On arrival in Berlin he cancelled the meeting with the Chancellor, cancelled the city tour, cancelled the Reception for the Russians.

Alison Lane had jumped out of his past, where she'd been shut up, bolted and kept out of sight. She didn't belong in the present.

And yet, how could he have missed her rise to power? The answer was immediate. Easily. He didn't know the names of three quarters of the British Cabinet, let alone any others. Wasn't any need to know, unless they came to visit or shot someone. Alison had done neither.

'I'm sick,' he told Till. 'Got the flu. Tell 'em I'll be OK tomorrow.'

But he had his doubts about that.

Alison Lane.

It was like opening a grave.

Remember that last afternoon? He did remember.

He was leaving Oxford to go into the US Army. He'd told her he didn't have a choice. *He* didn't. He wanted to stay with her because she was his home, she was the place he laid his head, where he stored his hopes and dreamed his dreams. But it was 1966. It was Vietnam. And he had to go. America's war. He couldn't sit in a library while his countrymen were going off to get killed. Couldn't drink himself silly at pubs and parties and read out essays in cozy tutorials. He'd drive himself completely insane. Just couldn't do it.

Vietnam. 'Nam.

He shook his head, tried to slow his breathing. Seemed like ten centuries had passed since then.

He could recall the anti-war movement, just getting up to speed, marching through the colleges of Oxford. Meetings, dem-onstrations, the sit-ins. And there he'd been, out on his own. The only one who couldn't see the big, bad Truth.

'But I have to do this,' he told her, the day before the summer term ended. 'And you have to think it through and find a way to accept it ...'

'I can't accept it. How many times do I have to tell you? It's morally indefensible. It's stupid. It's a waste of lives. And it's a waste of you. I thought you were cleverer than that. I thought you wanted to study and learn and be someone ... that's the person I've ... that's what you said you wanted ...'

And she'd been right, hadn't she? They'd all been right. Only he couldn't have done it any different.

Even if it happened again, he'd go. Stupid war, stupid motives, ideal for a stupid bastard like me.

'You'll see it my way in the end ...' he'd said as they walked across Magdalen Bridge that last afternoon.

'If I was someone else I would – but I'm not.'

'Try to understand!'

'I can't.'

Final footsteps to the coffee house, out again into the rain.

'Won't you say goodbye to me, Alison?'

'I ...'

'Alison?'

And suddenly he couldn't tell where the rain ended and the tears began, running together down her face as she held him for a few seconds and then broke away.

'Alison!'

Seeing the long dark raincoat, disappearing down the street, the crowd opening like a mouth, taking her in ...

You have to let her go. You have to ...

Thirty years on he felt the sweat break out on his forehead as the moment came back.

I made a choice, didn't I? Terrible as it was, I made a choice and I had to live with it.

Three decades with no letter, no phone call, because that was how she'd wanted it.

He could still remember the way the hurt had stabbed at him. Even in battle he hadn't been able to shake the thoughts of her. The softness of her. Not for so many years.

But when the hurt had blurred and blunted, there had still been the favourite memories.

Like the winter weekend they'd spent at her aunt's house in the middle of what would have been a field in any other country – but in England was a swamp.

'I've put you, David, in the attic,' Auntie had raised one meaningful eyebrow. 'And you, Alison are next to me.' The eyebrow had become a no-nonsense challenge.

And there it was. The England of old ladies with big mouths, of relentless wind and rain, of darkness by teatime, of jelly called jam. How, he had wondered, could it also have been the England of Alison Lane?

Bedtime was decreed by Auntie after the radio news at ten o'clock. 'Quite enough misery for one day,' she had observed. 'Alison?'

And that had been the signal for the long march upstairs.

He hadn't been able to hide his disappointment, sitting downstairs, reading over *The Times*, the dogs, snoring and farting beside the fire.

Alison hadn't given him a sign of anything. Three weeks since he'd met her at a college dance, written her notes that hadn't received an answer, met her in the street and been brushed off. And then a letter in the college mailbox ... 'I'm going to spend the weekend at my Aunt's. If you'd like to see some English countryside, meet me at the station, Saturday 12 o'clock.'

Jesus, what an adventure.

And now zero. Zilch.

Eventually he had creaked his way to the attic. The light was broken, and the room was freezing, so he felt his way to the bed and decided to sleep fully dressed.

But when he climbed in, someone else had got there first.

'Ouch. Who is it?'

'It's my aunt. Be quiet.'

'What are you doing here?'

'Writing an essay. What d'you think?'

'I think you get a kick out of danger.'

'Don't you?'

'But I can't even see you.'

'Then imagine.'

'I'm American. We don't do imagining.'

She had laughed.

'You seem to know a lot about this kind of thing.'

'I'm *good* at imagining. What are you good at?'

'Can't you tell?'

'Not so far.'

He had never thought it would be something to laugh about. He thought it would be something you took with great intensity, with a kind of hallowed reverence, with lots of heavy breathing and deep stares.

But laughter?

She had gone on giggling, silently for about ten minutes. And in the end he had joined in.

Only one Alison in his life.

And then one Elizabeth.

Admit it now, that it was never the same. Of course – not the same. But nowhere close. A different level, different planet.

Elizabeth had been so organised and ordered. Submerged in blood at the Field hospital. So full of goodness.

Stand them side by side in your mind.

And Alison was breathless and unpredictable. Elizabeth was steady and calm, with all the values and morals that would, assuredly, have taken her to a better place.

When they married, there had been no place for friendship with Alison. They could never have met as friends, sitting across a coffee table, politely holding forth about their families, or politics – done lunch, exchanged season's greetings, phone call for the birthday.

Better the break, sudden and complete. That's the way she wanted it. Better they try to pretend it had never happened, the way he did try, over the years.

So many times, though, watching an English film, reading an English book – he would see her face and try to blot it out.

There never was an Alison Lane. Never knew her, never wanted her. Never heard the name. Repeat after me. Learn by heart.

Like an atheist, going every Sunday to church – he had recited the words – and believed not a single one.

Chapter Fifteen

The Russian leader was in a hurry and a bad temper. The two were closely connected. He hated to be late, liked to spend time combing his thick, grey hair, liked to check his suits were pressed, shoes gleaming.

'When you've grown up in a pisshole in the Urals,' he would tell Katya, 'such things are important.'

And yet that morning he had been unable to get up. She had tried at eight and at ten, and then again in desperation at 11.30.

'Why didn't you wake me before?' he had bellowed.

And she had smiled at him and replied quietly that she had.

He remembered now – sitting through the night, as if in a long tunnel of vodka, swimming down it with his two old friends from the Party school. No Party any more. No school. Just two friends – and these days you were lucky to have any at all.

Shilov swore at himself in the mirror. He'd tied the tie wrong. Look at it – bright blue Italian silk – hanging like a rope round a cow's neck. I can't escape my past, he thought suddenly. I come from a country where, according to the old saying, people always clambered up your arse to remove a tooth. Everything done in the most difficult fashion.

Only now you had to maintain appearances. Take Russia's new armies of smooth, silky tongued capitalists – all suited by French tailors, all with tassles on their shoes, and judging by the country's performance, without a fucking idea between them.

'I'm damned if I know where they're getting their money,' he had told Katya. 'I haven't got any. The country's pissed it all away years ago, and yet these little bastards drive BMWs and gamble all night at the Hippodrome.'

'Strana Chudyes,' she had said to him quietly. 'Land of miracles.'

'We could do with some,' he had replied. 'Especially now.'

When he was dressed, she looked at him, brushing his collar, straightening the tie. He was still a good-looking man, overweight, suffering a little from what Russians call 'mirror-disease' – when you have to look in one to see your feet. But then, who wanted bones?

'So we leave in thirty minutes,' she said to him.

'I know. I know. Always you are the planner – the details.'

'Just as well, don't you think?'

'You are an extraordinary woman. I become president and yet it is you who has the brains. Brains and beauty. I just have a loud voice, so all I do is shout out the things you tell me to say. If anything ever happens to me, you should take over. The Parliament respects you. The intellectuals respects you ...'

'And the "narod" – the people? Did you forget them?'

'Ah, the people.' He grinned at her. 'The people will love you the way I do ...'

'You are a sentimental fool ...' She led him into the small kitchen of the private apartment. It was modern and comfortable, with pine units fitted the year before by a Finnish contractor.

'You're worried about this meeting, aren't you?' she asked, making coffee.

'The meeting – no. The meeting will be all friendship and smiles. I'm more worried by what happens after it – when none of the promises are fulfilled and it turns out we have brought home a piece of paper as worthless as the ruble. This is what worries me.'

'So why do it?'

'I had to suggest international mediation. Nuclear weapons are everyone's issue. The Ukrainians have surrounded most of the silos that we still have on their territory. They're refusing to let supplies in or personnel out. This is very dangerous.'

'So talk to Klimak.'

'I can't talk to Klimak. He makes no sense. Now he is president of Ukraine he has become even more insufferable. Sits in Kiev stirring his nationalists. The only hope is that the Americans and British will put some pressure on him – we all need dollars these days. Maybe Klimak will listen to that kind of reason.'

'And if he doesn't?'

'We are both threatening to leave our great commonwealth of independent states.' He snorted. 'A meaningless gesture, since without Russia and Ukraine – there can be no commonwealth.' He shut his eyes and fell silent for a moment. Then he reached for her hand. 'It's good that you are coming with me, Katya.'

'Why?'

'Because I love you.'

She smiled. 'You won't have time to love me on this trip.' And then she looked into his eyes and the smile left her. 'These worries inside you, I can feel them, my dear. There is something you don't wish to tell me.'

He got up and held her head against his shoulder. It was the way he had said goodbye to her the first time they had met, more than thirty years before.

'I'll tell you,' he said softly. 'But there is no reason for this, no evidence, no facts. And yet I have the strongest of all convictions that this is a one-way journey ... that I will not be coming back.'

The captain pushed away his food half-eaten, and decided to pick a fight with Chukovsky.

'So, Colonel, when is this pointless exercise going to come to an end?'

Chukovsky looked up expressionless from his book. The captain was an arrogant little pisser from Moscow, serving the last two months of his military service. Then he'd probably go home, borrow Daddy's Mercedes and drink himself into the ground. Our great élite, he thought. Same people, only now they had a lot more money to chuck around. Didn't just *dream* about it, sitting a couple of thousand miles away in bank accounts in France or Cyprus or Liechtenstein – now they could spend it out in the open. Like this little shit's family. Gold rings, gold watches, probably had a gold condom in his wallet. He went back to his book, only the captain wouldn't leave it there.

'I mean – here we are, Colonel, seventy metres below the Republic of the Ukraine, next to a missile that's spitting smoke and is fuelled up ready to go. Only problem – there's no one to fire it at any more. So why not just turn off the lights and go home?'

Chukovsky put down his book. 'Where were you before this, Captain? Lunatic asylum? Lavatory? Maybe you were in the zoo. You see, I'm trying to work out why you're such a fucking idiot. Finally, after all these years we're coming down the mountain. Can't you see that? Only it's hard, because we've never done it before –

and none of the ignorant bastards in power ever thought we would. So they quarrel like kids. Who's going to get the toys? Have you got more toys than me? The great cities of Moscow and Kiev, scrapping in the street, over a bunch of rusty missiles. No wonder there needs to be a summit in Berlin ...'

'And after that we'll get out of here ... ?'

Chukovsky went back to his book. 'Tell you what, Captain – give the chief of staff a call. No really! Ask him. He's probably got fuck all to do – same as you.'

The captain stood up. 'Think I'll open the tin can and have a walk up top. Volodya will be awake in half an hour. Then he can take over. Not that there's anything *to* take over.'

Chukovsky heard him get in the tiny lift, heard it rattle up the shaft, heard it clank to a halt on the surface.

On a television monitor above the console he could see the captain standing on the green metal platform, in the clearing. There was nothing to show it was a silo – or anything at all for that matter. He was always amazed the army could find it. And yet every day the unmarked buses brought the three-man teams for their twenty-four-hour shift, then picked them up when it was over.

Otherwise they were nowhere. A hundred and eighty miles south of Chernobyl, in a wood.

And now the captain was 'having a walk.' Chukovsky nearly laughed out loud. You couldn't have had a walk in the old days. You couldn't even have pissed against a tree, for fear of being spotted from a US surveillance satellite. Especially this silo. This was one of the ones they hadn't declared in the arms talks, slipped it in under the net, built it in a hurry when the US satellites were playing up, back in '86 after the space shuttle disintegrated. The Americans hadn't been looking at anything for a while.

He put his feet on the console. This was really the silo that got away. Just a hole in the ground with a great fountain pen sticking up inside. The captain had said it was ready to go. Chukovsky wasn't so sure. So many components, always something going wrong. Never the proper personnel to service it. Who was to say, it wouldn't behave like any other piece of machinery Russia produced? When you wanted it, it lay down and died.

Nearly three p.m. – half-way through the twenty-four-hour shift.

The air was stale and damp. He cleared up the plastic plates from the meal and threw them away.

Maybe the captain was right – turn the lights off and leave.

And then he glanced again at the monitor.

In the days that followed he realised he could easily have missed it. Why look again? Nothing to see. No one around. Nowhere to go.

For a moment he froze. And it's probably conditioning, he realised. You see all manner of strange things on television screens. You're used to it, you grow up with it . . .

But the sight of the captain, writhing in apparent agony, scrabbling at the lift button, a low line of armoured cars and troops in the distance – this was something you didn't see. Only in nightmares. Only for the mentally deranged.

Chukovsky snatched at the console, pressing the lift override, bringing it down fast, and then pulled the red lever to the side – the hydraulic mechanism that would swing a three-metre thick steel lid across the silo, blocking out the world, making the installation impregnable.

'Volodya – get in here,' he shouted to the sergeant in the sleeping quarters.

At the bottom of the narrow shaft, the open lift came to a halt. And as he leaned forward in the semi-darkness Chukovsky could see the captain had passed out. There was blood spreading across his open shirt . . .

Christ and the resurrection.

'Volodya!'

The docile sergeant appeared, dazed, still sleepy, staring at the captain as if not understanding what he saw.

'Help me lift him, man. Quick.'

They dragged the captain through to the control room and laid him on the floor. Chukovsky could feel a heartbeat – but it didn't seem strong, didn't seem regular.

Volodya brought the first-aid battle kit. 'What the fuck's going on here?'

'Shut up, and help me dress this wound. No, fix this. It's morphine. He'll need it if he comes round.'

He looked at the captain's inert face. The colour had gone. Sweat had formed on the forehead and upper lip. As they cut away the shirt he could see thick, dark blood coming from a hole, below the ribcage. How the hell do you stop it?

Chukovsky hurried to the central console and lifted the emergency telephone. His eye caught the television monitor.

'Yop tvayu mat!'

It was the Russian expletive that exhorts you to commit an unnatural act with a close relative.

But then that was understandable. To Chukovsky the sight on the screen was as unnatural as they came. A row of armoured cars, lined up around the silo shield, some fifty infantrymen bearing the blue and yellow colours of the Ukraine, and an officer who strode towards the camera with evident pleasure, removed his revolver and shot out the glass.

Seventy metres below, the screen flashed and went black.

Chapter Sixteen

The room was full of traps. Building blocks, a train, crayons and balls. Little landmines in the darkness. Harry Deval picked his way round them, pulled the cover over the boy's legs and watched him kick it off again in his sleep. A good reflex, he thought. Don't accept things from people who stand by your bed late at night. Now there was a lesson in life.

When he came out, Jane was waiting for him on the landing.

'You only see him comatose, these days,' she shrugged. 'When was the last time you guys had a conversation?'

Harry took a deep breath. 'Is this something new?'

'What do you mean?'

'Is this a new complaint, or are we going back to the old one?'

'I'm just saying ... I think you should see more of each other. Go to a ball game, roll around on the floor, go eat pizza ...'

'You're right.'

'So?'

'So nothing. You tell me how to put in less hours. What kind of job do you think this is?'

'You always say that ...'

'The job doesn't change ...'

'Well maybe I do.'

They didn't talk for a while. It was Jane who broke the silence.

'Did you reach David in Berlin?'

'Nope. I was tied up. He was sleeping. Besides he was pretty strange last night, hanging up on me like that. I mention this prime minister's name – and that's it, he's gone. I tried thinking what it was that freaked him out – but who the hell knows? He's an odd kind of guy these days.'

'So are you.'

'Yeah, but at least I'm getting better.'

She grinned at him. 'That's what you think.'

'Maybe there's something in her past.' Harry stared at the ceiling.

'Maybe he knows something about her. I should run her through the computers ...'

'You mean you don't have better things to do. Is that what I pay my taxes for, so you can check up on friendly leaders?'

He looked up sharply, but she was still grinning.

'You know there are times when you really piss me off.'

She got up and went over to him, running her hands over his balding head.

'Hey you know I don't like that.'

She took his hand and led him towards the stairs. 'Come on, Mr Sensitive. I'll make it up to you. Haven't seen that pathetically grateful expression on your face for a long time.'

They both lay awake for a while, not talking.

'Who are your friends, Harry?' she put her head on his chest. 'There must be people you do talk to.'

'Get serious. You don't have friends in this town.'

'I mean the people you eat with, drink with ...'

'They're not friends. Mostly I'd prefer to eat without them. They're the people who smile at me, want my job, want information, want access to the president ...'

'No friends among them?'

'Maybe one or two. But how do you tell?'

'And David?'

'David's a friend.'

'Why? Because he doesn't want your job?'

'Maybe.'

'Do you want his?'

Harry didn't answer. He glanced over to her, wondering what lay behind her question. He really hadn't looked at it that way.

The snow froze again during the night and at five he woke, realising the room was unusually cold. The ice had scratched patterns across the window panes – from inside! The power was out. Washington's fragile electric system had bowed once again to winter. That's what you got for having overhead power cables. Jesus, it was cold!

He dressed in a hurry and made his way downstairs. Every room was freezing. Coat, hat, scarf – and all the papers he had brought home and hadn't read.

On the street, he could see the Dodge, icicles hanging from the headlamps. Still dark, fresh snow on ice, no lights in the houses. Like the end of the world.

Third try and the car started, and he kept his foot on the pedal, till the heater clicked in and the temperature arrow began to rise. As he lifted the handbrake, there was a creak of protest from the frozen suspension, and a spin from the rear wheels.

Some fucking superpower, he thought, if I can't even get up the hill.

Swearing and stamping his feet, Harry coaxed the car to the top.

Five minutes later he was at the bottom of Massachusetts Avenue, and it was then that he saw her. Not her face. Just the hair that bounced thick and free down her back, the handbag over her left shoulder, the sheepskin boots that they had chosen together in a shop, well out of town.

He didn't look at her until he was past, until he could see her in the rear mirror. Had she recognised the car? She'd sat in it often enough. Jesus! She was too far away for him to see her expression.

It took Harry at least a half hour to calm himself. By then he had forgotten all about the check he'd intended to run on Alison Lane.

Chapter Seventeen

Ruth Bradley couldn't remember the last time she had woken up with a man on her mind. Over the years she had woken up with one or two in her bed – discreetly, of course – and for no other reason than a very passing infatuation.

But this was different. Pete Levinson had been so charming at the party, and seemed so interested in *her*, and hadn't gone droning on about the presidency, and the greater glory of the nation . . .

The point was she had been able to turn off the damned performance for a while, and when that little minx Emily had not been watching, she had actually managed to relax and talk normally.

After all, you can't spend your life, guarding against a chance word. You had to be able to trust someone. And anyway, the presidency *should* be more open. There were far too many secrets in this world. She would talk to David when he returned from Europe.

For once Ruth Bradley didn't feel like breakfast in her room. She went downstairs to the coffee shop and sat for an hour, glowing brightly, with a copy of the *Washington Post*, crumpled beside her plate of croissants, and a vague, watery smile, just in case anyone recognised her.

It reminded her of sitting in bars all over the world – mostly on her own. Jack would never leave the farm, and when David was a child she had decided that if they were to see anything of the world, they would have to see it together. That was when the loneliness had set in.

Wherever they went, David would be in bed by nine or ten and Ruth Bradley would be sitting at midnight in the hotel bar, the perfect image of the American tourist, her maps, guidebooks and camera laid out on the table, and her heart crying in the wilderness.

On his thirteenth birthday she had taken the boy to Paris. It was late summer and she diligently led him to the art galleries, to the Tuileries Gardens, to the Bastille. But after the first few days she could see that his heart was elsewhere. The tall, awkward teenager had become captivated by the daughter of an American couple, staying in the same hotel.

The girl must have been at least three years older than David – even wore a little make-up. Not a beauty, but a wild, smiley, do-anything kind of creature, hair in thick brown bunches, constantly on the move, curious about everything she saw.

Paris to David Bradley was suddenly the girl from Fort Worth, Texas, who told him that when he grew up, she'd buy him a fifty-ounce steak and take him to Billy-Bob's saloon, where he could try his hand on the rodeo.

And then one night, she pushed him up against the wall outside the hotel and ran her tongue over his teeth, telling him she was just checking his dentistry. And he informed his mother the next day that he wouldn't be going with her to the galleries, or the race track at St Cloud, but he and his girlfriend were going to take a riverboat from the Pont St Michel and wouldn't be back till dinner.

From that moment on, Mrs Bradley had looked on her son as a man, or rather a man-to-be. Little David, who was now big David, had acquired new confidence. When he walked he left footprints. When he touched lives, they stayed touched.

She looked round the coffee shop, remembering a newspaper article about the types of men who became first or second husbands.

David was always a first and only husband. A once-only husband. He wasn't nice and accommodating. He wasn't soupy and soft, didn't wear tassles on his shoes, didn't work out or eat bean sprouts. Didn't need to. He came ready-made, tough, decisive and fright-eningly bright.

For years after that Paris trip, the letters had kept coming from Fort Worth in Texas.

On his eighteenth birthday, David had flown down there, eaten his fifty-ounce steak at Billy-Bob's, and a week later flown back to Kansas.

His mother had stood at the airport barrier with her head on one side, and her eyebrows like question marks. 'Well?' she had asked, 'Aren't you going to tell me.'

'Can I put down my suitcase?'

They had got in the car and he had turned to her and said

simply ... 'didn't work out, Mom. She still wanted someone three years younger.'

So the letters had stopped coming. But Mother Ruth was proud of him.

Later, of course, David went away on his own or with his friends. And so did she. There were causes and charities, excursions with the Audubon Society, treks in search of moose or eagles – and when the self-pity inside her reached intolerable heights, then there was the occasional night of hurried and largely incompetent passion.

She never really knew what to do, she told herself. The basic outlines, yes. But the details. The fine tuning. There would be plenty of shifting and groaning, and the men would grab her hands and try to show her what to do with them. But it was like gardening. You could either get the thing to grow – or you couldn't. And mostly, Ruth Bradley couldn't. Not for them. And not for herself either. Where, she often wondered, were the dark, delicious secrets that people were supposed to take with them to the grave? All she had was the memory of a few embarrassed conversations like ... 'I didn't mean to hold it so tight.' 'Never mind. It was my fault.' 'No, no. I was on edge.' 'Just tired. Maybe it'll be all right in the morning.' Oh God, Oh God, Oh God!

Gradually, the glow left Ruth Bradley, as the sludge of memories drifted past her.

Idly she picked up the *Washington Post* and glanced at the front page. 'Party Coup Brings New British Prime Minister.' Another woman, it seemed – but then who cared about Britain these days?

The photo looked nice enough, blonde hair, kind of fixed smile, pretty enough ...

She turned the page, but then something made her turn back.

The picture was interesting. Must have been taken on a day out, for the wind had caught the woman's hair, thin, fine hair ...'

And then something caught Mrs Bradley's memory deep inside.

Wait a minute. Wait, wait wait.

I know this face. Somewhere I have met this woman.

She ordered fresh coffee and sat thinking harder than she had thought for a long time.

It was the set of the face – that was it. Determined. Forceful and yet there was a smile never far away, if you knew how to get it from her.

David's words. God Almighty – David's friend. The friend from Oxford they had met so many years ago when he was over there. The ghastly meeting with her parents ... Mrs Bradley's mind had started to race.

She checked the name in the paper. Alison Lane. That was it. Alison.

My God, My God – this is incredible. I have to tell someone.

She looked around the coffee shop but there was no one in sight.

She read the story through twice. This was so ex-tra-ord-in-ary.

The bill came and as she got up to leave, her eyes became fixed by the passage of a rose, seemingly in free flight above her head, a pink rose, on a long stem, its leaves still wet, falling so slowly towards her, on to the table cloth. She looked at it for a few seconds, before seeing the hand that was attached, the blue shirtsleeve and the silver cufflinks.

To be fair to him – and most people weren't – Pete Levinson had entertained strong reservations about going to the hotel. He hadn't much enjoyed the twelfth-night party either. Old ladies, he told Larry D'Anna, weren't his style.

'But this old bird is something else.'

'You mean this old bird's son is something else.'

D'Anna smiled agreeably. 'That's what I said.'

Of course there was something in it for Levinson. And Levinson was in a needy state.

At the age of fifty-three he had discovered that the world of the freelance reporter can suddenly turn cold and inhospitable. Charm and the suntan from the ultra-violet lamp in his bedroom, were no longer enough to run the Porsche 944, the apartment on Capitol Hill, and the precious club afternoons out in suburban Maryland and Virginia.

It hadn't helped much that Levinson, who wrote for the *Washingtonian* under the pseudonym 'Count D', had torpedoed his own career by writing a story so disastrously inaccurate, that a number of influential people had seriously considered cutting him into little chunks and serving them up at the Baltimore aquarium.

The story had begun with an impeccable rumour that a man of

high standing called Richard C Whittle was visiting massage parlours from Washington all the way to the Great Lakes, treating himself to the extras – even dreaming up a few of his own.

Levinson had names and addresses. With a little work on the story, he even got some credit card receipts, autographed by Whittle with unashamed, ballpoint clarity. All of which should have told him something. For if Mr Whittle was indiscreet enough to go round using his credit card at such establishments, then there was the slimmest of chances that he wasn't the same Mr Whittle, Levinson thought he was: that is Richard C Whittle, secretary of the Navy, and a close friend of the president.

Now the real Whittle lived on the East-West Highway in Chevy Chase, never married, indulged in pyramid selling for Amway, and thought the whole incident was hilarious. When all the reporters and cameras turned up at his door, he 'just couldn't see what all the fuss was about.'

But his namesake at the Pentagon took an entirely different tack. The magazine story landed on Washington like a giant cowpat, spattering the filth as it went; and lawyers for the Navy department went in search of colossal damages. By lunchtime on publication day they had secured well over a million dollars and a retraction statement, broadcast by WTOP throughout the day.

As for Levinson, the city's insiders said his arse had been kicked so hard 'he'd had to go look for it in Wisconsin.'

Only the intervention of Larry D'Anna prevented him from being cast into outer darkness. But then D'Anna never knew when he might need a journalist, particularly a poor one, the kind who would eat out of your trouser pocket, and insert his tongue into whatever crack or orifice you suggested. Larry's words. Larry's style.

What he needed, he told Levinson, was some intrusive surgery on Bradley's private life. The time as a student, the early childhood. 'I want smoking bimbos ... I want to know if this guy farted out loud at a cocktail party. I want all the cracks in the mirror – and if there aren't any, I want to put some there.'

'This was all done when he got the job,' Levinson had protested.

'Bullshit! The guy's wife was badly ill, so the press laid off. That was the unwritten rule. We know bupkus. Bradley had the softest ride of any president in history. They virtually left the past alone, out of respect for his lady, and the illness and all that.'

'What makes you think there's anything there?'

D'Anna had grinned. 'There's always something there. Look at your own life, huh? Just find it, Pete. I don't care how.'

Levinson could recall the conversation word for word. He'd told D'Anna he drew the line at old ladies. But who cared what he thought? There was a job to be done.

'Mrs Bradley – a wonderful surprise.' He bared as many teeth as he could.

'Are you in the habit of throwing roses around hotel coffee shops?'

'I was carried away . . .'

'Oh please!'

Levinson realised he was in danger of overdoing the treacle.

'Let me be honest with you, Mrs Bradley . . .'

'That would be nice.'

'May I sit down?'

She nodded towards the chair opposite. She was so excited by the news of Alison, that she'd have offered the doorman a seat.

'I was looking for you because I thought we might have dinner together?'

'Why would we do that?'

'Perhaps because we had such an enjoyable conversation the other night. I wanted to tell you more about the boy's club I'm involved with. It seemed to me that you might just welcome a simple dinner and some conversation – instead of all the gala performances you're required to give around town.'

Levinson had the gift of being able to blush at will, and so the colour was coursing like a torrent into his cheeks.

Ruth Bradley surveyed him thoughtfully. He really did talk bullshit . . . flinging roses around, having a simple dinner, some conversation. If that wasn't a come-on, she didn't know what was. And yet, she was in such an excited mood. Could she tell him? No, no, of course not. Out of the question. But why not have some fun, for God's sake? What was she waiting for? A man who would build her a doll's house full of light and pretty dresses, fields of happiness stretching away to the horizon? Who was she kidding? Life was three-quarters over and if she didn't go out and grab some good times, she'd lie in her box and regret it forever. She knew she would.

Besides, he had such good teeth.

She leaned across the table and lowered her voice. 'What are you doing now?'

They went on to have a wonderful lunch. Galileo's restaurant, off M Street, with all the Northern Italian dishes Ruth Bradley could have imagined, and there was Campari to start, champagne to follow, red wine to savour, and brandy for nothing more than the joy of the moment. Whichever it was.

They had laughed and talked. God how they'd talked! It was so easy to talk to a man like that. Such a wonderful listener, with no axe to grind and you didn't have to watch . . .

Oh God!

At six o'clock that evening, she sat upright on her bed in the Four Seasons. What the hell had she said?

Maybe she had just thought it. The name Alison Lane. Not said it out loud. But hadn't there been a moment . . . ?

She recalled David's lecture to her when he took office. Nothing about his former life. No loves, no friends, no cute little memories. Presidents don't have pasts, except the ones the White House press office authorises. Break that rule and no one is safe – no contact, no girlfriend, no distant relative. 'The public domain is infinite.' Those had been his words.

Ruth Bradley felt very sick. If she'd had a gun, she reflected, she would have blown her brains out in that very moment, all over Georgetown.

Chapter Eighteen

'How long have we known each other, Peter?'

The British ambassador in Berlin toyed with his brandy glass and wondered what was coming. He had known Clark Norton for more than fifteen years on the diplomatic circuit. Quite long enough to form a deep and enduring dislike of the man. But since when did that get in the way of a good contact? And good contacts didn't come much better than the US secretary of state.

He smiled across the study at Norton. 'Been a few years, hasn't it? Paris first I think. You were the rising star in the political section, while I was sent out to buy the bloody croissants.'

'But you did it so well.'

'You're very kind, Mr Secretary.' It was only half a joke. Norton really liked his title. Flattered him. Made him feel someone.

'Wonderful dinner, Peter. And wonderful to see you again.' His mouth expanded to approximate a smile. 'Perhaps we should join the ladies in a minute. But I thought it would be good to talk.'

'Of course, anything worrying you?'

Norton crossed his legs. 'There's no chance of us being heard is there, Peter?'

'What d'you mean?'

'I mean you haven't got any kind of devices?' His hand described a circle around the room and gestured to the old black labrador crumpled by the floor. Brits always had to have something to dominate.

Peter shook his head.

'It's just that I wanted to get your reaction to an idea. Kind of an international position, if you know what I mean.'

'Whatever I can do to help. You know that. We've done one or two trades in the past, I seem to recall.'

'I want to make a bid for the presidency.'

The ambassador tried not to move a muscle, but he could feel his hand tighten on the brandy goblet.

'That's ...'

'I wanna make a bid, because Bradley's weak and damaged, and I have to distance myself from him, before he goes down the can.' A thin line of moisture appeared on Norton's upper lip. 'For Chrissake Peter, we need some leadership round here. Bradley's never recovered from his wife's death. I'm sorry about that. But this country needs a firm grip, and if I'm to get in the right position, I have to start now.'

'What can I say, Clark? That sounds a ... er exciting prospect.'

'What about, internationally?'

'You know us. Special relationship and all that. Every support.'

'Every support?'

'Of course.' Peter frowned. 'When the time comes.'

'I may need your help before then.'

The dog stirred in the corner, and yawned.

'In what way?'

'Bradley was in England as a student.'

'So?'

'There must be records about his time there?'

'Hang on a moment, we went down that road once before, if you remember. Clinton never forgave us.'

'This is different, Peter. This time, the right guy's gonna win.' He rose abruptly and smoothed down his trousers. 'I'm glad we had a chance to see each other again. It's always good to know one has friends abroad. So much more trustworthy than those at home.'

'Politics, Clark.'

'Where would we be without them?'

Chapter Nineteen

He thought Cindy Tremayne was really something, sitting there in the restaurant, with tits that could re-float a battleship – bobbing and buoyant, two separate invitations to make a bloody fool of yourself. He grinned across the table – but she wasn't reciprocating.

To her Keith Harper was cheap and a bit brash. Got himself a new job in the Party, come up from nowhere very nice, didn't mind bragging to anyone who'd listen.

And she'd done plenty of that.

He'd taken her to the Carvery at the Tower Thistle Hotel, where the greedy bugger had stuffed himself with roast turkey and potatoes, biggest plateful she'd seen in her life. Looked as though he hadn't eaten for a year.

She hoped fervently he'd be too bloated to take her to a room after lunch, like several other MPs she could name. But, on reflection, it wasn't his style. He was too mean to pay for sex. His kind would would rather look for strays and pick them up when they were down.

Coffee came and Keith turned to business. He had called in some favours, he said, got her an interview at the physiotherapy clinic – the one that pampered the very influential, 'including,' he added, 'the lady I work for. It's a poncey sort of place, but they're professional. I take it you still know the moves?'

'They're not moves. It's technique, skill . . .'

He had a sudden image of Cindy, naked on all fours, tying the hands of an MP with a leather thong. 'Of course.'

She took a gulp from the wine glass. 'How close do you want me to get?'

'Where no human eye has been before.'

'You have to be joking.'

'Don't even think it. The aim is to cause considerable embarrassment . . . that's why we're having this conversation . . .'

'And you'll take the pictures to make sure of it.'

'We'll need evidence, that's perfectly true . . .'

She looked out over St Katharine's Dock – the play-boats, the toys for the rich. One or two of the MPs kept discreet little cabin cruisers moored along the jetty. That's when they weren't over at her place, being little boys again – or girls, dressing up and preening. So many times she'd wanted to burst out laughing, at the sight of their bare bottoms in the air . . .

Cindy turned back to Harper. 'It isn't going to work.'

'Why?'

'Because she's going to tell me to piss off – that's why. The moment I start pawing her, where I'm not supposed to, that'll be it.'

'I'm not so sure.'

'Well I am. And then what's going to happen to me – get locked up in the bloody Tower, I expect?'

'I said we'd take care of it. We did last time, didn't we?'

'Last time was different. I came to you. Besides, I've never done anything like this.'

Harper inclined his head slightly. 'That's not quite true, is it Cindy?'

'Of course it's . . .' and Cindy really had to think hard to remember this one. How many years ago? Christ, he had done his homework!

She had been eighteen when a female teacher had tried it on. 'A' level college in boring old Bournemouth, where everyone and everything seemed to have retired. Only not Miss Simpson, deputy principal, in her late twenties, with her wide-blue eyes and short tennis skirts. Cindy had been invited to play singles on a Sunday afternoon and when the game was over, she thought nothing of entering the shower with Miss Simpson, watching her long black hair matting under the warm water, feeling the hands soaping her back and then her buttocks and thighs – hands that were so assured, so knowing.

The older woman had moved round, just as competent with the front of her body – the nerve-endings, the paths to pleasure . . .

Cindy could still hear the urgent flooding of the water, still feel the fingers drawing patterns on her body – the sense of being engulfed by new and illicit ecstasy. Miss Simpson had used the erotic weapons for which Cindy had no defence.

'I've always found difficulty saying no,' she confided later to a friend, 'it was easier just to go along with things.'

And things had gone along pretty pleasurably until, three weeks later, the affair had become public. A male staff member had forgotten to knock at Miss Simpson's door one evening, and had entered to find the hand of the deputy principal embedded down the front of Cindy's jeans. Worse, Miss Simpson had been unable to extricate her hand, without first loosening Cindy's waistband – a fact that had only served to prolong the embarrassment.

Of course, Miss Simpson was asked to resign and did so, and Cindy, after a talk with the college doctor, and some pastoral care from the parish priest, was allowed to stay on. Scandal committed, scandal buried. The rite of passage through the British provinces.

And now, some twelve years later, the government chief whip was recalling the incident at lunch by St Katharine's Dock, which meant he knew how to dig dirt and wasn't fussy where he looked for it. And in that case, thought Cindy, maybe, just maybe he was ruthless enough to make the scheme work.

Looking up from the table, she smiled at Harper, as if to show him, she wasn't even vaguely surprised.

'I think all that history is my business,' her eyes locked on to him across the table. 'We can all handle confidential material. I expect my own records are just as interesting as yours. That isn't the point. What is – is that I've thought about it and I'll give it a try. But if it does go wrong, I want out, and I want money to start a life somewhere else. Long way, away.'

'Agreed.' Harper gestured at the waitress to bring the bill. 'Only it isn't going to go wrong.'

He paid in cash, and steered her through the tables, watching the heads turn, the jealous glances, tourist and businessman transported into instant fantasy. That's what Cindy did for people. Brought those fantasies to life. Perhaps, she'd do it for Alison Lane. Who could tell? Maybe *that* was her thing, after all.

As they got out through the swing doors, he held on to her arm.

'Excuse me . . .' she turned round sharply.

'I just wanted to say one thing, Cindy, before we go our separate ways. I wanted to emphasise the importance of not mentioning this to anyone – and I mean anyone. You do see that, don't you?'

Cindy freed her arm. 'I hardly think you have to remind me of that.'

'Because if you do,' Keith ignored her, 'I'll close you down for good. No work, no favours. And a lot of aggravation that a single girl in London would be wise to avoid.' He handed her an envelope. 'All the details you need are in here. Your appointment's tomorrow. Please be there on time. They appreciate that kind of thing.'

He watched her drive away in the taxi. Of course, if it did go wrong, he reflected, they'd both be on their bike.

Probably to a place where you couldn't even buy one.

'Cindy Tremayne? What a pleasant name!'

'Thank you.'

'I've had a look at your qualifications and the ah ... letter you brought with you. That all looks perfectly in order ...' The director of the Harvey Clinic gave a little cough. 'Of course we don't normally discuss these things, but I can't tell you how fortuitous your application is. Most fortuitous, in fact. One of our longest serving physiotherapists called in a few hours ago from hospital, I regret to say, to inform us she'd been in an accident. Apparently she was pushed to the ground by a mugger. Fellow tried to steal her handbag, and when she resisted, struck her on the knee with a cosh. I gather she's in great pain – may even have fractured the bone ...'

'How awful!'

'Looks as though she'll be out of commission for weeks.'

'I see.'

'Thing is, if you'd come yesterday, I'd have told you we had no vacancies, and to come back another time. So you see ... one man's ... or rather one woman's misfortune ...' He laid his hands on the desk, white hands, perfectly manicured, the tip of a handkerchief protruding from his sleeve, 'One woman's misfortune is another's er ... good luck.'

'I suppose it is ...'

'Yes, well.' He stood up straight against the side of the desk. 'We shall of course want to see you at work for one or two sessions. Shall we say ten o'clock tomorrow morning. A little trial period, if that's acceptable to you . . . just a week or so. And then we'll review things at the end of the month . . . Miss Primp will discuss the . . . ah terms of the engagement . . .'

Cindy stood up and held out her hand. The director smiled smugly. 'We don't shake hands in this establishment, Miss Tremayne. We work with clients who don't normally like that kind of familiarity, unless of course they happen to be from the ah . . . continent.'

'I quite understand.'

'Good day, Miss Tremayne.'

It took an hour to fill in the forms, under the painstaking direction of Miss Primp. Miss Fatarse, more like, thought Cindy. And it was only as she walked away down the drive that she reflected in any detail on the circumstances of her engagement. What a wonderful coincidence that a long-serving physiotherapist had been injured in an accident. What perfect timing. What organisation.

Of course it was further evidence that Keith Harper was a man who got what he wanted. And if you stood in his way, he would sweep you aside.

It wasn't that she minded any of that. Cindy enjoyed high stakes, always had done. She enjoyed the feeling of standing on a tightrope, beating the odds. That was her life. The risk. The subterfuge.

All the same, she told herself, it would be prudent to make some travel arrangements, should the need arise.

Chapter Twenty

Alison Lane barely noticed the landing in Berlin, or the bulky German chancellor with his hand outstretched in welcome, blue raincoat almost touching the ground, full of sincere greetings and profound hopes. And wasn't he always?

Dick Foster sat beside her on the short journey to the city – and she took refuge in his low mumble, going over the programme, the people she'd see, the agenda.

He was like a priest intoning a private prayer, as she stared out at the neon lights and the crowded cafes along the Ku-damm.

'Give me half an hour,' she said as they reached the hotel. And Foster had rightly interpreted the look ... Don't interrupt me. I've got things on my mind. You know what to get on with.

She had shut the bedroom door of the suite and sat by the window, feeling the flush spread out over her cheeks.

Don't know if I can do this, she thought suddenly. Don't know if I want to. The mind isn't supposed to remember pain. That's the safety mechanism. But why can I feel it now, advancing like an army?

She opened the window and the cold air leapt in at her, bringing the noise of traffic and sirens as another delegation arrived. Little Berlin on the street far below. Out of reach.

We're none of us supposed to have lives, she reflected. Not the leaders. Not the heads of government. We're offices, we're chairs. We can't feel and we can't react. People write to us in their thousands about poverty, injustice, unhappiness. And we get up in parliament and tell them how well we're doing. We pick up babies in a crowd and kiss them, because we haven't time for our own.

That's why I grasped this job. I didn't want to feel any more. I didn't mind missing out on happiness. I just wanted to avoid the pain. I can't go through it again. I have to be the armour-plated bitch, they all think I am. And maybe it's true.

She picked up the phone and called Foster.

'Where's Bradley staying?'

'Hilton, I think. Want me to fix up a call?'

'No. Just wondered.'

'Right.'

'That's all, Dick.'

'Yes, Prime Minister.'

'Call you when I'm ready.'

'Of course, Prime Minister.'

Lying on the bed she remembered the first time she had seen his picture after Oxford. A magazine article ten years earlier about the soldier governor, the Vietnam hero from Kansas – and where better they had asked, to find a real cowboy?

She had felt a physical jolt, felt his hands, felt the rain as it washed away her dreams on that early winter evening in Oxford. The city where you came to learn of what had been and what might be.

And she could hear that voice as if it were yesterday. The voice that always said to her ... 'I can reach you, Alison. Wherever you disappear in your mind, wherever you hide your thoughts, whenever some hurt or some disappointment sends you running deep into your imagined cave. I can always reach you. I always will.'

She remembered the two of them, promising things they didn't know about, giving gifts that weren't theirs to own. How could we have said those things, said them with all the certainty of true ignorance? We found answers where there are only questions. We made plans and dreamed dreams as if they were the currency that could buy us a future. If you voiced the words – they'd come true.

I always said that to him, she recalled. 'Tell me it'll happen, David, and it will.' Only he wouldn't. He'd play lots of games but he wouldn't play that one.

For him the plans were intentions – that life would honour or dishonour according to rules of its own.

He knew it – and I didn't. He said it would happen if it was meant to. Does he think the same now?

I really believed that when my studies were over, I'd go to America, I'd go to the war, I'd find my soldier, with a book in his hand instead of a machine gun – and I'd take him home. And we would live that ever-after kind of life, whatever it was, under the tall skies, in certain hope of happiness and light.

And then the feeling of pride when he'd been elected president. What a night it had been. Quiet, silent pride, for her alone. David, David, you did it!' ... said only to herself, as she stared at his face on the screen. Hadn't a little voice said to her even then ... 'If he can do it, so can you?'

She got up, went into the bathroom and stared at herself. I know who *you* are, she thought. I recognise you from the papers. You're Prime Minister Alison Lane, nobody's lover, not for a long time ... A life on the outside.

But I no longer recognise the person you were in Oxford and maybe that's why I'm here. I want to find that woman. I want to know if she's still around. Because she was happier than me – and she knew how to love. And I think I can learn from her.

When I move, he thought, a thousand people have to move with me. Half of them arrive before I do ... they build little communication cities all over the world, so I can talk to anyone I want. And if that's not enough, they spend days discussing where the nearest hospitals are, in case someone decides to shoot me.

If I want to step over to a crowd, then the people will suddenly find themselves abused and threatened by men with plastic earpieces, ordering them to take their hands out of their pockets.

That would be all right for four years. But it isn't going to stop there. When I finally kick the bucket, they'll want to know from the Almighty well in advance whether I'm going up or down. If they haven't sanitised the area first, they'll tell him to back off. The secret service can do that.

Bradley looked around the crowded, makeshift Cabinet room. They had taken over the entire ninth and tenth floors of the Hilton. He had filled the place intentionally. Didn't want to do any thinking. Didn't want to reflect on the reason he'd come to Berlin.

Everyone seemed to be talking. You couldn't think a single coherent thought with this crowd around; secretary of state, press secretary, deputy chief of staff, jackets off, ties loose, gin and tonics and beers in front of them. All boys together. Night away from home. In charge of a country, sure. But what the hell, they were going to have a good time.

He had asked if Alison Lane had arrived. Just an innocent inquiry. But why should it be anything else? There wasn't any guilt, was there?

Christ, thirty years earlier, it was she who had broken it off. She and the circumstances. He had finished his studies at Oxford and was heading for the Army. She was going to call. That was the deal. She would make contact. But she never did. Deal was off.

Funny people, us Americans, he thought. Life defined in deals. Deals made, deals broken. Round the corner, though, there'll always be another ...

'Wanna drink, David?' Clark Norton from State had a voice that could cut diamonds.

'I think we'll settle down, gentlemen,' Bradley addressed the whole room. 'As you know I have a morning meeting with the Russians. It's a friendly. That's fine, but let's agree a position.'

They straightened up, put down the drinks, pulled out folders and yellow pads. The class was back in session.

Bradley knew all about the danger of friendly meetings. It was like exhibition boxing. You still fought and you still wanted to win. And at this level a wrong word, a wrong impression, an emphasis or a nuance misunderstood – and the whole conference could jump off the cliff.

It would be the same with Alison. So careful, David. So careful. For when you've loved a person, they leave something inside you – a presence, powerful yet dormant. Only if it should ever wake, he thought, it has the potential to shatter your beliefs and certainties and drag you from your orbit, right out into the unknown.

Twenty minutes later, a political aide brought a note to the president.

'Gentlemen,' he interrupted Norton in full flight. 'I'm gonna stop you here. The British prime minister is on the telephone. We'll resume in ten minutes ...'

The words weren't an invitation to be silent – they were an invitation to leave. A clear order to get out.

Rapidly, the five Cabinet members shouldered their jackets, collected their papers and headed for the door, exchanging puzzled looks. Something was wrong because prime ministers didn't call without warning, and presidents didn't get rid of their staff when they did.

In the secretary of state's suite the Cabinet put down their papers and breathed a collective sigh.

'What the hell's he up to?'

'Did you see his face?' Norton stood by the window and gazed out. 'He looked nervous ... who knows ... ?'

'Who cares?' said Till. 'Let's deal with the Press. We need some stories and we need some photo-ops. This isn't a summit unless it's on television.'

Norton threw a folder at him. 'Make it up, fellah. You usually do!'

Till stared down at his yellow pad. Like all Press secretaries he considered it was better not to lie unless he had to.

But, hell – it made the job more fun.

Chapter Twenty-one

Only Foster stayed behind in the room. He had scheduled the phone call, completed the formalities. Yes, the president would be happy to speak with Prime Minister Lane. One moment please.

She took the receiver. 'Thank you, Peter.'

'Goodnight, Prime Minister. If you need anything ...'

What I need, she thought, is to put down the phone and stop shaking inside. I need to black out the past, and look only to the days ahead. I need to speak to the president of the United States about an international crisis – not because I loved him thirty years ago on another planet.

As she gripped the receiver, she saw herself standing, decades ago, in an old red phonebox off the Oxford High Street ... picture so clear.

David had returned to the States because his grandfather had died. And he had written to her saying ... on May 21st, I'll call you at the payphone beside the King's Arms, exactly midnight your time, seven p.m., Eastern Standard. Don't get drunk. Don't pick up anyone. Be there, OK?

She had been there. An hour early, in fact. Whether by Greenwich Mean Time or Eastern Standard, walking up and down in the sub-zero temperatures of an English spring.

Bloody country, bloody phoneboxes. What am I doing?

And she could hear everyone else's conversations through a broken window pane ...

God the things people *said* to each other!

Of course midnight found some little wimp, standing, pouring out his miserable, wimpish heart to a girl called Tiggy, who clearly didn't want to know. There were plenty of 'please, Tiggy's, and 'be reasonable, Tiggy's, and 'let's give it another go, Tigs.'

All so clear, even with such a distance in time ...

And then the wimp had given up and she took possession of the box, ready to defend it whoever came.

He would ring late on principle. She had been so sure of it. But he was right on time.

'Al!'

'Don't call me Al, David.'

'How about "Ally"?'

'What's wrong with Alison? Been all right up till now.'

'Too long. I think you're an Ally.'

'Sounds like a narrow passage.'

He laughed.

'I didn't mean it like that. Can't you raise your mind above waist level?'

'It's kind of stuck down there.'

'Oh, very nice. I'm not standing in this phonebox to practise pornography . . .'

'You got something better to do?'

'As a matter of fact, there's a guy waiting outside who looks really gorgeous . . .'

'Remember I come from a violent country . . .'

Her turn to laugh.

'I'm not good with rivals . . .'

'Then don't think about it . . .'

'Why did I call you?'

'No idea. Tell me.'

'Uh-uh. I've told you too much already. I want you to put down the phone, walk straight past this Adonis creature, or whatever his name is, go back to the room, lock the door, and read a book by the gas fire . . .'

'What are you going to do?'

'Oh take a walk past the red lights and the ladies with white boots . . .'

'Goodnight, David. Don't bother coming back.'

''Night. I'll see you next week.'

As she left the box, the wind had raced up Broad Street, grabbing at her hair and her coat. Only she didn't feel cold. She could move with the wind, sway with the wind, ride it all the way to the little room across town . . .

And now?

Calm in the room, suddenly. Little pieces of history moving out of the shadows. Berlin – where she had brought her memories.

'Alison?'
  'Yes?'
  'My God, I can hardly believe this ...'
  'I know.'
  'You sound exactly the same ...'
  'I haven't said anything ...'
  'But you do .....'
  'What ....sound like a silly student, you mean?'
  'Never that ... I don't know what to say ... am I going to have to
beg to see you?'
  She laughed. 'I might like that. Do you want to see me?'
  'D'you need to ask?'
  'We could go on throwing questions at each other all night.'
  'Is that a formal proposal?'
  'David, I'll see you in the morning, OK?'
  'Breakfast here is at seven ...'
  'I'm not sure ...'
  'I could have you forcibly detained.'
  She smiled at the phone. 'All right.'
  'You can bring your chaperone. But I don't bite in the mornings.'
  She knew all about his mornings. 'Goodnight, David.'
  'I'm glad you called.'

Only why had she called? He sat still for a long time, repeating each
word.
  She still fenced. Still had her edge. To Alison conversation had
always been a martial art. And she, such an elegant practitioner. It
made her attractive, sexy. She would lock on to you with her mind,
applying a little pressure here, little pressure there. It was intensely
physical.
  Now, after thirty years, she was rolling back history – a whole
lifetime – calling to see who he was. Old friend or adversary?
Business or personal? It was that simple – and that complex.

At two in the morning he telephoned Deval at home in Washington.
  'How's Jane?'

'Pissed at me because I work too hard.'

'How's Jason?'

'Asleep, thank Christ. Otherwise he'd be pissed at me as well.'

'Then work less.'

'There's a job to do, David ... and you're so fucking needy. By the way, you OK? You didn't sound so good on the plane.'

'I realise I've been a pain in the arse these last two years. Elizabeth's death hit me harder than I thought, harder than I could even admit to myself. But I feel stronger now. When I went out to Arlington, it seemed for the first time as if I could let her go. Almost as if she were telling me to let her go, and get on with being president.'

'David ... Jane wants to talk to you.'

'Put her on. I like talking to a pretty woman at night ...'

She giggled. 'And I like talking to a real man. Not the kind of animal I'm married to. What are you wearing?'

'Nothing. Can't you tell?'

'You want me to fix you up with someone?'

'Sure. You busy tonight?'

'You mean to tell me that the cast of thousands you employ can't even get hold of a couple of Frauleins. They're not trying. You should sack the whole crowd of them.'

'I intend to. Time I waved around my little wand, don't you think?'

'Depends which little wand you had in mind ...'

'Jane!'

'David!' She laughed. 'I'm a doctor, remember? I'm used to discussing these things ...'

'Are you going to bill me for this consultation?'

'Isn't that the American way?'

He paused for a moment. 'Jane what would you say if I told you I was interested in someone ... ?'

'If it isn't me, I'll tear her eyes out.'

They both laughed across the Atlantic.

'David, if you're interested in someone who you think could make you happy, I have only one thing to say to you ... go for it. You've been sad long enough. You deserve it – and you also need it. Too many nights on your own aren't healthy. And yes, this is a consultation, and yes I'll be billing you . . .'

'And what if she turns me down?'

'Am I talking to my eight-year-old son or the president of this God-fearing nation?'

'I've been out of the game a long time . . .'

'Then get back in. Who's going to turn you down?'

'The lady who just called.'

'Tomorrow's another day, honey.'

'Goodnight, Jane. Tell Harry not to work so hard.'

'Goodnight, Mr President.' She laughed softly and with evident pleasure.

Chapter Twenty-two

He didn't look much like the president of Russia, sitting on the bed in his shirt-tails and stripy underpants, scowling at the floor. All day long his energy had been flagging, through the plane journey, the buffeting by the winds, the meetings with all those extra bright diplomats Russia never knew it had . . . and finally his strength had collapsed.

Katya put on her nightgown and went over to him. She laid a hand on his forehead and felt the fever.

'You're not well. "*Ty ustal kak syem chertyay.*" You're as tired as seven devils. Sleep! Tomorrow's very important.'

'Of course, yes, how good that you reminded me. I was planning to play tennis in the morning and then take a swim in the afternoon . . . so thank God you told me.' The anger was barely controlled. It was not a tone Shilov often used with her. And then, quite suddenly, it had disappeared. He turned and gripped her hand . . . 'Katya, I'm very sorry. I don't know why I spoke like that. The journey . . . I . . . please forgive me . . .'

'Forgive you?' She smiled. 'Why should I forgive you? You're just as bad-tempered as when I first met you. Always getting drunk and apologising for it. Ahhh . . .' She put her arms round him. 'Go and bark at someone else. But if you don't go to bed, you won't be able to.'

She patted the presidential behind, and he walked stiffly into the bathroom. It was the size of a small swimming pool in Moscow. Suite of Honour or some such nonsense in the Grand Hotel. East Berlin, of course. Not that there was supposed to be a difference any more – but there always would be.

He looked round at the gold-plated taps, the Italian tiles, the crystal glasses. Ample proof that the East German authorities had been corrupt and insensitive on a massive scale – building vast, opulent hotels to impress Westerners, and making their own people stand in line for a lousy sausage. The Party had had it coming.

Only, what a legacy! Half-empty, overpriced guest houses – and a few thousand nuclear missiles, being squabbled over for ownership. And now they came to Berlin, not as proud possessors of the largest country in the world, but a selection of bankrupt bureaucracies, begging bowls outstretched to the British and Americans.

Christ, it was humiliating!

He splashed cold water on his face, and stared at the mirror.

Time was when he too had been a good and faithful Party member. Hardly something to be proud of. Hardly something to shout about, either.

All those years reciting nonsensical claptrap about the proletariat, and the victory of socialism. He was as much to blame as anyone else, wasn't he?

And yet, you couldn't fight the Party from the outside. Gorbachev had known that. You had to take it over and destroy its entrails from within.

Only now there were other dangers ...

'Come to bed for God's sake ...' he could hear Katya calling from the bedroom. 'Stop daydreaming.'

He shuffled back to the room and got into bed beside her.

'Did you read the report I gave you?'

In the darkness she turned towards him. 'You mean the shooting at the missile silo? Yes, of course ...'

'I'm amazed Klimak had the nerve to come here. He blatantly attacks one of our nuclear installations, claims it's his, and refuses to allow medical care for the wounded ...'

'That's merely his negotiating position. He would obviously try to seize some advantage before the talks. I had expected something like that.'

'But I have to respond. Don't you see? I have to send reinforcements. If I'm seen to be weak, then my position at home becomes even more dangerous. I have very little room for manoeuvre.'

'Wait a day. This will all come out in the conference.'

An hour must have passed, maybe more, when something woke Katya and she sat up in bed, wondering where he was, seeing his silhouette by the window.

The pale streetlamps led all the way down to Unter Den Linden.

Cars were swishing past in the light rain. Berlin, still alive in the darkness.

'What is it, my dear?'

He smiled and pulled her close. 'You know what I'd like? Now – this minute. Just to go for a walk – the two of us. Take a look at the Brandenburg Gate without the people there. I know we've seen it in the ceremonies, we passed it in the motorcade. But just to stand and stare at it for a few minutes. You and me. Is that so much to ask?'

'Yes.' She ran a hand over his face. 'Much too much. You wanted to walk on different streets, the secret ones, the dark ones, the ceremonial ones. You wanted big fanfares and television cameras. You wanted people to listen when you speak. There's a price for all that.'

'No more midnight walks?' He shook his head. 'When we were students we used to walk half way across Moscow in the rain, or the snow. We used to pass the Lubyanka in terrible fear, thinking what would happen if someone stopped us. D'you remember the day, a man came out and told us – we should get away from the building and quickly, and it would be the worse for us if we didn't ... D'you remember that? You didn't stop shaking for three hours.'

'It was like living in a minefield. We never knew when we might make a mistake – an unguarded word, a joke. How many times did we lose our friends because an unknown informer had reported something. My God ... when you think back, Dmitry. Whatever problems we face now ... it has to be better than the way it was. And to have a revolution without blood? This is something so extraordinary, for us, for Russians ...'

'You're right, of course you're right ... but I wish sometimes we were different people. I wish that we didn't have to create with one hand and destroy with the other. Always this has been our pattern. All through history.' He put both arms around her and gripped her tightly. 'You know something ... I don't believe in revolutions without blood. Oh yes, the communist party is dead, Gorbachev resigned, the Soviet Union is like a black hole in the history of the world – but the blood will flow again. You saw what happened with our parliament. Maybe in drips, like the rain, or the patter of a tiny stream, but in the end there will be a river, and rivers flow into seas with their waves sweeping over our country . . .'

'Stop . . . stop . . .' She could feel him shaking. 'It won't be like that. Not this time. This is different. Civilization has moved on. The other countries will help us. Never again, Dmitry. Never again.'

Katya got him back to bed and held him tightly beneath the blankets, and then she moved her hand up under his pillow and touched cold steel. Without hesitating she clicked on the light and stared at the small, black automatic pistol.

'What the . . . ?' he turned round, blinded for a moment by the bedside lamp. Then he saw what was in her hand.

'Put it away, Katya, and go to sleep.'

'Why did you bring this?'

'Why did I bring this . . . you know why I brought it. Look at the people around us. What have we been talking about? Our history, the violence . . .'

'There is a whole army out there to protect you . . . bodyguards, KGB, police . . .'

'And one night a man may come through them all, past the guards, through the security, and he may open this door and stand looking down at us. What then? Do I throw a pillow at him and say my prayers . . . ?'

'It can't happen.'

'That's what Julius Caesar thought.'

'It won't happen. Please get rid of it, Dmitry. I'm serious. Give it to security. Trust me.'

'I need . . .' But he caught the expression in her eyes and knew he couldn't refuse her. In all the forty years they had known each other he hadn't been able to say no. Not when she really wanted something. Not when she knew she was right .. '

'All right, all right. I'll do as you say. Now go to sleep and let me do the same.'

He turned off the light and listened to the rhythm of her breathing. After a while it became slower and deeper and he knew she was sleeping. Katya had always possessed such wisdom. She had saved him so many times when his temper got the better of him, when he would have alienated his friends, when he was unable to see the way forward. She had been the powerful one. Her intelligence and her intuition, married to each other, had made for an unbeatable combination.

Only this time he knew she was wrong.

Chukovsky had watched three people die. Friends, hit in a convoy that had come under attack in Afghanistan. And it hadn't really struck him until much later. So much had been going on – the scramble to the field hospital, the shouts and instructions, the hard committed faces of the surgeons fighting death on its own ground, body by body. That is hot death, he thought – where you die in a hurry, in uniform, for a cause. And everything that can be done *is* done.

Not like now. Not like the captain – stretched out, quiet, motionless on the floor of a missile silo, seventy metres below ground. No assistance. No flurry. Cut off from the world and now, clearly, about to depart it. That would be a cold death. The worst kind.

Chukovsky could still feel a pulse, weak and hesitant. He and Volodya had managed to stop the bleeding. But there was no more they could do. Their communications with the other silos were down. Even the ground-wave emergency network was inoperative, or perhaps, he thought wryly, had never worked at all.

Now the three of them were at the bottom of the silo, out of contact, probably surrounded by half the fucking Ukrainian army. And who was coming to their rescue? Who even knew about them? What the the hell did it matter to anyone if the Captain lived or died?

Only it mattered to him.

'Colonel, you should eat something.' Volodya appeared with a bowl of stew.

'What time is it?'

'Seven.'

'Is that morning or evening?'

Volodya laughed without humour. 'Morning, I think. Here,' he handed Chukovsky a spoon, 'it's not bad. A lot better than my mother used to make.'

'Doesn't say much in this country.' He went over to the captain and checked his temperature, and listened to his heart. They had given him shots of antibiotics, and tried to get him to swallow some water. Thank God, he was unconscious. At least he was out of pain. And if he had been awake, what could they have said to him? 'We're doing all we can. Don't worry, comrade. Help is at hand.'

He sat at the main console and ate the stew. You lost all sense of time below ground. But there were some things, he thought, that you could see with greater clarity. Like the sense of futility, the waste of the captain's life.

Not that he had known him well. They'd only met each other a couple of months ago. And yet there was something about him that he'd admired. Sure, he was brash and loud, and couldn't wait to finish his two years in the army, to get out and make some money.

But he was different from many of the Russians. He didn't just sit moaning about the prices in the shops, he had schemes and dreams. Each day seemed to bring a new one. Big talk. Wild talk. Fifty projects a second. And although most of them would be forgotten the day after, it was exhilarating to listen. The future meant a goal, an event, achievements – not a tragedy waiting to happen.

Russia needed people like that, if it was ever to climb out of the hole it had dug itself.

Chukovsky felt the anger rising inside him. Why should a man like that have to die, in some stupid, pointless confrontation? And if he died, how many others would die, and how would the youth of Russia ever realise its dreams? It seemed to him that the Captain was a symbol of the future they *could* have. And he went over and knelt beside him ... 'Don't die, young friend,' he whispered, 'don't die. We'll find a way. You have to go on living. You must.'

At the console he could see Volodya fiddling with wires and switches, a metal plate had been removed from the installation.

'What's going on?'

'Checking the communications.' Volodya put down his screwdriver. Instead of the usual blank indifference, his face showed genuine puzzlement. 'I can't quite work out why no one is replying to our signal.'

'Because we aren't sending one. That's why. Our own transmitter is fucked. You said so yourself, an hour ago. '

'That's the point.' Volodya shook his head. 'It isn't fucked. We're sending fine. We're even receiving.' He turned a dial. 'Listen to this.' And suddenly the tinny voice of Moscow radio filled the room. A woman's voice, clear and well-modulated, discussing the opening of a new play.

'I don't get it.' Chukovsky slumped in the chair. 'Why don't they check in with us. Brigade headquarters are supposed to signal every three hours to make sure we're on line.'

Volodya picked up the metal plate and screwed it back into the console. 'They don't want to know,' he said casually. 'For some reason,' he raised his eyebrows and sighed, 'they just don't want to know. Isn't that a scary thought, Colonel?'

Chukovsky shook his head. 'It wasn't till you mentioned it.'

Chapter Twenty-three

She awoke in a hurry. Hungry, but not wanting food. Her throat dry, but not thirsty. She could feel the sensation of a storm building from a long way, away.

Alison, you wanted this day for so long. What will you do with it?

She chose a dark skirt and crimson jacket. Red for action. Red because it was urgent and immediate. Red – to camouflage the blushes. She took a gold link necklace that Dad had given her when she'd come out of hospital, and a signet ring from Mum. And now you're on your own . . .

In the office suite, Foster was skimming through the traffic from London, the Press summaries, the transcripts of the late night news programmes. A garden room girl was taking notes.

'You'll have to give some interviews this afternoon, Prime Minister.' He was jotting notes on a pad, trying to get what he called 'an armlock' on the day ahead. 'Got to hit the evening bulletins. As you see, we're mostly on the inside pages and quite a long way down the TV running order. But we'll build on that. Since this is your first Foreign, we're going to make you 'super stateswoman' today. Start pushing a few themes. Perhaps it's something you and Bradley can agree on. Remember he'll be getting quite a bit of coverage from our lot, as well. Can't be seen to lag behind. No sudden initiatives that we haven't been told about. No rug being pulled from under our feet. Americans are good at that . . .'

He rambled on, crumbs from his toast cascading over the blue worsted trousers, mouth awash with ideas and coffee.

She heard most of it, forcing herself to concentrate, forcing the past out of her mind, willing the present to take its place. Power and responsibility. That's all there was to think about. The reason she'd been chosen. The reason for doing the job. The same discipline that had made her get out of a wheelchair thirty years ago and walk – that's what would see her through. What was she expecting from this meeting, from David Bradley? Nothing, she told herself. Nothing at all. She shut her eyes for a moment. I wish that were true.

Quickly out of the car, into the hotel lobby. One deep breath and just do it. Foster struggling to keep up. A wave from a familiar figure. Ignore it. Christ, it was the Italian prime minister! Too late, you're in the lift now, secret service escort . . .

And then she reminded herself . . . It's only David. A boy you once knew. Just a boy . .

On the presidential floor the morning rush hour was breaking around them, the quick and the late, the paper carriers, the shouters, the orderers, the deciders. Everywhere she looked the place was running on coffee in plastic cups.

A plain white door opened into a crowded room and she stood there, not hearing the noise, searching the faces. It wasn't the man in the White House photos, or the magazines, that caught her attention, but the voice that had never changed or varied. A quiet voice for a president, quiet for a military commander. But a voice that could carry endlessly across time. If you shut your eyes for just a moment, she thought, then the years in between might never have happened.

'David . . .' In the few steps it took him to reach her, she saw only the smile of honour . . .

'Prime Minister,' he took her hand. The room stopped talking.

She could feel the instant warmth, the strength behind it, always so open, so approachable, always touching and holding . . . And the sheer size of this gentle giant. 'You're like a house.' She could hear her own voice, laughing the words on a summer afternoon decades ago. Sounds from another time, the stirring of a wind.

He was saying something else, but she couldn't hear him.

I know why it happened, she thought suddenly. I wondered if I'd stare at him and ask myself . . . .was this the man I knew? But I don't. I know him. An old face is like an old map, drawn long ago. The landmarks don't change . . . it's all still there . . .

She hardly saw the other people, other hands shook hers, and David was leading her down the row of food, the silver trays, the fruits and rolls and scrambled egg . . .

Clear your thoughts, she told herself suddenly. Otherwise you'll be the breakfast . . .

For a moment, she seemed to lose her balance, but his hand was there, solid beneath her arm, and the smile never wavered, or the words of welcome, the constant stream of introductions.

They sat on sofas – all so deceptive, she thought. So low-key, almost casual. And yet each of us is like a guard dog. At any moment we can bare our teeth and fight to protect what's ours. Till then we're happy enough to jump up and lick each other's faces.

She looked down the row at the American Cabinet. Americans are very focused and very organised. When they sit at a table, it's expected there'll be a winner and a loser. And they don't play for the fun of it . . . all this he had told her so many years ago.

Think hard, Alison. Take it point by point. She could feel her concentration returning.

Norton was speaking, laying out the American position, sur-rounded by coffee cups and yellow pads and hangers on . . .

And David was watching from the sidelines.

It was a standard American approach. They set out their points as if everyone else had already agreed them, and twice she was forced to interject, to clarify, to diverge . . .

His eyes never seemed to leave her . . .

The talk was sharp and detailed. Thank God she had read all the briefs, thank God for Foster, thank God for . . . the man sitting at the end of the table . . .

And then Norton came down to the bottom line.

'OK, this is our position. We're not about to get involved in this dispute. No peacekeeping between Russia and Ukraine. No green line. No troops. Period. We tried that in Yugoslavia, we've tried it in lots of places since the cold war. Doesn't work, and no one thanks you for it. We're here to offer assistance if they can sort out their problems – or take it away if they can't. That simple.'

'We look at it differently,' Alison shifted on the sofa.

'And what way is that?' Norton threw a look at the president, but the president ignored him. He drained a glass of orange juice. 'Prime Minister, would you care to share your thoughts with us.'

'We have a lot of thoughts. And a lot of facts,' she looked straight at Bradley. 'Money, straight money, aid, handouts, whatever you want to call it – none of it buys stability or democracy. Never has done. Not in any of the regions it's been tried. And especially not here. We can threaten them with cutting off aid from now until Christmas – and it won't make the slightest difference. These people have their own agenda, which has nothing to do with putting food in the shops or balance of payments – or any of the things that get us voted into office . . .' she smiled, . . . 'or out.'

'What then?' Norton grimaced across the coffee table.

'Pride. Honour. Power. It's trying to persuade these people that their ultimate interest lies in peaceful relations with each other . . .'

'And the best incentive for that is the dollar. We *buy* their co-operation. That's the language they understand.'

'Wrong . . .' she could see Bradley begin to smile. He was enjoying the argument. 'Oh, they understand what dollars are. They'll take all you've got. And it may change what they eat, or what they drive around in, but not the way they think . . . '

'So what will?'

'Diplomacy, cunning, understanding.'

Norton pushed away his cup. 'Sounds pretty damn wet to me.'

He looked towards Bradley for support. But the president seemed deep in thought, a thin smile was threatening to appear at the edge of his mouth.

'I think we have to listen very carefully. We're not dealing with rational people. We're not dealing with people who grew up with good educations and plenty of liberal thinking. We're dealing with very biased, ultra conservative old foxes, who still think they can play small town politics, and use their missiles when things get tough. It's very tense . . .'

'I'm sure we're grateful for you bringing that to our attention,' Norton let out a sigh. 'You Brits . . . you always look at it from too many sides. We need some clear thinking here, not a dopey kind of wishy-washy approach . . .'

'Mine isn't.'

'The hell it isn't.' Norton laughed hollowly. 'We got enough talk-shops around the world. We don't need the British Labour Party opening up another. I seem to remember you guys would have given the missiles away to the Soviets years ago. So don't lecture me . . .'

'Clark . . .' The president's fist descended in a straight, conclusive line, and came to rest on the coffee table. 'That's enough, Clark. I think you should apologise to the prime minister …'

'What the … ?'

'You seem to have gotten carried away. Your language was undiplomatic.' The room had grown very quiet. It was unheard of for a president to rebuke a senior adviser in front of the Cabinet, let alone a foreign leader.

Alison sat up … 'I'm sure no offence was intended. I certainly took none. Please continue, Mr Secretary … .'

Norton opened his mouth and hesitated … 'I   .. I regret if I upset anyone. I merely wished to make a point.' He looked Bradley straight in the eye and stood up. 'Excuse me. I have some important arrangements to make before the conference gets underway.'

Bradley poured himself another orange juice and waited till Norton had left. 'That's it, ladies and gentlemen, thank you. We'll stop here for now.'

The Cabinet and their advisers shuffled out. Foster threw Alison a raised eyebrow, as if to ask … 'D'you want me to hang around?' She shook her head. And then quite suddenly a palpable feeling of rage burst inside her …

Not only had David embarrassed his own staff, he'd stepped into a battle she could easily have fought for herself. Fought *and* won. Damn, damn him! She didn't need his intervention. His patronage. Or his help.

He closed the door and turned to face her, seeing the anger alive in her eyes.

'Alison …' Take it slow, for something is terribly wrong.

'I appreciate your help out there. But I can look after myself …' Slowly, she says it, each word stressed.

'Alison.'

'What?'

'We haven't seen each other for thirty years. Do we have to start like this? I'd have said the same thing if it had been the chambermaid in there. Norton was rude and boorish. I won't tolerate that kind of behaviour …'

'You were patronising me. This is business. What you did was personal …'

'Alison, please sit down …' He tries to smile, but he can see the fury, taste it …

'This can't happen again. It was totally unacceptable. The past is past. We have jobs to do. There's no sign we're going to agree on anything at all . . .'

'Wait a minute!'

'What for?' And the anger is there, coloured on her face, white hot, stored for years.

'I don't understand why you're upset.'

'Then you don't understand anything.'

'Tell me!'

'I . . . I couldn't even begin.'

'Listen to me. For thirty years I've been asking myself . . .'

'Leave it,' the voice is cracking at the edges. And now for the first time there is almost unbelievable pain in the face. 'I don't want to open this box and nor do you. You should apologise to me and to Norton.'

'What I say to my Cabinet is my affair . . .'

Her mouth closes very tight. Bradley can feel her slipping away.

He tries a final plea. 'You're acting as if we're strangers, for Chrissake.'

'That's exactly what we are. So leave it at that.'

'I have to talk to you.'

She turns and moves away. 'Goodbye, David.' And the anger has gone, replaced by something much worse, indifference, ice-cold.

Her back is already turned, her body through into the doorway, legs in black stockings leading her to the lift.'

Christ, Jesus. I don't believe this.

As he stands there alone, shock and disappointment crowd into the room beside him.

'I haven't felt so insulted in my entire career.'

Cliff Till considered the secretary of state's words with some scepticism. Norton was a tough, old-style campaigner. He belonged to the backbone of the GOP. Floated around for years with the highest of the high. Dinners at the White House, trips and Martinis on Air Force One, all the badges, T-shirts and pens he could want. A lifetime of politics that would have taught him how to kick and be kicked. And yet the public dressing down of a Cabinet member in front of a foreign leader – that had to be close to a first.

'Well, there are two ways you can handle this.' Till blew out his cheeks.

'Continue.'

'Stay or go.'

Norton moved his lips in the kind of mechanical gesture, often associated with a smile. And yet there was nothing even remotely friendly, happy, or contented about it.

'I'll take the third option.' He stood up. The decision was made. As far as he was concerned, Bradley was for the cooking pot.

Chapter Twenty-four

The hurt came back to him.

Like the time she had once scorned him in Oxford. The day he thought he'd lost her.

They had gone to see *Clockwork Orange*, which he hadn't enjoyed. She, by contrast, had loved it.

In the pub opposite the cinema she raved on about the symbolism, the double meanings, art.

'I thought it was pretentious crap,' he said and instantly regretted it. He could still see her face tighten, see her flounce up from the table, pushing her way out of the crowded bar, him following, people looking round ...

'What's going on?' He had caught up with her on the street corner.

'I want a walk. I don't want to discuss it any more, OK?'

'You can't walk on your own. It's late.'

'I'll do what I bloody well want.'

She caught a bus into the town centre and he stood watching the vehicle lights rock away down Hedington Hill into the darkness.

At midnight, he was looking out of the bedsit window, in the terrace off the Cowley Road. No one knew they stayed together. She always said her parents would disapprove if they found out. So she kept on her room in College. Kept up appearances.

At 1.30 she turned the corner at the bottom of the road, and he hid behind the curtains hoping she hadn't seen his face and the concern that was stamped all over it.

'What happened?'

'Let's just go to sleep.'

She had turned her back to him, but he moved close in, his arms tight around her.

'Take no notice of me.'

'Difficult when you share my bed.'

'I expect too much. I've no right ...'

'Did it matter ... what I said about the movie?'

'Yes. No – it just shakes me when we don't think the same about things. I'm used to us sharing things. And then something like this happens and I start to have doubts.' She put a hand on his arm. 'Just forget it.'

Only you never do, Bradley recalled. Even with all they'd had, Alison was like walking on a glacier. There was always a chance the ice would crack.

He looked out of the window over Berlin, recalling the student in the bedsit off the Cowley Road. There was no way of knowing if, this time, she'd come back.

At his disposal was all the power the world had on offer. He could destroy markets, start wars, summon anyone he wanted. He had only to command and the genie would deliver. Anyone, that is, except Alison Lane.

'Prime Minister, the BBC are here for the interview.'

'I'm not doing the interview.'

'I'm sorry, Prime Minister, I don't quite understand. We *agreed* to it this morning. It's very important we put across our position.'

'You do it then. Something just came up. Do I have to tell you how to do the bloody job?'

'We need to make an impact on the main news tonight.'

'Then dream up another way. I'm not doing the fucking interview. Is that clear enough?'

Foster retreated in a hurry.

It didn't take much, she thought. Just a trigger. A hair's pressure and the control had gone. All the mental reconstruction of thirty years. Collapsed.

She breathed deeply, trying to make her thoughts stand still. How is it that he can do this to me? Why can David Bradley reduce me to behaving like a wounded animal?

She went over to her dresser and looked for a handkerchief. Her face was wet. Wet! She went into the bathroom and stared into the mirror. Tears had mixed in with the makeup.

'I don't know what's happening to me ...'

She rubbed her face with a towel and repaired the damage. There hadn't been any tears for a quarter of a century. This wasn't the day to start again.

Chapter Twenty-five

'Sir Henry.'

'My dear.'

The head of British counter-intelligence hadn't announced his arrival in advance, never did, never would. Simply turned up in Downing Street or Berlin or countless other places, when he wanted. And you don't say no to this man – not unless you feel yourself in a stronger position that most of the British prime ministers this century.

He perched his black-striped bottom on the coffee table.

'I thought I'd better bring this in person. It's a report from our ambassador here.' He got up and handed her a few sheets of paper from his pocket. 'There's no file – no numbers. You'll see why.'

She read the document through and handed it back.

'I have to let him read it, Sir Henry'.

'That wouldn't be clever.'

'He's ...'

'President of a foreign power.'

'An ally. The most important one we have.'

'Of course he's an ally. Insofar as there are allies these days. But he's also the leader of a country, that we know to be conducting industrial espionage on our soil, that we know to be attempting to put some of our companies out of business in the Far East, so that their own can take over, that deliberately withholds ...'

'And we're not?' Alison felt involuntary anger.

'You read the reports ...'

'Those you show me. What about those you don't?'

He looked away. 'We've known each other a long time, Alison.'

'That's not always a good thing.'

'This is background, my dear. An example of gross disloyalty from one of the president's closest colleagues. All right, his secretary of state. It's appalling, it's unpleasant, but it's standard politics. Nothing more. The reason I thought you should see it, is in case there's some impact on the summit. If you want my opinion – it could be useful in the future.'

'I see. You want to keep your options open.'

'I don't want to blow our sources, either our man here in Berlin – or Norton himself. There's our own interest to consider, beyond any notions of . . . how shall I put it, friendship between nations.'

'You wouldn't mind an operation against the Russians, would you?'

'I didn't say that.'

'You never *say* anything, Sir Henry. But you might want to leave open the possibility that it could be useful to your interests.'

'To our interests, Alison. To the National Interest . .'

'As you see it.'

'That is the duty I'm empowered to perform.'

She paused for a moment. 'I take your point . . .'

'Let me make a point about allies, my dear. They're always more trouble than enemies. Our problem is remembering which lie we've told to whom. And as far as the Americans are concerned, we really don't count for much these days. We need them a lot more than they need us. Their weapons, their intelligence, the satellites . . .'

'All the more reason to buy some credit.'

He smiled. 'All the more reason to exploit whatever leverage we have. Let's make sure we get the best price for our goods . . . your decision of course . . .'

'I said – I take your point. It's bad enough to be a Labour prime minister, dealing with a Republican president. We're not exactly natural allies . . .'

'I wouldn't say that . . .'

'Then you exceed yourself . . .'

He got to his feet. 'In that case, I apologise, Prime Minister . . .'

Alison turned away towards the window. 'Have no doubt that if it comes to a choice between my past friendship with David Bradley and my duty to this country – my duty will be paramount. I hope that's understood.'

'Perfectly.'

Sir Henry slept badly on the flight from Berlin, his mind turning new circles. He didn't need to be told that Alison had already seen

David Bradley – nor that the meeting had gone badly.

Even so, she had surprised him. The new edge in her authority. She was sharper, more combative. For years he had thought he controlled her, politically, even emotionally. Now he couldn't be sure. Her rebuke had caught him off guard.

And yet it emphasised something he had known all along – that power was nothing more than a matter of perception. You didn't need to prove it. Rarely if ever did you need to use it. The trick was in persuading people you had more than them.

Alison was trying that trick for herself, and when it came down to the wire, who controlled whom?

By the time he reached it, the house in Holland Park was in darkness and his wife had gone to bed, leaving a plate of cold meat on the kitchen table.

Sir Henry ate thoughtfully, scooped himself two wedges of Stilton from the sideboard, and sent it down with a brandy and ginger ale.

It had been his nightcap for years – his routine. Often the one constant in a life of shifting lines and allegiances.

And yet there was a strange contrast between his professional and personal lives. At home there had always been Wendy and *her* routine, her sessions as a magistrate, her concerts and the dinner parties she gave for her friends.

Although they still slept in the same bed, they had shared no intimacy for years. Neither of them missed it. They had simply moved on. Life was cushioned and comfortable. They were companions, talking to each other, sharing four walls, friendly but conspicuously unaffectionate. They had tiptoed away from their sexuality. She wouldn't come in when he was in the bath, he would stay outside while she dressed. After a while, if you didn't look, it wasn't there.

Which was perhaps why he had failed to anticipate the changes in Alison Lane.

Sir Henry had never possessed knowledge of a searing and urgent relationship. He knew all about manipulation. He knew about Swallows and sexual tempting. But the process by which two human beings can eat out their hearts in the search for one another – this was closed territory. Unfamiliar, and in his case, largely unexplored. He had no idea how an old and powerful liaison could drastically alter a person's outlook.

Alison had said that if it came to a choice between duty and David Bradley – the duty would hold sway.

How could he be sure?

He recalled her face in Berlin, flushed, motivated . . . moved. Yes, that was it – moved, the way he hadn't seen it for years.

How could she be sure, either?

In the darkness of the bedroom Alison stretched out her feet, as if to make certain there was no one beside her.

Tonight, she thought, as every night, the British prime minister tucks herself up, kisses and hugs herself, tells herself how well she's done and goes to bloody sleep.

'That's it. What did you expect?'

'I didn't expect anything.'

The conversation began way down inside her.

'If you didn't – why the big fuss? The great buildup? Mm?'

'I thought if I saw him again, I could let it lie, finally, bury it, once and for all.'

'And can you?'

'I want to. I tried earlier . . .'

'Can you?'

'I have to . . .'

'*Can . . . you?*'

'I don't know.'

Only then did the voices quieten and let her sleep.

Chapter Twenty-six

'So you want me to return to Washington, Mr President?'

'It would be best, Clark. Under the circumstances. You can announce a new initiative on the Far East talks if you wish. But I want you out of here.'

'May I ask why?'

'That should be obvious. Your comments to the prime minister were really quite offensive. They displayed the kind of inflexibility we've been trying to move away from.'

'I'm sorry you felt that way. If you wish me to offer my . . .'

'We'll talk when I come back, Clark.'

'Of course, Mr President.'

Norton chuckled to himself and relaxed as the Atlantic flowed beneath him. The more distance between him and the President the better he felt. He knew he'd sailed pretty near to the storm, but he didn't think Bradley would fire him. That would upset the right wing of the Party, and Bradley wasn't strong enough for that. No – it had gone just right. He'd keep away from the White House, but stay close enough to gather some dirt. That was the object now.

He shut his eyes and replayed the conversation. It was typical of the slide at the top. Bradley was a sap. If you couldn't speak your mind to the fucking allies – who could you speak it to? It wasn't even as if Britain counted for anything these days.

Weakness. Indecision. Those were the hallmarks. Maybe it was time for a gentle word with the approachable Harry Deval. Maybe he too was fed up with Bradley. Maybe he had his own ambitions. It would be worth finding out.

The stewardess arrived with lunch and Norton smiled down at the plastic tray and the fruits of a first class meal. He stuck a fork into the smoked salmon and rolled it around his mouth.

How nice that Harry had fixed things up, after that little affair he'd been so careful to hide. Of course it was stupid to get involved in the first place.

Norton shuddered for a moment at the thought of what would happen to him in similar circumstances. Darlene had told him she'd cut it off with a rusty knife if she ever caught him at it. And he believed her. Darlene was like that. Led with her mouth, and the rest of her tended to follow. She didn't threaten for fun.

But Harry, well Harry had been really dumb. Dumb to do it and dumb to shit on his own doorstep. Of course the lady had needed some comfort when it all ended. Ladies were like that. She had really needed to talk to someone. And so the little word had spread, as words so often do around buildings, and closed communities.

And in the way of these things the little word had eventually come to him. Not to be used, of course, but to be filed away as part of that Washington compendium of useful facts that you keep close by you for quick and easy reference.

His father had taught him that. Keep good records. Always keep records.

Norton smiled at the memory. His father had died six years earlier, but not before he had destroyed the records that could have gotten him indicted by a grand jury. Records about his dealings as a long-time Washington lobbyist. Records of the receipts and the payouts. Records of the famous people he had made rich. And the riches he himself had acquired.

Records were all very well, until the day someone else saw them.

Harry Deval would find that out.

Chapter Twenty-seven

A long line of BMWs and Jaguars stretched up Whitehaven Parkway towards St Patrick's – the Episcopal day school and parking lot for the children of north-west Washington.

Harry could see a senator from South Dakota gesticulating into his carphone. Young blonde mothers stood outside chatting in designer sweats, hairbands. What did they find to talk about? It wasn't as if they ever did anything. Washington's houses and gardens were tended by armies of central Americans and Filipinos – most illegal. The actual owners barely took off their gloves, except to sign cheques.

These days, of course, it was PC for mothers to stay home with their kids. Ten years ago they'd have been social outcasts without a salary. No salary. No status. No one to talk to at cocktail parties. Now all it took were a few medical studies, and the stay-home mums got rehabilitated ...

Washington and its fashions.

Jason was at the back of the homecomers, tall for his age, his jeans half way down his bottom, shirt out. Harry thought he looked like a businessman after too much dictation with his secretary, but he wasn't going to tell him that.

He opened the car door and handed him a tuna sandwich. There'd be no point in conversation until the boy had eaten. God knows what they did to them at the school. Their blood sugar levels were zero by the end of the day.

They turned off MacArthur Boulevard, through Foxhall, towards the American University.

'Where's Mum?'

'Working.'

'What?'

'She's a doctor, remember? You guys should talk more ...'

'I know that ...' Jason dropped a blob of tuna on the seat, hoping Harry hadn't seen it.

'Remind me to bring a towel next time.' He grinned at the boy.

'Look, Dad . . . it's just that Mum usually comes on a Friday. You never come . . .'

'I come sometimes.'

'Bull . . .' Jason stopped himself just in time.

Harry was about to rebuke the boy but he changed his mind. They saw each other so little, the last thing he wanted was a fight. He'd start shouting, Jason would clam right up, and they'd sit in Pizza Hut like an old married couple, not saying a word.

'How was the sandwich?'

'Fine.'

'You still hungry?'

'Sure.'

At least there were some certainties left in life.

They drove to the Cheesecake Factory in Chevy Chase. Harry ordered a hamburger and fries, Jason chose salad.

'What's with this salad?'

'Cholesterol, Dad.'

'I don't believe what I'm hearing. Sounds like a bad TV ad.'

'No really. You have to watch that. Mum said so . . .'

Harry folded his arms. And people thought the White House was tough. 'I'll think about it.'

Jason smiled. Like his mother he had the knack of knowing when he'd won.

The bill came and the boy leaned his head on Harry's arm.

I'd pay for moments like this, he thought . . . I swear there are times when I could tell David I'm finished. I'm done with the intrigue, gonna stay home.

And then he saw her, saw the hair, saw the profile, the same profile that he'd held and hugged and watched in the semi-darkness. She was sitting in an alcove table and an electric jolt seemed to be stabbing at Harry's chest, his hands and jaw frozen, his life in his throat.

'Dad . . .'

She was talking to a man, in blazer and green pullover and the worst thing of all was that he knew him too.

A journalist from the White House Press corps. Investigative type. Little digger, little ferret, little rat. The worst.

'Dad, are we going?'

They were sitting so comfortably. Warm and happy. Coffees and Danishes on the table in front of them.

And she was talking away, nineteen to the fucking dozen. And he was listening.

They had cleared away dinner and the television was fighting for dominance. Jane punched the remote and switched it off.

'What's up, Harry?'

'I worry about everything.'

'Why?'

''Cos everything's fucked up. All kinds of strange things going on.'

'Like what?'

'You don't want to know.'

'I'm your wife ...'

'That's why you don't want to know. If I had the choice I wouldn't want to know either.'

She stretched a hand out to his arm. 'I could help.'

'I wish that was true.'

It must have been three when the phone rang. He had it instantly in his hand. Christ Jesus, who the hell ... ? If it was her calling ... But the voice wanted Jane. It was the intern at Sibley Hospital. Jane gave some instructions, asked some questions. Harry could hear the names of drugs, doses, checks every fifteen minutes. Someone was having a far worse night than him. She hung up and lay down again, facing the wall.

'Is the patient gonna live?'

'For a while.'

'Doesn't sound very optimistic.'

She turned towards him. 'Never is, Harry. Not in this job.'

Chapter Twenty-eight

Way back in the seventies Ruth Bradley was said to have 'electrocuted' Kansas City.

That was the view of the exclusive Women's club she set up, and the deputy chairwoman – a lady with no less a name than Champagne Tripp – who had meant to say 'electrified', but was too far gone to notice.

The occasion had been the club's gala dinner, one summer evening in the Hilton Hotel and a Tribute to Mrs Bradley's skill and leadership.

'You have done for women,' Champagne had smiled down from the podium, 'what Werner Von Braun did for rockets. Put us in orbit – where we can't get kicked around any longer.'

Mrs Bradley cringed deep down in her soul. God, the woman was an embarrassment. Drunk out of her mind and ludicrous with it.

All these years later she could remember the stupid sequins groping across her yellow frock, her bosom pouring out like some creamy trifle and the piggy eyes, questing for a suitable male to take her home.

'Anything with three good legs,' Champagne would declare to anyone who was listening, and collapse in squeals of laughter.

The rule was that members could invite husbands or boyfriends – or neither. And a smattering of docile, compliant tuxedos would sit through the evening, grinning and hating it. But, mostly, the women came by themselves. After all the club was about female bonding, 'fellowshipping' – women with an identity of their own and nothing to lose but their men.

At least, Mrs Bradley reflected, it had filled up the years – or part of them. Filled the place that an interested and involved husband might otherwise have occupied.

When she thought back, the club had lasted no more than five or six years. People had married and moved away, married again and moved somewhere else. It had been an effort just to update the mailing list.

Take Champagne Tripp herself. She had used husbands the way most people used airline upgrades. Everytime she got a new one – the seat improved. 'Never marry for money, honey,' she would always say. 'Marry where money *is*.'

Somehow though, they never completely lost touch. Champagne was incapable of forgetting a birthday, an anniversary, even a mother's day. Gaudy cards would arrive with absurd, outlandish inscriptions – from Santa Fe or Sausalito, or Vegas. Evidence of the winding path on to which lust, or money, had led her.

In the end, though, Mrs Bradley stopped opening the envelopes, re-directing them instead to the garbage compactor, wishing the tiresome woman would leave her in peace. Until, that is, one arrived with a Washington postmark.

What the hell was Champagne doing in DC?

She prised open the scented red envelope and looked inside. No card this time, but a lengthy, rambling scrawl over three pages, also scented, in which Champagne had detailed her latest catch.

'My dear, he's like a tiger, leaping on me all times of the day and night. I'm thinking it's safer not to bother with clothes and simply walk round the house stark naked. What a delicious idea! Would you come for the weekend???! Oh, stop it, Champagne . . .'

Mrs Bradley skipped a page of antics . . . who in God's name was this tiger?

Her eyes halted at the top of the last page . . . 'Of course, he's very well connected. Well, he would be, wouldn't he? I mean – not like David, of course, speaking of *connections* (!!!), Mrs First Mom . . .'

And there it was – three lines down. Mr Tiger ran a large and very powerful firm of Private Investigators. He was the mole inside, but more often in the street outside, Washington's number one bedrooms. He *knew* the city, biblically, biologically, scandal by scandal. Knew its fancies and foibles. He had studied that quintessential link between power and indiscretion. The high risk business – and the people who loved to play it.

That, thought Ruth Bradley, was the reason she had been thinking of Champagne Tripp. And that was why she needed her.

* * *

It took five minutes of gooey platitudes, before they could get down to business.

'I've been a little indiscreet.' Mrs Bradley coughed delicately.

'A man?'

'Well, it wouldn't be a dog, would it?'

'You mean you fucked him, honey.'

'I did not.'

'Then what does this "indiscreet" mean?' Champagne gave a little giggle.

'It means . . .' she tried again. 'It means I said some things I wasn't supposed to say.'

'Oh. That kind of indiscreet. I thought this was gonna be the fun kind.'

'Is there a fun kind?'

'You better believe it. Keeps me and my honey in . . .' she nearly said champagne, but giggled again instead, '. . . in the pink, mmm?'

'I see.'

'Now you just tell me what I can do for my old chairwoman. You know Ruth, there's nothing I wouldn't do for you. That was the club motto. And that's how I feel still. Us club girls have to stick together.'

'You're so right,' said Ruth Bradley. 'You are *so* right.'

They met the next day in the bar of the Willard Hotel. Champagne was in a pink trouser suit with a zip down to the crotch, half-opened either by strain or omission.

Mrs Bradley thought strain. No one could be that obvious.

She ordered two Bloody Marys and bounced on to the seat. By the second bounce she was already talking.

'You're in trouble, honey. This check you wanted on Pete Levinson – looks like shit on a windy day.' She removed the giant celery stick from her glass and chewed at the end. 'I got them to do this one fast. He's not a nice guy, Ruth. I think you should know that.'

'How not nice is "not nice"?'

'Big time.'

'I tried calling the number he gave me. But there isn't even an answering machine . . .'

'There isn't even a Pete Levinson . . . I'm sorry, honey.'

'What do you mean?'

'I mean that Pete Levinson is a stoodge. A reporter, by trade. He screwed up badly a few months ago, with that Pentagon story. Case of getting the wrong man. You must have heard about it?'

'I try not to read newspapers – far too depressing.'

'The reason he's a stoodge is that he's friends with one or two of the old Republican crowd. People who got thrown out in the final years of Bush – people with grudges. Plenty of grudges.'

'Go on.'

'It seems there was this plan to get even with the Party. Get at David – and more importantly, use you to do it. Levinson was told to make goo-goo eyes at you and find out any dirt he could on the president. It seems you've been pretty forthcoming. He left for London yesterday.'

Ruth Bradley shut her eyes. 'Is there anything I can do?'

'How much did you tell him?'

'I said David had once been in love with the woman who's now prime minister of Britain. I said he probably still is.'

Champagne toyed with the remains of her celery stick. 'That could be very embarrassing,' she bit off the end, 'for both of them.'

Mrs Bradley stayed at the bar longer than she'd intended. Long enough to realise that she had now divulged her secret to two people. In Washington, just one would have been lunacy. Two was suicide.

Chapter Twenty-nine

From his first-class compartment Pete Levinson stared out at the frontal depression of south London.

He hadn't been to England before, hadn't expected the desolation of terraced houses and terraced faces, as the train tore past them.

And yet it fitted in with all he'd heard. Brits didn't matter any more, didn't work, ate lousy food. They were living proof that you couldn't cash in your history. The more you had, the more it cost you.

He took out a notebook and wrote the thought down. Catchy little phrase. If he found the time maybe he'd do a colour piece on the side. 'Ignorance,' he recalled his first editor saying to him, 'ignorance is liberating. You're not restricted by facts or knowledge. You're a free man. And frankly Levinson,' he'd added, 'You're just about the freest man I ever met.'

As the train rattled on, he shook his head at the window, checked his reflection, smoothed the hair. The good thing was being free of Ruth Bradley.

She had really tied on a few at the restaurant in Washington. But she hadn't enjoyed it. There was an air of desperation about her, loneliness. Dying to talk to someone – perhaps for years. It only took a man with a suntan, and a few doses from the coloured bottles. She'd have woken up later and realised what she'd said, poor old fart. But he didn't have much choice.

That same evening he'd gone to D'Anna and told him about Alison Lane, and watched as the most ridiculous of smiles had spread itself across the man's flabby face.

'Bradley knew Lane at Oxford? You have to be kidding.'

'That's what she said.'

'What d'you mean "knew"?'

'She loved him.'

'Jesus!'

'Really loved him – that's what she said.'

Larry had begun walking up and down the room. 'This is one hell of a fucking story. What happened to them. How d'it break up?' His eyes seemed to enlarge. 'Get yourself over to England and do some checking. And Pete . . .'

'Yes, Larry.'

'I said checking. No fuck-ups on this one, 'cos your arse ain't exactly bullet-proof these days. You with me? By the way what did you have to do to get her talking, uh? A little magic-in-the-sack, uh?'

Larry was a creep. And yet Levinson was well aware he hadn't landed this assignment because of his reporting talents. In that, he'd already proved himself pitifully incompetent. D'Anna had chosen him for one reason only – he knew how to ingratiate himself with women. He was a cheap charmer – and when it came down to it, he admitted to himself, a dick for hire.

'When you come back,' D'Anna had said, 'you can pump Mrs B some more. And I mean pump.'

'Anything but that, Larry.'

'Anything, including that.'

He dozed for a while, waking as the train pulled into Brighton station. The air smelt fresh and the wind gusted him down to the seafront, blowing away the tiredness from the journey.

It was going to rain. Maybe it was always going to rain. A few tiny women were out with dogs, too cold to lift their legs . . .

As he walked along there was something one-handed about the place. What sort of major resort had two piers – one working, with lights and music, the other broken up by the sea and the storms, a mass of rusting girders, sitting just along the beach.

Why didn't they do something about it? In the States they'd have built a leisure complex, bars, a casino. Americans would never tolerate crap like this on their doorstep.

He rented a car and took the coastal road to Newhaven. The wind never stopped and the rain came and went and came again, unable to make up its mind.

When he reached the port, he made his way to the headland and walked along the harbour wall. In the distance the white cliffs rose sharply like the roof of a warehouse, and the sea went from light to dark green, as it stretched towards the horizon.

At the edge of the beach was a sprawling amusement arcade, again half-working. The tea was only half tea, the hotdog was cold and he took a diet coke because they 'wouldn't have been able to fuck that up.'

Britain, he decided, wasn't for him. No sunshine. No suntan. No buzz in the air.

Back in the car he ran a comb through the ruffled brown locks, and studied the map. It was easy. Take the coast road again, west to Saltdean. Up a hill. First house on the left. Soon be dark.

'Who is it?' The old woman's voice was barely audible behind the front door.

'I'm an American. Pete Levinson. My car broke down. I'm sorry, can I use your phone?'

He could hear her whispering.

'What's that you say?' A man's voice now, hesitant, wary.

'My car broke down. May I ... ?'

The door slid open on a chain. Levinson could see an eye looking him over. Finally it opened all the way and the two old folks were standing there, sharing a nervous smile. Didn't want to seem inhospitable. Wanted to help. But wished he hadn't come. He could see it in their gestures.

'I'm sorry to disturb you.'

'That's all right.' The lady beckoned him in. 'Cold night. Here, I've got the number of a garage.'

'Thanks so much.' Into the sitting room and he was taking it all in, the awful flowery chairs, a couple of vases, dining table ...

'The telephone's here.' The old man in the green cardigan pointed to a little table. He'd seen him looking round.

Levinson dialled. 'I think it's the fan belt. Ford Escort ... where am I?' He turned to the couple. 'I'm sorry what's the address here? Right ... uh-huh ... twenty minutes. OK.'

He hung up and turned towards them. 'They say it'll be twenty minutes.'

There was a moment of silence. They really didn't want him to hang around.

'I guess I'd better ...'

'Would you like a cup of tea, Mr ... ?' The lady smiled thinly. She couldn't bring herself to be rude. The husband glared at her.

'Pete Levinson, Mrs ... ?'

'Lane,' the smile held. 'Margaret Lane.'

He combed his hair in the bathroom and by the time he came out there was tea on the narrow kitchen table. Careful Pete.

'Milk, Mr Levinson?'

'Pete, please.' And as he looked up to answer, he could see the pictures on the cork noticeboard beside the dresser. A girl in her early twenties, standard beach picture, awkward pose, sixties hair – the crooked smile. Yes, yes! Jesus, yes ... !

'Are you on holiday, Pete?' She poured milk from a small jug.

'Just a few days. Came down this evening. You know, just on a whim.' Cool Pete. Your hands are shaking. Slow it down.

'Where are you staying?'

'Haven't thought.'

'There's the Grand in Brighton or if you're touring inland, the countryside, the White Hart in Lewes is very good. I mean the food. Rooms as well, but ...'

'I'm sorry, Mrs Lane' and the little boy blush began to seep in over his cheeks, right on command, 'but I couldn't help noticing your picture up there. It looks like a lady who's pretty much in the news right now ...'

The couple exchanged a glance.

'I mean, you said your name was Lane, after all.' You could have bottled the silence in that kitchen, he thought. Bottled and frozen it.

'Mister Levinson.' The father didn't look pleased. 'I'd thank you not to mention this to anyone. Parents are supposed to be a little bit in the background in cases like this.'

'No, no. I understand. Of course I do. I guess I just wanted to say congratulations. And, and ... you must be very proud.'

The old lady flushed. 'We are jolly proud. Aren't we Jack? It's wonderful news. I don't mind telling you that at all. And simply marvellous for the country.'

She was a stalwart – this one. No Ruth Bradley beating in her breast. Wave your whistler at this one – and she'd chop it off.

The father shifted his chair back. 'Look I don't mean to be unfriendly, but we've an early start tomorrow . . .'

'Please. I understand perfectly. It was great meeting you all.'

Mrs Lane showed him to the door, and walked a few steps down the path.

'I hope you didn't think we were unfriendly. We've always been fond of Americans. It's just this sort of thing is so new to us . . .'

'You've been very kind . . .'

'Goodbye, Pete.'

He turned to go. And this, he knew, was his last chance.

'As a matter of interest, Mrs Lane, why did you say you were fond of Americans?'

'Well, a long time ago Alison . . .'

'Margaret!' The father was standing in the doorway.

She stopped in mid-sentence, awkward suddenly, embarrassed. 'Well, goodbye then.'

Levinson raised his hand to wave and let himself out through the little garden gate.

He didn't look back, until he got to the end of the road.

And then it was that wonderful feeling, where you know you've something so special in your pocket that it's beginning to burn your nuts off. A story that would motor its way into the headlines. Christ, a real-live, prize-pinching mother of a scoop. A gift seized from heaven itself. I love you, he told himself, checking his reflection in the car mirror. I really, really love you.

Levinson just had time to open up the bonnet up and check that he'd mutilated the fan belt sufficiently, for the mechanic not to become suspicious.

'I didn't like him.'

'He was nice. Friendly. Americans are like that. You've just forgotten.'

Alison's father hadn't forgotten at all. 'Different breed this one, if you ask me. Too slimy for his own good. Surprised he didn't slip on the path.'

'Jack, that's awful.'

'I think he was snooping.'

'What on earth for?'

'Because Alison's in the public eye. That's what happens. Reporters and people like that start digging ... she warned us.'

'But how would he get the address?'

The old man sat in his favourite armchair, thinking it through. 'You hire an enquiry agent for a day. Anyone can do it. We should tell someone, just in case.'

'But Alison's in Berlin. We can't ring her there.'

'I know that.' He slumped deeper into the chair. 'Who was that friend of hers? Fellow who's now chief whip. She always spoke well of him. Harper, wasn't it?'

'You worry me with this kind of talk.'

'I'm only going to tell him what happened.'

'I don't think you should. Not without talking to Alison.'

But the old man was already looking through the diary beside the telephone, hunting for the special code that would put them through to Keith Harper, or anyone else they wanted in Downing Street.

Chapter Thirty

'You did exactly the right thing. Thanks very much.'

Keith Harper put down the phone and returned to the kitchen. Denise had cleared away his plate.

'It was all cold.' She scraped the leftovers into the bin. 'Who was that?'

'Work.'

'And how is Miss Work?'

'Don't be stupid.'

'Well, someone keeps calling all hours of the bloody day and night.' She cut the raspberry ripple into slices and gave him one. 'Not that I care.'

'It may have escaped your notice, but I am chief whip.'

'Ooh, sorry, sir, sorry, Mr Whip, I'm sure. If you ever took me to any of the parties or all these other things you go to, then maybe it *wouldn't* escape my notice.'

He couldn't answer that. Couldn't tell her he was ashamed – ashamed of the seventies dresses for sixteen-year-olds, the talk of make-up and television. The baby-doll face that now only pouted or cried.

Of course he'd loved her in the old days. She'd been pretty and lively and funny. She used to go canvassing in outfits that would have got her arrested in the fifties. She had once stretched up to kiss a baby, enabling the party manager to remark that he now knew for certain she wasn't a real blonde.

But it had all been fun and light-hearted. Denise was a cuddly, affectionate little creature, knew bugger all about politics. But backed her man, got him dressed up, got him envied, flirted and joked and played around till they elected him for her sake. The local party in Wigan loved her. She was a shocker when shockers were in. In the old days.

Wasn't her fault Alison had come along.

Wasn't his fault either.

He put the remains of the raspberry ripple in his mouth. 'I have to go out for a while.'

'Go, then. I'm not stopping you.'

Cindy Tremayne had made progress.

Not only had she passed her initial tests at the clinic, but she had passed into the affections of the Director's secretary – Miss Primp.

She it was who insisted on scheduling the most important clients. She it was, who had to be impressed.

The breakthrough had came early that evening, when Cindy had finished an appointment with the bottom-heavy Mrs Riverton-Fforde.

Rivers, as she was known in the clinic, was loaded with most things, including cellulite – but a sense of humour was not among them. So it was with considerable relief that Cindy pummelled the woman into silence, rubbed her down like an old carthorse, and pushed her out into the evening, to spend money and complain somewhere else.

Exhausted, Cindy retired to the staffroom, lay on the sofa and shut her eyes – a state of grace that remained uninterrupted for at least ten minutes, before Miss Primp's otter-like moustache appeared round the door.

'I say, Cindy?'

'Yes, Miss Primp.'

'D'you have a moment?'

As she led Cindy to the consulting rooms, she explained the reason for the summons.

'My back,' she passed a hand round and tried to rub her cocxyx.

'Where exactly does it hurt?' Cindy felt for the base of the spine.

'Bit lower.'

'There?'

'Bit more . . .'

Cindy removed her hand. Any lower she thought and she'd be half way into the colon.

'You'd better take your clothes off and let me have a look.' A smile crawled across Miss Primp's face.

Cindy turned down the light to shield her eyes from the sight of the middle-aged carcass. Lord save us, she thought, the old bird was wearing cami-knickers.

'It's nice when you dim the lights like that,' Primp stretched out on her front, peach-coloured bra, ankle-stockings.

'Now what kind of pain is it?'

'Dull ache, mostly. Probably the way I sit. So uncomfortable these new chairs. I tried putting a cushion ... outch!'

Cindy's fingers dug towards the thoracic nerves. 'I think we're getting somewhere ...'

'I think it's ...'

'Lower. I know, you said so. Let me explain something about the spine Miss Primp. The nerves all connect up to various organs of the body. The cervical nerves do the head and neck, biceps, wrist extensors. Down here we have the lumbar nerves – they look after the leg muscles. Little further on – the sacral nerves.'

'What do they do?'

'Bowel, bladder, feet – and, of course ... the sexual function.' Cindy let the words drip off the end of her tongue. 'One doesn't go messing around down there.'

Primp had started to breathe heavily. 'Quite.'

'But to an expert, it's possible to diagnose the source of the strain and carry out a course of regenerative work ...'

'Yes ... ?'

'Yes. It takes time, and obviously each treatment has to be carefully planned.' Cindy left her hand on Miss Primp's buttocks and knelt down till her face was next to the older woman's. 'It's important not to rush these things, Miss Primp.'

'I ...' the breathing was coming now in jerks.

'I think we should plan your treatment together, and have a full session next week. You know my timetable. I shall be happy ... her hand carressed the buttock, 'to help in whatever way I can.'

'That's most awfully kind.' Primp sat up. Cindy could see the perspiration on her upper lip, the flush of excitement.

She recalled what a colleague of hers had told her a long time ago. 'People are like cars, Cin. Put the right key in and you can turn them on. No different at all. Just find the key.'

And now she'd found the key to Old Primp. When the time was right, she wouldn't hesitate to use it.

It was nine o'clock that night, after a long day on her feet, if you please, when Keith Harper called.

'You free tonight?'

'Why, are you lonely?'

'Not me. There's a man I want you to go and see. I'm not even sure you'll find him. But it's important.'

'Where'm I supposed to look?'

'He's either in Brighton or a town called Lewes. Sussex.'

'Sussex! You must be mad. D'you know what time it is?'

'It's worth ...'

'I'm not even dressed and you want me to drive down to Sussex. I couldn't even be there before midnight.'

'Just wash your hands and get going. I was about to say it's worth a grand.'

They settled for fifteen hundred.

Two cups of coffee and twenty minutes later, Cindy was sitting in her white Toyota coupé, heading south over Westminster Bridge. She glanced in her mirror. Big Ben was like a great lighthouse, warning of the dangers of London.

When she'd first come to the city, she had taken to walking round the square at night, wondering what sort of people worked there.

Only now she knew. That was the trouble. Knew more than she'd ever wanted.

Cindy plugged in the CD player and switched on Dire Straits. Fast now, through Kennington, Lewisham, Croydon – the car, cutting through the cloudy night. It wasn't going to work, she told herself. She wouldn't find the American, wouldn't deliver him to Keith Harper and worst of all – wouldn't pass go and collect the fifteen hundred.

What kind of world did these people live in?

And yet it wasn't any stranger than her own. Over-fed women who came to lie on a massage table, because they wanted company, and were scared of being fat. Politicians, who paid out crazy money to unbutton their pants in front of someone who wouldn't laugh. Now this fellow – who by the sound of it, had been snooping in the right place and needed to be 'talked to'.

'Gently, carefully, Cindy, the way you do so well.'

She had put on the soft, black leather trouser suit for this job –

white turtle neck, her long, black hair let down over her shoulders. A touch of foundation. No powder, for her skin was without blemish.

But where the hell was he? Would he think small or big?

She headed the White Toyota towards Brighton.

An hour and a half earlier, Pete Levinson had driven along the coast road, looking for somewhere to celebrate.

The Grand sounded just right, fitted his mood. It was a grand kind of day. After all, he'd found the parents, found the photo, got a hint of the American connection. By the time he'd written it up – his way – the story would sit up and bark from here to Cincinatti. He'd be back in the groove, ready to forget about creeps like Larry D'Anna.

The Grand was just the place – the white facade, the doorman, the please sir, yes sir, of course sir. This was more like it. Some respect. About time, Pete my love. You've earned it and you're back where you belong.

Then there was room service, a bottle of champagne and an ice bucket to cuddle.

Only one thing he still wanted – but then he always wanted that.

It must have been 11.30 when someone knocked at his door. By that time he was only half-drunk, toying with a lobster claw, wondering how he'd spend the riches that would surely come his way. The girl asked if she could trouble him for a couple of minutes – she was doing a survey of hotel guests – what they liked, what they didn't. How their visit could be improved. She was sorry it was so late.

In her hand was a clipboard and pencil, but the smile told Levinson all he needed to know. He didn't mind what bullshit excuse she gave. If she wanted to come in, he wasn't going to stop her. If she charged, what the hell? This was his day.

As she stood in the doorway, he could have sworn the black leather moved and stretched, as if it had a mind of its own.

Chapter Thirty-one

It was only the clock on the wall that told him it was dark. But for just a moment Chukovsky fancied he could hear the wind in the forest clearing high above them, the calling of the birds, the rustling of the night creatures in the undergrowth.

Sometimes on the dawn shifts, he had left the dank confines of the silo and gone up top to watch the stars. And it seemed the supreme irony of all ironies – that here, laid out for him, was the beauty of the universe – and he held in his hands the power to destroy it.

On a night three years ago, he had stood in that clearing and made himself a promise. If the order ever came, he would disobey it. If they threatened to shoot him, he would die where he sat. But there was nothing that could make him contribute to the ending of the world, and the extinction of mankind. Not he. Chukovsky. Not this man, out of all of them.

And yet now, that thought seemed so remote. Tonight there was violence all around them. And in a little while, laid out at his feet, in a rough, army blanket, the young captain with his big mouth and his big ideas would die. He had crossed the river many hours ago, and you couldn't get him back now. He was already on the other bank and he'd go without ever once looking back.

Poor captain. Or was it those he'd left behind who would find themselves the poorer?

'Volodya, buy me a coffee. Leave the fucking radio. Do something useful.'

The big sergeant sighed and stood up from the main console. 'I can't get away from the idea that they're ignoring us.'

'Why should they?'

'Easy. Here's the picture at Brigade Headquarters, OK? I've got it all worked out. They look at the map – and they see us fine. Silo 312. Bad scene. Sending out emergency signal on the hour, every hour. Ukrainians have marched on it – shot up the captain and now they're sitting on top of the place – like a hen laying an egg. What do they do? They hear you bleating away. Captain's about to shove it, you're hysterical. And they can't do a thing. They're not exactly going to ask you to open up the bloody lid and let in a doctor – are they? Uh? Be realistic, Major. They just don't know what to say. So they shut up.'

'Get me some coffee!'

'It's true. I'm certain of it.'

They couldn't have said when he died – which, to Chukovsky, made it all the more poignant. Somewhere between four and seven in the morning, when the first fingers of light would have been pointing through the trees from the east.

Volodya had checked him. 'He's gone.' The two-word epitaph. Soldier's tribute. 'Been there, done that, gone away.'

This one, though, the most meaningless of all the journeys.

For some reason he could remember the instructions they'd been given about death. 'Meet it head on. Climax of a glorious, courageous duty. Celebrate the departure of another exemplary patriot, whose name will be forever, and ever and ever . . .'

That was the great thing about the Soviet Army. There'd been instructions for everything. What to feel, what to say, how to direct your energies. Or not.

He remembered the way they'd leafed through the rule book, presented to each recruit with all the solemnity of a public lavatory. 'Don't masturbate in battle,' read clause 74A. They'd fallen about laughing at that one. Bound to be plenty of time for the old, right-handed two-step when the great push came and the shells started falling. First thing you'd think of, if things got tricky. Put down the Kalashnikov, whip out the dong. Doesn't every soldier do that? Battlefields of rhythmic wristing. What a hoot!

Only the laughter hadn't lasted. This wasn't a fun army. You'd only had to go to Afghanistan to realise that. Think of the sickos you met there.

Plenty of them had been on drugs – cure for fear, cure for boredom, cure for sex, cure for loneliness. The longer you could be parted from your mind – the better the system had worked. Even the officers had been at it.

By the time they'd come home, the only thing there wasn't a shortage of was narcotics. How else d'you get an army of brainwashed illiterates to go up into the hills to be shot at?

And now? Now at last there was something to fight for and the captain had been the first casualty.

Chukovsky sat in the chair by the main console and shut his eyes. Of course the fighting would have to go on. But finally there would be some accountability. Some justice. Instead of being screwed around by nameless bureaucrats, there was the chance to do something right.

For the moment they would wait for rescue. But when it came, there wouldn't be any official commissions, or diplomatic exchanges, there would have to be an immediate investigation into the captain's murder. Culprits handed over. Here on Ukrainian territory. Otherwise . . .

'Volodya!'

The sergeant looked up, disinterestedly.

'What kind of arms do we have here?'

'A little of everything. Pistols, sub-machine guns. For some reason there are even a couple of hand-held anti-tank missiles. Think someone was doing a private deal . . . .'

'Make sure it all works.'

'Why?'

'Because I tell you to.'

They took out the weapons and put the captain's body in the cabinet where they'd been stored.

They covered him with a sack – and as a last gesture, Chukovsky folded one of the army greatcoats and laid it beneath his head.

If they didn't do something now, he decided, that's what all of Russia would be like.

Not caring for the living. But disposing of the dead.

Chapter Thirty-two

He wasn't used to having doors slammed in his face. Didn't happen much to presidents. Not in the open, at least.

Hadn't happened much to plain old David Bradley, either. Came out of the army after Vietnam, married the nurse who'd stitched his arm. Service wedding, statutory kiss, walked beneath the sabres. Happy ever after.

No place for rejection.

Not until Alison Lane.

The elaborate convoy was heading out of Berlin for the first session of talks. Behind him all the secret service trucks, the 'wacko' car with the nuclear buttons, A Lincoln limousine, shipped out specially from Washington, just in case he wanted to stop by the roadside and launch a missile before lunch. What a fucking waste of taxpayer's money!

Lousy mood you have there, Mr Bradley. Can't forget her standing there, telling you to shove it; the past is past, and you should think of your duty.

This from the new Labour prime minister of Great Britain and Northern Ireland – the lady you used to buy sweet and sour pork from the Chinese take-out – the lady you took to bed on a Saturday night, or Sunday night, or Monday . . .

But what did you expect?

No, really – what? To bridge half a lifetime in a single day? And think of this . . . maybe she's right. Maybe you simply forget the past, get on with your lives and responsibilities . . .

Isn't that the rule?

There's no place for the leader of one country going soft on the leader of another. No precedent. Too many conflicts of interest. Too many judgements clouded.

The rules, Mr President. Remember the rules.

He looked out at the thick woodland, the narrow roads that had once belonged to the miserable, little state of East Germany.

Look at the way *they'd* obeyed the rules.

Wasn't the duty of a leader to re-fashion rules? To *set* precedents, not follow them?

If I want Alison Lane ...

But it doesn't work that way. Not with her. For there's a whole wagon-load of pain that's travelled with her for years.

What happened to you, Alison? Who happened to you?

The setting was not what he'd wanted. The bleak, 19th-century castle of Babelsberg, stuck on a hillside overlooking a lake. Like the backdrop to a Wagner opera.

For weeks now the advance security team had been crawling through grass and climbing trees. Not even a hostile crow had come their way. It was declared safe. The 'protectee' could come.

And yet the difficulty of bringing four world leaders to a single place was scarcely believable.

The US delegation was frankly a disgrace. He'd asked to see the list, despite Harry's reservations. Four hundred people, for Chrissakes, right down to the lady who did his makeup, and made sure his three clean shirts were out there and ready in the holding rooms.

No wonder Reagan had loved the job. It was all acting and image. It was the feel-good factor, the comfort zone – or any of the other wacky concepts the media men liked to fling at him when he rehearsed a public appearance.

'Mr President, you still look like a soldier going into battle.'

'That's what I trained to do.'

'We have to sell you as the man who went to battle and won. You have to look like a winner – at all times – the guy on top. Not the guy under fire.'

They talked crap. But then the business was crap. So they talked the truth. He'd learned all that during the campaign, watching the public chew up the ones who didn't have the body-language right.

'Not too hard, not too soft,' came the instruction. 'You don't want to be like Bush and remind American women of their first husbands.'

'I'm here now,' he would say. 'So let's get on with the job.'

'Say that in your second term,' they'd reply. 'This is just a practice run'

* * *

And when she came he couldn't help the smile, realising the contrast with his own arrival. No security blankets, no young, grey-suited agents, ready to throw themselves in front of a bullet. But just a woman, with an elegance and calm that set her apart – almost alone. She left the car by herself, with a dark blue coat buttoned to the neck, black leather boots – and the fine blonde hair, blowing all ways in the wind.

Elegance and calm. She'd always had them.

'Shall we do the cameras?' He waved a hand at the wall of lenses.

'Is there a choice?'

'Always.'

He watched her gradually release a smile and turn to the photographers.

'Should we shake hands?'

The smile fled.

'There doesn't seem much point.'

They entered the hall and at once whole clusters of aides and ministers and interpreters were crowding in on them. He wanted to pull her to one side, find a quiet room, ask what the hell was going on in her mind. But the Russian was arriving and the Ukrainian would be there any moment. And there was a block in her eyes that he couldn't surmount.

I need to reach you.

But in that moment, he was powerless to do it.

A large, square table occupied the raised centre of the room. Eight seats – two each side. It was like a chess game in a vast auditorium – only if anyone lost, the entire game would end in failure. Four winners or four losers. No draws. No extra chances.

He'd shaken Klimak's hand outside. Ukraine's president, with his brushed crewcut. A rough hand. Once belonged to a miner. Once to a communist. Now he was anything they wanted if it kept him in power. The man was small and wide, but it wasn't fat. There was bone and muscle – and a brain, said the briefing, that would understand power and pressure and politics, and wouldn't lie down.

'You talk, we'll listen. I understand that's the way our people have set it out?' Bradley looked round the table.

Shilov nodded.

Klimak grinned. 'Are we to understand ...' his hand took in the British and American delegations, 'that you are together or apart? We,' he glanced at Shilov, 'are apart.'

'We represent independent voices in an alliance ... .' Bradley leaned forward, but Alison took the ball.

'Our politics are very different – our rules are different ...'

'So are our capabilities.'

She stared at him sharply.

Klimak laughed. 'Perhaps we should mediate between the two of you ... uh? We have experience of alliances, my friends. Very bad experience. That is why we left. You would do well ...' he stopped himself.

Old habits, thought Bradley. Start of the old lecture. Hasn't yet learned the new script. 'We're here because you requested a meeting – shall we leave it at that.'

The Klimak grin.

Shilov shifted his papers. 'Mr President, Miss Lane, President Klimak,' he sighed. 'Let's not waste time on the jokes and pleasantries. Klimak may enjoy this, but the situation is serious. The argument centres on the twelve missile silos, currently located in the Ukraine ...'

'You told us there were ten,' Bradley's fist hit the table. 'What is it with you people ... ?'

'That was my predecessor. You didn't expect that the communists would tell you the truth ... '

'Should I expect it from you?'

'I am telling you now, Mr President.'

'How many more surprises are there?'

'Ask Klimak.'

There was silence for at least twenty seconds. Across the table Bradley caught the interpreters exchanging glances. He hoped Alison wouldn't break the silence. You had to create some tension. Let Shilov and Klimak find something useful to say by themselves ....

He watched her sit back in the chair. She understood implicitly.

The Russian opened his briefing book. 'Our position is very simple ...'

Bradley chuckled inside.

'We are willing to decommission the silos, remove the weapons and have them destroyed, according to our international obligations ...'

'They're not yours to decommission.' Klimak was still smiling. 'The missiles are on Ukrainian territory. Therefore they belong to the Ukraine ...'

'They belonged to the Soviet Union and Russia is now the legal successor ...'

'My friend,' Klimak looked pityingly at Shilov, 'we all belonged to the Soviet Union. Times have changed. Now we belong to ourselves. We're human beings again. What's left on our territory is ours.'

'That is presumably why you have surrounded our silos, and in one instance – shot and wounded our military personnel.'

'A local misunderstanding. The officer has been disciplined. You are free to send in a medical team at any time ...'

'And open up the silo, so that you can overrun it.'

'Our silo, my friend.'

Alison sat forward. 'What if the area were to be cleared and an international team came in – and decommissioned the silos?'

Klimak looked at Bradley. They both realised she had made a mistake.

Shilov shook his head. 'You will understand, Miss Lane ...' it was clear from his voice that he doubted she would ... 'the missiles contain certain examples of technology that are the property of the Russian people. We cannot therefore simply allow international personnel – however, well-intentioned,' he bowed his head in her direction, 'to examine the missiles at will and acquire this technology. We're not yet so far down the road. I hope I make myself clear.'

'But you're content to leave your soldiers wounded, and possibly dying ...'

'That's a matter for Klimak's conscience. If he withdraws from the area, we'll tend the injured ...'

'How can you sit here ... ?'

'Prime Minister Lane! I would remind you this is not a road accident in Chelsea!' He paused to let her see the anger in his eyes. 'You may be glad that we left the men where they are, since the choice is between that – and handing the missiles over to Klimak. We, at least have proved a certain responsibility ...'

'Responsibility ... At this moment you possess 176 nuclear-armed ICBMs, carrying roughly 1,240 warheads and anywhere up to 600 additional warheads ...'

'Impressive, isn't it?' Klimak smiled amiably.

It's like bloodletting, thought Bradley. You bring out all the poison, release it from the system – jab by jab. And either you find a cure, or the patient dies. Even with all the preparations, the briefings, the assessments and strategies – you often don't know what's down there until you start to probe.

'I've heard enough for now.' Klimak pushed his chair away from the table. It was like a boat casting off from the jetty.

'Before you go ...' Bradley raised an eyebrow. 'Before you go, President Klimak may I suggest we at least keep our ministers and experts busy. I believe there's a useful area for the working parties to explore.'

'What?' Klimak stayed where he was. But they were all watching him.

'The setting up of a joint Russian-Ukrainian scientific team, to handle transition arrangements ...'

Klimak turned away in disgust.

'Just one word of warning ...' Bradley stood up. There were times when they had to know where you were coming from. You had to remind them who was what in the big, outside world. 'The United States, at least ...' he glanced at Alison, 'is not prepared to see a nuclear confrontation that would endanger our interests and those of other countries. Not when the Cold War has ended and our people are looking forward to a new stability. That is not acceptable to us. Period. There must be a solution ... We are required,' he let the word hang for a moment, 'we are required to find it.'

'I made a fool of myself, didn't I?'

She sat in the ante-room. Bradley gestured Norton and Till to leave them.

'It's your first summit. And no, you didn't.'

'Thanks for not helping me.'

'I learn by my mistakes.' He gestured to the sofa. 'Sit down for a moment.'

'Will they come to the evening session?'

'Hell, yes. This was just theatrics. Plenty of politicians don't think it's a proper meeting unless someone walks out. It just opens the bidding. To them it's part of the ritual – like shaking hands.'

She coloured. 'I'm sorry I refused outside. That was churlish. I was still angry with you.'

He joined her on the sofa, but said nothing. You couldn't pressure Alison Lane. Neither the teenager – nor the adult. Questions only brought more questions. If you wanted an answer, you waited for her to give it.

She got up and went to the diamond-shape window. Outside, past the security cordon, she could see through the trees, down to the lake, an old iron bridge, its superstructure shaped in a semi-circle.

'The Glienicke Bridge,' Bradley had come up behind her.

'Where they used to hand over spies?'

'All the fun has gone.'

She turned to face him. They were closer, he realised, than they'd been in thirty years ...

'I can't go back, David.'

The voice and the unexpected kindness in it, took him off guard. 'I never said ...'

'Listen,' she said quietly. 'Don't say anything. Just listen to me. I know what I see in your eyes, and it wouldn't be fair if I didn't tell you this. Our meeting is chance. One in a thousand. But it's still chance. I won't read more into it than that. Last time I saw you, I was angry and I'm sorry for that. Maybe I was still working things out in my mind. Maybe I wasn't clear. Perhaps not even until the summit – when I saw what we had to do. How important it is ...'

She looked hard into his eyes. But she couldn't read them. He was motionless, silent, as if a shield had come down in front of him.

'There's also a degree of pain in this, which you can't guess at – and for the moment I can't tell you. One day. But now isn't the time, David. There's too much to do.'

'I think you should give us a chance ...'

'It couldn't be, my dear. Just couldn't.'

'I'll fight for my chance, Alison.'

She went over to the door and opened it. 'Then you'll be fighting yourself.'

★ ★ ★

Till knew what he'd seen.

He sat in the fifth car of the US convoy, waiting for the president – and the return to Berlin.

The private meetings, the phone calls. He checked his notes. But Bradley wouldn't be that stupid, would he?

And yet look at Kennedy.

That was the strange thing about politics. Despite all the checks and balances, the men and women involved in it, acted as though they were totally unaccountable. Professionally and personally. Do what the hell they liked.

Oh yes, they would say, we're accountable to the people. The great American public.

Sure.

Since when did the people get to hear what was going on?

So maybe it wasn't so far-fetched. Bradley and the prime minister. Double the risk, double the fun. Perhaps people got off on things like that.

Chapter Thirty-three

'I'll do the interview now, Dick.'

'I don't understand, Prime Minister. I told them it was off.'

'Then tell them it's on again.'

Alison disappeared into her room, sat at the dressing table, and retouched her makeup. Decision time. That was it. You make your decisions and you go forward. And she had told David Bradley, where she stood. No return to the past.

'I'll fight for my chance, Alison ...'

She wished he hadn't said that. A long time ago, so many, many years back she could recall telling him ... 'when you fight for something, David Bradley, you always seem to get it. Don't know what it is about you – but you always get your way. Always win in the end.' It had been a source of pride to her when she'd said it. Now it seemed like a curse.

The BBC had asked for the 'friendly' interview. Here she was, they said, just three days in the job, attending summits, caught up in the tussle of international politics. Long way from Education Secretary. How did it *feel*? This was the Sunday morning chat programme. Bit of news, bit of colour and informality. Plenty of *feeling*.

She didn't mind that. All they wanted was for you to resemble vaguely a human being, smile, laugh, and appear to know what you were doing.

Only, don't ease up. Every interviewer believes there's an extra nugget to be extracted – just by them. They want to make news. They want their name in the headlines – and you're the vehicle to get them there.

She knew all that. Five minutes in they had covered the 'meteoric' rise, looked at the dangers of Russia and the Ukraine – now they'd be heading for the final straight.

'Thank you, Prime Minister, etc etc ...'

But the interview was running longer than scheduled. Perhaps another item had fallen through. And then as if from a clear blue sky, she heard the question ... 'So how are you getting on with President Bradley? Things haven't always been smooth between a Labour prime minister and a Republican president, now have they, Prime Minister?'

'The world's moved on,' she stiffened slightly. 'Of course there are differences of opinion. That's healthy in an alliance. But we have many points of common ground. We share the same concern that the nuclear dispute between Russia and Ukraine, should be settled as a matter of urgency. That's why we're here.'

'I meant more on a personal level.' The interviewer crossed his legs. 'You both went to Oxford, roughly at the same time, I believe. So ...'

A thin, sharp blade seemed to enter her chest, below the heart.

'So, did you never meet, or have any contact?'

And there it was all plain and simple – the one question she should have expected, and hadn't. The interviewer was staring at her, his mouth slightly open in a half-smile. And you have only a split second, no time for thought on this one, Alison. This is live. And there are two or three million people watching you at this exact moment. *Answer the question.*

'I don't believe we ever did.'

She knew it was the wrong answer, even as she said it. She knew – with the utmost certainty – that she had made a crucial blunder. 'You don't lie,' the whips had told her, when she'd entered parliament. 'You feign ignorance, stupidity, you avoid the question, if necessary you throw a fit and roll about on the floor screaming. But you don't tell a lie when there are people around who know the truth.'

What have I done? she asked herself.

But she already knew the answer.

Sir Henry knew it too. After years of watching Alison, and watching all the other politicians, you know when there's a turning point. You see so many scandals break and wash away the people caught up in them. You almost get used to it.

And yet this one seemed so unncecessary.

He leaned across the breakfast table and reached for another piece of toast.

Wendy put down her coffee cup. 'I thought she was rather good. A lot more capable than some.'

He nodded and spread the marmalade in thick dollops. Wendy had never understood anything.

Pete Levinson saw it – out of the corner of his eye. He hadn't known whether to watch the show – or watch Cindy. So he'd looked at both.

Cindy had been going through her second, morning exercise routine, dressed only in an ankle chain and a headband, and a lesser man, he told himself, would have missed the brain-shocking importance of what Alison Lane was saying.

He sat up straight in the bed and hit the television remote control, trying to read her face, seeing the lie, as if imprinted in the middle of her forehead.

Cindy was now doing handstands against the wall.

Jesus Christ! It was enough to make anyone go crazy. He'd come back to Alison later.

In the bungalow, a few miles along the coast, Margaret Lane, got up and turned off the set.

'Why did she *say* that? She didn't have to. It was an old relationship, finished thirty years ago. Normal, natural. She could have told the truth, brought it into the open. No one would have cared.'

Alison's father got up and went to the window. 'It's not over. That's why she said it. It's never been over. She's my daughter. I know her.'

They didn't speak again. Margaret Lane disappeared into the kitchen and began peeling potatoes. He found her there a half hour later, her face streaked with red and distorted by the tears.

Chapter Thirty-four

At dawn, on his fifty-first birthday, Harry defined the rest of his life.

You will never again have so much power, so much anguish, so much guilt.

Two days since he'd seen her in the restaurant in Chevy Chase. Two days of waiting and asking himself. Why would she be talking to the little Ferret from the Press corps?

He fancied he had heard his name, whispered and sniggered across the table.

Christ it was humiliating.

He went into the bathroom and splashed cold water on his face. A worried, hunted creature stared at him from the mirror. So who do you blame Harry?

Fucking idiot that you are.

He could hear the dull thud as the two thick wadges of Sunday paper landed in their polythene covers on the front porch. And maybe there will come a day when I don't have to run down and tear open the pages, scanning each column like a thing demented, to see whether they've found me out.

But not today.

Only when he'd covered all the sections did Harry relax. A day of rest had been ordered by the doctor who lay beside him. Jane Deval, prescribing a family outing, morning till night. So he could throw away the papers, and forget about heading into the White House.

That's what she'd said.

By the time she came down it was eight-thirty and he was making french toast and frying bacon.

'Boy, even the smell of this is life threatening.' Jane opened a window and let some of the smoke escape. 'Did you have to start a fire on your birthday?'

Harry wasn't to be distracted. 'Your order, madam?'

'Go easy on the heart attack. I want juice, bran, and a cup of black coffee.'

'I'm sorry, madam, we don't serve crap like that. This is a restaurant for people who eat. Grass and other fringe dishes are sold down the street.'

'You're crazy. I have to do something about you. People keep telling me you're a lousy ad for my medical practice. They look at you and think, that's a hell of a doctor he's married to. She can't even put him on a diet.' She was grinning now. 'Why shorten your life? I could give you ten extra years ...'

'Yeah – it'd feel like twenty. I wanna go out in a blaze of calories. Like a kind of dietary supernova.'

'What's a supernova?' Jason had shuffled in, wearing pyjamas. 'And where's the french toast?'

They took the toboggan to Battery Kemble Park and watched the boy, falling all over the hill, chased by dogs, shouting to his friends.

They said hallo to a White House staffer and his family.

They nodded to a teacher from St Patrick's, his wife, ridiculously overdressed in a yellow ski suit.

'Fifty-one.' Harry shook his head. 'Where'd it go?'

'Your waist.' Jane laughed. 'C'mon it's at least twenty minutes since your last meal. Let's go eat lunch.'

Harry couldn't remember a happier day. They had brunch at Houlihans, with tables of food and pitchers of beer that seemed to stretch well over the State line. We'll do more days like this, he thought. When this is all over ... when I can start again.

Get yourself a life, Harry. Get it now, while you still can.

He had almost fallen asleep back home when the phone rang.

'For you.' Jason couldn't have cared less.

Harry put his hand over the mouthpiece. 'Didn't you ask who it was?'

'Some guy.'

'Hallo?'

'Harry, it's Clark Norton.'

Harry closed his eyes. 'I thought you were in Berlin.'

'I was. President asked me to return home. New Far East initiative ...'

160

'Right, right, right. I believe I heard something about that.'

'Can we have a talk?'

'Monday, ten o'clock suit you?'

'Now, Harry.'

'Clark, this is my birthday.'

'Congratulations. Give me half an hour Harry. I'll come round.'

He climbed into his oldest coat, two sizes larger than he was now and walked Clark Norton down the street.

'What's on your mind?'

'I got sent home, Harry, like a schoolkid who'd fucked up on his homework.' Norton's foot kicked at a ridge of snow. 'That's what's on my mind.'

'President's call, Clark. Nothing to do with me.'

Walking past sleepy, snowy houses, some kids throwing snowballs, only the temperature was rising.

'Harry, Harry.' Clark smiled and patted Harry's shoulder. 'We're in this together. All of us. It's the way things are.'

Harry stopped and turned face on to Norton. 'What the hell are you talking about? You get sent home ... and we're suddenly all in this together? What's that supposed to mean?'

'Part of the general malaise, my friend. A symptom of the way this administration is going. You know what I did? I talked tough to the new Labour prime minister ... Alison Lane. Labour for Chrissake. Half-pink, half-any colour they can find. And we're supposed to pussyfoot around these people? Jesus! Memories are short in this town. So what happens ... the President tells me my behaviour's offensive and I'm to go home in disgrace. For what? For Chrissake.' Norton pointed his gloved finger through the air at Harry's nose. 'That's why I say we're all in this together, because something is plainly very wrong with the guy. And you should know about it.'

Harry turned away and began to walk down the street away from Norton.

The older man slithered after him. 'Well, Harry?'

'Well what, Clark?'

'I think we should at least discuss some strategy here.'

'I have nothing to discuss with you. The president makes his decisions and as far as I'm concerned that's it. You want to make a case out of that, you go to him, tell him to his face.' He shook his head. 'Because I will, Clark. I'll go to him and tell him about our little conversation.'

And suddenly the mood had changed and Norton was smiling the little smile he saved for those occasional little Washington triumphs. They could have been two men enjoying each other's company, out for a stroll – suburban DC, little friendly argument, some banter. Only it was way past that.

'I don't think you will, Harry.'

'No?'

'I don't think so. Because I don't think you would want a certain story coming to light and upsetting that nice family you have back in there . . .' he jerked his finger in the direction of Harry's house, 'and that attractive and very competent wife of yours . . .'

Someone seemed to be squeezing Harry's stomach and he was fighting for breath.

'I'm sorry, Harry, did you say something?'

'Spell it out, Clark. Let's hear what you have to say.'

'Only to point out that we have certain things in common and that we might be able to serve each other's interests over the next two years. So it wouldn't be a good idea to go talking to teacher out of school. Do I make myself clear? The lady we haven't yet spoken of, is, as you can understand, in some distress and feels it might be cathartic to let her feelings out. I have, of course, counselled against this. I . . .'

'Get out of here, Norton.' Harry's stomach seemed to be expanding, tearing, some kind of hook deep inside . . .

'Think about it, Harry.'

'You're scum, Norton.' Harry turned and walked away. 'That's what I'm thinking about.'

'Be careful, my friend.'

He could hear the words, following him up the hill, settling on his back.

'Do you often keep secrets from me?'

He smiled. 'Course I do. It's my job.'

She turned away in bed and faced the wall.

'What happened today, Harry? With Norton.'

'We talked. He's a pain in the arse. Should be put down.'

'I said . . . "What happened, Harry?"'

She didn't use that tone very often.

He stayed silent for a moment, turning his body, pressing against her back.

What was he to say? Listen, it's all one big mistake. I'm not really the person you thought I was. But please keep your mouth shut and don't talk to any of our very influential friends. Dry your eyes and let's go back to being the statistical exception you always thought we were – a happily married couple.

Instead he ran a hand through the hair on the back of her head. 'I turned fifty-one. I had a wonderful birthday.'

But even as he spoke, the nausea was rising in his throat.

Chapter Thirty-five

In the late afternoon they switched on the special lights in the Babelsberg castle, as the temperature plummeted across central Germany. The clouds hung thick with snow and the wind beat around the chimneys, shaking the trees. From outside only the cars and the lighted windows could be seen. A tiny village, iced in, cut off from the outside world. Four leaders at a table – winter at the door.

He could see the deep trenches below Alison's eyes – the skin pale under the spotlights, hands too busy with papers and pens. Nervous, damp hands that left a ring of moisture on the leather folder beside her. Only the face betrayed no emotion. And this, he thought, is a trained, political animal. Knows how to behave, controls the mouth, the body language – only the fine blonde hair seemed to go its own way, curling in irregular tufts at the side, untamable, as it always had been.

And yet he knew what she'd said on television. They'd flashed it from the embassy in London. Full text, without comment. Had it in his pocket. The phrase that denied him once and for all. 'I don't believe we ever did.' Why in God's name had she said it? Sooner or later, someone would talk. A friend from the old days, a tutor. Sooner or later the Press would get on to it. And how do you answer then? What was he to say if asked the same question? Go along with the lie? Challenge her in public? This was a nightmare, scheduled and waiting to happen. Worst of all ... it needn't have happened. She could have said '... I knew him, we talked, had a few drinks.' Now it was the worst of all worlds.

In the middle of a summit.

The president turned his eyes towards the Ukrainian leader. The Russian sighed. Alison spoke first.

'I understand some useful ground was covered by the working parties, this afternoon ...'

'They speak in the dark.' Klimak tossed his head back. 'They talk about technical details, removal of warheads ... .but the essential questions have not been resolved ...'

'Ownership of the missiles and the technology.' Bradley put down the papers. It was time to open the bidding. The Russian and the Ukrainian were there as dealers. One had a product, the other didn't. They would now have to bargain to divide it or dispose of it. These two men hadn't come to Germany to start a war. They'd come to set a price. You have to keep that in mind. The only thing at issue was the price.

He rubbed his eyes. 'What do you want, President Klimak, President Shilov – what do you want?'

The two leaders looked at each other for a moment, expressionless. Shilov raised an eyebrow.

'I want our share of the missiles,' Klimak folded his arms.

'What for?'

'Because they belong to us.'

'What do you want the missiles for?' Alison leaned forward.

'To protect our security.'

'Guarantees would protect your security.'

Klimak laughed. 'Look at the Soviet Union. Full of guarantees. To you, to us, to everyone. What are they worth now? There is no Soviet Union. Tomorrow,' he looked hard across the table towards the Russian president. 'Tomorrow there may be no Shilov.'

We'll get a price, thought Bradley. But not this session. Maybe not tomorrow either. They'll play it as far as they can, posture, threaten, go through the ritual ... Not surprising since this is the only chip they can cash in. Seventy years of communist rule and all they can sell are the weapons. This is the last, best deal they can hope to make.

'I'm hungry,' he said simply and gathered his papers. 'What d'you think – our people will let us take a break for lunch?'

'Take the rest of the day.' Klimak wasn't smiling. 'Frankly I have become bored with this discussion.'

'We shall try to be more entertaining.' Shilov got up. 'I'll have some clowns sent over to your hotel. Or do you have sufficient in your delegation?'

'Be careful, my friend. This is more serious than you ...'

'Gentlemen ...' Alison was standing, looking round at the faces.

'Forget I said that. We have to do better than this. I think our people deserve better.' She left the hall before anyone else could move. Never mind entrances, she thought. Making a bloody exit is just as important.

'I needed to talk to you.'

He had knocked at the door of her delegation, and she had duly excused her staff.

'Good. This summit isn't going anywhere.'

'Forget the summit. I want to talk about you.'

'No deal. For God's sake, David. We have something fast approaching an emergency and you want to talk about me. No. I'm not available. I'm not even here. D'you understand? If you want to talk summit – fine. If not – I have work to do.'

He stood outside in the corridor.

You should give her up now. This is all the excuse you need. Agree with her, tell her she was right, tell her goodbye. We all make choices . . .

And yet after two years in the presidency, you get used to having your way, all ways. He knew that. Knew the strength of his authority. You're not encouraged to accept restrictions.

'Presidents are powerful men. They end up getting what they want.'

He'd heard that during the campaign. Advice from an old CIA agent, who'd spent years in the basements of Washington, working on projects, far away from all the oversight committees and special prosecutors – projects, that somehow, somewhere, a president had whispered he wanted.

This time Harry would tell him . . . 'Don't even think about it. She's outside limits. You can't do that.'

Only no one says 'can't' to the president. People have tried persuading, arguing, but in the end no one says 'can't'. The president is elected by the people. He's the symbol of the people's will and the people's authority. You don't say 'can't' to the people of America.

Alison was everything he wanted.

Including unattainable.

Chapter Thirty-six

'Been a lousy day, Dad.'

'I know.'

'You saw the TV interview . . .'

'What made you tell them that – about never having met him?'

'I've been asking myself all day. I panicked. It's too close, too intense. I suddenly felt that if I said anything, even the slightest thing, it'd all come tumbling out . . . and then they'd never leave us alone. Can't you see it? Unmarried prime minister, widowed president. They'd have us in bed together before tomorrow's headlines.'

She could hear the old man sighing. 'Would they?'

'I had to make a decision, then and there. Whatever I did would have been wrong.'

'I suppose we should have expected it. I mean they know you were at Oxford, same time and all that . . .'

There was silence for a moment. 'I think I'm losing it, Dad. The summit, David. It's like an overload, seeing him again. He's amazingly impressive in the negotiations. In everything really. Just the same. Only more. That's what's so difficult. I don't know how to . . . half of me seems to have gone back in time, keeps telling me . . . go get him, he's yours, nothing's changed . . .'

'Easy, love. Take it slow.'

'And then there's the bloody summit, going nowhere . . .'

'You'll do it.'

'I wish I believed that. I keep telling myself what I should be doing. And yet I don't quite get there.'

'Tell me, then.'

'I can't help being struck by him. God knows, the men since haven't exactly beaten a path to my door.'

'I seem to remember you slamming that door . . .'

'Did I? I sit here, thinking – look at what you've got. The job they'd all kill for. Leader of the gang, and then I go to bed at night.

And who do I talk to about it? I ring you. Maybe I talk to Dick Foster. But he doesn't talk back ...'

'It's the life you chose.'

'What? David in his castle, me in mine ... to be alone?'

'It's too late for David. You're on opposite sides of the world. You've got to accept that.'

'I have, Dad. I was only talking.'

'Are you all right, Prime Minister?'

'What if I said "no", Dick?'

He blushed. 'I, er ... I'd see if I could help in some way?'

'What if I said I wanted you to take me out on the town, candle-lit restaurant, jazz club, dancing till dawn? What then, Dick?'

'I would make all the necessary arrangements, talk to the protocol office. We could ...'

'I didn't mean that. Can I be very personal for a moment? I meant, would you like to take me out? On a date. You know ... you're a single man and I'm a single woman. There's nothing in the rules ...'

'But I work for you!'

'I know,' she smiled. 'But if you didn't?'

'I really ... erm, I never thought, Prime Minister.'

'Thank you, Dick, that's all I wanted to know. Thank you for being so honest.'

'Is there anything else I can do?'

'Goodnight, Dick. Get some rest.'

Chapter Thirty-seven

Dear Harry . . .

'Who's your letter from, honey?'

The moment he saw the handwriting, he had gone down to the den, well away from Jane, heart clumping down the stairs after him. He knew who it was, although she'd never written before, swore she never would . . . 'I couldn't do anything to hurt you, Harry. Not in a million years . . .'

Bitch.

Dear Harry,

'I didn't want to write, but Clark said you wanted to know how I was. I never realised you told him about us. I didn't think you told anyone. But in a way I'm glad you did. Well, I'm lonely Harry and I miss you, the times we had together, the dinners, the walks. I've never felt so intimate with anyone in my entire life and I don't just mean the *physical* . . .'

He shut his eyes.

'Couldn't we just meet for a half hour? I want to talk to you, not to get in the way. But we have so much, you and I. I can't believe you have that kind of relationship with your wife, and I know you need it. The magic that we made together. I can't stop thinking about it.

'Anyway find me just a tiny corner of your day. Meanwhile, with love . . .'

Christ, there was more the other side.

'PS . . . Clark Norton is such a nice man. I thought he was just passing on a message from you, but he's taken quite an interest in my career and says I'm under-employed for my talents in the EOB. Would I like a spell at State. Jealous?

'PPS . . . I love you.'

I hate you, thought Harry. Almost as much as I hate myself.

Chapter Thirty-eight

Keith looked out of the window. Far below, the Gloucester Road was blocked solid with traffic. Rain was spitting and jumping off the sidewalk.

'Who are you?' Pete Levinson threw the question at his back.

He turned and examined him across the clinical neutrality of Cindy's living room. She had done a good job, tracking him down, getting him to London – peeled and packaged.

'A friend.'

'I've never . . .'

'A new friend. Isn't that nice?'

'Depends.'

'On both of us, Mr Levinson. Let's just say I have some influence in this town.'

Levinson swallowed. 'Are you police?'

'More influence than that.'

'I'm leaving. You can't keep me here.' He stood up.

'I wasn't aware we'd kept you anywhere.' Keith smiled and nodded over to Cindy. 'I'd have thought our hospitality has been pretty generous.' He raised an eyebrow. 'So far.'

'So what do you want?'

'We have a proposal.'

'I'm listening.'

'First we want to listen to you. What you're doing here, who you're seeing, what plans you may have?'

'That's my business.'

Keith turned to Cindy. 'Can we have some coffee, love?' She detached herself from the sideboard and disappeared into the kitchen. He took out a notebook. The pages were empty, but Levinson couldn't see that from where he was sitting.

'Last night you visited a Mr and Mrs Lane, claimed your car had broken down. Snooped around, asked a lot of questions . . .'

'I'm a reporter.'

'Who for?'

'Magazine.'

'Good circulation?'

'Very.'

'I'm so pleased.' Keith's smile hadn't wavered. 'There's a procedure here, Pete – you don't mind if I call you Pete, do you? Have
you ever worked abroad?'

Levinson shook his head. Keith had guessed well.

'So you don't know about our regulations. Reporters,' he closed
his notebook. 'Reporters need accreditation.'

'I'll send an apology.'

'That may not be enough . . .' Cindy returned with a pot of coffee.
'But don't let's talk of things like that, Pete. Let's talk of how we
might help each other.'

He poured the coffee into tiny blue cups and handed one to
Levinson. There was something he recognised in the man – a
chancer, a trader, a man of the streets. Some people look at you
head on, others don't look at you at all. Levinson looked through
you – to the angle beyond. We're not so different, thought Keith.

He took a sip of coffee and put the cup down. 'You went to
Brighton to get information about the prime minister's parents, or
about the prime minister herself. Right Pete?'

'I . . .'

'Let me finish, Pete, and then we'll throw this open to the floor,
OK? You're doing a story about Alison Lane. Where she came
from, what her home was like, background. Quite understandable.
She's only just got the job. It's very simple. And what I'm proposing
to you is also very simple. You want a story and I want to give you
one. What could be a better arrangement than that?'

Levinson showed his much-vaunted teeth and grinned at both of
them.

Cindy couldn't help a little fondness for him. Pete was very good
at what he did, and very appreciative of what she did back to him.
A real meeting of bodies, she reflected. It was something that Keith
Harper, with all his party funds, couldn't buy, couldn't create and
probably wouldn't even recognise if it crawled up into his pants.
Pleasure.

* * *

They ate lunch in, Cindy showing skills she didn't often use, pouring claret and brandy, while Levinson drank himself into a happier and more talkative frame of mind.

He was a gift. Keith had known that instantly. Much better to leak a story through the American press than going to the British tabloids. Fleet Street was too tricky, too close. A tiny elite knew everything. Downing Street's Press office called them 'the sharp-shitters' and hid behind trees when they walked past. There was only one imponderable about them. Would they knee you in the groin – or stab you in the back? And could they do both at the same time? You didn't leak through them. Not the big stuff.

But if a damaging report on Alison were filtered through the Americans, no one would suspect the Labour Party. And even if they did, the route would be too circumspect, too difficult to trace. When you had a story that flew – then so did the dirt, the recrimi-nations, the bloody witch hunts. Much safer to come from the States.

As Cindy cleared away the food, Levinson began laughing quietly, as if enjoying a private joke.

'Yes, Pete?'

'Eating here, like this, the three of us ...'

'Why is that so funny?'

'You don't want to be seen out with me, do you? Uh?' Levinson's voice had risen slightly, but it wasn't the wine talking. 'It just kinda hit me. That must mean your face is pretty well-known outside this apartment.'

Keith didn't move.

'That's OK. I'd do the same if this was Washington.' He shook his head. 'But you're good. No, really. I mean it. You find me, you organise this stunt – both of you. OK, I don't know what your game is. You don't tell me. But I figure one thing, and maybe this'll surprise you. You guys don't know what I know – about your own prime minister.'

'Really?' Cindy leaned forward and filled the American's goblet. She'd seen it so many times before. Another half bottle of fine champagne cognac in the wrong throat. One of the oldest of the truth drugs, prising inhibitions away from worried minds.

* * *

Keith tried to steady himself in the lift on the way down. But the drink and the excitement seemed to boil over inside him. Pete Levinson hadn't just sung his heart out – he'd performed a fucking aria. Sweet, sweet music, and more lyrics than he could ever have dared to hope for.

'I've got you,' he whispered, opening the main door to the apartment block, stumbling out on to the wet streets.

'Who's been telling lies then Alison, my love? Who's been fibbing on television? "I don't think I ever met David Bradley." ' His voice reached an imitation falsetto. 'And now we have you, my little vixen. Fellow students at bloody Oxford, living and screwing together. Christ – what a story. It'll be the bloody crucifixion all over again, from hell till Tuesday.'

He hailed a taxi and took it all the way home.

'Denise! Denise!'

'Stop shouting.' She appeared in her dressing gown at the top of the stairs. 'You're pissed.'

'Let's go out to eat.'

'You're too pissed.'

'Make me a coffee. Then we'll go.'

It was all right until half way through the meal, when the thrill of vengeance seemed to wear off.

Denise had ordered the best bottle of white wine in the Italian restaurant, wouldn't go home, chattered incessantly about her sister's hairdressing salon. A wedge of veal had stuck between her front teeth and he couldn't take his eyes off it. Suddenly it all seemed so clear. Things weren't ever going to change. He didn't want Denise, he wanted Alison. The closeness that had developed between them during the election campaign. If she were here now, they'd be sitting, almost nuzzling, talking about the rat-pack, who was up or down, who was up whom – all that kind of thing, the lifeblood of British politics, the things that counted – not this nonsense about the price of a perm.

Even now, when he thought he could wreck Alison – something told him to wait. Maybe if he went to her, said he understood how she felt, but just to give him some time, and see how things panned out ... then maybe after a few weeks they could ...

Denise was smoking – she had that annoying habit of talking while the cigarette was between her lips. 'So why the dinner out then? What's the big celebration? Something gone right for once?'

'I don't know. I really don't. Just needed to get out.'

'Thought it might be that you wanted us to try again.' She hung her head. Question disguised as statement.

'I . . .'

'Don't say it if you can't.' She shrugged. 'But you're still the only person I care about. I wish I didn't.' She fumbled her wine glass but eventually got it to her mouth. 'You know the place where you could try, if you wanted to, don't you?'

He knew that all right. He could see the wide, bouncy bed, with the television opposite, the dressing table, crowded with her bottles and potions. That's where you tried and failed. And that's where you knew about it first.

And what if Alison turned him down again? Would he simply dump Denise and live on his own?

Could he leave the silly creature to fend for herself. What kind of bastard could do that? One like me. The answer was immediate. No hesitation.

'Let's go.' He helped Denise to her feet, put the coat around her shoulders, steered her through the door.

By this time she was quite drunk, so when they got home he carried her upstairs and laid her fully clothed on the bed. The face was a mess. Smudged lipstick, runny mascara – a mess outside and a bigger mess within. The mouth seemed to be moving silently, but there were no words coming out. He took off her shoes, switched out the light and went downstairs to the kitchen.

Night of decisions then, Keith Harper. What do you really want?

I want Alison Lane to call me and say she wants me to come round, that she needs me, that we could be happy together, after all.

That's what I want.

He sat there, maybe for an hour, listening to the kitchen clock. In the end he poured himself a whisky and by the time he had drunk it, he'd decided what to do.

He'd talk one last time to Alison. Just for himself. Just so he'd really know.

After that, for all the hurt and disappointment, and for the life that could have been and wasn't going to be – then and only then – he'd break her.

Chapter Thirty-nine

Shilov sat on his bed and worried about himself. Was it a new worry? An old one? Was the Slavic melancholy descending on him with the winter? Try as he might, he couldn't shake it.

'There have been three attempts on my life since I became President . . .' He turned to Katya.

'Two of them were entirely frivolous . . .'

'How can you call them frivolous?'

'My dear, a man who charges at your bodyguards wielding an ancient Cossack spear is hardly serious. Nor is a madwoman trying to throw a brick at your car as it passes beneath her flat.' She smiled.

'And the third?'

'The third was not frivolous, I grant you. A bomb discovered in anyone's car is not frivolous.' She chuckled. 'Even if it was incorrectly wired. My dear, with such skills available in our country I am convinced you have nothing to worry about.'

'I believe you.' He inclined his head towards her, eyebrows raised. 'I always believe you, my dear. I gave up the pistol, remember?'

She rose and walked around the bed. Little did anyone know that the wife of the Russian president had spent the morning, sewing a new zip on his trousers, because the Russian tailors that her husband had brought with him from Yekaterinburg insisted on using buttons. Buttons for the president! At a summit! And they had fallen off. Christ arise!

'Somehow I have not seen you worry like this before.' She frowned. 'Is there anyone in our group you don't trust?'

'Ha! I am at a loss to find someone I do trust. This is the great irony of all ironies. Everyone thought the plotters and conspirators in Russia were all communists. So what happens when the communists disappear? Just as much plotting as ever. More, in fact. Open season. Trust is a luxury we don't yet enjoy in our country.'

'It's not that bad.'

He smiled and stroked her hand. 'Let's hope so.' Leaning across, he kissed her cheek an inch below the right eye. His favourite place for more than forty years. 'Let's hope so.'

Harry Deval was known as a slab of genuine Washington. A tough, experienced lawyer, willing to offend all kinds of people if the cause was right. Over time he had represented the presumed crooked and the barely innocent, the sinned against, and the sinners, the people who inhabit the city's greylands – the legal-lands, where day is night if a lawyer says so and a jury believes it.

Law was life in Washington, Harry reflected. Lawyers did your business, they often did your family. They most certainly did your death, and frequently your taxes. 'Enter a law office,' he used to say, 'and it's one-stop shopping – all the pains of life under the same roof.'

The pain that day came in the shape of Clark Norton, ushered into Harry's west wing office, with minimal formalities.

'I don't have time for you.' Harry stood up.

Norton grinned. 'Then I'll come back later.'

'I won't have time later, or tomorrow, or at any time in the future, Clark. Do I make myself clear.'

'Perfectly.' Norton let his thin, blue-suited frame fall into a high-backed armchair. 'I want to know about Alison Lane . . .'

'British Embassy is on Connecticut Avenue. Four dollar taxi ride. I'm sure they can help.'

'No, Harry!' He sounded like a whining schoolboy. 'I want to know about Alison Lane and our president. Rumour has it, there was once some kind of relationship between them.'

'Ask her.'

'Someone did. On television in fact. She denied it. My information is that she lied.'

'Too many rumours in your life, Clark. Why not get yourself some facts? Can't help. Sorry.'

'Help is required on this one, my friend. Think about it, Harry. I'd like some answers please, by tomorrow.

Harry moved to the door. 'Get out of here, Clark.'

'I'm sorry you feel that way.'

Harry's secretary appeared in the doorway from the outer office. 'Sorry to bother you, Mr Deval.'

'What is it, Jean?'

Her eyes took in the presence of Clark Norton and flashed Harry a warning.

'Would you show Mr Norton out?'

She returned ten seconds later, without him. Her voice descended into whisper. 'There's a lady in tears in the outer office. She's from the administrative section, says she's a friend of yours. A Miss . . .'

'Show her in, Jean.'

Harry faced the window and clutched his stomach. He could feel his temperature rocketing, could feel all the walls of all the castles falling in on him, all defences breached. I can't do this, I can't go on like this . . .

'Hallo Harry.'

As he turned again, she was sitting in the chair Norton had vacated, hair long and lush over the plain white blouse, red eyes, red nose, handkerchief in hand.

A full-scale assault on his conscience.

'I didn't mean to cry. It was just the thought of seeing you again.'

'Why did you come here?'

She opened her mouth wide. 'Why did I come here? Harry, you asked me to. Clark Norton fixed the time and made the appointment on your instructions . . .'

Worse than he'd thought. The sound of more walls tumbling.

'Listen to me. I'm sorry for what happened. More sorry than I can tell you, but there's something strange going on with Norton. I made no appointment. I never mentioned you to him. I gave him no messages for you.' He drew in his breath. 'Which means he's playing some game of his own to get at me . . .'

'I don't understand.'

'Don't you? Don't you ever read the papers or the scandal sheets? That's what this town is about. Who's . . .' he nearly said 'fucking' but stopped himself. 'Who's dating whom, who was seen where, who's split up. Careers are broken that way. Lives irreparably altered. That's called sport in this city. That's how you play power. That's what's being done to you and me.'

'But why would Norton do that?'

'He's in trouble with the president, wants my help. I'm not playing along.'

'But he seems such a kind man.' She dried her eyes with the handkerchief. 'You seemed such a kind man.'

Don't get into that Harry. Lovely as she looks. Vulnerable. All the reasons you went for her. Don't touch that one.

'Listen, I have to ask you something. Did Norton introduce you to any reporters?'

'Only one. Guy from the *Post*. Peters, I think his name was. Only because he's doing a feature about White House staffers ... you know, like about the footsoldiers, the people who work away in the basement but never get any recognition ...'

'Did he ask about me?'

'Well, only in passing. You are the chief of staff after all ...'

'But no other references ... nothing about you and me?'

'No, Harry.' Hurt across the eyes. 'And I wouldn't have told him anything either. But that was only a pre-interview. We're going to meet next week and do a full interview then.'

'Cancel it.'

'Why?'

'I'm sorry to say this, but you have to leave town for a while.'

'But ...'

'I know I have no right. Now especially. If I could do anything to change what happened... But there are some strange political games going on at the moment. This could get really messy.'

'You mean, for you.'

'For both of us. For the president.'

She stood up. 'I want to tell you something, Harry ... aside from all this Clark Norton business ... you really hurt me, the way I would never have hurt you. You said the kinds of things that married people shouldn't say to anyone. Not if they intend to stay married. Of course I was wrong to get involved with you, so I have to blame myself. But I couldn't help it. I loved you. And you took my love and made me feel it was going somewhere.' She swallowed hard. 'And then you dumped me.'

She looked round for her handbag and picked it up off the carpet beside the chair.

'I'll think about what you've said. But there's no point making any promises. You and I made plenty of those in the past. And look what happened to them.'

He watched her walk through the door, couldn't help following the sleek shape, the sculpted legs ...

You're sick, Harry. You wrecked a beautiful woman and you still can't take your eyes off her.

Chapter Forty

By 6.30 most of the lights in the clinic had been doused. Cindy looked out of the staffroom window and caught sight of the director hurrying across the car park towards a white Jaguar.

Inside the car, she saw him lean over and kiss a bearded face, and for a moment she wondered if the shy woman, introduced to her as his wife, knew about the liaison. But what did it matter? Open anyone's life, really open it – and there'd be plenty to shock. People were always more than they seemed – more dangerous, more irritating, hungrier ...

She sighed and buttoned her white coat, ready for the last session of the evening – Miss Celia Primp, the clinic's appointments secretary, fawner and gusher to the rich and famous.

This was the promised hour when she would explore Miss Primp's spinal nerves – and beyond; when Miss Primp, would be at her most sickeningly persuadable.

From early morning Cindy had watched the woman blushing and simpering in expectation. The red cheeks, the moist lips, the pouting at her tiny mirror. Even the director hadn't known what to make of it.

'You all right, Primp? Seem a little hyped-up, today.'

'Nothing, Mr Thomas. *Really.*'

Cindy headed down the corridor towards the most private of the consulting rooms, a white, windowless square, often used for the trainees. The table was in the centre, under a narrow-beam spotlight that could be brightened or dimmed by a foot control. Like all the rooms there were pictures of Arcadian landscapes, mountains, lakes – and a CD system, complete with the sounds of whales calling to each other. Maybe the patients identified with them, thought Cindy. After all, one or two were about the same size.

In the old days, when she'd trained, Cindy had taken the job seriously. She had her regulars and favourites. It was a very private, even caring kind of work, based on trust. Many people felt vulnerable when laid out on the table. They wanted to confide, they wanted to release pain both from the body and the mind. Some would weep silently as she rocked them from side to side.

Even the men behaved in those days – once you laid down the rules.

'You have to get across the idea,' the instructor had declared, 'that this is massage. Just massage. Right? Not massage and a blow-job.'

And by and large things were all right after that. You had to remember, though, that the masseuse, by the nature of the job, held a powerful position. In many cases she was more intimate with a patient than their spouse. But as always, you trod a narrow line. Touch them in one place and it was therapeutic, move your hand two inches to the left, and you could end up in the Magistrates Court.

As she opened the door Cindy could see that Primp had let down her hair from the grenade in which it was normally housed. She was lying face down on the table wearing what looked like a silver 'body'.

To Cindy she seemed like the kind of furry toy, children refuse to throw away – some of the stuffing had shifted, some had come out, nothing was quite where it should have been, and where it had been twenty years before.

'You'd better get undressed,' Cindy turned up the lights. 'We don't do treatments with a 'body' on. Just step into the changing room here, take your clothes off and put on the sheet that's hanging up. I'll be with you in a moment.'

'Yes, of course.'

A cloud seemed to pass over Primp's sun. She hadn't been expecting the business-like tone. Nothing for nothing, thought Cindy, we have to play hard and soft. That's the only way it'll work.

Primp emerged from the changing room, looking like the ghost in a school play.

'Lie on your front, please,' Cindy suddenly wanted to laugh. 'That's right. I'll just work in some lotion and we'll take it from there. By the way, is there anything I ought to know about you health-wise? Injuries? Bruises, any areas I ought not to touch.'

'Oh, no.' Primp sounded breathless. 'Nothing like that. I mean I'm really fine ...'

'You were complaining of terrible pain in the lower back . . .'

'I meant apart from that.'

I'll bet you did, thought Cindy and bent to the task. With her foot she turned on the CD, and the mournful notes of Albinoni seemed to drip from the walls. Lights down a little. Dig deep around the spine. Come on, old bird. Let's get you in the mood.

'All right, Miss Primp? Don't worry if you fall asleep. Plenty of patients do, you know. And tell me if you feel cold.'

'Oh, I won't do that . . .'

Cindy began a gentle rocking movement. This was going to take time.

'I like to have a friendly relationship with my clients.' She poured more oil on to Primp's mole-infested back.

'I do so agree.'

'Trouble is some of my clients are so . . . well, withdrawn.'

'Then we must see you get some others . . . Ooh yes, Cindy,' Primp had suddenly felt the impact in the sacral nerves.

'I'd like that. I mean you have some pretty important clients here . . .'

'The most important in the country.' Primp's voice lapsed briefly into its tart professional mode. 'Only the cream, in fact. Mr Thomas is most insistent . . .'

'And then there's the prime minister, isn't there?'

'Yes, but she's . . .'

'Anyway, I'm sure there wouldn't be any chance of working with her.' Cindy let the music have its say for a few bars. She lifted the sheet from Primp's back. 'Would you like to turn over – towards me, please?' The furry animal, with the misplaced stuffing, rolled on to its back. 'That's better.' She replaced the sheet. 'Would there?'

Primp looked puzzled. 'Would there what?'

'Be any chance of working with the prime minister.'

'I'm not . . .'

Cindy lowered the sheet and let her hand mark out a line between Primp's newly-exposed breasts.

'I'm sorry, what did you say?' The hand seemed to be losing its way somewhere around Primp's navel.

The woman's breathing had grown almost louder than Albinoni, much louder than the little voice. 'I said I'm not sure that wouldn't be an excellent idea.'

Cindy's hand continued its downward path.

Of course, they had an agreement of the best kind. The unspoken kind. The kind of professional confidence and trust, between a medical practitioner and a patient, sealed in a top London clinic.

The details remained to be worked out, but it was all going better than she could have hoped.

Only that, to Cindy, was an uncertain sign. In her life something good was inevitably followed by something bad. And for that reason, and for that alone, she made her way the next morning to a travel agent in London's St John's Wood, paid in excess of 1,200 pounds, and purchased a round the world ticket through Air New Zealand, valid for a year.

It was good to have that in your pocket. Risk was all very well. In fact she knew she thrived on it.

But risk-takers had to be careful. Particularly those who would seek to lay a hand on parts of the British prime minister. And not just any hand. And not just any parts.

Chapter Forty-one

The dinner party had felt long and rugged like a walk in the hills. Sir Henry took off his jacket and sat in the kitchen looking at the floor.

It wasn't that Wendy's friends were dreadful – they were just so *good*. Came from good families, did good works, said good things about other people.

Of course they knew what he did. That was all in the public domain these days. And they assumed it was also 'jolly good' for the country, for the state, for the world in general. He had ended up longing to tell them that they used to cosh the bloody confessions out of Soviet illegals, and went around the world gayly blackmailing and suborning with the best of them. All *good* fellows, every one of them.

One day. He smiled inwardly. One day.

Wendy came in, after seeing out the last couple. 'Don't bother with the clearing,' she grinned, enjoying the joke. They both knew that he never helped with the chores. There were some things a man of the house simply wouldn't do. Not if he had to work like a dog. Not if he had a certain status. She'd understood that when they got married – and she hadn't sought to change him.

'Brandy?'

He nodded and opened his briefcase. The Director General is still the only member of the service allowed to remove files from the building, and he spread the grey covers on the kitchen table, because he was too tired to make it to the study. Wendy would no more look at them, than attempt a climb on the north face of the Eiger. After forty years it was just one of the many unspoken agreements between them. In fact they were all unspoken agreements. Some days, he reflected, they barely conversed about anything.

The files dealt with surveillance on Keith Harper and the girl – Cindy Tremayne. They were detailed, terse and included the transcripts of telephone calls, and intercepted mail. There was also a page devoted to the American, Pete Levinson, with some supplementary background supplied by the FBI, through the National Security Agency. Sir Henry made a note in the margin, to do the Americans a similar service over the next few days. Gone was the time when you chalked up favours – now you paid for them pretty much on the nose, otherwise they didn't come again.

He could see where it was going, see the plan. Harper was a ruthless bugger, ruthless and hurt – and that combination was ... difficult. Yes, difficult was the word. Unpredictable. Because the hurt drove the aggression. And hurt came in odd waves, subject to odd moods.

And yet it wasn't a bad setup. Without knowing it, Harper was running the kind of 'sting' operation in which MI5 had long specialised. He was good too. Could almost have been recruited a few years back ...

'You looking after your young lady then?' Wendy turned round from the draining board, stacking plates.

'What d'you mean?'

'Don't shout, Henry.' She smiled pleasantly. 'I only meant the prime minister. Isn't that the young lady you're supposed to be looking after?' She turned back. 'Must be odd for you, working for a woman, mm?'

'She's quite well-behaved ...'

'I assumed she would be.' Wendy finished the dishes and put away the tea towel. 'All your women are – aren't they Henry?' She kissed him lightly on the cheek. 'I'm going to bed. Goodnight, my dear.'

He stayed where he was for a moment, then reluctantly closed the files and replaced them in his briefcase.

He couldn't help it – the files gave him a buzz, Alison Lane gave him a buzz – but Wendy didn't. Not any longer.

When in God's name had it happened? At what point had the work and the fantasies taken over and the beautiful woman upstairs gone and sat in the shade? At what point had they stopped investing in each other and sought solace elsewhere?

You're a fool, he thought. You didn't even realise, until it was too late.

Such a waste.

Chapter Forty-two

'I don't understand.'

Dick Foster's face took on the colour and texture of well-cooked gammon.

'It's quite simple. I don't wish to take the call.'

'But it's the president of the United States.'

'I don't wish to take the call. Do I make myself clear?'

'Perfectly ... but I ... I don't know what to *say* to them. I've got the deputy chief of staff, telling me to expect the call. *Expect*. This is really quite irregular.'

'Point out I'm engaged in very difficult domestic negotiations. There's a crisis in London. I'll see him later at the talks. Does that sound better?'

Foster's mouth described a few strange, but voiceless movements.

'Thank you, Dick.'

She closed the door on his departing back.

I can't speak to Bradley. Not now. He doesn't want to talk about the summit. He wants to talks about us. What us? Everytime I think about him it's like standing in quicksand. Sometimes I'm proud, sometimes I'm angry, sometimes I just wonder how he could have got where he has without me. Why didn't his life fall apart when we split up? Why was I the one, slammed into the gutter along the High Street in Oxford?

There's no forgetting him. Not after all this. But I have to find somewhere in my life to put him, somewhere safe and out of the way – like an old field at the bottom of the garden, with trees around it, so I can't see him from the house – and he can't see me.

She brushed her hair and tried to punch the summit into her mind.

Keep in mind the central idea. They've come for a price. They've come to deal.

And then she remembered. Even that thought belonged to David Bradley.

* * *

The telephone buzzed to tell her the car had arrived. In ten minutes they'd be moving out again to the Babelsberg Castle.

'Security's been tightened.' Foster sounded tired. 'They've already cleared the hotel foyer, guests are being kept behind barriers and those here already, have to stay in their rooms. Germans have laid on extra police outside and the crowds are under video surveillance.'

'What's going on?'

'No idea. Maybe some hoax calls. You always get them at summits.'

She hung up and checked her briefcase.

Downstairs Foster did the same.

If you'd taken the bloody call from the president, he told her in his mind, we might have found out what it was about. Bloody woman. Bloody prima donna.

He couldn't help the old prejudices rising to the surface. True, she was clever. True, she was attractive. But she wasn't consistent. Women never were.

He remembered his mother warning him about minxes in skirts. And she should have known.

Shilov glanced out of the ninth-floor window of the Grand Hotel.

'It's so odd to hear them talk about German security.' He turned to Katya. 'The last time we talked about German anything – it was the Nazis. That's what I grew up with. Hitler's Germany.'

'You of all people have to move with the times.'

He laughed. 'What is it with you? Always, you have to keep my nose on the path. Plenty of wives would say simply ... yes, darling, or whatever you say, darling. You've never said that.'

'If I did you would go even softer and sillier than you are.'

'That's not how the country sees me.'

'They don't know you like I do.'

He pulled her towards him. 'Katya, Katya ...'

Her eyes softened. 'There's no time for that Katya nonsense. You have a summit to think about. How long is this bastard Klimak going to hold out?'

'The working parties have made some progress ...'

'Then maybe he will deal.'

'We will both deal. That was never in doubt. Neither of us can go back with nothing. It's just a question of how much we pay ...'

He broke off as his personal bodyguard appeared in the doorway. 'The foreign minister wishes to see you urgently.'

'Then show him in. Must I sign a form?'

The minister hovered in the doorway in double-breasted suit.

'Katya Borisovna,' he bowed briefly towards the president's wife.

'Speak, man.'

'Most interesting news. The defence ministry reports Klimak has begun pulling Ukrainian forces away from the missile silos ...'

'Ha!' Shilov turned and beamed at Katya. 'You see, you see what I was saying. The bargaining's begun.'

Bradley's call reached her in the limousine as it pulled away from the hotel. There was no preamble. No preparation. Out of the corner of her eye she could see Dick Foster trying to disappear at the edge of the seat.

'I hope this isn't a bad time.'

'It feels like it.' She shifted uncomfortably.

'I'm sorry. You're the only identifiable human being on this planet, who's so far refused to take my call.'

'What's it like being God?'

'I didn't mean it that way. I wanted to tell you I'm sorry. I was behaving like a kid. It wasn't the time to be talking about relationships.'

'Nor is this. You have to see that. It shows we have duties which go beyond ...' she looked at Foster's profile, 'it shows there's no place for other things ...'

'I can't accept that ...'

'I suppose gods find it difficult to accept what mortals tell them ...'

'That's not what you feel ... you forget, I've done a little exploring inside your head.'

'Old paths, David, they're out of date. And now I have a summit to go to ... so do you.'

'I'll get back to you one of these days. If it kills me.'

Official tone now. 'Thank you, Mr President. I'll let you know when there's some progress.'

She replaced the handset, and looked over at Foster. He had shut his eyes in the hope he could feign sleep. But his breathing gave him away. Short, nervous gasps, like a spaniel having a bad dream.

'Dick . . . ?'

The eyes opened a fraction.

'Must have dozed off, Prime Minister. Sorry.' He sat up.

Alison raised an eyebrow. 'You're going to have to lie a little better, Dick, now that you've heard the conversation.'

Chapter Forty-three

They liberated the silo on a cold afternoon, with the sun standing sullen in the corner of the clearing and the cool dampness of death on the trees around them.

There's no triumph here, thought Chukovsky as he blinked into the grey daylight, and grasped the hand of the air corps major. But there is shame and anger. And there's payment for both of them.

The body-bag came out, Volodya, directing the soldiers ...

'This is a great day,' the major wore his smile tight like a belt. 'They've pulled back to within two or three kilometres of the silos, leaving us a corridor, and permission to fly three helicopters in.' He chuckled. 'We brought six – the Hinds, gunships.'

Chukovsy hadn't known what to think when the radio message came through. Was it genuine? Who was giving the orders? Finally there had been confirmation from the other silos in the region. And he had taken the lift to the surface and gone back to the world with a vengeance.

The commandos had set up a tent. Inside it – a map table, communications post, canteen – all rudimentary.

'Right.' Chukovsky sat down in the only available chair. 'As the senior officer here, I'm taking command. Notify Moscow that my captain was killed in an act of cold-blooded murder. Representations must be made to the Ukrainian foreign ministry and the culprit handed over for court martial within forty-eight hours.'

The major didn't move.

'Why d'you wait?'

'You exceed your authority, Colonel. This is my command, my post, my men ... .'

A flush had started to spread across Chukovsky's face. He could feel the beginnings of a fever. 'Damn you – we have to secure the area. We need more troops. More helicopters ...'

'I can't do that without direct authorisation from Moscow.'

'Then get it.'

'They won't agree. It's too sensitive. For God's sake, there's a fucking summit going on in Berlin ...'

Chukovsky slammed his hand on the table. 'If we don't act now, then by the morning the supply route could be closed again, and we'll be trapped inside. You can't go on hiding in silos. My God – we're the forces of the Russian Federation. Doesn't that count for something?'

'You play with dangerous toys, my friend. You should show more responsibility.'

'An officer of mine has been killed in an act of war. What more d'you need to ... ?'

'Soldiers die – even in peacetime, Colonel, or have you forgotten some of the little adventures we used to carry out in the name of the great Socialist motherland? Uh?'

'Then now is the time to force a stop.'

The major shook his head. It struck him that the two of them were like pots, boiling side by side on the same stove.

Risky.

He hadn't been so happy since God alone knew when. The news from Ukraine was the breakthrough he'd almost stopped believing would happen. Now the summit could move.

Me and my premonitions, he thought. I'm too Russian. Too dark. I've forgotten how to be content. We'll get the session over, then Katya and I will slip away, lose the bastards, take a little journey with a bottle of wine and some chicken. An adventure. A night-time feast – like the old days.

He stood in front of the mirror and rubbed his hands in delight.

This time she tied the tie for him. 'You never get it right.'

'Still not bad for a fellow who used to drive a tractor ...'

'And might do again soon.'

He grinned. 'If I do, you can sit on my knee.'

'Your stomach has beaten me to it.'

They opened the suite door and moved out among the body-guards.

No more doom. Thank God.

Into the lift. One of the bulky men seemed to have bathed in eau de cologne. Shilov caught his wife's eye and winked. Just because they were in the West they had to smell like French whores.

Outside, can you believe it? Sunshine even. Not a trace of cloud. The kind of day you killed for in Moscow.

Through the empty foyer – out under the canopy. Wait a minute. The way I feel. Look at the crowds. Listen to the cheering. I'm a popular guy. Man of the people. He looked at Katya, this would be fun.

Shilov bypassed the car. The tallest of the security men blocked his path. 'Not a good idea, sir. Extra security. You know the American warning . . .'

'I'll judge the warnings. If you can't talk to people – you shouldn't be in power . . .'

Out there on his own suddenly, the security men hurrying to keep up. And they tell you the biggest nightmare of all is a man in the crowd, with bad intentions . . . .

Katya's face borrows a frown. The security chief turns to her . . . 'Please get him back.'

And he's over by the barrier, heart expanding with all the goodwill of the moment, Russian hospitality and peace to all mankind.

Down the line he goes, like a small tank, elbowing his own security, thinking he'll kick them later for getting in the way. Child's hand, woman's hand, a camera, two cameras . . .'

He hears Katya's voice in the background. Wonderful! After all the dark days, the crises, this is why I went for the job. A little adoration isn't a bad thing.

More hands and cameras.

And then he stops for a second because the sound drowns out and it isn't a camera in front of him, four feet back, not in that shape, with the eyes beside it, looking beyond this world, and way too far into the next.

And Shilov – trained as he is by years of Soviet treachery and danger – reaches into his jacket to the gun he always carries, and knows in that second that it isn't there.

Katya, he wants to say. Katya, I gave it up because you asked me to. Katya I need . . .

But there's no time for him to turn, as the eyes in the crowd find their focus and the bullet travels . . .

That this should happen to the President of Russia, he thinks, just a few yards from his wife, on the best day, for so many, many months.

Please, just an hour, a field, bottle of wine, Katya ... please!

But the thoughts were silent, and lost in the screams and the terrible shouting, as they closed around him, the sudden violence and the shock reverberating along the street.

No one heard them except Katya, running, running towards him.

It came at them on the emergency defence channel.

Unreal. So unreal when you sit in a wood and learn that the world has thrown itself out of the window.

'Can't believe this ...' The major kept repeating it, the words slurring round and round.

'They're saying injured. Badly injured. Christ! Taken to the Charite hospital in Berlin ... Fuck!'

'Quiet, I can't hear ...'

They had all gathered, drawn by the alarm in the voices, soldiers, officers, the commandos on guard, standing in the half-dark clearing, knowing they'd remember the moment.

Same bulletin, repeated, minute by minute. And they waited for the orders. Countdown, thought Chukovsky. He could just picture the chaos in Moscow, the scramble to take power, the shouting, the garbled orders given and withdrawn, no one knowing what to believe. Panic across the jagged, snowy rooftops. Good city not to be in that night.

And then it came, authorised by a whole clutch of them, because no single man had the power any longer to take a decision. Not these days, when power was shared, when power was a broken instrument that might or might not work on the day you wanted it.

There it was – general state of alert ... 'To all the Forces of the Russian Federation, to the border units, the internal troops, to the airforce and navy, both in and outside Russian territorial limits ...' The voice droned on, reciting the endless units.

Chukovsky stood up. 'That's it, Major. I think we know who's responsible for this. And now I'm *taking* command and securing our position. Time we got some responses from the Ukrainian authorities, may be with a gun or two up their backside.'

The major said nothing. Out over the clearing the darkness had come in and lain across them. There were many hours to go till morning.

Chapter Forty-four

Katya stood up, straight and proud, as Alison entered the hospital waiting room.

'I'm Alison Lane.'

'Thank you for coming, Alison Lane.' The English was effortless. Katya gestured to the row of chairs.

To Alison it was a macabre little room – the place where you sit waiting for news of lives and deaths. Like the departure lounge in an airport – who's leaving, who's delayed. Only here, no one's hurrying to catch their flight, and any delay is welcome. 'Travelling today?' people ask. 'Hope not,' is the best response.

Contrast the stillness here, she thought, with the clamour now being raised across the planet, people in all countries, shot out of their daily routine by the news of a single bullet in Berlin.

Beyond the partition wall lay the man it had struck, and beside her the woman.

'Today he was very happy. That's why he went out to the crowds. He loves to do that; says it's the best part of the job. He thought there'd be a breakthrough at the summit.'

Katya had stopped crying. Or maybe, it occurred to Alison, she hadn't yet begun.

'I'm being asked to make a statement.'

'What are the doctors saying?'

'The doctors say nothing.' Katya sat up. 'That's because they know nothing. They're still assessing the extent of the wound. It may be some time.'

'Then there's little you can say.'

'I have to say something. He's the president of the largest country on earth. Anyway ...' she shrugged, 'the days of silence are over. The people elected him. He belongs to them. They've a right to know.'

'D'you know what's happening in Moscow?'

'Some of it. The rest, I can guess. Of course they're already blaming Ukraine and Klimak ...'

'He's left for Kiev.'

'Good. For now I'm more worried about our own people. We've got to prevent any reprisals. I don't trust the vice-president. He blows in so many winds he can no longer stand straight.' She shook her head. 'He even asked me what I thought he should do ...'

'So you told him?'

'Of course. Dissolve the parliament, I said. Call in the military and intelligence chiefs, make sure the country stays calm and disciplined, that nothing is done in haste .... He said yes, yes, yes. Which means no, no, no. I may have to return to Moscow myself and carry a message from the president.'

'But he's unconscious ...'

'Exactly.' She gave a thin smile. 'Isn't it fortunate that I can read his mind?'

They called her away to visit the visitors – the German chancellor, the mayor, the chief of protocol, like schoolboys, she thought, come to confess they've broken your window. No, they hadn't detained the person responsible. But they would. They really would. Rest assured. And then the head-hanging ritual ... 'So very sorry,' 'thank-you,' 'if there's anything ...,' 'Thank you again,' 'anything at all ...'

Just turn the clock back an hour or two, she told them silently. Not much to ask. Give him back to me, without the stains on his shirt, and the sightless eyes. Give him back.

But they simply bowed in their collective helplessness and looked at the floor.

'May I suggest something?' Alison leaned forward.

'Please.'

'That you go in and talk to him.'

'Why?'

'I said I knew something of what you're going through. And I do. Many years ago, when I was a student, I was hit by a truck and not expected to live. My parents gathered at my bedside and talked to me, and refused to let me die. I heard what they were saying. I couldn't move, but I heard almost every word. I believe it was that which gave me the strength to pull through.'

'You recovered well.'

'Not entirely.'

'Why?'

'It's another story.'

'Ah.' It was Katya's turn to stretch out her hand.

'He *will* make it.' Alison got up to leave.

'You're right. He's certainly obstinate enough.' A smile appeared in Katya's eyes. 'Besides, he always said he wouldn't trust me if I were left too long on my own.'

Outside the hospital Alison tripped and fell getting into the car, twisting her back, wincing at the pain.

'I'm fine, I'm fine ...' But Foster was already racing round to help her up, two German security men bearing down, out of nowhere. You could see it in their faces – please God, not another accident.

'Really. It's perfectly all right.'

But the pain travelled with her to the airport.

It sat there, bringing back that sense of utter despair which had hit her thirty years before.

She recalled the first time she'd tried to sit up in bed after the accident. 'Why can't I? What the bloody hell's going on? Je—sus!!' The shrieks had summoned the ward sister, two nurses, a houseman on duty on the floor below. 'I can't do it. I can't do it.'

Trouble was, the mind doesn't leave it at that. Body's failed, it says, tut tutting, standing all smug beside you. Only maybe it's your failure, in some small way. After all, you didn't look where you were going. So you brought it on yourself. Your failure, miss. So what does that make you?

There were times when she could cheerfully have cut off her head, just to drown out the voice.

But which was worse? That shrill, little voice inside, or the deadening solicitations from the people around you.

They could never leave you alone with your infirmity. Suddenly you were everyone's parcel, marked fragile. The chorus followed you ... 'you all right, dear? Everything all right? You must be so tired. Take the weight off your feet.' You weren't just your own cripple, you were everyone else's as well. The moment they caught sight of you, you were elevated to cause of the day. Public cripple No. One.

That's why she'd forced herself to mend.

That's why she'd hated her own weakness.

And she had promised herself there'd be no more displays of that weakness – or any other.

On the runway the RAF VC10 reared its head and lifted out of Berlin. Foster was mumbling about the Cabinet meeting on her return, the statement to Parliament, the need, he 'honestly felt', to get a grip on the colleagues closest to her, assert authority. After all, her first days as PM had been out of the country. Foreign Secretary was better. He could take over the gallivanting . . . time of crisis. She tuned him out.

On board was a message just in from Air Force One. David Bradley, already on his way to Washington, intended calling for a meeting of the security council. Heads of government invited.

Then she remembered. In the chaos after the shooting, she hadn't even had time to tell him goodbye. He'd simply made his arrangements and she'd made hers. Officials had communicated. The master and mistress had been swept up by their delegations and sent home.

She held the message up to the light and read it again.

Every time she cleared him from her mind, he put himself back.

Chapter Forty-five

Crises had always done a great deal for David Bradley. To him they made the difference between showman and president.

He wasn't angered or upset by the attack on the Russian President. It simply focused the mind.

Piece by piece his timetable was constructed as he crossed the Atlantic – the day like a slab of meat, carved and re-carved into tiny slices. Phone calls to world leaders, emergency Cabinet meetings, Defence, the national security. All the implications to be weighed and assessed.

Washington would be running on its favourite fuels – black coffee and hype.

Bradley wasn't like his predecessors, wasn't a concensus builder. Didn't see the job as being chief American mediator, didn't much favour Clinton's informality – the pressure groups and the kids wandering in, discussing, discussing ... and then the next day's headlines ... 'Still no decision from the White House.'

Didn't want Jimmy Carter's isolation. The guy who preferred reading it all on paper to dealing direct with humans.

Had little time for Ronald Reagan's good natured bonhomie, which inspired only back-biting and disloyalty from his closest colleagues.

Nor did he want an army. He'd served in one of those and was glad to leave it behind.

David Bradley considered his role was to make decisions. The more crises you confronted, the more decisions you made.

Sure you consulted. But each day you had to press buttons. Send signals.

The public had to know that if ninety odd missiles came up on a radar screen, inbound on Washington, the main man wasn't going to wake up half the lobby groups in the city to establish a view.

He was damned if he was going to run his administration like that. And he was damned sure the staff was going to know that.

By five a.m. Air Force One had landed him at Andrews, more awake than he had been in months. By seven he had his diary cards, his press reviews and the news from Berlin. Shilov was hanging on. Harry had phoned Moscow to confirm it.

'Good flight?'

The butler served them breakfast in the family dining room.

'Best in the world, Harry. What you got?'

'Trouble. Listen, David, this is going to be a crazy day so I'll say what I have to and then leave you in peace. I'm not qualified to talk about this nuclear thing, or Shilov, but you have a serious domestic problem, that we need to address right now.'

'What's it called?'

'What's *she* called?' His shoulders hunched. 'She's called Alison Lane.'

Bradley reached for a slice of wheat toast, smearing it with butter. 'OK, let's have it.'

'When you upset Norton at the summit – you seem to have made a good job of it. If you searched his house, you'd probably find it full of your effigies – with pins in them. Anyway, Norton has powerful friends. Larry D'Anna – for one. Magazines, newspapers ...'

'So?'

'So they're asking questions. They've put out feelers.'

'Let them.'

'OK, David. OK.' Harry laid his hands on his lap. 'I suppose I'm asking the question as well.'

Bradley drew a line under his scribblings. 'I'm not going to let them or anyone else dictate how I live my life. Alison Lane is an unmarried woman, who I once fell for in a big way and might ...'

'So it's true.'

'That much is true. We had an extraordinary relationship. It was in Oxford. 1966. We were gonna get married. Then Vietnam came along. I went off and left her.'

'End of story?'

'Yes. Except that now I want her back.'

Harry looked at the floor. Once you cross the line from honesty to hypocrisy, he thought, the lies come easy. The deceptions. They're like bricks. Build one, and then there's another on top of it. All of a sudden you've got the foundations for a whole life of lies. Hard to go back and start again.

'The problem is, David, they want to find some way to use this story against you ... And she's helping them. That interview where she said you'd never met ...'

'It was a slip ...'

'It was a lie. It happened and she said it. No instant corrections afterwards – the way Reagan used to churn them out. She's saddled with it. A pure eighteen-carat lie, out there on the record. And sooner or later someone'll ask you the same question.'

'So I tell them – no comment. Presidents don't comment on their personal life. You know that ...'

'She's a prime minister for Chrissake. This isn't some bimbo – the kind your predecessors indulged in. It's a prime minister. I know it was years ago. But she's denied it – that's why it's dangerous. She's made it dangerous. I've been in this city a long time. I've watched snowflakes turn overnight into avalanches. And that's in summer! I'm telling you ... I sense trouble with this one.'

'What do I do about it?'

'Don't see her for a while. Communicate by telephone. People are already noting the long looks between you guys and a lot of very private conversations behind closed doors. Don't add to it, David. You both have a lot of enemies, especially her. You're not just giving them the ammo, you're loading the gun for them.'

Bradley got up from the table and put on his jacket.'I have to tell you ... that's not going to be easy.'

Deval sighed. 'What can I tell you? I'm not so old and worn out that I can't see her attractions. She has authority, she has charm – she's a lot better looking as a leader than you ...' He grinned. 'Listen, it comes down to the person you are. In the old days you always pushed the boundaries. You did it in Vietnam. That's why you're sitting in this office right now.' He drank the last dregs of his coffee. 'In my experience presidents fall into two categories – those who don't believe they can do anything – they're in the minority, always whining about oversight committees, terrified that if they turn out the light, they'll trip over a special prosecutor; and the others who believe the world's up for grabs. Mandate, schmandate – I'm here and you're there – like Kennedy. The Charles Atlas brigade – kicking sand in people's faces, and enjoying it. Right?'

'Right.'

'Which are you?'

'D'you have to ask?'

Deval took off his gold-rimmed Dunhill glasses and rubbed his eyes. It was a punctuation mark – nothing more.

'Let me put this in context, David. This could blow over. It could. But I doubt it. There's a lie on the table. A lie from a world leader, about a very personal and unusual subject – a love affair thirty years ago between two people who went on to lead their countries. That's big time. Be assured that if you're ever forced to answer the same question she did, you either compound the lie – or finish her completely. What I'm saying is that if the scenario develops you may be obliged to choose between her . . .' he paused for a moment and replaced his glasses, '. . . and this job.'

Bradley didn't answer.

'The only thing you have going for you right now, is that with Shilov shot, there's an international emergency. So people are looking at other things. That may not last long.'

Bradley put his arm on the chief of staff's shoulder. 'You know, there's a funny thing about this story. I really believed that with all the leaks in this place, all the kissing and telling and kissing again – that this thing was safe. Why? Because only two people knew about it. Me. And I didn't tell anyone . . .'

'And?'

'And my mother.'

As Harry promised, the day was truly crazy. For everyone. Even Emily Laurence at the quiet end of the administration, had felt the heat. Now, close to 7.30 at night she was enjoying a cup of coffee, the size of a small bucket. Mrs Bradley was thankfully out of town, so the duties of shepherdess, cash-carrier and chief muzzler had fallen to someone else.

On her desk lay the latest edition of the *Washingtonian* and she was scanning the In Search Of columns, because one day, according to her best friend, there'd be a description that would 'leap out and french-kiss her to the ground.'

Hadn't happened of course, but it was a nice thought on a snowy morning.

When the door opened she had expected almost anyone except the person who entered, looking remarkably like the president of the United States, in his shirtsleeves, and minus the winning smile that had won him so many electoral college votes two years before.

She stood up hurriedly, unable to disguise the page she'd been reading.

'Good evening, Mr President.'

'Was never going to be.' He stood in front of her desk, lips pursed, eyes unimpressed. 'I want to talk to you, Miss Laurence. Maybe you can shed some light on what my mother has been doing, recently.'

Emily blushed.

'Doing and saying.' Bradley leaned forward and closed the magazine on her desk.

Chapter Forty-six

London felt deeply unwelcoming and proud to be so.

To Alison there were no concessions from the winter night. When the rain stopped, the wind would start, when the wind died away there was always the drizzle. Insipid. Incessant. You could live a lifetime on interval wipe.

And Foster never seems to leave my side, she thought, except when I'm lonely, when I could do with the company, when I don't want to talk politics.

Where are my friends? I mean, I've had so many over the years. Only this is the strange thing about Britain. When you get on, when you really make it, so many of them drift away. They don't like to say 'well done' or 'terrific stuff' – sticks in their craw, because you've made it and maybe they haven't. They're afraid to ask what it's like, in case it's really wonderful. That'd undermine their own lives. They couldn't bear it, going round believing someone else is having an amazing life – and they're not. We can be so mean-minded.

Such a contrast with the political managers. To them everything you did was 'bloody amazing.' 'You really got 'em going with that speech, knocked 'em dead in the debate.' No praise too overdone, too fawning, too outlandish.

So it's the parents you call, isn't it? They're the ones who'll tell you if you were great, or simply average. Not Mum, because she's star-struck by the whole thing. But Dad's still got a sharp knife. He can cut through the crap.

And what had he told her? 'It's too late for David. You're on opposite sides of the world. You've got to accept that.'

No one else would tell her the truth.

If she wanted to hear it.

'Welcome back, Prime Minister.'

'Prime Minister.'

'Prime Minister.'

There's a moment when she wonders if they're addressing *her*.

And then you're back in the study, gazing out on to Mountbatten Green, the oak desk looks so small, and the room is so ordinary. And there's no power there, of any kind – except what you bring to it.

'Don't you want to go home, Dick?'

But he shakes his head. Doesn't he have a home? Maybe all he possesses is a collection of pin-stripe suits, white shirts, flowery ties. Goes out at night to the park, changes behind a tree, comes back in the morning.

'Shilov's condition's the same,' he's holding up a news agency report. 'Wife's gone back to Moscow, though. Mounting unrest among politicians ...'

And in that moment she can see Katya quite clearly, sitting on the Aeroflot plane, heading back into the Russian night. She didn't know if her husband would live, she didn't know what she'd find when she got to the Kremlin. But she'd be sitting so straight and dignified, emotions tied up in a bundle for later, working through the options.

Why can't I be like her?

'I've sent the messages you wanted.' Foster looks awkward. 'But there's no reply from either Sir Henry or Mr Harper. I ...' he blushes slightly, 'I took it on myself to call the clinic and arrange for the physiotherapist to come round, er ... seeing that you hurt your back.'

'That's very thoughtful.'

'Different lady, they said ...'

'Oh.' Alison looks down at the stack of red boxes on the carpet by the desk. 'Listen, Dick, I think I should go to New York tomorrow. The security council ...'

'If you want my opinion ...'

'Situation's very serious, very fluid ...'

'I was about to say that the political secretary thinks it'd be a bad idea ...'

Her eyebrows lifted. 'You've spoken to him?'

'I thought it prudent. His feeling is that since your sudden appointment there's been no time to consolidate your position at home. Naturally the news from Berlin has dominated, the shooting ... but you haven't yet made any Cabinet changes, and he felt there was a need to stamp your personal imprint quite quickly. In fact ...'

'In fact, let the rest of the world get on with it. Is that what you're saying?'

'We just felt that in order to prevent any murmurings ...'

'Which've doubtless begun already ...'

'But before they take on any momentum.'

'How many murmurings, Dick?'

'Preventive action, Prime Minister, that's all we had in mind ...'

'I said how many?'

He shook his head. 'Five, six. I don't know ...'

'And Harper?'

'I just don't know, Prime Minister.'

Even for Cindy Tremayne, blessed with the acquaintance and favours of a Cabinet minister, an opposition front bench spokesman, assorted MPs and advisers, this was the ultimate playground.

Not nervous, she told herself, recalling Primp's breathy phone call. 'You've got your chance. Seven p.m. Downing Street.' But keyed. Poised. There was a lot to remember.

They had her name at the big iron gate on Whitehall. 'Any identification? Fine. Someone'll meet you inside.'

Up the street and the clouds have cleared. Moon's come out to play, she tells herself – and haven't we all. Past the big iron barrier in the road, the black front door, already open because they radioed ahead. Shirtsleeved security, perched inside on the right.

'Miss Tremayne? This gentleman will show you the waiting room, if you wouldn't mind, for just a few minutes. You can leave your coat there.'

It's quiet. Hardly anyone about. Place is so much bigger than you think from the outside. Long corridor to the back, waiting room on the left. She hung up the raincoat, plain white uniform underneath. Starched, professional. 'Nurse Tremayne.' That's what one of the MPs liked to call her. 'Nursey.'

She put down the blue holdall. Few towels inside, lotion, and a closed metal compartment that Keith Harper had said was none of her business.

'Just stand it as high as you can, turn the side towards her and open the catch. When you've finished, close it up again and walk away. You'll have done the business.'

Cindy checked her handbag. Passport inside, money. She could go now. Should go now. But then if you buy a ticket, you have to take the ride. The story. The experience. You couldn't pass up a thrill like this. She couldn't.

The messenger's back and it's up the wrought-iron staircase, past the portraits and photos of all the old PMs, seen off by mortality, or treachery or the whim of an ungrateful public.

More stairs.

He knocks at the door.

'Come in, be right there.' And it isn't just any voice. It's her. Head girl – as the papers have started calling her.

Now there's a bloody thought on a winter's night.

'You're Miss Tremayne, aren't you? I'm Alison Lane. Thanks for coming.'

'Very pleased to meet you.' And Cindy looks hard at her. For she's younger than the early fifties they've given her. Very blonde. Strong face, strong body. And wouldn't she have to be, to survive?

'Sorry to hear about Lillian. She all right?'

'Fine now. Nothing serious.'

So normal.

'I had a slight fall while I was away. Couldn't get to the clinic ... they told you about my back, didn't they?'

'I read the file before coming.'

'Oh good. Tea? Coffee?'

So normal.

'No thanks. Where would you like me to unpack?'

She's standing just inside the door with the picture of a ship on the wall, and the moon staring through the skylight.

'Why don't you come into the sitting room? I set up the portable table the way Lillian's done a couple of times.'

'That'll be fine.'

Too bloody normal. This woman is very deceptive. Dressed in a simple red tracksuit. Nicely spoken. Could be Kensington. But there's an edge to her that comes from somewhere else. A sharpness. An economy. Means she's trained in a rough school and still works there. She doesn't just look. She's working out the angles. Yours and hers. Eyes seem to go everywhere.

She's put a couple of sheets on the table. 'Shall we get going then?'

'Right.' Cindy turns away, hears the track suit coming off. Admit it, you're excited by all this, aren't you? Admit it – it's a hell of a thrill, a prime minister undressing behind your back.

She's settled on her stomach, sheet pulled across the back. There's nothing awkward about her. She's in charge.

Cindy lays the holdall on the floor, unsnaps the clasp. Clear view of everything. And now you move.

Almost immediately she can feel the woman's pain.

She can see the heavy, multiple tracks they left on her spine. Miracle that she's walking.

'You mess around with people's backs and you're never sure what will happen.' Words from a class many years ago.

'How long've you been with the clinic?'

'Not that long. Few months.'

'Like it?'

'Very much'

'Why?'

Cindy poured some lotion on to the lower back. 'Why do I like it?'

'Mmm.'

Clever question, that one. Casual but not. Forces me to show who I am.

'The people. It's extraordinary what some women will say when they're on the table. They get relaxed. They want to talk. Some even cry. I could write a book.'

Alison coughs. 'But you won't.'

'I take the trust very seriously.'

Pile it on – the pressure. Five minutes, ten, fifteen, and she's close to sleep. Practically exhausted. Ask how she feels.

'Fine.' Languid moan. Very sensuous, this woman. She enjoys it. Odd that you never think of prime ministers as sensual, the same way you can't imagine your parents having sex. But Alison Lane is intensely physical. She's letting her body take a walk with me. No inhibitions.

There's silence in this sitting room with its pleasant striped wall-paper, the beige carpet, oatmeal sofas. No clocks to tick. Just her breathing – and mine.

'Would you like to turn over – away from me?' You always add that phrase to cover their sensitivities – except with Primp.

But Alison just turns towards her, showing a body, full and cushioned, a luxurious body, thinks Cindy, a place where people would want to make a home – in the warmth and the light freckled skin, curving like a mountain road. And who has the run of you?

'Just the shoulders and legs now,' Cindy's voice rises . . .

'Fine, whatever you think. Feels really good.'

She closes her eyes and Cindy starts on the feet and ankles. And the patient's breathing is deep, relaxed. From the calves up to the knee, sheet rising as we go. Take it very gently. Thighs need a little work, very English there. But she's soft, and they're slightly apart, and just once the skin trembled with the touch, just the hint of a chain reaction, lights turning on across the body, deep inside . . . keep walking with me, very, very slow now.

And you're an inch away, move her thighs, rock them gently, ride the sheet up . . . touch once as if by mistake, just a finger brushing at the door . . .

She's still breathing hard, eyes closed.

Go on. Again.

And then a rock out of nowhere smashes the atmosphere. 'I think we'd better stop there, Cindy.' Voice suddenly firm and level.

Oh God. Oh God. Oh God. 'I'm terribly sorry Miss Lane. I don't know what I was thinking of.'

'Don't you?' She sits up. Sheet pulled up to the neck 'Would you step outside for a moment, while I get dressed.'

Cindy reaches for the holdall.

'Leave that, would you.' Command not question.

And Cindy can't help feeling like the schoolgirl, banished from class by the headteacher.

Back in the safety of the red tracksuit, Alison glances round the room.

I don't believe this. I don't believe someone would go this far. But then if you have strangers in the queen's bedroom, this is minor league.

She opens the holdall, seeing the metal compartment, the glass eye, the tiny window that housed God knows what . . .

Little bitch. Bloody little bitch. A cheap, cheap shot. The cheapest of all.

'Come in, Cindy.' She doesn't look at all contrite. Confident, experienced. How the hell did she get into the clinic?

'Talk to me, Cindy.' She goes up very close to her. 'I've no interest in threatening you, or making a scene, although I could – and maybe I will. I just want an answer to a question, and then you can go on your sordid little way, pick up where you left off. I don't give a damn what you do. I want to know who organised this. That's all.'

Cindy shrugs. She's not nervous or upset. Very confident, in fact. They chose well with her. Whoever 'they' are.

'Nothing to say?'

'I've got plenty to say. Just wouldn't do me much good to say it.'

'You've been threatened?'

'Something like that.'

'Just a name, Cindy.'

'I think it's past that. I'm leaving anyway.'

'Then leave behind the name.'

'This is so strange.' Cindy shakes her head. 'You know I didn't mind the idea of it all. I knew it was a risk. But I thought . . . hey, it'd be a real lark. After all, I know politicians. I mean 'know'. OK? I thought you'd be the same. Hot air. Lot of pompous crap. And look at you! You don't shout, you don't scream, although by rights you should, after what I've done.'

'So?'

'So what do I owe any of them? Not much. Nothing. You're different. You don't seem to me to be polishing an image. I'm not sure what you're doing here. Yes, you're tough. You probably play the game, same as the rest of them. We all play games. But you seem to know the difference. There seems to be a person still in there. Anyway,' she shrugs, 'you don't need this from a tart like me, do you?'

Alison doesn't answer.

'Keith Harper,' says Cindy and raises her eyebrows.

Chapter Forty-seven

'Why didn't I shout at her?'

I know why.

I have to admit something to myself. Something I never thought I'd feel. But I did – I enjoyed it. Put me at rest for the first time in … God, days. Truth is, she turned me on, for just a moment. Not in a way that challenges my sexuality. But there was one moment …

She snapped shut the folder on her desk and went over to the sofa. You don't think of this again, Alison. Once and once only. Now it's over. You have urgent business. Urgent, right?

Sir Henry had called. Sir Henry was on his way. Together they had more important things to consider – like the immediate future of Mr Keith Harper. Call your mind back. Go on, it's wandering. Get it back.

She sat and stared at the gold-framed mirror above the fireplace. This wasn't a warm room. The ceilings too high. Narrow and white and clinical. And the desperate presence of Keith Harper was still there, hard to shake, the smell of anger and desperation.

Not that he'd surprised her. For thirty years she'd known politicians every bit as prepared to crawl around in cesspools and garbage. Harper was the rule – not the exception. You only had to take the whip's office that he so ably managed. There, intimidation was dish of the day. Oh, it could be subtle. Could happen over a sherry in the club. Might be just one of those soft, lilting voices from the Welsh valleys, reminding you of a little indiscretion you'd long ago forgotten; or, a couple of the big boys to kindly help you through the correct voting lobby, when – oh, dear – you might have forgotten which one to go for.

Not long ago, she recalled, those same kind-hearted boys had all but broken down a lavatory door in the Commons, where a diminutive Labour MP had been crouching to avoid a vote. Forced him into the lobby with his shirt caught in his zip. Fine moment for the mother of parliaments.

Keith Harper fitted well within *that* establishment.

Now, of course, there'd have to be the ritual revenge. The destruction of the man's political career, his removal from the government. That wasn't in doubt; only the manner of it needed careful planning.

Sir Henry was shown in shortly before 9.30.

'My dear.' He took off his raincoat, showering the carpet in the process. You could see it on his face. He liked the off-duty calls, the grand doctor summoned to an emergency, the only one who'll do. Routine was all very well, but it was in the hours of darkness that you earned your money. 'Filthy night, isn't it?' He retrieved a handkerchief and blew his nose.

'In more ways than one.'

She offered him the sofa she'd vacated and watched his reaction as she spoke. He was no more surprised than she'd been. In fact, she'd never known Sir Henry surprised by anything. It was a face that took in, but didn't give out. Neither warmth, nor information – just the social mask, as and when circumstance demanded. A little small talk, a grin, a wink. He knew the tricks – when he chose to use them.

'So.' Alison finished the story and stood with her back to the fire. 'I should simply sack him outright, shouldn't I?'

'Of course you should, *should*, I emphasise ... but you can't afford to. He's the centre of your power base.' Sir Henry frowned. 'Such as it is. He got you the job – or at least he was one of the prime movers. Brought you the trade unions, didn't he? Anyway, confirms what I've always known. It's your allies you have to worry about. If I were you I'd sack him in a week's time, in a month, when you've had time to bring in some of your own people. But get them there first. Sack him now and it'll be suicide. I'm afraid those are the practical limits of power.'

'I have to go to New York tomorrow. The security council ...'

'Not a good time, my dear ...'

'Maybe there are no good times.' She grimaced. 'There is, believe it or not, an international emergency. Shilov may well die. In which case the emergency will rapidly become a crisis. I should be there ...'

Sir Henry inclined his head in deference. She turned and looked out of the window.

'I take it – you know about my little slip on television.'

He nodded. 'You didn't help yourself, if I may say so.'

'Will you watch my back, while I'm away?'

Sir Henry moved his hand to the coffee table and put the metal device from the holdall in his pocket. 'Haven't I always?'

'Will you, this time?'

She turned round and he met her gaze with what he hoped was a sincere expression. Of course, it wasn't good to lie to a prime minister. But if you had to, it was best to choose one who was unlikely to hold the office much longer.

Keith Harper knew it had gone wrong. Cindy didn't show at the restaurant beside Victoria station. He waited an hour, walked twice round the concourse and thought about going home.

Bugger Cindy. She and her antics would have been the icing on an already tasty cake. A wonderful headline for the tabloids. 'Who strokes the PM?' What the hell? He still had plenty.

Inside the station he rang Levinson at the Baker Street hotel where they'd installed him.

'We're getting close, OK? Something went wrong with Cindy. But we still have plenty to go on. Are your people ready in Washington.'

There was silence for a moment. 'Right. They're sitting on the edge of their seats.'

'Did I wake you?'

'Uh-Uh. Just reading. Story's ready to go when you say the word. We can top it with the political implications, as seen by a high, and very unnamed, government source.' He chuckled. 'You up for this?'

'What d'you think I've been doing it for?'

'Right.'

'I'll call you later.' Levinson was really lightweight. Or maybe that was just the manner. He was oddly wide-eyed for someone clearly so devoid of scruples. The kind of person who could shatter lives with a smile and a shrug, as if to say – hey, this is nothing personal. Just business, fellah.

Keith would have been surprised, though, to see Levinson put down the receiver and smile towards the light in the bathroom. Surprised too, at the figure who emerged and came over to him. She was outrageously overdressed in a silver ankle chain, with a silver tag, that only the influential and acrobatic had ever been in a position to read. 'To Cindy with love from Cindy,' it said.

Footnote from an admirer.

They were all long nights. That was the abiding feature of Downing Street. The government had a thousand leak points. And they all leaked late. Someone would open their mouths or their trousers too wide and suddenly, wherever you looked, there was a cat peering out of a bag.

Then the night news editors would be on the phone, the political correspondents, the dawn reporters – who was going to rebuff the latest, slur, smear or inaccuracy?

Foster sighed. This might be one of those nights – with the comings and goings, the closing of doors, and now a wild-eyed chief whip, waiting in the hall downstairs, demanding an audience.

He hurried down the corridor to meet him. 'I phoned your home hours ago.'

'I didn't go home.' Keith removed his coat. 'Is she in?'

'I'll have to see.'

'Bollocks! I'm going up.'

'Haven't you had a bit too much to drink?'

'What if I have?'

And yet, by the time he reached the study door, Keith had calmed himself. I have only one chance, he thought. One chance left to get close to this woman. He knocked quietly and went in.

'Alison?'

She didn't look up. A single lamp was illuminated on the desk, shadows lay across the striped wallpaper.

'I ...'

'Sit down, Keith – before I have you thrown out.' The words were controlled, quiet.

He tried to speak but his voice didn't seem to be where he'd left it. 'Listen, love I ... I actually came to say I'm sorry. Isn't that ludicrous, me coming here to apologise? This whole thing ... it was so stupid and unnecessary. I was so hurt. Believe me I didn't know what to do. I just wanted to lash out ...'

'I'm glad you did. Shows me what worthless scum you really are. Now get out of my sight.'

'Alison, listen to me ... there has to be some way we can piece this all together .... I just want to make it work, to be with you ...'

'You make me sick.'

He swayed for a moment, but the words seemed to pull him upright. In that moment she could see the flame ignite in his eyes, the dirty, ruffled collar, the cheap pretensions, as the anger gripped him. The index finger of his right hand shot out towards her. 'And you ... you're finished. Finished.' She could see him transforming before her eyes. The monster, shedding its cloak. 'D'you understand that? I can pull the plug on you anytime I want. Your lying on television, your cosy, private sessions with David bloody Bradley. You're in this office because I and my people put you here ...' The voice was little more than a croak.

'Get out, Keith ...'

'Don't think that we won't get little Cindy to dress up a story as well, by the time I put the papers on to her. There's enough muck and innuendo to bury you ...'

Alison got up from the desk and went over to the door. 'If that's what it takes to stay in power, stroking the egos of creeps like you, I don't want it. Not now, not in the future, either.' She opened the door and stood aside. 'It's not necessary for you to come here again. I hope I make myself clear?'

Eleven o'clock. In the study you got the time from Big Ben. Upstairs in the bedroom there was the clock over the arch at the Horseguards Barracks. No shortage of chimes. Like calls to battle.

It was good to have this one in the open.

Less good, though, to go away.

So stay and fight your corner, said the voice. That's what you've always done. You like fighting. They all say that. You fought your body. Made life so tough for it, that eventually it gave in and got better. You fought for this job.

But in New York, I can do something, she told herself. In New York I can have a say in the whole crisis. I *can* make a difference.

Oh yes?

And in New York there'll be one David Bradley. My oasis.

You're not going for him, are you?

I'm not going to make a choice between him and my job. I'll see him and come back. Then I'll turn the bloody Labour Party inside out, on its head.

But I need to see him. I need the strength.

She stared at the White House telephone on the desk, only it wasn't the one that began to ring.

'Yes, Dick.'

'Another visitor, I'm afraid.'

'Shop's closed. Goodnight. No more visitors. I'm going to bed . . .'

'I think you'll see this one.'

And in the seconds that followed she was running down the stairs, taking them two at a time, not caring about protocol or decorum, shrieking the way few, if any British prime ministers have ever been known to do, within the confines of the building.

Chapter Forty-eight

He had put on his best suit, like a Sunday boy home from school, standing in the hall, red-cheeked, unsure what to do, where to go.

Dad.

'What are you doing here?'

'I had to come.'

'I don't believe it.' She led him upstairs to the flat. Dad with the unfailing antennae, always knowing when to call, when to be there, all through her life, especially the times when the candle was flickering low.

'Right.' She flung open the sitting-room door. 'Let's have a drink. C'mon, Dad, take off your tie. Relax. It's me – Alison. I'm not the bloody Queen.'

Shy smile. Sunday boy on special outing. 'Can't stay long. I promised your mum I'd get back tonight.'

'You drove up all the way?'

'Your mum and I ... we thought ... I don't know, we just thought you might need a friend.'

He looked round the room. He's cowed by it, she thought. They all are. I can't just have a person in and say ... let's be normal. Even Dad. They all behave as though it's Disneyworld and I'm Mickey Mouse.

'Listen, stay the night, for heaven's sake. I'll show you round. We'll do the tour.' She poured him a whisky. 'Bring your glass.'

Alison on his arm, leading him from darkened corridor to darkened landing, pointing out pictures and inscriptions, the sword in the Cabinet room, the table shaped like a whale, brown leather chairs, yellow carpet, blue pencils and pads, the trees of St James's Park spiky like witches' fingers against the skyline.

Back in the flat she cooked him an omelette, and when he'd eaten he perched uncomfortably on the armchair, startled momentarily by the noise of the front door opening and closing.

'Just the boxes, Dad. Papers. They bring them all through the night when things are going on. It's probably stuff on Russia and the Ukraine.'

'Don't you ever sleep?'

'So pampered I hardly need it. Stewards doing my shopping, taking the cleaning, typing the diary. Like being married to thirty people at the same time. They're all wonderful wives.' She laughed. ''Specially the men.'

'Not lonely?'

'No time. You forget Dad, Alison and I are used to each other. Had to be.'

Later, they sat in front of the fire, each with a second glass of whisky to distance them from their thoughts.

He took her back to her childhood, the fairy tales and sunny days, the teachers and friends, the landmarks of a little life in a London suburb. And she too, began turning the pages.

'You remember the Christmas dances? Us girls at one end, the boys at the other . . .'

'You didn't put up with that for long,' he grinned. 'Always the first to rush over and take your pick . . .'

'Was I?' She laughed. 'I never told you about this bloody awful dance at my first Party conference. I still had that limp, and I got paired off with this northern lad. Well, I thought everything was going fine till he looked at me halfway through the Twist and said . . . "you're a pretty lass, but I never seen such bloody dancing in all my life." He was so embarrassed when he found out why. Sent flowers to my room. He'd have married me next day, if I'd smiled at him.'

Uh-oh. Wrong turn, she thought suddenly, getting up, switching on the television. *Newsnight* was showing her picture, quoting her statement on arrival from Berlin, someone else speculating about her hold on Foreign Affairs . . .

'Popular girl, aren't I? Talk of the town.'

'D'you mind?'

'Not yet. I expect I will, when they get it wrong.' She laughed dryly. 'I should think I'll mind even more when they get it right. For now I can't quite believe they're talking about me. Alison this, Alison that. Who the hell *is* this Alison Lane?'

'I'm beginning to ask myself that as well.'

The tone caught her off guard. 'She's a lot tougher than she used to be. She wouldn't have survived otherwise ...'

'And one day they'll take it away from you, love. What then?'

'Jesus, Dad. How much forward bloody planning d'you want? I've got a job to do. *The* job. Number One. Most important handbag in Britain. See ...' She pointed to the screen. It was a picture of her coming down the steps of the plane. 'Look at me. Talking. Talked about. Analysed. Probed. I'm the bloody evening meal for each and everyone in this country – to be chewed up, or left on the side. But for the little time I may have here ... I'm it. OK. So don't tell a climber who's just reached the top of Everest, that one day he'll have arthritis and won't be able to make it up the stairs.'

His eyes turned down towards the floor. 'I shouldn't have come.'

'Maybe you shouldn't have.' She got up and stood in front of the fireplace. 'I know I've been a single girl all my life. So in your eyes I've probably never grown up. No ties. No kids. But in some ways, I've lived ten lives – the kinds of lives you and Mum couldn't even imagine. The things I haven't done have been a lot harder than the things I have. They've required some pretty difficult decisions over the years. So when you come in here and tell me ...' she stopped and looked down at him. He seemed suddenly like the family Labrador, kicked hard in the balls and sent to its basket for chasing sheep. How can you do that? The man's your father. Not an aide or a flunky, or a worm from the other benches. Can't you turn it off?

She waited a moment, letting the sharp taste drain away. 'It's been a hell of a day, Dad. And you don't know the half of it.'

It was about two in the morning when someone stuck a blade into her chest. And she sat upright in bed, knowing instantly what was wrong.

In dressing gown and slippers she hurried down to the study, unlocked the door and stared at the coffee table, where she knew she had placed Cindy's metal box.

The coffee table gleamed back at her – bare.

Keith had taken it. Had to have done. Nobody else had been in the room. Nobody. Must have slipped it in his pocket when she wasn't looking. How the hell could she have been so stupid? Keith was the only one to come into the room. Except, of course, Sir Henry.

She stood still for a while, mouthing his name over and over again, not knowing why.

Chapter Forty-nine

'Is that your final answer, Harry?'

'Isn't ... "go to hell" clear enough for you?'

'I hoped you'd be more sensible.'

'Just fuck off, Clark. Do the world a favour.'

'You're a stupid man, for someone who was once so clever. The ironic thing is that at this point, I know far more than you do about the whole affair. David Bradley, Alison Lane. You haven't even got a clue, Harry. But I'll break you anyway, because you deserve it.'

The phone went dead and Harry sat at his desk, counting the now familiar symptoms of guilt. The eyelid that wouldn't sit still, the creeping nausea – and the growing need to tell someone.

But he couldn't have told David. Didn't want to admit he'd been stupid enough to have an affair. At his age. In his position. Just another Washington idiot, like so many others. And he had prided himself on being different. Pride? Now it would come out in the worst of all ways and they'd be joking that the whole White House had its dick hanging out ... and Jane? Oh God! Too awful to contemplate.

Norton had said ... 'You haven't even got a clue.' What did that mean?

Somewhere in all this, there were details he'd missed. Something else. Something about Lane.

It peeved him, niggled him, sat in front of him on the desk, daring to be addressed.

Harry knew he couldn't leave it alone.

As a lawyer he had become a formidable researcher. Never went to court without digging a hole in his case. And then he'd dig deeper and again and dig around the first one.

There's no such thing as a complete picture, he would tell his juniors. But you're either more or less complete than your opponent. You work harder, you go to bed later. You suffer for your work, just as artists suffer for their art.

So he knew how to pick up a telephone, knew how to use a library, knew how one document led to another – and with age had come the delight of remote control.

Six calls, four of them transatlantic had set the hunt in train. If there was any delight at being fifty-one, he reflected, it was that your friends started moving into useful positions. A journalist in London, a visiting professor at Oxford, a doctor in Harley Street, and an enquiry agent who had retired to Britain to escape all the clients he'd upset. Then an archivist in Army Records at Quantico.

There were dates and times to be discovered, there were biographies half-written, half thought about.

He would get it, he promised himself.

The only question was whether it would get *him* first.

Harry didn't see the president until much later. He put on his coat and together they stepped on to the Truman balcony. The sun had begun grilling the capital in defiance of winter tradition. Across the south lawn large tracts of snow had melted into swamp.

'It'll freeze again tonight.'

The chief of staff shook his head. 'Time was when the climate did what it was supposed to do. Froze your pipes in winter. Bleached your hair in summer . . .'

'And Washington was a sleepy, southern town.'

'Still is – in some departments.' Harry shrugged. 'So why the smiles?'

'Miss Lane says she'll join me at Camp David tonight and we'll fly on to New York tomorrow.'

'She agreed just like that?'

'I told her several other leaders would be there.'

'And they won't.'

'Right.'

'Jesus, David.' He breathed deeply. 'So you're celebrating?'

'It's kind of premature. Shilov is still in a coma and the news from the Russian border with the Ukraine is lousy. For now I think celebrations would be unwise.'

'So to take your mind off all this, you invited her – with a straight lie.'

'Let's not kid ourselves, Harry. We didn't exactly lose our virginity today.'

Right, he told Bradley silently. Never more right than that, my friend.

The president looked sideways at his friend. 'I want to have some time with her.'

'You'll have an evening,' he winked. 'Until midnight.'

'That's exactly what my landlady once told me in Oxford. If you can't do what you want by midnight ... you're no bloody good. Whenever I had a girl in my room, she used to climb the old narrow staircase with her squeaky, flea-infested dog, and shout outside the door. 'Time up – out you go.'

'Maybe I should play landlady.' Stupid, thought Harry. Stupid thing to say. 'Be careful, David. Please,' he added.

Which of course was even more stupid.

'I'm not invited to Camp David. Can you believe that? The fucking secretary of state doesn't get to go to Camp David when the British prime minister flies in. What in Christ's name's going on?'

Norton stood up. He wore his anger in the shape of two bright red patches that stood out from each cheek, as if they'd been sewn on.

'The guy doesn't like you.' Till's merit in the White House was that unlike many people he could see the obvious. The disadvantage was that he would tell everyone.

'Makes me feel like some kind of leper. And there's a ripple effect. Once it gets out that I don't have the president's ear, let alone even his courtesy, I'm finished inside State. They'll be using my office for the fucking discotheque. And I'll still be there.'

Till burst out laughing.

'I'm serious. If I had any pride I'd resign.'

'We're not in it for the pride ...'

'Yeah, well right now, I'm barely in it, at all. I get about as much time with the President as the Burmese ambassador. We'll meet in New York tomorrow ... I won't have spoken to him, he won't have spoken to me, there won't be any kind of agreed position ... I might as well take round the tray of fucking doughnuts.'

'Ain't that bad.'

'Sure. The only guy Bradley sees is the White House counsel.'

'Fox dressed in human clothes.'

'Same guy.' Norton swung himself a half circle in the easy chair. An ideal time to sound out Till. The house in suburban Maryland was quiet. The family away, thank Christ. Otherwise his wife would be shoving it up his arse, that he was being walked all over and he ought to fight back. What the hell did she think he did?

She'd find out though, soon enough.

He reached over and poured Till a bourbon and a mound of ice. 'I've been talking to an old friend of mine ... .you know Larry D'Anna?'

'That guy's a friend?'

'I use the term loosely.'

'Larry's pretty loose himself. At least he was with the Party finances ...'

'Still a powerful guy. The newspapers he has ... you should know that.'

'So what's his angle?'

'He's taking a very personal interest in the affairs of the president. And I mean affairs ...'

Till grinned. 'So that's why you're pissed at not going to Camp David ...'

'I'd give plenty to know what happens out there.'

Till looked thoughtful. 'What exactly would you be prepared to give?'

Norton caught his eye. 'Favours, recognition, still the only usable currency in this city.'

'How far have you thought this through?'

There was a line of sweat on Norton's upper lip. 'I want to expose him, destroy his credibility, limit his options for manoeuvre. I want more than a lame duck. I want a laughing stock duck; a can't-get-himself-out-of-bed-on-crutches duck; the biggest duck casualty since records began.'

'That's a lot of wanting.'

'Look at it this way ... We're midway through the guy's first term. It's time to start positioning yourself. If you want to come along for the ride?'

Till nodded, drained the bourbon and got up to pour himself another.'

Norton frowned. 'Make yourself at home.'

'Thanks. I will.' He grinned. 'As a matter of fact I'll be at Camp David myself tonight.'

'I know, you beautiful little putz.' The secretary of state smiled for the first time that day.

It was nearly twenty-four hours later that Harry saw Jane. She had been working nights at the hospital. He had been working nights. Jason had been baby-sat to distraction.

He tiptoed in and sat in the kitchen, listening to the silence.

And then as he looked up, he saw her standing in the doorway, with an expression she'd never worn before.

She knows. She knows. And that silence is the sound of my life coming to an end.

'I got a letter today, Harry.' So quiet, so level. 'It told me you'd been seeing someone, even gave me a name and a few other details as well ...'

'Jane ...'

'Listen to me Harry. I don't believe everything I read. After all I'm a doctor, aren't I? I make my own diagnoses. Set my own questions and then answer them. I even checked with the White House to see if there was someone by the name I'd been given ...'

Harry, like time itself, is a thing of the past.

'They told me there used to be but she'd just left town. For good. Gone back home to California. Couldn't take Washington. People are very understanding. They like to help.'

'Listen, Jane ...'

'Don't, Harry. You see that's good enough for me. I don't own you ...'

'Maybe you do, more than you think.'

'If you ever meet someone, Harry. Just tell me about it, OK. Lies – I can't deal with, but the truth I can handle, however bad. I give it to my patients' families, and they cry and they weep, and then they go home and somehow as the days go by, they get on with their lives. I cried and wept a lot today, Harry. Now I'm getting on with my life. With our life.' She kissed him on the cheek. 'Goodnight, Harry.'

He fell asleep where he was, head cushioned by his arm on the kitchen table.

Chapter Fifty

Katya knew she should return to Moscow.

She leaned over the inert body of her husband and looked hard into his face. 'You'd want me to go, wouldn't you? At least I can try to get them talking, keep the old bastards at bay, make them see reason. I've known that little pisser of a vice-president since he was six ...'

But Shilov didn't answer, half-buried as he was under wires and bandages. Half-alive.

She touched his hand, as if that might stir him, force him to make the connections. And yet the hand seemed strangely cold.

'I need your strength to help me do what must be done. Please!'

She sat back in the chair and dried her eyes. The last thing he wanted was a snivelling cry-baby. He'd never had one before. He wasn't going to get one now. Not when so much had to be done. Not when Russia seemed to be hurrying towards a black hole.

Such a terrifying country, she reflected. Like a violent, uncontrollable horse. Everytime you loosened the reins, it would gallop towards the cliff, bent on its own destruction. There was no kinder, gentler Russia. There was a manageable Russia – with the lid shut tight. Or there was no Russia at all.

She looked at the clock. Another half hour and then she'd leave him, order up the presidential plane, shout her way on to it – loud and angry. As long as he lived, she'd possess his authority. They couldn't refuse her.

Watching him, it occurred to her that she hadn't seen him that peaceful for so many years. Not since their student days, when they would lie for hours in the woods on the outskirts of Moscow, because that was the only place you could be alone.

There you could imagine you lived in a beautiful country, far away from the red banners and the slogans, the deadening pettiness that went with them, the food queues, the scavenging and dishonesty.

But it required great imagination. It was as if the magnificent Russian soul that her husband spoke about, wasn't really so magnificent after all. It was a fragile, capricious being, always hostage to the abuses and corruption of its people.

Maybe a part of it still existed somewhere. Maybe it had died, like so much else. Maybe she would find out in the days to come.

In the distance, Katya heard a door slam shut.

She had always believed in signals. The little things of life, pointing the way to the bigger things. Everyone had a path to follow. All you had to do was read the signposts correctly along the way.

She got up, aware that the atmosphere inside the room had changed. Shilov lay more still, more peaceful than before.

'I'm leaving now,' she said quietly, and bent to kiss him.

Yet, at the last moment something stopped her. Somehow a kiss like that seemed too final.

What had he said once? ... 'If it hurts to say goodbye, then don't say it. Just walk out. Go. But leave the door open. Then anything is possible.'

'The only doors that ever close for good are in the mind. Others – you can force open, pick the lock, smash them down with an axe. But not the ones inside the head ... So leave the door open.' She could still hear the words, the way he had uttered them.

Rapidly now, Katya turned away without looking at her husband, and went in search of the doctors.

She spoke to them for no more than two minutes, holding herself so straight and calm, that they marvelled at her self-possession. And yet they seemed genuinely shocked by her words. One of them stared after her in disbelief, as she walked away down the corridor, past the nurses and the trolleys. He was still staring long after she'd disappeared.

'You think,' he told his colleagues, 'that you've seen it all. Until the day – like this day – when you haven't.'

Through the trees around the clearing, the moonlight sketched shadows over Chukovsky's encampment. The six helicopter gunships had turned into fifteen – dragooned together, their missiles slung beneath them. For now they were lifeless and awkward. Once ordered into the air they were the favoured killing machines of

Russia's forward units, on special operations.

'Colonel, you should see this.'

The young major handed him a computer print-out. Chukovsky read it briefly and passed it back.

'Is that all, Colonel? No reply?'

'What d'you want me to say?'

'For the sake of Jesus Christ, say something. And pretty fucking quickly. What I gave you was the official Ukrainian communique issued in Kiev forty minutes ago. It accuses you of an act of war against a Sovereign state and demands the withdrawal of all forces, within twenty-four hours. Still nothing to say? Uh? Where is this little adventure to lead. Perhaps you'd like to share this State secret . . . ?'

'They won't do anything.' Chukovsky's voice was calm.

'How can you be sure?'

'Because they want the missiles intact. Anyway it's out of my hands. I'm now obeying orders from Moscow. Or hadn't you noticed?'

The major snorted. 'There aren't any fucking orders out of Moscow. No one has a clue who's in command. They're running around, scared out of their wits that Shilov will die, or they'll be a coup, or God knows what else might happen . . . The only reason they haven't told you where to get off, is because no one's strong enough to issue the order. And besides, the hardliners are quite happy for you to make a point. Mother Russia baring her teeth. You're just playing into their hands . . .'

'Maybe. That's not the point.'

'What is?'

'I told you. We have to defend the missiles. If we clear out. If we remove the troops, they'll seize the silos and the missiles, and we'll have lost everything.'

'Meanwhile, you're content to start a war?'

'I didn't attack the silo in the first place . . . I didn't kill a twenty-year-old captain.'

'But you're escalating the conflict. Ukraine . . .'

'Somebody has to solve the question of these missiles. Finally. The leaders got nowhere in Berlin. Maybe this will focus their minds. It's vital. We need the world's attention. Now.'

'So you hold the world to ransom.'

Chukovsky got up and went over to within a few inches of the major's face. 'I force the world to see this issue. Now. In daylight.'

'A fine argument, my friend.' The major spat on the ground. 'I wonder if the history books will manage to see it that way.'

He must have slept for an hour. No more. And yet he knew that the sleep had gone.

In the forest you were never alone. Birds, animals, all moving to the rhythm of their night.

He could well remember the time he had climbed up from the silo and surveyed the universe beyond the clearing. He remembered the promise he had made himself, never to use the weapons, never to destroy the beauty that he saw around him.

Chukovsky didn't think of himself as a religious man. True, he had been baptised in secret, soon after birth ... but he had hardly made the decision himself. To him the church had always been part of Russia's folklore. A cultural heritage, irrelevant to the life around him.

So he didn't know what made him kneel down on the forest floor, and pray to a God he had never spoken to, and never even imagined.

Chapter Fifty-one

'Why do we have to keep on meeting like a couple of old queens out of school?'

Tom Marks, the Trade and Industry Secretary, glared at Harper across his double espresso.

'Speak for yourself, my friend. It's Ms Lane you should be asking.' Keith made a point of the Ms.

'Still bitter and twisted, I see. For God's sake, Keith give it up. I'm not surprised she won't jump into bed with you. Can't say I know many who would. Look at yourself, man. You're no oil painting, are you?'

Keith sat back and surveyed Marks with evident enjoyment. He had chosen the café well. A small brasserie, just behind Oxford Street. The place full of guide books and Italians. Not a soul speaking English. Even so, he leaned forward almost whispering, watching the colour ebb away from Marks's face, the fingers begin a little dance on the table. Rage, incredulity. It was all there, thought Keith, building nicely.

'Christ, Jesus, Almighty!' Marks pushed away his cup in disgust. 'I can't bloody believe it. Alison Lane? Cool as a mountain stream. You've *got* to be joking . . .'

'The Americans say Bradley's crazy about her. This morning she went haring off to Camp David. Told everyone there was going to be a crisis meeting of foreign leaders there. I happen to know she's the only one. And if what I think will happen, happens . . .'

Marks looked round to make sure no one was listening. 'It's the lies I don't like. Combination of lie and innuendo. And then there's this being in bed with the Americans – in more ways than one – that's going to piss the Party off mightily. Most of them loathe Bradley and everything he stands for.'

'There's also the film.'

'What film?'

'Delivered to me, this morning. Film of a little incident between Ms Lane and her masseuse.'

'I don't believe . . .'

'You want to see it?'

'Dirty bastard.' Marks shifted his bottom off the plastic seat, from where it appeared to have stuck fast. 'I don't get this. Any of it. I just don't . . . whole thing smacks almost of a concerted campaign. But who . . .?' He put his hands together on the table. 'We're going to have to bury this, and bury it now. There's too much at stake. We've got the Party faithful out all over the bloody country, swearing undying allegiance to her, selling her on every bloody soapbox from here to Flugga Mugga. Historic change of course. Bloody hell!' He wiped his forehead on his sleeve. 'If you don't get rid of this, she isn't going to make it. New prime ministers are fragile enough as it is. We couldn't take this amount of scandal. Party's been out of power too long. Seventeen years and now this. There's no other way, Harper. You'll have to kick it under the nearest rug and sit on it.'

'Too late for that.'

'What?'

'I said it's too late. The Americans have the story and they're not exactly blushing virgins. They've got the film as well. Don't you see what I'm saying?'

'So what do we do?' Marks's voice climbed into descant.

'Stay calm in the first instance.'

'We have to do something, man. Fast.'

'I can't save her, Marks. I've tried thinking of everything. But it's not in my power. You've got to know that. Talk to the rest of the Cabinet. Talk to the Unions, the party managers. Get everyone prepared, because she's going down – and there's not a thing I can do about it.'

Marks had begun flapping his head up and down, like a rag doll.

'Listen to what I'm saying. There aren't any quiet ways – she's got to go in a blaze of publicity. Get it out. Get it over and move on. Otherwise the story will never go away. It's too close. Too sensitive. Too many ramifications. If she's hit with this at the start of her term, she'll never recover . . . you know that, as well as I do.'

Marks's face twisted into a sneer. 'I'm not blind, my friend. Don't think I can't see your role in any of this.'

Keith put on a choirboy expression. Calm Keith. Reasonable

Keith. 'I'm simply warning everyone to be prepared, learn their lines, so we're not all caught looking even more stupid ... It'll be a bad week. Course it will. I'm not saying it won't. An awful week. But it doesn't have to be a mass grave for everyone. Think about that.' He shrugged. 'As for me ... I stand ready to serve the Party in any way I can.'

'You pompous shit.'

Marks got up and left the café without another word.

Keith could see Levinson in the cinema queue, just as they'd arranged. But he wouldn't greet him. They stood separately as the dismal matinée audience shuffled in out of the daylight. He couldn't remember the last time he'd seen a movie in daytime. God, not since they'd played truant from school and got a clout round the ear for it.

He hadn't even looked at the film's title. Something like Black Dogs, or Red Dogs.

Didn't matter anyway.

It was funny to think this was how Denise spent her time. Whatever it was at the local flicks, she saw it. Lined her stomach with coffee and sat bug-eyed as one film blurred into another and one more day got clocked up on life's meter. No wonder she'd become so boring. Her whole existence took place on a screen. Bugger all in the way of participation.

Levinson joined him in the neighbouring seat, Coke in hand. He offered a wet hand.

'So are we ready?'

Keith surveyed the auditorium. 'Let's get the story out of Camp David. If it comes, you can go for the next day's papers. Understood?'

'My people have already psyched up some of the editors ...'

'Did you hear what I said? Only if we get something out of Camp David ...'

'I hear you. I hear you. This isn't the slither of cold feet, I hope?'

'Keep your bloody voice down.' Keith could see a couple of heads turning in their direction. 'I'm the one who set all this up, if you remember. So don't talk to me about cold feet.'

They sat in silence for a few moments. On the screen Keith could see a train bearing down a mountain pass. Anxious faces. Just like his.

In the past, he reflected, he'd never been the one to press the big button. Not by himself. Of course he'd helped. Any number of ritual muggings. MPs set on in the parliamentary equivalent of a dark alley. Careers and reputations beaten up for the greater good. Fighting the good fight.

'Look at this place,' a fellow MP had told him, his first day in the Commons. 'Look at the building. Grand isn't it? Then take a look at the buggers walking around. Half of them would be better off managing a public pisshole. Be more honest, wouldn't it?'

Rough game you played, in your suits and ties, in the bars and tea-rooms and on the terraces. All the honourable members, shafting each other with a cucumber sandwich in one hand and a young blonde researcher in the other ... if they could get it. Bloody rough game.

He turned towards Levinson. 'All right. But Camp David's got to be the lead. If you get it – ring the number I gave you. If you don't, we'll have to think again. But either way we don't have to meet any more. That's one advantage, I suppose. Just don't mess it up.'

Levinson offered his hand again, but Keith ignored it. He knew perfectly well where that hand had been.

'May I speak to you, Prime Minister?'

'Of course, Dick. Sit down.'

They were three quarters across the Atlantic, 35,000 feet high. Every hour putting them another six hundred miles further from London.

'What's on your mind?'

'This is difficult, Prime Minister.' The face once again gammon pink. 'I don't know how to begin really ... but it's something I feel I have to say ...'

'Then you'd better say it.' Alison gestured to the cabin around her. 'I'm not exactly going anywhere.'

'That's just it, I'm afraid. I don't think I'm going anywhere, with you. Not in this job. I just feel it's not going to take me in the right

233

direction ... and I have my future to consider, my children ...' His voice trailed away.

'I see. May I ask what's brought you to this realisation? After all, we've only been working together for a week now. I wasn't aware I'd presented a major threat to your children during that time – nor any other members of your family, come to think of it. Not so far, anyway.'

'I don't think it's going to work. I mean I feel very nervous about some of the things I'm hearing ...'

'From me?'

'Not just from you. But there's some talk among the Press. Some kind of groundswell against you. It seems to be building ... .'

'When does it not build? Have you ever known a prime minister who didn't have to watch out for the Ides of January, February, March and then all the way to bloody Christmas and back again. What d'you think politics is ... ?'

'I just think this is different.' He bites a piece of gammon from the lower lip. 'This ship doesn't seem to have a direction ...'

'And you want my permission to bravely jump before it capsizes.'

'I don't mean it that way.' Foster's cheeks are carrying a film of sweat, embarrassment and fear. 'This is all so awkward ...'

'But you need to think of the future. That's what you said. Your children. My goodness I never realised I was so life threatening. According to you, staying with me is just about as healthy as a weekend in Chernobyl. Well ... Dick Foster.' Her fingers locked together under her chin. 'This is your immediate future. You will work with me during this trip, because I don't have anyone else. When we return to London, you can draw up a shortlist of replacements, preferably people who have a little more backbone and loyalty in them, than you. After that you can dig a hole in the ground and live in it, as far as I'm concerned. Is that understood?'

'I ... I'm very sorry, Prime Minister.'

'So am I, Dick. I had no idea you were as weak and pathetic as this. Perhaps politics isn't for you at all. Maybe you should give the hole in the ground serious consideration. You could possibly find work as a gardener. Something quiet and intellectually untaxing.' She smiled sweetly. 'That should suit your talents.'

* * *

So what am I doing? Chucking it all away?

It's Harper and his friends. They got me in. Now they want me destroyed with rumour, and a lie I should never have told.

Why did I?

I could so easily have said, yes, Bradley and I knew each other. Course we did. Not well, mind. But we had a drink a couple of times. Why not. What would have been so astronomically mundane as that?

And yet I couldn't let the genie out. That moment, in the middle of the interview – I thought – if anybody learns of this, even the barest details, then the whole thing'll be public property. The pain, the memories. The realisation of what I lost. I couldn't have gone through that.

So what now? Sir Henry will look out for me. Do whatever he does below the surface – pressure, suborn, threaten . . . who knows?

'Haven't I always?' he said, when I asked him to watch my back. And he has. That's true.

Only this time, it wasn't much of an answer, was it?

Chapter Fifty-two

From Dulles airport in Virginia the presidential helicopter carried her north over the state line into Maryland, where the snow lay speckled and uneven across the landscape, patterned as if by the paw-prints of a giant beast.

They bent low over the forests with the rotors slashing at the wind. As the machine banked hard towards a clearing, Alison could make out the toy people in parkas and fur hats, the snow driving at their faces.

She knew him instantly, the giant in blue, at least three inches taller than the others, laughing as his cap was torn off in the slipstream, springing after it.

Alison felt a pang of embarrassment. They were all in jeans and rough boots and she had worn a suit – a bloody suit for God's sake – with patent leather shoes. The prize cow from England. Trust a Brit to get it wrong.

Doors open and she was making excuses in her mind. This was what you got when your Party'd been out of power for seventeen years. No one knew these things. No one had the faintest idea how you dressed at Camp David. Last time Labour had been in government, they'd gone into the ark two by two. Bugger! The other woman hadn't made mistakes like this. That at least was certain.

Carefully she let herself down the steps, as the Marine guard saluted. Bradley stepped forward and for a moment it seemed she almost fell into his arms.

'Prime Minister . . .' he grinned. 'Great welcome.'

Introductions through chattering teeth as the cold swirled around them. Presidential aides, a pool camera, White House lenswoman. Bags of American informality and ease, while her own sphincter squeezed ever more tightly.

Bradley's arm cossetted her through. 'I was going to treat you to the presidential golf cart. It was the only thing Ronald Reagan was ever trusted to drive. But it doesn't go too well in the snow. Walk?'

The wind bit at her face and legs. 'Of course. That'd be very nice ...'

'I mean you Brits don't feel the cold, I seem to remember.' His eyes laughed at her.

They walked in silence for a while, feet crunching on ice.

'We have a lot of work to get through tonight.' Business now. Business first and last, she thought. 'Have the others arrived yet?'

'Ah.'

She stopped and turned towards him. About fifty yards back three secret servicemen slithered to a halt. 'Ah' was not the answer she wanted.

Bradley seemed to be hiding behind a tree of his own making. 'They ... uh ... cancelled at the last moment.'

'I see. They just ... uh, cancelled. All of them. One by one.'

A quiet 'Yup.'

'You liar!' Came out just like that.

'Yes. I'm afraid so.'

'You admit it?'

'Can't deny it.'

'God! What's the matter with you? Don't you hear anything I've been saying ... ?'

'Everything. Every word, Prime Minister.' More teeth. 'I just had a query or two on interpretation ...'

She turned away from him and took a few steps off the path between the trees. But then, quite suddenly, she didn't want to fight. She could see the image of a little girl stamping her foot in the snow, because someone had taken her toboggan, yelling out loud across the park, trying to throw rocks at the sky. You can't go on like that. Not when all your friends have run away. In the grown-up world, he lied and she lied. But on a snowy day in Maryland, there was a single truth. She was glad to see him.

'You like my coat?'

He peered at her as if from the trenches. 'Sure.'

'Can you lend me some jeans?'

Camp David is an upmarket holiday village, a series of guest cottages, with tiny kitchens and bars and televisions and all the freedom of a zoo.

When the president is there, air-space in the region is closed to all but the official. Noisy dogs and very silent human beings patrol the forests around. The seat of power becomes a high-tech log cabin, like a wooden white house – a tree house. Birds eat crumbs from your table while the man with the Great Seal turns sausages on the barbecue and discusses what he wants to do with the rest of the world, for the rest of the day.

Jeans and sweats *are* the order of the day – any day. For long ago American presidents gave up wearing ties simply to prove they were gentlemen. Fashions changed – and real gentlemen went and did other jobs.

Bradley led her to the cabin and pushed open the door. Someone had already placed her luggage on a rack. I expect, she thought, that someone would hang up my clothes if I asked. Someone would polish my shoes, or lick them if I really wanted it, turn down the bed, fasten my dress – or unfasten it, if it ever came to that ... no doubts on that score. But everything in front of her spoke simplicity and warmth. The country-bright sofas. Wooden sills, wooden floors polished to a diplomatic sparkle. Little house on the prairie, it said. Only the outsize white telephone hinted at power and the world beyond.

'If you need your people, they're somewhere out there.' He pointed vaguely through the windows, but she could see only the trees, sagging under snow. 'If you want a maid or a butler, we have those too. If you need me ...'

I do. Something inside her spoke the words, but they didn't come out.

'If you need me, just pick up the phone.'

He stood there, uncertain what to say next.

When you speak, she thought, you use your eyes, and you angle your head, and you hold your hands in front of you, feeling for the cuffs that aren't there. Some people make decisions when life rules out all the other options. You make them right up front. Choices. And yours are different from mine.

'I shouldn't be here like this. Nor should you. Not when there's a spotlight on us, when people are talking and sniffing and looking for evidence ...'

'People always talk ...'

'It's more serious than that,' she interrupted. 'It's damaging and it's painful, for all sorts of reasons ...'

'But you're safe here. For just a night. Nothing's going to happen, Alison ...'

She shivered slightly. 'If you leave the door open the warmth will go.'

'I could close it from the inside, or shut it behind me on the porch.'

'Is that a question?'

'If it were, would you answer?'

She couldn't help smiling. 'If I answered, would it be the one you wanted?'

Gently, almost imperceptibly, he licked the side of his mouth and it reminded her the way she used to do that in the darkness of the cinema, a teenager sitting next to her boyfriend, getting ready in case he kissed her. You didn't want your lips too dry. You had to be prepared.

The scene changed again and she could see him in her room at Oxford in the middle of the night, twenty years old, eyes peaceful, heart peaceful, only his hands moving. You've loved once and you know you'll do so again before morning.

And she would run her finger down his chest, as if it were a zip, releasing the energy below, watching him stir, hearing the breathing become more urgent.

Like the tide, he was, coming in, slamming against the shore.

'What do you want from me, David?'

'I want to find the person I knew.'

'What for?'

'Because I cared very much for her.'

'And if she's gone?'

'Then she's gone. But what if she hasn't?'

'It may not matter.' Her eyes left him, as if to look into herself. 'If she has another life.'

'She could have both.'

'Is that the American way, to have it all ways, and death is just an option ... if you want to go?'

'I don't want to take anything away from her ...'

'Then how does she keep what she has ... ?'

'By adding to it.'

Dialogue in the third person. Always safer. The fiction that you're talking about other people. 'You used to be so good.' Her eyes seem to find him again. 'So plausible. You could argue a case.'

'And this one?'

I'm so tired of fighting.

'You still argue well.'

Outside the window a pile of snow cascaded softly from the trees. If their eyes could reach out, she thought, then they would touch. There was a moment when they dared each other to step forward. Like standing in the sea thirty years before, wondering who'd be the first to strip. Only neither moved. Then or now.

A moment that sits forever in the space between you.

And you can spend a lifetime wondering why you never went for it. When it was there on offer and you wanted to.

Why didn't he move?

Why didn't I move?

Moments are just that.

And this one has passed.

Dinner comes. Simple and large.

They sat at a farmhouse table. Till and Foster on hand, talking cameras and press pools and a scattering of others. The Brits had removed their ties as a concession to informality – the Americans in designer leisure, as if born in it.

There's another difference, thought Alison. They have expectations. They expect to succeed, expect to be happy, expect things to work. And we're always surprised if they do. We trail around, head held low, palms on the ground, waiting for a brick to drop on us. That's why it does. What brick can resist the temptation?

They talked Russia. Shook their heads over the turkey, basted and glistening, tutted at the pecan pie, sighed long and loud over the cognac. Life was hard and likely to prove it once again.

Bradley did the carving himself. 'We have to involve the security council. Has to be an international concensus on this thing.'

'Why?' Alison's sharp little word. Sharper than they'd expected. 'Look at Bosnia. Whole thing winds up in a talk shop. A few UN troops get sent out to provide target practice for the warring parties.

And they settle it on the ground anyway.'

'What would you do?'

They all seemed to be munching more quietly, ears extended to pull in her answer – if she had one.

Bradley collected a sliver of white meat, smothered it in mashed potato, and was about to despatch it, when he put down his fork and stared at her quizzically.

'As I understand it, your Party generally favours the use of sanctions in these circumstances. Right?'

'Right.' She tilted her head in acknowledgement. 'But times are different. And maybe, Mr President, I'm different. There isn't time for resolutions, for condemnations. Right now there's a missile silo in the Ukraine that the Russians and Ukrainians may be about to fight over. If we don't sort out *this* silo, there are dozens of others waiting to flare up in our faces.'

'So?'

She looked down the two rows of faces, and at David Bradley at the other end.

'I'll announce my proposal in New York tomorrow.' She caught David's eye. 'Meanwhile, your turkey's getting cold.'

Till has a friend in the secret service. One of the friends Till tries to have everywhere.

Pressman's friend is Till. Anyone's friend. Listen and spin. Listen and spin. That's the job. Can't do it without friends in all the places. High and low. Especially low.

Till sits in his cottage with the head of the secret service detail.

Truth be known, they're not too fond of Bradley either. Doesn't do what he's told.

And to think they have him for life. Not just the four-year term. This guy gets a nanny in dark glasses and a plastic earpiece until the day he croaks. If he doesn't behave now, think what he'll be like when he's a crochety old fool, curmudgeon – or the way Till puts it – 'pain in the butt.'

Secret serviceman is bitter because he was told to get lost. Presidents can do that. Most of them don't know they can. But if the commander in chief tells you to back off, you shrivel up and die. And Bradley did just that. Tonight.

And I know why, Till thinks. My knowledge is my power.

'I shouldn't be telling you any of this.'

But she does.

And he sits where he was at the end of the table, now that everyone has shuffled away into the forest and the peace of the night lies around them.

She tells him about the foreboding she feels, about her lie on television, about Harper and Cindy – about the row with Dad.

If she leaves out anything – then she leaves out Sir Henry, not knowing why.

'Nature of the beast,' he says. 'You always feel you're on the brink.'

'In Britain you are. I could be gone tomorrow. You at least know you have four years in office. You're also head of state. That's like dry land. I don't have that refuge. My feet are wet all the time. Even Foster, born into slavery by the look of him – even he wants to desert.'

'I can have him shot.'

She smiled. 'Does it ever get to be fun?'

'Moments. In retrospect.' He gets up, turns down the light, leans against the wall, notes the fullness of her breasts against the blouse. Breasts to feed men, not babies, he thinks, wondering where the thought has come from. 'What will you do?'

'Fight. What else can I do?'

'D'you have enough friends?'

'Maybe. Early days. Depends if they think I'll make it. Coups like mine are notoriously unstable. I shouldn't be here. Shouldn't have left Britain. Not now. Certainly not for any international crisis.'

'Why did you?'

'Wanted to show off. Always easier to score goals away, than at home. Thought I could make a difference. I still think that.'

'Then you will.'

Not an awkward end to the conversation. Quite a natural pause – the way two travellers might stop along a country road to check directions.

David Bradley went over to Alison's chair, knelt beside it and touched the fine blonde hair and the dimpled face. Somehow his hand found hers and the fingers locked.

In the darkness of the forest an animal pauses to sniff the night, drawn by the lights and the sounds from the big house.

There's no thought for the cold – only for the prey, for the victims.

When you watch someone, you join their life. You leave your world and attempt to enter theirs. You read their intentions, and actions. From then on, they talk to you. They act for you. They belong in part to your vision.

When he rose from the frozen ground, the animal became a man, who shuffled away from the big house and went looking for his friend.

He wakes up Till, who wasn't sleeping anyway.

It's as good as anything they'd imagined.

In his mind David's rushing back down the path, same feel, same sensations, hurrying as if, after all this time, the same person will be waiting at the other end.

'Don't move me too fast.'

'It's been thirty years.'

'I'm an old lady. I need careful handling. I'm not used to being pawed.'

'I'm not pawing you.'

'Maybe we should wait.'

'What for? The millennium?'

'Maybe we've forgotten how to do it.'

'We used to do little else.'

'I don't remember.'

'Think back to the bathroom, old lady. Things you used to do with a bar of soap.'

'Only 'cos you asked me to.'

'I'm asking again.'

'Nicely?'

'Nicely.'

'Haven't got any soap.'

And then the white phone on the bureau starts buzzing and the rest of the world seems to walk in and watch.

'This isn't going to work.'

'Yes, it is.'

'No,' she says. 'I have to answer it.'

Chapter Fifty-three

Katya put down the phone and stared out over the traffic of central Moscow.

They didn't live in the Kremlin. Her husband had insisted on keeping their three-room flat from the old days, and she'd agreed. Image was vital. Nowadays the president was poor and the crooks were rich. So things had changed.

And other things had stayed the same.

All morning she had held court among the powerful and the corrupt. How was the president, they salivated? How serious were his wounds, what could they do for him and for her? And for the cause of peace?

And as she answered, she could see their eyes making the calculations. Where did they stand in the order of succession? Would they rise or fall? Could they claw themselves an extra slice of power while the larder was open?

To each she had conveyed what she termed 'the president's instructions.' Stay calm, stay loyal, prevent retaliation.

And in mock solemnity they had nodded back their assent. One or two had even stooped to wiping perfectly dry eyes with a handkerchief. Of course they understood. They would obey the president without question. Only ... only the silo in the Ukraine refused to back down. For now, dear lady, it was out of contact. Out of reach. They could do little except wait. Russia, did she know, was a big country ...

Maybe it was the smile, barely repressed on the lips of the armed forces chief, Marshal Tenko, that made her lose her footing. Made her realise the presence of men without care or restraint. Men of bad will.

And now in the last few hours they had made sure the new reports were brought gleefully to her door; men and material had poured over the border into Ukraine ... and Russia was once again on the cliff, getting ready to jump.

Katya didn't know what brought her the image of Alison Lane. Perhaps it was the expression of sympathy and understanding she had seen in Berlin. Only she couldn't let it go. Without thinking she had ordered the Kremlin operators to locate the British prime minister as a matter of great urgency, wherever on the planet she might be.

'I have to go to the Ukraine. I need you to come with me. A symbol of international concern and resolve. The situation is deteriorating very rapidly. I need your presence. Will you come?'

The voice, bounced by two satellites to the Russian Far East, downlegged, as they like to put it in Seattle, and beamed through White House communications to the State of Maryland, losing none of its brittle control.

To a cottage in the woods.

And even allowing for the fact that politicians fear a direct question like the onset of typhoid, the answer had been unambiguous.

'I'll return your call in thirty minutes. Please wait beside the phone.'

So Katya knew she was dealing with a woman of unusual decisiveness. A serious woman. And for a moment she felt relief.

Only when she caught sight of herself in a mirror did she see the avalanche of pain the other side of her eyes.

How long before it smashed through her defences and broke her?

The room at Berlin's Charite hospital had been sealed. And yet two plain-clothed guards from the Russian embassy sat outside day and night.

No one entered or left, and they asked no questions. The shifts changed every eight hours, and the hospital administration continued to give twice-daily bulletins to the reporters and television crews, installed at the front of the building.

Only a handful of doctors knew where the president had been taken. They had arranged the transfer by themselves, in the low hours of the night, when the corridors had been all but deserted, when death moves quietly about its business. They had used a tunnel once reserved for the East German communist leaders. No nurses or orderlies had assisted. They had kept their word. And it was they alone who supplied the information about their patient.

Of course, they had misgivings. But then, they reasoned, they had had those before. Plenty of them, during the twenty-eight years when Berlin had lived with a wall, and its citizens had died trying to cross it.

What they were doing was strictly against the ethics of the medical profession.

And yet, once you started down such a road, it is virtually impossible to turn back.

The president's wife had known that when she looked at each of them in turn and extracted their promise.

I can't think of him lying in a tiny room in Berlin. I mustn't. I may only think of him when it's over.

And yet that figure was no longer my husband. The face, plain and white like cardboard. The body immobile. The mind, gone on a journey, who knows where. Not the man I have carried in my hands and my heart.

When I knew him he possessed the force of ten devils, pulled by a train. A man machine, energised by all the could-be visions that might have so changed the world.

Now silent. But not at peace. Never at peace.

I will return to you soon.

Chapter Fifty-four

'You don't want my advice, do you?'

'No. Yes.'

'Which?'

'You tell me.'

He pulled away from her. The flushed cheeks made her seem younger, more vulnerable.

'I know what I have to do, David.'

'Great. Then do it.' Back away into a corner. See if she'll follow.

'I don't have too many choices any more . . .'

'We could talk about that.'

'For Chrissake, I'm being squeezed by the bloody snakes. All about you and me. Mainly. Thirty years ago. This is what gets me. And I had to lie about it. D'you believe that? I don't know any more if I'm going to be sleeping in Downing Street or under Charing Cross Bridge.'

'Then go home . . .'

'And lose the chance to make a difference. In Russia I might be able to *do* something . . .'

'Too risky. Too unprepared. Could easily blow up in your face . . .'

'So you're saying forget it . . . ?'

He nodded.

'I can't.'

Somewhere, he thought, I've played this scene already. Only the roles were reversed, and the issues were just as blurred . . .

'Listen to me, Alison . . .' He saw her head shake. 'All right, don't listen, but I'll say it anyway. World leaders, and you're one of them, can't just go jetting round the world – like some kind of do-gooders tour. Doesn't work that way. Can't work that way. This Russian woman could be lying. They could have set a trap for her. She doesn't know what she's getting into. And you don't either. Bottom line, Alison. You can't afford to bet on less than a pretty-damn-close-to certainty. And you don't have it here.'

'You went off to Vietnam. Bush went to Panama. Mitterrand went to Bosnia. People do this ...'

'When it's prepared ...'

'No! When it's important. How many times do leaders sit on their fat arses on fat cushions and order people into war? Tell me. You've done it. If I stay in power much longer, maybe I'll do it too. Who knows? But just sometimes you've got to set an example, David. You have to get out of the sleaze bucket of party politics and opinion polls and lead from the front. Not from some armour plated fucking car with bodyguards.'

'Jesus! How you can even think about something as stupid ... ?'

'I haven't seen you this angry for a few years ...'

'I haven't had so much cause ...'

She sat up on the sofa and draped her feet over the side. Her blouse stayed half-open, the way it had been when the phone rang. Even angry, David required a serious effort to pull away his eyes.

'Call her back, Alison. Offer tea and regrets. Advisers. Blankets. Offer her anything she wants, except your presence. You're not a mediation service, you're a leader.'

'I don't want your advice.'

'Then why are you here?'

She looked away. 'I don't know, David. I really don't know.'

He'd give it one more try, he thought. Moving closer, despite the imminent storm warnings ...

'You're not elected to take risks like this ...'

'I took enough risks to get here.'

'That's different. When you get the job, things change.'

'They shouldn't ...'

'They have to. It's called responsibility.'

'Not in my world. I didn't take the job to sit in a chair. Didn't you ever have any sense of what you wanted to achieve ... ?'

'Yes.'

'And did this sense involve any risk-taking – albeit in the cause of truth, liberty and the pursuit of happiness?'

'Don't patronise me. Of course it did ...' He could see where she was taking him.

'So risks are fine under certain circumstances?'

248

'Right.'

'You mean when they pay off.'

'Yes.'

'When the world holds its breath, and you come home with the trophy. Against all the odds, all the predictions. Our boy shoots the apple off a baby's head at a thousand yards, and becomes the hero of the day . . .'

'Yes, yes, yes . . .' He couldn't help feeling a grain of admiration.

'So all it has to do is work. That's your bottom line. That's how you get from being idiot to genius, from fool to sage, from coward to a citation for bravery. All it has to do is work.'

'It won't.'

'It will.'

And there was the wire.

There were the words, he thought, that stop time in its passage.

He could see it in her. Still, after so many years. The Alison who would always stand up from the crowd, spear in hand, who'd argue with all the finesse of a battering ram, who'd always go after just one more dragon. He'd seen it in Oxford at the political meetings, in the lectures when she'd argued with the tutors. There had to have been thirty years in which she'd refined the art, developed it, channelled it into the lady who *would* win. The lady with her blouse unbuttoned and the fine blonde hair in all directions. In a cabin in the woods.

'Then call her,' he said.

She put out her hand and touched his forehead.

Something mundane about the final act of betrayal. It's the plotting that's fearful, the steps, the intention. The nights when you wonder where your soul will go.

And then the thing builds a life of its own. And you, the creator, can only sit back and watch it grow.

As he dialled the number on his cellphone, Till felt no remorse and no trepidation. He was calm. He felt good about himself. At peace with the final move.

He could picture Norton in the front room of his colonial, just over the DC line. Guarded voice, because the pushy wife was back. She of the rasping Southern stiletto, she of the ambition. Only now he'd have something to tell her, and it would be plum pie and he could do it up, down, and kissing her kazoo all night long, if that's what he wanted. And anything else he wanted. So long as she got it first.

In turn, Norton would make a call of his own. To the prize skunk Larry D'Anna who would get the printing presses spinning for the devil himself, and all who would smile at his works.

Till lay down on the bed, and pictured the first of the White House news conferences that he'd be facing in just a day and a half. 'I'm sorry guys, I have nothing for you on this one. We do not, repeat not comment on the president's personal life, nor his past, nor any sleazy innuendo that happens to be circulating.'

And then they'd tear him to pieces and the crews would be out, and they'd be digging into every crumb of dirt they could lay their hands on. And he'd love it.

Wouldn't be long before someone talked. A someone in London, or from the Oxford days, or from Camp David or Berlin. The networks would throw dollars at anyone who even whistled the right tune. He'd see to that. Stoking the fire, if it were needed. He'd help it along.

Norton's call rang more than one telephone in the nation's capital.

By means of an extraordinary chain reaction, it activated the pearly-grey, see-through box that Champagne Tripp kept beside her bed, for those special conversations.

What she loved most about it was the classically understated, banana-shaped receiver. For if that 'tiger' of a husband ever called when he was away on business, and wanted a little caressing by remote, she could nestle it against her ear, coo softly into the mouthpiece – and leave her hands perfectly, but perfectly free.

Which was exactly what Tiger wanted that night.

'You ready?' he croaked, when she picked up the phone.

'Chrissakes, honey. Gimme a moment – I was just writin' a letter. Can't be spread out on the bed, stark naked, twenty-four hours every day, just in case you call.'

'Well drop 'em and get movin'.'

Tiger could be an arsehole when he wanted, she reflected, as she moaned distractedly down the telephone. But it was a small price to pay for the luxuries, heaped upon her. In any case, on this occasion, it was over before it had begun.

She pouted down the line. 'That was quick, honey. Didn't you want to wait for me?

'How long d'ya need? Haven't got all day. Busy man. Things to do, people to see.'

Jerk.

She mouthed the word at the telephone, hearing the rustling of tissues and clothes in the background ...

'Wanna know something?'

She smiled. 'Only if you tell me you love me.'

'Listen. Remember you asked me to find out about Ruth Bradley? Well, now there's more.'

And so he told her what he was hearing. What someone influential had taken the trouble to phone in, just in case he needed to know. Just a rumour. Not to be spread around. But watch the papers next day. And no calling the lady to warn her, OK? Things were pretty delicate, and might just backfire.

Champagne reached for her address book and opened it at B. 'Don't worry. You know I never tell anyone your little secrets.'

' 'Bye, honey.'

' 'Bye, sugar.'

Please, Mr Jack Daniels, tell me I didn't do this.

The bottle was on the sideboard and Ruth Bradley was on the bed.

Her first thought after hearing from Chamapgne Tripp, was to buy an air ticket, go to Europe that night and disappear. Turkey or Egypt. Someone would take her in, give her sanctuary. Hide a stupid old fool, until the fuss had died down.

But David would find her.

And she was too old to go chasing round foreign countries where they didn't speak American.

She'd just have to face him and admit what she'd done. A ghastly, ghastly error.

Only he wouldn't see it that way. He'd look at her, the way he used to when he was a boy, with deep pools of disappointment in his eyes, and a kind of unspoken blame.

And when she thought about it, that was the most upsetting thing of all. For she had so wanted David to be proud of her, because no one else was, or ever would be again. He was the last person she had. The very last in the world who still loved her. And now he would despise her, just the same as everyone else.

Outside the window, it was snowing all over again in Georgetown.

Please, Mr Jack Daniels. Tell me I didn't do this.

And gradually Mr Daniels did as she requested, the way he always did.

In a while she pulled up a chair to the window, watching the snow, feeling nothing at all.

Chapter Fifty-five

The helicopter lifted off at first light, sucking the snow from the treetops, turning towards a sunrise, pale as a watercolour.

'If it goes wrong,' she'd told him, 'you'll read about it in the papers.' Standing in the wooden holiday home, coat on, bags already gone. 'I have to go and do this.'

'You said that.'

'D'you understand why?'

'Does it matter?'

She shrugged. 'Maybe. Thirty years ago you went to Vietnam because you had to. Now I have to.'

'And afterwards?'

'I'll either be prime minister or you can look for me under the Bridges ...'

'I didn't mean that.'

'I know you didn't.' She reached up and put her arm round his neck. It was like pulling on the branch of a tall tree. 'Don't count on me, David. I don't know what I'll be able to do, when all this is over.'

And then a formal handshaking in the clearing.

'By the dawn's early light,' he said quietly, removing his right glove and pulling hers off as well, so that skin touched skin. I remember him doing that, she thought, the night when the gloves were all I wore ...

Alison climbed on to the steps but he wasn't releasing her hand.

'Let's do lunch one of these days, Prime Minister.'

'I know a little place in Oxford.'

'Perfect. I expect I'll find it on the map.'

Only their eyes said goodbye.

'So who's coming, Colonel?'

Chukovsky sat in the tent, watching the troops go through the exercises. One thousand men, and Moscow kept sending more. His command, his operation and yet someone else was now giving the orders.

The major went and stood looking down into Chukovsky's face. 'No one's coming, Colonel. Isn't that right? We have twelve hours before the Ukrainian ultimatum runs out. And no one is fucking backing down ...'

'You forget yourself, major ...'

'And you forget where you are, Colonel Chukovsky. Even now, even at this ludicrously late stage, you can inform Ukraine that we're withdrawing. You can order the troops back to Russia. You can close down this encampment. You can terminate this pathetic farce. You. Commander fucking designate, Russian land forces, Ukraine.'

'I suggest you keep such thoughts to yourself, unless you wish to be removed from further duties and arrested.'

'You're mad.'

Chukovsky stood up. 'Wrong, major. I'm desperate, and the world ought to be desperate with me. To settle this question once and for all, and bring this long-suffering planet a little peace and a little confidence. Do I make myself clear?'

Clear?

He watched the major's departing back. Somehow the prayers he had whispered, kneeling on the floor of the forest, had given him a new sense of determination. The weakness had passed.

Keith Harper gave it the final push.

Alison *seen* at Camp David; so very close to the president of the United States; touching, cuddling little escapade; late at night in one of the guest cottages; blouse undone ...

Jesus Christ!

He couldn't help the stab of jealousy that seemed to pierce right into his head. It had taken half an hour to get a grip.

So he'd talked to them one by one. The Cabinet. The young, the Scottish, the Trade Unionists, the anxious and ambitious. Some had ranted. Others had sat across from him, eyebrows scraping the ceiling in disbelief. One woman, the chief secretary to the Treasury had wept. One friend for Alison, he thought. Maybe two at most. When they know you're down, and about to be carried from the ring, there aren't too many people to cry for you. They backed you.

They betted on you. But they're not impressed when you lose.

Salutary lesson, he thought, for the time, when I'm the one out there ... and the final right hook goes in.

There's no such thing as a bulletproof politician. They don't make them, so you can't buy or sell them. And just when you think you beat the system, you, the first of your kind, the only one ever to do it – the system will bring you down.

You're a glorified temp. That's what someone had told him. Bloody 'here today, gone tomorrow'. Country run by temps. Called a democracy.

'Funny, old ...' he wasn't going to say it out loud. Not like the last woman PM, crying her eyes out all the way to Buck House and back.

And yet she'd had a point.

Marks had been the last one in. Stayed behind, like the prefect after school. Talked to his people, he said. But the damage went deep. Party was already lining up for therapy. Thrown off one leader, about to throw off another. 'What the bloody hell's going on?' was the cry coming down from the regions.

'They want it done rapidly. They also want it done on medical grounds.' Marks spoke very quietly and slowly. 'Nervous exhaustion, spinal complications brought on by stress.'

'Bollocks! That went out with the Kremlin.' Keith pointed his index finger at Marks's nose. 'She resigns because her personal life has got in the way of her politics. Best interests of the Party and the country. Happy to serve in any capacity. Maybe at some future date ... etc, etc. Anything else, and the country'll throw up all over us, and the Tories'll be in for the next fifty years. Grow up, Marks, for God's sake. She's going to have to take it. All there is to it.'

'And what about you, Keith. What's going to happen now to Mr Keith Harper, eh?'

'The National Executive will meet, the general secretary will call for a one-day emergency conference at Queen Elizabeth Hall. And the Party will choose itself a new leader.' He smiled. 'Just the way we did a few days ago.'

'And with all your intimate knowledge of the candidates ...'

'The Party will choose ...'

'But who, Keith? The candidate of the Left, the safe pair of hands, the bold image ... which is it to be? Which one are you?'

'You don't seem to be hearing me, Marks. I said the party'll choose.'

'Tough lady, your prime minister.'

Harry had flown to New York to chaperone Bradley at the United Nations. Not before he'd made his calls again, done the rounds. Answers soon they'd told him. Any moment. But in the interim things weren't going well.

'Ambition.' The president nodded his head. 'That's what always turned her on. That and some other things.' He stood at the sideboard and poured the coffee.

'Ambition or desperation?'

'Maybe both. But you didn't come here to discuss that.'

'No. I didn't.' Harry took a sip from the tiny espresso cup. 'My newspaper friends tell me there's an article that isn't exactly going to make your day – slated for tomorrow's tabloids ...'

'Just the tabloids?'

He shook his head. 'There's a head of steam on this one. The networks are already trying to decide how they'll handle the thing. It's scheduled to come up at the Affiliate meetings in a couple of hours' time. So far nobody knows the strength of the story. Nor do I, by the way. But they're working out contingencies.' He put down the coffee cup. 'So what are yours?'

'State of denial.'

'You mean ignore it, laugh at it, hope it'll go away? Uh-uh, not this one, David. Each time you get out of a car, or walk through the Rose Garden, or wave at a passing pigeon, they'll be shouting the questions at you. Until there's an answer that works and an answer that satisfies. You can't do a Reagan and pretend you don't hear.'

'I can for a while.'

'And then?'

'Then's another season. No news conferences scheduled for a while. And when there are, there'll be something else to worry about. Plenty to choose from. Somalia, Bosnia, violence on the streets. Besides we'll get one of our guys on *Time* magazine to do a piece knocking the thing down ...'

'They don't get a story like this every day.'

'They're not getting it any day. Not from me.'

'And Alison Lane?'

'Right now, the best thing I can do for her is shut up. Period.'

'This isn't gonna be easy, David.'

The president rose to signal the meeting was over. 'That's why they pay us.'

Chapter Fifty-six

In the stale, endless hours of Sunday, Alison Lane drops down through clear skies on to Moscow's Vnukovo airport.

Even as the plane taxis in, Russia pulls its curtains and goes to bed. The runway lights are doused and the plane sits alone and untended in the moonlight as if it's come to the wrong place.

She can see there's no guard of honour, no flowers from the rented schoolgirl. Only a lady in boots, frail and small at the bottom of the steps, blown there by the wind.

Katya reaches out to grasp Alison's hand, and her gratitude comes in short, cold sentences. The exhaustion has attacked her English. She's running on emergency power, way beyond her limits.

Inside the VIP reception only half the neon strips are working, half the room closed off. Little clusters of mineral water, some steps of bread, smeared with red and black caviar. Regulation welcome kit, it says, for visiting inconsequentials.

'We leave in twenty minutes if that's convenient.'

Convenient.

As if, thinks Alison, we're off to a tea-party in the Ukraine – and don't want to miss the cakes.

While they watched in silence, a miniature tanker emerged from the darkness to fuel the plane. Only when they boarded did Katya feel like talking.

'You are so good to come, my dear Miss Lane. I did not think you would. Not for one moment.'

'Can I help?'

'They are playing political games with me. I knew it would happen. Now they say I can't use the presidential plane, because he's not with me. Tomorrow it'll be something else . . .'

'How is he, Katya?'

For a moment she looked puzzled as if she hadn't understood the question. 'Nothing changed.' Staring straight ahead, somewhere else. 'Nothing. Doctors, you know doctors. I ...' She stopped as if arriving at a roadblock. Perhaps there was simply nothing else to say.

'And you?'

'What can I tell you, dear friend? I try to follow where the days take me. I try to put out fires by blowing on them. It's not so effective.'

Foster came through to the forward cabin, bringing the outside world on his clipboard. 'We've got clearance for a military airfield, south of Kiev. After that, seems we're on our own. No facilities on offer. Ukrainians are telling us they're facing an emergency, an armed incursion by Russia, so we have to take sufficient fuel for a return flight. No guarantee of safety.' Monotone delivery, message and messenger become indistinguishable. 'Foreign Office is of course strongly recommending not going. Secretary of state requests an urgent radio linkup. Insists it's far too risky.'

'How many Press are we carrying?'

'Twelve, including a TV crew.'

'Why don't you tell them what you've told me, in case anyone wants to get off.'

'They won't.' He looked at his notes. 'Met report forecasts lousy weather down there. Drifting snow. High winds. Pilot says it's borderline for an old bus like this. Your call, of course.'

'I'll talk to him.'

'One last thing, Prime Minister.' He handed her an envelope. 'Came just a minute ago over White House communications. I'll leave you in peace, for now.'

Alison broke open the seal, but stopped before unfolding the paper inside. There was a time when David had written to her almost every week. How many letters had she collected during that year? Collected and later destroyed. Only one had been stored, deep inside, where the mind refuses point blank to tear up its memories. 'There's not a city been built where I can't find you, not a forest where you can lose me, not a river where you can submerge, but that I will see your shadow in the water.' She hadn't recited those words in decades, but they were still there, still familiar.

As she opened up the single sheet, Alison could see them in the same order, just as she had remembered, clustered together on the page.

Not a city been built, not a forest, not a river ... thoughts from another time ...

'Good news?' Katya raised an eyebrow.

She folded the paper and put it in her bag. 'No news. On the contrary – a very old story.'

'I prefer old stories.' Katya stared out into the darkness. 'The endings were happier.'

For the first time since his liberation, Chukovsky had returned to the silo, taking the lift to the control room, checking the systems as he went. You didn't become a colonel in the Strategic Rocket Forces Command, without acquiring unbreakable habits. Like staring at the thin pencil-shaped killer, standing, spitting smoke on its haunches, just a wall away from you.

Even now the Ukrainians would be attempting to break the launch codes that were held in Moscow.

It might not be long before they did.

As he made his way to the surface he could see the major's face peering down at him. What was that strange expression? Not a smile, surely.

'What's happened? Fresh food arrived?'

The young officer shook his head, a child with a secret, dying to tell. 'Visitors. Important ones.'

'Dracula.'

'The president's wife, for God's sake. She's on her way here, left Moscow about an hour ago, says she's bringing a message from the president ...'

'I'm sure we'll all be very excited to hear it ...'

'No, but listen, Colonel – there's someone travelling with her. They just announced it on the radio – British Prime Minister, Alison Lane, of all people, two women ...' he began to giggle. 'Did you ever believe ... ?'

'Quiet man! Wait a minute ...' His thoughts had begun sprinting in different directions. Why Lane? Why the president's wife?

'Colonel ... ?'

'Listen to me ...' Maybe he was missing something. He had to look at all the angles. Nothing was ever what it seemed, or where it seemed. No one lied until they actually opened their mouth. A gift was nothing but an object whose price tag was hidden. Catechism from Soviet life. Think hard.

And then he saw it.

An idea that caught fire in his mind and started to burn.

'Colonel . . . ?' Much louder now.

But Chukovsky wasn't listening.

In that moment he had decided what he'd do. And maybe he *was* crazy. Maybe that's what happened when you slept and worked next to a nuclear warhead.

Only he knew he had never thought more clearly in his life.

Out over the English Channel the storm clouds had merged, drawing a curtain towards the south coast.

The elderly couple could feel the dampness in the air as they hurried out of the bungalow with their suitcases and loaded the car. The cat was packed squealing into a box. Last of all came a plastic bag with the supper they would have eaten in tired tranquillity in front of the television – if it hadn't been for the call from Sir Henry.

'Mrs Lane? Alison asked me to give you a ring. Going to be a little bad publicity breaking in a few hours. Might be as well if you went somewhere else. Only a couple of days. Soon blow over. It's just that you'd have to deal with quite a few reporters, and that wouldn't be pleasant, as I'm sure you already know. Fact of life, I'm afraid. Very little we can do about it.'

'But what's happened?'

'Much ado . . . as usual. Old story plus a bit of new innuendo. Typical tabloid stuff. One gets used to it after a while.'

'What?'

'Just let the Downing Street operators know where you are. Don't worry. It'll all be fine.'

So they hadn't waited. Margaret Lane had rung their friends the Taggarts who lived along the coast in Sidmouth. Met on a cruise years before, swigged back the rum and oranges like nobody's business. Bloody good times, they'd been. And yet somehow never saw much of each other. Devon's finest, they were. Two old clotted creams. Daft as brushes.

'Of course you can come. Must come.' Taggart in organisational mode. Thirty years as a tax inspector behind him. 'Climb into the old jalopy and get a bloody move on. If I were you, I'd stay the night somewhere and we'll see you lunchtime for a wee dram. What's that? Course we won't say anything. Quiet as a pigeon's piss. Sorry. Yes, yes. Stay as long as you like. Best news we've had in months.'

Only it wasn't the best news at all.

Not when they turned on the car radio and heard the midnight bulletin, with the trickle of poison running right through it.

Chapter Fifty-seven

Sir Henry stared at his toast, seemingly unsure what to do with it.

Across the breakfast table the radio held court, and Wendy could see her husband pretending not to listen as the reports from Washington poured into the dining room.

Along the US Eastern Seaboard, it was three a.m. and yet the coffee cups were already rattling. First editions of the major papers were in the television and radio newsrooms. The story was on the runway, cleared for flight.

Sir Henry chose marmalade over butter. A large dollop from a silver serving spoon.

This was different from all the other scandals and rumours. Too much meat on this animal, too many legs. Too big a mouth.

This time the Press had done a number, just as he'd known it would.

In his mind he ticked off the points as they came up. Relationship in Oxford. Love that had never died. Alison's denial, broadcast and re-broadcast. Shots from the Berlin summit. Little bricks to build a scandal. You could see it being constructed, statement by statement, times and places, places and times, looks and handshakes and the damning indictments of all those 'highly influential sources', interviewed on condition of anonymity.

'Car's outside, Henry.' Wendy got up from the table.

But he didn't answer, sitting there, watching the structure rise.

Of course there were tell-tale signs. But who would spot them? The Labour party, just a little over-rehearsed, the lines a little too finely-honed, the message off pat. Surprise on their lips, but no surprise in the tone. No rush to defend their precious lady, no counter-accusations of smear and slur, no 'too ridiculous for words.'

Go on like this, he thought, and she'd be sentenced and hanged by midday.

'Poor taste. Dangerous precedent. Lack of judgement.' And from one Labour MP . . . 'If it's true it's crap. If it isn't it's crap.'

As for Downing Street, the Press office had run up the No Comment flag and was waving it wildly from the chimney pots. All around town, the government's officials and advisers were coming to work, and lying down beneath their desks.

'What does it mean, Henry?'

'Haven't got a clue.'

'Balls.'

'I beg your pardon.'

Wendy leaned across the table, daring him to look away. 'Is it true?'

'I've no idea.'

'Yes you have. According to the papers you bring home. You were well aware this was going on.'

Henry's hand had been reaching for a fresh piece of toast, but it stopped in mid-air. 'You looked at those papers?'

A smile began creeping across her face.

'But they're secret. They're some of the most confidential documents that exist in this country.'

The smile completed its journey. 'I know.'

'For God's sake, Wendy. I thought we had an understanding.'

'You had an understanding. I didn't. What have I ever had? Certainly not you.' She sat down again. 'Oh God, Henry, as if it bloody mattered. Just a lot of stupid papers ... games, all of them. I used to think ... what kind of job is that? You go to the office every day in a big shiny car, in a smart suit, with the shirt I've ironed the night before and the cufflinks I've put out, and then you play ... games. That's all they are ... until someone loses.'

'I don't believe this. I simply don't believe after all these years you could do a thing like that ...'

'It's exactly because of all these years, as you put it, that I could.'

He sat silent at the head of the table, not knowing how to answer.

'You can tell me one thing,' she said. 'And then we'll drop the subject, and I'll go back to being the dutiful, boring wife you married to do the washing up.'

'What?'

'Why didn't you protect her, watch her back, as you always put it? I thought that was part of your function.'

'Wasn't in the plan this time.'

'Why not?'

'Just wasn't.'

And that, she thought later, was the real turning point. Slowly she began clearing the plates and cups from the table, but after a few moments she stopped and went over to the dining-room door empty-handed.

'What's in the plan for me, Henry? I think I need to know that.' The voice was sharper than he'd ever known it. 'What's going to happen to me?'

'You've handled it well so far.'

'Thanks.'

'It's not a compliment, Harper. There aren't any prizes on this one. For any of us. Let's just get through it, OK?'

'People seem to have learned their lines.'

'Yeah, including the bloody Tories. It's more fun than most of them could dream of . . .'

'Not so much.' Keith smiled into the receiver. 'They're a little surprised to find we're not defending the castle. Wait and see, worst'll be over in forty-eight hours.'

'And the lady herself?'

'Who cares? Somewhere in the Ukraine. One of our people is going to ask a question in the House this afternoon . . . Does the prime minister intend to return to this country in the near future, and in what capacity?'

Marks snorted.

'Thought you'd like that one. All my own work.'

'Don't get too cocky, Harper. If she comes back with a triumph from the Ukraine . . . peace in our time . . .'

'She could come back with bloody Noah's ark, but it wouldn't make any difference. Ever heard anything as stupid – PM dashing off to a crisis zone? No protection, no planning, no clear aim in view. You think this is the way prime ministers are supposed to act? You wouldn't catch the bloody Tories sticking their necks above the parapet. No, my friend. No more. The moment she's back, the National Executive will call an emergency conference, and Miss Lane'll be invited to step aside . . .'

'Invited?'

'Carried out on a pig's back, for all I care.'

Cindy Tremayne was changing planes in the scrum of Karachi airport when she caught the picture on the television screen. The face and the caption . . . 'Special Relations?'.

She couldn't make out what the BBC Asia newsreader was saying but she didn't need to.

Bloody hell, she thought. It's happened and I was a bloody part of it.

And she could see the attractive blonde woman in the small cramped flat on the top floor of Downing Street, lying there, with her back being massaged and her reputation already slipping away.

Hard to believe, when you thought back. Being right there, at the centre. The power, the dignity. All the fine words used by all those fine people. You imagined they'd be so different from everyone else, at least in their private lives. But they weren't. Just more so. More insecure. More desperate. More needy.

It had been fun for a while. But it wasn't right. Alison had done nothing wrong. Not in Cindy's eyes. Just got caught up with the hard crowd – the Keith Harpers, the aggressives, the ones who always wanted more.

She'd get a new life once she arrived in New Zealand. She'd heard it was green and pleasant and maybe wouldn't ask too much of her, or about her. Just another Brit wanting twelve and a half thousand miles of scandal-free distance from the old country. Not the first.

'Well, thanks for coming with me this far.' She turned and held out her hand to Pete Levinson, and then laughed a little nervously and hugged him, because it was ludicrous just to shake hands, after all the other kinds of shaking.

'I could ride further, if you want. They told me to get lost for a couple of months.'

'Let's just leave it here, while we still like each other.'

He smiled. 'You're the best, Cindy. Best ever.'

'That's the problem.' She pulled away from him.' I was too good, wasn't I? Don't ever get too good, Pete. People don't like that. OK? Just remember I said so.'

Taggart got up from the sofa, switched off the news and turned to the Lanes.

'I think they're all shits ...'

'Jim, really.' His wife looked at the wall.

'No, I think it's got to be said the way it is. The bloody BBC should be ashamed, broadcasting that kind of character assassination. Cos, that's what it was. Make no mistake. Wouldn't be surprised if they're jamming the bloody switchboard with protests all over the country. Got a good mind, myself ....'

'It's all right, Jim.' Margaret Lane went on calmly sipping her whisky. A woman to whom all problems had solutions, all evil would be vanquished. She could never believe, she once said, that bad people would win in the end. 'It's really all right.' She shrugged. 'That's what happens in politics. Alison can look after herself ...'

'But what about you?'

'What about us, Jim?'

'I just meant all the scandal and everything. Bit difficult to cope with, I'd have thought, having to go to ground and all that ...'

Margaret Lane sat up in the chair and fixed him with her finest British Empire smile. 'If you think we're going to hang our heads and start weeping because people are telling lies about Alison, you've got another think coming. We're proud of our daughter, Jim Taggart. Always will be. And we're going to tell that to anyone who asks, and go on telling it, till this nonsense is dead and buried. I hope I make myself clear.'

She turned and looked at her husband for reassurance. He shook his head at her and thanked God silently for the thousandth time that he had married the right woman.

Deval was on the phone soon after six a.m.

'I was about to call you.' Bradley turned down the TV sound. He hadn't slept for most of the night.

'They're crucifying her. All sides.'

'I know.'

'They're going to turn on you by the time the morning shows get going.'

'Till's been briefed. No comment on the president's personal life. We never comment on former relationships, real or imaginary. Nor on personal rumours or speculation. The press knows the rules.'

Deval snorted. 'Since when? There haven't been any rules I can remember for years.'

'Come up with something better, Harry, and we'll go for it. OK? For now there aren't too many other fig leaves that fit.'

Till couldn't help enjoying himself as the 9.30 White House briefing approached.

If Bradley thought he could hold them off with a little sign saying 'No Go' – he'd think again in a while. All the TV networks had requested permission to carry the briefing live. They were turned down, reminded tartly that it was off the record – as usual. If there were any special announcements to be made they'd be notified in the normal way.

The long narrow room was crowded. Winter outside, the heat of the chase within.

From the veteran UPI correspondent came the 'what you got, Cliff?' that set it all off. And from then on Till could barely hear himself speak.

He stood smiling for a full half-minute while the tremors subsided and the reporters realised they were shouting solely at each other.

'We've no further news from Berlin on the condition of the Russian leader.' Till looked meaningfully at his notes. 'The president is being kept fully informed. I understand he has spoken to Mrs Shilov during the night.'

'Jesus Christ, Cliff' A gasp of frustration came out of a hundred mouths as the dogs sensed their quarry slipping out of reach.

'The relationship, Cliff. The relationship.' ABC's White House correspondent rose, face contorted, an inch away from his trade-mark tantrum. Immediately after the briefing he'd have to go live into the network with fuck all to say, which meant his contract negotiations would be even more dicey . . .

'Quit stonewalling.' An ageless blonde from the rival CBS, stood up shaking her perfect perm at the presidential spokesman. 'You've seen the papers, you've heard the bulletins. Start giving. The nation expects, Cliff. Bring the president out. Let's hear what he's got to say.'

'The president is spending the morning in telephone discussions with our allies,' he smiled, 'including the British. We're monitoring developments in Russia with the utmost care.'

He gathered his papers. 'That's all guys. Thanks for coming. No further announcements expected today. It's a wrap.'

He turned to his right, stepped down from the podium and disappeared through the door, as the howling followed him.

Back in his office, there were phone calls from sixteen of the country's principal editors, the presidents of the four major networks, twenty-three foreign news moguls – and the list was mounting.

'Way to go,' he muttered. The phone calls would keep coming. The more Bradley ducked, the better they'd learn to shoot.

Chapter Fifty-eight

The reports, coded from London, were received in flight over the Ukraine. Maybe a little worse than Alison had expected, more barbed and vindictive. But then, she told herself, you shouldn't be surprised in British politics. The mother of parliaments could be a real bitch when she chose.

Skimming through the lines, she noted the absence of any robust defences, any smoke screens, any standard ministerial diatribes against the Press. This was a frontal attack, with the party fully behind it. Foster had been right. Tricky, clever, little Foster. Only even he hadn't jumped in time.

'I'm sorry, Prime Minister. For what it's worth.' He was sitting opposite, having brought her the papers, gauging her reaction.

'For what it's worth, Dick Foster, don't go away thinking this is the end of Alison Lane. Tell that to anyone who asks. It's an authorised comment, OK?'

She shut the papers away in her briefcase and stared into the clouds. They were flying into a gulley, between two walls of solid grey. Nothing could be done about events in Britain. Not from this distance. But in the Ukraine, by contrast, she still had a small chance to make an imprint, to leave a mark.

If there was some point to it all, to the struggling and suffering and pushing of the last thirty years – then maybe it was here.

Standing by the open door of the plane, they could see the airport stretching away in stagnant desolation. At the perimeter the control tower seemed to lean on a single leg, its plaster facing half crumbled away, old signs and notices ripped from the wall and stacked against it. Broken windows, empty hangars, their mouths frozen open in shock. Dirty snow. The crows in sole possession, calling out to each other across the emptiness.

At the foot of the steps were the only visible signs of life –

two ancient minibuses, spattered with mud, ragged curtains at the windows, and a single black Volga sedan, its bonnet coated up against the chill. It was like an invalid who should have stayed in bed.

'This is one of the old Soviet bases. You see the long runways. They were for the heavy transport planes, closed up when the Union disintegrated.' Katya had put on a red fox shapka, pulled tightly down over her head. 'There are many like this – relics, you say?'

'Relics. Just like us.'

'Better let me go first, Prime Minister,' Alison's detective pushed past them to the top of the steps. 'Just clarify the situation. Think it'd be wise.'

But even as he reached the ground, a figure in a long black leather coat swung easily from the Volga and approached the plane. The young, swaggery walk of the nouveau powerful, she thought, thug of the day, with a voice that scythed through the wind.

'Prime Minister, Mrs Shilov. I come from the president's office.'

Alison stayed where she was. Let him shout, let him come to me.

'The president regrets he was unable to meet you. He is, as you understand, in the midst of a crisis but you are free to go where you wish.'

She nodded.

'You'll be aware that our ultimatum to the Russian government runs out in just over six hours. Please give yourselves time to leave the area and be out of Ukrainian airspace by then. This is for your own protection. The matter is, of course, up to you.' He spread his hands like a priest offering absolution. 'I hope your mission is successful, Prime Minister. For our part there's nothing more we can do.'

'I wish to talk to your president.' Her own voice seemed so frail by comparison. A tiny echo across the airfield.

'I regret that's not possible.'

'Then make it possible. We are trying to negotiate. That means talking. Everyone. No communication barriers.'

He smiled. 'The Russian military commander knows where to find us. He is, after all, situated on our territory. We are listening on all frequencies ... when he wishes to announce his withdrawal.'

'You are not helping the situation.'

The hands returned to the black leather pockets. 'Forgive me, Prime Minister, but you are arguing with the messenger. I convey what I am told – no more, no less. I can make no deals.' He looked at his watch. 'I may only observe that time is still passing – and there is very little left.' His eyes flicked towards the vehicles. 'The drivers know where you wish to go. You'll understand if I don't travel with you.'

The detective, Katya and Alison in the first car. The others in the minibuses. Crew on the plane. The little expeditionary force on its way into the Ukraine.

You couldn't see where the fields ended and the snow began, the roads cleared only by the tracks of the other vehicles, skidding, slithering across the country.

'You are new to this job.' Katya leans towards Alison.

She nodded.

'You are an adventurer?'

'I never thought so.'

'But you have struggled.'

'Yes.' And she could remember hearing that a conversation in Russia is always a grope towards the meaning of life. No small talk. History has never given them that luxury. Your subjects are death and freedom and lies because you must confront them each day. You bump into them on the street. They are all around you.

'Is the truth important to you, Alison?'

'It has to be.'

'So you try always to tell it?'

'I try ...' she could see the television screen back in Berlin, the colour spreading out across her cheeks. The simple denial of a simple fact. 'I don't always succeed.'

'So there is a place for lies in government?'

'There's a place for confidentiality.'

'May I share a confidence with you?'

Cold suddenly in the car, limping along in the slush.

'If you wish.'

'And you will inform no one.'

'Of course.'

'Then I will tell you when this is over. For now you will need your strength and your concentration.' Katya stretched out her hand and Alison felt the force of the fingers, like tensile claws.

As she did so, the Volga slid to a halt in the forest clearing and the engine fell silent.

'You're keeping watch on her?'

'The Pentagon, the DIA, half the agencies we possess. The plane was tracked throughout Ukrainian airspace.' Harry spoke softly, easily, trying to reassure the president.

'And on the ground?'

'Difficult. Satellites are still being re-tasked and there's heavy cloud over the region.'

'I want her tracked, dammit.'

'They're working on it, David.'

'They'd better be. If she clears her throat, I want to know about it.'

'David . . . this close interest of yours . . . you've seen the reports. Hour by hour. A pundit here, a pundit there, TV, radio, the Press, they're talking about nothing else. I haven't seen this level of hype since Iran-Contra. If you want her monitored so closely, there's going to be a leak. I can guarantee it. Hundred per cent . . .'

'Do it, Harry. Every move she makes. No questions on this one. Just do it.'

Chapter Fifty-nine

There are helicopter gunships, missiles, there are troops encamped beneath the trees. Straight out of the briefing books, straight off the pages of Nato threat assessments – and they shouldn't be here.

Someone has let them out.

Alison can see the silent, fair-haired colonel, standing at the entrance to the field tent, apart from the others, a danger all on his own.

He walks towards them, eyes armed with a cause.

He talks quietly to Katya in Russian and she listens, probing, not pushing, not insisting. Simple enquiries.

'This is Colonel Sergei Chukovsky of the Strategic Rocket Forces Command.'

'Yes.' Alison is motionless.

'He welcomes you to Silo 318. A tent has been prepared for you and your advisers . . .'

'I don't need a tent. I want to talk. Now.'

'He says we should wait a while.'

'He's in no position to make demands.'

'On the contrary, he claims to be in the best possible position.'

Alison looks into the large, tired eyes. Know your opponent. Know your target. If you can see how he's put together, then you can see how to take him apart. That's politics. But not here, beside a missile. All the rules are different.

'We've come as a sign of international goodwill. You can't order the leaders of the world around. Doesn't work like that.'

Look at him, though, as the words reach him in Russian. He doesn't care what works or what doesn't. Couldn't care a fig about leaders or protocol. He has an idea. A light to see by, and a path to follow.

And me? I'm prime minister of Great Britain and Northern Ireland. I hold the highest political office in the land, I'm supposed to make the decisions others carry out.

I shouldn't be here.

Behind her in the trees a group of commandos snaps to attention. But there's something wrong, something out of place. Only as her eyes accustom to the dying light of the forest, can Alison see the machine guns in their hands – pointed straight at her.

Three hours go by and David Bradley takes calls from a satellite station in California. It's a grey windowless warehouse, sitting beside a six-lane highway, and the name on the sign is 'Keep Out.'

There are little specks of doubt on the things he is hearing.

They have pinpointed the silo and the helicopters. But it's too quiet and too inactive.

The hours are inching past. The sun is moving out of the Ukraine, and they don't like what they don't see.

'She's in talks, David. Long and difficult.' Harry leans against the desk. The hotel suite is forty-eight floors above the reporters and TV trucks gathered in the streets.

'You believe that? They don't all sit there navel-gazing. People take breaks, walk around, communicate. The press are with her. What about them? They should be filing reports, clamouring for phones. And they're not. No calls. No radio traffic. There's nothing from Klimak either.'

'What d'you mean? We've tried hotlines, faxes, even our ambassador in Kiev has been round to the Presidential residence, but they turned him away.'

'So you're telling me there's silence on this, right across the world. And we, the United States, can't get any answers.'

'David, for now there's nothing you can do.' In that moment, Harry catches sight of the president's expression, eyes staring into the middle distance, calculating. Shouldn't have said that, he tells himself. Not to this guy. Should've kept my mouth shut. This one time.

'We haven't met before.'

Keith Harper tried to place the voice before turning round. It was certainly more polished than the other drinkers at the bar, more rounded. Always happened when he needed peace – some doddery, old fool from the constituency would crawl out of the furniture, wanting to talk about schools or the bloody health service. Only now, when he looked at the face, he knew this was different.

There was confidence in there, an in-built superiority. The mottled after-dinner skin, the manicured hands, the hint of a handkerchief protruding from the sleeve. Power.

'To whom do I have the pleasure?' he had to raise his voice to be heard. But the figure seemed to draw him impercptibly towards the corner of the bar. Only when the light hit Sir Henry's face full on did Keith know who was with him.

'This is a surprise.' He took a sip of beer and licked his lips.

'A pleasant one, I hope.'

'I'm not sure you're the kind of person associated with pleasant surprises.'

Sir Henry smiled. He took that as a compliment.

'You seem to be heading ever onward, ever upward, if I may say so.'

'Kind of you to notice.'

'Oh, but I do.'

'Well the Party has been forced to make changes. That much should be clear today of all days.'

'Yes, of course. So nice when a Party can agree and come to democratic decisions . . .'

Keith took another swig of beer and seemed emboldened by it. 'So what did you want?'

'To pay my compliments.'

'Why?'

'You've played it very cleverly.' He raised his eyebrows.. 'If I may say so.'

'I'm not sure I get your drift. I said *the Party* had been making some changes . . .'

'Suggested by you.'

'Some of them.'

'And some of them seem to have paid off. Don't they?' Sir Henry's eyebrows lifted the barest fraction.

'Listen,' Keith smiled for a moment. 'Why don't you and I play a little game? I start a sentence like this . . . 'I've come here today because . . .' and you finish it for me. OK? Shall we have a go?'

'So black and white?'

'So black *or* white, Sir Henry. Let's finish the sentence and then decide, shall we?'

Sir Henry inclined his head. It was good to be reminded that Harper was far from stupid.

'As you wish. I simply wanted to tell you, as I tell all prospective candidates for the leadership that they can count on our unbiased support. You are, I take it, a candidate for the leadership?'

'News to me.'

'I see. Well, perhaps it won't be news for much longer.'

'Is that the kind of assurance you gave Alison Lane?'

'You're quite a politician, Mr Harper.'

'My constituency seems to think so. I've been their MP for twenty-six years.' Harper finished his beer and put the glass on the ledge beside him. 'Anyway, how do I know you're on my side? You people haven't exactly put yourselves out for Labour in the past, have you?'

Sir Henry grinned. 'Those pictures you received, the ones featuring Alison Lane and her physiotherapist. Your pictures, in fact. Who do you imagine sent them?'

Chapter Sixty

Alone in his room above New York, Harry Deval assembles his bag – the enquiries, the little unanswered questions and the big ones.

Only now can he think himself back to the city of Oxford. End of the summer term, 1966. Vietnam building steadingly into the headlines, the counter movements learning to tie their shoelaces and going for walks.

You'd think everyone was involved – at least from the newspaper cuttings. But not David Bradley.

He's a volunteer, by golly – one of a kind, recorded in Army archives at Quantico as a committed soldier-to-be. So they paid his air fare home and cut him a uniform. Didn't get many like that. People with a brain, willing to use their hands.

And there's the High Street, warm and crowded on a summer night. Bottles of booze in every fist, students ebbing and flowing away. Careless, they were. As if the future were simply an open door, admission free.

David stays outside the celebrations. Hasn't got anything to feel good about. He's making the supreme sacrifice for a young guy, kissing his girl goodbye, the girl he promised to marry, the girl who won't wait for him, because she can't love a fool in a stupid war.

You see ... Harry's friend had found a friend of hers. And eventually she'd talked.

Time: 7.30, perhaps. Bags already packed in the college. The London train ran at eight, in those days. Said his piece, had young David, walks back to his room, calls a cab from the porter's lodge.

Funny how everyone keeps records. Old, half-eaten by time and termites. The more trivial, the more there are. You don't pass through life without leaving paper behind.

Only Bradley's state of mind is unclear. No papers for that.

And yet by 9.30 that night he's in London's Paddington station. And there's nothing to show that he ever phoned back, went back or looked back to Oxford, ever again.

Alison?

She's in there too. One more year to go. Heading for a First Class degree. Straight A student – only they don't use the term in England.

Last meeting with her tutor – 6.30, same evening.

Says she can't stay long, the old bag remembers. Always in a hurry but more so that day. Hurried and sad.

How does she remember?

Well, she remembers because of what happened later, and what Alison became. And because a wasp flew in the open window and stung her.

Christ knows how, but the local police records have made it.

7.40. pm. Not 7.41. Not 7.39. Exact time of incident. Female student, Alison Lane, hit by van, registration so and so, driver so and so.

Ambulance is summoned, 7.46. Admitted Casualty, Radcliffe Infirmary, 7.59.

And they don't hang about.

Casualty sister, houseman, professor of surgery. All the reports in there.

All bleak.

Pulse barely there. Shock trauma. Severe spinal damage.

A young woman who isn't going to see night turn to day.

Prime minister-to-be. A. Lane. Miss.

Harry takes off the Dunhill spectacles and listens to New York, as the certainty comes to him across the miles and years. The complete and utter conviction that David Bradley knows nothing of this. Not the accident, not the injuries, not the struggle young Alison Lane undertook in order to rise and walk.

Bradley has no idea.

I could junk this, he tells himself. Bin it, pretend I never knew, and so he'd never know, and the world can take its own course.

But Harry can't do that.

Not this time.

After all the lies and obfuscations of his own life – he decides that a little piece of truth deserves to be heard.

Chapter Sixty-one

Her own thoughts travelled that way in the hour between sunset and dusk.

A time to wonder what might have been.

'I refuse to wait any longer,' she had said. And that was an age ago, before they had posted sentries around the cars, taken her with her advisers to a field command post, and the others somewhere else.

'I demand to begin negotiations. I demand communications equipment.'

And the silence had seemed so conclusive. Served as it was with the evening stew in tin pots, with a bucket of water and a pile of plastic mugs.

She sat in a corner of the tent with Katya, while they examined options that weren't. And realities.

Odd thing about power, she decided. It wasn't real. It relied on other people giving it to you. Recognising you. An acceptance that you're the one.

Withdraw it and suddenly you're stuck back down in the world of the ordinary; protesting, demanding – to no avail.

Like judgement day. When the powerful find out they're not. And the meek inherit, the way they were promised.

'What's their aim?' This to Katya, just a whisper.

'World attention. Blackmail, possibly. But I doubt it.'

'The deadline has passed . . .'

'That too, they have calculated. Ukraine will not attack with you here. You've bought them some time.'

'You too.'

'The purpose, Colonel. This is what I'm asking myself.'

'That should be clear enough.' Chukovsky bit the end of his thumbnail. 'In a few hours' time, the world community will realise that a prime minister is here, and held against her will. They'll put unbearable pressure on Moscow and the Ukraine, there'll be meetings in the security council and a settlement will be forced on all the parties concerned.'

'Will, will, will . . . what makes you so sure?'

'What would you do, Major?'

'You asking me? Personally I'd infiltrate a single agent into this command and kill you. That's what I'd do. And the moment you become too great an embarrassment to our so-called leaders in Moscow, the moment they stop fucking around and decide something – that's exactly what they'll do.'

'I'm grateful for your thoughts, Major.'

'I thought you would be.'

As they watched the television news the Lanes and the Taggarts could see the little bungalow near Brighton, with the reporters staking out the road.

'Neighbours say they have no idea where Alison Lane's parents have gone. They left no forwarding address, simply took the car out of the garage and slipped away into the night.'

Taggart pressed the remote and blacked out the screen.

'Look at the bastards. Like bees round the proverbial . . .'

His wife threw him a warning glance. She'd already warned him his language was 'on the fruity side' and after all, these *were* the prime minister's parents.

Margaret Lane got up from the sofa and smoothed her skirt. 'I'm away to bed, if nobody minds. Seen enough news for today. Although I'm a little surprised there was nothing from the Ukraine. I know they mentioned communications problems. But there should have been a report about what Alison's doing, instead of all this speculation . . . you know. I mean it's very unusual, isn't it? Shouldn't we ring the BBC or Downing Street.'

'Everything's unusual these days,' said Taggart, gazing philosophically towards the window. 'Bloody unusual, if you ask me. Still, I'm sure there's nothing to worry about.'

'Why, Jim?' Mrs Lane was staring at him.

'Why what?'

'Why are you sure there's nothing to worry about?'

'Well, of course there isn't.'

'No, but how do you know?'

Taggart sniffed. 'Stands to reason.'

'Let me tell you something, Jim,' Margaret Lane opened the door to the hall. 'I never realised what an awful windbag you are. Thanks for putting us up. But we'll be leaving in the morning.'

'What are the Brits saying, Harry? She's their prime minister.'

'Not worried. Not concerned. Fault with her radio system. They'll let us know.'

The president ran a hand through his hair. 'So they're doing nothing.'

'Right.'

'You contacted the Ukrainian ambassador here.'

'He promised to call within one hour.'

'One hour then. That's all I'm waiting.'

'David.' Harry produces his file from the briefcase – the little bag of facts on Alison Lane, the little pieces of history that he's fitted together.

'What's this?'

'Just read it. Spend an hour of your life. I think you should.'

Chapter Sixty-two

The Ukrainian ambassador has called Deval. He has failed to make contact with Kiev. He wants to explain, wishes he could, perhaps in another hour ...

Harry takes the elevator to the forty-eighth floor, past the secret service, along to the presidential suite. And for a moment it seems like a different man at the desk. Different colours in his face. Different lines. Something inside him has re-arranged.

'You didn't know about it, did you David? The accident? All the rest ...'

And Harry can see him trying to play back the day. Retrieve the sights and the voices.

'Nothing. Thirty years and nothing. Wouldn't she have said ... ?' He closes the file and pushes it away from him. 'Listen, I'm not going to go back over everything. I'm going to act on it.'

'Right. We've got to discuss all this, bring in the Cabinet, take soundings.'

'Not this time.' And if you look carefully, Bradley's eyes are carrying a decision. An impetus that wasn't there before. 'I want you to call the networks. I'm going to make an announcement in two hours.'

'What the ...?'

'I'm announcing the resumption of the summit ...'

'Jesus Christ! The summit's over, David. There's no venue, no agenda, and there's no one to sit down with. Listen to me. Listen very carefully ...'

'No, Harry. Make the arrangements.'

'What arrangements? We've had no contact with State. Congress has no idea what's going on. The allies need to be called. You're not just one man with a plane. You're an office, for Chrissake. An institution, the highest, most protected and most valuable on this planet. Do I even have to be telling you this?'

'I wasn't elected to be an office, Harry. I was elected to do something with it. That means taking action. What're we gonna do? Wait a year for the UN?' He shakes his head. 'You talk about the presidency as if it's some kind of divine relic ...'

'It is.'

'Well, I'm not.' Eyes already travelling.

'Your judgment's clouded, David. I can't put it more strongly than that.'

'You're saying I'm doing this for Alison?'

'Of course I'm saying it. Everyone's gonna say it. You risked the security of the United States for a woman you love. That's what the American people will say. The truth.'

'Let them say it, Harry. But I left this woman for dead, thirty years ago and never knew anything about it. I'm not going to do that again.'

'You don't have the right to take that risk.'

'It's why I was elected. Remember? The man who took risks and won. What did I do in Vietnam? Disobeyed orders right from the top, saved lives. The people elected that person. Remember the campaign, the commercials ...'

'You're starting to believe your own propaganda ... that's dangerous ...'

'You get paid for results, Harry. That's the only propaganda that matters. If I don't bring them home this time, then I'll take one final executive action ...'

'Why, David? You have to make a choice. Her or the job. Choose her, if that's what you want. But make a choice.'

'No choice. I want them both.'

'You can't ...'

'Look at my predecessors. Look at the crap they did and got away with. Most of it illegal. Why d'you think Bush overwrote so many of the White House computer discs before he got out of office? You've seen some of it. Jesus, this doesn't even rate next to Nixon or Kennedy. I'm not doing anything illegal, Harry.'

'There are worse things than illegal. There's ill-advised. There's imprudent. Hair-brained. Want me to go on?'

'So tell me the stakes aren't high.'

'Course they are.'

'So you take drastic action.'

284

'You order drastic action. You're commander in chief. You order – they do.'

Bradley got up and poured two whiskys from a decanter on the sideboard.

'Seems to me I've been away from the action far too long. Seems to me I've lived in the dark. This woman nearly died because of me. D'you understand, Harry?' He drained the whisky and poured another. 'It's not enough to make decisions from the safety of a big chair, behind bullet-proof glass. I've never in my life been paid to sit around while others do things. Never led from the back. Not me. Not on this planet.'

He handed his chief of staff the other glass.

'Make the calls, Harry. We can't wait any longer.'

'Now I know he's crazy.' Norton sat on the edge of his chair, watching the network special.

David Bradley in a New York studio, dark suit, plenty of Max Factor, seemed normal enough. Summit back on, where better to hold it than at the site of the missile silo in the Ukraine?

Take the medicine direct to the patient.

This time they wouldn't leave without a solution.

Mrs Darlene Norton sat scraping her nails with an emery-board. 'Looked pretty damned convincing to me.' The low drawl was deceptive. 'Why did you tell them you were ill, for Chrissake? You should be on that plane same as the rest of them.'

'I told you why.'

'Tell me again.'

'Because he's gonna fall flat on his arse, and I don't want to be part of it. I have to keep my distance . . .'

'Yeah.' She stood up. 'I might just keep some distance of my own for right now.' She let him stare at her slim, tanned legs, disppearing all the way up into the short, silk nightgown. Let him look all he wanted. She wasn't going to give him any tonight. Not after a damn fool trick like that.

Clark, she reckoned, could be a real schmuck when he dropped his guard.

Sir Henry heard it all on the BBC World Service. Two a.m., London time, alone in the downstairs kitchen.

So Bradley didn't want to play it safe. Must be really hooked. Much more than he'd realised. If he was going to risk everything for her.

Why did these leaders all think they were gods?

So many of them did.

Believed all the hype and the praise, the trappings of power. The special lifestyle, removed from normal people and normal considerations.

In the end they all lost their judgement. Became overwhelmed by their own self-importance.

Thought they could have it all.

Funny thing was ... the more they talked about accountability, the less there was.

People didn't know what went on. And if they knew what, they seldom knew why.

Not the real reasons.

Bradley's mistake was to think he could get away with it.

When the broadcast was over, Sir Henry took his solemn thoughts up to the bedroom and sat in darkness on his side of the bed.

Not, of course, that he had played it any better than Bradley.

Wendy was gone, and there was nothing to indicate whether she ever intended to return.

'You spoke to Klimak?'

'The message has reached him. I know that.'

'What did it say?'

'It said you'd be arriving to continue the summit beside the missile silo. And if he wasn't there he could forget about Ukraine's international reputation, forget about aid. We'd blacken his name and that of his country for all time. By fair means or any other.'

'Those exact words?'

'More or less. And to the Russian vice-president.'

'And Norton?'

'Says he's sick. Deputy secretary will stand in. Defence and NSA are going with you. They're really sick – with worry, but privately wouldn't miss this for the world.'

'Congress?'

'Shock from the senate majority leader and a few others, but most are on board. Plenty of God speeds and good lucks.'

'That simple, Uh?'

'There are still people in this country who like decisions. Any decisions. Plane's at Kennedy, fuelled and ready. Some Press on board. Secret service. Counter assault. New wash cloth. Amazing what you get when you ask for it. Trouble is, nobody says "no" to the president. Maybe some day we'll learn.'

'Thanks, Harry.'

Deval has to stand almost on tiptoe to touch Bradley's shoulder. 'For what it's worth, David, I'd do the same thing.'

Chapter Sixty-three

Katya woke her before dawn and for a moment she thought she heard a different sound. A low, persistent rattle in the distance, the grind of heavy machinery on the move.

She opened the front of the tent, but the noise had gone. Above the trees, thick clouds were pulling hard from the east.

'When it's light, I'm going to demand transport to the plane. We're going to walk to the cars and buses and drive away. What'll they do – shoot us? I can't allow myself to be a virtual hostage. That's the worst of all options. For everyone.'

'I regret very much that I brought you here.' Katya's voice just a whisper in the dark.

'You shouldn't. People face this kind of lawlessness all over the world, every day of their lives. And governments never hear about it or never do anything. The leaders all go off in protected convoys, on so-called familiarisation trips, exchanging one set of luxuries for another. But this time it's different. I get to make a stand, where it counts.'

She lay down again and tried to sleep. But now there was a face in front of her that she couldn't shake.

And what would you do, David?

You'd do the same, wouldn't you? Always said so. Can't get others to carry your convictions.

And maybe for the first time in thirty years I understand why you went to Vietnam, why you felt involved. Everyone else was having parties and celebrating the end of the summer term in Oxford – and you walked the other way.

Without me.

You threw away the person you loved. And now I've thrown away my career.

Perhaps there's some sense to it, somewhere.

He couldn't explain it to anyone on the aircraft. Just how good it

288

felt to have the leash untied, to be going out of a sanitised, protected, cushioned little world – and into trouble.

Felt like the first time they'd been helicoptered into battle inside North Vietnam, over the jungle, low over the treetops, the wind and the rotors tearing at your tunic, the hunt in your blood.

And we're not killers at all, because right is on our side. The mantra, repeated over and over again to ward off conscience.

Should I be here, now? Was Harry right? Could I have done this differently?

Not when I look back.

Not when I see Alison Lane, student of mine, lying in the gutter of an Oxford street, that soft summer day, with the rain crying gently over the city.

I don't have a choice.

I made one thirty years ago. And it was wrong.

Now there's no choice at all.

Wherever Air Force One travels it is the most closely monitored flight on the planet. That night it was shadowed into Ukrainian airspace by F-14 fighters, with US airbases on alert throughout the European continent, and governments warned that the protection of this one aircraft was their duty, and America's right.

The president was on an emergency peace mission. No hostile action would be tolerated. And US armed forces world-wide stood ready to enforce the threat.

Throughout the night, Harry had been busy.

Chapter Sixty-four

David Bradley looks back on this time as the best and the stupidest thing he ever did, brushing aside the secret service to stand by the open door of Air Force One, smelling the damp cold, hearing the snow falling from the trees.

He says it was the longest two minutes he ever waited, before the line of black cars emerged from behind the hangar, the Ukrainian colours in full view, doors opening, security men running hard to keep up, and the Ukrainian president, stepping towards the aircraft, the short squat body slipping on the tarmac.

Bradley took hold of Klimak's hand and felt it start to crush his own, in something more than diplomatic enthusiasm.

He remembers telling him ... 'how good it was to re-start the talks.'

And Klimak, jaw frozen, muttering simply, 'Do you always threaten weaker countries?' Do you think this is acceptable behaviour for a superpower? Bradley answering 'yes' to both.

There's a picture he likes to recall of Klimak scowling, while two secret servicemen force their way into his limousine to sit either side of their president, rejecting all efforts to have them removed.

Such an uncomfortable ride across the countryside, with the counter assault team right behind and Bradley in bullet-proof vest, no room for his legs, jammed as they were against Klimak's. No conversation between them.

And you don't attend public events and the glittering international occasions without savouring those moments of delicious embarrassment.

Klimak again, exiting from the car, stiff and awkward, confronted on his own territory by a Russian colonel, informed that the summit is about to begin and that all the other participants are ready.

'You're very welcome,' says Sergei Chukovsky, newly-shaved and luxuriating in false modesty. 'I am most grateful you could be here.'

And as Bradley's eyes scout the territory, he can see a blonde lady in a coat, pencils and files under her arm, scribbling notes on a paper in front of her.

He remembers what she said. Probably always will.

'You're late, David. I expected you hours ago.'

And as he tells the story, himself, there wasn't anything else that needed saying.

Most of this is in the public record, thanks to the cameras. The six-hour talks, the minute details, the lengthy and laborious route towards an agreement.

Nobody ever gives in at a summit and says ... 'OK, you've won. I change my mind.' Each concession is dragged from the sections and sub-sections of draft after draft, that the experts on both sides agree to put before their leaders.

So it was in the Ukraine.

But there are two meetings that didn't get recorded.

Sergei Chukovsky taking the American president into the silo that he had commanded on behalf of the Strategic Rocket Forces. Just the two of them.

Seventy metres below ground they inspected the launch control, and the missile, still fuelled in the shaft beside it.

Bradley leaned on the table and examined the colonel in the dim neon light.

'You took a big risk.'

'So did you, Mr President.'

Bradley grinned. 'I guess I'm paid to take them. What's your excuse?'

Chukovsky paused and looked around the narrow complex. 'I watched my captain die here in this silo. A boy, but a boy with good ideas, big ideas, all about the new Russia. He saw a different future. This was for him.'

'Would you have used the missile?'

'No. I promised myself that years ago. Way before the cold war ended. But I thought we waited long enough for an agreement. No more people were going to die.'

They emerged into sunlight, more cameras, and the signing of an agreement in principle.

The four summit powers to guard the silos in the Ukraine, until new arrangements could be concluded. All disputed missiles ceded to the control of the United Nations.

'Peace in our time?' A reporter shouted at Bradley.

'It's a start. That's all.' He searched for the requisite soundbite cliché. 'Peace isn't a destination. It's a journey. We travelled a way today. No more than that.'

And then they cordoned off a section of the wood. Alison Lane and David Bradley once again in protected space.

'So you came to get me.'

'I came for a summit. Your idea.'

'And released me in the process.'

'I can leave you if you want. The fact is we did what we couldn't do in Berlin.'

'That's not the way it'll be seen back home.'

'How so?'

'The Press were with me. They know what really happened. They know I was a hostage till you arrived. "Bradley releases Lane." That'll be the headline. Then the ... so-called love story. Then down at the bottom of the page, that we got an agreement on nuclear missiles which may or may not hold. I know Britain, David. I know the Press.'

'I shall tell it another way.'

'I shan't.'

They walked for a moment, conscious that the space and time were restricted.

'Why did you never mention the accident in Oxford?'

She shrugged. 'You *have* been busy. Why? What for, David? It was a long time ago. Everything was a long time ago. Would it have made any difference if you'd known?'

'Yes.'

'No. You had something you wanted to do with your life. Something you needed to do. I wasn't going to show up, like a cripple and say ... hey, remember me?'

They stood for a moment, and then a thought pierced her.

'Is that why you came? Because of the accident?'

'No.'

'Yes.' She smiled. 'Doesn't look as though we'll ever get the same answers, will we?'

'I don't need any answers. I know what happened thirty years ago and I know what happened at Camp David.'

'It was like re-visiting an old house, where we were once happy. It was the past. Not the future.'

'I don't accept that.'

'You have to David. You have to return to Washington and go back to being a president, and I have to go to London.'

'You said we'd do lunch in Oxford.'

'Did I?' She took his hand. 'Then we will.'

Only when Bradley had gone, did she get the chance to see Katya.

They sat in an empty Field-tent, while the summit set was cleared behind them.

'So, my dear. It worked.'

Alison leaned against the long table. 'It worked because David Bradley flew in, like the knight of old. Let's not kid ourselves.'

'You remember, I asked if I could share a confidence?'

'Yes.'

'Perhaps now is the time.' And as Alison looked there were tears, freshly squeezed from her eyes.

'What is it?'

'My husband . . .'

'So go to Berlin, Katya. Now. He's strong. He's holding on.'

'My dear, he died four days ago, while I was with him.' Tears flowing free down the steep, grey cheeks. 'I couldn't tell anyone. Russia would have broken apart if they had known.'

'I don't . . .'

'I had no choice. I knew that. It was almost as if he were telling me what to do. The moment I was about to kiss him goodbye, he'd already gone. Like he couldn't bring himself to part. You know what he once said . . . if it hurts to say farewell, then don't, just walk away. And that's what he did.'

'But the doctors . . . and the bulletins . . . ?'

'I made them promise. They're good when it comes to questions of life and death. They're used to that. They'll announce the death tonight and I'll go to Berlin and take him home.'

Alison could see the first hint of darkness, the forest closing in around them.

'You're a remarkable woman, Katya.'

'You won't break my confidence?' Tears and more tears, like a river bursting its banks, sweeping away the levy.

'I won't break your confidence.'

They held each other for a long time without speaking, until the advisers moved in quietly behind them and suggested it was time to leave.

Chapter Sixty-five

'Harper?'

'D'you know what time it is?'

'It's Marks. We have to talk.'

'Go to sleep.'

'But she's got an agreement in the Ukraine. What about that? What about public opinion?'

'Don't be stupid. Why d'you think I called in the Lobby correspondents last night? I told them what the Americans are telling their people, privately of course. That she blundered into something she couldn't handle, and Bradley had to rush in after her. The agreement's OK as far as it goes – but the experts say it's full of holes.'

'You hear the Russian leader's died?'

'See? That'll keep any thoughts of triumph off the front pages. Now the whole nuclear thing'll be up in the air again. That's the line I'm flogging and I suggest you do the same.'

'So we go ahead as planned?'

'You've got a bloody short memory. There's an emergency conference fixed for the Queen Elizabeth Hall, day after tomorrow. It's all been decided. Get some sleep and stop panicking. You're like a little girl.'

'You can go now, Foster. I expect you want to get back to your children.'

They had reached Downing Street way after midnight. A single light in the study, Mountbatten Green and St James's Park deserted in the middle distance. The first editions of the national papers covered the coffee table.

Foster hadn't taken off his coat, hadn't been asked to. 'I'm sorry things turned out this way. But you know, even now you could go to the people. That was a very brave thing you did back there. You deserve some credit, really . . .'

'Maybe ...' she gestured towards the pile of newsprint. 'But they've already sold their version. And what would I achieve? Split the party. More scandal. At the end of the day, I told a lie in public. And that's still on the record. My record. I also took a dangerous, foolhardy decision, had to be rescued by a foreign leader who has more experience and sense than I do.'

'I don't ...'

She stood up. 'Listen, Dick, this was a caretaker administration at a time of crisis. Let's leave it at that, shall we?'

'If only there'd been more time.'

'How d'you mean?'

'Time to make enough friends. You don't need much time to make enemies. They're all around you in politics. Come with the job. But real friends – the people who'll back you when it's tough, who'll go out on limbs for you, who'll take some heat on your behalf – takes years to cultivate those kinds of relationships. Years, if ever.' He blushed. 'I wish I'd done better by you.'

'Goodnight, Dick.' She held out her hand.

'Goodbye, Prime Minister.'

'What's up, Harry?'

The satellite link to Air Force One was clear as a local call.

'*You're* up for one thing. Jesus, David. Talk about returning hero.'

'Tell me.'

'In the last hour calls to the White House are running fifteen to one in your favour. Congress is going crazy – both parties. The Cabinet wanted to give you a ticker-tape parade along Pennsylvania Avenue. Anyone'd think you'd found Elvis. Did you?'

'Harry ...'

'I can't tell you ... every five minutes they're bringing flowers here. Lee Greenfield's re-recording "Proud to be an American" ...'

'Finest taste, as always.'

'Don't knock it, David. Been a long winter.'

'They'll get over it.'

'Let's hope they don't. You could ride this all the way to the next convention. Reagan would've killed for the part – flying in like that, rescuing Lane ...'

'Is that how the story's playing?'

'Isn't that the way it was?'

'And in London?'

'They're killing her.'

'How bad?'

'The embassy thinks she'll be out – day after tomorrow. Labour's calling a special conference, where she'll be forced to step down – health reasons, maybe. And if she doesn't go quietly, they'll push her. She doesn't have many friends. Papers cite lack of judgement, foolhardiness, lying about her personal life . . . I'm sorry to dampen your landing, but you asked.'

'That's always been my problem.'

'I'll be there to hold your hand at Andrews.'

'Thanks, Harry, but I'll hold my own.'

Darlene woke Norton on the sofa where he lay.

She flicked on the television.

'You better watch this.'

And he hadn't got much choice. Seeing the turnout at Andrews, the congressional leaders out there in force, a band, well-wishers, streamers. Messages of congratulation pouring in to stations all over the country – and the president's approval rating, like a summer in Washington – well into the nineties.

'Gonna fall flat on his face, huh? Isn't that what you said?' The Southern drawl was right up against his ear. 'You fucking idiot. Had to distance yourself from the president, didn't you? Arsehole! Know something, I'm wondering why I wasted so much time on you in the first place. You really piss me off.'

He watched her turn the magic, tanned thighs away and flounce out of the room.

If he hadn't been scared of her, he'd have gone upstairs and bent her over the side of the bed.

In your dreams, he told himself. In your dreams.

Chapter Sixty-six

She had been home for three days when Sir Henry visited.

Even the Press had got tired by then. Gone off, leaving their tripod marks in the front garden, and mother shaking her head over the plants.

She'd told them there were errors of judgement, the Party had made its decision, she was stepping down, would resign her seat at the next election.

What else was there to say?

They walked beneath the chalk-white cliffs at Saltdean, dodging the waves that hurled shingle on to the pathway. The air was bright and good, and she wanted him to feel the cold.

'Why didn't you watch my back ... ?'

'I tried ... This time it didn't work. You can do almost anything except when a straight lie is sitting there on the record.'

You're a glib bugger, she thought. Always got the answer ready.

'What are you going to do now?' he asked.

'Find something.'

'I'm sure you could find something the other side of the Atlantic.'

'I've already turned that down, thanks. I can find my own occupations.'

'He rang, didn't he?'

'Of course he did.'

'So why did you turn him down?'

'Don't want the job. Not good with consolation prizes. Winning or nothing really.'

'That's pretty arrogant if you don't mind my saying ...'

'I bloody well do ...'

'You want a function. I'll give you one. You go there and watch out for your country. You watch for the intelligence operations they mount against us, the secrets they fail to give us, the way they play us off against their other allies. You care for your country – you do something for it.'

298

'Lousy, twisted argument, that one.'

'They're all lousy arguments. You want to do something useful. Then do it. You want to make a difference to this country, then do it . . .'

'Wouldn't work. Too many split loyalties.'

'They all are, my dear. That's the trouble with loyalties.'

'It's no way to start a life together.'

'It's a way to make a difference.'

'And go through all the pomp of being First Lady . . .'

'Tell me another way you can do more for your country.'

'I can't do it.'

'Then bury yourself in the country. Write your memoirs. Raise flowers.'

She could have slapped his face then. Wanted to for the first time since they'd known each other.

'What have you fought for all these years . . . to be an ex-prime minister, to hug babies for the UN? You pick yourself up and you take the crap, because you want to do something. Use what you have, use his position. But at the end of the day . . . *do something* that makes a difference. Or is your petty pride too great?'

And then she did slap him, full and hard on the red, right cheek, the kind of satisfying clap that imprints all five fingers on the skin.

So that he knew he'd got through to her, made her think.

'Wouldn't he come back for tea?'

'I didn't ask him.'

Her mother always seemed to find something to do in the kitchen.

'It's the first day David hasn't rung.'

'I told him not to, any more. He's there, I'm here. And he, at least has a job to do.'

Her mother and father exchanged glances.

'You seem to be shutting all the doors, love.'

She wasn't going to get into that.

'I'm going to New York tomorrow. Interview at the United Nations. There's talk of some kind of ambassadorship. I think it'll be worthwhile.'

'You didn't mention anything . . .'

'Wasn't confirmed until this afternoon. But I'll go up to London tonight. Plenty of things to sort out with the flat.'

'Anything we can do, love?' Hurt emblazoned on the two elderly faces.

'Stop worrying both of you. I'm alive and well. Life goes on. OK?'

'Come to bed, Keith. I want to christen it.'

He stood by the window, looking out over St James's Park. Still couldn't believe it. You worked and you schemed and then you schemed again ... .and suddenly it was there in your hands. The unthinkable. Crown Jewels. King of the world. You of all people, Keith Harper.

It had been some arrival. Denise leaping around the building, flirting with all the staff, yelping like a puppy and threatening to invite all the relatives. They wouldn't take long to reduce the place to the dignity of a Happy Eater on the M4.

Have to keep them well out of sight.

As if there wasn't enough to think about.

He sat on the bed and swung his legs under the blanket, aware suddenly that Denise was naked, pressing her body against his side.

'I said I wanted to christen it.'

He turned away. 'I'm really tired, love. OK? Tomorrow.'

'Listen, Keith Harper, you only ever get one First Night. So why don't we put on a real show?'

'I told you love. Lot on my mind ...'

'But it's been ages.'

And then he knew why. Even now, even after all that had happened, he would have given the last change in his pocket to have Alison lying beside him. This had been her bed, and she had lain on this same mattress, staring at these same walls. The imprint was hers, the smell. Part of her lingered on.

After a while, Denise gave up, switched off her body and went to sleep. As the hours passed, he couldn't help wondering if the longing and the disappointment would ever leave him alone.

Chapter Sixty-seven

Alison could hear the police sirens all the way down Lexington Avenue. But they meant nothing to her.

As she returned to the hotel her mind was full of the interview she'd attended at the UN. One down – and a second scheduled for the morning with the Secretary General. The questions had been sharp, incisive – so had the answers. And she'd found herself enjoying the chance to flex her claws again. You didn't want to lose your edge.

From what they'd told her, she liked the sound of the job. Liked the idea of troubleshooting flashpoints and crises. There'd be sacrifices and tradeoffs, but it was well away from the ritual muggings of Westminster. And she needed that. Once the dogs had been turned loose on you, it took a long time to return to normality. You kept finding scars you never knew you had – ones they'd opened and left behind.

Three times that day she had picked up the phone to call David Bradley, but each time she had replaced it. He wasn't the answer to her problems. He was part of them.

The only solution, she decided, was work. Work would fill the gap that he left in her. Had done for thirty years. She'd have to hope it would do so again.

She undressed, put on a bathrobe and ordered her dinner from room service.

And it failed to occur to her when she heard a knock on the door just three minutes later, that even by the superfast standards of New York, this might be a little hard to credit.

So it was a full five seconds extra before she recognised the face of David Bradley.

'What the hell are you doing here?'

He smiled and moved past her into the room.

'I thought it was time you bought me dinner.'

'But how did you get here?'

'I took a plane and about sixty motorcycle outriders helped me through the traffic. "The President," it says on my schedule, "is having a private dinner with friends in New York."'

'What friends?'

'You.'

'I don't even need to ask how you knew I was here, do I?'

'No.' He sat down in an easy chair. 'I don't suppose you do.'

She stayed where she was, beside the door. 'I'm not even dressed, David. And you shouldn't be here. What about your army of secret servicemen?'

'They're fine. They've closed off one of the elevators. They're staked out along the corridor, and most of them have already eaten. So don't worry about them. If you could just order for me, that'd be quite sufficient.'

'I don't know what to say?'

He leaned across and took the menu. 'I'll have the grilled chicken, if that's OK. And some wine. Say that.'

They ate by a candle-light on the dinner tray, Alison still in her bathrobe, fastened by the single cord. She could see his eyes, distracted, the hint of another appetite, his hands unable to stay still.

Bradley finished the chicken and pushed away the plate. 'So what are you going to say to me?'

'I thought we'd said everything, David. I couldn't be happier about the way this all turned out for you – but I can't be part of it. I have a life of my own. And what's more I have my pride.'

'You can have more than that.'

'That's not the way it'd be seen.'

'That's the way you could see it.'

'Listen to me. I fight for what I have. I've always fought. I had to. So I don't want gifts. Not even one . . . .' she stopped for a moment. 'Not even one as generous as this.'

His little finger touched hers. 'I'm asking you to carry my ring, that's all. Everything else is your own. Your job. Your life. Come and go as you please. Hell, you're going to be away a lot anyway . . . .'

'But even so, I'd be judged simply as your wife.'

They both seemed surprised by the feel of the word. For a moment, neither of them spoke.

And strangely she didn't mind the way it sounded, leaning forward, doing nothing to prevent the opening of the robe. Was she daring him, she wondered, or daring herself?

'Things have changed,' he said, voice much quieter. 'White House women aren't the same as they used to be.'

'I'm British.'

'I'm very happy you are. Means you can't challenge me for the Presidency. There are some compensations.' He could see the faintest swing of movement below the robe.

'Why, David? What am I to you?'

'I'll show you.'

She couldn't help laughing as his hands undid the cord, couldn't help the pleasure being squeezed from inside her, couldn't help the sounds and rhythms that he brought out of her, played and played again. And she went on grinning to herself, eyes tight shut, just as she had done in the rooms of Oxford.

It seemed as if three more decades were to pass before they spoke.

'You feel just the same.'

'There's more of me.' She turned towards him and ran her hand down his stomach. 'And there's less of you.'

'That's not very flattering.'

She giggled again. 'I didn't mean there. I meant your waist.'

'You still laugh in bed.'

'That's because you're still funny in bed.'

'Why?'

'You treat me like a meal. Only not everything was meant to be eaten.'

'That's what you used to say in Oxford.'

'You're better than you were in Oxford. You don't rush your food any more.'

'And you taste better.'

'Couldn't you put away your tongue for a moment? I haven't seen your face for the last fifteen minutes.'

'Can't you take it?'

'Too much pleasure for an old lady. I might overdose. I'm not used to it.'

They got up for a while and finished the wine, and then she

began to laugh again, low down . . .

'Where are you now, for God's sake?'

'Last outpost of the empire.'

'Well, come back to Rome for a moment.'

'Why, do I get an answer to my question?'

'Yes.'

'What is it?'

'The answer's no.' She smiled at him in the darkness. 'But ask me again in a few minutes.'

Chapter Sixty-eight

They all went to the same place. But they all remember that day for different reasons.

Champagne Tripp remembers the day, because it was the last time she squeezed herself into her pink outfit. And she still believes the outspoken senator from Wyoming made an assignation, that he intended to follow up.

Ruth Bradley remembers the day because her son forgave her – over breakfast in the family quarters – the way she never thought he would.

David remembers the day, for the beginnings of a question mark that somehow never went away.

Shortly before six a.m. Alison Lane, as she still was, dodged the cameras and the satellite trucks, and the twenty thousand reporters, and thirty thousand police that filled the capital. And she met Sir Henry at a metro station half way up the line to Shady Grove, in Maryland.

Washington's suburbs still dozed in the snow. Only the very early and the very cold saw her, scarf about her head, knee-length black boots, grey sheepskin coat. Not a bride-to-be. Not out there in sleepy-town USA.

They walked for a while around the empty parking lot, until he broke the silence.

'Thank you for seeing me. I realise it couldn't be a busier day.'

'You said it was urgent.'

'I thought it important that we clarified our arrangement. Since you're going to be pretty well protected after today.'

She didn't answer for a moment, just listened to the boots on the soft snow, watching the lights turn on in the blocks along the Pike.

'I don't think we have an arrangment any more, Sir Henry.'

'I'm sorry, my dear. I don't follow. I thought our conversation on the coast a while back was pretty clear.'

'You made me an offer and now I'm turning it down.' She stopped in the snow and faced him. 'Our arrangement is over, terminated. I'm not doing this for you. I can't. I know that now. I'm not going to burrow and ferret for you, as I have done over the last thirty years. This is where it ends. It has to.'

Even in the dawn light, she could see the surge of anger, the way it burst inside him, the way he sought instantly to control it. The pleading, reasonable tone that took its place.

'I think you should see this in context, my dear. In the context of the relationship that we've enjoyed for a very long time.'

'What does that mean?'

'I'm offering you a chance to do something of the utmost importance.'

'That's exactly what I'm doing. I have a new career at the UN, and for the first time in thirty years I'm going to have a personal life. Can you understand how much that means to me? All of it on my terms. Not for you. Not for anyone else.'

'I still don't think you've grasped what I'm saying. Our relationship has been based on a number of mutual favours. Without my help ...'

'Get to the point, Sir Henry.'

And the anger was returning to him. First in the eyes, now spreading outwards, tightening the face and the lower lip.

'The point, my dear, is that I made you, your career, your chances and I'll be the one to decide when this is over. Is that clearer ... ?'

'So that's where we've got to, is it? Threats, little tantrum perhaps, intimidation. Good old weapons, tried and tested.' She took off her glove and rubbed her eyes. 'Go home. Go on. Go back to London. It's over. The time has moved on. And ...' the voice seemed to hold a threat of its own 'don't let me hear this again. D'you understand? It's finished.'

'Not for me.'

She shrugged and walked away, back to the metro, not knowing or caring what happened to him.

Harry Deval remembers the day with considerable trepidation. For the fourth time that morning he was tying Jason's tie, standing him up against the wall of his west wing office, while Jane made final adjustments to her hair.

It was past eleven o'clock, when his secretary knocked at the door.

'What is it, Jean?'

'There's a man been calling for you all morning. I've explained the circumstances. You'd think he'd understand.'

'Who is he?'

She lowered her voice. 'He's from one of the British Services ... you know ...'

'So put him on to NSA. For Chrissake there are channels to go through. I don't meet with these people. Period.'

'I tried. But he won't speak to them. Says it's vital he sees you. Can't wait. National Security. He's at the south-west gate. Now.'

'Jesus, there's a wedding in the East Room in forty-five minutes ...'

'It's OK, Harry.' Jane touched his arm. 'Do what you have to do. I wanted to go up anyway and make sure David's all right.'

Harry made two phone calls and then sat at his desk and waited. Even as he replaced the receiver, there was a knock at the door and the elderly man was shown in.

'A thousand apologies, Mr Deval, I'm ...'

'I know exactly who you are. What you don't seem to realise is what the hell's going on here today. Don't you read the papers, watch television? What in Christ's name is the matter with you people? You have your own contacts, your own channels. If it wasn't for the fact that the president is marrying a Brit ...'

'A British national?' The man took off his hat. 'That's precisely why I thought you ought to see the file I have with me and communicate the contents ...'

'I'll look at it later.'

'You'd do well to look at it now. I understand you've been conducting a few researches of your own recently in England. There are one or two details here, which I believe you missed.' A folder seemed to make its own way across the desk to Harry. 'I didn't want there to be any question about our commitment to the Special Relationship, in the years to come.'

He put his hand on the door and was half-way through it before Harry caught him.

'Where you going?'

The old man waved the gold embossed card in front of him. 'I have an invitation.'

All of them have one peculiar recollection.

Of seeing David Bradley moving through the crowd in the East Room, surrounded by glitter and smiles, a mass of hands shaking almost all his movable parts. A little bit of White House magic in the air, the kind that accompanies every great occasion in the capital of the Americas.

And then Harry Deval catches his arm, still smiling and joking and leads him firmly to the exit, back to the Cross Halls, into the shadows where he can't be seen.

'Just signing a piece of paper,' the word goes out. 'Only take a second.'

Then, just as suddenly, he's back into the crowds, with the winter suntan and the campaign smile, trying not to step on everyone's feet as he makes it across the room to Alison.

She too, remembers that moment, thinking she heard her name being called. Just as she thought it, thirty years before on a street in Oxford. Only this time she doesn't turn, catching sight instead of the elderly man in the crowd – the red face, the studiedly ill-fitting morning coat, a rose in his lapel, half-smiling, because he only ever had half-emotions; half there, half somewhere else.

'Alison!' David's hand tight on her arm, a new urgency in the grip.

'What is it?'

His eyes taking a moment to decide.

'Nothing.'

ONE NIGHT IN PARADISE

MAISEY YATES

Maisey Yates was an avid Mills & Boon Modern Romance reader before she began to write them. She still can't quite believe she's lucky enough to get to create her very own sexy alpha heroes and feisty heroines. Seeing her name on one of those lovely covers is a dream come true.

Maisey lives with her handsome, wonderful, nappy-changing husband and three small children across the street from her extremely supportive parents and the home she grew up in, in the wilds of Southern Oregon, USA. She enjoys the contrast of living in a place where you might wake up to find a bear on your back porch and then heading into the home office to write stories that take place in exotic urban locales.

CHAPTER ONE

CLARA Davis looked at the uneaten cake, still as pristine and pink as the bride had demanded, sitting on its pedestal. A very precarious pedestal that had taken a whole lot of skill to balance and get set up. Not to mention have delivered to the coast-side hotel that sat twenty miles away from her San Francisco kitchen.

Everything would have been perfect. The cake, the setting, the groom, well, he was beyond perfect, as usual. And everyone who had been invited had come.

There had been one key person missing, though. The bride had decided to skip the event. And without her, it made it sort of tricky to continue.

Clara eyed the cake and considered taking a slice for herself. She'd worked hard on it. No sense letting it go to waste.

She sighed. The cake wouldn't make the knot in her stomach go away. It wouldn't ease any of the sadness she felt. Nothing had been able to shake that feeling, not since the groom, who was now officially jilted, had announced the engagement in the first place.

Though, ironically, watching him get stood up at the altar hadn't made her feel any better. But how could it? She didn't like seeing Zack hurt. He was her business partner—more than that, he was her best friend. And also, yeah, the man who kept her awake some nights with the kinds of fantasies that did not bear rehashing in the light of day.

But secret fantasies aside, she hadn't really wanted the wedding to fall apart. Well, not this close to the actual ceremony. Or maybe she had wanted it. Maybe a small part of her had hoped this would be the outcome.

Maybe that was why she'd agreed to bake the cake. To stand by and watch Zack bind himself to another woman for the rest of his life. There wasn't really another sane reason for it.

She blew out a breath and walked out of the kitchen and into the massive, empty reception hall. Her heart hit hard against her breastbone when she saw Zack Parsons, coffee mogul, business genius and abandoned groom, standing near the window, looking out at the beach, the sun casting an orange glow on his face and bleeding onto the pristine white of his tuxedo shirt.

He looked different, for just a moment. Leaner. Harder than she was used to seeing him. His tie was draped over his shoulders, his jacket a black puddle by his feet. He was leaning against the window, bracing himself on his forearm.

It shouldn't really shock her that after being left at the altar he looked stronger in a strange way.

"Hey," she said, her voice sounding too loud. Stupid in the empty room.

He turned, his gray eyes locking with hers, and she stopped breathing for a moment. He truly was the most beautiful man on the planet. Seven years of working with him on a daily basis should have taken some of the impact away. And some days she was able to ignore it, or at least sublimate it. But then there were other days when it hit her with the force of ten tons of bricks.

Today was one of those days.

"What kind of cake did I buy, Clara?" he asked, pushing off from the window and stuffing his hand into his pocket.

She forced herself to breathe. "The bottom tier was vanilla, with raspberry filling, per Hannah's instructions. And there was pink fondant. Which I hand-painted, by the way. But the vanilla cake in the middle was soaked in bourbon and honey. And not a single walnut on the whole cake. Because I know what you like."

"Good. Have someone wrap up the middle tier and send it to my house. And they can send Hannah her tier, too."

"You don't have to do that. You can throw it out."

"It's edible. Why would I throw it out?"

"Uh…because it was your wedding cake. For a wedding that didn't happen. For most people it might…take the sweet out of it."

He shrugged one shoulder. "Cake is cake."

She put her hand on her hip and affected a haughty expression, hoping to force a slight smile. "My cake is more than mere cake, but I get your point."

"We've made a fortune off your cakes, I'm aware of how spectacular they are."

"I know. But I can make a new cake. I can make a cake that says Condolences on Your Canceled Nuptials. We could put a man on top of it sitting in a recliner, watching sports on his flat-screen television, with no bride in sight."

The corner of his mouth lifted slightly and she felt a small bubbly sensation in her chest. As though a weight had just been removed.

"That won't be necessary."

"That could be a new thing we offer in the shops, Zack," she said, knowing business was his favorite topic, aborted wedding or no. "Little cupcakes for sad occasions."

"I'm not all that sad."

"You aren't?"

"I'm not heartbroken, if that's what you're wondering."

Clara frowned. "But you got left at the altar. Public humiliation is…well, it's never fun. I had something like that happen in high school when I got stood up by my date at a dance.

People pointed and laughed. I was humiliated. It was all very Carrie. Without the pig's blood or the mass murder."

"Not the highlight of my life, Clara, I'll admit." He swallowed. "Not the lowest point, either. I would have preferred for her to leave me before I was standing at the altar, with the preacher, in a tux, in front of nearly a thousand people, but I'm not exactly devastated."

"That's…well, that's good." Except it was sort of scary to know that he could be abandoned just before taking his vows and respond to it with an eerie calm. She reacted more strongly to a recipe that didn't pan out the way she wanted it to.

But then, Zack was always the one with the zenlike composure. When they'd first met, over a cupcake of all things, she'd been impressed by that right away. That and his beautiful eyes, but that was a different story.

She'd been working at a small bakery in the Mission District in San Francisco, and he'd been scoping out a new location for his local chain of coffee shops. He'd bought one of her peanut-butter-banana cupcakes, her experiment du jour. His reaction, like all of Zack's reactions, hadn't been overly demonstrative. But there had been a glint in his eye, a hint of that hard steel that lay just beneath the outer calm.

And he'd come back the next day, and the next. She'd never entertained, not for a moment, the idea that he'd been coming in to see her. It had been all about the cupcakes.

And then he'd offered her twice the money to come and work in his flagship shop, making the treats of her choice in his gorgeous, state-of-the-art kitchen. It had been the start of everything for her. At eighteen it had been a major break, and had allowed her to get out of her parents' house, something she'd been desperate to do.

In the years since, it had been a whole lot more than that.

Roasted's ten thousandth location had just opened, their first in Japan, and it was being hailed a massive success.

Conceptualizing the treats for that shop had been a fun challenge, just like every new international location had been.

She and Zack hadn't had a life since Roasted had really started to take off, nothing that went beyond coffee and confections, anyway. Of course, Zack was the backbone of the company, the man who got it done, the man who had seen it become a worldwide phenomenon.

They had drinks, coffee beans and mass-produced versions of her cupcakes and other goodies in all the major grocery chains in the U.S. Roasted was a household name. Because Zack was willing to sacrifice everything in his personal life to see it happen.

Hannah had been his only major concession to having a personal life, and that relationship had only started in the past year. And now Zack had lost her.

But he wasn't devastated. Apparently. She was probably more devastated than *he* was. Again, cake related.

"I didn't love her," he said.

Clara blinked. "You didn't...love her?"

"I cared about her. She was going to make a perfectly acceptable wife. But it wasn't like I was passionately head over heels for her or anything."

"Then why...why were you marrying her?"

"Because it was time for me to get married. I'm thirty. Roasted has achieved the level of success I was hoping for, and there comes a point where it's the logical step. I reached that point, Hannah had, too."

"Apparently she hadn't."

He gave her a hard glare. "Apparently."

"Do you know why? Have you talked to her?"

"She can come and talk to me when she's ready."

Zack would have laughed at the expression on Clara's face if he'd found anything remotely funny about the situation. The headlines would be unkind, and with so many media-hungry witnesses to the event, mostly on the absent bride's side, there would be plenty of people salivating to get their name in print by offering their version of the wedding of the century that wasn't.

Clara was too soft. Her brown eyes were all dewy looking, as though she were ready to cry on his behalf, her petite hands clasped in front of her, her shoulders slumped. She was more dressed up than he was used to seeing her. Her lush, and no he wasn't blind so of course he'd noticed, curves complemented, though not really displayed, by a dress that could only be characterized as nice, if a bit matronly.

She did that, dressed much older than she needed to, her thick auburn hair always pulled back into a low bun. Because she had to have her hair up to bake, and it had become a habit. But sometimes he wished she'd just let her hair down. And, because he was a man, sometimes he wished she wouldn't go to so much trouble to conceal her curves, either.

Although, in reality, her style of dress suited him. They worked together every day, and he had no business having an opinion on her physical appearance. His interest was purely for aesthetic purposes. Like opting for a room with a nice view.

That aside, Clara was all emotion and big hand gestures. There was nothing contained about her.

"I'm fine," he said.

"I know. I believe you," she said.

"No, you don't. Or you don't want to believe me because your more romantic sensibilities can't handle the fact that my heart isn't broken."

"Well, you ought to love the person you're going to marry, Zack."

"Why? Give me a good reason why. So that I could be more broken up about today? So that I could be more suitably wounded if she had shown up, and we had said our vows, when ten years on the marriage fell on the wrong side of the divorce statistics? I don't see the point in that."

"Well, I don't see the point at all."

"And I didn't ask."

"You never do."

"The secret to my success." His tone came out a bit harsher than he intended and Clara's expression reflected it. "You'll survive this," he said drily. "Breaking up is hard to do."

She rolled her eyes. "I'm worried about you."

"Don't be. I'm not so breakable. Tell me, any big word on the Japan location go up online while I was busy getting my photo taken?"

"All good. Some of the pictures I've been seeing are showing that it's absolutely slammed. And everything seems to be going over huge."

"Good. That means the likelihood of expanding further there is good." He sat down in one of the vacant, linen-covered chairs. They had pink bows. Also Hannah's choice. He put his hands on the tabletop, moving his mind away from the fiasco of a wedding day and getting it back on business. "How are things going with our designer cupcakes?"

"Um…well, I was pretty busy getting the wedding cake together." Clara felt like her head was spinning from the abrupt subject change.

Zack was in full business mode, sitting at the trussed up wedding-party table like it was the pared-down bamboo desk he had in his office at Roasted's corporate headquarters.

"And?"

"I have a few ideas. But these are pretty labor-intensive recipes and they really aren't practical for the retail line, or even for most of the stores."

"Cupcakes are labor intensive?"

She shot him a deadly look. "Why don't you try baking a simple batch and tell me how it goes?"

"No, thanks. I stick to my strengths, and none of them happen to involve baking."

"Then trust me, they're labor intensive."

"That's fine. My goal is to start doing a few boutique-style shops in some more affluent areas. We'll have bigger kitchens so that we'll have the capability to do more on-site baking."

"That could work. We'll have to have a more highly trained staff."

"That's fine. I'm talking about a few locations in Los Angeles, New York, Paris, London, that sort of thing. It will be more like the flagship store. A bit more personalized."

"I really like the idea, not that you'd care if I didn't."

"I am the boss."

"I know. I'm just the Vice President of Confections," she said, bringing up a joke they'd started in the early days of the company.

A smile touched his lips again and her heart expanded. "A big job."

"It is," she said. "And you don't pay me enough."

"Yes, I do."

She gave him a look. One she knew was less than scary, but she tried. "Anyway, go on."

"I had made an appointment to speak to a man who owns a large portion of farmland in Thailand. Small clusters of coffee and tea. All of his plants receive a very high level of care and that's making for extremely good quality roasts and brews. My goal is to set up a deal with him so we can get some limited-editions blends. We'll sell them in select locations, and have them available for order online."

Her mind skipped over all the details he'd just laid out, latching on to just one thing. "Weren't you going to Thailand on your honeymoon?"

"That was the plan."

Clara couldn't stop her mouth from dropping open. "You were going to do business on your honeymoon?"

"Hannah had some work to do, as well. Time doesn't stop just because you get married."

"No wonder she left you at the altar." She regretted the

words the moment they left her mouth. "Sorry. I didn't mean that."

"You did, and that's fine. Unlike you, Hannah had no romantic illusions, you can trust me on that. Her reasons for not showing up today may very well have had something to do with a Wall Street crisis. There's actually a good chance she's at her apartment, in her wedding gown, screaming obscenities at her computer screen watching the cost of grain go down."

She had to concede that the scenario was almost plausible. Hannah was all icy cool composure, and generally nice and polite, until someone crossed her in the corporate world. Clara had overheard the other woman's phone conversations become seriously cutthroat in tense business situations. Threats of removal of tender body parts had crossed her lips without hesitation.

She admired her for it. For the the intense way she went after what she wanted. She'd done it with Zack. It had been sort of awe inspiring to watch. Mostly it had been awe-inspiringly depressing. Because Clara wasn't cutthroat, or intense. And she hadn't been brave enough to pursue what she really wanted. She'd never been brave enough to pursue Zack.

"I doubt that's what happened," Clara said, even though she couldn't be certain.

"There was a reason I asked how the designer-cupcake thing was going."

"Oh." Back to business.

"I was trying to make sure you didn't feel swamped by the amount of work you have to do."

"No. Creating recipes is the best part of my job. I've been having fun with this one. I've actually done most of the experimental baking and tasting with our panel, and I have a few standout favorites, plus some that need to be improved. And then I'll have to narrow down the selection, because it just won't be feasible to have too many different kinds on the menu at once."

"So that was the long, detailed version of you telling me you aren't too busy at the moment?"

She shot him a deadly look. Jilted or not, he didn't need to be a jerk. "No, I'm not too busy."

"Good, because everything was set for me to head to Chiang Mai tonight."

"And you need me to make sure everything is running smoothly at corporate?" That wasn't usually the role she ful-filled. She wasn't an administrator, not even close.

"No, I want you to get packed, because you're coming with me."

Her stomach honestly felt like it plummeted, squeezing as it made its way down into her toes. "You're not serious. You're not actually asking me to come on your honeymoon with you?"

"The trip is booked. I have appointments made. I'm not canceling the honeymoon just because my bride neglected to show up." He looked at her, like he had thousands of times, but this time felt... It felt different. The inspection seemed closer somehow, his gray eyes more assessing, more intimate. She swallowed hard and tried to ignore the fact that her heart seemed to be trying to claw its way out of her chest. "I think you'll make a more than fitting replacement."

CHAPTER TWO

IF he had physically hit her he couldn't have possibly hurt her worse. A replacement? The consolation prize. The stand-in for tall, lean, angular Hannah who possessed the cheekbones of a goddess. Not that Clara had noticed, or compared.

Well, she had. And in some ways, on some days, the fact they were so different made it easier because there was no question of what the other woman had that she didn't.

But she had never, never put herself in the position of trying to vie for Zack's attention, not in that way. Because she'd known that she would be the consolation prize if he ever did decide to look in her direction. And she'd decided that was one thing she couldn't do to herself. The one thing worse than watching the man who meant the world to her tie himself to another woman. Being the one he'd settled for.

And now Zack was shoving her into that position. It made her want to gag.

"I'm not a replacement for anyone, Zack. And if you're suggesting I am, then I think we've become a little bit too comfortable with each other."

She turned and walked out of the reception hall. She left the cake. She didn't care about the cake. The staff of the hotel could have it for an early, sugary breakfast when they came in tomorrow morning.

She breezed through the hall and out the front doors, into

the damp, salty air. It had been a cool day, but now, with the sun dipping down below the horizon, the air coming in off of the bay was downright chilly. Which was good, because now, if anyone saw her lip tremble a little bit, she could blame the cold.

She didn't want to be emotional, not over something that wasn't even intentional, and with Zack, she knew it wasn't. Zack wasn't mean, more than that; he simply wasn't all that emotional, so he never assumed that anyone else was.

Everything was so surface to Zack. Nothing seemed to get under his skin. Nothing seemed to throw him off, even for a moment. Not even a canceled wedding.

Anyway, she'd had enough intentional digs taken at her in her life to know that things could get far too dramatic if she didn't make people have to work at hurting her feelings.

But since her feelings for Zack were a constant jumble, her reactions to anything involving him were always strong. Most of the time, though, she managed to keep that fact hidden from Zack. A lot of the time, she kept the extent of her feelings hidden from herself.

"Clara."

She turned and saw him standing just behind her. She didn't say anything. She crossed her arms beneath her breasts and fixed him with her best glare.

"You're the second woman to abandon me today."

Her face flooded with prickly heat. "See, that comparison is not very flattering, considering you've already used the word replacement in regards to me."

"That's not what I meant."

"Then what did you mean?"

"That I need someone to come with me, and actually, under the circumstances you're a better fit than my ex-fiancée."

For a full second she could only think of one thing his statement could possibly mean. Images clicked through her mind like close-up still-shots. Tan hands on a pale, bare hip.

Masculine lips on a feminine throat. Blood roared through her body, into her cheeks, making her face burn. She was sure they were the color of ripe strawberries, broadcasting her thoughts to anyone who looked at her.

"What?" she asked.

"Hannah's smart, don't get me wrong, but she doesn't know this market quite like you do. Prices on stocks, maybe, but it will be nice to have you on hand to offer an opinion about marketing and flavor."

Business. He was talking about business. And somehow, to Zack, business was more important than romance and making love on his honeymoon?

At least he was pretending it was. There was something different about his expression, a dark light behind his gray eyes. She'd seen Zack nearly every day for the past seven years. She knew his moods, his expressions as well as she knew her own.

And this was a different Zack. Well, she thought it was. For some reason, the hardness, the intensity, seemed more true than what she thought she knew of him.

Strange. But then, the whole day had been strange. Starting with the interminably long silence after the strains of the Bridal March had faded from the air and the aisle remained vacant.

All right, he'd made her mad. It wasn't the first time. He was bullheaded and a general pain in the butt sometimes. He was also the smartest man she knew, with a cutting wit that always kept her amused. He was one of the few people who'd never doubted that her ideas were good.

If she didn't go with him, she would spend her evenings hanging out by herself, reading and experimenting with cupcake recipes and licking the batter off the spatula. Fun, sure, but not the kind of fun she could have in Thailand.

Again, those images, erotic and explicit, assaulted her. No, that wasn't the kind of fun she would be having in Thailand.

Zack had never looked twice at her in that way and for the most part, she was fine with that. She'd had a crush on him at first, but even then she hadn't expected anything to come of it.

And, yes, Hannah had come in and stirred up some strange feelings. Because as long as Zack had simply been there, at work every day, and available for dinner meetings and a lot of other things, it had been comfortable. Zack was in every space in her life, at work and home.

But then along came Hannah, and she took up his time, and, Clara had assumed, that he loved her. And having to share Zack's emotion with someone else had felt… It had felt awful. And it had made her jealous, which didn't make sense because she'd never even tried to cross the boundaries of friendship with Zack. So it wasn't like Hannah had been encroaching on her territory or anything. But she'd been so jealous looking at Zack and Hannah she'd felt like her stomach was turning inside out, and she knew, that even if she could never have Zack, she didn't want anyone else to have him, either.

Which was just stupid and childish. About as stupid as going with a man on his honeymoon, platonically, in place of his bride, to conduct business with him. Platonically.

She needed her head checked. She needed some sanity. Maybe the problem was that Zack did take up all the spaces in her life. Maybe it would have to change.

Just the thought of that, of pushing him away, sent a sharp dose of pain through her system. She was addicted to him.

"All right. I'll go. Because I would rather have a paid vacation in Thailand than spend the week hanging out in the office and orchestrating the return of all your wedding presents."

"I'm not returning my wedding presents."

"You can't keep them, Zack."

"Of course I can. I might need a food processor someday. What does a food processor do?"

"I'll teach you sometime. Anyway, yes, I'll go with you."

The corner of his lip curved up into a wicked smile that

made her stomach tighten in a way that wasn't entirely unpleasant. "Excellent. Looks like I won't be spending my wedding night alone, after all."

It probably wasn't nice of him to tease Clara. But he liked the way her cheeks turned pink when he slipped an innuendo into the conversation. And frankly, he was in need of amusement after the day he'd had.

But amusement hadn't been his primary goal when he'd given her the wedding-night line out in front of the hotel. He'd been trying to atone for his ill-spoken remark about her being a replacement. In truth, he had more fun with Clara than he did with Hannah. It wasn't as though he disliked Hannah; quite the opposite. But he hadn't been marrying Hannah for the company.

She'd needed a husband to help her climb the corporate ladder, a little testosterone to help her out in a male-dominated field. And a wife…well, a wife like her was a convenience for a lot of reasons.

But Clara was not his wife. In a lot of ways, she was better. And he hadn't intended to hurt her feelings. She'd been quiet on the ride from the hotel back to her town house by the bay, and once they'd gotten inside to her place she'd dashed into her bedroom to pack a few things "real quick" which, in his experience with women meant…not quick at all.

He sat in her white leather chair, the one that faced her tiny television. Not state of the art at all, nothing like his place. The home theater had been one of his first major purchases when Roasted had become solvent. Clara's had been an industrial-grade mixer for her kitchen. That was where all *her* high-tech gear was. She had a stove with more settings than his stereo system.

"Ready." He looked up and his stomach clenched.

Clara was standing at the end of the hallway, large, pink leather bag draped over her shoulder, dark jeans conforming to the curve of her hips, and a black knit top outlining the contours of her very generous breasts. He hadn't gotten married today, so he was going to allow himself a longer look than he ever did. He'd noticed her body before, but he'd never allowed himself to really look at her as a man looked at a woman. He didn't know why he was letting himself do it now. A treat in exchange for the day, maybe. Or exhaustion making him sloppy with his rules.

Clara was an employee. Clara was a friend. Clara was not a possible lover, and normally that meant no looking at her like she could be.

But tonight wasn't normal. Not by a long stretch.

"Good." He stood up and tried to keep his interest in her body sublimated. But he was just a man. A man who had been celibate for a very long time. A man who had been expecting a reprieve on that and had been sadly disappointed.

"Are we taking the company jet?" She smiled, her perfectly shaped brow raised.

She really was beautiful, and not just her curves. He didn't stop to notice her looks very often. She was like…not furniture, but a fixture for sure. Someone who was always there, every day, no matter what. And when someone was always there, you didn't stop and look at them very often.

But he was looking at her now. Her face was a little bit round, her skin pale and soft. Her eyes, dark brown and wide, were fringed with dark lashes, surprising given her auburn hair color. And her lips…full and soft looking, a very delicate shade of pink.

Looking at her features was a nice distraction, especially since he was about to make her very, very angry. Normally he didn't care for other people's feelings. Not enough to lose any sleep over. He was in command of his world, and he didn't question his decisions.

But Clara was different. She'd always been different.

"There's something I didn't tell you yet." And it might have been wise to save it until she was safely on the plane. And had had a glass or two of champagne.

"What's that?" she asked, eyes narrowing.

"I was supposed to get married today."

Her eyes became glittering, deadly slits. "Right."

"I was meant to be going on my honeymoon with my wife. And now, here I find myself jilted. No bride. Barely any pride to speak of."

She arched her brow, her mouth twisted into a sour expression. "What, Zack?"

"I need you to come with me. As more than my friend. Not really more than my friend, but more as far as Amudee is concerned."

She shook her head and let her pink bag slip off of her shoulder and onto the hardwood floor. "That's…that's insane! Who would believe you'd hooked up with someone else already?"

"Everyone, Clara. I'm a man who, as far as the public is concerned, is in the throes of heartbreak. Everyone knows about our business relationship. About our friendship. Is it so insane to think that, after suffering heartbreak, I looked to my closest friend and found so much more?"

Oh, it was sick. It really was. To hear him saying something that was…that was so close to her real-life fantasies it was painful to listen to the words fall from his lips. "No. No, I am not playing this game. That's ridiculous, Zack. Go on your own."

"I can't."

"Why?"

"Look, my pride will survive. But if I show up alone, and without my wife, looking the part of lonely loser who couldn't hold on to his woman…well, who wants to cut a business deal with that guy?"

"So offer him more money," she hissed.

"That's the thing with Amudee. Money isn't the main objective. If I could throw a bigger check at him, I would. But it's not only about that. It's about people, the kind of people he wants to do business with, and for the most part, I am that man. I care deeply about fair trade, about the work he has going on there in Thailand. I have to look like I call the shots in my own life, and I will not let an inconsequential hiccup like Hannah's cold feet affect that."

She shook her head. "No. Zack just…"

"If I lose the deal because of this…"

"I'm fired? I doubt it. And I can't imagine him passing this up just because you aren't getting married now."

"This growing project is a huge thing for him, his life's work. He's poured his entire fortune into this. He has high principles, and, yes, a lot of it does have to do with bringing money into Northern Thailand, for the people that live there, but he won't go into something if he doesn't feel one hundred percent about it. I can't afford to let it slip to ninety-nine percent. And if you tip the deal over, then I need you."

"So buy your beans from someone else," she said. "Someone who doesn't care what your personal life looks like."

"There is no one else. Not with a product like this. He understands the foundation I've built Roasted on. That it's always been my goal to find small, family run farms to support. He's a philanthropist and what he's done is give different families in the north of Thailand their own plots to cultivate their own crops. Tea and coffee is being grown there, of the highest quality. And I want the best—I don't want to settle for second."

Clara bent and picked her bag up from the floor. She really hated what Zack was proposing. Not just because she didn't exactly relish the idea of lying to someone for a week; there was that, but also because the idea of playing the part of his lover for a week made her feel sick.

She'd done a good job, a damn good job, of pretending that all she felt for Zack was friendship, with a very successful working relationship thrown into the mix. She'd pretended, not just for him, but for herself.

Because she didn't want to desire a man who was so out

of her league. A man who dated women who were her polar opposites in looks and personality. Women who were tall and thin, blonde and as cool and in control at all times as he was.

Wanting Zack was a pipe dream of the highest order.

Yes, it had been harder to ignore those sneaky, forbidden feelings when his engagement was announced, but she'd still done it. She'd baked his wedding cake, for heaven's sake.

But this, this was one ask too many. Even for him. To go to a romantic setting, pretend she was experiencing her deepest fantasy, all for show, just seemed too masochistic.

And yet, it was hard to say no to him, too. Not when, as much as it galled to be asked to do this, it would give her this sort of strange, out of time, experience with him.

And definitely not when the whole thing was such a big deal to the future of Roasted. Her wagon was well and truly hitched to the company, and in order for her to succeed, the company had to succeed.

Her wagon was hitched to more than the company, if she was honest. It was Zack. Zack and his wicked smiles, Zack and that indefinable thing he possessed that made her want to care for him, even though he never let her.

Zack was the reason she didn't date. Not because, as a boss he kept her so busy with work, though she'd pretended that was it for a long, long time. It was Zack the man. Because her feelings for him were more than just complicated. And she was… she was a doormat.

She'd baked the man's wedding cake. And then what had she thought would happen? She was going to stay at Roasted, after Zack married? Play Aunt Clara to his kids? Watch while he had this whole life while she died a virgin with nothing but her convection oven for company?

Sick. It was sick.

And now she was really going with him to Chiang Mai to play the part she knew he'd never really consider her for?

She needed to get a life.

She was right. What she'd thought earlier at the hotel had been right. A moment of clarity. It wasn't healthy to have him in everything. He was her boss, her best friend. He filled her work and personal hours, and even when he wasn't around, he was in her thoughts. Zack had dates, he had a life that didn't include her and she…didn't. She couldn't do it anymore.

"If I do this… If I do this, then it's going to be the last thing I do at Roasted." She thought about the bakery, the one she'd been dreaming of for the past few months. The one she'd drawn up plans for. It had been in her mind ever since Zack and Hannah got engaged. Just a mere fantasy of escaping that painful reality at first, but now…now she thought she needed to make it happen.

She needed to make some boundaries. Have something that was hers. Just hers.

"What?" he asked, his dark brows locking together.

"If I go with you and play arm candy then I'm done. It's not…it's not the first time I've thought of this." It wasn't. When he'd come into the office with Hannah and announced that the whole thing was official, well, she'd just about handed in her resignation then and there.

But of course his smile and his innate Zack-ness had stopped her. Because in her mind, it was better to have crumbs from him than everything from someone else. Because he was so enmeshed in her life, so a part of her routine. Her first thought in the morning, her constant companion throughout the day. And it was his face she saw when she drifted off to sleep.

He was everything.

And the real truth of the situation was that while Zack cared for her, and even loved her, possibly like some sort of younger sister figure, she wasn't everything to him. And he didn't want her the way she wanted him.

"What the hell?" he asked.

"I'm…I'm having a revelation, hold on."

"Could you not?"

"No. I'm sorry. I'm…I'm sorry, Zack. This really has been… It's been brewing for a while and I know it wasn't the best day or the best way to say it, but…it does have to be said."

"Why?"

"Because… Because it's eating my life!" The words exploded from her. "And if that isn't made completely obvious by the fact that I'm agreeing to drop everything at the spur-of-the-moment to fly to Asia to go on your honeymoon in place of your fiancée and pretend to be your *new* girlfriend…well…I can't help you."

"No. No, I don't agree."

"And what, Zack? You can't force me to stay at my job."

He looked like he was searching for some loophole that would in fact give him that authority.

"I need a good severance, too. I want to open my own bakery."

"The hell you will!" he said, his voice hard, harsher than she'd ever heard.

"The hell I won't," she returned, keeping her own voice steady, though, how she managed, she wasn't sure.

"Non-compete."

"What?"

"You signed a non-compete."

"A bakery would not compete with Roasted, not really," she said, planting her hands on her hips.

"It could, on a technicality, especially as we'd likely share a very similar desserts menu, seeing as you planned all of mine."

"I'm not talking about a worldwide bakery chain, I'm talking… I want to open one up that I run myself. Here in San Francisco. Something personal, something me. Something that would give me a chance to have a life."

"No."

It was shocking, Zack's transformation from unaffected, jilted groom, to this. She would have expected this kind of reaction from Hannah not showing up to the wedding, not to her asking to quit the business. Where was his control? Zack always had control. Always.

Except now.

"Then I won't go with you. And I get the feeling that a female companion is a bit more important than you let on. I know you too well for you to hide it from me."

His gray eyes glittered in the dim light of her apartment. "There is some competition. Sand Dollar Coffee is competing for the chance to get these same roasts, and Mr. Amudee, traditionalist he is, is very likely to give preference to their CEO. They were just there for a week in the villa, Martin Cole, his wife and their four children. Mr. Amudee was charmed."

"So you do need me. You need me to give you an edge. To make sure Amudee knows you're a macho man who can have his way with whomever, whenever. We're friends, Zack. I don't know why it has to be like this…."

"You were the one leveraging," he bit out.

"Because I can't do this anymore. The beck-and-call thing. I need more. *You* were getting married, you should get that."

"You want to get married?"

Her stomach tightened. "Not necessarily. But I don't even have a hope of it as long as I'm working sixty-hour weeks. And since I don't believe in practical arrangements, like the one you and Hannah have, that will keep me from having a successful relationship."

"Fine," he said, the word stiff. "But you stay on until the deal with Amudee is done. Got it? I'll need you to be around, at the business, my assumed lover, until the ink is dry on the contract."

It was cold and mercenary. And it was tempting. Tempting to play the part. To immerse herself in it for a while. Just thinking about it made her stomach tighten, made her shiver.

No. You can't forget. This is just a game to him. More business. "Yes. I won't let you down. If I say I'm going to do something, I'll do it."

"I know."

"And when it's over?"

"You can open your bakery. I'll make sure you're compensated for your time here."

Clara stuck out her hand, her heart cracking in her chest. "Then I think we have a deal."

CHAPTER THREE

ZACK was in a fouler mood than he'd been when the double doors of the hotel's wedding hall had opened to reveal, not his bride, but a very panicked wedding coordinator who was hissing into her headset.

He leaned back in his seat on his private plane and stared at the amber liquid in the tumbler on his tray. Turbulence was bouncing the alcohol around, sending the strong aroma into the air. He wasn't tempted to take a drink. He didn't drink, it was just that his flight attendant had heard about the disaster and assumed he might be in need.

He looked across the wide aisle at Clara, who was, sitting on a leather love seat in the living-room-style plane cabin, staring fixedly at her touch-screen phone.

"Good book?" he asked.

Her head snapped up. "How did you know I was reading?"

"Because you always read."

"Books make better company than surly bosses."

"Do they make better company than bitchy employees? If so, perhaps I should read more."

She looked at him, her expression bland. "I wouldn't know."

"No. You wouldn't. Look, I gave you what you asked for."

"After a big ugly fight."

"Because I don't want to lose you."

A strange expression flashed in her brown eyes. "Right."

"You've been here since the very early days of Roasted, and you've been key to the success of the company, of course I don't want to lose you."

She looked back down at her phone. "Well, I can't live my entire life to make you happy."

He frowned. "That's not how it's been, is it?"

"No," she said, her tone grudging. She put her phone down and stretched her legs out in front of her and her arms straight over her head, back arching, thrusting her breasts forward. His body hardened, his blood rushing through his veins hotter and faster.

That was a direct result of the fact that he was supposed to break his long bout with celibacy tonight, on this very plane, and it wasn't happening now. Still, his body hadn't caught up with his mind yet. Damned inconvenient considering he was now fixating on his friend's breasts. Breasts that he was not supposed to fixate on. Basically two of the only breasts on earth that were off-limits to him.

More inconvenient, considering they were about to spend the week in Chiang Mai in a very secluded and gorgeous honeymoon villa. Even more when you considered that she was leaving the company soon after.

Well, that wasn't happening. He would make sure of that. He would offer her whatever he had to offer to get her to stay, and until then he would simply nod whenever she brought it up.

He wasn't sure how he would convince her, only that he would. He'd successfully stolen her away from her bakery job back when he'd only had a handful of coffee shops to his name. He had no doubt he could do an even better job of keeping her now that he had so many resources at his disposal. He could give her whatever she wanted, more freedom, more time off. And she was his friend. She wouldn't leave him.

She was just mad about the whole fake fiancée thing. But she would get over it. She always did. It wasn't the first time he'd made her mad. Likely it wouldn't be the last. But that was just how it was. She wouldn't really leave him.

He was a master negotiator. And he didn't lose. He was good at keeping control, of his life and of his business.

"The property we're staying on is supposed to be amazing. It borders a Chiang Mai, and there's a spa right on site. It's more of a resort than anything else, but you have to be invited to stay there by the owner. Very exclusive." He got nothing but silence in response.

"They have unicorns, I hear," he continued, "with golden hooves. You'll love it."

He heard her try to stifle a very reluctant snicker.

He leaned in and looked at her face, at the faint shadows marring the pale skin beneath her eyes. "Are you tired?" he asked.

She leaned back in the chair. "You have no idea."

"There's a bedroom." His blood jumped in his veins again, like the kick-start on a motorcycle. "You could lay down for a while if you want."

"How long have we got?"

"Ten more hours."

"Oh, yeah, I need sleep." She stood up and did another little stretch move that accentuated her breasts.

Clara needed more than sleep. She needed to get out of the tiny, enclosed space with Zack and all of his hot, male phero-mones that were wreaking havoc on her good sense. If she had any at all to wreak havoc on. Well, she did have some. She'd used it to ask for her out.

For a little bit of a chance to move on and forward with her life. Because Zack hadn't married Hannah today, which was fine and good, but he would marry someone. He'd decided to, and when Zack put his mind to something, he did it. That meant it would happen, sometime in the very near future, she imag-ined, now that she knew love wasn't necessarily on the docket. Heck, if he smiled just right at the flight attendant they would probably be engaged by the time they landed in Thailand. And then she could sleep in the guest room in the villa.

She snorted.

"What?" he asked.

"Nothing."

"The scariest word known to man when issued from the lips of a woman."

Her lip curled voluntarily at his statement. "Sexist."

"I prefer realist, but you're free to call it as you see it."

"So tell me this, Zack."

"What?" he asked, one dark eyebrow arched.

"I assume you'll attempt marriage again."

"If I find the right woman."

"And by that, you don't mean the woman you love?"

Something in Zack's posture changed, subtle but obvious to her, his shoulders straightening, his muscles tensing beneath his expertly tailored shirt. His eyes changed, too. There was something dark there, haunted, something she'd never seen before, not this clearly. She'd felt it before, an intensity lurking beneath his cool exterior, but she'd never seen it so plainly.

It was almost frightening in its intensity, transforming a man she'd seen every day for seven years into a cold stranger.

"I don't do love, Clara. Ever." He turned his focus to the newspaper that was folded on his lap. "Good night."

Clara turned toward the bedroom, exhaustion burrowing beneath her skin, down into her bones. Yesterday, everything had been the way it had always been. It had sucked; it had been heading in a direction she hadn't liked, but for the most part, it had been the same.

Today everything felt different. Most of it was her fault. And even though she wouldn't change it, she hated it.

"We just landed."

Clara sat up and pushed the wild mass of auburn curls out of her eyes. She blinked a few times and Zack's face came into focus. For a moment, she didn't do anything. She didn't move, she didn't breathe, she just concentrated on his face being the first thing she saw.

She'd never woken up next to a man before. And, yeah, this wasn't really waking up next to a man in the traditional sense. And he was more leaning over than next to her. But it was a really nice thought, and it was a very nice sight first thing in the morning. If it was even morning. She had no idea.

"What time is it?" she asked.

"It's 10:00 p.m. local time."

She flopped backward. "Oh, no. Why did you let me sleep?"

"I tried to wake you."

"No, you didn't."

"I did, you were out."

She felt a strange sort of disappointment curling in her stomach. She wished, well, part of her did, that he had woken her up. She swallowed hard. Her throat felt like it was lined with cotton. It was far too easy to think of a lot of very interesting ways he might have woken her up.

No. Bad.

"I'm going to be a wreck."

"Sorry."

"I take it you didn't sleep?" She looked down and realized she was still wearing her jeans.

"No. But then, I don't sleep all that much."

That didn't surprise her. She'd never really quizzed him on his sleeping habits, but honestly, he just didn't seem like the kind of man who could sleep at all. He had too much energy and drive to stop even for a moment. Whenever she'd thought of him in bed…well, it hadn't been images of him sleeping plaguing her.

"We're at the airport?" she asked, peering out one of the windows, confused by how dark it was outside.

"Don't know if I'd say airport so much as landing strip.

We're on Mr. Amudee's property. It backs the city, but there's a lot of forest in between his land and civilization."

"Oh."

"There's a car waiting for us, and your luggage, such as it was, is already loaded in it."

She stood and her breasts nearly brushed his chest. She'd misjudged the distance. Her breath caught in her throat and nearly choked her.

Zack didn't seem affected at all. He just smiled at her, one of his wicked smiles, all of the ghosts she'd glimpsed in his gray eyes before she'd gone to sleep were banished now, leaving behind nothing but the glint that was so familiar to her.

"I didn't have—" she had to take in another breath because being so close to him had kind of sucked the other one out of her "—that much time to pack. Otherwise I could have had just as many bags as your high-maintenance ladies."

"You aren't like the women I date. You aren't high-maintenance. I like that about you." He turned and headed out the bedroom and she followed him, her chest suddenly feeling tight.

What he meant was, she wasn't beautiful. Not like the women he dated. The women who were all high-fashion planes and angles. And cheekbones.

Her mother was like that. Her sister, too. Tall and leggy with hip bones that were more prominent than their breasts. And that was the look that walked runways. The look that was fashionable, especially in southern California.

And she just didn't have the look. She had curves. An abundance of them. If any of the chi-chi boutiques had bras with her cup size, they were very often too small around, meant for women who'd gone under the knife to give them what nature had bestowed upon her so liberally. And her stomach was a little bit round, not concave or rippling. She wasn't sure if she'd ever seen her ribs.

Standing next to the women in her family just made her

feel…inadequate. And wide. And short. She'd tried to subsist on cabbage and water like her mother and sister, but frankly, she'd felt like garbage and had decided a long time ago that feeling healthy beat being fifteen pounds lighter.

Of course, that decision didn't erase a lifetime of insecurity. And that insecurity wasn't all down to weight, either.

"Great. Glad to be so…easy."

The door to the plane was standing open, and a staircase had been lowered to the tarmac. Zack stood and waited for her to go in front of him. She passed him without looking, trying not to show the knockout effect the slight scent of his cologne had on her as she moved by him.

"I wouldn't call you easy," he said.

She stopped, third stair from the top, and whipped around to look at him. "That's not what I meant."

"Not what I meant, either," he said, his expression overly innocent.

"Yeah. Right. Are you determined to drive me absolutely insane for this whole trip?" She continued down the steps and hopped onto the tarmac, the night air balmy and thick with mist, blowing across her cheeks and leaving its moist hand-print behind.

"We are supposed to be a couple."

"Fair enough."

She was reluctant to get into the glossy black town car that was parked right by the plane. Because she'd only just gotten Zack-free air, and she didn't really relish the thought of getting right back into a tight, enclosed space with him.

She needed to be able to breathe. To think. And she couldn't do it when he was around.

That realization alone reinforced her crazy, spur-of-the-moment decision to move on with her life, and away from Roasted.

The idea made her slightly sick and more than a little bit sad. Roasted had been her life since Zack had hired her on. The day-to-day of it, the constant push to invent more and more goodies, to push the flavor profiles, to push her creativity... there would never be anything else like it.

But she needed to stand on her own feet. To move on with life. She'd gone from her parents to Zack, and while she didn't feel familial about Zack in any way, he represented comfort and safety. And other stuff that wasn't comforting or safe. But being with him, like she was, wasn't pushing her to move forward.

So she was pushing herself. It was uncomfortable, but that was the way it worked. She hoped it would work.

He opened the door to the town car for her and she slid inside, and he came in just behind her. "So, do you and your boyfriends have fights?"

He must know she never had boyfriends. The odd disastrous date that never went past the front door. Emphasis on the odd, since half the men picked her up while she happened to be in the flagship store. And, in her experience, men who picked you up at ten in the morning in coffeehouses were a bit strange.

"How many long-term relationships have I had, Zack?"

"Well, Pete was around a lot until he moved for work."

"Pete? He was a friend from high school. And I was not his type, if you catch my drift."

"You weren't blonde?"

"Or male."

"Oh."

"Point being, I haven't done a lot of long-term." Any, but whatever. "And if I'm ever going to...move on, go into that phase of life then I need to be less consumed with work."

A muscled in his jaw ticked. "But you won't make this kind of money running your own bakery."

"I know. But I have a decent amount of money. How much do I need? How much do you need?"

There was a pause. Zack's hand curled into a fist on the leather seat, then relaxed. "More. Just...a bit more."

"And then you're never done."

"But if not for that then what am I working for?"

She swallowed. "A good question. Good and scary. Though I suppose adding a wife will add...something. When you find a new prospect, that is. Did Hannah have an equally efficient and driven sister, by chance?"

"Not that I'm aware of."

She snapped her fingers. "Darn."

"Don't lose sleep over it."

"I won't be sleeping tonight, anyway. Because you didn't wake me up on the plane." She couldn't resist the jab.

"Because you sleep like a rock and snore like a walrus."

"Might be why my relationships aren't long-term," she said drily. Not that any man had ever heard her snore but she was so not admitting to that.

"I doubt that."

"Do you?"

His eyes locked with hers and something changed in the air. It seemed to crackle. Like a spark on dry leaves. It was strange. It was breathtaking, and electrifying, and she never wanted it to end.

"Why?" she asked, pressing. Desperate to hear more. A little bit afraid of hearing more, too.

"Because a little bit of snoring wouldn't deter a man who'd had the pleasure of sharing your bed."

She sucked in a sharp breath and looked out the window, and into the inky-black jungle. She felt dizzy. She felt...hot.

"Well, thanks," she said.

He chuckled, low and rich like the best chocolate ganache. Just as bad for her to indulge in as the naughty treat, too. "You seem uncomfortable with the compliment."

"You and I don't talk about things like that."

"Only because it hadn't come up."

"Do you snore?" she asked.

"Not that I'm aware of."

"Then your lack of long-term relationships doesn't really make sense at all."

He arched one dark brow. "Was that a compliment?"

"More a commentary on the transient nature of your love life."

"I'm wounded."

She winced. "Well, maybe in light of all that happened today it wasn't the best thing to say."

"You've never pulled punches before, don't start now."

"I don't know any other way to be."

"Now that may account for your own short-term relationships."

She whipped around to face him and her heart stalled. He was looking at her like she was a particularly interesting treat. One he might like to taste.

The car stopped and she nearly breathed a prayer of thanks out loud. She needed distance. She needed it desperately.

"Well," Zack said, opening the door. "Time to go and have a look at our honeymoon suite."

CHAPTER FOUR

THE honeymoon villa was the epitome of romance. The anterior wall of the courtyard was surrounded by dense, green trees, clinging vines and flowers covering most of the stone wall, adding color, a sense that nature ruled here, not man. There was a keypad on the gate and Zack entered a code in; a reminder that the man very much had his fingerprints all over the property.

"Nice," she said, as the gates swung open and revealed an open courtyard area. The villa itself was white and clean. Intricate spires, carved from wood and capped in gold, adorned the roof of the house, rising up to meet the thick canopy of teak trees.

"Mr. Amudee had planned on giving Hannah and I a few days of wedded bliss prior to meeting with me, so he made sure I had the code, and that everything in the home would be stocked and ready."

Clara tried not to think about Zack and Hannah, using the love nest for its intended purpose. More than that, she tried not to think of her and Zack using it for its intended purpose.

She really did try. There was no point in allowing those fantasies. Those fantasies had led to nothing more than dateless Friday nights and lack of sleep.

"Well, that was...thoughtful of him."

"It was. I believe he has some activities planned for us, too."

Oh, great. She was going to be trapped in happy-couple-honeymoon-activity hell.

She followed Zack through the vast courtyard and to the wide, ornately carved double doors at the front of the villa. She touched one of the flower blossoms etched into the hard surface. "These are gorgeous. I wonder if I could mimic the design with frosting."

"I will happily be a part of that experiment." He pushed open the doors and stood, waiting for her to go in before him.

"You do seem to hang around a lot more when I'm practicing my baking skills."

"I don't know how."

"I could teach you," she said. "Maybe sometimes after I can teach you how to use a food processor."

"I think I'll pass. Anyway, I'm a bachelor. Have pity on me. I wasn't supposed to be a bachelor after today, but I am, and now I still need my best friend to cook for me."

"And probably do your laundry."

"I wouldn't mind."

Basically he wanted her to be his wife with none of the perks. She nearly said so, but that would sound too much like she wanted the perks, and even if a part of her did, she'd rather parade naked through the Castro District than confess it.

"I'm not doing your laundry."

Zack closed the door behind them and a shock of awareness hit her, low and strong in her stomach. She felt so very alone with Zack all of a sudden that she could hardly breathe. And it wasn't as though she'd never been alone with him. She had been. Hundreds of times. Late nights in the office, at her apartment cooking, at his luxury penthouse watching a movie.

But this wasn't San Francisco. It wasn't their offices; it wasn't one of their apartments. It felt like another world entirely and that was...dangerous.

She looked up at the tall, peaked ceilings, at the intricately carved vines and flowers that cascaded from wooden rafters.

Swaths of fabric were the only dividers between rooms, gauzy and sexy, providing the illusion of privacy without actually giving any at all.

And in the middle of it all was Zack. He filled the space, not just with his breadth and height, but with his presence. With the unique scent that was so utterly Zack mingling with the heavy perfume of plumeria. Familiar and exotic all at once.

This was like one of her late-night fantasies. Like a scene she'd only ever allowed herself to indulge in when she was shrouded in the darkness of her room. And now, those fantasies were coming back to bite her.

Because they were mingling with reality. This was real. And in reality, Zack didn't want her like she wanted him. But in her fantasies he did. There, he touched her like a lover, his eyes locked with hers, his lips...

She needed her head checked.

"I have a housekeeper, anyway. I was teasing," he said.

"I know." She hoped she didn't look as flushed as she felt.

"I don't think you did. I think you were about to bite my head off." He looked...amused. Damn him.

"Is there food?"

His lips curved into a half smile. "I can check."

He wandered out of the main living area, in search of the kitchen, she imagined, and she took the opportunity to breathe in air that didn't smell of Zack. Air that didn't make her stomach twist.

She walked the opposite direction of Zack, through one of the fabric-covered doorways and stopped. It was the bedroom. The bed was up on a raised platform, a duvet in deep red spread over it. Cream colored fabric with delicate gold vines woven throughout hung from the ceiling, shielding the bed. It was obvious that it wasn't a bed made for one, or for sleeping.

She swallowed heavily, her eyes glued to the center of the room.

She heard footsteps behind her and turned. "I found food."

"Good," she said, trying to ignore the fast-paced beating of her heart. Zack and the bed in one room was enough to make her feel like her head might explode. "There is… I mean, this isn't the only bedroom is it?"

"I'm not sure."

"Oh," she said.

"I set dinner out on the balcony, if you want to join me."

"Don't you want to go to bed?" she asked, then immediately regretted the way the words had come out. Heat flooded her face, and she was certain there was a very blatant blush staining her cheeks. "I mean…well, you know what I mean. That wasn't… I meant you. By yourself. Because I slept and I know you didn't."

"At least let me buy you dinner first, Clara," he said, his mouth curved in amusement, his eyes glittering with the same heat she'd noticed earlier. It made her uncomfortable. And jittery. And a little bit excited.

She laughed, a kind of nervous, fake sound. "Of course."

Zack ignored the jolt of arousal that shot through his veins. For a moment at least, he and Clara had both been thinking the same thing. And it had involved that bed. That bed that was far too tempting, even for a man who prided himself on having absolute control at all times.

Things with Clara had always been easy. No, he'd never been blind to her beauty, but their relationship had never been marked by moments of heavy sexual tension. Not until today.

And knowing that, even for a moment, she'd shared in the temptation, well, that made it all worse. Or better. No, definitely worse, because in his life, he valued boundaries. Everything and everyone had a place and a purpose. Clara had a place. It was not in his bed.

Or this bed.

It was important that his life stay focused like that. Controlled. That nothing crossed over. He'd been rigid in that, uncompromising, for the past fourteen years.

"This way, beautiful," he said, clenching his hand into a fist to keep from putting it on Clara's lower back. He would have done it before. But suddenly it seemed like far too risky of a maneuver.

Clara shot him a look that was pure Clara, his friend, and it made the knot in his chest ease slightly. Though it didn't do much for the heat coursing through his veins.

He was questioning why he'd thought bringing her was a good idea. And he never questioned his decisions. Not anymore. Because he thought everything through before he acted. Not thinking, letting anything go before reason, was a recipe for disaster.

And bringing Clara had been the logical choice. At least until thirty seconds ago.

He moved in front of her, under the guise of leading her to the deck, but really just so he wouldn't let himself look at her butt while she walked. Occasionally he allowed himself the indulgence of looking at her curves. Harmless enough. He was human, a man, and she was a beautiful woman. But it seemed less harmless after a moment like that.

"This is really nice," she said when they were outside.

Her words were true, banal and safe. He'd set the table and turned on the string of lanterns that were hung above the table. A moderate effort, but he had wanted it to be nice. Now it felt strangely intimate.

He couldn't remember the last time a dinner date had seemed intimate. He couldn't even remember the last time that word had seemed applicable to something in his life. Very often, sex didn't even seem all that intimate to him.

Of course, it had been so long since he'd had sex maybe that wasn't true. That was likely half of his problem now.

Clara wandered to the railing and leaned over the edge, tossing her glossy copper curls over her shoulder and sniffing the air. Or maybe the sex wasn't the problem. Because being alone with Hannah hadn't made him feel this way. And there were days when the scent of Clara's perfume hitting him when she walked past made his stomach tighten…

But he ignored that. He was good at ignoring it.

"What are you doing?"

"It smells amazing out here. Like when you bake bread and the air is heavy with it. Only it's flowers instead of flour." She turned to him and smiled, the familiar glitter back in her eyes.

The knot inside him eased even more.

"I would never have thought of it that way." He pulled her chair out and nodded toward it and she walked over to the table and took her seat.

He sat across from her, ladling reheated *Tom Yum Ka* into her bowl and then into his. She smiled at him, the slight dimple in her rounded cheeks deepening as she did.

Things seemed to have stabilized, even if her sweet grin did have an impact on his stomach.

"So, tell me more about this deal with Mr. Amudee."

He put his forearm on the table and leaned forward. "I think we covered most of it. Although, another reason it's nice to have you here is your palate. I'd like you to taste the different roasts and come up with pairings for them. It would be particularly nice to have in our boutique locations."

"Pairings!" Her eyes glittered. "I love it."

"Good coffee or tea really is just as complex as good wine. There are just as many flavor variations."

"I know, Zack," she said.

"Of course you do. You appreciate good coffee. It's one reason we get along so well."

Clara took another bite of her soup and let the ginger sit on her tongue, enjoying the zip of spice that hurt just enough to take her mind off the weird reaction she was having to Zack. Yes, being attracted to him was nothing new.

But this was different. The attraction she felt at home was like a sleeper agent. It attacked her when she least expected it. In dreams. When she was looking at other men and contemplating accepting a date. It wasn't usually this shaky, limb-weakening thing that made her feel tongue-tied and exposed in his presence. Maybe it was the feeling of utter seclusion. Or maybe it was because she knew just what that big bed was here for, what he'd been planning on doing with it.

"That and I bake you cupcakes," she said, swallowing the tart and spicy soup.

"There is that." Zack looked toward the railing of the deck, off into trees, the look in his eyes distant, cold suddenly. "Tell me about your bakery."

"The one I hope to have?"

"Yes. And the life you're going to put with it."

Her chest constricted. "It will be small. I'll have regular menu items and daily specials. I'll have more time to make fancy little treats with a lot of decorations. I'll have a hand in everything instead of just conceptualizing and farming the instructions out to hordes of employees."

"And that's important to you?"

"It's how we started. Me in the flagship store, you going back and forth between your— What did you have when I met you? Fifteen stores up and down the West Coast? It was fun."

"Yes, but now we have money."

She nodded. "We do. And it's great. You've done this incredible thing, Zack. The growth has been…amazing. Way beyond what I imagined."

"Not beyond what I imagined."

"No?"

He shook his head. "It was always the plan. Planning is key. It's when you don't plan, when you drift, that's when things are a surprise. Good or bad."

"You didn't plan for Hannah to opt out of the wedding."

"I didn't plan for you to leave Roasted, either. Sometimes other people come in and mess with your plans," he said, his dark eyebrows locked together.

"This doesn't mean I won't see you anymore," she said.

Though she probably shouldn't. But the thought of that made her chest feel like there was a hole in it. Still, she'd baked the man's wedding cake. She was such a pushover, such a hopeless case, it was obscene. It had to end.

She didn't want it to. But if she didn't see him at work every day…it would be a start.

"I know you'll still see me," he said, his mouth curving. "You'd have withdrawals otherwise."

If only that weren't true. "Right. Can't live without you, Zack." She felt her throat get tight. *Stupid.* So stupid. But Zack really did mean the world to her, and she had a very strong suspicion that her statement was nothing but the truth. He had offered her support when no one else in her life had. He still did.

She regretted saying she wanted to leave Roasted. Regretted it with everything in her. But she couldn't change her mind. The reasoning behind the decision was still sound. And she really would still see him. He just wouldn't fill up her whole world anymore. She couldn't let feelings for him, feelings that would never be returned, hold her back for the rest of her life.

Zack's arm twitched and he reached into his pocket. "Phone vibrated," he said. He pulled out his smart phone and unlocked the screen, a strange expression on his face. "Hannah texted me."

"Really?"

"She's really sorry about the wedding."

"Oh, good," Clara snorted. The weird jealousy and protectiveness were back together again. She was still righteously angry at Hannah for what she'd done, even while she was relieved.

"She met someone else."

"What?"

"Yes." He looked up, his expression neutral. "She's in love apparently."

"And she's texting this to you?"

He shrugged. "It fits our relationship."

"No, it doesn't. Love or not, you still had a relationship."

"We weren't sleeping together."

Clara felt her stomach free fall down into her toes. "What?" That didn't even make sense. Hannah was a goddess. A sex bomb that had been detonated in the middle of her life, making her feel inadequate and inexperienced.

And he hadn't slept with her? She'd assumed—imagined even, in sadly graphic detail—that half of the meetings in his office had been rousing desk-sex sessions. And…they hadn't been? So much angst. So much stomach curling angst exerted over…nothing, it turned out.

"Why?" she asked, her voice several notches higher than usual.

"Hannah's kind of traditional. Because we weren't in love… well, she needed love or marriage. We were going to have marriage."

"Hmm. Well, then maybe texting is appropriate. I don't understand how you were going to marry this woman."

"Marriage is a business agreement, like anything else, Clara. You decide if you can fulfill the obligations and if they'll be advantageous to you. Then you sign or you don't."

"Cynical."

"True."

"Then why bother to get married? I don't understand."

He shrugged. "Because it's the thing to do. Marriage offers stability, companionship. It's logical."

"Good grief, Spock. Logical. That's not why people get married." She snorted again. "Did your parents have a horrible divorce or something?"

Zack shook his head. "No."

"You never talk about your family."

He looked down at his soup. "Not on accident."

"Well, I figured. That's why I never ask."

"This isn't never asking."

She looked at him, at the side of his head. He wouldn't look at her. "We've known each other for seven years, Zack."

"And I'm sure I don't know everything about you, either. But I know what counts. I know that you lick the mixer. Even if it's got batter with raw eggs on it."

She laughed. "Tell anyone that and I'll ruin you."

"I have no doubt. I also know that you like stupid comedies."

"And I know that you put on football games and never end up watching them. You're just in it for the snacks."

He smiled, his gray eyes meeting hers. "See? You know the real truth."

Except there was something in the way he said it, a strange undertone, that told her she didn't. She wasn't sure how she'd missed it before. But she had. Now it seemed blatant, obvious. Zack had a way of presenting such a calm, easy front. In business, she knew it was to disarm, that no matter how easygoing he appeared, he was the man in charge. No question.

Now she wondered how much of the easy act in his personal life was just that. An act.

His eyes lingered on her face for a moment, and she suddenly became acutely conscious of her lips. And how dry they were. She stuck out the tip of her tongue and moistened them, the action taking an undertone she hadn't intended when she'd begun.

This week was going to kill her. Eventually the tension would get too heavy and she would be crushed beneath the weight of it. There was no possible way she could endure any more.

"I'm really tired," she said, the lie so blatant and obvious it was embarrassing.

To Zack's credit, he didn't call her on it. "The inner sanctum is all yours. I'll make do with the couch."

She wasn't going to feel bad about that for a second. "All right, I'll see you in the morning."

Maybe by morning some of the surrealism of the whole day

would have worn off. Maybe by morning she wouldn't feel choked by the attraction she felt to Zack.

Maybe, but not likely.

CHAPTER FIVE

"MR. Amudee has extended an invitation for you and me to have a private tour of the forest land."

Zack strode into the kitchen area and Clara sucked coffee down into her lungs. He was wearing jeans, only jeans, low on his lean hips, his chest bare and muscular and far too tempting. She could lean right in and...

"Coffee for me?" he asked.

"Oh, yes. Sure." She picked up the carafe and poured some coffee into a bright blue mug. "It's the shade-grown Chiang Mai Morning Blend. Really good. Strong but bright, a bit of citrus."

"I love it when you talk coffee to me," he said, lifting the mug to his lips, a wicked grin curving his mouth.

There was something borderline domestic about the scene. Although, nothing truly domestic could have such a dangerous, arousing edge to it, she was certain. And Zack, shirtless, had all of those things.

"All right, tell me about the tour," she said, looking very hard into her coffee mug.

"Very romantic. For the newly engaged."

Her stomach tightened. "Great."

"I hope you brought a swimsuit."

Oh, good. Zack in a swimsuit. With her in a swimsuit. That was going to help things get back on comfortable footing. She looked at Zack, at the easy expression on his handsome face. The ridiculous thing was, the footing was perfectly comfortable for him. Her little hell of sexual frustration was one hundred percent private. All her own. Zack wasn't remotely ruffled.

Typical.

"Yes, I brought a swimsuit."

"Good. I'll meet you back here in twenty minutes."

"Right." Unfortunately it would take longer than twenty minutes to plot an escape. So that meant Zack and swimsuits.

She tried to ignore the small, eternally optimistic part of her that whispered it might be a good thing.

Clara tugged at her brilliant pink sarong and made sure the knot was secure at her breasts before stepping out into the courtyard, where Zack was standing already.

"Ready. What's the deal? Give."

"You have to wait and see," he said, moving behind her, placing his hand low on her back as he led her to the gate and out onto a narrow path that wound through a thick canopy of trees and opened on an expansive green lawn.

"Are you kidding me?" she asked, stopping, her eyes widening.

There were two elephants in the field, one equipped with a harness that had small, cushioned seats on top. He was large enough he looked like he could comfortably seat at least four.

"Elephant rides are a big tourist draw in Chiang Mai," Zack said, the corner of his mouth lifting. "And I've never done it before, so I thought I would take advantage of the offer."

"First time for you?" she asked. She'd intended it as a joke, but it hit a bit to close to that sexual undercurrent they'd been dealing with since they left San Francisco.

A slow smile spread across his face. "Just for the elephant ride."

"Right. Got it." She was sure she was turning pink.

"You?"

She just about choked. "The elephant?"

"What else would I have been asking about?"

Her virginity. Except, no he wouldn't have been asking about that. It wasn't like she had a neon sign on her forehead that blinked red and said Virgin on it. Unless she did. Maybe he could tell.

She really hoped he couldn't tell.

"Yes, first time on an elephant," she said drily, aiming for cool humor. She wasn't sure she made her mark, but it was a valiant effort.

"Mr. Parsons." There was a man in white linen pants and a loose white shirt approaching them, his hand raised in greeting. "Ms. Davis, I believe," he said, stopping in front of her, his dark eyes glittering with warmth.

"Yes," Clara said, extending her hand. He bent his head and dropped a kiss on it, smiling, the skin around his eyes wrinkling with the motion.

"Isra Amudee. Pleasure." He straightened and shook Zack's hand. "Very glad you could make it. Especially after what happened."

Zack put his arm around Clara's waist and Clara tried to ignore the jolt of heat that raced through her. "Really, it didn't take me long to discover it wasn't a problem. Clara…well, I've known her for a long time. I don't really know how I missed what was right in front of me."

Mr. Amudee's smile widened. "A new wedding in your future, then?"

Zack stiffened. "Naturally. Actually I've already asked."

"And she's accepted?" Amudee looked at her and Clara felt her stomach bottom out.

Zack tightened his hold on her. "Yes," she said, her throat sandpaper dry. "Of course."

"And you, I bet, will have the good sense to show up. Now, I'll leave you to the elephants. I have to go and take a walk around the grounds. But I'll see you later on."

Clara watched Amudee walk away and tried to ignore the buzzing in her head as the man who was with the elephants introduced himself in English as Joe. He explained how the ride would work, that the elephant knew the route through the forrest and up to a waterfall, and she wouldn't deviate from that.

"They're trained. Very well. Safe. You'll be riding Anong." Joe indicated the elephant who was harnessed up. "And I'll follow on Mali. Just as a precaution."

He tapped Anong on her back leg and she bent low, making it easy for them to climb up onto the seat. Zack went first, then leaned forward and extended his hand, helping her up onto the bench.

"Seat belts," he said, raising one eyebrow as he fastened the long leather strap over both of their laps.

"Comforting," she said, a tingle of nerves and excitement running through her.

"Ready?" their guide called to them.

"I have no idea," she whispered to Zack.

"Ready," Zack said.

The elephant rose up, the sharp pitch forward and to the left a shock. She lurched to the side and took hold of Zack's arm while Anong finished getting to her feet, each movement throwing them in a different direction.

"I think I'm good now," she whispered, her fingers still wrapped, clawlike around Zack's arm.

"Just relax, he said this is a path she takes all the time. New for us, but not new for her."

She didn't actually want to know the answer to the question, but she asked it anyway. "Accustomed to calming the nerves of the inexperienced?"

"No. I don't mess around with women who need comforting in the bedroom. That's not what I'm there for."

She felt a heavy blush spread over her cheeks. "I guess not."

She was alternately relieved and disappointed by that bit

of news. Relieved, because she didn't really like to think of her friend as some crass seducer of innocents, and she really couldn't picture him in that role, anyway.

If he was the big bad wolf, it would be because the woman he was with wanted to play Little Red Riding Hood.

But it was disappointing, too, because that pushed her even farther outside the box that Zack's "ideal woman" resided in.

Ideal bedmate.

Sure, maybe it was more that than any sort of romantic ideal, but she would like to just fit the requirements for that. Well, really, being the woman he was sleeping with was very far away from what she actually wanted, but it would be a start.

A wonderful, sexual, amazing start...

She jerked her thoughts back to the present, not hard to do with the pitch-and-roll gait of the elephant rivaling a storm-tossed boat. It was a smooth, fluid sort of motion, but it was a very big motion, to match the size of the animal.

It also wasn't hard to do when she remembered that, as far as their host was concerned, she and Zack were now engaged.

"A tangled web, isn't it, Parsons?" she asked.

"What was I supposed to say?" he countered. "Ah, no, this is just my best friend that I brought along for a roll in the hay."

"The truth might have worked. He seems like a nice man."

"Look, it's done. I'm sure his assumption works even more in my favor, in favor of the deal, and that's all that really matters, right? We know where we stand. It's not like it changes anything between us."

She felt like the air had been knocked out of her. "No. Of course not."

They moved through the meadow and down into the trees, onto a well-worn path that took them along a slow-moving river, the banks covered in greenery, bright pink flowers glowing from the dark, lush foliage.

She tried to keep her focus on the view, but her mind kept wandering back to Zack, to his solid, steady heat, so close to her. It would be easy to just melt into him, to stop fighting so hard for a moment and give in to the need to touch him.

But she wouldn't. She couldn't. Nothing had changed between them, after all. His words.

There was a reason she'd never made any sort of attempt to change their relationship from friends to more-than-friends. The biggest one being that she didn't want to jeopardize the most stable relationship she had, the one closest to it being unable to stomach the thought of being rejected by him.

Of having him confirm that everything her mother said about her was true. Of having her know, for certain, that a man really wouldn't want her because she just wasn't all that pretty. Her mother had made sure she'd known men would still sleep with her, because of course, men would sleep with anyone. But she wasn't the sort of woman a man would want for a wife. Not the type of woman a man could be proud to take to events.

Not like her sister. Gorgeous, perfect Lucy who was, in all unfairness, smart and actually quite sweet along with being slender, blonde and generally elegant.

Lucy actually would have looked more like Hannah's sister than like *her* sister.

A sobering thought, indeed.

She should make sure Zack never met her sister.

The sound of running water grew louder and they rounded a curve in the path and came into a clearing that curved around a still, jade pool. At least twenty fine steams were trickling down moss-covered rocks, meeting at the center and falling into the pool as one heavy rush of water.

Anong the elephant stopped at the edge of the pool, dropping slowly down to her knees, the ground rising up a bit faster than Clara would have like. She leaned into Zack, clinging to the sleeve of his T-shirt as Anong settled.

"All right?" he asked.

She looked at where her hand was, and slowly uncurled her fingers, releasing her hold on him. "Sorry," she said.

He smiled, that simple expression enough to melt her insides. He was so sexy. Time and exposure, familiarity, didn't change it. Didn't lessen it.

Just another reason for her to leave Roasted. If exposure didn't do it, distance might.

Zack moved away from her, dismounting their ride first and waited for her at the side of their living chariot, his hand outstretched. She leaned forward and took it, letting his muscles propel her gently to the ground. Her feet hit just in front of his, her breasts close to touching his chest, the heat from him enticing her, taunting her.

"Do you want me to wait for you?" their guide asked.

Zack shook his head. "We'll walk back. Thank you for the ride. It was an experience."

He nodded and whistled a signal to Anong, who rose slowly and turned, going back with her owner and friend. She watched them round the corner, a smile on her lips. Yesterday, she was at a beachside hotel in San Francisco, expecting to lose half of her heart as Zack married another woman.

Today she was with him on his honeymoon. Riding elephants.

"An experience," Zack said, turning to face the water.

"It was fun," she said.

"Not relaxing exactly."

"No," she said, laughing. "Not in the least."

"Mr. Amudee informed me by phone this morning that this is a safe place to swim. Clean. They don't let the elephants up here and the waterfall keeps it all moving."

She made a face. "Good to know. I liked the elephants, don't really want to share a swimming hole with them. It looks pristine," she said, moving to the edge, looking down into the clear pool. She could see rocks covered in moss along the bottom, small fish darting around, only leaving the cover of their hiding places for a few moments before swimming behind something else. "Perfect."

Zack tugged his black shirt over his head, leaving him in nothing more than a pair of very low-cut white board shorts that, when wet, she had no doubt would cling to some very interesting places.

Her mind was a filthy place lately. And the sad thing was, it was hard to regret. Because it was so enjoyable.

"Swimming?"

"No." She shook her head and gripped her sarong.

"Why?"

"It looks cold."

He put his hands on his lean hips and sighed, the motion making his ab muscles ripple in a very enticing fashion. "It's so hot and muggy out here it could be snowmelt and it would feel good. And I guarantee you it's not snowmelt."

"It just looks…cold." Lame. So lame. But she didn't really want to strip down to her swimsuit in front of him, not when he looked so amazing in his. She was… There was too much of her for a start. She was so very conscious of that. Of the fact that she had hips and breasts, and that she could pinch fat on her stomach.

Zack's girlfriends had hip bones and abs that were just as cut as his.

"Ridiculous." He walked over to her and scooped her up in his arms, her heart climbing up into her throat as he did. His arms were tight and strong around her, masculine. Lifting her seemed effortless. His large hands cupped her thigh and her shoulder, his heat spreading through her like warm, sticky honey, thick and sweet.

She realized what was happening a little bit too late, because sexual attraction had short-circuited her brain. She put her hand flat on his chest, another bolt of awareness shocking her even as Zack took two big steps off the bank and down into the water.

The hot and cold burst through her, her body still warm from his touch on the inside, the water freezing her skin.

"Zack!"

He looked down at her, smiling. She sputtered and clung to his shoulders, his arms still wrapped tightly around her. His skin was slick now, so sexy, and it took everything in her arsenal of willpower to keep from sliding her palms down from their perch on his shoulders and flattening them against his amazing, perfect pecs.

She wanted to. She wanted to press her lips to the hollow of his throat, lick the water drops that were clinging to his neck.

She wiggled against him and managed to extricate herself from his grasp. Fleeing temptation.

She walked up to the shallow part of the pool, her pink sarong limp and heavy now, clinging to her curves like a second skin. She untied it and looped it over a tree branch. There was no point in it now.

She felt exposed in her black one-piece. It was pretty modest by some suit standards, but anything that tight tended to make her feel a bit exposed.

"Well, that's one way to get me in the water. Brute force," she sniffed, walking back to the water and sinking into the depths quickly, desperate for the covering it would provide.

"Brute?" Zack swam to where she was, treading water, his eyes glinting with amusement.

"Uh...yeah. You took advantage of me."

He paddled closer, his face a whisper from hers. "I didn't take advantage of you. If I had, you'd have known it, that's for sure."

Strangely, with her body half submerged in water, her throat suddenly felt bone-dry. "I feel um...taken advantage... You... picked me up and threw me in and I'm...wet."

His expression changed, his eyes darkening. "Interesting."

"Oh, *pffft*." She dunked her head, letting the cold water envelop her, pull the stinging heat from her cheeks. She paddled toward the waterfall, away from Zack. Away from certain mortification and temptation.

She surfaced again and looked back at Zack, still treading water where she'd left him.

Nice, Clara. Next time just tell him straight up that you're hot for him and would like to jump him, if that's all right with him.

She pulled a face for her own benefit and climbed up one of the mossy rocks that sat beneath the slow flowing falls, water trickling down, mist hovering above the surface of the cool, plant-covered stones.

She pulled her knees to her chest and looked up, squinting at the sunlight pouring through the thick canopy of trees.

"You're like a jungle fairy."

She looked down into the water and saw Zack, his hair wet and glistening.

"You're startling me," she said. More with his statement than with his presence, but she didn't intend to elaborate.

He planted his palms flat on the rocks and hoisted himself up, the muscles in his shoulders rolling and shifting with the motion. He sat next to her, the heat from his body a welcome respite from the cold. But that was about all it was a respite from. Because mostly he just made her feel edgy.

And happy. He made her so happy that it hurt. Just being with him made everything seem right. Like a missing part of herself was finally in place. Like some of her insecurities and inadequacies didn't matter so much.

And that was just stupid. Not to mention scary. Because it was an illusion. He would never be with her in the way she wanted, and watching him marry another woman, give someone else everything she longed for, *that* would turn her happiness into the bitterest pain.

The kind she wasn't sure she could withstand.

"You're beautiful," he said.

She turned sharply to look at him, her heart in her throat. "What?"

"Just stating a fact."

"It's not one you typically state. About me, I mean."

He put his hand out and brushed a water drop from her cheek with his thumb, the motion sending an electric shock through her body, heat pooling in her stomach and radiating from there to her limbs.

"Well, I thought it needed to be said."

It was so tantalizingly close to what she wanted. But to him it was simply an empty compliment, or maybe he even meant it. But not in the way she would. He didn't mean she was beautiful in the same way she found him beautiful. The way that made her body warm and her heart flutter.

"Thanks for that. You aren't so bad, either." She tried to sound casual. Light. Like a friend. Like she was supposed to sound.

He smiled and lifted his arm, curling his fist in, showing off his very, very impressive biceps.

"You're shameless," she said, somehow managing to laugh around her stubborn heart, still lodged firmly in her throat.

"Sorry."

"About as sorry as you are for dumping me in the water?"

"Yeah. About." He leaned in, his arm curving around her waist and everything slowed down for a moment. He tightened his hold on her, his face so close…

And then they were falling.

She shrieked just before they hit the water. And surfaced with a loud curse, unreasonable anger mingling with disappointment. "Zack! You jackass!"

She moved to him and planted her hands on his shoulders, attempting to dunk him beneath the water. He put his hands on her waist and held her still in front of him, her movements impotent against his strength.

"You can touch bottom here, can't you?" she asked, her feet

hovering above the sandy floor of the pool while Zack seemed firmly rooted.

"Maybe."

His hands slipped down, resting on her hips, the heat from his touch cutting through the icy chill in the water. He kept one hand there, the other sliding around to her back, his fingers drifting upward, skimming the line of her spine.

She shivered, but she wasn't cold. And he didn't let go.

His eyes were locked with hers, the head there matching the heat he was spreading over her skin. Her hands were still on his shoulders. And since he'd just moved his hands, it seemed... somehow it seemed right to move hers.

Her heart thundered in her chest as she slid her hands down, palms skimming his chest hair, the firm muscles beneath, as she rested them against his chest. She could hardly breathe. Her chest, her stomach, every last muscle, was too tightly wound.

His fingers flexed, the blunt tips digging into her flesh. His hands were rough, strong, everything she'd ever imagined and so much more.

Zack loosened his hold, a muscle in his jaw jerking. She pulled away from him, the water freezing where his hands had been.

"We should go," Zack said, his words abrupt.

"I... We haven't been here very long." She felt muddled, as though the mist from the waterfall had wrapped itself around her, making everything seem fuzzy.

And she was glad. Because she had a feeling that when the reality of what had just happened, of how stupid she'd been, hit, it was going to hit hard.

"Yes, but I have some things to take care of before tonight. We have dinner reservations at the restaurant down in the main part of the resort."

He reversed direction and swam to shore, walking out of the pool, his muscular legs fighting against the water pressure, his swim trunks conforming to his body. A hard pang hit her in the stomach when she looked and saw the outline of his erection. Had she really gotten him hot? Was that about her?

He turned away from her and pulled his shirt on.

And was the arousal why they were leaving now?

So he felt something. Even if he was running from it. Something that was at least physical.

Her hart hammered, echoing in her head, making her temples pulse.

Maybe she did matter to him, like that, at least a little bit? Maybe… Yes, she knew men were excited by women but this had to be personal. It had to be about her, at least a little bit. Did he think she was sexy?

She followed him to shore, scrambling onto the sandy ground, her feet picking up grains of dirt, clinging to her toes. She shook her foot out, grateful to have something else to concentrate on for a moment.

She looked back up and saw Zack, his eyes on her, his jaw locked tight.

She swallowed hard and grabbed her sarong. "So we're having dinner out tonight?"

"Yes," he bit out. "I have to go and pick up a package down in town and then I'll meet you back up at the villa. The car will be by around seven."

"Okay." She wished she could come up with something better than the bland, one-word answer, but she just couldn't.

Something had changed. The air around them seemed tight, the way Zack looked at her new and strange. And for the first time, she felt power in her beauty, in her body.

And she wondered if maybe he could want her. If she could be the sort of woman he wanted.

Maybe tonight she would actually try.

It was criminal. The dress that Clara was wearing should be illegal. She certainly shouldn't be allowed out in public. It was tight, like that black, second-skin swimsuit, accentuating curves that, until this afternoon, he hadn't realized were quite so…lush.

Breasts that were round and perfect, firm looking. They would overflow in his hands. And her hips were incredible, nothing like the androgynous, straight up-and-down supermodels that were so in style. Not even like Hannah, whose image he was having trouble conjuring up.

Today, at the river, with her body pressed against his, wet and slick, soft and feminine, he'd had a reaction he really hadn't counted on. He hadn't counted on touching her like he had, either. Exploring the elegant line of her back. Holding her to him. It had been a big mistake.

Getting out of the water, in front of his best friend, sporting an erection inspired by her, hadn't really been his idea of a good time.

He put his hand in his pocket, let his fingers close around the velvet box that was nestled there. The one that Hannah had had rush delivered to the resort. Because it was the right thing to do, or so she'd said. He hadn't really cared whether he got the engagement ring back or not. But he could use it.

The thing with Amudee, his assumption, had been unexpected. But Zack was good at reading people and the older man's delight at the thought had been so obvious, there had been no way he would disappoint him. Not with so much riding on things going well this week.

His other plans had all gone to hell. He wasn't sending this one there with the rest of them.

"What exactly is that?" he asked. They were in the car, being driven up to the main area of the resort, and being closed in with her when she looked like that and smelled, well, she smelled sweet enough to taste, was a bit of torture.

"What?" she asked.

"What you're wearing."

Her cheeks colored. "A dress."

"But do you…call it something?"

"A dress," she said again, her voice low now, dangerous.

"It's a nice dress."

She looked straight ahead. "Thank you."

The car stopped in front of an open, wooden building that had all the lights on despite the late hour. There were people sitting at a bar, musicians set down in the center of the seating area, and dancers out on the grass, candles balanced on their hands as they moved in time with the music.

He opened his door and Clara just sat, her posture stiff. "What?"

"Now I'm not sure if I should go back and change."

"I don't even want to understand women," he said.

"Why?"

"You just changed into that dress, so clearly you thought it was a good choice, and now you want to change back?"

"Because there must be something wrong with what I'm wearing. Although, you didn't seem to have a problem with my bathing suit, and it showed a lot more than this." She put a hand on her stomach. "It's too tight."

His body hardened. "Trust me, it's not. Every man in the bar is going to give himself whiplash when you walk by."

She frowned. "Really?"

She looked…mystified. Doubtful.

"Did you not look at yourself in the mirror?" he asked, completely incredulous that she somehow didn't see what he did. That she didn't realize how appealing a dress that was basically a second skin was to a man. It showed every bit of her shape, while still concealing the details. Made him feel desperate to see everything, the tease nearly unbearable.

She looked away from him. "That's the trouble, I did, and I chose to wear it anyway."

"What makes you think it doesn't look good?"

"You reacted…funny."

"Because I'm not used to seeing so much of you. But what I can see is certainly good."

"Really?"

He took a lock of her silky hair between his thumb and fore-finger. A mistake. It was so soft. Like he imagined the rest of her would be. "Didn't I tell you any man would put up with your snoring for the pleasure of having you sleep with him?"

His eyes dropped to her mouth and he felt an uncomfort-able shock of sensation when, for the second time in the past hour, she stuck her pink tongue out and slicked it across her lips, leaving them looking glossy and oddly kissable.

Clara felt like there was someone sitting on her chest, keep-ing her from breathing. The knot of insecurity that had tied up her stomach was changing into something else, something dangerous. A strand of hope she had no business feeling. A kind of feminine pride that didn't make sense.

Zack was a charmer. He could charm the white gloves off a spinster, and what he was saying to her was no different. Empty charm that had no real weight behind it. It was easy to say that some other man would like to share her bed. It didn't mean he did. Or that anyone he even knew would.

All right, in reality, she knew how men were about sex. If she was willing to put out they wouldn't care if she had a pinch of extra flesh around her middle, but that wasn't really the issue. She didn't want to be a second choice. Second best.

She was even second-guessing the physical reaction Zack had had to her down at the river. Because that could simply be a man overdue for sex. Nothing more. She'd made it personal because she'd been desperate for it. But in reality, he was sup-posed to be here, with his wife, having lots and lots of sex, and he wasn't. But she doubted he'd forgotten.

She was tired of being in the shadow of someone else. Even tonight, she was the consolation prize for Zack. Rather than spending the night with Hannah, he was with her, watching tra-ditional dancing instead of having hot, sweaty, wedding night sex. Ah, yes, all fine and good for him to say those things to her, but he wasn't really backing it up.

She forced a smile. "You did. All right, let's go…drink or something."

He chuckled. "Sounds like a good idea to me."

They both got out of the car and walked over to an alcove, shrouded in misty fabric, like everything in the whole resort property. It was designed for people to take advantage of the perceived privacy. It was an invitation to some sort of heady, fantastic sin. Traditional values her fanny.

She sat down on one of the cushions, positioned in front of a low table. Zack sat next to her, so close she could feel the heat radiating off his body.

"So what about my comment spawned the dress edition of twenty questions?" he asked.

"I don't usually wear things that are this tight, so you…your reaction made me think it looked… You've met my mother, right?" She changed tactics.

"Yes."

"She's like a model. And my sister…well, she takes after my mom. I take after my dad."

"Something wrong with that?"

"Well, I'm just not…not everything Lucy is. And my mother let me know that. Let me know that I was second best in nearly every way. She didn't just get beauty, she had a perfect grade-point average without even trying. I was just average. I liked school, but I didn't excel at it. The only thing I've ever excelled at is baking, which in my mother's estimation contributes to my weight issues."

Zack swore and Clara jumped. "Weight issues? You don't have weight issues."

"I did. More than I do now, I mean. It was a whole…thing in high school. Remember, I mentioned the time my date stood me up?"

He nodded and she continued on, hating to dredge up the memory. "Asking me was a joke in the first place, not that I had any idea, of course. And I was supposed to meet him by the stage in the gym, which is where the dance was, and he walked up with his real date, and the guys doing the lights knew to put a spotlight on me right then. And I was all chubby and wrapped up in this silly, tight pink dress that was just so… shiny. That stays with you. Sometimes, for no reason, I still feel like the girl under the spotlight, with everyone looking at all my flaws."

He swore sharply. "That's bull. That's…kids are stupid and that's high school." He swallowed. "It's not real life. None of us stay the same as we were back then." His words ended sounding rough, hard.

"Maybe not. Still, even though I've sort of…slimmed out as I've grown up, as far as my mom is concerned, since I'm not six feet tall and runway ready, I'm not perfect. I have her genes, too, after all," she said, echoing a sentiment she'd heard so many times. "And that means I could be much thinner if I *tried*."

"Let me tell you something about women's bodies, Clara, and I know you are a woman, but I'm still going to claim the greater expertise. Men like women's bodies, and there isn't only one kind to like, that's part of the fun. Beauty isn't just one thing."

She tried to ignore the warm, glowy feeling that was spreading through her. "I know that. I mean, part of me knows that. But it's hard to let go of the second-best thing."

"Better than feeling like you're above everyone else," he said slowly. "Like nothing can touch you because you're just so damn perfect life wouldn't dare."

"I don't know if Lucy feels that way, my mother might but…" She trailed off when she noticed the look on his face. There was something, just for a moment, etched there that was so cold, so utterly filled with despair that it reached inside her and twisted her heart.

"Zack…"

He shook his head. "Nothing, Clara. Just leave it." The dancers had cleared the area out on the lawn and there were couples moving out into the lit circles, holding each other close, looking at each other with a kind of longing that made Clara ache with jealousy. "Care to dance before dinner is served?"

Yes and no. She felt a bit too fragile to be so close to him, and yet a part of her wanted it more than she wanted air. Just like in the water today, she'd wanted to run and cling at the same time. She was never sure which desire would win out.

He offered his hand and she took it, his fingers curling around hers, warm and masculine. He helped her up from her seat and drew her to him, his expression still strange, foreign more than familiar. He looked leaner, more dangerous. Which was strange, because even though Zack was her friend, she always felt an edge of danger around him, a little bit of unrest. Probably because she was so attracted to him that just looking at him made her shiver with longing.

"Just a warning," he said, as they made their way out onto the grass. "People will probably stare. But that's because you look good, amazing even. And you certainly aren't second to any woman here."

"Flatterer."

"No, I'm not, and I think we both know that."

"Okay, I suppose that's true," she said, kicking her shoes off and enjoying the feeling of the grass under her feet. Although, losing the little lift her shoes provided put her eyes level with Zack's chest.

He pulled her to him, his hand on her waist. She fought the urge to melt into him, to rest her head on his chest. This wasn't that kind of dance; theirs wasn't that kind of relationship. That didn't mean she didn't want to pretend. It was easy, with the heat of his body so close to hers, to imagine that tonight might end differently. To imagine that he saw her as a woman.

Not just in the way that he'd referenced, that vague, sweet, but generic talk about women and their figures. But that he would desire her body specifically. She kept her eyes open, fixed on his throat. She knew him so well, that even looking there she knew just who she was with. And she didn't want to shut that reality out by closing her eyes. She wanted to watch, relish.

For a moment reality seemed suspended. There wasn't time, there wasn't a fiancée, one more suited to Zack than she was, looming in the background. There was only her and Zack, the heat of the night air, the strains from the stringed instruments weaving around them, creating a sensual, exotic rhythm that she wanted to embrace completely.

She loved him so much.

That hit her hard in the chest. The final, concrete acknowledgment of what she'd probably always known. A moment that was completely lacking in denial for once. She loved Zack. With her entire heart, with everything in her. And she was in his arms now.

But not in the way she wanted to be. She breathed in deeply, smelling flowers, rain and Zack. Her lungs burned, her stomach aching. She wished it was real. So much that it hurt, down to her bones.

Maybe, just for a moment, she could pretend that it was real. That this was romance. That he held her because he wanted her. Because after this, after the fake engagement, after the ink was dry on the contracts, there would be no more chances to pretend.

She would go her way, and she would leave Zack behind. Why couldn't she ignore it now? Just for now.

She didn't want the song to end, wished the notes would linger in the air forever, an excuse to stay in his arms. But it ended. And that was why she shouldn't have said yes to the dance in the first place. Playing games wouldn't come close to giving her what she wanted with Zack. It just made her aware of how far she was from having what she really wanted.

He took her hand and pulled her away from the other dancing couples, and for one heart-stopping moment, she thought he might lean in and kiss her. His lips were close to hers, his breath hot, fanning across her cheek. Her body felt too tight, her skin too hot. She needed something. Needed him.

"I have something for you," he said. "For tomorrow."

"I like presents," she said, trying to keep her voice from sounding too shaky. Too needy. Too honest. "It's not a food processor, is it?"

He chuckled, a low, sexy sound that reverberated through her. "I told you, I'm keeping my food processor."

She tried to breathe. "All right then, I can't guess."

He reached into his jacket pocket and pulled out a small velvet box. Everything slowed down for a moment, but unlike before, when the gauzy, frothy film of fantasy had covered it all, this was stark reality. She shook her head even before he opened it, but he didn't seem to notice.

He popped the top on it and revealed a huge ring, glittering gold and diamonds. She sucked in a sharp breath. Such a perfect ring. Gorgeous. Extravagant. Familiar. The ring he'd given to Hannah. The exact same ring. The ring for the woman who was supposed to be here. The ring for the woman he should have danced with, the woman he would have kissed, made love to.

A well of pain, deep, unreasonable and no less intense for it, opened up in her, threatened to consume her. What a joke. A cheap trick. And the worst part was that she'd played it on herself. Letting herself pretend that he'd wanted *her* at the river, playing like he wanted her in his arms tonight.

Letting hope exist in her, along with the futile, ridiculous love she felt for him. Ridiculous, because for half a second, her breath had caught when she'd seen the ring, and she'd forgotten it was fake.

"No," she said.

"Clara…"

"I don't…" She was horrified to feel wetness on her cheeks, tears falling she hadn't even realized were building. She backed away from him, hitting her shoulder against one of the bar area's supporting pillars. But she didn't stop. "I'm sorry."

She wasn't sorry. She was angry. She was hurt. Ravaged to her soul. Maybe it had been ignorant of her not to think all the way to the ring. To think that the farce wouldn't include that. Of course it would. Zack didn't cut corners and he didn't forget details. So of course he wouldn't forget something as essential to an engagement as a ring.

But it hurt. To see him, impossibly gorgeous and, in so many ways, everything she'd always dreamed of, offering her a ring, a ring he'd already given to another woman, as part of a lie, it killed something inside her.

Maybe it was just the fact that it pulled her deepest, most secret fantasy out of her and laid it bare. And made it into a joke. Designed to show her that there was no way he would ever consider her. Not with any real seriousness. That she was nothing more than a replacement for the woman he'd intended to have here with him.

That she was interchangeable.

She was hopeless. She needed a friend to tell her what a head case she was. To tell her to get over him. To take her out to pie and tell her she could do better, have better.

But Zack should have been that person. *He* was her best friend. He was the one she talked to. The one she confided in. And she couldn't confide this, couldn't tell him that he'd just shredded her heart. Couldn't tell him she was hopelessly in love with a man she couldn't have, because he was the man.

The crushing loneliness that thought brought on, the pain, was overwhelming.

Her stomach twisted. "I have to… I'm sorry."

She turned away from him, walking quickly across the lawn, back to into the lobby area to find a car, an elephant, whatever would get her back to the villa the fastest.

She was running and she knew it. From him. From her hurt. And from the moment she knew would come, the one where she'd have to explain to him just why looking at the ring had made her cry.

It was an explanation she never wanted to give. Because the only man she could ever confide her pain in, was also the one man she could never tell. Because he was the man who'd caused it.

CHAPTER SIX

Zack's heart pounded as he scanned the villa's courtyard. It was too dark to see anything, but he was sure this was where she was. Unless she'd called the car service and asked them to come and get her, which, if Clara was really upset, he wouldn't put past her. She could be on the next plane back to the States.

His plane.

Which, he had a suspicion he might deserve.

There was a narrow path that led from the main area of the courtyard into an alcove surrounded by flowering plants and trees. And he was willing to bet that, if she was still in the villa, she'd gone there.

He was right. She was sitting on the stone bench, her knees pulled up to her chest. She was simply staring, her cheeks glistening in the moonlight. The sight made him ache.

He was all about control, all about living life with as few entanglements and attachments as possible. But Clara was his exception. She had been from the moment he'd met her.

She was the one person who could alter his emotions without his say so. Make him happy if he really wanted to be angry. Make his gut feel wrenched with her tears.

"Are you okay?"

She dropped her knees and put her feet on the ground, straightening. "I'm sorry. That was stupid. I overreacted."

He moved to the bench and crouched down in front of it, in front of her. "What did I do?"

"I was just...I told you, it was an overreaction. It was nothing, really." She sucked in a breath that ended on a hiccup and his heart twisted. "I can't really...explain it."

The confusion he felt was nearly as frustrating as the pain he felt over hurting her. He didn't really understand exactly what he'd done, but not understanding it didn't make it go away.

Without thinking, he lifted his hand and curved it around her neck, stroking her tender skin with his thumb. It was a gesture meant to comfort her, because he'd upset her somehow, for the second time in forty-eight hours, and he hated to upset her. She meant too much to him.

But something in the touch changed. He wasn't sure exactly when it tipped over from being comfort to being a caress, he wasn't sure how her skin beneath his fingers transformed from something everyday to something silky, tempting.

She looked at him, her eyes glistening, the expression in them angry. Angry and hot. And that heat licked through him, reached down into his gut and squeezed him tight.

It was close to what he'd felt down at the river, but magnified, her anger feeding the flame that burned between them. And he couldn't walk away from it. Not this time.

Without thought, without reason or planning, without stopping to think of possible consequences, he leaned in and closed the space between them, his lips meeting hers. First kisses were for tasting, testing. They were a question.

At least historically for him they had been. This kiss wasn't.

Something roared through him, filling him, a kind of desperation he'd never felt before. He didn't ask, he took. He didn't taste, he devoured. The hunger in him was too ravenous to do anything else, so sudden he had no chance to sublimate it. He wrapped his arms around her, and she clung to his shoulders, her lips parting beneath his.

He growled and thrust his tongue against hers, his body

shuddering as his world reduced to the slick friction, to the warmth of her lips on his.

Clara was powerless to do anything but cling to Zack. Powerless to give anything less than every bit of passion and desire that was pouring through her. To do anything but devour him, giving in to the hunger that had lived in her, gnawed at her for the past seven years.

This was heaven. And it was hell. Everything she'd longed for, still off-limits to her for the same reasons it always had been. Except for right now, for some reason, it was as though a ban had been lifted. For this one moment, a moment out of time. A moment that she needed more than she needed air.

His lips, firm and sure, were everything she'd ever dreamed they might be, his hands, heavy and hot on her back even more arousing than she'd thought possible.

This was why there had been no one else. Because the idea of Zack had always been more enticing than the reality of any other man. And the reality of Zack far surpassed any fantasy she'd ever had. Maybe any fantasy *any* woman had ever had.

She slid from the bench and onto the stone-covered ground, gripping the front of his shirt, their knees touching. He pulled her closer, bringing her breasts against his hard, muscular chest. She arched into him, craving more. Craving everything. All of him.

When they parted, he rested his forehead against hers, his breathing shallow, unsteady, loud in the otherwise silent night.

She didn't know what to say. She was afraid that he would try to say something first. Something that would ruin it. A joke. Or maybe he'd even be angry. Or he'd say it was a mistake. All valid reactions, but she didn't want any of them. She didn't want to deal with anything. She simply wanted to focus on the pounding of her heart, the swollen, tingly feeling in her lips. On all the really good, fizzy little sensations that were popping in her veins like champagne.

Zack let out a gust of air. "Damn."

She laughed. She couldn't help it. Of all the reactions she'd expected, and dreaded, that hadn't been it. That he would allow an honest reaction, and that his reaction would match hers, hadn't seemed likely.

"Yeah," she said.

He braced his hand on the bench behind her and pulled himself up, then extended his hand to her. She gripped it and let him help her to her feet. She brushed some dried leaves from her knees, ignoring the slight prickle of pain and indents of small twigs left behind on her skin.

Her eyes caught his and held, and all of the good exciting feelings that had been swirling through her dissolved. The cushion of fantasy yanked from under her, there was nothing but cold, hard reality. She'd kissed Zack. More than kissed, she'd attacked him.

And there was nowhere for it to go from that point. If she leaned in again, if she kissed him again, then what? They might go to bed together. And where would that leave her after? Where would it leave them?

No, he hadn't slept with Hannah, but he'd slept with other beautiful women. Lots of them. She'd met a good number of them. And she was…she was inexperienced, unglamorous. And she was here as a replacement. If something happened between them now, on a night that was meant to be his wedding night with another woman, she would always feel like she'd been second.

He was a man, and the pump was well and truly primed. He'd been promised sex after what had been a lengthy bout of not having sex, so of course he was hot for it. But he was hot for it. Not for her.

He'd never kissed her before tonight. That, if nothing else, cemented the point.

She wasn't going to cry again. She wasn't going to let him know how vulnerable she was to him. Wasn't going to let him know how bad it hurt to pull away now.

"This has been a bit of a crazy day," she said.

"I can't argue with that."

"Sorry. About this." She gestured to the bench. "All of it… I don't…I don't really know what that was about."

The flash of relief she saw in Zack's eyes made her heart twist. She would finish now. Make sure he'd never want to talk about it again.

"I mean…how do you feel?" She'd said the magic feel word. Zack didn't like to talk about how he felt. Not in a way that went any deeper than happy, or angry, or hungry.

"Fine. Good, in fact. Kissing a beautiful woman is never a bad thing."

She felt heat creep into her cheeks. She shouldn't respond to the compliment. It was empty, an attempt to smooth things over. But it affected her, and she couldn't stop it from making her stomach curl in traitorous satisfaction.

"I might say the same. Not the woman part but the… You get it."

"I did something wrong. With the ring. I'm sorry. I'm not hitting them out of the park with you today, am I?"

"I don't think either of us is at our best right now," she said. That at least was true. Of course, she hadn't been her best since the engagement announcement. Her safe little world had been chucked off-kilter in that moment and she'd felt out of balance ever since.

"Probably need sleep."

She forced a laugh. "You probably do. I got that extra sleep on the plane, remember?"

"But you should sleep again. Otherwise you'll be off for even longer."

She did feel tired suddenly. And not a normal tired, an all-consuming sort of tired that went all the way down into her bones. "Yeah. You're right. I can sleep on the couch tonight."

"I'll sleep on the couch again. After being left at the altar, sleeping alone in the honeymoon bed is just a bit depressing, don't you think?"

For a moment, she thought about inviting him to join her. To play the vixen for once. To say to hell with all of her insecurities and just be the woman she wished she could be.

But she didn't.

"Yeah, maybe a little." She swallowed and stuck her hand out. "I'll take that ring though."

"You sure?"

"I told you, I was being stupid. Emotional girl moment. The kind specifically designed to boggle the minds of men. Actually, a little secret for you, they occasionally boggle our minds, too. So, ring, give."

She held her hand out and he took it in his, turning it over so her palm was facing down. He took the ring box out of his pocket and took the ring out of its pink silk nest, holding it up for a moment before sliding it on to her ring finger.

She looked down at it, then curled her fingers into a fist, trying to force a smile.

"Looks good," he said.

"It's a diamond, it can't look anything else," she said, trying to sound breezy and unaffected. Both things she wasn't.

"Perfect. And now we're ready for tomorrow. I hope you brought shoes you can walk in."

"Of course I did."

"That's right. I forgot."

"Forgot what?" she asked.

"That you're different. Come on, let's go try to get some sleep."

She followed him out of the courtyard, trying to leave everything behind them, all the needs, desires, pain, back in the alcove. But his words kept repeating in her head, and she could still feel his kiss on her lips.

And she felt different. Like a completely different woman

than the one who had walked into the garden with tears streaming down her face.

One kiss shouldn't have that kind of power. But that kiss had. She felt changed. She felt a a tiny bit destroyed, and a little bit stronger. And she wasn't sure she would take it back. Even if she could.

Sleep had been a joke. An elusive thing that had never even come close to happening. Zack looked at the tie he'd brought with him for meetings with Mr. Amudee, and decided against putting it on. Not twice in one week.

He left two buttons undone on his crisp white shirt and pushed the sleeves halfway up his forearms. That should be good enough. They were spending the day looking at where the coffee and tea plants were grown.

Maybe spending the day outdoors would clear his head. Would lift the heavy fog of arousal that had plagued him since the kiss. Not just the kiss, since that strange, tense moment at the lake before the kiss.

But the kiss… A few more minutes and he would have had her flat on her back on the stone bench with more than half of her clothes stripped from her gorgeous curves.

He bit down hard, his teeth grinding together. He shouldn't be thinking of her curves. But he was.

"Zack?"

The sound of her voice hit him like a kick in the gut.

"Here," he said, sliding his belt through the loops on his pants and fastening the buckle as she walked around the corner, into the bedroom. Her pale cheeks colored slightly when she saw him.

"How did you sleep?" she asked.

"Great," he lied. "Thanks for letting me use the room to get ready."

"Yeah, no problem. I got up pretty early. Wandered around in the garden. There are so many flowers here."

And she'd put a few different varieties in her hair. It was silly. And it was cute. She had a way of making that work for her.

"I didn't know you liked flowers so much."

She shrugged. "I always have some on my kitchen table."

She did, now that he thought about it. He wondered if anyone ever bought them for her. He wondered why he'd never really stopped to notice before. Why he'd never bought her any.

Because, bosses don't buy employees flowers. And friends don't buy friends flowers.

Friends also didn't kiss each other like he and Clara had done last night. His pulse jump-started at the thought, his blood rushing south. He tightened his hands into fists and tried to will his body back under control.

"Ready to go?" he asked, his voice curt because it was taking every last bit of his willpower to keep his desire for her leashed.

She frowned slightly. "Yeah. Ready."

"Good. Remember, you're my fiancée, and we've been very suddenly overcome by love that can no longer be denied."

One side of her mouth quirked up. "Is that the story?"

"Yes. That's the story. As Amudee created it, so he'll believe it. He's the one who assumed."

"A romantic, I suppose. Either that or he just thinks you move fast."

"I'm decisive. And we've known each other for years." He studied her face for a moment, dark almost almond-shaped eyes, pale skin, clear and smooth. Perfection. Her lips were pink and full and, now he knew, made for kissing. And he had to wonder how he'd known her for so long and never really looked at her.

Because if he had he would have realized. He would have had to realize, that she was the most gorgeous woman. Exquisite. Curved, just as a woman should be, in all the right places. Beautiful without fuss or pretension.

"Yes, we have," she said slowly, those liquid brown eyes locked with his.

"So it stands to reason that after Hannah decided not to go through with things…"

"Right."

The air between them seemed thicker now, that dangerous edge sharpening. Now that he knew what it was like to touch her, to feel her soft lips beneath his, well, now it was a lot harder to ignore.

"So let's go, then," he said.

"Right," she said again.

He moved to her and slid his arm around her waist. It was more slender than he'd imagined it might be. "We have to do things like this," he said, his voice getting rougher as her hips brushed against his.

She nodded, her eyes on his face. On his lips. She would be the death of him.

"Lovely to see you again, Ms. Davis," Mr. Amudee said, inclining his head. "And with a ring, I see."

Her heart rate kicked up several notches.

"Oh. Yes. Zack…made it official last night. It's lovely to see you, too." She touched the ring on her finger and Zack tightened his hold around her waist. She nearly stopped breathing, her accelerated heart rate lurching to a halt with it. From the moment they'd arrived at Mr. Amudee's house, he had put his arm around her and kept it there. She'd assumed she would get used to it, to the warm weight of his touch. But she wasn't getting used to it. If anything, she was getting more jittery, more aroused with each passing second.

The sun was hot on the wide, open veranda that overlooked rows of coffee trees with flat glossy leaves and bright red coffee cherries. But Zack's touch was the thing that was making her melt.

"I had not met the other woman you intended to marry,

Zack, but I must say that comparing the photos of the first one, to Ms. Davis, I find I prefer Ms. Davis."

Clara's heart bumped against her chest. "That's kind of you to say." She knew her face had to be beet-red, it was hot, that was for sure. Because it was nice of him to say, but there was no way it could be true.

There was no comparison between her and Hannah. Hannah was…well, sex bomb came to mind yet again.

"Not kind," Isra said. "Just the truth. I was married, a long time ago, to the most wonderful woman. I have a good judge of character. Unfortunately I was too busy to see just how wonderful she was. Don't make that mistake."

Zack cleared his throat. "Clara is also very knowledgable about our product. I know we'll both enjoy getting a look at the growing process today. And we're both excited about the tasting."

Back to business. Zack was good at that. Thank God one of them was.

"I'm excited to share it with you. Come this way." They followed him down the stairs that led to the lush, green garden filled with fragrant foliage. He moved quickly for a man his age, his movements sharp and precise as he explained where each plant was in the growing stage, and which family was leasing which segment of the farmland, and how the soil and amount of shade would affect the flavor of each type of coffee, even before it was roasted.

The tea was grown in a more remote segment of the farm and required walking up into the rolling hills, where the leaves were in the process of being harvested.

"A lot depends on when you pick them," Mr. Amudee said, bending and plucking a small, tender-looking cluster of leaves. "Smell. Very delicate."

He handed the leaves to Zack and he did as instructed. Then he held them out for Clara. She bent and took in the light fragrance. She looked up and her eyes clashed with Zack's and her heart beat double time.

"And this will be…what sort of tea will it be?" she asked, anything to get her mind off Zack and his eyes.

"White tea," Zack said. "Am I right?"

Mr. Amudee inclined his head. "Right. Ready to go and taste?"

Her eyes met Zack's again, the word tasting bringing to mind something new and different entirely. Something heady and sexual.

She swallowed hard.

"Yes, I think we are," Zack said slowly, his eyes never leaving hers.

And she wondered if he'd been thinking the exact same thing she was. And if he was thinking the same thing, if he wanted to kiss her again, she wasn't sure what she would do.

No, that was a lie. She was sure. She would kiss him again. Like nothing else mattered. Like there was no future and no consequences. Because she'd had enough of not getting what she wanted out of life. Quite enough.

She looked at Zack again and she wondered if she'd only imagined that momentary flash of heat. Because his eyes were cool again, his expression neutral.

She tried to convince herself that it was better that way.

Clara spent the next few days carefully avoiding Zack. It was easier than expected, given the cozy living situation. But during the day he had meetings with Mr. Amudee and when she wasn't needed, she took advantage of all the vacation-type things that were available in the resort.

There was a spa down in the hotel, and also some incredible restaurants. Her favorite retreat was up on the roof of the villa that gave her a view of the mountains, and the small town that was only a short walk away, the golden rooftops reflecting the sunlight like fire in the late afternoon. It was the perfect view for yoga, which kept her mind focused and relaxed at the same time.

She even managed to forget about the kiss. Mostly. As long as she made a concerted effort not to think of it. And as long as she didn't get into bed before she was ready to fall asleep instantly. Lying awake for any length of time was a recipe for disaster. And for replaying that moment. Over and over again.

Clara took a deep breath and tried to focus on the scenery, on the sky as it lightened. Orange fading into a pale pink, then to purple as the sun rose from behind the sloping hills. She would focus on that. Not Zack. Because that door was clearly closed. He hadn't touched her again, unless it was absolutely necessary, since the night in the garden. Since the kiss that had scorched her inside and out.

The kiss that didn't even seem to be a vague memory to him.

"Got plans for today?"

She turned and her heart lodged itself in her throat. Zack strode onto the roof in nothing more than a pair of low-slung jeans, his chest, broad and muscular, sprinkled with the perfect amount of chest hair, was streaked with dirt and glistening with sweat.

She had to remind herself to breathe when he came closer. And she had to remind herself not to stare at his abs, bunching and shifting as he moved.

"Do I…" She blinked and looked up at his face. "What?"

"Do you have plans? You've been busy. Remarkably so for someone on vacation."

"Well, down in the village they have these neat classes for tourists. Weaving and things like that. And one of the restaurants in the hotel has a culinary school."

"I thought you wanted to relax."

"Cooking is relaxing for me." And it had been conducive to avoiding him. "Anyway, now I can make you some killer Pad Thai when we get back home."

"Well, I support that."

"What are you doing up so early?"

"Working. Before the sun had a chance to get over the mountains and scorch me. Part of the deal. I need to understand where it all comes from. How important the work is to the families. I'm really pleased we're going to be part of this process."

"Me, too," she said. Although, she wouldn't be. Not once everything was in place. This was it for her.

"I'm going up to Doi Suthep, to see the temple. I thought you might want to come with me."

She did. Not just to see the temple, although that was of major interest to her, but to spend some time with him. It was that whole inconvenient paradox of being in love with her best friend again. She wanted to avoid him, because she felt conflicted over the kiss. She wanted to be with him, confide in him, because she felt conflicted, too.

"I…"

"Are you avoiding me?" he asked, hands on his lean hips. "Well, I know you're avoiding me, but I guess I don't know why. Does this have to do with you leaving Roasted?"

"No!"

"Then what the hell is your problem?"

Hot, reckless anger flooded her. "My problem? Are you serious? You asked me to come here, and play fiancée, and I have. I don't have a problem."

"When you aren't avoiding me."

"I have done exactly what you asked me to do," she said. "I have played the part of charming, simpering fiancée, I've worn this ring on my finger, and you can't, for one second see why that might not be…something I want to do. And then you kiss me. Kiss me like…like you really are on your honeymoon, and you want to know what my problem is?"

He looped his arm around her waist and drew her to him, his eyes blazing. She braced herself against him, her palms flat on his bare chest. "I think I do know what your problem is. I think you're avoiding me because of the kiss. Because you're afraid it will happen again. Or because you want it to happen again."

She shook her head slightly. "N-no. I haven't even thought about it again."

"Liar." He dipped his head so that his lips hovered just above hers. "You want this."

She did. She really did. She wanted his lips on hers. His hands on her body. She wanted everything. "You arrogant bastard," she said, her voice trembling. "How dare you?"

"How dare I what? Say that you want it again? We both know you do."

His lips were so close to hers and it was tempting, so tempting, to angle her head so that they met. So that she could taste him again. Have a moment of stolen pleasure again.

"You do want it," he said again, his voice rough, strained.

"So?" she whispered.

"What?"

"So what if I do?" she said, finding strength in her voice. "What then, Zack? We'll kiss? Sleep together? And then what? Nothing. You and I both know there won't be anything after that. We'll just ruin what we do have."

He released his hold on her and took a step back, letting his hands fall to his sides. "Sorry."

"You've been apologizing to me a lot lately," she said, her voice trembling. "You don't need to do that."

He nodded. "I'm going to take a quick shower."

"Not going to the temple?"

He smiled ruefully. "Still am. And you can come if you want. Provided you've worked the tantrum out of your system."

"That was your tantrum, Parsons, not mine."

"Maybe." He tightened his jaw, his hands curling into fists. "Just tense I suppose. Coming with me or not?"

She hesitated. Because she did want to go, but things

weren't…easy with him at the moment. And the scariest thing was she wasn't sure she wanted them to be easy again. She was sort of liking this new, scary dynamic between them. The one that made him touch her like she did something to him. Like he was losing control.

"I'll be good. I promise," he added.

She laughed, a fake, tremulous sound. "I wasn't worried."

Zack wasn't the one who worried her. She hesitated because she wasn't sure she trusted *herself* to behave.

"I was," he said, turning away from her and walking back into the house. She watched him the whole way, the muscles on his back, the dent just above the waistline of his jeans, and his perfect, tight butt.

She let out a slow, shaky breath. Yeah, it was definitely herself she didn't trust.

The temple at Doi Suthep was crowded with tourists, spiritual pilgrims and locals. Clara and Zack walked up the redbrick staircase, the handrails fashioned into guardian dragons with slithering bodies and fierce faces.

They were silent for the three-hundred-step trek up to the temple, Clara keeping a safe distance between them, in spite of the crush of people all around them. She was mad at him.

And fair enough, he'd been a jerk earlier. That was sexual frustration. Sexual frustration combined with the desire to give in to the need to kiss her again. To do more than kiss her.

Damn.

He could still remember the first time he'd seen Clara. She was working behind the counter at a bakery, flour on her cheeks. She was cute. Not the kind of woman he was normally attracted to. But she'd fascinated him. Utterly and completely. It had turned out she'd made great cupcakes, too. And that she was smart and funny. That it felt good to be with her.

The emotional connection to her, when he'd been lacking a connection with anyone for years, had been shocking, instant, and had immediately found him shoving his attraction to her away.

A friendship with her was fine. Anything else…he didn't have room for it. Anything else would go beyond the boundaries he'd set for himself. And he needed his boundaries. His control. He valued it above everything else.

Just another reason he'd intended to marry Hannah. Marriage brought stability, a sort of controlled existence that attracted him. One woman in his bed, in his life.

And now that that had gone to hell, it seemed his feelings for Clara were headed in the same direction. He'd done with her, for seven years now, what he did with everything in his life. She had a place. She was his friend. She didn't move out of that place in his mind.

His body was suddenly thinking differently. He'd made a mistake. He'd allowed himself too much freedom. He'd indulged his desire to look at her body. To touch her soft skin when they'd gone swimming. And that night, he'd given in to the temptation to allow her to feature in his fantasies. To find release with her image in his mind.

He'd allowed himself to cross the line in his mind, and that was where control started. He knew better. Yet it was hard to regret. Because wanting her was such a tantalizing experience. Just feeling desire for her was a pleasure on its own.

Her sweet, short, sundress was not helping matters. Though, thankfully she'd had to purchase a pair of silk pants to wear beneath it before they could head up toward the temple.

Still, even with her legs covered, there was that bright, gorgeous smile that had been plastered on her face since they'd arrived. She was all breathy sighs and sounds of pleasure over the sights and sounds. It was the sweetest torture.

"Incredible," she breathed, her voice soft, sensual in a way. Enough to make his body ache.

"Yes," he agreed. Mostly, he was looking at her, and not the immense, gold-laden temple.

He forced himself to look away from Clara. To keep his focus on the gilded statues, the bright, fragrant offerings of flowers, fresh fruit and cakes left in front of the different alters that were placed throughout the courtyard. A large, dome-shaped building covered entirely in gold reflected the sun, the air bright, thick with smoke from burning incense.

Monks in bright orange robes wove through the crowds, talking, laughing, offering blessing.

It *was* incredible. And still nowhere near as interesting as the woman next to him.

"Have you been enjoying yourself here?" he asked.

"More or less," she said, looking at him from the corner of her eye, color creeping into her cheeks. Probably not the smartest question to ask. Why was he struggling with his words and actions? That never happened to him. Not anymore.

"The less would be me being a jerk and planting my lips on you, right?" Might as well go for honesty. Clara was the only person in his life who rated that. He didn't want to violate it.

She blew out a breath. "Um…mostly the being a jerk. You're a pretty good kisser, it turns out."

"So you didn't mind that?"

"Not as much as I should have." Her words escaped in a rush.

"Glad to know I'm not the only one," he said, forcing the words out.

"Not sure it helps anything." She walked ahead of him, straying beneath the overhang of a curled roof, her eyes on the murals painted on the walls of the temple.

"Maybe not." He leaned in, pretending to examine the same image she was.

"So…is there a solution?" She put her hand on the wall, tracing the painting of a white elephant with her finger.

He covered her hands with his, his heart pounding, his hand shaking like he was a teenage virgin. "Let me see."

He leaned in, his mouth brushing hers. He went slow this

time, asking the question, as he should have done the first time he'd kissed her. She didn't move, not into him or away from him. He angled his head and deepened the kiss and he felt her soften beneath him, her lips parting beneath his, her breath catching, sharp and sweet when the tip of his tongue met hers.

He pulled away, his eyes on hers.

She released a breath. "How do you feel?"

"I was going to ask you the same thing."

She looked up. "The roof didn't fall in."

"No," he said, following her gaze. "It didn't."

She leaned into him, her elbow jabbing his side, a shy smile on her face. "Good to know anyway."

"Glad it comforts you."

She laughed, her cheeks turning pink, betraying the fact that she wasn't unaffected. "Comfort may not be the right word."

He looked around the teeming common area, at the completely unfamiliar surroundings. And he found he wanted to pretend that the feelings he was having for Clara were unfamiliar, too.

But he couldn't. Because they had been there, for a long time, lurking beneath the surface. Ignored. Unwanted. But there.

"No. Comfort is definitely not the right word."

They'd spent most of the day at the temple, then taken a car back to Chiang Mai where they'd wandered the streets buying food from vendors, and watching decorations go up on every market stall for a festival that was happening in the evening.

Now, with the event coming close, the streets were packed tight with people, carrying street food, flower arrangements with candles in the center, talking, laughing. It was dark out, the sun long gone behind the mountains, but the air was still thick, warm and fragrant. There was music, noise and movement everywhere. The smell of frying food mixed with the perfume of flowers and the dry, stale scent of dust clung to the air, filled her senses.

It almost helped block out Zack. But not quite. No matter just how much it filled up her senses, it couldn't erase Zack. The imprint of his kiss. It had been different than the first one. Tender. Achingly sexy.

It had made her want more. Not simply in a sexual way, but in an emotional way. It didn't bear thinking about. Still, she knew she would.

She kept an eye on the food stalls, passing more exotic fare, like anything with six legs or more, for something a bit more vanilla. Maybe food would help keep her mind off things. At least temporarily.

"I definitely don't need this," she said, stopping to buy battered, fried bananas from the nearest food stall.

"But you bought it," he said, breaking a piece off the banana and putting it in his mouth.

"Well, that's because sweets are my area of expertise. You're here for the beans and tea leaves, I'm here for the pairing, right? This is research. It's for work. I need to capture the new and exotic flavor profiles Chiang Mai has to offer," she said, trying to sound official. "Maybe I can write off the calories?"

They dodged a bicycle deliveryman and crossed the busy, bustling street, moving away from the stalls and toward the river that ran through the city. "You don't need to worry about it. You're perfect like you are."

She looked down at the bag of sweets. "You're just saying that."

"I'm not."

She sucked in a sharp breath and looked at the lanterns that were strung from tree to tree, glowing overhead. "We should do this more. At home."

"Eat?"

"No. Go do things. Mostly we work, and sometimes I feed

you at my house, or we watch a movie at yours. Well, we do go out to lunch sometimes, but on workdays, so it doesn't count."

"We're busy."

"We're workaholics."

Zack frowned and stopped walking. He extended his hand and took a lock of her hair between his thumb and forefinger, rubbing it idly. "Is that why you're leaving me?"

She looked up at him. "I'm not leaving you. I'm leaving the company." And she was counting on that to put some natural and healthy distance between them. Roasted had brought them together, and because they got along so well, after spending the day at work together, half of the time it felt natural to simply go and have dinner together. Watch bad reality TV together. Once they weren't involved in the same business it would only be natural they would drift apart. And with any luck, it would only feel like she was missing her right arm for a couple of years.

"What do you need? I'll give it to you."

"You're missing the point, Zack. It's about having something of my own."

"Roasted isn't enough for you? You've been there from the beginning, more or less. You've helped me make it what it is."

"No. I just bake cupcakes. And there are a lot of people who can do my job."

"But they aren't you."

She closed her eyes and let the compliment wash over her. She'd say this for Zack; he gave her more than most anyone else in her life ever had, including her family. But it was still just a crumb of what she wanted.

"No," she said, "some of them are even better."

She wove through the crowd to the edge of the waterfront. People were kneeling down and putting the flower arrangements with their lit candles into the stream. The crowd standing on the other side of the waterfront was lighting candles inside tall, rice paper lanterns, the orange spreading to the inky night, casting color and light all around.

Zack was behind her, she could sense it without even turning around. "I'm glad we came tonight," she said.

Zack swept his fingers through Clara's hair, moving it over her shoulder, exposing her neck. He didn't normally touch her like that, but tonight, he found he couldn't help himself. Things were tense between them. The kiss at the temple certainly hadn't helped diffuse it.

He wondered if most of the tension had started in the bedroom back in the villa. That moment when they'd both looked at the bed and had that same, illicit thought.

If it had started there, they might be able to finish it there.

Temptation, pure and strong, lit him on fire from the inside out. She turned, and his heart slammed hard against his rib cage, blood rushing south of his belt, every muscle tensing. He could feel the energy change between them, like a wire that had been connecting them, unseen and unfelt for years had suddenly come alive with high-voltage electricity. He knew she felt it, too.

"We broke things, didn't we?" she whispered.

It was like she read his thoughts, which, truly, was nothing new. But inconvenient now, since his thoughts had a lot to do with what it might be like to see her naked.

"Because of the kisses?"

She nodded once. "I can't forget them."

"I can't, either. I'm not sure if I want to."

She took a deep breath. "That's just what I was thinking earlier."

"Was it?"

"Yes. I should want to forget it, we both should. So we can get things back to where they're supposed to be but…"

He leaned down and pressed his lips to hers, soft again. "Do you think we could break it worse than we already have? Or is the damage done?"

"I have no idea."

Everything in him screamed to step back. Because this was an unknown. A move that would affect his life, his daily life, and he couldn't see the way it would end. And that just wasn't how he did things. Not since that night when he'd been sixteen and he'd acted unthinkingly, impulsively, and ruined everything.

He wasn't that person anymore. He'd made sure of it. If he didn't walk away from Clara now, from the temptation she presented, if he didn't plan it out and look at all the angles, he was opening them both up to potential fallout.

He stepped forward and kissed her again. Deepening the kiss this time, letting the blood that was roaring in his ears drown out conscious thought.

Clara knew she should stop this. Stop the madness before it went too far. It already had gone too far. It had gone too far the moment she agreed to come. Because the desire for this, for the week to turn into this, had been there. Of course, she'd never imagined that Zack would—could—want her.

The breaking of things wasn't just down to the kiss. It was the day at the river, the intense moment on the balcony. The fact that she'd realized she was deeply, madly, irrevocably in love with a man who was just supposed to be her friend.

He kissed the tip of her nose, then her cheeks. "Zack," she whispered.

"Clara."

"Are we trying to see if we can break things worse?"

"Actually, I'm not thinking at all. Not about anything beyond what I feel right now."

"What is it you feel?" she asked, echoing what she'd said after they'd kissed.

"I want you."

She hesitated, her heart squeezing tight. "Do you want me? Or do you want to have sex?"

He looked at her for a long time, the glow of flames across

the river reflected in his eyes. "I want you, Clara Davis. I have never slept with one woman when I wanted another one, and I would never start the practice with you. When I have you, I won't be thinking of anyone else. I'll only have room for you."

His words trickled through her, balm on her soul. Exactly the right words.

The real question was, did she want to accept a physical relationship when it was only part of what she wanted?

You only have part of what you want now. A very small part.

"Just for tonight," she said, hating that she had to say it, but knowing she did. Because she knew for certain that there could be no romantic future for them. She loved him, she was certain of it now. She had for a long time, possibly for most of the seven years she'd known him. It had been a slow thing, working its way into her system bit by bit. With every smile, every touch.

And he didn't love her. Looking at him now, the light in his eyes, that wasn't anything deeper than lust. But if that was all she could have, she would take that. Right now, she would take it, and she wouldn't think about the wisdom of it, or the consequences.

Because she was staring hard into a Zack-free future, and she would rather have all of him tonight, and carry the memory with her, than be nothing more than his trusty sidekick forever, standing by watching while he married another woman. Watching him make a life with someone else, someone he didn't even love, while her heart splintered into tiny pieces with every beat.

"One night," she repeated. "Here. Away from reality. Away from work and home. Because… We can't keep going on like this. It can't be healthy."

The people around them started cheering and she looked around them, saw the paper lanterns start to rise up above them, filling the air with thousands of floating, ethereal lights.

"Just one night," he said, his voice rough. "One night to explore this." He touched her cheek. "To satisfy us both. Is that really what you want?"

"I want you. So much."

He kissed her without preliminaries this time, her body pressed against hers, his erection thick and hard against her stomach as his mouth teased and tormented her in the most delicious way. She wrapped her arms around his neck and gave herself up to the heat coursing between them. When they parted she felt like she was floating up with the lanterns.

One night. The proposition made her heart ache, and pound faster. It excited her and terrified her. She didn't know what she was thinking. But one thing she did know: he wanted her. He wasn't faking the physical reaction she'd felt pressed against her.

The very thought of Zack, perfect, sexy Zack wanting her, was intoxicating. Empowering. She wanted to revel in the feeling. One night. To find out if her fantasies were all she'd built them up to be. One night to have the man of her dreams.

One night to make a memory that she would carry with her for the rest of her life.

CHAPTER SEVEN

BACK at the villa, Clara started to question some of the bravado she'd felt down in the city. It was one thing to know, for a moment, in public, fully dressed, that Zack was attracted to her. It was another to suddenly forget a lifetime's insecurity. To wonder if it would be Hannah on his mind.

They were in the bedroom. And her eyes were fixed on the bed, that invitation to decadence, to passion unlike anything she'd ever known. With the man she loved.

She sucked in a breath. She wasn't going to worry about how attracted he was to her, where she ranked with his other lovers. This night was for her. It was the culmination of every fantasy, every longing she'd had since Zack had walked into the bakery she worked at seven years ago and offered her a job.

He pulled her to him and kissed her. Hungry. Wild. She felt it, too, an uncontrollable, uncivilized need that had no place anywhere else in her life. No one had ever made her feel like this. No one had ever made her want to forget every convention, every rule, and just follow her body's most untamed needs.

But Zack did.

"I want you," she said, her voice breaking as they parted. She had to say it. Because it had been building in her for so long and now she felt like she was going to burst with it.

"I want you, too. I've thought of this before," Zack said, unbuttoning his shirt as he spoke, revealing that gorgeous, toned chest. "Of what it might be like to see you."

"To…to see me?"

"Naked," he said.

"You have?" she asked, her voice trembling now, because she'd hoped, maybe naively, that he would want the lights off. She didn't want him to see her. Touch, yes. Taste, sure. But see?

"Of course I have. I've tried not to think about it too hard. Because you work for me. Because you're my friend. And it's not good to picture friends or employees naked. In my life, everything has a place, and yours was never supposed to be in my bed. And I was never supposed to imagine you naked. But I have anyway sometimes."

"I have a hard time believing that."

"Why?" He shrugged his shirt off and let it fall to the floor, then his hands went to his belt and her breath stuck in her throat.

"Because I'm…average."

He chuckled, his hands freezing on the belt buckle. "Damn your mother for making you believe that garbage." He took a step toward her and put his hand on her cheek, his thumb sliding gently across her face. "You are exquisite. You have such perfect skin. Smooth. Soft. And your body." He put his other hand on her waist. "I thought of you last night. Of this. Of how beautiful you would look."

Reflexively she pulled back slightly.

"What?" he asked.

"I'm not… What was Hannah? A size two? I'm…I'm not a size two."

"Beauty isn't a size. I don't care what the number on the tag of your dresses says. I don't care what your sister looked like, or what your mother thought you should look like. I know what I see. You have the kind of curves other women envy."

He reached around and caught the tab on her summer dress with his thumb and forefinger and tugged it down partway.

Her hands shook, her body trembling inside and out. She felt like she was back beneath the spotlight again. Just waiting to have all of her flaws put out there for everyone to ridicule.

"Wait," she said.

His hands stilled. "I don't know if I can."

"Please. Can were turn the lights off?"

There was only one lamp on. It wasn't terribly bright in the room, but she still felt exposed already, with the zipper barely open across the top part of her back. She felt awkward. Unexceptional. Especially faced with all of Zack's perfection. He didn't have an ounce of spare flesh, every muscle perfectly defined as though he were carved from granite.

He put his hands on her hips and pulled her to him. She could feel his erection again, hard and hot against her. "You are perfect." He moved his hands around to her back, to her bottom, cupping her. She gasped. She'd never been this intimate with a man. She wondered if she should be more or less nervous that it was Zack she was finally taking the step with.

No one had seen her naked, not since she was in diapers. She didn't even change in public locker rooms. She would hide in bathroom stalls, needing the coverage of four walls and a door. And Zack wanted...

"Please."

"Let me see you first." Her eyes met his and she drew in an unsteady breath. "It's me, Clara."

"I know," she said.

"When you're ready."

She took a breath and turned away from him, catching the zipper and tugging it down the rest of the way, letting her dress fall to the floor. Zack moved behind her, his arm curving around her, his palm pressed flat against her stomach.

He swept her hair to the side and pressed a kiss to her neck. "As I said. Perfection."

He turned her slowly, keeping his arms around her, holding her against him, his hard body acting as a shield. Cocooned in his arms, she didn't feel quite so naked.

She looked at his eyes, so familiar, yet different at the same time. Zack's eyes, filled with a kind of raw lust she'd never had directed at her before. Not by him, not by any man. The enormity of the moment hit her then. She was about to be with Zack. About to make love to him.

She started shaking then, her hands, her entire body, from the inside out. He wrapped his arms around her and held her against him. "Are you okay?"

"Yes," she said, her voice shaking. "I'm okay."

"Why are you shaking?" She couldn't answer. "Be honest," he said.

"Because it's you."

He tilted his head to the side and kissed her. She closed her eyes determined to do nothing more than luxuriate in the moment. The heat of his mouth, the slide of his tongue. She was going to believe, in this moment, that she could be the woman he wanted.

He reached around and unhooked her bra. He pulled back from her for a moment so he could remove it the rest of the way, leaving her exposed to his hungry gaze. "I said you were perfection, but I didn't know just how true that was."

A hot flush spread over her entire body, heating her. Embarrassment battling with desire.

He cupped her breasts, sliding his thumbs over her nipples. And that was when desire won. She shook with pleasure, her stomach tightening, her internal muscles pulsing, her body ready, demanding, more of him. Demanding climax. She was close to finding it, with just the touch of his hands. Maybe it was because in her mind she had found pleasure with him so many times, in reality, it was effortless to get close to the peak.

A hoarse sound caught in her throat and she felt herself go over the edge. She gripped his forearms, her fingernails digging into his flesh. As soon as the numbing pleasure washed away, embarrassment crashed in on her. She couldn't believe she'd come so quickly. Telling in so many ways. She hadn't realized just how impossible it would be to keep secrets when they were like this, hadn't realized just how intimate it would be.

"I…" She looked at his face, and his expression stole the words from her lips. A look of pure masculine satisfaction, combined with total arousal. The embarrassment dissolved. She reached forward and put her hands on his belt buckle, undoing it and pulling his belt from the loops.

He pulled her to him again, kissing her like a starving man. She reached between them and undid the closure on his pants, pushing them down his hips, along with his underwear. She felt his bare flesh against her for the first time, so impossibly hot and hard.

She wrapped her fingers around him and squeezed. She wasn't sure why, only that she wanted to. That she wanted to touch him, taste him, everywhere. To make him feel half of what he'd made her feel.

So this would be about him, a little bit. But mostly, she was just going to enjoy having the man she'd dreamed of having for so long, completely available to her. For tonight, he was hers.

He put his hand on her thigh and pulled her leg up over his hip. She held on to his shoulders and he curled his fingers around her other thigh, lifting her off the ground and walking her to the bed, up the step, laying her down on the soft mattress, his body over hers, making her feel small. Feminine. Beautiful.

He dipped his head and slid the tip of his tongue around the edge of one of her nipples. She arched into him and he sucked the tip into his mouth, his eyes never leaving hers.

"You're so sensitive there," he said, his voice sounding different, strained. "I love it."

"I like it, too," she said. It was the first time she'd ever really liked her body.

He tugged her panties down her thighs and she helped kick them off of the bed. "I stand by what I said earlier. Perfection." He kissed her ribs, just beneath her breasts, down to her belly button. "Designed to take pleasure. For me to give you pleasure. Exquisite." He moved lower, his lips teasing the tender skin. He parted her thighs and slid his tongue over her clitoris. White heat shot through her body, a deep, intense pleasure tightening her muscles. She gripped the sheets, trying to hold herself to the bed.

He slid one finger inside her and she thought she might explode. Then another finger joined the first and a slight stinging sensation cut through the pleasure. She held her breath for a moment and waited for it to fade. It would. She knew it would. And all the better if he took care of it this way.

He worked his fingers in and out of her body, each time, the discomfort lessened. And he didn't seem to notice. Which was fine by her.

"I can't wait anymore," he said, his voice rough, broken.

"I don't think I can wait, either."

He moved up so that the head of his erection was testing the entrance to her body, his arms bracketing hers, his biceps trembling slightly. He was as undone as she was. It was such a wonderful, incredible feeling. It made her truly believe that she was beautiful.

He pushed into her partway then pulled out completely, swearing sharply.

"What?" she asked, hoping it had nothing to do with her virginity. Because she couldn't stop. Not now.

"Condoms," he said, his hands unsteady as he opened the drawer to the bedside table. He opened the box and pulled out a packet, getting the condom out and rolling it on to his length quickly.

"Oh. Good." She didn't know why she hadn't thought of

it. She should have. But there were so many things filling her head. So many emotions. She'd almost forgotten the most important thing.

Then he was back, poised over her, ready to enter her.

He slid back in as far as he'd already been, then pressed in the rest of the way. It was tight, but it wasn't painful, the evidence of her virginity likely dealt with earlier.

He flexed his hips, his pelvis pressing against her clitoris at exactly the right angle, the sensation of him being inside her as her muscles clenched tight around him so incredible she couldn't stop the moan of pleasure from escaping her lips.

She gripped his tight, muscular butt, so much more perfect than she'd even imagined. Everything so much more perfect than she'd imagined.

She wrapped her legs around his calves and held him to her, moving in rhythm with his thrusts, the pleasure building low in her stomach, emotion swelling in her chest, threatening to overflow. It came to a head, pushing her until she was certain that unless she found release, she would break apart into tiny little pieces beneath the weight of the pressure inside of her.

Then she was falling apart, splintering, release, pleasure, love, pouring through the cracks, filling her, washing through her. She dug her fingernails into his back, squeezing her eyes closed tight. She didn't even try to stop the sharp cry that was climbing her throat, couldn't feel embarrassed that she was arching and moving against him with no control at all.

Because he was right with her, his entire body trembling, his fist gripping the comforter by her head, a low, intense growl rumbling in his chest as he found his own release.

He lay above her, his breathing harsh, his heart pounding so hard she could hear it. And she was pretty sure he could hear hers, too.

"Wow," she said.

He moved to the side, withdrawing from her body, one arm resting on her body. He was watching her closely, like he wanted to ask her something. Or like he thought he should but didn't want to.

"You've never been careful about what you said to me before," she said. "Don't start now."

He huffed a laugh. "Clara…"

"Actually I changed my mind," she said. "We have one night. Why talk about anything?"

Something in his expression changed, hardened. "I think that's a good idea." He rolled to his side and stood up. "I'll be back in a minute."

He went into the bathroom and came back out a moment later.

"What do you propose we do, if we aren't going to talk?"

She got up on her knees and went to the edge of the bed, wrapping her arms around his neck, uncharacteristic boldness surging through her. "I'm sure we can think of a few things."

This was her night to have all of the man she loved. And she wasn't going to miss out on a single experience.

Morning came too quickly, light breaking through the gauzy curtain that surrounded the bed, bringing reality in with the sunbeams.

She didn't want the night to end. She didn't want to face reality. She'd felt like a princess last night; beautiful, desired. She'd felt like her dream was in her grasp. And this morning she felt like she'd turned back into a pumpkin. Reality sucked.

She looked at the man sleeping next to her, the only man she'd ever really wanted. The only man she'd ever loved.

And today, she would have to get up and forget that last night had happened. She would have to consign it to the "perfect memories" bin along with other things she pulled out when she was feeling lonely, or when things weren't going well.

The thought made her whole body hurt.

"I arranged to have the plane leave in an hour or so," he said, his eyes still closed.

"Okay," she said, swallowing thickly and sliding out of the bed, clutching the sheet tightly to her breasts, desperate to cover herself now, in the light of day. It was one thing to feel sexy, to be all right with her nudity when he was looking at her like he was starving and she was a delicacy. A lot less easy when he seemed...uninterested.

"I'm going to take a shower real quick."

He made a noise that might have been a form of consent, but she didn't ask for confirmation before beating a hasty retreat to the bathroom. She turned the water on and sat on the closed toilet lid, letting the tears fall down her cheeks, hoping the sound of the water hitting the tile would drown out the sound of her sobs.

Zack sat up, a curse on his lips. Last night...last night had been an aberration. A hot, amazing aberration, maybe, but it could never happen again. He had been careless. He'd nearly forgotten to use a condom. And she'd been a virgin.

If he'd thought about it, if he'd thought at all, he would have guessed that. He knew her well enough to have picked up on how nervous she was, to understand what that meant. He also knew her well enough to know she wasn't really a one-night-stand woman. She was sensitive, emotional. Sweet.

His stomach twisted, nausea overtaking him, spreading through his limbs. She probably wasn't on birth control, and there was a possibility that in that moment, when he'd been inside of her without protection, that he'd made a very big mistake.

No, he knew he'd made a mistake. He hit his fist on the top of the nightstand and stood, stalking through the room collecting his clothes. Had he learned nothing? Was he as stupid now as he'd been fourteen years ago?

His heart froze for a moment, the events of what sometimes felt like a past life, playing through his head from start to finish. Like a horror film he couldn't pause.

No. He'd worked way too hard to leave that person behind. That boy, who had been so irresponsible. Who had caused so much damage.

Last night he'd lost control. With Clara, of all people. She shouldn't have tempted him like that. But she had. She'd made him shake like *he* was the virgin.

It couldn't happen again. It wouldn't. He might have lost his control for a moment, but he wouldn't do it again.

Clara appeared a few moments later, her face scrubbed fresh and pink, her hair wet and wavy. She was dressed, a fitted T-shirt and jeans meaningless now since he'd already seen her naked and his mind was doing a very good job of envisioning her as she'd been last night.

All pale skin and soft curves. Pure perfection. Better than he'd ever imagined.

"Hey," she said, trying to smile and not quite managing it.

"Are you all right?" he asked. He'd never slept with a virgin before, but that was only part of the foreign, first-time feeling he was dealing with. The other part of that was because it was Clara. And the rest was because of his carelessness.

Carelessness that had to be addressed.

"I'm fine," she said.

"Are you on birth control?" he asked.

She narrowed her eyes. "No."

He tried to get a handle on the gnawing panic in his gut. Condoms were reliable. He knew that. But there was the matter of his impatience, of his entering her, even briefly, without protection. He swore. "Why not?"

"What?" She crossed her arms beneath her breasts. "I'm sorry, was I supposed to start taking the pill just in case you invited me on your honeymoon and we hooked up? I was a virgin, you jackass."

"I know," he shouted, not sure why he was shouting, only that his blood was pumping too fast through his veins and his heart was threatening to thunder out of his chest. "I know," he said again, softer this time.

"You used a condom," she said, her cheeks flushing pink.

"Yes, I did, eventually. There's a chance that kind of carelessness could have gotten you pregnant. It's not a big chance, but there is a chance."

"I...I seriously doubt that I'm pregnant. Well, obviously I'm not pregnant yet since things take a while to travel and...well, that's high-school health, you know all that."

"But there's a chance. I'm usually more careful."

"Zack, I think you're overreacting."

"Is that what you think, Clara?" he asked, his voice deadly calm. "You think I'm overreacting because you think it can't happen. But then, you've never been pregnant, obviously. And I have gotten a woman pregnant, so I think I might be a bit more in touch with that reality than you are. Do you know what it's like? To know that everything in your life is going to have to change because for one moment you were so utterly selfish and consumed with one moment of pleasure that you didn't think about anything else?"

Clara's heart was in her throat. She felt like she couldn't breathe. It was like a shield had been torn away from Zack, like his armor had dissolved, crumbled around his feet, leaving nothing but the man he was beneath his facade. A facade she hadn't realized was there.

This was the man she'd seen glimpses of. The reason for the darkness that she saw in his eyes sometimes. And she was afraid to hear the rest. But she had to.

His chest rose and fell sharply. "I was sixteen. And I was more interested in getting some than thinking about using a condom. Turns out you can get someone pregnant after just one time, regardless of the idiot rumors floating around the high school saying otherwise."

She didn't ask him what happened. She didn't interrupt the break. She just let his silence fill the room, and she felt his pain. Felt it in her, through her. She didn't have to know what happened to know that it was bad. Devastating. To know that knowing it was going to change her. The way it had changed Zack.

"I didn't want a baby, but we were having one. She wanted it. I didn't want him," he said. "But I got a job so that I could pay for the doctor bills. So I could help her raise him. Because at least I knew that I should do the right thing." A muscle in his jaw jerked. "He came too early. And by the time I realized how badly I did want him, it was too late. By the time I realized that a baby can very quickly mean everything in the world to you, he was gone."

She tried to hold back the sob that was rising inside her. His face was blank now, void of emotion, flat. Like he was reading a story in a newspaper, not telling her about his life.

"Another reason Hannah was so perfect for me," he said. "She didn't want kids."

"You don't… You don't want kids?"

"I had one, Clara. I would never…I will never put myself through something like that again. I nearly died with him. I don't make the same mistakes twice. I'm always careful now."

Except last night, he wasn't as careful as he usually was, obviously. And she wasn't sure how she felt about that. Or what it might mean. And right now, she wished they had never slept together. Because she wanted to comfort him as a friend. To tell him how much her heart ached for him. But she wasn't sure if it was her place now. She wasn't sure what she was supposed to do. What he expected. What he would allow.

Because now she saw just how much he had always hidden from her. She saw a stranger. She wondered if it was even possible that this man, hard and angry, was the same man she'd seen every day for the past seven years.

"How did you…how did you cope with it?"

"I don't need to talk about it, Clara. I don't talk about it, ever. This isn't an invitation for you to psychoanalyze me. But now you know why I insist on being careful. That's the important part of the story. And you'll tell me, if you're pregnant."

"I'll let you know," she said. "But I'm sure everything will be fine."

He turned away from her and shrugged his shirt on.

"Everything will be fine," she repeated. That assurance was just for her. And she wasn't certain she believed it.

CHAPTER EIGHT

THE plane ride back to San Francisco was a study in torture. Zack was hardly speaking to her and she felt battered from the inside out. Her body was a little bit sore from her first time, and her heart felt like it had been wrung out and left to dry.

Zack was acting overly composed. His focus on work, not on her. Not on the revelation that had passed between them, both in bed and out.

She didn't feel like the same person. She felt changed. She wasn't sure if Zack was the same person, either. Or maybe he was; maybe it was just that she saw him better now.

"I think I'll probably take a couple days off," she said, looking over at Zack who was engrossed in his laptop screen. "Recover. From the jet lag."

"Fine."

The chill in his response made her shiver. "And I'm thinking of buying a pony."

"You don't have anywhere to keep one," he said drily, still not looking up.

"Just a small one. For the rooftop garden."

He did look up this time. "Your neighbors would complain."

"I don't like my neighbors." That earned her a slight smile. "So, what's the plan when we get back to civilization?"

"With any luck, things can go back to normal."

Two questions flitted through her mind. Luck for who? And, what's normal? She didn't voice either of them. "Okay."

"I still need you there, at Roasted, until Amudee signs off on the deal."

"Right." She looked down at her hand. The ring was still there. "You'll want this back, I assume." She pulled the ring off and got up, walking over to his seat and depositing it on the desk in front of him. "Since we won't need it."

A relief. Wearing another woman's ring made her feel weighted down.

"No. We won't." His eyes met hers and held. She felt heat prickle down her arms, her nipples tightening as a flash of arousal hit her.

"Great. I'll um…I'm going to try to sleep."

As she drifted off in the plane's bedroom, she tried not to be disappointed that Zack didn't join her.

"Amudee is coming here."

Clara looked up and saw Zack. For the first time since they'd landed in San Francisco three days earlier. She'd taken a couple of days to get over her jet lag, and had sneaked around the office yesterday like a cat burglar, trying to get work done without encountering him.

Because ultimately, avoiding him was simply easier than trying to juggle all the emotions she felt when she saw him. Cowardly? Yes, yes, it was. But she felt a bit yellow-bellied after all that had happened between them, and she was wallowing in it.

"What?"

"He's coming here to see how we run our operation. He wants to talk to employees, to see where we work. If we truly do conduct business in an ethical manner."

Zack reached into his pocket and took out an overly familiar velvet box. He set it on the edge of her desk, his expression grim. "And now it continues. And every single person working in the this office has to believe it, too."

"Zack this can't… It has to end."

"It will. After. And you can take as much money as you need for a start-up. You can have my blessing, hell, you can have free Roasted coffee for the first five years. But I want this deal to go through."

"Ironic that you're trying to convince him of your business ethics by using a lie," she said, annoyance spiking inside her.

"Odd that it's necessary, too, don't you think?"

"He's a nice man."

"And a romantic, it seems. He loves you. He wants to make sure he sees us together as a couple again while he's here."

"Tangled web," she snapped, putting her pencil down on the desk.

"Isn't it?"

The air between them seemed to crackle, everything slowing for a moment, the silence so tense and brittle she was certain she could splinter it into tiny pieces if she spoke.

"Put it on," he said, looking at the ring.

"I gave it back," she said tightly.

"Clara, I need you to do this for me."

She fought the urge to make a rude gesture with a different finger than the one meant for a ring and grabbed the box, opened the lid and slid the ring on. "There."

"Come on."

"What?"

"We have to make an announcement."

"Zack…"

"We're going to see this through, right? Then you can leave. Whatever you need to do, you can go do it, but finish this with me."

"Fine." She stood up and rounded the desk, he wrapped his arm around her waist and drew her to him. Heat exploded in her, stronger than she remembered, more arousing than anything had a right to be.

Instantly she was assaulted by images of their night together. His mouth, his hands, the way it had felt when he was over her, in her. It was torture. She clenched her hands into fists and the heavy ring band bit into her fingers.

There was a small group of employees who worked on her floor, their desks clustered in the center of the room. Roasted's office had a social atmosphere, which Zack had always believed made for optimum creativity. Because Zack was a great boss, the kind who made everyone feel appreciated, all the time.

And he never, ever showed the dark, tortured side of himself she'd seen in Chiang Mai. He never showed the intense, sexual side of himself, either. But she'd seen it. She'd felt it.

"Clara and I have an announcement to make."

Ten heads instantly popped up, eyes trained on her and Zack. Her heart started pounding, her palms sweating. It was one thing to lie to a man she'd never met before. A thing she hated. But it was really quite another to lie to people she worked with every day. People who she considered her friends.

"We're getting married," he said.

"Pay up." Cynthia, a woman with gray hair and pronounced smile lines turned to Jess, a twenty-something computer whiz who did their online marketing.

Jess swore and took his wallet out.

"What is this?" Clara asked.

"Congratulations," Cynthia said, beaming. "We had bets placed on this. I bet you would get married. Most everyone changed sides when Mr. Parsons got engaged to someone else. But I held out. And now I'm collecting."

"Unbelievable," Clara muttered. She wasn't sure how she felt about this revelation, either. A little bit flattered that people believed it was possible.

"Clearly I'm not giving people enough work to do," Zack said.

"Kiss her!" This from Jess, who undoubtedly considered it a consolation prize.

Everything inside Clara seized up, her muscles locking tight. Zack looked down at her, his fingers brushing her jaw. He dipped his head and kissed her. A perfectly appropriate kiss to give her in front of his employees. Nothing scandalous or overly sexual. But it grabbed hold of her world and shook it completely. Shook her.

When he lifted his head there was a smattering of applause. "Feel free to spread the news," Zack said, lacing his fingers through hers and leading her toward his office.

He closed the door tightly behind him, taking long strides to the far window that overlooked the bay, his back turned to her.

"Good show," she said icily.

He looked over his shoulder. "You could have been a little less stiff," he said.

"You…" She strode across the room, embracing the anger, unrest and desire that was rioting through her. "You…" She grabbed the lapels of his jacket and stretched up onto her toes, kissing him with every last ounce of passion and frustration that she felt.

He locked his arm around her waist and drew her up tight against his body, his erection hard and hot against her. He spun them around and backed her against the wall, pressing her against the hard surface, his lips hungry as he tasted her, feasted on her.

She wrapped her arms around him, sifted her fingers through his thick brown hair, holding him to her as she returned each stroke and thrust of his tongue. The days of not touching him, thinking of him and denying herself the pleasure of even seeing in him, crashed in on her, fueled her desperation.

She growled in frustration, needing more, faster. Now. She pushed his jacket down his arms and onto the floor, grabbing the knot on his tie and tugging it down as he put his hands on her thighs and pushed the hem of her skirt up. She wrapped one leg around his calf and arched against him.

He tore his mouth away from hers and put his palm flat on the wall behind them, a short, sharp curse punctuated by heavy breaths escaped his lips.

The full horror of what she'd done hit her all at once, like getting a bucket of freezing water dumped in her face. She echoed his choice of swear word and ducked beneath his arm, leaning forward and bracing herself on his desk.

"That shouldn't have happened," she said.

"For more than one reason."

"Why don't you list them?" she said sharply.

"Fine. I'll list them. We said one night. And that kind of kiss doesn't stop at just a kiss. The second reason is that you mean more to me than this," he said.

"Than what?"

"Than an angry make out session against a wall. Than you sneaking around, avoiding me, because we slept together. You mean more to me than sex."

That cut. And maybe it shouldn't have, but she couldn't separate having sex with Zack from the emotions she felt for him. She loved him; sex had been an expression of that. Being joined to him, intimate with him, it had been everything.

But not to him. To him, the sex was separate from the feeling.

"Great. But I apparently don't mean so much to you that you won't use me as a pretend fiancée." Her argument was thin, because frankly, if her feelings for him were platonic, the engagement thing would be nothing big at all.

But her feelings weren't platonic. Not even close.

"Then leave, Clara. If you don't want to do it, don't do it. I'm not holding you hostage. But understand this. I will likely lose the deal with Amudee, and then I won't be able to get the product I need to start the boutique stores. And my search for an acceptable product will continue. It will cost everyone time and money, lots of it. That's just stating a fact—it's not emotional blackmail or anything else you might be tempted to accuse me of."

Clara looked at his face, at the familiar planes and angles. The mouth she'd seen smile so many times, the lips she'd kissed just now. She knew him differently now than she had a week ago. She knew his body, she knew his loss. And as hard as it would have been for her to walk away then, it was impossible now. Impossible to leave him when she'd promised she would see this through.

"I'll do it. I'll play the part, I'll keep playing the part, I mean. But I didn't expect for it to go this far."

"I know. But we had a deal." He probably thought she meant the farce, but she was thinking of the sex. Or maybe he knew what she was really talking about and he was content to leave it ambiguous, just like she was.

"When the ink is dry on the agreement, it can be finished. You gave me your word," he said.

"That's low, Zack," she said, sucking in a deep breath, trying to make her lungs expand.

"It's true. I've been there for you when you needed me. I held your hair while you…"

"I know. Food poisoning. Please don't bring that up." It was right up there with her high-school humiliation. Zack watching her vomit. But he had taken care of her. There hadn't been anyone else. Truly, they were the key players in each other's lives. They were there for each other, at work and at home.

"My point is, I've helped you. Help me. I'm asking you as a friend, not your boss. Your friend."

She gritted her teeth, raw emotion, so intense she couldn't identify it, flooded her. She swung her arms back and forth, trying to ease the nervous energy surging through her limbs. "So when does Mr. Amudee get here?"

"Soon. He'll be in the office tomorrow morning, so it would be good if we came in together."

If they spent the night with each other, it would be even easier for them to commute to Roasted together, but she didn't say that. And she wouldn't. One night, that was all it was supposed to be and that was all it would be. Make-out sessions against the wall would be immediately stricken from record and forgotten. Completely.

"Then I'll see you tomorrow."

"We should probably leave together, too," he said.

"Probably." That would mean an evening waiting around for him to leave. "I'm going to go down to the kitchens and fiddle around with some recipes."

"I'll see you down there."

"See you then." Hopefully a little baking therapy would clear her mind. Because if not, they were both in trouble.

By the time Zack made it down to the kitchen he didn't have a handle on his libido or his temper. He'd figured a couple of hours separation for him and Clara would be a good idea, but it hadn't accomplished anything on his end.

No, he wouldn't feel satisfied until he was in bed with her again. Or just against the wall. That was why he had stopped kissing her, though. He didn't have a condom.

As an adult he hadn't had all that many lovers, mostly because he believed in taking things slowly, and making sure everything was completely safe. He liked for the woman to be on the pill, and he still used condoms, every time.

Already with Clara he'd been lax, skipping steps he hadn't since high school, and then he'd been ready to forgo any sort of protection in his office so that he could be with her again. In her. Because the truth of the matter was, he hadn't stopped thinking about how amazing that night had been since they'd arrived back in California. Not even close.

He'd dreamed of it, or rather, fantasized about it since sleep had eluded him. And when he hadn't been thinking about making love with her, he'd been replaying the moment he'd told her about his son. Over and over again.

He never talked about Jake. Ever. Not since he'd died, still in the hospital he'd never had a chance to leave, only a couple of days old. Sarah had never wanted to talk about it, and they hadn't had a romantic relationship at that point, anyway.

His parents…they had been horrified that their star football-playing son was going to give it all up to raise a child. If anything, they'd been relieved.

That day had changed everything. He'd been nothing more than a spoiled brat. An only child, destined to skate through college on a football scholarship. He'd taken everything, the adoration of the girls at his school, the free passes the teachers had given him, as his due.

But when Jake was born, he'd felt the weight of purpose. And when he died, it hadn't gone away. He hadn't fit anymore. In one blinding, clear moment he saw everything he'd done that was wrong, selfish, careless. He saw how his stupidity had cost everyone so much.

And he'd left. Left who he was. Left everyone he knew. And every day that passed was one day farther away from that awful day in the hospital. That day that had felt like someone reaching into his chest and yanking his emotions out, twisting them, distorting them.

He had never wanted to feel that way again. Ever. Even more importantly, he'd never wanted to have anything unplanned happen ever again. He wanted control. To plan, to consider the cost of his actions. To be in charge of his life.

He wasn't sure why he'd told Clara about it. Although she had asked why the birth-control lapse was such a big deal to him. But then, a few of his girlfriends had wanted to know why he used every method he could think of to prevent pregnancy. It had cost him relationships since the women involved had taken it as a sign of just how much he didn't want to be with them.

And while it was true he hadn't been looking for forever, his reasoning hadn't quite been what they'd assumed. Still, he hadn't felt compelled to tell them the story. Maybe it was because Clara was...Clara. She was the one person who had been in his life with any regularity for the past decade.

And now he'd likely screwed it up by sleeping with her. Or by kissing her. Or maybe he'd screwed it up the moment he'd asked her to play fiancée and go on his honeymoon.

He pushed open the stainless-steel double doors that led to the baking facility and saw Clara, bending down and looking in one of the ovens.

He took the opportunity to enjoy the view, the way her skirt hugged the round curve of her butt. It was a crime that she'd been made to feel insecure about those curves. He flashed back to the heady moments in his office, when he'd had her skirt pushed up around her hips, when he'd been ready to...

She straightened and turned, her brown eyes widening. "Oh! I didn't know you were here."

"Just walked in. What did you make me?"

"I think you'll like them. I have some cooling. I'm going to pass them out at lunch hour tomorrow."

"No walnuts?"

"None. They're Orange Cream. Don't look at me like that, they'll be good." She handed him a vaguely orange cupcake with white frosting, coated in bright orange sugar crystals.

"It has orange zest in the cake, and there's a Bavarian cream in the center. And the frosting is buttercream."

"All things I like." He took a bite, relishing the burst of sweet citrus and cream. She really was a genius. She'd hooked him with her cupcake-making skills the first time he'd met her, and he'd known then he had to have her for his company. That with her, his line of baked goods would be a massive success. And they had been.

And now she was leaving him.

"Good," he said, even though now he was having a hard time swallowing the bite.

"See? I told you."

"And I told you you wouldn't be easily replaced. You're the best at what you do."

She smiled, a sort of funny smile that almost made her look sad. "I do bake a mean cupcake. I'm glad you like them."

He wasn't going to ask her what was wrong. Because he wasn't sure if he could fix it, and he was afraid he might be the cause of it. "Ready to go?"

"Yes, ready. Oh, wait." She stopped and moved toward him, her eyes fixed on his mouth. His entire body was hot and hard instantly. Ready for her touch, her kiss. She extended her hand and put her thumb on the corner of his mouth. "You had some frosting there," she said, her tone as sweet as her cupcakes, her eyes filled with a knowing, sexual expression that told him she was tormenting him, and she knew it. It was going to be an interesting few weeks.

CHAPTER NINE

"I'm not going to bite you."

Clara glared at Zack from her position in the passenger side of his sporty little two-seater. She was clinging to the door handle, her shoulder smashed against the window. As much space between them as was humanly possible in the tiny metal cage.

The first words that bubbled up were *well that's a shame.* But she held them back, because she was not going to flirt with him. Was not. And she was going to forget about that lapse in the kitchen when she'd wiped the frosting from his mouth. She hadn't licked it off and that had been her first inclination, so really, her self-control was pretty rock solid.

"I know," she said. Much more innocuous than an invitation to bite her, that was for sure.

"Then stop clinging to the door handle like you're planning on jumping out when there's a lull in traffic."

She laughed, somehow, even though most of her felt anything but amused by the entire situation. "I'm not, I promise." She relaxed her hold on the door.

"Good." They pulled down into the underground parking lot of Roasted and into the spot that was second closest to the elevator. He'd given her the closest spot years ago. Some sort of chivalrous gesture, silly, but at the time she'd loved it.

He put the car in Park and killed the engine, getting out

and closing the door behind him. She watched him straighten his shirt collar through the window. He hated ties. He didn't wear them unless he had to. It was sexier when he didn't, in her opinion. It showed a little bit of his sculpted chest, a bit of dark hair. Of course, it was sexier when he didn't wear a shirt at all.

She felt the door give behind her and she squeaked, tightening her hold on the handle. Zack had opened it, just a bit, and was looking down at her, the expression on his face wicked.

"Are you going to sit in there all day? Because we have a meeting," he said.

"Creep," she said, no venom in her tone.

He winked and darn it all, it made her stomach turn over. "Only during business hours."

She released her hold on the door and he opened it the rest of the way, waiting for her to get out before pushing the up button on the lift. When they got in and the door closed, the easy moment evaporated.

The tension was back, and so thick she could hardly breathe. Judging by the sharp pitch of his chest when he drew in a breath, he felt the same. It made her feel better. Slightly.

"So, when is he coming in?"

"Soon," Zack said, his eyes fixed on the doors.

"Oh."

The elevator stopped and the doors slid open. Clara nearly sagged with relief as she scurried out of the elevator, eager to get back into non-shared air space.

When she and Zack walked into the main reception area the employees milling around, scavenging on last night's baking efforts stopped and clapped for them. She ducked her head and offered a smile and finger wave. She didn't know if Zack made a reciprocal gesture or not. She was far too busy not dying of humiliation.

The gleaming, golden elevator doors that would take them

up to their offices were just up ahead. She made a dash for it, and Zack got in behind her, the doors sliding closed.

"So many elevators," she said.

"Is that a problem?"

"Not at all," she said.

Two interminable minutes later they were on the floor that housed both of their offices. "I have work to do," she said, heading toward her own office. A little sanctuary would not go amiss.

"No time, Amudee is in the building. My office."

He put his hand on the small of her back and directed her into his office, closing the door behind them. A horrible, hot, tantalizing sense of déjà vu hit her. Their eyes clashed and held, his all steel heat and temptation. He took a step toward her just as the intercom on his desk phone went on.

"Mr. Parsons? Mr. Amudee is here to see you."

Zack leaned back and punched a button on the phone. "Send him in."

She wished she were relieved. She wasn't. She was just disappointed that she hadn't gotten to experience the conclusion of Zack's step forward. Of what he might have intended to do.

Zack's office door opened and the reason for their charade walked in, looking as personable and cheerful as ever, the lines by his dark eyes deepening as he smiled. "Good to see you again. Zack, I stopped by one of your locations here in the city on my way in, I was very impressed."

"Thank you, Mr. Amudee," Zack said, his charm turned on and dialed up several notches.

She watched Zack work, a sense of awe overtaking her. He was good, and she knew that, but seeing him in action was always incredible. He was smart and he was savvy. And the best part was, he really was a man of ethical business practices.

That, she knew, was the thing that made working with Amudee so important to him. Because he didn't just want to import coffee and tea from any farm. He didn't want to get involved in a share-cropping situation. He didn't want anyone being taken advantage of so that he could turn a profit.

Unfortunately Amudee seemed just as picky about who he did business with. And when money wasn't the be all and end all…you couldn't just throw dollars at it to solve everything. Dollars Zack had. It was the fiancée he'd found himself short of.

She toyed with the ring on her finger, her secondhand ring. The one that had belonged to Hannah. She would be a happy woman the moment she could get it off her finger and keep it off, that was for sure.

"So, dinner tonight, then?" Zack said. "Clara?" he prompted.

"Oh, yes. Tonight. Dinner."

"And as for today, I'd be happy to give you a tour of the corporate office. You can see how we run things here."

Mr. Amudee nodded in approval and started to head out the office door with Zack. "So," she said, "I think I'll go to my office and get some work done then."

"Great." He leaned in and kissed her cheek before walking out of the room.

She knew it was an empty gesture, all part of the show. But it still made her feel like she was floating to her office instead of walking. And no matter how much she tried to tell herself not to think about it, her cheek burned for the rest of the morning.

"What is this?"

When Zack had seen Clara's number flash onto his cellphone screen, he'd heard her sweet hello before he'd even answered. So being greeted by a venomous hiss was an unexpected, unpleasant surprise.

"What is what, Clara? I'm currently battling traffic on North Point so I have no idea what you're talking about."

"This dress. This… Do you even call it a dress? I mean it's

short and slinky and I think the neckline is designed to show skin all the way down to a woman's belly button."

"I saw it, and I liked it, so I had my PA send it over."

"I agreed to a lot when I agreed to play fiancée, but I did not," she growled and paused for a moment before continuing, "agree to stuff myself into a gown that has all the give of saran wrap like a Vienna sausage!"

"I like the visual, but your attitude needs work."

"Your head needs work," she shot back.

"Wear the dress." He hung up the phone and tossed it onto the passenger seat before maneuvering his car against the curb in front of Clara's apartment.

He didn't bother to wait for the elevator. He took the stairs two at a time and knocked on her door, beneath the pretty, pink flowery wreath thing she had hung there. A clever ruse to make people think the owner of the apartment was sweetness and light when, at the moment, she was spitting flame and sulfur.

The door jerked open and he met Clara's glittering brown eyes. And then he looked down and all of the blood in his body roared south.

She was right about the dress. A deep scarlet, it would draw the eye of everyone in the restaurant. And while it didn't show her belly button, it did put her amazing cleavage on display. The soft, rounded curves of her breasts were accentuated by the sweetheart neckline, the pleating in the waist showing off just how tiny she was, before her hips flared out, the fabric conforming to that gorgeous, hourglass shape of hers.

"I am not going out in this."

"It's too late for you to change," he said, barely able to force himself to raise his eyes to her face. He had to admit, the dress was counterproductive as when it came to trying to put Clara back into the proper compartment she was meant to be in in his life, he didn't want her to change.

He wanted to look at her in that dress for as long as he could.

And then, he wanted to lower the zipper on the back of it and watch it slither down her body. He wanted to see her again, soft, naked and begging him to take her.

"Zack…"

"Do you have something against looking sexy?"

"What? No."

"Then what's the problem? If it honestly offends your modesty in some way, fine, change. But otherwise, you look…"

"Like I'm trying too hard?"

He took a step and she backed away from the door, letting him into the apartment. He shouldn't touch her. Not even an innocent gesture. Because with the thoughts that were running through his brain, nothing could be innocent.

He did anyway, and he ignored the voice in his head telling him to stay in control. He was in control. He could touch her without doing more. He was the master of his body, of his emotions.

He put his finger on her jaw, traced the line of it down her neck, to her exposed collarbone.

"You look effortless. As though bringing men to their knees is something you do every day of the week without breaking a sweat. You look like the kind of woman who can have anyone or anything she wants."

"I…I…well, I don't appreciate you dressing me," she said. "It's demeaning."

"I don't know if it was demeaning, but selfish, perhaps."

"Selfish?"

"Because I'm enjoying looking at you so much."

She bent down and picked up a black shawl from the couch, looping it over her arms before grabbing a black clutch purse from the little side table. "You shouldn't say things like that."

She breezed out the door ahead of him, clearly resigned to wearing the dress.

"Probably not," he said, his tone light.

"But you did anyway," she said, turning to face him.

"I did. There are a lot of things I shouldn't have said or done over the past couple of weeks, and yet, it seems I've said and done them all."

"I haven't," she said, turning away from him again and heading down the stairs, eager to avoid being in an elevator with him, he imagined.

"Oh, really?"

"Mmm. I have been virtuous. I've wanted to say and do many things in the past week that I haven't."

"Why do I feel disappointed by that news?"

"I don't know. You shouldn't be," she said, her stilettos clicking and echoing in the stairwell. "You should be thankful." She pushed open the exterior door and they both walked out into the cool evening air.

"I find I'm not."

"I can't help you there."

Something hot and reckless sparked in him. She must have noticed because she backed away from him until she bumped against his car. That was a picture, Clara, in scarlet silk, leaning against his black sports car. The fantasies that were rolling through his mind should be illegal.

"I wish you could," he said, taking a step toward her.

She shook her head. "There's no help for either of us."

"I'm starting to think that might be true."

He wanted to kiss the red off her lips. He wanted to take her back upstairs and do something about the unbearable ache that had settled in his body more than a week ago and hadn't released him since.

"Let's go. We have a dinner date," he said, his voice curt, harsher than he'd intended.

She nodded and went around to the passenger side and he let out a long, slow breath, trying to ease the tension in his body.

Being with her once hadn't helped at all. One night hadn't been enough.

But there wouldn't be another night. There would be no point to it.

CHAPTER TEN

"Thank you for doing that," Zack said, once they were back in the car and away from the presence of the man they were putting on the show for.

Dinner had gone well, and it looked like everything was on track for Mr. Amudee to sign the exclusive deal with Roasted. It turned out he was thrilled that Zack was marrying a woman he worked with, a woman who understood and shared his passion for the business. It was one of the things, they'd found out over dessert, that had placed Zack slightly ahead of his rival at Sand Dollar. Because Amudee felt Zack and Clara were working together, and the owner of the other coffee-shop chain would be spending more time away from his family.

So, just another way their farce had helped. She still didn't feel good about it.

"You're welcome."

"I'm serious. I should have thanked you before."

"Gourmet dinner after a week in Thailand? I'm not all that put out by it." A big lie, and they both knew it.

"I'm sorry about earlier," she said. "About freaking out about the dress."

"Not a big deal."

Tension hung thick in the air between them. She just felt... restless and needy. The kiss, the one they'd shared in his office, still burning her lips.

It was only supposed to be the one time. Just once. In Chiang Mai, not here.

"I really liked my…salmon," she said. It was lame but she didn't want to leave Zack yet. Didn't want to get into her cold, empty bed and slowly die, crushed beneath the weight of her sexual frustration.

A dramatic interpretation of what would actually happen, but she felt dramatic.

"You didn't have salmon."

"I didn't?" she asked.

"No. You had…I think you had chicken."

"Oh."

The only thing she could remember about dinner was trying not to melt every time Zack looked in her direction.

"So…I guess I'll see you tomorrow, then," she said slowly, reaching for the door handle.

"Wait." She froze. "I have a nice vintage wine at my house. I've been meaning to have you come and try it," he said.

She moved away from the car door, letting her back rest against the seat again. "Really?"

"Yes. Do you want… You could come over and have some?"

Zack could have cut his own tongue out. As pickup lines went, it was a clumsy one. He shouldn't be handing her pickup lines at all, clumsy or otherwise. They'd committed to only sleeping together one time, and the fact that he was so turned on his entire body had broken out into a cold sweat shouldn't change that. Once should have been enough. But it wasn't.

He watched her face, watched her eyes get round, her mouth dropping open. As if she'd just realized what the hidden question was.

It was hidden. If she said no, they could both pretend that it wasn't another night he was after. They could brush it under the rug. Simple.

"Now?" she asked.

He nodded once.

"I don't…" She looked at her apartment building for a moment, her hands folded in her lap, toying with the fabric of her skirt, twisting it. "I'd love some wine."

"Good."

He turned the key over and the engine purred as he pulled away from the curb and headed out of the city, toward the waterfront.

Zack's house was a marvel, grand and pristine, massive windows with views the bay and the Golden Gate Bridge. It was a physical testament to the wealth he'd accumulated since he started his business. How much he had done. How far he had come on his own.

Every time she came over, she stopped and looked at the gorgeous, stained-glass skylight in the entryway. Not this time, though. This time, she didn't have energy to focus on anything beyond Zack and the desire that was roaring through her body. Desire that was finally going to be satisfied tonight.

A week without him, without him inside of her body, had been far too long of a wait.

He closed the door behind them and stood still, poised near the door. He looked like a predator lying in wait. The thought of it, of being the object of his desire, heated her from the inside out.

When he moved, it was quick and fluid. He wrapped his arms around her, kissing her deep and long, his tongue stroking against hers, the evidence of his arousal hard and tempting against her body.

"You're sure?"

"No," she said.

"I'm not, either."

"But I want to."

"Me, too. You know where the bedroom is," he said.

"I do. But I haven't spent that much time in it."

"You'll be lucky if I let you out of it tonight," he said, his voice a low growl. Feral and uncontrolled. It sent a shiver of pure need all the way down to her toes.

It was crazy. Stupid crazy and not at all what they'd agreed to.

Just one more time. One more night.

"I don't mind."

She walked ahead of him, to the winding staircase that led up to his room. She heard him following behind her as she walked up the stairs, and she knew the action was making her dress ride up, made it hug the curve of her bottom, and barely covered it at all.

He grabbed her arm and turned her to him. He was on the step below her, which, with her heels, made them close to the same height. He put his hand on her lower back and pressed her to him, kissing her again, his mouth hot and hungry on hers.

She cupped his face, his stubble rough on her fingertips, a potent, sexy reminder of his masculinity. He reached up and took her hands, lacing his fingers through hers and backing her against the wall as he stepped up onto the stair she was on.

He pressed his body against hers, hard and long, perfectly muscular. She started working the buttons on his shirt, popping a few of them off in her haste to get him undressed. He helped with the sleeve cuffs and tossed the shirt down to the bottom of the stairs.

"Oh, yes," she breathed, running her hands over his bare chest, the crisp hair tickling her palms. "You're so hot."

He chuckled. "I could say the same." He gripped the zipper tab of her dress and tugged it down, letting her dress fall off her body. She hardly had time to think about it, to worry about how she looked to him.

She kicked the dress down to the next stair, still wearing her heels, a strapless bra and a pair of underwear that may as well not exist for all that they covered.

But tonight, she really did feel sexy. She didn't feel the need to cover herself, to hide anything. And she really didn't want him hiding anything. She made quick work of his slacks, pushing them down his muscular thighs, her body heating when she looked at him, dressed in nothing more than a pair of tight black boxer briefs that revealed the outline of his erection in tantalizing detail.

She put her hand on him, sliding her palm over his cloth-covered length, reveling in his harsh, indrawn breath.

"Do you know how many times I thought of you?" she asked, the question requiring a whole lot of boldness she hadn't realized she possessed. "Of touching you. Having my way with you. You've kept me up a lot of nights, Zack. Imagining what it would be like if you kissed me."

"You thought of me?" he asked, his words rough.

"I did."

He didn't have to ask why she hadn't acted on it. Because what would the point have been? They didn't want the same things. He wanted a loveless marriage, no family. She wanted more. There was still no point to this. No point beyond trying to satisfy the sexual hunger that was burning between them.

And the burning hope in her that she couldn't quite snuff out that wondered if he could change his mind…

"Do you know what *I've* thought about?" She pushed his underwear down and he kicked them down with the growing pile of clothes on the staircase. She started to kneel down in front of him and he forked his fingers through her hair, halting her for a moment, the sting from the tug on her hair sending a sharp sensation of pleasure through her.

"Careful," he said. "I'm close."

"We have all night. I'm not worried. And I've had a lot of fantasies about this. You wouldn't deny me a little fantasy fulfillment, would you?" She leaned forward and flicked the tip of her tongue over the head of his shaft. He sucked in a breath, his hold on her hair tightening again.

She took him into her mouth, loving the taste of him, the

power she felt. That she could make his thigh muscles shake, make his hands tremble. He kept one hand in her hair, one on the staircase railing, bracing himself as she continued to explore him.

"Clara…I need…not like this."

She raised her head, her heart nearly stopping when she saw his face. He had sweat beads on his forehead, the tendons in his neck standing out. He looked like a man who'd been tortured with pleasure.

And she'd been the one doing the torturing.

"I don't mind."

"I do. I need to have all of you."

"Maybe we can make it the rest of the way up the stairs?"

"If we hurry," he growled.

So she did, walking in front of him, knowing her thong and high heels were making a provocative visual for him. The feeling of confidence she felt, the absolute certainty that he enjoyed looking at her, that, for now at least, she was the woman he desired, was amazing. New.

His bedroom door was open, and she walked inside and sat down on the bed, waiting for him. He stood in the doorway, his eyes hot on her. The lights were off, moonlight filtering through the window. The darkness felt like a cover, made her feel more confident.

"Take everything off," he bit out.

She undid the front clasp on her bra and was gratified by the sharp rise and fall of his chest as she revealed her breasts to him. She stood and tugged her underwear down her legs, leaving the high heels for last.

"Want to help with these?" she asked, sitting again, holding her foot out.

He smiled and walked over to the bed and knelt in front of her, putting his hands on the curve of her knees, sliding them down her calf, he bent his head down and kissed her ankle as he took one of her shoes off and dropped it onto the carpet.

He did the same with the other one, slow, erotic movements making her shiver all over. And when he leaned in and pressed his mouth between her thighs she nearly came apart with the first stroke of his tongue.

"I'll confess, I didn't think about this very much until recently," he said. "But I haven't stopped thinking about it since last week. Every night, I dream of you," he said, his voice rough as he continued to pleasure her with his hands.

"Me, too," she said, panting, her body on the brink of climax, so close she felt it all through her, tension drawing all of her muscles tight.

Zack stood up, his smile wicked as he looked at her. He leaned over and took a condom from the nightstand. He tore the packet open and rolled a condom onto his length before joining her on the bed.

He put his hands on her thigh and pulled her over him so that her legs were bracketing his and his erection poised at the entranced to her body. Her eyes locked with his, she lowered herself onto him, a low moan climbing in her throat as he filled her.

She gripped his shoulders, enjoying the feeling. Enjoying the moment of being joined with him completely.

She moved slowly at first, trying to find the right rhythm, her confidence increasing as his grip on her hips tightened, as she started to move closer to the edge of climax.

She was saying things, words, about how good it felt, how much she cared about him, but she wasn't sure what she was saying exactly. She didn't care. She couldn't think, she could only feel.

Could only hold on to Zack as her orgasm pushed her over the edge and into an abyss of light and feeling, where there was nothing, no one, except for her and Zack. There was no past, and there was no future. There was only the two of them.

In that world, in that moment, everything could work. Everything was perfect.

The ascent back to reality was slow and fuzzy, and she almost regretted it when it happened. But even reality, his skin hot and sweaty beneath her cheek, his chest hair a little bit scratchy, was pretty near perfect.

She didn't have the assurance of a future. But for now she had Zack. And she would take him. She felt tears sting her eyes and she squeezed them shut, trying to hold them at bay.

She had him tonight. And it would be perfect. She wouldn't ruin it by crying.

"I'll go and take care of things," he said.

Clara sat up and let Zack get out of bed and go into the bathroom. He came back a couple of moments later and slid back into bed. She looked at his profile. Strong, set. So handsome, so special to her. For so long she'd imagined that she knew everything about Zack. Now she found out there was a huge piece missing.

"Zack…" She knew she probably shouldn't say what was on her mind, but they were naked and in bed together. If they couldn't be honest now, when could you be honest with anyone? "What happened?"

"I told you," he said, his voice stilted. He knew what she meant. No need to clarify.

"Sort of."

"You want to hear more?"

"I want to know what happened. Have you ever told anyone?"

There was a long pause, Zack shifted next to her. "I don't talk about this, Clara. Not ever. Not with anyone."

She put her hand on his shoulder. "And I don't let men see me naked. Not ever. But I let you. So tell me."

He paused and she thought, for a moment, he wasn't going to say anything. "We named him Jake. He lived for forty-eight hours. No one at the hospital thought, even for a moment, that he had a chance. But I did." Silence hung between them, heavy and oppressive. She didn't interrupt it.

Zack breathed in deeply. Faintly, in the dim light filtering in through the windows, she could see a single track of moisture shining on his cheek. "I was wrong. There was no miracle. No beating the odds. I'd thought…I was sure he'd have to be okay. I'd changed all my plans, in my head, my whole future was different. And then it was back to being the same, except it wasn't. It never would be again. And my parents…I think they were relieved. They'd been so angry that I was throwing my future away. I think they were relieved when my son died, Clara."

"Zack…" She started to offer something. Comfort maybe. But she wasn't sure if there was any comfort for that kind of pain. She wasn't sure if it was a wound that could heal.

"Sarah didn't want to talk to me again and I don't blame her. Every time I looked at her I just remembered. I think it was the same for her. So I just left. I couldn't stay there." He paused for a moment. "He would be fourteen now. Just two years younger than I was when he was born. Maybe he'd play football, like I did. He'd be close to the age where I would be teaching him how to drive and telling him about girls. I think about it still. About him. I didn't understand how one person could, even for such a short amount of time, became my whole world. For those two days, I breathed for him. And when he stopped, I almost forgot why I was still trying. Rock bottom is…something else. There's a lot of alcohol there, let me tell you. But not even that fixes it. It just makes you pathetic. But I got hired on at a coffeehouse here, even though I was an aimless wreck. Once I had that job, I had a new focus. I got my GED, I found out I loved coffee. I worked my way up in the company, and I bought it from my boss when he retired. I think that's the beginning of what you, and everyone else, already knew."

She wiped at a tear that was sliding down her cheek, her heart aching, her entire body aching, real, physical pain tearing at her. She turned to the side and rested her head on his shoulder, her hand on his face. He wrapped an arm around her and held her to him.

"But that changed me," he said, his voice strong. "It made me grow up. Made me move forward. It taught me to value control. Responsibility and planning. It's why I'm here. Why I'm so successful and not some burned out, ex-college football star has-been."

He believed it. She could tell he did. But the road to success had been hard. It had hurt. And along with conviction, she heard the pain in his voice, too.

"Arrogance, impulsiveness. That leads to disaster. It creates grief. Needless grief," he said.

She wished she could tell him how much she loved him, but she knew that it was the last thing he wanted to hear. So she just held him, and let him hold her. Let him offer her comfort, so that he didn't realize she sas offering him everything.

"So," she said after a while, "do you want me to go?"

"I want you here," he said. "Spend the night with me."

"Sure, Zack," she said, breathing a sigh of relief.

He tightened his hold on her and neither of them spoke.

Tonight they were together. She hoped she didn't fall asleep. She didn't want to miss a moment.

Clara rolled over and stretched in the morning, her eyes opening to a familiar sight. Zack's room. Though, it wasn't familiar at all to wake up in Zack's room. Even less familiar to wake up in Zack's room after making love with him all night.

A slow smile spread across her lips, followed by a pang of sadness when she remembered their conversation. When she remembered his story about his son.

She looked at Zack, his eyes still closed. She wished, more than anything, that she could take his pain from him. His grief was something she couldn't begin to understand, the kind of cut it would leave so deep she wasn't sure if it could heal. She knew it couldn't, not really. It would never disappear. He'd said himself it had changed him. Had changed the course of his entire life.

His eyes opened and he smiled. "Good morning."

"Morning."

"So, I guess we should get ready to go to work," she said.

"You think so?"

"Well, it's almost time."

"True," he said, wrapping his arms around her and rolling her beneath him. "But you might be able to go in late today. I know the boss."

"So do I," she said, wiggling underneath him. "He's kind of intense about people being at work on time. A bit anal, even."

His eyebrows shot up. "Really? Well, I have a feeling that he'll look the other way today."

CHAPTER ELEVEN

"I got an invitation in the mail. For me and my wife." Zack walked into her office and tossed a cream-colored envelope onto her desk.

She grimaced. "Don't people read the news?"

"Well, I called the charity putting the event on and I explained to them what happened. Of course, they would still like me to come and buy two dinners at four hundred dollars a plate, so my new fiancée is more than welcome."

"Well, hopefully the deal will be finalized by then," she said, looking down at the spiteful ring. "And I'll be off the hook."

"Good for both of us, but even if you are, you still might like to come. As my friend."

"Right." Yes. They were friends. First and foremost, before the sex stuff. At least in his mind. She was his friend, and he was hers, her very best friend. But he was so much more to her than that.

"It's for charity. Something I've been planning on for a while, though, thanks to everything that's been happening the timing slipped my mind. And I can't take anyone else until all of this is finished."

She noticed he didn't say that he didn't want to take anyone else. Only that he *couldn't*.

Being a bit oversensitive, aren't we? Maybe. Or maybe not.

"When is it?" she asked.

"Thursday. How are things going today? Have you come up with anything to go with the white tea from Amudee's? I'm thinking of a gourmet tea cake. Wondering if we could start making our own preserves. That has definite mass-market appeal. Are you closer to reaching a deal?"

"It looks that way. I'm optimistic. He's a hard man to read but he seems reasonably satisfied that Roasted is run to the sort of standards he likes to see."

"Good." She fought the urge to reach out and touch him, to forge a connection. That would just come across as needy and she didn't want to seem needy. Even if she did feel a little bit needy.

"What's this?" He took a sheet of paper off her desk and she cringed.

"Uh…a list I was making. For my bakery."

Her bakery. The dream that wasn't really her dream. She loved her job at Roasted, but if things didn't work out with Zack she was going to need her escape more than ever.

"Oh. Right." He set it back down. "Working on it during business hours?"

"Or during lunch. Or maybe during business hours, but you know I put my time in," she said stiffly.

"I'm not going to give you special treatment just because we slept together."

His words hung in the air, too loud in the small office, and far too harsh for her already-tender insides.

"Of course not. That would be ridiculous," she said, picking up a stack of unidentified papers from her desk and walking over to the industrial stapler. She punched it down in three places and hoped that they were at least documents that went together. "Why would you do that?"

The truth was, he had always treated her like she was special, and having him say something like that made her feel demoted.

"You know what I meant."

"I guess I don't."

He rounded her desk and cupped her chin with his thumb and forefinger, tilting her face up so that she had to meet his eyes. He leaned in and pressed a light kiss to her lips. He didn't apologize. He didn't say anything. Even so, all of the fight drained out of her.

"I'm going to be busy tonight," he said.

That was probably for the best. Distance was probably a really, really good idea. Because she desperately didn't want it, and that meant she very likely needed it. Because last night was proof neither of them were thinking clearly where the other was concerned.

They'd done it again. And there could be no more sex. None. It was too dangerous for her, too stupid. Too little. It was physical only for Zack, and she wanted more. She needed more.

"All right. Me, too, actually." She'd find something to be busy with. She would. Except, the only people she ever hung out with, besides Zack, were the people she worked with. And it would be hard hanging out with them now when she was lying to them.

Maybe she'd work on some of the tea pastries she'd been thinking of.

"See you tomorrow, then. At work," she said, feeling very accomplished that she was managing to seem cool and aloof about the whole thing.

"See you then," he said, nodding and walking out of the room.

When he left she blew out a breath. The affair, fling, whatever, was supposed to ease some of the tension between them. But if anything, it seemed more intense than it had before.

She looked back down at her list. The items she was choosing for if she opened her own bakery. For if she had to leave Roasted so she could get away from Zack.

She was starting to hope she wouldn't need it.

* * *

Clara put a pan of twelve cupcakes into the oven and closed the rack with her foot. They were pineapple cupcakes which she was intending to pair light, whipped frosting and candied mango on top. They might very well taste like a Caribbean vacation gone wrong, but she was feeling risky.

She was also feeling restless and sad.

It was Monday and normally Zack would come over for a football game neither of them would pay attention to. He would bring takeout, she would provide all things baked and sinful.

She missed that. And she wondered if the status quo hadn't been so bad after all.

Right. Because you were such a sopping, sad mess you made his wedding cake even though it destroyed you to do it. And you've barely had a date since you met the man.

All true.

She growled into the empty room and turned her focus to whipping her frosting. That, at least, was physically satisfying. She dipped an unused spoon into the mix and tasted it. She hit Play on her kitchen stereo system and turned to the pantry humming while she rummaged for a can of pineapple juice.

She heard a sharp knock over the sound of her acoustic-guitar music and she stopped rummaging. She frowned and walked over to the door, peeking through the security window at the top.

Zack was there, looking back down the hall, like he was thinking about leaving. He had a brown paper bag in his hand, his work clothes long discarded in favor of a gray T-shirt and a pair of dark fitted jeans.

Her heart crumpled. Seeing him was almost painful. A reminder of how close they'd been physically. How far apart they were emotionally.

She braced herself for the full impact of his presence and opened the door.

He turned to her, smiling. "Hi."

"I thought you were busy."

That wasn't what she'd intended to lead with, but it had sort of slipped out. Things just seemed to be "happening" around him without her permission a lot lately.

"It turns out it could wait." He slipped past her and stepped into her apartment, depositing his bags of food on the counter and pulling white boxes from it without even asking for permission.

"Why are you...here?"

"It's Monday."

"And?"

"Football." He shrugged as he opened the first container, revealing her favorite, Sweet and Sour Pork. Like nothing had changed.

It was comforting in a very bizarre way. And a tiny bit upsetting, too. She wasn't sure which emotion she was going to let win. She'd give it until after dinner to decide.

"Right." She turned and made her way around the counter, taking plates and utensils out of the cupboard and drawers. Zack dished up the food and neither of them spoke as they took their first few bites.

"You could turn the game on," she said.

Zack walked across the open room and took her remote off the couch, aiming it at the TV and putting it on the local channel broadcasting the event.

"Who's playing?" she asked.

"No idea." He tossed the remote back where it had been and crossed back into the kitchen, taking a seat at one of the bar stools that lined the counter.

"Important enough to come over for, though," she said, looking down at her plate and stabbing a piece of meat with her fork.

"I missed you," he said, his voice rough.

"What...me? You missed me?"

"Yes. We always get together Monday. And I found myself wandering around my house. Thought about turning the game on. But you're right. I don't really care about football, probably a side effect of coming down from the high of being the world's most entitled high-school jock. I didn't really want to watch sports, but I did want to eat dinner. With you."

"I missed you, too, Zack," she said.

His smile. His presence. His arms around her while she slept. But she wasn't allowed to miss that last part. That had to be done. Over.

As for their friendship…she didn't know what she would do without him. But she didn't know if she would ever get over him if he was always around, either.

But she had to be with him, at least until she left Roasted. She would worry about the rest then.

"Making cupcakes?" he asked.

"They're going to be very tropical." She took a bite of fried rice and stood up, walking back into the kitchen to grab the can of pineapple juice she'd been after when he came to the door. "Not sure about them yet."

She punched the top of the tin and drizzled some juice into her frosting, stirring it in slowly.

Zack leaned over the counter and stuck his finger in the bowl. She smacked the top of his hand. "I will frost your butt, Parsons. Keep your fingers out of my mixing bowl."

He held his finger near his lips and gave her a roguish smile. "Is that what the kids are calling it these days?" He licked his frosting-covered finger and her internal muscles clenched in response.

She snorted. "No. I don't know. You know what I meant."

"Yeah."

Her heart fluttered, but it was a manageable amount. "Behave."

He arched one eyebrow. "Can't make any promises."

She rolled her eyes and sat back down to her dinner.

"Heard anymore about the store in Japan?" she asked.

That got Zack rolling on statistics and sales figures and all sorts of things he found endlessly fascinating. She liked that about him. Liked that his job sometimes gave him a glint in his eye that made him look like an enthusiastic kid.

Then he launched into a story about the street performers that had been out in front of the restaurant tonight when he'd picked the food up, which reminded her of the time they'd been all but accosted by a street mime on their way to lunch one day.

She really had missed this. Sharing. Laughing. She loved that he knew her, that he knew all of her best stories, her most embarrassing moments.

The timer pinged for the cupcakes and she got up to check them.

"Finished?" he asked.

"Yes," she said, pulling them out with an oven mitt and setting them on the counter. "But hot." She nearly laughed at his pained expression. "I have some cool ones, though. I know you don't bake, but if you want to frost them you're welcome to."

"I think I can handle that."

"Bear in mind they are highly experimental."

He smiled. "Sounds exciting, anyway."

"Or a potential disaster of epic proportions, but we won't know until we taste them."

She loaded up a frosting bag and handed it to Zack while she set her own up and got started on leaving little stars all over the surface of one of the cupcakes.

Zack sneaked his hand past her and dipped it into the bowl again. She grabbed the spatula and smacked the back of his hand, leaving a streak of white frosting behind. "I said stop!" she said, laughing as he examined the mess she'd left behind.

"But the frosting is the best part."

"You didn't try the cake yet."

He shrugged and raised his hand to his lips cleaning off the frosting she'd left behind, then he moved his finger near her mouth. "Taste?" he asked.

In that moment, it felt like her vision tunneled, reduced to nothing but Zack. The game, the sounds of the whistle, the crowd, the announcers, faded, blood roaring in her ears.

It was innocent. Or it should have been. She tried to tell herself that for about ten seconds. Because there was no female friend on earth, no matter how close, who would have offered what Zack was at the moment.

So it wasn't innocent. She looked up, her eyes clashing with his.

They were dark, intense. Aroused. The air between them seemed to thicken, the only sound her breath. Too loud. Too obvious.

It wasn't innocent at all.

She'd promised herself it wouldn't happen again. That their last night together had been exactly that: their last night together.

It won't happen again. I just need a taste.

She leaned in and slid her tongue along the line of his finger and her entire body tightened when a rough groan escaped his lips. The salt of his skin gave bite to the super-sweet frosting. If her cupcakes were a bust maybe she could just spread it all over Zack…

No.

She pulled back sharply, shaking her head. "Sorry. Just… sorry, I…"

He wrapped his arm around her waist and kissed her, deep and long, his tongue still coated in icing. When he released her, she felt dazed in the very best way.

She licked her lips. "You taste like a pineapple," she said, her breath erratic, her heart pounding.

"Is that a good thing?" His voice sounded strained, like each word was an effort.

"I might have to…test it out again."

He smiled and her stomach curled in on itself. "I'm more than willing to aid you in the testing."

He dipped his head and she closed the distance between them, sliding her tongue over his bottom lip, reveling in the rough groan that rumbled in his chest.

He dipped his fingers back in the bowl and tugged at the hem of her shirt, drawing it over her head. "I feel at a disadvantage," he said, sliding his fingers over her stomach. "Because you got a chance to taste me this way, and I haven't gotten to do the same."

He bent down and slid his tongue over her stomach. She shivered, gripping his shoulders, knowing they were going too far, not sure if she wanted to stop.

He stood and reached behind her, unhooking her bra with one hand. "You're better at that than I am," she said, her voice shaking.

"Good. That's kind of the idea. I'd hate to think you'd be better off doing this for yourself." He cupped her breast and slid his thumb off her nipple, leaving a faint dusting of icing covering her there. He bent his head and circled the tightened bud with his tongue before drawing it into his mouth.

She forked her fingers through his hair, holding his head to her as he continued to lavish attention on her breast.

"Oh, no...I could not do this by myself," she breathed.

He lifted his head and captured her lips, sweetness clinging to his tongue, his grip tight on her hips as he tugged her body against his. "You're beautiful," he said, abandoning her mouth to skim kisses down her neck, across her collarbone.

"You make me believe it."

He raised his head, his expression serious. "You should never doubt it, not for a moment. You make me lose control."

The words hung between them, an admission that held power. Because she knew Zack, and she knew what he prized. His control. Above everything. She knew why now, too. She even understood it. And he was saying that her beauty, her body, took it from him.

"Me?" she asked.

"You," he repeated, his voice hard. "Everything about you." He moved his palm over her breast and she shuddered. "Now that I'm allowing myself to look…I can't stop myself. I can't stop at just looking, I have to touch you, then I have to taste you. And it's still not enough."

Zack's heart raged out of control. It was more than just arousal. His chest burned, the need going so much deeper than sex. It was pleasure and pain, heaven and hell. But he couldn't turn away from any of it. He didn't want to.

This wasn't what was supposed to happen tonight. He'd missed Clara, Clara his friend. The companionship she provided, the safety. She was the one person he ever let his guard down with. The one person he laughed with. Relaxed with.

It wasn't supposed to turn into this. But his desire for her was like a storm, devastating everything in its path. Devastating his control.

And he'd admitted it to her. Because what else could he do? She'd brought him to his knees.

"It's a nice apartment," he said, trying to lighten the moment, to bring himself back to earth. "I bet the bedrooms are really nice."

She snorted a laugh and buried her face in his neck. "You've been in my bedroom."

He sifted her hair through his fingers. "I've never slept in your bed."

"Do you want to?" She posed the question as though she was asking if he wanted something purely innocent.

"After we get some other business taken care of."

"I'm in complete agreement with that."

He swung her up into his arms and she squeaked, looping her arms around his neck and laughing as he dashed to her bedroom.

Zack set Clara down when they got inside her room. A room he'd been in more times than he could count. But never like this. She kissed him, her mouth hungry, pulled his shirt off him in one swift motion. Trading piece of clothing for piece of clothing until they were both naked, limbs entwined, her full breasts pressed against his chest.

It was almost enough for a while, to simply lay on the bed with her, moving his hands over her bare curves, kissing her. Doing nothing more than kissing.

It was almost enough, but not quite.

He swore sharply. "I don't have anything. I didn't plan this."

"It's okay," she said, wrapping her hand around his length, squeezing him. He groaned, her soft flesh against his almost making up for the fact that he couldn't be inside her. Almost.

He put his hand between her thighs and drew his fingers over her clitoris, then repeated the motion.

She gasped and arched against him, tightening her hold on his arms, fingernails digging into his skin. "Oh, Zack," she breathed, his name on her lips like balm to his soul.

Everything after that was lost in a frenzy of movement, sighs and graphic words that he'd never heard come from Clara's mouth before. But it was only more exciting, because it was her. Because he knew that he was able to do that to her, to make her say things, feel things no other man ever had.

They reached the peak together, his body shaking down to his bones as he found his release.

He held her soft body against his afterward, a sort of strange contentedness spreading through him that he'd never felt before.

"You're beautiful, you know?" he asked, pushing her hair to one side and kissing her neck.

She turned to look at him, rolling to her side, making the curve of her hip rounder, her waist smaller. And her breasts…

"You keep saying that."

"So that you can't doubt it."

"I'm starting to believe you, actually," she said, a smile curving her lips. She reached out and put her finger on his biceps, tracing a long line up to his shoulder. "You're not so bad yourself."

"I'm flattered." He leaned forward and kissed her nose, the contentedness morphing into something else. Something that felt light and...happy.

He wrapped his arms more tightly around her and rolled onto his back. She planted her palms on his chest, her body half on his.

"Hi," she said, smiling.

"I just want you to know that you're not second to anyone," he said, cupping her cheek. "There's no other woman on earth I would rather be with."

Her brown eyes glistened. "You really are good for my ego."

"I'm glad. Someone has to be."

He wanted to say something. Something bigger than he should, than he could. He just wanted more. In that moment, with her body, so soft and bare and perfect, pressed against his, with her smiling at him like he could solve all of the world's problems, he wanted to offer her the world. He wanted more than temporary, more than distant for the first time in his memory.

She rested her head on his chest, her fingertips moving lightly over his skin until her breathing deepened and her eyes fluttered closed.

It wasn't until she was asleep that panic slammed into him. The full enormity of what had happened. He'd lost control. More than that, he'd been letting go of it, inch by inch, with Clara for the past seven years.

With everyone else he was guarded. He never dropped his defenses. He never talked about his past.

He'd cried in front of her. He had allowed real, raw weakness and emotion to escape in her presence when he never even let himself give in like that in private. She was under his skin. So much so she felt like she was a part of him.

A necessary part.

What if he lost her? No, it wasn't even a matter of if, it was when.

The terror that thought evoked, the absolute, gut-wrenching horror was a sobering as a punch to the jaw. He was playing a game he had no business playing, flirting with things he shouldn't be. Tempting feelings he couldn't risk having.

He slid out of her hold and she stirred briefly, stretching, arching her back. His mouth dried. He shook his head and bent to collect his clothes, dressing and walking out of her bedroom, closing the door quietly behind him, ignoring the continual stab of pain in his chest.

He paused in her living room for a moment, the weight of the familiarity of his surroundings crushing him, a feeling of claustrophobia overtaking him.

He had to leave. He had to think. He had to find his control.

He walked out her front door, closing it behind him and making sure everything was locked so that she would be safe. He walked out into the cold night, sucking in a deep breath and blaming the cold for the pain that came with it.

"Where were you this morning? When did you leave?" Clara whispered the words when she went into Zack's office in the early afternoon. He'd been out of the office all morning, and he had been very noticeably not at her apartment before that.

"I had some things to do," he said, his voice flat. "Could you bring me a coffee?" His phone rang and he picked it up. She stomped out of the room and picked up the freshly brewed pot that was sitting in the main area of the office. She poured a half a cup and dumped powdered creamer in, no sugar, and stirred it halfheartedly with one of the little wooden sticks that was on the coffee station.

There were still little lumps of powder floating on the top.

She went back into his office and plunked it onto his desk, letting some of it slosh over the side. He didn't flick her or the coffee a glance as he continued his phone call. He picked it up and took a sip then grimaced and set it back down, shooting her an evil look. She responded with a wide, saccharine smile.

"I'll call you back," he said into the phone, hanging up. "Do you have something on your mind?"

"Yes. Where were you this morning, and do not give me another half-assed answer."

"Clara, there's a way I conduct physical relationships. I don't always stay for the whole night."

She felt like he'd slapped her. Like she was just the same as every other physical relationship he had. But she wasn't. She knew she wasn't.

Anger made her scalp feel prickly. "Don't give me that. Don't even try. I made you shake last night. Made you lose control." Boldness came from anger, and she could't regret it.

His eyes glittered and he looked like he might pounce on her. But he didn't. "I just went home, so that I could get a good night's sleep. I have to go over some legalese in the contract I'm having drawn up for the deal with Amudee. That's all."

That wasn't all. She knew it wasn't all. But she didn't know what the rest of it was, either, so that didn't help.

"And that looks like it's going to go through?" she asked, looking down at the ring again, the ring she was starting to hate, willing to let the subject drop, for now.

"Looks like, but nothing is finalized. So we're still in this until the ink is dry."

She nodded. "I know."

It was all about the contract to Zack. Last night…she could have sworn that last night something had changed. There had been more in their lovemaking. There had been fun. Their friendship had been in it.

It had been special.

Well, today things felt different. It just wasn't the sort of different she'd been hoping for.

"I'll be down in the kitchen," she said, eager to get away.

It was going to take a whole lot of cupcakes to make this day feel okay.

The next few days Zack really did manage to be busy and stay busy. He didn't stop by her apartment late at night, or any time of day. Her head hurt and her bed felt empty. Which was silly, since her bed had been empty of anyone other than her for twenty-five years.

It was just the past couple weeks she'd had Zack sometimes. And she found she really liked it, and it wasn't just because of the orgasms. It was just listening to him breathe. Feeling his body heat so close to hers. Just being with him, finally, finally able to express how much she wanted him. To not have to hold such a huge part of herself back from him anymore.

She loved the way he made her feel about herself. That he wanted her in a sexy red dress, or yoga pants, or nothing. That he made her feel beautiful. That he made her see things in herself she hadn't seen before.

And if she told him that he'd undoubtedly run away screaming.

Tonight, the contracts remained unsigned and that meant they still had plans to go to the big charity event. Something to do with a children's hospital. She wondered if that was by design. If it would bother him. Make him think of his son.

Her heart hurt every time she thought of Zack's past. Of what that false front of his was created to hide. To hide what he'd been through, who he really was. He had perfected a persona, controlled, light, charming, and even she had bought into it. Not even *she* had seen everything.

But she was starting to.

Tonight was going to feel more like a real date. A public event with just the two of them, not with Mr. Amudee sitting by, watching their performance as a couple. She was dressing up in a dress she'd selected this time. Something between her usual fare and that screaming, sex-on-a-hanger number Zack had picked out for her.

It was a full-length gown with a mermaid-style skirt that conformed to her body before flaring out around her knees. It swished when she walked, and a halter-top neckline showed her cleavage. And she felt sexy in it. She felt like a woman who was ready to conquer the world. One who could outshine other women, at least for the man she was with. And that was what mattered, anyway.

She heard a knock on her door and she tried to shove her feet into stilettos, while standing, and fastening dangly diamond earrings. "Coming!"

She opened the door and all the air rushed out of her body. Zack was a wearing a suit, black jacket, crisp white shirt and a perfectly straight black tie. He was the epitome of gorgeous. He always was, half dressed, all dressed or completely naked. But there was something about a man in a suit...

It sort of reminded her of his wedding. The wedding that wasn't.

"You look...you look great," she said.

"So do you. I brought you something," he said.

There was something strange about his tone, something formal and distant. It matched his clothing. Cool, well-tailored, nothing out of place. And yet, that in and of itself felt out of place. Zack wasn't formal with her. Why should he be? They'd known each other for years. They had slept together for heaven's sake.

She held her hand out and smiled, trying to make him smile. It didn't work.

He took a flat, black box from his jacket and opened it.

"Oh, my...Zack this is...it must have cost..." None of her words would gel into a complete sentence, everything jumbling and stalling half thought through.

It was a necklace, a truly spectacular necklace, not the sort you saw under the display case of just any department store.

Not even the sort of thing you saw at Saks. It was too unique, too extravagant.

She reached out and touched the center stone, a deep green emerald, cut into the shape of a teardrop and surrounded by glittering diamonds.

"I don't think I can accept this."

"Of course you can," he said, his voice still tinged with that unfamiliar distance. "Turn around."

She did, slowly, craning her neck to look at him. He swept her hair to the side and took the necklace from the box, draping it over her, the stone falling between her breasts, the chill making her shiver. He clasped the necklace, his fingers brushing the back of her neck as we worked the tiny clasp.

"This isn't…this isn't a friendships gift," she said, her voice trembling.

That did earn her a short chuckle. "Maybe tonight friendship isn't what I want."

His words made her shiver, the sensual promise in them turning her on. The underlying, darker meaning she couldn't quite grasp making goose bumps break out on her arms. "It really is too much," she said, turning to face him, her nose nearly touching his.

He straightened putting some distance between them. "It's a perfectly fitting gift for a lover. Are you ready?"

"Yes," she said, turning his choice of word over in her head. Yes, she was his lover, in the sense that they'd slept together. But there was something in the way he said it, something that seemed cold, when a lover should be something warm. Something personal.

She touched the necklace, the gems cold beneath her fingertips.

CHAPTER TWELVE

THE charity ball was crowded already when they arrived, a sea of beautiful people dressed in black positioned around the ballroom, chatting and eating the very expensive canapes.

Heads turned when she and Zack walked down the marble staircase and down into the room. Everyone was looking at Zack, because it was impossible not to. She was fully appreciating just how he was viewed in the community now. A man of power and wealth, a man of unsurpassed beauty. If you could call what he possessed beauty. It was too masculine for that, and yet she wasn't sure there was another word for it, either.

Pride flared in her stomach, low and warm. All the women in the room were looking at Zack with undisguised sexual hunger. And Zack was with her. Touching her, his hand low on her back, possessive.

She turned and pressed a kiss to his cheek. He looked at her. "What was that for?"

"Because," she said.

He looked at her for a moment, a strange light in his eyes. "Let's go find our table."

"Okay," she said, trying to ignore the tightening in her throat.

There was a table, for two, with place cards set on each empty plate. Zack held her chair out for her and she sat, her heart slamming against her ribs as she read the name that had been written in calligraphy on her place card.

Hannah Parsons.

With Zack's name tacked on to hers, even. Clara felt dizzy. She looked down at the ring. Hannah's ring. Hannah's seat. Hannah's man. She had to wonder if the necklace had been meant for Hannah, too.

She wrapped her fingers around the card and curled them into a fist, crumpling it and tossing it onto the marble floor.

"What the hell?" Zack asked.

"It had the wrong name on it," she said stiffly.

"Does it matter?"

That hit even harder than seeing the name. "I suppose not." She put her foot over the crumpled paper and squished it beneath the platform of her stiletto.

"You're the one who's here with me." He stretched his hand toward hers, covering it, stroking her wrist. "No one else."

She knew it. And in some ways she knew his words were sincere. But there was also something generic in them. There was something strangely generic to the whole evening and she couldn't quite place what it was or why.

"Of course." She looked into his eyes, tried to find something familiar now. Something of her friend. But she didn't see it. She only saw the man as he presented himself to the world. Aloof, put together, charming. But there was no depth there. No feeling or warmth.

It was frightening.

Dinner was lovely, tiny bits of sculpted beauty made to be admired before being eaten. Of course it was marked up extravagantly, because the whole point of the evening was that the charity received donations.

A woman in a long, flowing dress walked up onto the stage, her air of authority making it obvious that she was the coordinator of the event, and a hushed silence fell over the crowd.

"Thank you all for coming tonight," she said. "And for the

very generous donation of your time and money to the Bay Area Children's Hospital."

She turned and looked toward their table, a smile on her face. "And tonight, we would also like to give special acknowledgment to Mr. Zack Parsons, who has donated enough money to revamp the entire Neo-Natal Intensive Care Unit. Everything in the unit will be state of the art. It will be the best equipped facility in the state of California. There have been major advances in the field of Neo-Natal medicine over the past few years. We're able to offer hope to babies, to families, who wouldn't have had any as little as five years ago. And now, we're able to offer even more. So, thank you, Mr. Parsons."

The room erupted into applause and everyone stood. Except for Zack. Except for her. Her eyes stung, her entire body feeling numb.

Zack lifted his hand and nodded once, his acknowledgment. Her heart broke for him. What a wonderful gift he was giving to so many families. A gift he hadn't been able to give to himself, to his own son.

She wanted to howl at the universe for the unfairness of it all. And yet there was no point. And Zack was there, broken, and probably in pain. She could be there for him. It was all she could do. And she would. Because she was his friend. His lover.

The speaker went on to talk about some more donations and then invited everyone to stay for dancing and an open bar.

After the applause died away, people started to wander around the room, talking and laughing, some people came to talk to Zack. She wanted to tell them to go away. Because she could feel the dark energy, the grief, radiating from him like a physical force. How was everyone else missing it?

She didn't understand how they could miss what was so clear to her.

"Let's go." She put her hand on his, felt his pulse, pounding hard in his wrist. She ran her fingers along his forearm.

She didn't think he would accept loving words, but she could offer him comfort in another way. A way he could accept.

There was no question where things would end up tonight. No fighting it. They both knew it.

He nodded once and stood, she stood, too, and went to him, putting her hand on his back. He wrapped his arm around her waist as they headed out of the ballroom.

Zack's chest felt too full. Everything felt like too much. The whole day. He shouldn't have brought Clara with him tonight. It was one thing to sit in a room full of strangers and have them talk about his contribution to the NICU, but it was another to have someone sitting there, knowing why he'd done it. Someone else thinking of Jake. It was hard enough to be alone in it. Sharing it made it seem more real. It made him feel exposed.

It made him feel like everything, his failures, his pain, was written on him. Something he couldn't hide, or scrub off no matter how many layers of control he tried to conceal it with.

Clara saw him.

When he'd picked her up tonight, he'd fully intended on keeping her at a distance, putting her in her place. A new place. Because he had mistresses, women who were with him for the sole purpose of warming his bed and accompanying him to events.

He wasn't friends with those women. He didn't eat their baked goods, he didn't know that they wore yoga pants to bed when there wasn't a man around. He didn't know that they were insecure about their bodies, or that their favorite band was still that group of long-haired teenage boys that had been so popular in the nineties.

He didn't know anything about them beyond what they looked like naked.

He knew the other stuff about Clara. And he knew the naked stuff. And tonight he'd been determined to focus only on the latter. If he couldn't keep her as only a friend, and he'd proven he wasn't doing a very good job of that, then he would have her as a mistress. Because what had happened at her apartment, the way they'd shared dinner, jokes, then made love, him holding her while she'd slept…he couldn't do that. It was too reckless. To out of his control.

He had to move her into the compartment he could deal with. And she seemed determined to push her way back out.

The expression on her face when she saw the wrong card in her spot had been so sad, stricken, as though someone had slapped her.

And he'd felt it in him. As though her emotion was his. He'd always felt connected to Clara, but this was different. Sharper. Impossible to deny. Beyond his control.

He should have taken her home. Yet he'd still taken her back to his house. Because he had planned on having her tonight, had been obsessed with it all week. If only to prove that he could sleep with her without having his insides flayed. Sex was only sex. It didn't have to be personal, it didn't have to mean anything. It didn't have to be related to the awful, tight feeling in his chest.

She was beautiful tonight, incredible in that form-fitting black dress and the gem, enticing in the valley of her cleavage, drawing his eye, tormenting him.

She was standing by the massive living-room windows, the bay in the background, city lights glittering on the inky surface of the waves. He wanted her. Here and now. A good thing he'd planned for it. It wasn't spur-of-the-moment, it wasn't beyond his control.

He had condoms and everything else he needed. He was in control. He desperately needed the control. He tightened his hand into a fist, steadied it, ignored the tremor that ran through his fingers and skated up his arm, jolting his heart.

Ignoring the strange tenderness he felt when he looked at

her. This wasn't about feeling, not in an emotional sense. This was physical. It was sex.

"Take off your dress," he said.

She reached behind herself and unzipped the gown, letting it fall to the floor. She wasn't wearing a bra, only a small triangle of lace keeping her from being completely bare. That and the necklace, the emerald heavy and glittering between her breasts.

She reached around to remove it, her breasts rising with the action, pink tipped and perfect.

"No," he ground out. "Leave it on." A reminder. A reminder that she was the same as every other woman he'd ever been with. The exchange of gifts, jewelry, that was how it worked. It was invariable, it was safe. It was unchallenging.

She dropped her hands to her sides and he walked closer to her, loving the way the moonlight spilled silver over her pale curves. The way the deep shadows accentuated the dip of her small waist, the round fullness of her hips and breasts.

She was a woman. There was no denying it. And he was starving for her.

But he would wait. He would draw it out. Because he was the master of this game. He was always in charge. He had forgotten that sometimes over the past few weeks, had allowed her inexperience, the nature of their friendship, to change the way he approached it.

Not now.

She's a woman. Only a woman. The same as any other.

No. Not the same. His mind rebelled against that thought immediately. There had never been a more exquisite woman, that much he knew for certain. There had never been a figure, not since Eve, better designed to tempt a man.

She was the epitome of sensual beauty, more seductive simply standing there than any other woman could have been if she'd been trying.

Clara.

Her name flashed through his mind, loud, a reminder.

No. He didn't need it. He wasn't thinking of her. Only of his own need and how she might fulfill it. He would pleasure her, too, as he did all of his lovers. But it wasn't different. It couldn't be different. Not again. Not after that night in her apartment.

"Turn around for me," he said. "Face the window."

She obeyed again. She was like a perfect hourglass, the elegant line of her back enticing. He walked over to her, extending his hand and tracing the dip of her spine. She shivered beneath his touch.

"Do you like that?" he asked.

"I've liked everything you've ever done to me." Her voice, so sweet, a bit vulnerable. Not a temptress.

Clara.

He put his hands on her hips and tugged her back against him, let her feel the hard ridge of his arousal, the blatant, purely sexual evidence of what he wanted from her. Her indrawn breath, the short, sweet sound of pleasure that escaped her lips, let him know that she was tracking with him. Important.

He would never do anything she didn't want.

He put his hand on her stomach, soft, slightly rounded. He liked that about her, too, that she was so feminine, curved everywhere. Absolute perfection.

He cupped her butt with his other hand, her flesh silken beneath his palm. "You're beautiful," he said. She leaned back against him, her head against his chest. Her slid his hand up to palm her breast, teasing her nipples as he continued to stroke her backside.

He gripped the side of her panties and drew them down her legs.

He move his hand back behind her, moving it forward, teasing her slick folds before parting them and sliding his fingers deep inside of her. She gasped, spreading her thighs a bit wider to accommodate him.

The line of her neck was so elegant, irresistible. He bent his head and kissed her there, tasting the salt of her skin, so familiar now, as he slid his free hand up to her breast and squeezed her nipple tightly between his thumb and forefinger. She arched against him, her breathing growing harsher, more shallow.

He had her pleasure in his hands, how he touched her and where, dictating everything she did. Everything she felt. This was like everything else. Every other sexual encounter he'd had as an adult. He was in charge of their pleasure, both of them. He decided when things happened and how.

This thing with Clara hadn't been right from the beginning, because he hadn't managed to put her in her place for their affair. He hadn't separated their friendship from it. That was why he'd shared with her, held her while she slept. That was why he'd started feeling things.

But he knew it now. He knew what he had to do. He could still have her. He could get a handle on everything, and then he could have her. He touched the necklace between her breasts, fingers sliding over the gem. A reminder of exactly what they had between them.

She tried to turn and he held her so she was facing the window, away from him. He reached over and picked up a condom sheathing himself and turning her to the side so that she was standing in front of the couch.

"Hold on to the back of it," he said. She obeyed, bending at the waist, gripping the back of the couch. She looked back at him, her eyes round, questioning. Familiar.

He chose not to focus on her face. He gripped her hips, looked at the curve of her hips, how her body dipped in beautifully, perfectly, at her waist.

He positioned himself at the entrance to her body.

She made a short, low sound that vibrated through her. "Okay?" he asked, his teeth gritted tight, every ounce of control spent on moving slowly, on not thrusting in to her the rest of the way and satisfying the need that was roaring inside of him.

"Yes," she said.

He pushed into her the rest of the way, her body so hot and tight it took every ounce of his willpower to keep from coming the moment he was inside.

"Oh, Zack," she breathed. "Zack."

His name on her lips, her voice, so utterly Clara. So familiar and still so exciting.

Clara. Her name was in his head on his lips, with each and every thrust, with each sweet pulse of her internal muscles around his shaft.

And suddenly there was no denying it. It didn't matter that he couldn't see her face. Her smell, the feel of her skin beneath his fingertips, the way it felt to be in her body, all of it was pure, undeniable Clara Davis.

The woman who baked orange cupcakes and had a pink wreath on the door. The woman knew about his past, about the darkest moments of his life. The woman who smiled at him every morning. Who could always make him smile, no matter what. Who put powdered creamer in his coffee when he made her angry.

The woman who lit him on fire, body and soul.

He couldn't pretend she was someone else, or that it didn't matter who she was. There was no way. No one had ever been like her before, no one ever would be.

He had no control. He had nothing. He was at her mercy. If he'd had to get on his knees and beg her for a kiss tonight he would have done it, because he needed her.

Not just in a purely sexual sense. He needed *her.*

His climax built, hard and fast, the pitch too steep, too unexpected for him to control. He put his hand between her thighs and stroked her, trying to bring her with him. Her body tightened around him, her orgasm hitting hard and fast. When she cried out her pleasure, then he let go.

"Clara," he whispered, resting his forehead on her back as he gave in. As he let the release crash through him, devastating everything in its path.

He released his hold on her hips, his body shaking, spent as though he'd just battled his way through a storm. Sweat made his skin slick all over. His hands were trembling, his breathing sharp and jagged.

He looked at her. At Clara. There were red marks on her hips where his fingers had pressed into her flesh. Where he had lost all control. He brushed his fingers along the part where he'd marked her, his chest tightening, regret forming, a knot he couldn't breathe around.

She turned to look at him, a smile on her lips. She straightened, naked and completely unconcerned about it. Nothing like she'd been at first. Her confidence, the fact that she felt beautiful, shone from her face.

Her beautiful face. Unique. Essential. So damn important.

"I'm sorry," he said.

She blushed, looking away from him. "Didn't I tell you not to apologize to me all the time?"

"What about when I need to?" he asked, moving toward where she was standing, brushing his fingertips over her hips. "I was holding on to you too tightly," he whispered.

She met his eyes and they held. He saw deep, intense emotion there. A connection, affection. Something real. It wasn't part of a facade, or a game. It was the way she always looked at him, whether they were in his office, in her living room or in bed. She was the same woman. She cared for him. She looked at him like he mattered to her.

The realization rocked him, filled him. Every piece and fiber of his being absorbing it. It made it easier to breathe, as though he hadn't truly been drawing in breath for years and now he was again.

For the first time in fourteen years. Since he'd lost his reason for breath, his desire to give any sort of emotion, to give of himself. He felt like he'd found it again. In Clara's eyes.

"I didn't mind," she said.

The moment, the tiny sliver of freedom he felt evaporated, chased away by a biting, clawing panic that was working from his stomach up through his chest. He had felt this way before and it had ended in utter destruction.

He knew what this was. And he knew he couldn't have it. Wouldn't allow himself to have it. Not ever. Not ever again.

He took a step away from her and bent down, picking her dress up from the floor, rubbing his fingers over the sequins. He felt choked, like his throat was closing in on itself, like his chest was too full for his lungs to expand.

He could do it. He could have her still, keep her where she belonged in his life. In his bed.

He had been careless again. He had lost control. He could find it again. He had to.

"Get dressed," he said, handing her the gown.

"What?"

"I'll drive you home."

"What?" she said again.

He didn't look at her face. He couldn't.

"You and I are having an affair, Clara, I made that clear the other day. I don't cuddle up with the women I'm having sex with at night, and I damn sure don't have their toothbrush on my sink. That's just how it works."

"And I think I told you, I am not just one of your mistresses."

"When you're in my bed…or my couch, you are."

"I am your friend," she said, her voice ringing in the room.

"Not when we're here, like this. Now, you're just the woman I'm sleeping with. We aren't going to curl up and watch a chick flick after what just happened."

She jerked back, pulling her dress over her breasts. "I'm going to go get dressed. Send the car. I'm not riding back with you, and I'm not staying, not now so I think the decent thing to do, if you still remember decency, would be to arrange me a ride."

"Clara…"

"We'll talk tomorrow. I can't now."

She turned and walked away, her steps clumsy. She ducked into his downstairs bathroom and closed the door. He heard the click of the lock.

And he didn't blame her. But he had to define the relationship, as much for her benefit as for his. Yes, he had lied. She was different. But she couldn't be. It couldn't happen.

He would fix it. He'd gotten it wrong tonight, by denying the one thing that had been there from the beginning. His feelings. The sex…he would pretend it hadn't happened. Whatever he had to do to fix it, to have her never look at him like that again. As if he was a cold stranger, as if he'd physically hurt her.

It would have to go back to how it was. Because he could live without sex. He wasn't sure he could live without Clara.

It was the longest car ride in the world. No one was on the streets, and it technically took half the time it normally did to get from Zack's place to hers, but it seemed like the longest ever.

Because everything hurt. And she was wearing a really fabulous gown that had already been torn from her body once, during the most intense, emotion-filled sexual encounter they'd ever had. There had been something dark in Zack tonight. A battle. She wasn't stupid. She knew something had changed, she knew, at least she hoped, that he wasn't as horrible as he'd seemed when he'd sent her away.

She bunched up the flaring skirt of her gown when the car stopped and she slid out, letting the dress fan out around her. She gave the driver a halfhearted, awkward wave. He knew her. She'd used his services quite a few times with Zack. Having him be a part of this, the most awful, embarrassing, heart-wrenching moment of her life wasn't so great.

Because it was two in the morning and it was completely obvious what had just happened. That Zack had had sex with her, sex, at its most base, and had her go home rather than have her spend the night in his bed.

She curled her hands into fists and let her nails cut into her palms, tears stinging her eyes. She almost hated him right now. It almost rivaled how much she loved him.

Almost.

If she didn't love him, it wouldn't hurt so bad.

You're my mistress.

Like hell she was. He might be the only man who'd seen her naked, but she was certain, beyond a shadow of a doubt, that she was the only woman who'd ever seen him cry.

CHAPTER THIRTEEN

SHE really hoped everyone wanted cupcakes for lunch. Because there were cupcakes. Nine varieties of them, and someone had to eat them.

She didn't think she could eat and she was *not* sharing them with Zack, which meant they would be going straight into the break room. On the bright side, she'd found a few new varieties that had worked out nicely.

The sea-salt caramel one was her favorite. She just couldn't force down more than two bites at a time. Anything beyond that stuck in her throat and joined the ever-present lump that made her feel like she was perpetually on the edge of tears.

She was just too full of angst to eat anything. She hadn't been able to eat anything since she'd been dropped at the front of her building by Zack's driver.

Zack.

She put her head on the pristine counter of the office kitchen and tried to hold back the sob that was building in her chest.

Something had broken in him last night. It had started after their time together at her place, the night he'd left. And last night it had snapped completely. But she didn't know what it was. She didn't know how to pull him out of it. If she could, or if she even should.

"Clara."

Clara looked up and saw Jess standing in the doorway of the kitchen. "Zack is looking for you."

"Oh," Clara straightened and wiped her eyes. Normally Zack would come and find her himself. Because there was a time when he'd wanted to be with her simply to be with her. Now she wondered if she had any value when she wasn't naked. "I'll be there in a second. Take…" She gestured to the platters of cupcakes. "Take some of these with you. I can't eat them by myself. If Zack comes near them, tell him they have walnuts."

Jess's eye widened. "They all have walnuts?"

"No. But tell him they do. All of them."

Jess gave her a strange look and picked two of the platters up, heading back out the door.

She had no choice now. She had to go face the man himself. And figure out exactly what she was going to say. As long as it didn't involve melting into a heap, she supposed almost anything would do.

"You sent Jess after me?" She looked inside of Zack's office, waiting to be invited in. Silly maybe, since she hadn't knocked on his office door in the seven years since she'd started working at Roasted. But she felt like she needed to now.

"Yes. Come in." His tone was formal, like it had been the night before when he'd given her the necklace. Distance. Divorced from emotion.

That was the strange thing. He'd been aloof the night of the charity, until they'd made love. Then he'd been commanding, all dark intensity and so much emotion it had filled the room. It had filled her. It hadn't been good emotion. It had been raw and painful. Almost more than she could bear.

It had caused the break. That much she knew.

But he was back to his calm and controlled self now, not a trace of last night's fracture in composure anywhere. She almost couldn't believe he was the same man whose hands had trembled after they'd made love.

She almost couldn't believe he was the same man she'd known for seven years. The same man she'd watched movies with, shared dinners with.

But he was. He was both of those men.

He was also the cold man standing before her, and she wasn't sure how all of those facets of himself wove together. And she really wasn't sure where she fit in. If she did at all.

She stepped into the office, watching his face for some sort of reaction. He had that sort of distant, implacable calm he'd had on his wedding day, standing and looking out the window as though nothing mattered to him. As though he had no deeper emotion at all.

She knew differently now. She saw it for what it was now. A facade. But she wasn't certain there was a way through it, unless he wanted her to break through.

"I'm about to sign the final paperwork for the deal with Amudee. I wanted to thank you for your help."

For her help. "Of course."

They were talking like strangers now. They'd never been like strangers, not from the moment she'd met him. They'd had a connection from the first moment he'd walked into the bakery.

Now she couldn't feel anything from him. Now that they'd been so intimate, she felt totally shut off from him.

"Once everything is finalized we can let everyone know that our engagement has been called off," he said.

"Right," she said, clenching her left hand into a fist.

"That's all." He looked back at his computer screen for a moment, then looked back up. "Are you busy tonight?"

Her heart stopped. Did he want sex? Again? After what he'd done last night?

"Um…why?"

"Because I thought I might come over and watch a movie."

His words were so unexpected it took her brain a moment

to digest them, as though she was translating them from a foreign language. "And?"

He shrugged. "Nothing."

He was behaving as if…as if nothing had changed. As if they'd gone back in time a few weeks.

He was pretending, she was certain of it, because he certainly wasn't acting normal, whatever he might think, but she was insulted that he was trying. After what he'd said to her last night. After the way he'd objectified her.

She wanted to yell at him. Maybe even hit him, and she'd never hit anyone in her life. But she wanted a reaction. She didn't want his control.

"Are you going to pretend last night didn't happen?" she asked, her voice low, unsteady.

Zack remained calm, his control, that control he claimed to have lost, the control she witnessed in tatters last night, firmly in place. "I think we both know that's not working out. But you're right. You're my friend, and I didn't treat you like a friend last night."

"An understatement," she spat. "You treated me like your whore."

She saw something, an emotion, faint and brief, flicker in his eyes before being replaced by that maddening calm again. That same sort of dead expression he'd worn when he'd been jilted on his wedding day.

"I apologize," he said. "I wasn't myself."

She curled her hands into fists, her fingernails digging into the tender skin on her palm, the pain the only thing keeping her from exploding. "Do you know what I think, Zack? I think you were yourself. This? This is the lie. This isn't you. It's you being a coward. You can't face whatever it is that happened between us last night and now you're hiding from it."

"It isn't working. That element of our relationship." The only thing that betrayed his tension was the shifting of a muscle in his jaw. "But we've been friends for seven years. That works for us. We need to go back to that."

"Are you…are you crazy?" she asked, the words exploding from her. "We can't go back. I've been naked with you. You've been… We've made love. You can't just go back from that like it never happened. I don't care what we thought, we were wrong. That one night, that one night that's turned into four, it changed everything. You can't just experience something like that with someone and feel nothing."

"I can."

"Do you really think this is nothing? That we're nothing?"

"We're friends, Clara. You mean a lot to me. But it doesn't mean I want to keep sleeping with you. It doesn't mean I want this kind of drama. We need things back like they were so that the business can stay on track…."

"I'm leaving Roasted. You know that."

He tightened his jaw. "I didn't think you would really leave."

"What? Now that we've slept together? You can't have it both ways. Either it changed things or it didn't."

"I care about you," he said, his tone intensifying.

"Not enough." She shook her head, fighting tears. They weren't sad tears. She was too angry for that. That would come later. "I am your sidekick, and that's how you like it. As long as I give you company when you want it, eat dinner with you when you're lonely, bake your wedding cake when you decide it's time to have a cold, emotionless marriage, well then, you care about me. As long as I'm willing to pretend to be your fiancée so you can get your precious business deal. But it's on your terms. And the minute it isn't, when I start having power, that's when you can't handle it."

He only looked at her, his expression neutral.

"I'm done with it, Zack," she said, pulling the ring, the ring that wasn't hers, from her finger. "All of it."

She put the ring on his desk and backed away, her heart thundering, each beat causing it to splinter.

"We have a deal," he bit out.

"You'll figure it out. If that's the only reason you don't want me to go…if that's all that's supposed to keep me here… I can't."

Zack stood, his gray eyes suddenly fierce. "So, you're just going to walk out, throw away our friendship over a meaningless fling?"

"No. It's not the fling, Zack, it's the fact that you think it's meaningless. The fact that I've realized exactly where I rate as far as you're concerned."

"What do you want?" he exploded. "Why is what we have suddenly not good enough for you?"

"Because I realized how little I was accepting. That everything was about you. I'm just willing to take whatever you give me, whether it's a spot in your bed or a job baking your wedding cake and it's…sick. I can't keep doing this to myself." She turned to go and he rounded the desk, gripping her arm tightly.

"I'll ask you again," he said, his voice rough. "What do you want? I'll give it to you. Don't leave."

"So I can wait around for you to decide you want to try a loveless marriage again? So I can bake you another cake? Maybe I'll help the bride pick out her dress this time, because, hey, I'm always here to do whatever you need done, right?"

"Does it bother you? The thought of another woman marrying me? Then you marry me." He reached behind him and took the ring off the desk, holding it out to her, his hand shaking. "Marry me. And stay."

She recoiled, her stomach tight, like she'd just been punched. "For what purpose, Zack? So I can be the wife you don't love? Your stand-in for Hannah, different woman, same ring. Doesn't matter, right? You're still doing it. You're trying to keep me from leaving, trying to keep control. You'll even marry me to keep it. That's not what I want."

He took her hand in his, opened it, tried to hand her the ring.

She pulled back. "Don't," she said, her voice breaking. "Don't. I'm going to clean my desk out now."

"Clara."

Zack watched as she turned away from him and walked out his office door, closing it sharply behind her. Everything was deathly silent without her there, his breath too loud in the enclosed space. The ring too heavy.

Had he truly done that? Offered her Hannah's ring? Begged her to marry him just so she would stay?

He had. She had gone anyway and there had been nothing he could do to make her stay. All of his control, all of his planning, hadn't fixed it. He had lost the one person in his life who had given things meaning.

He'd been pretending, from the moment he'd met Clara, that she was only his friend. Only one thing. Because he'd known she could very easily become everything. How had he not realized that she'd been everything from day one?

Pain crashed through him, a sense of loss so great it stole the breath from his lungs.

His chest pitched sharply, his body unable to take in air.

He dropped the ring and it fell to the floor, rolling underneath his desk. He left it. It didn't matter.

He'd just broken the only thing in his life that did matter.

Control. She spoke of his control, how he tried to control her, keep her in his life on his terms. And she was right. Because he'd known instinctively that if he ever let go of that control she would take over.

She had. His control was shattered now, laying around his feet in a million broken pieces he would never be able to reclaim.

And if finding it again meant losing Clara, he didn't want it, anyway.

He hadn't chosen to lose his son, it had been a tragedy, one that had painted his life from that moment forward. He'd let

Clara leave, because he'd been too afraid to give. Too afraid to let his barriers down.

Because he'd been certain he couldn't live with the kind of pain love would bring, not again. But now he was certain he couldn't live without it. Without Clara. He loved her so much his entire being ached with it.

And if he had to lay down every bit of pride, every last vestige of control and protection to have her back, he would.

CHAPTER FOURTEEN

CLARA had looked at nine buildings in the space of four hours. She'd hated them all. The idea of having her own bakery... it had been so great before. But she realized now that when she pictured it, when she saw the image of a shop filled with people enjoying her cupcakes, Zack was there. At a table that she knew, in her imagination, anyway, was the one he sat at every day.

And she would come and sit with him when she took a break. And ask him what his favorite confection was. How his day had been. If he'd run in to any mimes. Because in her mind, in her heart, she'd never truly thought he would be gone from her life altogether.

The truth was, a life without him had been impossible to imagine.

In the three days since she'd walked out of Zack's office, it had changed. She didn't have a vision when she viewed the potential bakery locations. She saw nothing more than brick and wood. There were no visions. No warmth.

There was no Zack.

When he'd handed her the ring...the temptation to say yes had been there, and it had sickened her. That she would continue to be the void filler in Zack's life, while she let him be her everything. It was wrong. And she knew it.

Still, a part of her wished she could go back and say yes. She despised that part of herself.

She sighed and walked up the narrow staircase that led to her apartment. She hadn't taken the elevator in three days, either. Because it reminded her of the elevator rides with Zack, the ones rife with sexual tension. It was almost funny now.

Almost. She'd discovered a broken heart made it mostly impossible to find things funny.

When she reached her floor she walked slowly down the hall. She was exhausted, but going back to her apartment wasn't a restful thought. Because he was everywhere there. Memories of him. On her couch, in the kitchen, most recently, in her bed.

She stopped midway down the hall, her eyes locking on the small pink and brown box placed in front of her door. She eyed it for a moment before making her way to it, kneeling down and lifting the lid.

Her breath caught in her throat when she saw the contents. Cupcakes.

The ugliest cupcakes she'd ever seen. The frosting was a garish orange, the cake a sort of sickly pale gray. There was a note tucked into the side and she took it out and unfolded it.

I know I said I don't bake. I did, though. For you. Because it means something to you and I wanted to try it. It made me feel close to you to do it. Please don't eat them, they're terrible. I miss you.
Zack

She traced the letters with her fingertips, his handwriting so familiar. So dear to her. The note was scattered, funny. Sweet. She could hear him reading it to her.

A tear slipped down her cheek. "I miss you, too," she said. "But I couldn't let things stay the same."

"Don't cry. I know they're awful, but they aren't that bad are they?"

Clara looked up and saw Zack standing in the doorway of the elevator. He looked tired, the lines around his mouth deeper.

She wiped her cheeks. "They're pretty bad."

"Almost as bad as their creator." He took a step toward her. "I'm sorry. About the other day. About the past few weeks."

"Zack can we not do this? I don't think…I don't think I can."

"Well, I can't walk away. I won't. So if you don't mind me camping out here in front of your door until you're ready, then I can wait."

Clara crossed her arms beneath her breasts, curling her hands into fists, trying to disguise that she was shaking, trembling from head to toe. "What is it?"

"I told Amudee that I lied."

"And?"

"We still have a deal, but not based on how he feels about me as a human being. More about my corporate track record."

"Why did you do that?"

"Because I had to clean this up. I used you. I didn't want to gain anything from that."

Clara tried to smile. "I appreciate that, Zack, but…"

"I'm not finished."

She blinked and tried not to cry. She wasn't ready for this. Wasn't ready for him to try to repair their friendship, not when she needed more.

"You were right. About me," he continued. "I have been trying to control everything in my life, including you. Because I felt like there was safety in control. I felt like it was responsible, and I never wanted to deal with the consequences of a lack of control again."

He took a step toward her, put his hand on her cheek, and her heart stopped. "Clara, from the moment I met you I felt a connection with you. And I had to make a very quick decision about where to put you in my life. It was conscious. It was controlled. So I decided you would be my friend, my employee, but never anything more. Because I think part of me knew that if I let you, you could mean everything to me. If I didn't keep you in your place you would fill my life, every part of me. That I would love you. But then in Chiang Mai, being near you like that, I couldn't deny it anymore. I couldn't pretend I didn't want you. And we gave in. I lost control. So then, I thought maybe if I put you in that same place in my head I put my lovers, I could have you in my bed, without risking anything more. Without things getting deeper."

Clara's entire body trembled as she looked up at Zack, as she watched his face, so tired and sad. Mirroring her own, she knew.

"But they got deeper," he said, his voice rough. "And I couldn't stop it. Then I tried to reset things, and that didn't work, either. Not just because you told me where to stick it, which I absolutely deserved, but because things changed too much. Because knowing what it is to be skin to skin with you, has changed me. And it terrified me to admit that, even to myself."

"Zack…"

"You have every right to be angry at me. To hate me."

"I don't hate you."

"That's good, because it makes this next part easier. Because as terrified as I was the first time we kissed, I'm even more afraid now." He took a deep breath, his nerves visible, his control absent. "You're right, Clara Davis, you do make me tremble. You have been my friend, my partner, my lover. I want you to be all of those things to me for the rest of my life. I'll understand if you don't want the same from me. But no matter what, you have to know that I love you."

Clara felt dizzy, her fingertips numb. "You…you love me?"

"With everything. After we made love at my house, the last time, I felt like I could breathe again for the first time in fourteen years. For the first time since I lost Jake, I felt something real, something bigger than myself. Do you have any idea how much that scared me? But I realized something, the other day as I was reaching for a bottle of alcohol, to drink away the pain for the first time in fourteen years. That love can make you strong. I've always thought of it going hand in hand with loss, with weakness. But being with you…it makes me better. That's just one reason I love you so much. One of the reasons I had to tell you. Because all of my control, all of my pride, was just to cover up how scared I was. How weak I was. You've made me stronger. You've made me stop hiding."

A sob worked its way up her throat. "Zack, I thought I knew you. For seven years I thought I knew you. I thought you were this suave, together guy who had an unshakable calm that I really, really envied. And then I found out how broken you were, how messed up. I loved you before. I loved that guy I thought I knew. His jokes, his company, everything."

She pressed on, her voice cracking. "But do you want to know something? I love this man more." She stepped forward and put her palm flat on his chest, her hand unsteady. "Because this is you, and this is real. And I know you've been hurt. I know you've hurt in ways I can't imagine. And I know you aren't perfect. But you're perfect for me."

And then he was kissing her, his lips hot and hungry on hers. Her chest expanded, love, hope, filling every fiber of her body. When they parted, they were both breathing hard.

"Do you really love me?" he asked, wiping away tears she hadn't realized were on her cheeks.

"From the moment I met you."

"What a fool I was."

"I wouldn't trade the time, Zack. I wouldn't give back those years of friendship, not for anything. They made us who we are. They made us right for each other."

"I don't know if you can ever know how much your friendship has meant to me, how much your love means to me now. You're the only person I've shared myself with in so long, the only person I've wanted to share with. Without you…there would have been nothing in my life but work. You brought color, flavor."

"Cupcakes."

"That, too. And as you can see, I need someone to provide them for me because I'm useless at doing it myself. You make my life worth living, Clara. You make me better."

"I can say the same for you. I never felt beautiful, never felt special, until you."

"You're all those things. Never doubt it."

"I never will again."

"I have something for you," he said.

She smiled through a sheen of tears. "I love presents."

"I know." He reached into his pocket and pulled out a box. This one wasn't black and velvet. It was pink silk with orange blossoms. "Because you like flowers. And pink." This was for her. Only for Clara.

"I do," she said, opening the lid with shaking fingers. The ring inside was an antique style, a round diamond in the center and smaller diamonds encircling the band.

"It reminded me of you," he said. "Mostly just because it's beautiful. And so are you."

She laughed through new tears and held her hand out. "That's so lame, Zack."

"I know. It is. It's really lame. I make bad jokes sometimes, but you know that. You know everything there is to know about me, and if you can do that and love me anyway, I consider myself the luckiest man on earth."

"I do," she whispered. "Put it on me."

He took the ring out of the box and got on his knee in front of her. "Will you marry me? Clara Davis, will you be my wife, in every way. Will you understand that you are first for me, in every way. Will you love me, and let me love you?"

She wiped a tear away that was sliding down her cheek. "I will."

"And will you bake me cupcakes for as long as we both shall live?"

A watery laugh escaped her lips. "Without a walnut in sight."

He stood and kissed her on the lips. "I love you. As my friend, my future wife, my everything."

"I love you, too." She kissed him again.

"Would you mind if I stayed the night with you?" he asked, his lips hovering near hers.

"One night only?" she said, turning to him.

"No. It would never be enough. I want you every night for the rest of our lives, does that work for you?"

"Yes, Zack. I think a lifetime sounds about right."

EPILOGUE

CLARA Parsons looked at the mostly uneaten cake. Three tiers of blue frosting that had been perfectly smooth just a few hours earlier, before two, chubby hands had taken some fistfuls out of the side.

"That was the most extravagant cake I've ever seen at a one-year-old's birthday party," Zack said, looking down at the crumbs all over the kitchen floor. "And I don't think Colton ate half of it. He mostly just spread it around."

"That's what kids do, Zack."

"He's asleep. I think we put him in a sugar coma. Anyway, you only get one first birthday, I suppose. You might as well live it up."

Clara looked at the cake again. "This reminds me of another cake I made that didn't really get eaten. A wedding cake."

"I'm still very thankful that one didn't end up being used for its intended purpose."

"Oh, so am I. Because then we wouldn't have had our wedding cake, or our wedding."

"Or our son," Zack said.

"So, all things considered, it was a pretty important uneaten cake."

Zack advanced on her and pulled her up against his body, resting his forehead against hers. Her heart stopped for a moment, like it always did when she looked at him. Like it had from the moment she'd first met him.

"A lot has changed since that day," he said, dropping a kiss on her lips.

"A whole lot," she agreed.

"Do you know what's stayed the same?"

"What's that?"

"You're still my best friend."

She kissed him, deeper this time, love expanding her chest. "You're my best friend, too."

* * * * *

PIRATE TYCOON,
FORBIDDEN BABY
JANETTE KENNY

To my three wonderful daughters.

For as long as **Janette Kenny** can remember, plots and characters have taken up residence in her head. Her parents, both voracious readers, read her the classics when she was a child. That gave birth to a deep love of literature, and allowed her to travel to exotic locales – those found between the covers of books. Janette's artist mother encouraged her yen to write. As an adolescent she began creating cartoons featuring her dad as the hero, with plots that focused on the misadventures on their family farm, and she stuffed them in the nightly newspaper for him to find. To her frustration, her sketches paled in comparison with her captions.

Though she dabbled with articles, she didn't fully embrace her dream to write novels until years later, when she was a busy cosmetologist making a name for herself in her own salon. That was when she decided to write the type of stories she'd been reading – romances.

Once the writing bug bit, an incurable passion consumed her to create stories and people them. Still, it was seven more years and that many novels before she saw her first historical romance published. Now that she's also writing contemporary romances for Mills & Boon she finally knows that a full-time career in writing is closer to reality.

Janette shares her home and free time with a chow-shepherd mix pup she rescued from the pound, who aspires to be a lap dog. She invites you to visit her website at www.jankenny.com and she loves to hear from readers – e-mail her at janette@jankenny.com

CHAPTER ONE

KIRA MONTGOMERY pressed her forehead against the massage table's padded face cradle and shifted again to loosen the tension knotting her shoulders and neck. Impossible.

Her masseuse had "stepped out for a moment." The term obviously meant something different to her than it did to Kira. Leaving a client waiting fifteen minutes was unsuitable.

Chateau Mystique couldn't afford more bad press. The tragic deaths and ensuing scandals associated with the five-star hotel on the Las Vegas strip had hurt business. Hurt her in ways she'd never imagined.

To make her life more of a jumble, her doctor had confirmed the one thing she'd never anticipated. She was pregnant.

Her insides quivered and she took a deep breath. Held it. Let it out slowly. It didn't help. Nothing helped.

Ever since she'd heeded her solicitor's advice and traveled to the Caribbean island of Petit St. Marc for a closed meeting with André Gauthier, her life had tumbled into a chaotic nightmare. The devastatingly handsome billionaire had denied ever knowing of their meeting, and had refused to divulge how he'd gained stock in her hotel. Though she'd been frustrated and angry, she'd been captivated by the sheer power of his persona and his rapier-quick ability to debate an issue.

He'd mentally stimulated her and physically aroused her more than any man she'd ever met. But she wouldn't be swayed by his staggering offer to buy out her shares. He owned minority stock, and that was all he'd ever have.

The Chateau was her home. Her dream. Her legacy. There'd been no reason to tarry on the island any longer.

No reason except desire. She hadn't been able to deny the passion blazing between them and the raw hunger he stirred in her. And why should she?

She was an adult. Surely she could engage in a brief affair and walk away?

But thirteen weeks later she hadn't been able to forget their stolen night of passion. Or the scandal that had erupted the following morning to rip them apart. Or André Gauthier, the father of her child, the man who'd recently made headlines with his ruthless attempt to break Bellamy Enterprises.

Would the shareholders force Peter Bellamy to sell his father's empire? Would they decide to defy André and set the stage for a hostile takeover?

Perhaps they'd agree to a merger. Yes, a nice peaceful working arrangement, like the one she'd thought to forge with André before she learned of his perfidy.

How naïve she'd been. Where she'd only worried about dealing with André over the Chateau, she now fretted over the merger of them as parents. How did one tell a chance lover that he'd soon be a father—a chance lover she'd parted with on hostile terms?

The nausea that had been her constant companion the past few weeks threatened to return. She concentrated on the doctor's instructions instead of dwelling on ringing up André again to relay her news.

One dragon at a time. That was the only way she'd come out of this debacle intact. She'd left a message for him to contact her. And if he didn't. If he chose to ignore her…

The door opened behind Kira, and she quickly pushed her worries about André to the back of her mind to confront the tardy masseuse. "I trust you have a good excuse for leaving me here waiting for so long?"

Silence answered her.

Kira frowned at the floor, willing away the dark premonition that crept into the room like a cold London fog roiling off the Thames. But her trepidation only grew, because she knew someone stood in the doorway, watching her.

Someone, she sensed, who shouldn't be here.

She stilled, her breath catching in her throat as a wedge of light arrowed across the plush carpet and darted beneath the table to inch up the wall.

A chill born of anxiety hopscotched up her spine, and she shivered despite the luxurious blanket draped over her bare body. "Who's there?"

"Bonjour, ma chérie," he said, his deep, rough-edged voice causing her heart to race so fast her head spun.

André Gauthier! Instead of returning her call, he'd come to her. Her first impulse was to scramble off the table and launch herself into his arms, just to assure herself this wasn't a dream. Just to touch him, kiss him.

"I suggest we wait to talk until later, when I'm presentable," she said, in an effort to gain control of her rioting emotions.

"I didn't come here to chat."

A pair of obscenely expensive men's loafers stepped into the view afforded her through the face cradle, the hem of his charcoal trousers breaking perfectly on his vamps.

He splayed a hand on the small of her back, the heat of his palm sensuously electric, branding her, reminding her that the last time he'd touched her thusly she'd been awash with passion. Not that she needed a reminder.

But where she'd sensed his ardor before, she perceived his antagonism now. All directed at her.

His anger didn't bode well for what she must tell him.

"Then why are you here?" The tremor in her voice conveyed her trepidation and confusion.

"To claim what is mine."

She dug her fingernails into the armrest, likely scoring the butter-soft leather. Of course. He was here to haggle with her over the Chateau again.

Kira had expected this quarrel. Yet in her imaginings she'd been dressed and in control of her emotions, at the board meeting scheduled two weeks from now, not naked and quivering with apprehension and need. Surely she didn't wish to feel sexually receptive to him? But his presence commanded all her senses.

He glided a hand up her spine, sliding the blanket over her sensitized skin slowly, and the desire churning to life within her silenced the protests in her head. She gritted her teeth, fighting the feelings erupting in her: annoyance, desire, need.

It was a losing battle.

From the very first time they'd met she'd been in tune to his every breath, to the way he filled a room with his intensity. To the way his unique scent of spice tempered with the tang of the sea called to her, stripping her inhibitions bare.

His long fingers danced over her bared back in a silken caress, flooding her with unbidden memories of the intoxicating kisses that she'd craved, of masterful hands that had brought her to the pinnacle of pleasure and beyond, and lovemaking that had been more intense, more consuming than anything she'd experienced in her life.

That firm, yet gentle caress muddled her thinking. Her body reacted to him with shocking welcome, her breasts growing heavy, the sensitive nipples peaking.

She bit back a sigh of pleasure, her emotions roiling in utter turmoil. A heavy ache of want converged at the apex of her thighs, spreading upward, making her quake with desire. Damn him!

One caress had reduced her to a quivering wanton, sweeping her away on a wave of raw need. She detested his power over her. Hated the magnetism that drew her to the powerful throb of his touch.

Kira forced her voice to remain steady when her emotions were anything but. "This isn't the place to discuss business."

"I disagree."

The crackle of paper echoed in the tense stillness. A pristine white sheet was thrust beneath the face cradle.

She huffed out an annoyed breath, expecting another decadently outlandish offer for the Chateau. Her gaze skimmed the header, and her stomach plummeted as her world tipped on its axis.

No! This couldn't be! She read each damning word, her racing heart nearly stopping as the meaning sank into her soul. How could she have believed her future was safe from his power, from his dominance?

"What trickery is this?" she asked.

"No tricks, *ma chérie*. I own majority shares in Chateau Mystique."

Impossible! Edouard's shares were to pass into her hands after his will was read in two weeks. He'd promised she'd have majority control of the hotel then.

Yet the document proved Edouard's shares had fallen into this arrogant billionaire's hands. She doubted its validity, even though her solicitor's signature was there, a signature she'd seen countless times. This couldn't have happened, yet it had.

She felt betrayed. Used. Abandoned all over again.

André controlled her hotel. Her home. And he'd control her if she let him.

His hand glided over her shoulders in a mock caress, the fingers playing her skin like a fine instrument. Only the dirge sang her doom. She trembled, her mind reeling, more furious than she'd ever been in her life.

He laughed, no doubt gloating over his conquest and her reaction to him, and her humiliation was absolute. "Get up."

Kira sprang up so fast the room spun. She clasped the blanket around her heaving chest and shook her head to toss her heavy hair away from her face, too gripped with shock and anger to feel satisfaction when his eyes flared with sensual awareness, with masculine appreciation.

At least they were alone. She'd read that whenever André

left his island compound his trusted guard accompanied him. The brute was undoubtedly in the hall, making sure nobody interrupted his decadently wealthy employer.

Her gaze climbed André's tall, muscular form, clad in an impeccably tailored charcoal suit that shimmered in the artificial light. French, of course, the cut emphasizing his long powerful legs, lean hips and broad shoulders.

His snow-white shirt was a startling contrast against his darkly tanned skin, and his silvery tie complemented his platinum watchband that had probably cost more than what she earned in a year. His thick black hair was combed off his brow, his clothing meticulous, his bearing indomitable.

Her heart did a traitorous flutter as she remembered how much she'd savored having his powerful body molded to hers, those elegant hands bringing her to pleasure again and again. Drowning in the passion in his eyes as they'd made love.

It had been this way from the start. Less than two hours after she'd met him they'd had sex: hot, wild, urgent. There had been no love involved, only an overpowering attraction and an intense demanding need.

She'd never behaved so recklessly in her life. Never thought of the consequences of falling into André's bed.

Tell him the result of the affair, her mind screamed. Get it out in the open now.

Hands trembling, she dug her cold fingers into the blanket and met his eyes, such an intense dark brown they gleamed black. A dizzying rush of emotions slammed into her, staggering her with their strength. No, now wasn't the time.

"Get dressed," he said.

Kira turned her back to him and slipped a blue silk sundress over her flushed body, hating the way her hands shook and how her body pulsed and quivered with awareness of him. Though the garment she donned was modest, she felt exposed under his knowing stare. Vulnerable.

"I assume you expect to buy my shares now?" she said.

"Oui."

"They aren't for sale."

"You haven't heard my offer."

"I don't need to." She faced him, head high, her insides tangled in a riot of emotions. My God, he was an extraordinarily gorgeous man—tall, bronzed, strong, like a god come to life. And he was just as arrogant, just as domineering.

"I'm not selling," she said.

One dark eyebrow lifted, as if challenging her statement. "Everyone has a price."

"I don't."

"We shall see." André nodded to the door. "After you."

"I'll say my goodbye to you here, and see you at the board meeting in two weeks."

His smile was glacial. "You're coming with me, *ma chérie*."

Her skin pebbled as a cloying sensation settled over her. "In your dreams," she said, hating the tremor in her voice.

A muscle pulsed madly in his cheek. "I'll carry you if I must, but we are returning to Petit St. Marc."

The island? Her heart stuttered, then began racing. "Why?"

"To trump your lover, *ma chérie*."

Had he gone mad? "Then you are wasting your time, because I don't have a lover."

"I know you've been doing Peter Bellamy's bidding from the start. Now it stops."

"Peter?" A hysterical laugh bubbled from her. "I assure you that I'm not his lover."

"Spare me your lies. I know the truth."

No, he couldn't be more wrong. But she realized that if he didn't believe her in this, he'd never believe he was the father of her child.

"I'm not going anywhere with you. Leave now or I'll—"

He snapped his fingers and she jumped, slamming her back against the wall. "That's all it would take to have this hotel razed. Your shares would be worthless. Is that what you want?"

This was blackmail. Kidnapping at the very least! But to balk would bring about the destruction of her hotel.

"No," she said, knowing he wasn't bluffing. "But I can't leave the Chateau without making arrangements."

"You can and you will." His long fingers curled around her bare arm and he guided her out the door, his touch surprisingly gentle.

Yet she felt the underlying steel and rage in him and knew fighting was futile. And she was so weary already.

André was a man who took what he wanted, when he wanted. He'd proved that when he'd seduced her on Petit St. Marc. Proved it again when he'd swum in from the Caribbean like a great white shark and gobbled up control of the Chateau.

Yet she'd glimpsed another side of him on the island—a tenderness that had called to her heart, and a vulnerability she hadn't understood.

Yes, for now she'd return to the island with him. Perhaps there she'd find the right time to tell him about their child. Perhaps there she'd be able to reason with him about the Chateau—convince him she'd been robbed of her birthright. Perhaps in time they'd be able to start over.

André Gauthier stared at the deceptive woman walking down the corridor before him, her rounded hips rocking in an invitation that any red-blooded man would accept. No wonder Bellamy had given her forty-nine percent of Chateau Mystique.

Kira Montgomery was sex personified. She had certainly beguiled *him* with the oldest trick in the book.

He'd prided himself on his cool control under duress, nurtured it until it was second nature. It had never let him down—until Kira had invaded his island three months ago.

André hadn't been surprised when Bellamy had sent a female employee to Petit St. Marc to charm him after his last offer to buy the Chateau had been turned down. The excuse that she'd come for a prearranged meeting had been a lie.

The old man had banked on Kira's charms and André's

moment of grief to alter his ultimate goal. Or so André had believed.

It had worked. For that one night. Kira had pleaded her case with passion, and André had found himself caught up in the most stimulating debate of his life.

He hadn't realized the extend of her deceit until much later. The elder Bellamy hadn't sent her—his son had. Peter. His most fierce rival. Peter—the man he now suspected had set in motion events that had brought about the accident that had killed Edouard's mistress and landed Edouard in a hospital.

Kira was not only Peter's mistress, she was his accomplice as well. *Oui*, she was the brains of the maneuver that had ultimately eliminated the old man—that had earned her control of Chateau Mystique.

But her treachery had robbed André of something far more valuable than property. She'd had a hand in destroying the last of his family.

Kira had deceived him in the worst possible way.

She deserved no less in return.

Retribution coursed through his blood like a molten river.

Peter Bellamy would chaff, knowing that André held Kira on Petit St. Marc. She in turn wouldn't be able to contact her accomplice—her lover.

She'd be at his mercy when he launched the final takeover of Bellamy Enterprises.

His revenge wouldn't be satisfied until he'd bested Bellamy's conniving son at his own game—until he'd made Kira regret that she'd set out to destroy him.

André joined her in the lift and they rode up in silence to the fifth floor. He wondered if she'd entertained Peter Bellamy there while the old man had dominated his mistress in the penthouse.

The dark thought stayed with him as he followed Kira to a fifth-floor door. She slid a card key in the slot and stepped into a small but cozy suite. He noted the room bore quaint personal touches, typical of an English parlor, and carried her light floral fragrance. It seemed too benign. Too cozy.

"Pack light," he said, annoyed by the thought of her entertaining Peter Bellamy here.

Her shoulders stiffened—proof the order had grated. Good. He wanted to keep her off balance, keep her wondering what he planned to do to her.

"Do you plan to keep me locked in a room?" she asked.

"If I must."

The color leached from her face, only to return in a rosy flush that hinted of righteous anger. He ground his teeth, annoyed she could project such a quality.

"This is wrong of you to force me to leave here," she said.

How dared she accuse *him* of wrongdoing? "You should have thought of that before you agreed to do Bellamy's bidding."

She stared at him, her expression guarded. "As I've said all along, I was told you'd agreed to meet me on your island to discuss the Chateau."

"Save your lies," he said. "I have proof of your part in his scheme."

Her lovely mouth fell open, as if she was shocked by his claim. "I have absolutely no idea what you're referring to."

His smile was as tight as the tension bouncing off the jade brocade walls. "It amazes me that people shred the paper trail but forget the electronic one."

"There is none," she said.

"Don't be too sure."

"But I am certain."

"Then you're a fool."

She flushed, but instead of continuing her defense she looked away from him. Guilt? It must be.

André smiled. He'd caught her. Her game was over, and his was just beginning.

"Enough wasting time," he said, eager to leave this place that pulsed with bad memories.

She moved into her bedroom like someone walking to the guillotine. Soundlessly she rolled a case from the closet. The damned thing was half as tall as she.

When he realized her intent, he took it from her and hefted it onto the bed. "Take only the essentials."

"I'll pack what I wish to," she said, her amber eyes too bright with moisture.

Her tears had no effect on him. He'd learned long ago from his mother and sister that women cried over everything and nothing just to get their way. He certainly wouldn't allow Bellamy's mistress to beguile him again.

His mobile phone chirped and he immediately answered it. The tone signaled it came from his guard. "What?"

"Peter Bellamy just arrived."

André cut a sharp glance to Kira, who seemed preoccupied packing her bag. She'd not been out of his sight, so either Bellamy was making a surprise visit to the Chateau to see his lover, or someone on Kira's staff had phoned him.

"Watch him." André slipped his mobile in his pocket. "How much longer are you going to dawdle over what to take?"

"I only need a few more things, and my files." She moved to a desk and secured a laptop. "Everything is here so I can keep abreast of the hotel."

"You cannot mean to continue working?"

"I'm not one to sit around and while away my time." She flicked him a defiant glare and slipped the laptop in a carryon. "And I don't require your permission."

"Do not be too sure of that."

André had the satisfaction of watching her face drain of color before his mobile chirped again. He answered it curtly.

"Paparazzi just arrived," his guard said. "They're swarming around Peter Bellamy."

Damn. The last thing André wanted to do was engage in another public confrontation with Kira and the media at the start of his takeover.

He met her questioning gaze. "We need to leave without the gossipmongers seeing us. Unless you prefer a repeat of our last encounter?"

She flushed crimson and shook her head. He feared she'd balk—that she'd court the media's attention again. "The service entrance is our best choice."

He repeated that to his guard. "Meet us in five minutes."

"But I'm not ready yet," she said.

He swore and checked his watch. "You have three minutes. Then we leave, no matter your state of dress." He gaze slid over her body, openly appreciating her curves. "Or undress."

She stiffened, as if ready to argue.

He fed on his annoyance and tapped a finger on his watch. "You're down to two minutes and forty-five seconds."

Mumbling an oath, she grabbed lacy undergarments from a drawer and ran to the walk-in closet. He made to follow.

"Don't you dare come closer," she said, making him wonder if she could read minds.

"I wouldn't dream of it." He strode to her suitcase, zipped it shut and heaved it from the bed.

With five seconds to spare, she stepped from the dressing room wearing a floral skirt that hugged her firm bottom and thighs and stopped above her knees to accentuate the curve of her calves and dainty ankles. A fashionable summer sweater in a clear turquoise molded the full bosom he knew filled his hands. She stepped into sling heels that were sexy as hell, and tossed a smaller bag into her carryon.

She zipped it shut with impatient finality. Her small hand closed around the reinforced handles, her intent clear.

"I'll take that." André slung the strap over his shoulder.

She grabbed her purse and slipped a mobile inside it. He took the bag from her and removed the phone, setting it high on a shelf. "So you managed to ring Peter after all?"

"I left a message for my solicitor."

"I trust you bade him *au revoir*, for we leave now, Kira."
André held the door for her.

She glanced once at the shelf, then swept past him, her head
high. He smiled and followed. She moved with a staccato
click of heels and a beguiling sway of her hips down the
corridor to the lifts.

Oui, enjoying her luscious body would assuage his rage.

She stepped inside the lift and he joined her, wrestling the
baggage behind them and forcing her closer to him.

The doors started to shut. The ones on the car directly across
from theirs opened in perfect synchronization.

In that split second, when each had a full view of the
opposite lift, André locked gazes with Peter Bellamy. His rival
fixed a black scowl on him, then looked sharply to André's side,
where Kira stood.

Bellamy stared, then his mouth dropped open as he realized
his lover, his deceitful accomplice, was at his enemy's side. His
furious gaze snapped back to André.

André smiled, draped an arm around Kira's slender shoulder,
and gave his arch rival a smart salute.

CHAPTER TWO

KIRA wondered if this day would ever end as she exchanged André's private jet for the limousine waiting for them at Aimé Césaire International Airport. And what had her solicitor made of the harried message she'd left him?

She had no way of knowing. At least the flight from Las Vegas to Martinique had gone smoothly, but nearly fourteen hours of travel had exhausted her.

André's stony silence had drained the last of her energy. She'd hoped to talk with him rationally on the flight, but he'd closed himself off from her. Now she was in no mood to engage in heartfelt conversation with him.

Her summer-weight sweater smothered her, and the skirt she'd thought would be refined and comfortable hung like a limp rag. The island humidity, vastly different from the dry Nevada air, urged her heavy hair into the natural curl that she'd struggled to straighten all of her life. She was sure the make-up she'd applied before André dragged her from the Chateau was gone.

But she had the satisfaction of not being the only one wearied by the trip. Though André's perfectly tailored suit retained the crisp lines that complemented the brooding intensity of his dark eyes and matched his arrogance, dark stubble delineated his arrogantly handsome face.

That rogue's shadow emphasized the grim set of his mouth and gave him a dangerously sexy look. She caught herself remembering how those firm lips had felt moving against hers, tearing down her defenses and arresting her fears. How his hands and mouth and powerful body had brought her to her first shattering climax, and then continued to do so more times than she could recall, until she'd been deliciously sated and more happy than she'd ever been.

That had been the calm before the storm. What she couldn't fathom was what tempest now brewed in André, as the limo raced past fields of sugar cane toward Fort-de-France.

Three months ago, on his island, they'd both expressed that they never wished to see the other again in the heat of anger. Yet she'd rung him, and he'd come for her. Or had he planned to come to the Chateau anyway, to steal her away?

She suspected that was the case, as he hadn't even asked why she'd contacted him. And with his anger heating the very air she breathed, it was better she hold her secret a bit longer.

Too weary to make sense of this nightmare, she stretched her legs to ease the dull ache in her back. Like the other drivers racing down the boulevard in a hurry to get to their homes, she was anxious to get settled for the day.

This extended close proximity to André wreaked havoc on her senses. Every subtle shift of his powerful body, every heated glance, each casual touch, muddled her mind more and more.

A dozen times she'd nearly blurted out that she was pregnant with his child. Let him deal with *that*! But his brooding silence had stopped her.

He barely resembled the teasing rogue she'd met on Petit St. Marc. The man who'd baited and lured her into rousing debate, who'd flirted shamelessly with her. Who'd made love to her with unbridled passion and made her feel wanted, if only for a moment.

He'd withdrawn from her like a wounded animal. She debated scooting closer and taking him into her arms. Intuition told her he wouldn't welcome her gesture of comfort and empathy.

Kira bit her lower lip, exhausted and pensive. She'd never been this undone by a man, and her lack of control over her emotions mortified her. But then, she'd never been plunked into the middle of a dark drama without a script either.

She shifted on her seat as traffic slowed and the sleek white limo crawled past La Savane. Palms towered over the public gardens, lush with greenery and a profusion of flowers. How sad she'd not had time to visit the gardens when she was here before. She certainly wouldn't ask André for a tour now.

As they neared the harbor, quaint shops and houses were stacked against the hills like colorful children's blocks in bright crayon colors. A reggae beat from the market area danced in the air, yet the silence in the limo throbbed to the weary cadence of her heart.

"How much longer?" she asked, glancing at the harbor, where the docked sailboats resembled a denuded forest.

André gave a terse shrug, drawing her attention from the impressive breadth of his shoulders to the fatigue lines etched under his eyes. His was an intense gaze that seemed to look right through her. "An hour and a half at the most."

No rest or respite anytime soon, then. She took small consolation in the fact he looked as weary as she felt.

Not for the first time she suspected he'd left near midnight to arrive in Las Vegas early this morning. Perhaps, like she, he'd had a sleepless night.

But where he'd likely dwelled on blackmailing her to leave the Chateau, her mind had spun with the miracle of motherhood. For the first time in her life she'd no longer be alone.

Kira rested a hand on her stomach and smiled. Last night she hadn't been concerned about the hours ticking by while she lay in bed in wonder, awed by the precious baby growing in her.

She'd tried to envision how her life was about to change— had debated how she should let André know. She'd naïvely believed impending fatherhood might mellow him, that what they'd shared once could grow into something meaningful.

Love? Yes, the possibility of that blooming between them

had played over in her mind as well, teasing her with how good her future with him could be.

For the first time in ages she'd taken a peek at the school-girl imaginings she'd painted in the dark of night back in the days of her youth, when she'd dreamed her prince would ride in on a white horse and whisk her away to his castle, where they'd live happily ever after. When she'd fall in love forever, and not just for a stolen moment.

Not once had she thought André would sail back into her life this morning like a bloodthirsty pirate, with pillaging and revenge burning in his soul. That he'd accuse her of joining forces with Peter to ruin him. If he only knew the truth.

No, if only he'd *believe* the truth!

She shut her eyes against cold, hard reality. Instead of a white horse bearing her to a castle, a white limo raced her toward an uncertain future. Instead of her prince gazing at her with loving eyes, André barely spared her a glance.

What would he do when she told him she carried his child? Accept his responsibility with resigned indifference, as her father had done? Surely he wasn't that cold, that callous?

"What's wrong?" André asked, his warm breath fanning her face. "Are you ill?"

I'm pregnant. She looked up at him, prepared to tell him, but his eyes were as dark and turbulent as a winter storm. She was simply too weary to brave the gale now.

"I was just—" Caught in a fairytale. But they never come true. Never. "I'm just tired. It's been a long journey."

He stared at her for a tense moment, his expression shifting to the hard, indifferent mask she'd come to hate. "You can rest on the boat."

Kira laughed to herself as he moved to his side of the limo again, though the space between them afforded her no comfort. The express ferry she'd taken to and from the island before had provided seating, but no place where she could put her feet up.

Right now her ankles felt hot and swollen. Strange, since

she'd refrained from satisfying her thirst so she wouldn't spend the whole flight in the tiny restroom.

She stared at the glistening expanse of Flamands Bay, where a cruise ship dwarfed the catamarans and yachts that bobbed lazily in a turquoise sea. A welcoming breeze sent the palm fronds swaying, and gentled the tide to a mesmerizing ripple touched with gold. But she feared she couldn't tolerate much more travel without succumbing to motion sickness.

That certainly wasn't the way she wished to alert André of her condition. In fact, she was totally lost on how to broach the subject in light of today's shocking events and his aggressive mood.

André exited the limo the second it stopped, as if anxious to get away from her. Fine. She welcomed the reprieve. But it was short-lived again. Instead of the driver helping her out, the handsome billionaire, unyielding and resolute, opened her door.

He extended an exquisitely manicured hand to her. She stared at it, at the fingers long and graceful, the tanned skin smooth and dusted with black hair.

Memories of those hands skimming over her naked flesh and bringing her to pleasure time and again tormented her. There was nothing of her body he hadn't touched. Including her heart?

"I won't bite," he said, the arrogant tilt to his mouth hinting the opposite.

Not that she needed to be reminded. "You did before."

She saw her own burning need flickering in his eyes and gasped. A flush stole over her, and she chided herself for reminding him of their night together.

"I wasn't the only one with teeth, *ma chérie*." He took her hand, and the electricity that zinged from him staggered her.

Kira wanted to jerk away, but couldn't. She wanted to lean into him, but didn't dare.

The warmth of his skin and his steely power made her feel safe when she was anything but. How pathetic she must be.

Only a fool would fantasize about the man who'd accused her of bringing the paparazzi to his island. Who'd somehow acquired majority shares in her hotel. Who'd forced her to return to his island, where she'd experienced blazing passion. Where they'd created a child.

Kira forced her feet to move, grateful the setting sun had taken the heat out of the day. Yet a more dangerous warmth replaced it as she kept pace with André toward the waterfront, his hand firmly grasping hers, his narrowed gaze seeming to look beyond the people around them.

A few native workers near the boatyard glanced their way as they passed, speaking in a rich patois accented with French. She could only make out a word or two—greetings, mostly, interspersed with his name. Obviously the billionaire was known here, but no one attempted to engage him in talk.

Several express taxis were moored at the ferry terminal, their gangplanks crowded with a blend of tourists, transplanted islanders and native Caribs. The thought of joining that mass of humanity made her break her out in a nervous sweat.

At the dock, André guided her away from the larger craft. All she saw were small speedboats, bobbing wildly in the water. Her stomach lifted, then slammed down again as she scanned the jetty for a larger vessel.

None were moored along its length. None!

"Please tell me you don't expect me to ride in one of those little boats?" she asked.

"*Oui*, a dinghy. It is the fastest way."

She held back—not easy, considering his strength and the way her knees knocked. "No, I can't."

He stared down at her, his lean features resolute, his dark eyes intense. "You've no choice."

She swallowed her panic and closed her eyes, struggling to calm the riotous beat of her heart. "Small boats terrify me."

"You've nothing to fear."

Was he joking? No, the taut line of his jaw shadowed with stubble told her he was dead serious.

Panic clawed at her throat. As a child, she'd nearly died in a boating accident on Lake Mead. That memory and its devastating aftermath still haunted her.

She wouldn't, couldn't, get in a small boat.

Kira jerked free, but before she could bolt up the pier he swept her into his arms. She squirmed, then went still as death as he stepped down into the rocking boat.

She flung her arms around his neck and clung like a sandbur, her heart beating so hard she knew he must feel it too. Each gasp for air drew the spicy scent of him deeper into her lungs, further muddling her senses.

A laugh rumbled from him, at odds with the ferocious temperament he'd shown thus far. "Relax, *ma chérie*. See that cruiser anchored in the bay?"

She reluctantly lifted her face from the shelter of his warm neck. A sleek white cabin cruiser gleamed like a pearl against the caramel-tinged sunset. But it was so far away.

"You'll be perfectly safe on the *Sans Doute*."

Her mouth formed a soundless "oh."

André set her on her feet, his own braced wide as the boat rose and fell with the tide. He rattled off instructions in French to the boy manning the motor.

The engine powered up. André sat on the bench and pulled her down beside him. Her stomach pitched and her skin turned clammy, despite the refreshing seaspray.

She trembled with bone-deep fear. Her hand gripped the single handhold so tightly her fingers went numb.

He stared at her, his brows slammed together. "*Mon Dieu*, you *are* afraid."

She gave a jerky nod.

He wrapped an arm around her shoulders, one hand making soothing circles on her arm. "Relax."

If only she could. The dinghy raced away, the hull rising as they picked up speed. Her insides quivered and snapped like the nautical flags on nearby boats. She buried her face against his chest, her mind trapped in a nightmare.

"Look at me. *Mon Dieu*, look at me!"

She met his penetrating gaze, knowing hers was wide with fright, but uncaring what he thought of her. "I hate you."

"I would expect no less from you." His eyes blazed with dark emotion as his head lowered to hers.

Kira knew he intended to kiss her, and she knew it wouldn't be gentle. She knew she should push him away—at the very least turn her head. And she knew she would do neither. For she wanted him to kiss her with a desperation that shocked her.

His mouth closed over hers with a hunger that devoured what remained of her will. She shuddered violently and held herself impassive for a heartbeat, knowing capitulation would signal her doom. Then the kiss changed, softened, and a different type of tremor swept through her, stripping her of reason.

She splayed her free hand over his heart, marveling at the strong rapid beat so in tandem with her own, kissing him in kind. He tasted of exotic spices and seduction, and she suddenly craved both so much she knew she'd die of want if he denied her.

As the boat cut across the waves, the rhythmic duel of their tongues and the ravenous glide of lips on skin consumed her with memories. She was lost. Adrift at sea with her corporate pirate. Enslaved to the sensations she'd only known with him.

His long strong fingers played an erotic melody on her back that made her heart sing and her body hum with need. Like a rosebud caressed by the sun, she blossomed in his arms, kissing him back with all the hunger she'd denied for so long.

He'd done nothing to earn her trust, yet she felt safe in his arms. Wanted. So she simply gave up rational thought and relished this moment.

Too soon he pulled away, when she would've begged him to touch her breasts, her sex.

"We've reached the *Sans Doute*, *ma chérie*, and you are safe."

It was a lie. As long as she surrendered to his slightest touch she was in mortal danger of losing her heart and soul to this enigmatic man.

André prided himself on his rigid control in the boardroom and the bedroom, yet kissing Kira had been a mistake. He'd done it to take her mind off her crippling fear. But he'd come close to losing control of the situation.

She wasn't an innocent, yet he'd felt hesitation ripple through her, felt her lips tremble against his, felt her fear of the sea. Then that whispered moan of surrender had sung through his blood and instinct had taken over.

She was an enchantress. A sea witch. Now she was his.

He helped her climb onto the aft deck of the *Sans Doute*, mindful of her shaky posture and her frantic hold on his hand, the nails digging in so deep they'd leave a mark. He was gripped with the sudden urge to hold her, protect her, make love to her until her fears dissipated.

Mon Dieu, he hated this raging desire that threatened to burn out of control for her. Hated the role she'd played in Bellamy's life. Hated that he admired her pluck, that she hadn't resorted to tears, threats or seduction once.

He escorted Kira up the circular stairs and propelled her through the main salon, dressed in the richest golden sateen and deepest burgundy velour, then up to the observation salon. His hand rested at the beguiling curve of her back—in part because he enjoyed touching her, and also because he knew it bothered her. He wanted her hot and bothered.

The bullet lights in the ceiling shot platinum and bronze streaks through her wealth of mahogany hair that his fingers itched to sift through. But she would not welcome his touch now. She was as flighty as a hummingbird, the pulse-point in her throat warbling to a frantic beat.

Still he ached to draw her close, to press his mouth over that spot, feel the beat of her heart match time with his. She'd not fight him. No, she'd melt in his arms—if only to take her mind off her fear.

That was reason enough to bide his time. It was imperative she crave his touch. That he earn her trust.

It shouldn't be difficult to do, considering she'd been groomed to pleasure a man. *Oui*, before he was through she'd beg him to bed her.

It was inevitable—a fact Bellamy must be aware of. So why hadn't his enemy contacted him yet?

"Make yourself comfortable." He strode across the lounge to the bar. "Would you care for a drink before we get underway?"

"Water, please."

He slipped behind the granite-topped bar and slid her a look. She'd taken a seat on the circular sofa, her legs curled beneath her and an overstuffed pillow hugged to her stomach. Her complexion was paler than before.

A spark of alarm hit him again. "Are you all right?"

"I'm just thirsty." She flicked him an uncertain glance. "It's been too long since I drank any water." She shook her head as if dismissing the matter.

Another ploy to gather sympathy? To heap guilt on him for dragging her to the island against her will?

Of course. She'd only had to ask at any time and he would have made sure she was refreshed, that she was comfortable. He wasn't an ogre, determined to make her suffer physically.

He poured sparkling water into a glass, added a twist of lime and took it to her. Annoyance burned his soul as he handed her the glass.

She took it, a telling gasp escaping her as their fingers brushed. "Thank you."

"My pleasure," André said, which was far from the truth.

He stalked back to the bar and prepared a simple rum daiquiri with the barest squeeze of lime. Thoughts of Kira making love with Bellamy sped through his mind and left a white froth of rage in its wake.

Instead of savoring the heavy, rich swirl of rum, André tasted bitter revenge coating his tongue. Spending half a day with her had sharpened his senses to a razor's edge.

Kira portrayed the *ingénue* when she was anything but innocent. *Oui*, he knew her for what she truly was, for he'd tasted her passion. One sip demanded more.

Every nuance of her was branded on his mind. The occasional tremor that rocked her, leaving her shaken. The pensive look he glimpsed in her eyes when she thought nobody was watching. Those odd moments when she rested a hand on her stomach and the most beauteous expression came over her.

It was as if she was sharing a secret with someone.

Well, he had secrets of his own. Dark, disturbing ones that robbed him of sleep.

"Do you have reliable internet on the island?" she asked.

"*Oui*. I have a private satellite connection in my office." *She* would have limited access, at his discretion, and monitored. He prowled the carpeted salon and sipped his drink, her question spiking his suspicion. "Thinking of begging Peter to rescue you from the situation you've both created? Or do you need his instructions on how best to spy on me?"

Color streaked across her high cheekbones and her amber eyes snapped, her anger and defiance charging the air. "I intend to run my hotel from my prison."

"You mean *my* hotel."

"You are the majority stockholder now, but the Chateau will always be mine."

His fingers tightened on his glass. She couldn't be more wrong, but he'd let her hold her confidence for now. He took no pleasure in beating someone who was so near the edge.

The dark smudges beneath her eyes attested that she was close to exhaustion. Yet her narrow shoulders remained squared and her chin high, as if she was refusing to accept that she stood on thin ice regarding the Chateau—regarding him.

Her quiet strength intrigued him. He'd expected her to use

her delectable body to court his favor, to deceive him more. But though she'd responded instantly to his touch, his kiss, she hadn't attempted to take the initiative with him. Yet.

He tossed back his daiquiri as his anger burned anew. What was her game?

It didn't matter. He'd have his revenge in the end. He had proof Peter had sent her to Petit St. Marc to seduce him, *and* alerted the paparazzi, and he now held documents proving her part in the deadly plot she and Peter had instigated.

The latter was enough to make him despise her. He hated that she'd acquired the Chateau with her deceit. Hated that she was Bellamy's mistress. Hated that her solemn amber eyes had the power to make him question his plans.

He set his glass on the bar with a thunk and strode to her, his annoyance sparking like lightning when she lifted her chin and stared up at him, wide-eyed but unflinching. She was driving him mad, for he'd never wanted to intimidate a woman until now.

In one fluid movement he rested a knee on the cushions before her curled legs, braced one hand on the sofa's arm and the other on its back. "I own Chateau Mystique and I own you. Never doubt you are both in my control."

Her full lips thinned. "That is barbarous."

"Perhaps you were unaware the blood of pirates courses through my veins?" He yanked away the pillow shielding her and splayed his fingers on her stomach, his thumb resting on her *mons* and his fingers grazing the swell of her breasts.

She gasped, eyes huge and dark, with awakening desire. The pulse in the ivory column of her neck throbbed to a savage tempo that mirrored his own erratic heartbeat.

Oui. She didn't fear him. She wanted him as much as he wanted her. In this they were equal. But not for long.

André affected a rapacious grin. "What? You have nothing to say?"

A tremor vibrated through her into him as she shoved his

hand from her, but her eyes were still smoky with passion. "Nothing that you'd believe."

"Save your professions of innocence." He lurched from her and stared at her expressive eyes that challenged him. "Relax, *ma chérie*. I have no intention of ravishing you. At least not yet."

She looked away, satisfying him that she understood his dismissal as well as his promise. The inevitability.

"Not ever," she said, the words whispered, yet fierce.

The challenge hung between them—a cold, invisible wall that he longed to tear down.

André stalked across the salon and bounded up the stairs to the sundeck, knowing he was a hair's breadth from toppling Kira back on the sumptuous sofa and showing her just how much she hungered for his touch. How easily she'd capitulate.

Now wasn't the time. They were spent from the journey. In thirty minutes they'd land at Petit St. Marc. That wasn't nearly enough time to enjoy her charms, and he fully intended to savor every inch of Kira at his leisure, for bedding her would enrage Peter Bellamy. Never mind that it would satisfy the savage beast within him as well.

For a moment he paused at the starboard side and simply soaked in the breathtaking view of the silvery disk of the sun as it slipped into the rippling mocha waters.

The horizon gleamed like buttered rum. Golden glimmers tinged with red skipped over the waves as if they were ablaze, glimmers of light that matched the highlights in Kira's long luxurious hair.

Kira. Why did she bring out such poetic yearnings in him?

Out here was nothing but the sea, mistress to many of his ancestors. Mistress to him in many ways.

He shook his head at his own fanciful musings and took the stairs to the fly bridge. A stocky old sailor, wearing cutoff jeans and a tattered T-shirt, manned the helm.

"How's she sail, Captain?"

The old salt flashed him a cunning grin. "I'd ask the same

of you if I thought you'd tell me who that tempting gal is that you stowed on board."

André scowled. "It's a long story."

The Captain chuckled. "Most interesting ones are."

He shrugged. Though their friendship spanned a decade, he was loath to explain his association with Kira.

"Just keep it steady," André said. "The lady isn't accustomed to the sea."

"Aye, aye, boss."

André gave the horizon one last look, then hit the stairs. Annoyance bobbed within him like a storm-tossed buoy. Thanks to the scandal, every moment away from his desk cost him a fortune.

He hadn't intended to make any changes at the Chateau as yet, for he wanted Kira to squirm, to wonder what he planned to do, to get comfortable in her role as his lover. Then he'd swoop in and exert his will over the hotel—and her.

Oui, he'd not soften toward Kira. He would not make the same mistakes his father had made. No woman would rule *him*.

André slammed into the master stateroom and dropped onto a tufted leather chair at his desk, even though he ached to pace the confines like a caged tiger scenting fresh meat. He grabbed the phone and put in a call to his private detective. The man answered on the second ring.

"Is Bellamy still at the Chateau?" André asked, dispensing with pleasantries.

"No. He left an hour after you did."

"Back to Florida?"

"To California, to inaugurate a new hotel," he said. "Do you want me to continue surveillance?"

"*Oui*. I want to know every damned thing he does. Who he talks to, who he does business with."

"You got it," the detective said.

André ended the connection and rocked back in his chair, his mind sifting through this startling news. Why was Bellamy carrying on as if nothing had happened instead of rushing back to his compound in Florida? It didn't make sense, for Bellamy had seen André leave with Kira. The deception was over.

Had she simply been Bellamy's pawn, used to publicly humiliate André? Used as needed and then discarded? Paid off with shares in the Chateau? It was a possibility he'd considered.

His fight with Edouard had been personal, rife with emotions André deemed crippling. Simple revenge. He was David going up against Goliath.

His feud with Peter was strictly business. One corporate raider battling another. But over the last six months Bellamy had turned vicious. Personal attacks on André that the media fed on.

Where Edouard had regarded him as a pest, Peter Bellamy set out to destroy him. And Kira had sided with the enemy to bring about his ruin.

Yet he desired her.

Mon Dieu! Sleep deprivation was warping his mind. He rubbed his gritty eyes and winced. His body screamed for rest, yet he couldn't afford it yet.

André threw the pen on his desk and stormed from his stateroom. In moments he'd reached the main salon. His gaze sought and found the object of his scorn.

She lay curled on the sofa, napping, her hair spilling over a pillow in a waterfall of mahogany curls. He wasn't sure how she managed to look innocent and provocative at the same time. Nor could he understand why he wanted her, knowing she was a calculating liar.

But his pulse quickened all the same. He longed to run his fingers through her hair as he covered her body with his. Would she welcome his caresses? Melt in his embrace? Sigh as he thrust inside her?

He undid the knot in his tie and gave it a savage jerk. The silver-gray silk whistled free in the quiet. He'd know soon.

CHAPTER THREE

KIRA stirred, awakened by the crushed-velvet voice of her dreams. She understood very little French, but her body recognized the sultry promise his tone evoked.

She frowned, annoyed. It was always this way—André's voice rousing her from sleep as if to taunt her about the passion they'd shared once. Passion she'd never had with another man. Passion she missed with a soul-deep ache that never left her.

As always, she was helpless to stop the desire radiating in her belly, spreading low and leaving her hot and throbbing and so restless she couldn't lie still. She thrashed and arched in mute supplication for his touch, his kiss.

His hand glided under her skirt and up her inner thigh, his fingers splaying over her skin, so close to where she wept for his touch. Sensations exploded in her in dizzying colors and she moaned as she was drawn into the kaleidoscope of desire.

A soft laugh shattered the dream. She froze, knowing before her eyes popped open that the intimate touch was as real as the man. André loomed over her, his eyes dark and his features unreadable, his fingers inches from the juncture of her thighs.

Her heart careened crazily, for in that second she wanted him to touch her there like he had before. Wanted him to see her as a woman with dreams and hopes, not just as a sexual partner.

The knowledge that wouldn't likely happen snapped her from her sensual haze.

She slammed her hands against his shoulders. Mistake. Electricity arced into her as his muscles bunched and quivered. Her hands shifted over his chest, and she marveled at the power pulsing beneath her palms that she ached to explore.

"Stop it," she said, as much to herself as to him, shoving against him to scoot away, only to have the sofa's marble-topped divider table stop her. "What do you think you are doing?"

His lips pulled into a predatory smile that made her shiver with sexual awareness. "That should be obvious."

She shook her head, shocked he'd taken advantage of her while she was sleeping, stunned that she'd nearly begged him to take her. Hard. Fast. Deep.

"I'm not making that mistake again."

Something akin to pain flashed in his eyes, a lightning strike of emotion she couldn't read. "Yet you desire me, *oui*?"

"No."

"I know when a woman is faking and when she is gripped by passion."

One bold hot finger slipped beneath the lace trim of her silky panties and traced the sensitive crease of her leg. She couldn't stop the tremor that bolted through her, leaving her quivering with need.

She drew on every ounce of courage she possessed to defy his potent masculinity and preserve what remained of her dignity. "You're wrong. I don't want you."

André slid his finger from her, depriving her of his touch, giving her false security. He flashed a beautifully masculine smile and skimmed that same finger over the desire-dampened crotch of her panties.

Her body jerked of its own volition. She bit her lip to stifle a moan of raw pleasure, and her face flamed with embarrassment and anger for he'd proven his point.

She was putty in his hands. Helpless to resist him.

"I knew you were ready before I touched you," he said.

"André, don't," she said, curling her fingers into fists so she couldn't clutch him and draw him to her.

"Why? We have nothing to lose."

"You're wrong." She was already in danger of losing her heart to him—which made no sense, considering how he'd taken over her hotel and was dragging her to his island lair.

"Is that a challenge?" His hand slid down her calf and lower, sending hot quivers of sensation spiraling up her leg.

"No." She'd be a fool to square off against André when her defenses were so low, when she was so weary she could barely think straight.

He didn't play fair, and she did. Even now, with her emotions stretched thin, she became lost in his touch. Her breath hitched and her heart raced, and she willed his hand to glide back up her leg, to—

His palm cupped her foot, the fingers curling beneath the arch to skim the ball of her foot. A burning pain shot up her leg and her pleasure popped like a child's balloon.

"Don't! That hurts." An exaggeration. The skin burned hot all over.

He examined her foot, his frown darkening. His finger lightly traced the strap indentations cutting across her skin and she set her teeth against the fiery pinpricks that danced across her skin.

He spat out a torrent of French that she was sure were curses, yet his touch remained gentle. "You are a fool to sacrifice comfort for fashion. How long have your feet been like this?"

"They began hurting as we walked from the car to the dock."

"You should have told me."

She glared at him and tried pulling her foot free of his hold. "You were not exactly in a friendly mood."

He moved faster than lightning, pressing her deeper into the sumptuous cushions, blanketing her with his powerful body. His arms bracketed beside her head kept some of his weight off her, but not his groin. She felt the steely length of his sex against her belly and bit back a moan, afraid he'd ravish her, and equally afraid she'd not find the will to stop him.

"Discovering I had been tricked by my fiercest rival's mistress puts me in a bad mood," he said, his mouth tantalizingly close to hers, his eyes dark and mercurial.

"I'm not Peter's mistress," she said, willing him to believe her this time.

His features changed, hardening more than she'd thought was possible. "Why do you persist in lying?"

"Why won't you believe me?"

He snorted. "Because I know what you are."

Hot color stained her cheeks, her anger mounting. "No, you only think you do."

"Then tell me. How did you gain control of the Chateau?"

The truth was poised on her tongue, burning to be released. There was no reason to keep the promise she'd made Edouard. No reason except to weigh the danger in confiding in André. For if he hated her now, he'd despise her when he knew the rest.

"Having trouble sorting out your lies?" he asked.

No, the truth. "Nothing of the sort."

Kira looked away from the anger flashing in André's eyes. She was tired of working long hours to earn her rightful place at the Chateau, only to have a stranger step in and take it all away from her. Tired of living on the fringe of Edouard Bellamy's life so his family would be spared the stigma of knowing that he'd sired and provided for his bastard. Tired of receiving only crumbs of Edouard's affection. Tired of fighting this same argument with André.

"I'm simply an employee who invested wisely in Bellamy Enterprises," she said at last, repeating the excuse Edouard had devised.

"Did you receive a bonus when you came to my island and seduced me?"

"Of course not. I came to talk with you," she said.

"So you said. Yet you found your way into my bed."

"It was a mutual seduction."

"*Oui*, but I wasn't the one who invited the world to witness our affair the next morning."

Kira shook her head, having nothing to say in her defense. He wouldn't believe her anyway. She wouldn't rail at him, because he volleyed her barbs back with the ease of a tennis pro—only his shots drew blood.

"Neither did I."

"Perhaps you didn't issue the order," he said. "But you were aware that was Peter's intent before you came."

"If I had known, I assure you I'd never have come," she said, furious that he doubted her at every turn. "And, for the last time, my solicitor had assured me that you'd requested a meeting between us."

"Bravo, Miss Montgomery, for sticking with your story. Perhaps later you can entertain me with the story of how a new employee managed to buy a forty-nine percent holding in a multimillion-dollar Las Vegas hotel."

Before she could think how or if she should respond to that, a shrill whistle echoed in the salon.

He surged to his feet, his features rigid with anger. "We've arrived at Petit St. Marc."

Kira intended to do little more than rest for the remainder of this day, and maybe the next as well. She'd deal with André and the baby that tied them together later.

She watched him shrug into his suit jacket and give the lapels a tug. Except for the shadow of a beard lending him a roguish look, he looked no worse for wear.

Kira was sure she looked as weary as she felt. She swung her legs off the sofa and tugged down the skirt he'd rucked to her thighs. Her checks burned hot with mortification.

In London she'd spent her days working in a hotel and her evenings devoted to night classes. Edouard Bellamy had paid for her hospitality degree, but he'd insisted that was all the education she needed. She was, as her father had reminded her often, only suited to be a hospitality manager. But she'd had higher aspirations.

She needed a business degree to run a hotel. *Her* hotel!

Kira picked up her sling heels, hooked her purse over her shoulder and started across the main salon. The carpet felt good underfoot, but the onyx floors were sheer heaven, cooling her feverish feet like nothing else had.

No matter what else she did when she settled into a cottage, she intended to soak her abused feet. She descended the steps with care and moved across the carpeted deck to the railing. Her first look at the island took her breath away.

The lush rainforest on Petit St. Marc covered the humped dome of an extinct volcano. The knot of trees was so lush and dense that the forest appeared black at its heart—much like André's must surely be.

Palm trees close to the water swayed in the gentle southeasterly breeze that was refreshing her heated skin as it skipped over the expanse of sea, carrying with it the tang of salt and the intoxicating sweet scent of exotic flowers.

She tensed as his shadow fell over her, but as the island came into sharp focus her temper mellowed. "It's breathtaking."

"Oui," he said.

She looked away from the men mooring the yacht with quiet efficiency to André. Instead of staring at the island he frowned at her, as if he couldn't believe she'd seen beauty here. As if he couldn't believe she was here again.

Not by choice. And not for long, if she had anything to say about it.

"Come. The hour grows late." He motioned toward the short gangplank being secured to the aft deck.

Kira moved down it with care, and stepped onto the weathered boards of the dock. Heat burned the soles of her feet. She hissed in a breath and took a cautious step.

"Do you need help?" he asked.

"No. I just need to put on my shoes."

She gripped the railing and tried to don her slings. Impossible. Her feet were too swollen to fit under the straps.

Strong arms swept her off her feet.

She grabbed André's shoulders and felt a frisson of heat shoot through her. "You don't have to carry me."

"There is much I don't have to do, *ma chérie*." He carried her with effortless grace down the length of the dock.

Kira wanted to upbraid him for his Neanderthal ways, but she couldn't bring herself to knock his kindness. The closeness to him was to her detriment, though, for resting against the stalwart wall of his chest not only teased her with erotic memories, but incited the desire to create new ones.

Dangerous thoughts. Hopefully when she was in her own quarters she'd be able to control this bizarre attraction to André. She wasn't fool enough to believe she could remain indifferent to him.

André deposited her in the front seat of a canopied utility cart, his hands lingering on her bare skin for a charged fraction before deserting her. She tugged her skirt over her knees, annoyed that her body still throbbed with desire.

The utility cart dipped slightly as he eased his big frame behind the wheel, power and sensuality radiating off him in waves that rivaled the golden-tinged ones rolling toward the shore. He'd removed his jacket and rolled up his shirtsleeves, revealing tanned forearms corded with muscle and sprinkled with black hair. The breeze flattened his fine shirt against the hard planes of his chest and upper arms.

He was all power and dominance, a king in his kingdom. But it was that sultry gleam in his eyes as they undressed her that took her breath away. For just one look had her forgetting about the tenuous position she was in.

Disgusted at her weakness for him, she turned her head to watch a young Carib jostle her luggage onto the rear deck of the cart. Unlike his decadently rich employer's, his smile was kind and respectful.

Kira returned the gesture. Though the Caribs treated her like a guest, she suspected none of them would help her escape.

What unnerved her was that her captivity was two-fold. For the child growing within her bound her tighter to André than any lock or key.

The vehicle jolted forward, the electric hum of its engine fading as the peaceful sigh of the island took dominance. "Do you ever grow weary of it here?"

"Only during hurricane season."

He maneuvered the utility cart up a winding path paved with crushed seashells, the fat tires crunching them into a finer roadbed. The smooth surface was a welcome surprise.

Kira scanned the area anew. The first time she'd come here she'd been too incensed to appreciate the resort. And now? Her gaze took in the red-tiled roofs of the cottages almost hidden in the forest, and moved down to the secluded white beach below.

She caught a glimpse of a couple strolling hand in hand, naked as the day they were born. "You have a nude beach here?"

"Four natural beaches, all private, and all reserved beforehand by the guests." A hint of a smile touched his mouth. "Tops are optional on the public beach. We are very European here."

"I'm too British to appreciate it."

"You'll learn to enjoy it."

Never. Unlike her mother, she didn't flaunt her body.

Kira closed her eyes to the beauty around her as the ugliness of her past tried to intrude. No, she wasn't like her mother at all. She slid a hand over her belly. The past was just that—past. This baby was her future.

The utility vehicle whirred past another lane leading to another cottage and sped up an incline beneath a canopy of trees alive with birds. Through the light flickering through the foliage Kira caught a glimpse of the big house, nestled into the hillside.

She gripped the handrail and swallowed the panic building in her chest. He *couldn't* mean to move her into his dwelling.

But as the vehicle emerged from the trees into an area

cleared behind the old plantation house, she was certain that was his intention. Living on his island would be taxing enough. But to stay in his home and endure his temper? Impossible.

"I'd prefer my own quarters." Away from him and temptation.

"The cottages are for paying guests." He stepped from the cart and pocketed the key.

"Fine. I'll pay," she said, craning her neck to see where he'd gone. "I won't live with you."

"You don't have a choice, *ma chérie*."

She whipped around to find him at her side. One arm rested on the top of the canopy and the other gripped the support pole.

At first glance his was a casual pose. But one look at his white knuckles, at the corded muscles in his arms and the grim set of his mouth, dispelled that thought.

"I won't be your mistress," she said.

"I didn't offer you the position."

It was true. He hadn't said a word about her being his lover. She should feel relieved, not disappointed. What was wrong with her?

His enigmatic gaze held hers another long moment before he straightened and extended a hand to her. "It has been a taxing journey. Come. I'll help you inside."

"I can manage myself." Kira swung her legs out and stood.

Her sensitive feet settled onto the crushed shells and her breath hitched, but she was determined to walk into his house under her own power.

"Mon Dieu!" André stepped forward and swept her up in his arms again. "Are you always this stubborn?"

She planted her hands on his shoulders to force a minute distance between their bodies. "Are you always this domineering?"

"Only with you."

Kira didn't believe that for a moment as he strode up the walk, his shoes crunching the walkway. She resisted the urge to rest her head against his shoulder, refused to relax against the comforting wall of his chest.

He climbed the two steps to the front terrace with ease. The temperature was refreshingly cooler beneath the roofed porch. His housekeeper stood at the open door, the white ruffle on her peasant blouse and the hem of her orange floral skirt fluttering in the breeze that filtered through the house.

A smile wreathed her face. "*Bonjour*, Monsieur Gauthier."

"*Bon après-midi*, Otillie." André shouldered through the door with Kira in his arms, speaking rapidly in the island patois which sailed right over Kira's head.

Otillie volleyed back with what sounded like affronted questions, and stepped in front of André, bringing him up short.

After a few choice words from him, Otillie tossed her hands in the air and quit the living room, muttering under her breath.

"What was that about?" Kira asked.

"Otillie is annoyed with me for not telling her I was bringing a guest home."

"You should have let me rent a cottage."

"I should have kicked you off my island when you first came here to play out your vengeance."

"Why didn't you?" she asked, refusing to be baited into the same argument about her reasons for coming here.

"Because you intrigued me."

That feeling had been mutual. She'd never met a man like André. Never felt such a strong connection to another man. It had been more than sex to her, yet she suspected that was where their similarities ended.

He climbed the steps with apparent ease and continued down a hall swathed in shadows. Her blood heated and her heart quickened, for she knew there were only bedrooms on this level.

And she knew exactly which room was his.

Tingles of awareness streaked through her, sending her heart into a crazy rhythm. Was that where he was taking her? Would she be a prisoner in his bed?

Surely not? Even André couldn't be that barbarous. Yet he'd taken her from the Chateau and brought her here. She was on his island. In his house. At his mercy.

Mercy? She gave in to a shiver. He had none.

He was a ruthless corporate pirate and a master of seduction. She might not be a match for him in business, but she'd proved she was his carnal equal. In that they were well suited.

That admission terrified her more than anything, for she was fatally attracted to him—like a moth to a flame. She'd been burned once by tumbling into his bed. The next time the flames of desire would consume her—if his quest for vengeance didn't destroy her first.

He passed the door to his chamber without pause—the room where they'd made love, the room where the world had intruded on their ideal, the room she'd fled in anger and shame.

She shook off those memories as he shouldered open a louvered door midway down the hall, and pushed into a cool, dark room. A gorgeous canopied bed dominated the space, its mosquito netting rippling in the refreshing breeze that filtered through the room.

André headed straight toward the bed, his features so hard and unyielding they looked carved from stone. Yet he laid her on the bed gently, his touch lingering a telling moment.

Instead of pouncing on her, as she'd half expected he'd do, he stood back and stared at her with cold derision. She sensed he waged a war within himself, and a part of her commiserated, for she was fighting her own private battle to remain unmoved by him. It had been so good between them that one glorious night.

Though her heart pounded louder than the drums that had greeted them on their arrival, she sat up and faced him. And waited for him to break the tense silence.

"I'm a private man," he said, pacing before the foot of the bed. "I guarded my business and my private life. But in one night you stripped me bare and invited the world as witness."

"I had nothing to do with that swarm of paparazzi."

He sliced a hand through the air. "Of course you *would* deny your part in that."

"What about you?" she asked, having learned after Edouard's death that André wasn't a man to be crossed—or trusted. "You're as much to blame for the dissolution of your engagement."

He released a cold, hard laugh. "As much as I value privacy, my former fiancée cherished it more. You destroyed that and humiliated her."

"I didn't do it alone," she said, in a burst of irritation.

He slammed both hands on the footboard, making the bed shake. "Don't remind me."

His eyes burned into hers, a mixture of anger and desire that made her light-headed. She looked away, breaking the spell.

At least André was no longer in the limelight. Just two weeks ago, a new celebrity upheaval had dimmed the spotlight on André Gauthier and his equally rich ex-fiancée. And the hunt to find his mystery lover—Kira—had finally lost its appeal.

But Kira would always regret being "the other woman"—a role she'd vowed never to assume. "I'm sorry your fiancée was hurt."

"Are you?" he asked.

"Yes! I'm not a homewrecker. If I'd known you were engaged I never would have let you touch me."

"But of course you have manipulated this in your mind, so I am to blame for not telling you."

"Why didn't you speak up?"

An awful quiet hummed between them. The muscles and tendons in his face were stretched so tight she feared they'd snap. He looked angry enough to kill her with his bare hands, and at that moment she wouldn't have blamed him.

She was furious at herself for listening to her solicitor and coming here for the meeting that André had always denied requesting. Though they'd tumbled into bed soon after, he surely had to admit he was as much at fault as her—maybe more so.

For he'd been affianced. He should have sent Kira away instead of seducing her.

"Do you have any idea what you did to me?" he asked, his voice lethally soft.

She bit back the desire to ask him the same, for that would lead to questions she wasn't prepared to answer yet. "I exposed you for what you are. It was you alone who broke her heart."

"Are you really that naïve?"

Anger sparked in her—again directed as much at herself as at him. "I know what I saw. When your fiancée found us together she was devastated that you'd broken your pledge to her. If she hadn't loved you, your infidelity wouldn't have bothered her."

He shook his head and his mouth pulled into a grim smile. "*Oui*, she was furious that my affair was made public. So furious she rescinded the offer that would have merged our companies. You, Miss Montgomery, cost me a fortune."

Kira blanched, certain he was exaggerating. "You make it sound as if your impending marriage was just a business merger."

"It was."

"You can't be serious."

"But I am. You did more than create a scandal," he said. "You interfered in a lucrative deal. But then Peter must have made you aware of that. That's why you must suffer the consequences of your actions."

That was why he'd struck now to acquire the Chateau—why he'd blackmailed her into leaving with him. The corporate raider with meticulous timing. The father of her child.

A man who broke his vows—just like her father. A man who took pleasure exacting revenge.

Without another word he turned and stormed from the room, closing the door behind him with a demoralizing click.

Kira leapt from the bed and raced to the door, not done with this argument yet. She spied his shadow through the louvers and grabbed the knob, but it wouldn't turn. Locked.

She pounded the doorframe so hard the louvers rattled. "Unlock this door! We need to talk."

"I've said all I intend to say for now."

"Wait! You can't keep me in here."

"*Oui*, I can."

It was a fact she detested. She was marooned on an island with a man who burned with revenge—and she was pregnant with his child. He likely believed he'd rendered her helpless.

But then, André really didn't know her.

"If you don't unlock this door, I'll—I'll—"

"Do what?" he asked, his voice smug. "Throw a tantrum?"

Kira seethed and scanned the room. Her gaze fell on a pair of rococo vases adorning a shelf. Old Paris Mantle vases, she was sure. Lovely. Delicate.

"No, something far more valuable," she said, and heaved both vases at the door. The porcelain shattered in a million rose-hued shards—just like her dreams.

CHAPTER FOUR

ANDRÉ stood in the hall, chest heaving and fists shaking at his sides. He'd not intended to lock her in her room, but the moment he'd held her in his arms and kissed her he'd wanted her so badly he throbbed with need. Knowing she was receptive to him only made the urge to possess her again stronger than ever.

So he'd locked the door to keep her from charging from the room and challenging him. For this time he'd not be able to walk away. It was a chilling admission to make.

He'd never experienced this sensual intensity with another woman. He'd soared to a summit with Kira that he'd not known existed. A place he'd feared going all his life, for he'd had to relinquish control to get there.

It had been just one night of passion. One damned night. But he recalled every detail. The taste of her skin, the silken strength of her muscles straining with his, her lusty response to each intimate stroke of his hands, his mouth, his body.

Mon Dieu, her anger was as fiery as her desire—the flint to ignite his passion. Knowing she'd flung a set of exquisite rococo vases against the door had awakened a primitive side in him. Like the passion-crazed hero in *La Valse Chaloupée*, he was tempted to kick down the door, grab her by her hair, and drag her into his bedroom.

But this was life, not a facsimile of the Apache Dance.

Though he was his father's only son, he'd be damned if he'd let a woman blind him to reason. Not again!

History would not repeat itself through him. Never.

Yet it had, for he'd been lenient with her from the start. That would end now.

Though Kira was the object of his baser desires, she'd been his enemy's mistress. She'd come here to seduce him, to drag his name through the muck. Her success had ruined the most lucrative deal of his life, and made a fool of him.

His enemy had won that battle through her. But he'd not be deterred from his goal this time.

Biting off a curse, he strode the length of the hall to his room. The southeasterly breeze drifting through his chamber failed to refresh him.

He was weary and hot, and disgusted with himself. Spending the better part of a day in Kira's close company had driven him mad with lust.

André strode into his *en suite* glass-enclosed shower and turned the jets on full blast. Cold water rained down on his body, pelting muscles that had grown so tense and knotted they ached.

He flattened both hands on the ceramic-tiled wall and put down his head, welcoming the water coursing over his body, cooling his ardor, his anger. The intense feelings warring within him were new, and he hated that he'd lost control with her again.

Yes, this had to be similar to the hell his father had endured throughout his marriage. André would have none of it.

The water spurting from the jets beat his savage jealousy for Kira to a manageable level. He'd run on pure adrenaline the past few hours. But he'd accomplished what he'd set out to do.

He'd brought Kira to Petit St. Marc and he'd exact his revenge. Peter Bellamy would be livid by now, knowing that he held Kira here, that he'd use whatever means necessary to access any secrets she held about Bellamy Enterprises. Yet Bellamy had been deceptively silent, going about his life as if nothing out of the ordinary had happened. What was his plan?

Perhaps Bellamy had anticipated André would strike back, that he'd go after Kira to bring Bellamy to heel? Perhaps that was why Kira hadn't put up much resistance to leave the Chateau. Perhaps the plan was to ensure that lightning struck twice—she was to seduce him and create another media nightmare.

It was a possibility he couldn't ignore. Paparazzi could be on their way to the island now, in hopes of catching André availing himself of Bellamy's tempting mistress again.

The thought pulsed in his blood like lava, thick and scalding hot.

André pushed away from the shower wall and turned off the water. The cold dousing had cooled his temper, but he was still semi-aroused.

He stalked into his room, his body dripping water, his sex heavy. He stared at the security panel, smiled, then punched in numbers to deactivate the lock on her door.

Bellamy's feigned uninterest in André taking Kira from the Chateau roused his darkest suspicions. If she made no attempt to escape, then it was likely she and Bellamy already had an ulterior plan in place, should André try to use Kira to crush Bellamy.

He wouldn't be played for a fool again. He'd alerted his guards to bar anyone except their guests from the island. He'd set men to patrol the shoreline as well, for the same reason.

New game. New rules. One winner—him.

Kira pressed one hand to the *en suite* bathroom door while the other tightened around the knob, her pulse racing with a sense of dread and anticipation. She'd just decided she might as well take a shower to cool her anger when she'd heard the lock on her door click. But she hadn't heard the door open.

She strained to hear, but the only sound she detected was the soft whir of the ceiling fan and the pounding of her own heart. André must have returned.

Good. She was ready to confront him, for the longer she put this off the worse it would be. Or was it already too late?

She pressed a hand over her still-flat belly, her emotions more tangled than before, her anger cooling. André believed she was Peter's mistress. Believed she'd come to the island before to ruin him. Believed she was his enemy.

Kira could produce a document to debunk that claim. But, short of a DNA test, she feared she'd never convince André of his paternity. Not unless she earned his trust first.

Taking a resigned breath, she opened the bathroom door and stepped into the room. A glance proved she was the only one in residence. She eased to the entrance door and peeked through the louvers.

Her brow creased. No masculine shadow in the hall.

Yet someone had thrown open the heavy curtains in the hall and opened the windows to let the refreshing ocean breeze riffle in. She strained to hear sounds of life, and caught a faint murmur of voices echoing from below stairs.

Kira closed her door and paced the luxurious bedroom. Why had he locked her in, only to set her free soon afterward? Why had he left her in peace?

Peace? That was a laugh.

There'd be no peace until she and André came to amiable terms regarding their child. Though, considering who she was, it was likely he'd regard her with hate. And what of their child?

Surely the island tycoon who'd loved her to distraction wasn't as cold as her own father? André would insist on playing a vital role in their child's life. And hers as well?

If she was honest with herself, she wanted the fairy tale dream of a loving husband and family.

She wanted André.

This dangerous fascination she had with him made no sense to her. He was all wrong for her. She detested his infidelity. His arrogance. His ruthless intention to take what he wanted without a care for her feelings.

He believed she was Peter's mistress—his enemy. What did he intend to do with her? What would he do when he learned the whole truth?

Restless energy pulsed within her, leaving her thoughts scrambled and her stomach alive with butterflies. She crossed to the window, where cream voile curtains fluttered like gossamer wings.

The vista was a feast: sky bathed in the richest bronze and edged in an ethereal glow. Like André's tanned skin, smooth, unblemished, potently sensual.

She frowned, annoyed she couldn't enjoy a pastoral thought without him crowding into her mind. Like a thorn, André Gauthier was embedded in her, festering, painful when poked.

Her hand stole to her belly and her eyes stung with tears she refused to shed. André was in her, his blood coursing in their child, mixing with hers. The child bound them together. But what would the future hold for them all? Could they find a way to resolve their differences for the baby's sake?

Kira shook her head, apprehensive and weary. She'd worked so hard to gain confidence in herself, yet in less than a day he'd rendered her poise nonexistent.

He was too dominant.

Too virile.

Too addictive to her senses.

She didn't want to want him. Didn't want to think of him. Yet he remained constant in her mind. He kept her worries alive, churning like a whirlpool.

She needed to unwind, to work off the tension coiling and striking like maddened vipers within her. Because as long as her emotions were this frayed, she remained vulnerable to André.

Around the plantation house the rainforest had been cut back to allow a garden paradise. Lanterns outlined the fence, and more strategically placed lights spotlighted fabulous floral displays.

Nearly in the center lay a large swimming pool, awash in

soft light. Several small thatched shelters strung with inviting hammocks stood nearby, the encroaching shadows of dusk lending them more privacy.

The pool beckoned to her. She licked her lips, debating.

Nothing had been said regarding an evening meal, though she caught a tantalizing spicy aroma drifting from below. She didn't know if she was expected to dine with André or eat alone in her room. She wasn't sure of anything. But she reasoned she had time for a quick dip in the pool.

Kira dug through her luggage and found her simple coral maillot. In another month her pregnancy would make her hesitant to wear anything this revealing. So she might as well enjoy this opportunity while she could.

Once she'd donned her swimsuit, she stood in front of the mirror and critically studied herself. She wasn't showing yet. Still she hesitated, until she'd borrowed a large bath towel. She wrapped it sari-fashion around her and slipped from the room.

For a moment she stood there, listening, afraid André would appear. Or worse. That he'd take her in his arms. Kiss her. Melt her resolve.

But not a soul stirred, and the quiet bolstered her flagging courage. She hurried across the cool beechwood floors to the stairs. Again she paused, listening, heart hammering.

Nobody was about, so she padded down the steps and hurried to French doors thrown open to welcome the prevailing breezes. She stepped onto a terrace facing the forest and breathed in the exotic perfume of flowers.

The lights lent a fantasy glow to the garden, and in no time she'd padded down the terracotta stones to the pool. It seemed too good to be true that this enchanted garden was all hers to enjoy this evening.

Kira undid the towel at her waist and let it drop, then stepped to the deep end of the pool and dived into its turquoise depth. The water was almost too warm and drugging, but she forced her arms to slice through the water, her legs to scissor and propel her across the pool.

One lap and turn. Then two, three, four...

She stopped counting after that. Though she was tired to her core, the repetition was the nirvana she sought to banish André from her mind.

André watched the monitor, transfixed by the woman cleanly navigating his Olympic-sized pool. He'd not taken time to study her body impartially. If he had, he'd have recognized she possessed an athlete's physique.

Her sleek suit was designed to minimize drag. It molded to her and left nothing for the imagination. Not that he needed to guess what was beneath the suit.

He remembered every nuance of her body. Every curve, every dimple, right down to the sexy mole on her derrière.

Yet his research into Kira Montgomery had failed to tell him she was an expert swimmer. Not a leisurely one either. No, she swam with speed and power, the defined muscles in her arms and shoulders attesting that she was fit. That she was a competitor.

He smiled, pleased to discover a reason for the aggressive tendency which had drawn him to her. Though he could see she was used to challenging others in the pool, she was far out of her league in trying to best him.

He was a shark, whereas she was a sleek dolphin. Graceful, swift and desirable. Cunning as well?

Heat pooled in his groin as he watched her slice through the water, over and over. A sea nymph come to life, luring him to come to her. That was likely her plan—to seduce him again.

But this time he was alert to her scheme. This time he'd use her own desire against her. This time he'd turn the tables on her.

He pushed from his chair and strode from the room, the cutoff jeans he'd donned barely clinging to his hips, his chest and feet as bare as his rising need.

With Bellamy's help she'd succeeded in breaching his

defenses. His lust for her had eroded his control, for he'd never been so attracted to a woman before. Never enjoyed such sensual sparring.

But he'd not make the same mistake twice. This time he was aware of the depth of her deceit.

Oui, when he was done with Kira Montgomery she'd be financially ruined and humiliated. As for her benefactor—he'd strip Peter Bellamy of his fortune and his empire.

Only then would his revenge be complete.

Kira felt the pressure of water swelling behind her, followed by the tingling sensation that she wasn't alone. She faltered midway to glance back at the tiled edge.

She recognized the circle of ripples for what they were—someone had dived in. André?

The thought of him in the pool with her drugged her limbs and muddled her thoughts. It had to be him, for even the water was charged with an energy that hadn't been there before.

Kira went hot and cold and hot again, her heart drumming too fast. She pulled herself through the water, determined to outdistance André. She found a burst of renewed speed and concentrated on reaching the far wall before him.

She had to get out of the water. She had to be on firm ground when she encountered him again.

Doing laps had cleared her head, and she was glad she hadn't blurted out the truth earlier. He was too mired in anger to reason with, too set on seducing her out of some misguided sense of revenge to deal with the reality of their future.

There would be time later to explain everything. She'd make time. She'd somehow make him understand that she'd played no part in Peter Bellamy's schemes. That she was the injured party in this—just like him.

That, despite the feud between the Bellamys and André, they'd created something beautiful together. That they had a chance for a bright future.

But now wasn't the time to discuss it. The day had exhausted her and strained his patience.

Tomorrow. She'd deal with all this then.

Her arms sliced the water with precision, her shoulders burning from the exertion, her thighs growing tighter, her lungs starting to burn.

The intricate mosaic design on the tile edging the far end of the pool became clearer, the bright red, blue and yellow more intense. Almost there. Almost.

She felt the pressure of water pushing at her from below. Panic nipped at her, for she knew he was a heartbeat away from colliding with her.

A great white shark chasing her, poised to attack. She chanced a look down, faltering when she saw him.

His long powerful body surged upward to meld with hers, his hands on her waist anchoring her to him. Before she could think to fight him, he broke the water and shot upward, taking her with him.

The night breeze whispered over her body, pebbling her skin. She slammed both palms on his wet chest to push him away, but the raw hunger in his eyes paralyzed her.

He smiled, arrogant and potently sexy. Then his mouth captured hers and she surrendered with a whimper.

They fell back into the water, the splash noisy and ungraceful. Her hands slipped around his neck, her fingers memorizing the play of muscle flexing beneath warm smooth skin.

She'd missed this connection to him so much.

The water lapped over them as they sank in the pool, and she clung to him. The kiss deepened, breathing life into her.

He was her anchor and her damnation. As before, his kiss was unlike any she'd experienced. Deep, wild, intoxicating, dragging her through hell to glimpse heaven.

Each glide of skin against skin sent shockwaves of need vibrating through her, crumbling the walls of restraint she'd hastily erected. Just like that and she capitulated to him.

There was no reason to continue fighting when he'd won this battle. She wanted him, and she hated herself for being so weak around him, hated this intense need that coursed in her for him.

With just a kiss he'd reduced her world to her and him and the child in her womb, nestled between them. But he didn't know that, or realize her concern at holding her breath too long.

He pushed off the bottom of the pool and propelled them upward. Toward air.

And another confrontation with André.

He held majority shares in her hotel as tightly as he held her life in his hands. She should fear him. But she believed that he'd protect her, even though her intuition warned she'd come out the loser in any personal war with him. Even knowing the danger ahead of her, she let him woo her heart without effort.

They broke the surface, each dragging in air—another form of torture, for her breasts rubbed his chest with each indrawn breath, teasing the nipples into aching peaks. And lower his sex pressed against her belly, separated only by her swimsuit.

A languid heat coiled in her at knowing he was naked. Knowing that it would be so simple to reach down and stroke his exquisite length, to guide him where she ached for him.

"You're an expert swimmer," he said, forcing her mind from sex—a blessing that part of her cursed.

"It's good exercise." No longer a passion.

Her dream to compete in watersports had died long ago, derailed by an injury, then later crushed beneath Edouard's plans for her.

She'd not relinquish another dream to please a man, no matter how much she ached for his touch, his possession. Yet even as the thought crossed her mind she admitted that was a lie. She ached to have a family. To be wanted. Loved.

He moved, lifting her to nuzzle her breasts through the thin Spandex of her swimsuit. Fire shot through her. She dug her fingers into his strong wet shoulders, trembling and arching her back to press her bosom closer to his mouth.

"I want you," he said, his teeth grazing one sensitized nipple before moving to the other. "You want me."

She moaned, awash in need, refusing to fight what they both wanted. "That's obvious."

He scowled, as if angered by her admission. "I won't take you now."

Had she heard him wrong? No, even as he spoke with biting conviction he pulled away from her, putting her at arm's length, slamming the door on the hot emotions she'd seen flickering in his eyes.

"Then why the foreplay?" she asked, disgusted that her face was flushed and her body trembled with desire.

"I was ravenous for an appetizer." He left her standing in the water and strode to the edge. "We will indulge in the sensual entrée later."

He hoisted himself from the pool, water sluicing down his naked and aroused body. He was tanned all over, though a slightly lighter hue banded his groin and his firm, sexy behind, indicating he wore a brief swimsuit on occasion.

The sight of his magnificent body intensified the ache in her. "I won't have sex with you."

"*Oui*, you will. But tonight I need rest and I need food." His gaze slid over her with a hunger that made her breath catch. "When we make love it will be leisurely and very thorough."

She trembled at the promise, at a loss as to what to say that wouldn't betray her wants, her needs.

"Dinner will be served in fifteen minutes," he said. "We'll dine casually tonight."

He stepped into his cutoff jean shorts, but left them unbuttoned, clinging to him like she longed to do. Then he walked away, his long strides taking him further from her. Just like that he could shut off his need for her, while she still quivered with want.

Damn him!

Kira slapped both palms on the calm water as anger danced

up her limbs. He didn't look back once, didn't pause. He stepped onto the terrace and into the house.

Frustrated beyond words, she launched into a breaststroke that took her the length of the pool and back. Yet even though her muscles screamed for rest as she climbed from the water, a part of her was still ravenous for André's touch.

She had to gain control of her emotions and her libido. For if she wasn't very careful her weakness for him would be the downfall from which she'd never recover.

After a quick shower, Kira donned a simple sundress patterned in aqua and a rich brown the color of André's eyes. That she could make the comparison confirmed she was still on dangerous ground around him. It didn't help that her emotions swung wildly due to her pregnancy.

One moment she hated him, the next she craved his touch, his kiss. She'd even pondered engaging him in a debate, but quelled the urge. Their first and last verbal clash had led them straight to the bedroom.

Considering how she'd melted in his arms in the pool, she dreaded sitting across from him at the dinner table. But her fears were for naught. Soon after they'd sat down to dine and their meal had been served, André was called away—an urgent conference call he must take.

Alarm bubbled in her. Her first fear was he'd made good on his threat to destroy her hotel. "If this concerns the Chateau—"

"It doesn't." He drained his glass of wine, his features remote. "Enjoy your meal, Miss Montgomery."

Without a backward glance, he strode from the room. His plate remained untouched.

Worry nipped along Kira's nerves, leaving her edgy. She didn't trust André to tell her the truth, for he was convinced that she was in league with Peter Bellamy.

He swore he had proof. So what did he have that condemned her? Or was it a bluff?

She speared a wedge of orange and trailed it through her serving of chicken, tomato and pepper and into a bed of wild rice. The subtle aroma of garlic and citrus that had appealed earlier deserted her. Yet she knew that she must eat something for the baby's sake.

She forced herself to eat and let her mind roam. What electronic proof could he have that tied her to Peter Bellamy?

It couldn't be genuine. So who'd manufactured this proof?

There were those at the Chateau who disliked her. Since she'd taken over things had gone awry. Items she'd needed hadn't been ordered. Reservations were often jumbled.

But even if one of them took their dislike of her beyond reasonable in an attempt to ruin her, nobody there had the power to sell Edouard Bellamy's shares.

No one except Peter. Edouard's son. He'd been made executor of Edouard's will. He'd inherited his father's corporation. Had *he* set out to strip her of her inheritance?

She dropped her fork on her plate and rubbed her aching temples. It was very possible that he'd discovered the role she'd played in Edouard's life. That Peter resented her with a towering hatred—just as Edouard had predicted would happen should the truth ever come out.

Everything had been a jumble since the accident. Edouard had clung to life while his mistress had lost hers. The dissolution of her stock had been swift and secretive, with André buying those shares in the Chateau.

That was what had sent Kira here to confer with André. A meeting André swore he'd never agreed to. Had she been set up from the start?

André believed she'd conspired with Peter to ruin him. Not true, but she had no idea how to prove her innocence. She didn't know what to do, who to trust beyond Claude, her solicitor.

Kira slumped back in her chair, her appetite and what little remained of her energy gone. She wanted to crawl in bed and sleep. Wanted to forget this nightmare that had become her life.

Her hand stole over her belly and, despite her annoyance and fears and worries, she smiled. More than anything she wanted to protect her baby. The best way to do that was rest.

She put her napkin on the table and rose. Her gaze collided with André's.

As before, his stance was deceptively casual as he leaned a shoulder against the doorjamb, arms hanging loose at his sides and one foot crossed over an ankle.

But his expression was dark and forbidding, and censure burned in his eyes. He was angry, and she wondered if that ire was the result of his conference call or with her.

"How long have you been there?" she asked.

"Long enough. You didn't eat enough to keep a bird alive."

"It's enough for now."

He snorted. "But of course you must ensure your figure remains desirable, *oui*?"

His handsome face had graced many a business magazine, but she'd only seen this ferocious expression once before. Three months ago, when she'd fled Petit St. Marc.

So much had happened, so quickly. It seemed surreal that she'd gone from being the hospitality manager at Edouard Bellamy's elite Le Cygne Hotel in London to stockholder of Chateau Mystique to André's impromptu lover.

But that seemed a lifetime ago.

Now fury ruled his features. From the rigid set of his lean jaw to the grim slash of his firm full lips. As ruthless as he'd seemed when she'd escaped the island, he appeared menacing now, like a bloodthirsty pirate instead of a renowned island tycoon.

Whatever had taken him away tonight had put him in a dangerous mood. But she was too tired and emotionally spent to spar with him tonight.

Still she asked, "Is something wrong?"

He shrugged, but his body remained tense. Wary. "My guards intercepted paparazzi off the coast."

"That should please you," she said, suspecting that diverting the media was a common occurrence on the island.

He pushed away from the doorjamb and prowled the room, like a predator stalking its prey. "What is he paying you to continue this charade?"

She gave a brittle laugh. "Am I to assume you mean Peter again? Because, if so, the answer is the same as before. I've never met Peter Bellamy, and I've never taken any directives from him."

"*Oui*, just from Edouard. He selected well when he chose you for his son," he said, and she debated lobbing the water carafe at his arrogant head.

"Why do you hate him?" she asked, thinking she should know what drove André before she said anything more. Certainly before she divulged her secret.

"Why?" André released a caustic laugh, his features devoid of humor. "Edouard Bellamy destroyed my family."

A sickening chill swept over Kira. "That's why you engineered the takeover of the Chateau? Why you want to break Bellamy Enterprises?"

"Revenge, *ma chérie*."

"But Edouard's dead."

His smile was so cold she felt as if she'd been plunged in ice water. "You are familiar with the concept of the sins of the father being visited upon his children, *oui*?"

Kira managed a weak nod, though her knees nearly buckled. "What has Peter done to you?"

Again the negligent shrug. "He's a Bellamy."

And that answer said it all. For she was a Bellamy as well, Edouard's daughter. And her baby—their baby!—had Bellamy blood.

She had to escape Petit St. Marc before he discovered the truth—before his vendetta against the Bellamys destroyed her and their child.

CHAPTER FIVE

ANDRÉ watched Kira. The skin at his nape was hot, his muscles bunched to spring forward and catch her should she faint. It seemed imminent. She swayed slightly and her face was leached of color again. All because he'd told her that he intended to destroy Edouard Bellamy's empire.

"It's been a trying day," she said at last, her voice strained and tinged with weariness. "I need sleep."

So did he, but he was too livid at his investigator's initial report to shut off his mind. "I have just discovered that Edouard Bellamy paid for your education and your efficient Mini Cooper car. And how interesting that you moved into the spacious flat that Peter had called home for over a year."

"You had me investigated?" she asked, features suddenly tense and expressive eyes wary.

"*Oui.*" She was the product of a single parent, and raised in an elite boarding school. Illegitimate, with "father unknown" marked on her birth certificate. "Bellamy gave you your first job as the hospitality manager at Le Cygne. Were you Peter's mistress by then?"

An angry red flush mottled her cheeks. "No! Edouard offered me a scholarship to further my education, but I landed that position at Le Cygne because of my high marks. I had no idea that his son had once lived in the flat I was lent."

He didn't believe that for a heartbeat. "What did you do to acquire forty-nine percent of Chateau Mystique?"

"We've been over this once—which was quite enough. Nothing has changed. Nothing *will* change. Because I've never been any man's mistress!"

She whirled toward the door and stumbled. He caught her, alarmed by her too-pale complexion and near faint.

"You should have eaten more," he said.

"It wouldn't stay down."

His brows slammed together. "You're ill? Should I send for a physician?"

"No, I'm just tired and thirsty. The doctor stressed I need to drink more fluid in my condi—" She broke off, her lips parting and her eyes going wide. It was the look of someone who'd said more than they'd intended.

His gaze narrowed on hers, his heart beating too fast as his mind found the only appropriate word to finish her thought. "What is your condition?"

She swallowed hard, her gaze locking on his. "I'm three months pregnant."

Mon Dieu! He drove his fingers through his hair, his mind reeling with that news. Had he known, had he suspected, he never would have taken her from the Chateau.

"But of course—you are *enceinte* with Peter's child."

"No, I'm not," she said, jerking free of him. "You are the father."

It was a lie. It had to be. But even as he thought it his mind replayed a vivid image of the one time he'd neglected to use protection. He'd wanted Kira so much that he'd not even thought about birth control until after the fact.

Now he would pay for that consequence. If it were true.

"When did you plan to tell me, *ma chérie*?"

She shook her head, hating that she'd blurted out the truth. But at least that secret was out. "I hadn't decided."

"Convenient." His gaze narrowed on her. "Was this part of

Bellamy's scheme to further smear my reputation, or your ticket to gain a greater fortune?"

Kira stared into dark angry eyes that flashed as fierce as the desert lightning storms that terrified her. She was crushed he believed her so mercenary. But she couldn't—wouldn't—explain herself, for she'd only incur his wrath.

"Answer me! Whose idea was it to steal my heir?"

A glint of longing softened his features, so brief she wondered if she'd imagined it, so real she nearly spoke with her heart. But no, it was too soon to trust him without question—never mind that she longed to do just that.

She'd been an unwanted child, disowned by her mother and regarded as an obligation by her father. She wouldn't let her child be treated so dispassionately by a rich father.

"Your heir?" She forced a laugh, the sound harsh to her own ears. "Is that all our child means to you?"

How dared she ask that? André's jaw throbbed from clenching his teeth. "There are tests that will prove if the baby you carry is your lover's or—"

"I won't risk my child's life to satisfy your curiosity," she said, a hand pressed protectively to her belly.

His temper flared. "*Mon Dieu*, do you think I'd put the baby's life at risk?"

"I don't know. You've done nothing to earn my trust."

"*Touché.*"

André ran a hand over the stubble on his jaw, damning the tremor streaking up his arm. The baby was likely Bellamy's.

But it was possible the child was his.

"My baby's health is more important than anything," she said, and he silently agreed with her. "Let me return to the Chateau. I need to see my doctor regularly—"

"I will arrange for an obstetrician from Martinique to visit you weekly here on Petit St. Marc."

"Weekly? You can't mean to keep me here."

"*Oui*, you will stay on the island for the duration of your pregnancy."

Until paternity could be proved, Kira realized with renewed annoyance.

Petit St. Marc would be her prison for the next six months. Unless she could break through the wall of resistance and hatred André had erected. Unless she could finally gain his trust. And if not—

"I never meant for you to find out this way," she said at last, to fill the awful silence that roared in the room.

He let out a course bark of laughter. "Forgive me for not believing you."

The thought of being unable to bridge this impasse made her queasy. "I'm going to my room."

André cut her a sharp glare and cringed at the dark smudges beneath her eyes. She looked ready to collapse.

Guilt niggled at him, for he was responsible for her long, arduous journey here. He'd gone to Las Vegas to kidnap a scheming mistress, not an expectant mother. What the hell had he brought on himself?

Time would tell. For now he'd err on the side of caution. "Come. I'll escort you to your room."

She glared at him. "So you can lock me in again?"

He affected a negligent shrug as he longed to throw something—ah, she *did* speak to his inner beast. He waited until she'd started up the stairs before following her up.

"My apology for doing so earlier." His fit of anger had been so reminiscent of his father that he still longed to rail at himself.

"But you did it anyway," she said.

"You have my word that it won't happen again."

"Your word?" She laughed, a glacial sound vibrating with anger. "Why would I believe you?"

He grabbed her arm and tugged her to him, wanting to see her face when he replied. "Because, unlike your previous protector, I stand by my promises."

She jerked free, her arms banding her middle to hug her tiny waist as he longed to do, amber eyes condemning him. "Tell me, André. Did you vow fidelity to your fiancée?"

"No."

Clearly his admission was the last thing she'd expected, for the flush of anger left her cheeks, leaving her exhaustion plain to see. He huffed out an annoyed breath at himself. Continuing this war of words served no purpose tonight.

"Seek your bed, *ma chérie*."

She stared at him, as if trying to see into his heart, his soul. A waste, for the lock to both was rusted shut and the key lost to painful experience.

"I don't understand you, André," she said.

"There is no reason why you should."

André turned and sought his own room, leaving her to think what she would of him. It mattered little to him that she didn't understand his motives.

Anger boiled in him—at himself, for he'd believed her when she'd admitted she was *enceinte*. He'd taken her at her word, which showed how dangerous she was to him.

He needed more than an admission. He needed proof.

Even then he wouldn't tie himself to a woman who stirred such fiery passion in him. A woman who'd deceived him.

Just because she might be the mother of his child, it didn't mean he had to include her in his life. If the child proved to be his, he could easily gain custody of his heir and banish Kira Montgomery from their lives.

She was a schemer. A puppet of Bellamy's who'd thought nothing of doing the unthinkable. She didn't deserve to be in charge of an innocent life.

Kira had smoothly lied to him from the start. He had proof. Proof didn't lie, didn't deceive.

She bore watching closely, for her will was strong. So were her wiles, and she knew how to use them to get her way. While her *femme fatale* act had won Bellamy over, it wouldn't work on him.

But it had—and that shamed him.

He should not find her desirable—shouldn't want her for his own. But he craved her with a hunger that startled him.

His body burned with need, even knowing what he did about her, knowing she would betray him the first chance she got. He loathed the crippling emotion and refused to be ruled by it.

As he'd watched Kira gain control of her emotions earlier, he'd realized she hated the attraction she had for him as well. She pulled him to her, a powerful, sensual magnet that he struggled to resist.

Oui, André was not alone in his passion. She wanted him with a fierceness that rivaled his. She would have given herself to him in the pool if he'd pushed. He'd come close to doing just that!

She was his for the taking. He knew it, and she did as well. He could have had her tonight if he chose to, but she'd expected that. Planned it! The damn paparazzi had even circled his waters like sharks!

Though he believed she was with child, he knew better than to trust a woman—especially one who'd deceived him before. Was still deceiving him.

He'd buy a pregnancy test kit in Martinique tomorrow and verify her condition. And after that?

After that, they'd wait to learn the baby's paternity.

And while they waited she'd be his willing mistress, for there'd be no reason to deny what they both wanted.

Kira woke well past the first blush of dawn, stretching in the downy bed like a sated cat. She couldn't recall when she'd felt so rested. Sleep had been a stranger to her of late—she'd endured weeks of minimal rest even before her arduous journey to Petit St. Marc.

She sighed, lulled by the distant crash of the sea to the shore and the foreign caw and trill of exotic birds. Most were distant or muffled, but all were soothing. She could lie in bed for hours—something she rarely did.

The creak of the rattan chair in her room seemed overly loud. Her nerves tightened, the calming mood gone.

She wasn't alone.

Kira gathered the sheet to her chin and stared toward the chair. Her pulse quickened when her gaze lit on André's tall form lounging negligently across from the bed, watching her.

"Bonjour," he said, rising with fluid grace to cross to the bed with lazy purpose.

The closer he got, the clearer she read the impatience in his dark eyes. What now?

"Good morning," she replied, and hoped it would be.

He sat a box on the bedside table. "I have it on good authority that these tests are reliable."

Her gaze flicked from his to the box, then back to him. "You want me to take a pregnancy test?"

"Oui. It is suggested one should take it first thing."

A fact she knew well, since she'd gone through this procedure when her cycle had been uncharacteristically late. Her doctor had confirmed the test was right—she was pregnant.

Yet André demanded proof again.

She shrugged, hiding her annoyance that he distrusted her so. "As soon as you leave I'll take it, and satisfy your curiosity."

"I'll wait."

He had to be kidding. But one look at the firm set to his mouth confirmed he was dead serious.

"Fine. Just give me a moment." She left the bed and padded to the *en suite* bathroom. "Alone," she added, when she sensed him following her.

She took the test, as prescribed, then carried the stick out into the room. "It takes five minutes."

He checked his watch and nodded, his features a stony mask of indifference. An odd tension hummed between them to keep her on edge. What went through his mind? And, more importantly, could he love their baby?

Thirty seconds before time was up, he strode to her side and stared down at the test she held. As if it had awaited his arrival, a pink line materialized in the window.

"It is positive," he said. "You are *enceinte*."

She shook her head as she disposed of the test stick, her smile rueful. "I admitted that."

He stared at her for a long, uncomfortable moment, as if expecting her to say more. And she wanted to talk to him, for she had no idea how he felt about having a child.

"But who is the father?" he asked.

"I've told you already."

"*Oui*, once."

"Once is enough." He could either believe her, or wait six months for the test that would prove she'd told him the truth.

"You surprise me, *ma chérie*. I expected you would *insist* that the baby you carry is mine and not Bellamy's," he said, his eyes dark and accusatory.

"Why should I bother? You don't believe a word I say."

"For once we are in agreement." He strode to the door, back straight and broad shoulders stiff. "You will remain my guest until you have the baby."

"Your prisoner, you mean," she said.

"If you choose to look at it that way."

"Fine—play the tyrant," she said, so angry she could scream. But he'd expect that, and she'd not surrender to hysterics. Not now. "I can work on my laptop from here as easily as I can from the Chateau."

He stopped at the door, his expression incredulous. At last she'd gotten some reaction from him. But in a flash it was gone, replaced by the hard look she'd come to hate.

"Your only job until you give birth is to take care of yourself and the baby," he said.

"I can do that and continue working."

"Out of the question."

"Why? Have you fired me?"

"You have a new job now," he said, leaving her to wonder. "Or have you so quickly forgotten your condition?"

She glared at him, chafing at the order. "Not likely. I'll be pregnant for another six months. If I don't have something with which to occupy my time I'll go out of my mind."

His smile came slowly—a thief of passion, sneaking in unaware. The sensual curl to his mouth sent heat unfurling in her and reminded her just how much she craved his touch, his kiss. Just how responsive she was to him.

"I will endeavor to keep you busy, *ma chérie*." And with that he was gone.

Kira pressed her fists to her temples, so frustrated with André's high-handedness she could scream. If she stayed she'd become his mistress. But no matter how appealing it would be to lose herself in his arms again, to stay placed her in a dangerous game she feared she'd not win.

For once André discovered she was a Bellamy, he'd treat her with the same hatred he harbored for Edouard and Peter. He'd hate her *and* their child.

She had to contact her solicitor today. She had to find out who had set her up to look like Peter's accomplice.

Perhaps when the truth was out in the open she and André could reach a rational decision regarding the future of the Chateau and their child? And their own relationship? She could only hope.

Kira paced her room, wondering how she'd manage to sneak into André's office and ring up her solicitor. It would have to be when he left the house. Even then she'd have to be careful, for Otillie was always around.

Kira dressed quickly in khaki capri pants and a floral blouse that made her eyes gleam like rich amber and enriched the auburn highlights in her hair.

She slipped into comfortable espadrilles and made her way downstairs to the dining room. Otillie appeared almost immediately, which confirmed what Kira feared—the housekeeper was watching her closely.

She took a seat and forced a casual mien. "Will André be joining me for breakfast?"

"No," Otillie said, as she set an assortment of thinly sliced baguettes topped with ruby-tinted jelly and chocolate-filled croissants on the table. "Monsieur Gauthier ate earlier."

"Perhaps I'll see him at lunch, then."

Otillie frowned as she poured coffee that smelled rich and strong. "*Monsieur* will not return until this afternoon. He requested dinner at seven, and will join you then, *oui*?"

"Of course. I'll enjoy the beach, then," she said, hoping Otillie would take her at her word.

The older woman looked her up and down, then nodded. "*Bonjour, mademoiselle.*"

Kira ate a croissant, though her appetite was nil, then left the table. She resisted the urge to rush into André's office, and waited until Otillie disappeared into the kitchen.

Her nerves twanged a discordant beat as she slipped into his masculine domain. She hadn't been in this room in three months, yet it looked the same. With one exception. There was no telephone evident.

She searched everywhere, her frustration rising. He must have anticipated she'd try to place a call and removed the phone. He'd trumped her plan. Or so he thought.

Kira was not to be deterred—not on something as important as discovering who was set on discrediting her. She knew none of the cottages had telephones, yet there must be one at the restaurant.

Fifteen minutes later she slipped into the only restaurant on the island. A guard sat at the bar, which was manned by a tall thin Carib.

"*Bonjour, mademoiselle,*" the bartender said. "What is your pleasure?"

"Sparkling water with a twist of lime," she said as she claimed a stool at the end of the bar.

From here she had a good view of behind the bar. But the

only telephone visible was the mobile hooked to the bartender's belt.

Feeling defeated, Kira grabbed her glass of water and took a stroll along the beach. She saw more guards positioned at the dock. Though they appeared to be resting, she knew they were watching her.

Kira continued onward, down the leeward side of the island away from the public beach, so frustrated she wanted to scream.

Petit St. Marc was a beautiful prison, a verdant green rainforest surrounded by white sand. The turquoise sea rolled in an endless expanse toward the horizon, broken only by a passing ship that was soon out of sight. She walked around the spit of land that jutted into the froth of water and stepped into a protected cay.

She caught a glimpse of a guard patrolling the beach before he disappeared around an outcropping. Closer to her, a Carib boy stood on the crescent of sand, staring out to sea. Kira followed his gaze.

Not far offshore she spotted a sleek kayak, slicing through the water with apparent ease. And far out in the water she spied the unmistakable green of trees. Another island?

Of course. The kayak must have come from there.

A daring plan teased her mind as she stood in the protection of the rocks while the mariner rowed toward the shore. Just before the lime-green kayak reached the beach the young Carib bounded out and pulled the shallow boat the rest of the way onto the sand.

The two boys ran up the track and disappeared into the forest. Her gaze flitted from the kayak to the other island. There'd be a telephone there—one that was not guarded.

If she left immediately she could ring her solicitor and be back on the island before anyone missed her. She'd know what Claude had found out in her absence. But she'd have to journey there in the kayak first.

Her stomach knotted at the thought of riding such a distance in a small watercraft. Her terror of small boats tended to paralyze her with fear. But this was her best chance to speak at length with her solicitor.

With Claude's aid she could get to the bottom of this deception. But first she had to overcome her phobia.

She closed her eyes, trembling from head to toe, her stomach tossing like a storm-tossed sea. Dark memories of the boating accident darted from their shadows to taunt her. The pitch of the boat on Lake Mead. Her mother's squeal of laughter as her newest lover drove the speedboat at a reckless speed. The sharp turn that had pitched Kira from the boat. The suffocating water that had rushed over her head, the numbing cold, the blackness that had seemed eternal.

Kira opened her eyes on a gasp, the wedge of green lying before her a blur through her tears. She couldn't do it. Her fear was too great.

Yet even as she admitted it she knew she had to try.

Kira darted an uncertain glance at the forest. The boys had yet to return. Nobody else was around. This was her chance to slip away. Now.

Her stomach quivered and her knees trembled as she inched toward the kayak. One step. Two.

She had to think of her child. Of convincing André she wasn't the conniving tart he believed her to be. This was the only way.

Yet even as she maneuvered the light vessel around and jumped in, she wondered if she could trust her solicitor with this request.

What if he was the one who'd set her up for this fall? Kira wondered as she put to sea. Who could she trust? Nobody.

André, her heart whispered.

No! It was too soon to trust him. She concentrated on rowing the kayak.

The first swell propelled the craft high on a wave and dropped it. Terror coursed through her in electrifying ripples. Her hands tightened so on the rounded handle of the paddle, fighting the waves that threatened to force her back to Petit St. Marc.

A young boy had managed it. Surely she could as well?

Kira focused on making the paddle work for her instead of against her. But reading about kayaking and doing it were two different things, further complicated by her numbing fear of sitting so low on the sea.

The salt spray stung her skin. The strong lap of the waves against the fiberglass kayak kept her on edge.

She dipped the paddle in the turquoise brine and thought of the men in her life. The promises made. Broken. The love she'd hoped to find that remained elusive.

The soul-searing passion she'd shared with just one man. André. The precious baby they'd created.

The past month she'd thought of coming back to him. Having lived her life embroiled in secrets, she'd grown to despise them. And now that he'd brought her back she was cloaked in more secrets that could destroy their future.

She kept her gaze trained on the island ahead. It still seemed small and remote. How long would it take to get there?

Hopefully not long. She needed to be back on Petit St. Marc when André returned.

Kira longed to give her weary arms a rest from rowing, but the sudden change in the wind was whipping her off course. It took all her strength to keep the kayak headed toward her destination.

She glanced back at Petit St. Marc. Though she was far from the island, it still loomed large and mysterious, much like its owner.

Her stomach rolled like the sea, growing angrier by the second. So did the wall of clouds hunkering on the horizon, stretching high and ominous in a blue sky that was quickly growing black.

A storm was approaching fast. Being out on the water in the small kayak doused her in renewed fear.

She'd made a mistake setting to sea. The clouds boiled into a tower that looked more ominous than André's temper. She'd never make it to shore before the squall broke.

As if in agreement, a gust of wind hit her, lifting the kayak and sending it shooting a good ten feet in the wrong direction. Panic squeezed a scream from her. She shook so badly her knees knocked against the fiberglass hull of the craft.

The swell crashed over her, drenching her to the skin. Then again as it tossed the kayak further off course.

Kira forced her weary arms to work the paddle, slicing in the choppy water. Again and again. Fighting against the storm and her choking panic, knowing if she gave up she would die.

She was close enough to see details of the island's shoreline. Her heart sank and new fear exploded within her.

The island was minuscule compared to Petit St. Marc—a heavily wooded dome that crashed into the sea, leaving a shoreline littered with treacherous rocks.

Her arms shook so badly with fear and exhaustion she could barely row. But she couldn't stop. She couldn't put ashore here.

It was too dangerous. She had to push on.

Surely she'd find a village on the other side?

Lightning streaked overhead and she jumped, nearly dropping the paddle. Her heart pounded so hard she grew light-headed.

Kira tried to skirt the side of the island. Her arms ached, her shoulders burned, and her stomach lurched with dread. But it was her mind that taunted her the most, chiding her for making a mistake that could kill herself and her child.

The sky opened. Rain pelted her, blinded her. Her clothes molded to her. Her long hair was plastered to her face and back. Water filled the small kayak.

Still she fought the paddle, fought the swell of the waves, fought her panic. She couldn't stop, couldn't rest until she got past the last cluster of jagged rocks that had turned black and sinister in the deluge.

The whine of a high-powered engine sliced through the rumble of a storm. Someone else was out in this weather. Coming closer. Perhaps the Carib boy's father? Perhaps someone who could help her?

She whimpered with exhaustion and darted past the last out-cropping, knowing to stop would send the kayak crashing into the rocks. But her strength was deserting her.

The engine's whine grew closer. Closer. Apprehension skipped down her spine.

Nobody should be out in this weather. Yet she was, and she wasn't alone.

She risked a quick glance back, hoping to see who was there, catching a glimpse of a man riding the crest of a wave.

André? No!

How had he found her so quickly?

It didn't matter. He was here. She had absolute trust he'd save her, if only to upbraid her for setting to sea in a storm.

As if mocking her attempt to stay alive, a gust of wind broadsided the kayak. The paddle was ripped from her hands. The wind stole her scream. In a blink, the kayak flipped over.

Sea water was shoved into her face and enveloped her, dragging her down. Down. Down.

Dark.

Suffocating.

And her nightmare came back to life.

André's heart stopped, only to start with a vengeance and race with the fury of the wind. He'd kill her for doing something so foolish, for putting herself and his baby in harm's way.

But first he had to rescue her and see them safely onto Noir Creux. First he had to play the part of a fool again.

He cut the Jet Ski's engine and dove into the spot where he'd seen her go down. He ticked off minutes in his mind, knowing time was precious. Crucial.

He died by centimeters as he searched the murky depths churned by the storm and didn't find her. He stretched out, swimming fast and hard, pushing through the black water until his lungs burned.

Finally his fingers grazed skeins of silk. He wound a hand

in the thick mass of hair and reeled her to him, then anchored her close and pushed them both to the surface at the same time.

Her fingers digging into his arms gave him hope, energy, profound relief. His choking fear died, only to give birth to an anger that made the storm pale in comparison.

They broke the surface together, pounded by rain and battered by waves, limbs entwined, gazes locked on one another. He read the fear and need and relief in her eyes. He recoiled from the odd tangled emotions that sank into him.

He didn't want to feel more for her than lust. All he wanted was to capture her desire. But she took more. More than he had to offer. More than he wanted to give.

After his jaunt to Martinique to meet with his solicitor he knew why. For her impassioned vow that the Chateau was her home was a lie. She was an opportunist, flitting from one bene-factor to another.

But not with him. He had the upper hand now, and he didn't intend to relinquish it.

It was just as well she didn't understand the turmoil eddying within him. She was an enchantress who wouldn't hesitate to use his weakness toward her to further her goal.

He wrapped an arm around her tiny waist and struck out for shore, aware of the pitfalls he'd memorized years before. The press of her body against his was sheer torture.

Before his private hell had enveloped his life she'd been the type of woman he'd desired. Not just as a lover. No, as his mate.

But that had been an eternity ago.

He wasn't the same man he'd been back then.

He'd lost patience with the gentler side that demanded trust, fidelity. Love.

He couldn't give any woman those things. All he could offer was his protection. Money. Unbridled passion.

André certainly would never offer even that to his enemy, no matter how much he desired her. No matter that she likely carried his heir.

After an eternity, André felt the black grit of volcanic sand beneath him. He pushed from the surf, dragging her with him, her fingernails digging into his arm attesting to her fear.

She was his for the taking. One word, one touch, and she'd tumble into his arms.

That would be too easy, stripping him of any satisfaction of conquering her. Of catching her at her own duplicity.

The rain battered them now, as merciless as his feelings toward her. He trudged through the churning surf between towering rocks slicked by rain, her by his side, her essence coursing through his blood, luring him in.

A black hole loomed ahead and he ran into it, pulling her in beside him. Only then did he draw a decent breath. Only then did he look at her. Only then did he realize his heart was close to beating out of his chest.

Fury. That was why. Any other reason was unacceptable.

The deep shadows in the cave obscured her features. So he focused on each indrawn breath, each stutter of sound, each ripple of sensation that sped from her hand into his.

"Do you feel all right?" he dared to ask.

"Yes. Fine." He heard her swallow, felt another tremor go from her, and he cursed the span of concern he felt for her. "We are all right."

She and the baby were alive. He was alive. And they were marooned together until the storm abated.

He detested the fact she'd ensnared him in such seclusion. Even though he knew what he knew about her, she made him feel things that made no sense to him, that he'd never experienced before. That scared the hell out of him.

Yet he ached to make her his right now. Again. Alone in this primitive cave while the storm raged outside and his own tempest battered within him, when nothing and nobody could interrupt them this time.

He wanted to pound into her with the same intensity as the

storm pummeled the islet. He wanted to break down her defenses and for once hear her admit the truth.

Mon Dieu! She'd drive him mad with her stubborn nature and siren's body. She was a contradiction that defied reason.

How could she be terrified of small boats, yet risk her life in one today? To escape him. That was why.

She'd have done anything to flee the trap she'd ended up in, for a fortune awaited her. Yet how could she have known?

Damn her! "Have you no regard for my child?"

He felt her stiffen, sensed her muscles bunching as if to pull away from him. "I—I only meant to find a telephone here, then return to Petit St. Marc."

No doubt she'd been desperate to contact Peter and confirm if the deal had gone through. If so, she'd have found a way to disappear. Her error in seeking help here, coupled with the storm, had thwarted that plan. It had dumped her right back into André's lap. Just where he wanted her.

"You would've waited an eternity. Noir Creux is uninhabited. A nature sanctuary under the protection of France." He hauled her against his side, stopping her retreat. "And me."

"You watch over a nature sanctuary?" Incredulity rang in her voice.

"I watch over many precious things." Like her?

The thought came unbidden and was met with immediate resistance. She was more dangerous than a hurricane. Her carnal sting more lethal than a scorpion's.

"Noir Creux is unique," he said at last, when his pulse had ceased hammering in his veins, when his need to take her had abated. "An extinct volcanic dome is attached to a coral reef. Both are ancient."

"Any buried treasure?"

"Oui," he said, attuned to her every word, to every subtle shift of her body, to the wild scent of the storm mingling with warm woman. "But to attempt to remove it would destroy something far more valuable than doubloons."

"You surprise me, André." The comment was soft. Intimate, yet tinged with awe.

His fingers curled into fists. He didn't want her admiration, her praise. He didn't want to think that she'd be more than willing to tumble into his arms now that he'd proved he cared about something other than making millions. Or was it just another act?

It didn't matter anymore. He wanted her.

Here.

Fast.

Hard.

Kira was his booty, fetched from the sea. His prize to savor. His to command. Yet the life within her tempered him like nothing else had. Life they'd likely created.

She'd gotten to him, breached his defenses, made him deal with emotions he'd vowed never to feel. He hated the doubts that crept into his mind. Hated second-guessing himself. Hated that she had lied to him from the start.

It would stop now.

He wouldn't be swayed by her excuses.

He had to throw up walls again.

He had to gain the upper hand.

He had just the means to make her hate him.

"You could have asked more for your shares, *ma chérie*," he said.

"Shares?"

"*Oui.* Your stock in the Chateau."

He heard her breath catch, felt tension eddy from her in icy waves. "I didn't put a price on my shares because they aren't for sale."

Mon Dieu, was all that came from her mouth lies? "I received a call early this morning, giving me first chance to buy your shares. Just like Edouard's were offered to me."

"This can't be happening," she said. "Who called you?"

"It doesn't matter."

"Yes, it does, because I won't sell."

"You can't change your mind now."

"I most certainly can. I never approved a sale. My God, I have to call my solicitor, stop this before—"

"It's too late. I paid your price," he said. "As of an hour ago, Chateau Mystique is one hundred percent mine."

CHAPTER SIX

KIRA moved toward the mouth of the cave, her feet leaden, feeling cold and hollow inside. She'd thought she'd survived the worst life could fling at her. How naïve she'd been.

When Edouard had promoted her from hospitality manager of his elite Le Cygne Hotel in London to significant minority stockholder of Chateau Mystique, she'd been terrified and anxious. She'd wanted to please Edouard. Wanted to prove to him that she could run a luxury hotel, that she was worthy of his attention at last.

But she'd barely settled in when tragedy had struck. A car accident had taken the life of Edouard's mistress and left him in critical condition.

That was when André Gauthier had struck, offering an outrageous sum for the whole of the Chateau. Edouard, through his solicitor Claude, had delivered a firm no—the Chateau wasn't for sale. But André had persisted, and Kira had feared for Edouard's recovery in the face of so much turmoil.

She'd said as much to Claude, who'd quickly arranged that meeting between Kira and André on Petit St. Marc. A meeting André still swore he'd known nothing about.

That was when she'd engaged in the most bracing debate of her life. That was when she'd lost a bit of her heart to André Gauthier.

Not once had she surrendered her stance on the availability of the Chateau, but she'd caved to his sensual demands.

The day after she'd returned to Las Vegas Edouard had died. Kira had mourned him in her own way, for though he'd been her father, she'd barely known him.

He'd made it clear when she was very young that he would provide for her, but he'd never give her his name. He would keep her apart from his legitimate family—the two would never become one. She was never to admit her paternity to anyone, and if she did he'd disinherit her.

She'd done as he'd asked because she'd been a child and alone. Because she'd known no better.

He had educated her and given her a job at his London hotel, but the biggest surprise had come when he'd brought her to America and given her shares in the Chateau. He'd made it clear that this was all she'd get from him, and his own shares wouldn't pass to her until his death.

It had been enough. She'd had great plans to improve the hotel on the Vegas strip, and she'd had a chance to finally know her father.

But tragedy had struck first. And now, through an act of deceit, André owned it all.

And she had nothing but false promises.

She stared out at the rain sheeting over the islet. Had the person who'd trumped up documents to make it appear as if she'd conspired with Peter Bellamy to ruin André also forged her name to dispose of her shares? Had they done the same with Edouard's shares as well?

Who had that much corporate power? Peter Bellamy?

According to Edouard, when Peter had discovered Kira's existence his legitimate son had resented her. Had her half-brother sought to ruin her? If so, he'd done a good job of it, for both acquisitions had gotten past Claude, her and Edouard's solicitor.

It could take years of litigation to regain her shares. She had no money. No resources. Nothing but a baby growing in her. While André had wealth and control on his side.

How utterly foolish she'd been to think she could come to terms with him. "How much did you pay?" she asked.

"You know the answer."

"How much?" she asked, her voice cracking.

His pause stretched an eternity. "Two million."

A fortune. *Her* fortune.

Kira pressed her head against the damp stone wall of the cave, feeling dry and burned up inside. Used and tossed aside like refuse.

She doubted the funds had gone into her account. No, whoever had plotted this embezzlement would have escaped with it.

Kira pressed a palm over the cold stone, so chilled by her bleak future that she barely felt the dampness seep deeper into her. She didn't know what to do now. Didn't know what she could possibly do.

She stared at the rain coursing over the rocks, each droplet knowing its destination. Gravity guided it, though the water was happy to stay its course, to rush on and join a larger pool, its identity lost in the community of water, joining the mass for the common good of the sea.

Kira envied those droplets, for as of now she had nowhere to go. No one to turn to for help. No family waiting to take her in. No purpose. Nothing.

All because of a traitor at the Chateau and André Gauthier's thirst for vengeance.

She'd known André was ruthless, that he was a corporate raider who attained whatever he set out to conquer. He'd never lied about wanting the Chateau.

But she hadn't guessed he'd be so relentless in his pursuit of it. That he'd abduct her in his quest for vengeance, then cut her out of her inheritance without remorse. That it would be so easy for him to achieve his goal with the destruction of her own.

Her own naïveté was much to blame, for she'd believed the

trouble she'd faced at the Chateau had stemmed from a few disloyal employees who'd resented her sudden elevated status. She'd never dreamed someone was plotting her ruin.

Or were they? Could she truly believe André? Had *he* paid the traitor to do this bit of nasty business?

Her heart said no, that he'd simply been waiting for the opportunity to present itself. But her heart was too hungry for love to be trusted. Her heart was too open, too innocent—easy bait for the sly and cunning of the species. Like André?

He had the power to engineer such a takeover. The ruthless bent to take what he wanted by any means.

"Who is the conspirator?" she asked, too heartsick to cry or raise her voice. "I have a right to know his name."

"How would I know?"

She whirled on him, blinking once, then again, before she saw him in the gloom. The shadows fit him well.

"Don't lie to me," she said. "You must have paid someone at the Chateau to do your bidding. Someone who would forge my name on documents so nobody would question why my stocks were offered to you, making your takeover complete."

"I don't resort to underhanded dealings."

She jerked her chin up, willing him to read the movement as defiant. Livid. "Just kidnapping?"

"Don't bait me, *ma chérie*."

"Why not?" She moved toward him, trembling with anger as well as anxiety, tired of his bullying. "You stripped me of my home and my job. My dream. I have nothing left to lose."

"No?"

He flung an arm around her and jerked her to him. Her breasts flattened against his chest, her stomach rubbing his taut belly. His powerful arms banded hers to her sides.

His captive. His desire. His!

She felt his dominance in every breath he took. Felt his savage need course from him into her, fueling her own wants which she could barely contain.

Kira knew the folly in trying to break free, so she stood as stiff as a statue and braced herself for a kiss meant to dominate. To punish.

Let him take. She could give no more.

For surely an arrogant man like André, who was this close to the edge, would take her now? He'd be driven to punish her for challenging him. He wouldn't be satisfied until he controlled everything about her.

Like the last time they'd ended up entwined in each other's arms? Making love with a fever that had threatened to consume them? That had created a life?

His head bent to hers, slowly, his gaze afire with need and something else she couldn't recognize. She trembled, wanting him so badly she shook.

But she had to be strong—for her child. For her self-respect. That was all she had left. Kira turned her head, denying him.

Instead of his expected spate of anger, one strong, masculine hand slipped between their bodies and splayed on her belly. Tremors coursed through her with terrifying force, mocking her with a sense of rightness she was loath to admit. Firing her blood and her anger in turn.

But it was her heart that paused, warmed, softened. For surely that protective palm, pressed where their child thrived, meant he cared?

"I will file for complete custody," he said, his lips grazing the tender skin behind her ear. But instead of heat, she felt chilled to the bone.

He couldn't be that cold. That heartless. Yet he wasn't a man to make idle threats either.

"You can't mean that," she said.

"But I do, *ma chérie*. The baby binds us together now, but after the birthing that will change."

The forewarning speared her heart and soul, honing her maternal instincts to protect her baby however she must. How could she have thought she had nothing more to lose? That she had a chance for a future with André?

She'd do anything to keep her child. Anything.

She would not lose this battle.

Kira turned her head, her gaze seeking his in the minimal light. His resolute features confirmed he knew her weakness as well. And he knew how to use that against her.

Certainly whoever had sculpted his beautiful mouth had seduction in mind. She felt her own lips tingle, remembering the firmness of his mouth molded to hers, the provocative bow that tickled and teased and tempted her to shed her inhibitions. She had only to shift a little and lift her face to his to steal a kiss, to take the initiative again. She wouldn't. She couldn't. But, oh, how she longed to!

And his eyes—my God, she could drown in their mesmerizing depths.

"You can't seriously mean to take my child from me." Because it was wrong and cruel. Because it would kill her to be cut from her child's life.

"It is for the best," he said, his voice lethally low and as impassive as his gaze. "I am wealthy and can provide for my heir."

"I'll fight you."

"You will lose."

She didn't doubt that he was right, that he'd pull strings to get his way. But she wouldn't capitulate either. Not on this. Not ever.

"Then I'll seek joint custody—"

"No. After this reckless stunt you pulled today, you can't be trusted to care for my baby."

Unbidden tears stung her eyes and she looked away, feeling frantic now, refusing to give him the satisfaction of knowing he'd brought her low again. She gathered her courage around her, ready to plead with him to have a heart, then reminded herself he had none. For no man possessing compassion would attempt to rip a child from his mother's arms.

"I'll fight you until my very last breath," she said again, her fingers bunching his wet shirtfront. "I'll never willingly give up my child."

A charged silence rebounded off the cave walls, the tension punctuated by the rain that had reduced to a gentle patter, as if hushing to hear what he'd say. But time crawled by and he didn't respond. Didn't so much as move a muscle.

Slowly, sunlight crept into the cave, as if the heavens were rolling up their blinds. Even the air had become heavy and still, as if holding its breath in anticipation of his reply.

"Nor will I," he said at last, his arms tightening a fraction in a parody of a hug before releasing her.

Kira stepped away from him, knowing things would only get worse when the truth came out, certain that whatever bargain she struck with André must be done soon. "I'll never accept being a passing moment in my baby's life."

Some emotion flickered in his eyes—something beyond hate or lust or cold calculation. Something that gave her a thin thread of hope. She grabbed onto to it and held tight.

She trusted that André would never be so cruel as to rip her baby from her arms, from her heart. But if she was wrong…

André ran a hand over his hair, slicking the wet strands back off his tanned brow, his features unreadable as he motioned to the cave entrance. "It's time we returned to Petit St. Marc."

"How?"

She doubted she had the strength to paddle the kayak back to the island, even if she could find it. Most likely the small craft was lost to the sea.

"With luck, my Jet Ski rode out the squall."

"And if it didn't?" she asked.

He lifted one broad shoulder in a negligent shrug and left the cave. She took a deep breath, stretching her hands forward and then tightening her fingers into fists. Once. Twice.

But it did no good. Her hands still trembled, her stomach still pitched, and her heart still ached with old worries and new. For if she couldn't reach his heart, she'd have to escape the island before her baby was born. She'd have to disappear. Start over. Hide the rest of her life. For a man like André would never let her best him.

Kira quit the cave and stepped onto the rain-soaked black sand beach. As she'd expected, there was no sign of the kayak.

Its burial at sea was fitting, since a pirate had seized control of her hotel. Her life. Her future.

Out with the old.

In with the new.

Her gaze flitted to André, knee-deep in the frothy surf, inspecting a long, sleek Jet Ski. His hair glistened blue-black in the now blinding sun, the thick mass waving in artful precision over the strong column of his neck.

He'd removed his shirt to reveal a bronzed back beautifully chiseled with muscles that bunched and bulged with each movement. She remembered the feel of that power beneath her fingers as she ran her hands up and down his back, clinging to him, scoring his flesh as he took her beyond any passion that she'd known. The firm smooth texture of his skin beneath her palms. The hint of salt on her tongue that had made her thirsty for more of him.

Her fingers flexed, her body quickening as her gaze flicked over him and she remembered more. His jeans rode low on his lean waist, yet his limbs still looked long and graceful.

Once with him had not been enough.

It never would be, she admitted.

That traitorous ache of want pulsed between her legs, radiating upward to turn her limbs languid, her blood thick and hot. It scared her to be that receptive to any man. That dependent. For it allowed him to dominate her thoughts and keep her on edge.

Just like she'd been all her life. The cycle had to end.

She was so tired of being dominated by powerful men. So weary of having no say in anything.

Oh, Edouard had given her *carte blanche* for implementation of new services at the Chateau. But the long hours she'd pored over the plans had been for naught.

The Chateau was lost to her. It was just another cherished dream that had failed. All because André had chosen to exert his iron control over her.

But he was wrong about one thing. Taking her child from her wasn't for the best. She'd prove it to him. And if his heart still remained hardened, she'd simply disappear.

Talk was nonexistent on the trip back to Petit St. Marc. Not only did the whine of the Jet Ski make conversation nearly impossible, André suspected Kira was too engrossed battling her fear of an even smaller faster sea vessel.

André knew her fingernails would leave marks on his belly. She clung to him, pressing her face to his back, as if branding herself to him there as well.

Her terror rippled through her, tempering his speed as surely as the heat of her passion had burned him earlier. He felt her in every fiber of his being, each indrawn breath, each telling beat of his heart.

He wanted to hate her. Did hate her for siding with Peter Bellamy against him. Yet he desired her with an intensity he'd never felt before.

The admission worried him, for it had been that way from the beginning. When she'd first walked into his study on Petit St. Marc he'd been gripped with lust. He'd had to have her.

Even now, knowing she was in league with his enemy did not lessen his desire. He had the proof of her role in this charade tucked away in his safe, yet he wanted Kira Montgomery in his bed. Wanted his name on her lips when he brought her to climax.

And then what?

The question nagged at him as he killed the engine and beached the Jet Ski. He climbed off and helped her alight, reluctant to release her hand. So he didn't.

For once she wasn't pulling away from him either.

That glint of determination he noted in her eyes intrigued him. Now that they were on firm land, he imagined her mind was busy thinking of ways to convince him she needed to remain an integral part of her child's life.

She didn't need to bother.

He already knew she'd be a good mother.

The thought had embedded itself in André when she stood up to him, fire in her eyes, chin lifted proud, despite the telling tremors that streaked through her. He'd experienced a moment's shame for tossing out the barbarous threat that he'd bar her from their child's life.

But how could he endure her closeness either? Dare to trust her knowing that she'd repeatedly lied to him?

He didn't know. The fact he was not ready to leave her company when he had things to do in his office annoyed him, but it was the truth nonetheless.

"Monsieur Gauthier!"

André looked up at the young boy running pell-mell toward him, one brown hand raised high and waving a snow-white envelope. The mail must have arrived, and Georges had determined this missive demanded his immediate attention.

He allowed a fleeting smile. The boy was eager to earn another euro for hand-delivering his mail. André knew the boy would use the money to help support his ill mother and younger siblings.

"Pour vous, monsieur," Georges said, thrusting the envelope at him with a toothy smile.

The missive was from his detective, sent to the island by courier. It must be the final report on Kira Montgomery.

Unwilling to trek to the house to reward the boy, he tossed him the keys to the Jet Ski. "Take it. It is yours."

George's eyes rounded. *"Merci—merci."*

André turned to Kira and motioned to the gate leading into his private beach. "Walk with me."

"You're going to let that boy borrow that dangerous thing?" she asked.

"No, he can have the Jet Ski."

"Why?"

"Because he is loyal. Because it pleases me."

She tipped her head back and stared up at him curiously. The angle was just perfect for the sun to streak highlights in her vibrant hair. The mass hung in rebellious curls, giving her that just-pleasured-by-a-man look.

He caught himself on the verge of smiling and shook his head, surprised again by the contradiction that was Kira Montgomery. She portrayed a refreshing innocence at times, like now, with a flush tinting her cheeks and her eyes wide with wonder.

It was a quality he'd never seen in a mistress before—certainly in none of the women he'd employed! Was it possible that Bellamy had been her first lover?

The thought of her lying with the old man rankled. He entwined his fingers with hers, his chest tightening with annoyance.

A woman with Kira's passion deserved a virile man who could match her in bed, who'd boldly explore the myriad ways they could pleasure each other, who knew how to give and take in bed.

A man who treasured a woman instead of beating her.

He had it on good authority that Edouard Bellamy's finesse in *amour* was lacking, that he was given to bouts of unparalleled jealousy and rage. He knew it was true, for he'd seen the bruises on the old man's former mistress.

André had listened in silent rage as Suzette had made excuses for Bellamy's inexcusable behavior. But she'd stayed with the old man because he had showered her with everything she wanted. She'd chosen Bellamy over her family. She'd loved their enemy.

Had Kira fallen into the same trap? Was she fatalistically loyal to Edouard Bellamy? Would she stab André in the back too?

"What makes you so angry?" she asked, breaking the silence.

He glanced at her and shrugged, pushing the past into the recesses of his mind where it belonged. "After your adventure to Noir Creux, I have reason to be angry, *n'est-ce pas?*"

"Perhaps. I just thought——" She shook her head, her expression pensive. "We need to talk, André."

He frowned, knowing she sought reassurance. It was beyond him to offer comfort, yet he was hesitant to crush her spirits again. Nothing could be gained by beating her down more.

His win was her loss. He'd bested her. So where was the feeling of satisfaction?

André motioned to a massive hammock strung between poles and shaded by a canopy of palm fronds. "This way. I'll join you in a moment."

She bit her lip, as if hesitating, then set off toward the shade without argument.

He watched her, noticing her wet clothes no longer clung to her like his hands longed to do. That was his most challenging problem, for though she'd lied to him, deceived him, he wanted to believe her. His desire for her had blinded him to her perfidy.

André shook his head and tore open the letter from his detective, his impatience with himself escalating. His gaze flew over the short message that ended with a cryptic "more to follow when I receive proof."

He scanned the note again, then read it slowly, absorbing every word. His body tensed as his ire blazed to life again. Could this be some mistake?

But, no, the detective was meticulous in his findings, checking and double-checking everything he uncovered. Which made this bit of news all the more troubling.

Just what the hell was going on? He stuffed the note in his pocket and headed across the sand that was bleached white under the sun's glare.

He'd known from the start Kira was doing Bellamy's bidding, having had proof of her involvement. He'd deduced that she'd now sold her shares in the Chateau so she could embark on a new life—escape his grasp out of fear of retaliation should the child be Bellamy's, or entrapment if the baby was his, as he suspected.

But the two million André had paid for complete control of the Chateau had never showed up in her account in Las Vegas or in England. Likely she'd had the money funneled into a Swiss or offshore bank account. But as soon as the thought crossed his mind he doubted its validity.

Kira hadn't had any access to a telephone—so she couldn't have made the transaction. No, the only way she could have had a hand in this sale was if she'd set it up before he took her from Las Vegas.

It was plausible, for she had admitted to ringing her solicitor, but even so she'd had no idea of his plan. Then, too, why had she refused his earlier offer to buy her shares and then turned around and given him the first crack to acquire them for the price he'd offered earlier?

It made no sense.

She wasn't a flighty businesswoman—of that he was sure. Yet this offer made it seem that way.

Everything she'd queried him about on Noir Creux came back to him. Her surprise at his acquisition and at the amount he'd paid for her shares. The anger, panic and defeat when she'd realized it was a done deal.

Her admission that she'd risked her life just to phone her solicitor to find out the truth. She wasn't lying—of that he was sure.

His mouth pulled into a grim line at that admission. Whether she was the injured party or not, there was nothing he could do about it now. If his detective turned up anything that nullified Kira he'd take action then.

André scanned the beach for Kira. He spotted her, staring forlornly out to sea.

A chill tripped up his spine when he thought how close she'd come to dying. *Mon Dieu*, he had nearly lost them both!

His woman. His child.

A strange warmth expanded in his chest as he allowed himself to believe the truth in his heart. If she was to be believed he'd soon be a father. Not Bellamy. Him—André Gauthier.

It was sobering.

He and his former fiancée had discussed having a family once. She'd wanted two—no more than that! And she hadn't wished to start a family until they'd been married at least three years. No exceptions.

He'd agreed, simply because it was a solid plan. Controlled, like every facet of his life. Because his impending marriage had been nothing more than a business deal.

Then Kira had burst into his life, vibrant and fiery as the morning sun. Her blinding light had exposed the rigidity of his life—she'd roused his anger and his lust. But her sharp mind had been the spark to ignite his interest.

Even knowing she was his enemy's plaything, he'd wanted her then.

Even knowing she'd conspired to ruin him, he still wanted her.

And, damn, he'd have her now.

André ducked under the canopy, pleased Kira was stretched out on the hammock. He kicked off his shoes and pulled his shirt over his head, letting it fall where it might. His cutoffs went next, and he heaved a relieved breath as his sex sprang free.

Her lips parted on a gasp. "What are you doing?"

"Getting comfortable." He moved toward her. The darkening glow of passion in her eyes confirmed she was battling desire without success. "Take your clothes off, *ma chérie*."

"Absolutely not! Someone could come by—"

"Not here. This is my private beach. Nobody will see you but me."

André had the satisfaction of watching her eyes widen, the pupils dilate, her breathing grow heavy. She wanted him as much as he did her, but she was clearly hesitant to shed her inhibitions or her clothes.

Contrary behavior for a mistress. But he'd come to realize Kira wasn't ordinary. *Oui*, she was a contradiction.

Sexy, yet shy.

Passionate, yet refined.

Savvy, yet reserved.

He leaned over her, noting the quickening of her breath, the flushing of her skin. His mouth grazed her soft flushed cheek, nuzzled her neck, moving slowly to where a telling pulse hammered in the slender column of her throat, keeping pace with his own wild heartbeat.

He'd never wanted a woman as much as he did her. Had never exercised such restraint in seducing a woman. But though the chase made the anticipation all the more sweeter, his patience would not last much longer.

"I've seen you naked," he said. "Why hesitate now?"

He heard her swallow, felt a shiver rip through her. "You dare to ask after you threaten to bar me from my child's life?"

He read the resolute determination in her eyes and almost smiled. Almost. She possessed more power than she realized.

"One has nothing to do with the other, *ma chérie*," he said, his fingers releasing the tiny buttons on her blouse.

She grasped his hand, stopping him. "It has everything to do with this—this passion between us. I won't be removed from our child's life, André. Not now, not ever."

She'd thrown down the gauntlet, giving him the choice to refuse to bend, to acquiesce to her demand, or to lie. "Very well. You have my word that I won't mention it again."

"I—" She swallowed. Stared straight into his eyes. And he saw her acceptance for what it was. Trust. "Thank you."

He didn't want her gratitude. Didn't want to tie anything to this moment but mutual desire. No strings, no promises.

"Now we will make love *à la Caribbean Française, oui*?"

"Yes," she said.

Triumph surged through him, along with emotions he didn't want to face. Not now. Not when these new disturbing sensations were hammering away at him.

He pushed her blouse wide and traced a finger over the lace trim on her demi-bra, surprised his hand trembled. Stunned that with her he felt like an untried youth again.

She moaned and splayed her hands on his chest, the small

fingers flexing over his muscles. An electric jolt shot through him, his muscles snapping taut, his body quivering with need. *Mon Dieu*, but he'd never experienced such sexual awareness from a simple touch.

He stared at her, his gaze ravenous as it swept over the creamy swells of her breasts pushing above the lacy scrap of her bra. A growl of annoyance rumbled through him, for he hated the barrier. With a flick of his fingers he released the clasp.

She moaned as her bosom spilled free. He palmed a globe, intrigued by the pale silken texture of her breast against his tanned skin, of the taut puckered nipple begging for his kiss.

"You are beautiful."

The tip of her tongue flicked over the lips he longed to taste and tease. But it was her eyes, lifted to his, that sent his heart racing into overdrive. Desire, longing, trust.

"I am average," she said. "But you—you're extraordinary."

"You needn't resort to flattery to win my favor."

"I'm not," she said, her voice breathy. "It's just that I've never met a man like you before."

"Nor will you," he said, driven by a fierce possessiveness.

Raw need coursed through him, his own blood pooling hot and thick in his groin. He ached to have her. Protect her. To make her his and his alone.

The erotic drumbeat in his ears matched time with her erratic pulse as he removed the last of her clothes, until she was as naked as he. He stood there feasting on the pale curves and hollows of her body, knowing that for now she was his.

Oui, the time for waiting was over.

He'd have her here. Now. And damn the consequences.

Kira shivered with nervous energy and a good dose of shock. She'd never imagined she would enjoy lying naked beneath a man's scrutiny. And in broad daylight on a beach, no less!

But the sultry promise in André's eyes captivated her. She was under his spell, ensnared by the onslaught of his passion, a willing slave to his desire.

More than that, she trusted that he would make things right. That sometime he'd listen to her. That he'd believe she wasn't the calculating woman he'd accused her of being.

She trusted him in this. It was enough. For now.

Warmth swept over her like a welcoming summer breeze, kissing the skin he'd just bared. He was going to make love with her and she would welcome him.

She ached for him to kiss her, to touch her. But he just stood by the hammock, his gaze devouring every inch of her. And her body reacted to his scrutiny as if the touch were real, her skin pebbling and flushing, her muscles tensing, her breath growing heavy as her pulse raced out of control.

The sensations were new and intense, robbing her of will, of restraint. She couldn't push him away, not when her arms had ached to hold him to her again. Not when she'd dreamed of this moment for three long months.

Her body had throbbed in the dead of night, just remembering the wonder of his gloriously powerful form fitted to hers, moving in hers in a harmony she'd never felt before. When he'd made love to her before she'd felt their hearts beat in tandem.

She wanted that again. Had to have it.

The sensations he wrought in her defied description, but her soul knew this joining was right.

He was the flesh-and-blood man of her dreams. The father of her baby. She wanted him with a keening ache that overrode caution.

She smiled, her arms reaching for him, knowing she'd die if he didn't kiss her, touch her, love her. Knowing she must steal this moment, this memory, now, before he learned the truth.

His mouth quirked, his eyes gleaming. He rolled into the hammock, the net dipping precariously as he settled beside her.

In the perfect synchronization of the lovers' dance, her body shifted to fit against his. She focused on every nuance of the moment, skin touching skin, hard unyielding muscles pressing against soft flesh.

His hand rested on her hip, unmoving, light, yet his touch sent heat spiraling to her core. Her hand found a natural perch on his broad shoulder.

It felt right. Perfect.

It felt like forever.

But all it could ever be was now.

For the passion blazing between them would be doused the moment he learned she was Edouard Bellamy's daughter.

CHAPTER SEVEN

KIRA shifted to make more room for him, her muscles clenching deep inside her as he slid a hair-roughened thigh between hers. She trailed a hand up his muscular arm and over his shoulder, savoring the bunch of strength beneath his hot, smooth skin.

"Make love with me," she said, her hand trekking down his chest to rub a palm over his hardened nipples, feeling his body quicken.

His eyes flared with lust, his hand shifting to caress her with slow, agonizing strokes. "But of course."

Yet he made no move to hurry things along. Desperation sizzled in her. She wanted all he had to give *now*, to sink into him before she had time to analyze this driving need building and building within her. But he was clearly in no hurry.

His big hand glided down the back of her thigh and she squirmed, begging for him to touch her intimately. Instead, his hand meandered back up to her waist, and she dug her fingers into his shoulders as need rocked through her again, her body quivering like jelly.

His fingers splayed over her stomach and a different emotion gripped her, so sharp and new that it shrank her world to what mattered most: him, her and their child.

The tense expression on his face made her wonder if he felt the same. If he felt anything at all except lust and the need to maintain control.

Their child. Could he love their baby?

She closed her eyes, wishing she knew, wishing her emotions weren't so intense and raw with André, wishing what they'd shared was based on love instead of passion.

A child didn't have to be conceived in love to be loved. She would adore her baby—she already did. For once in her life, she'd have someone to love her in return.

But how would André fit into this tidy family?

Kira bit her lip, fearing he'd regard their child much like her father had treated her. She'd been a responsibility he hadn't wanted, yet he'd assumed her care at a young age and placed her in boarding school.

Strangers had raised her, praised her, nourished her as best they could. When the other students had gone home on holiday, she'd been shuffled off to a posh hotel in London and watched by a nanny. She'd never shared a birthday or Christmas with family. Never had anyone who cared about her.

That was why her child would know that he or she was loved. Her child would have a home. Security. A mother. A father?

"What is going on in that pretty head of yours?" he asked.

Us, she wanted to say, but knew that would spoil the moment. So she tucked that truth away with her other secret, that made this dream a challenge to attain.

"I was thinking how good this felt," she said, and it did.

"It gets better."

His hand swept up her ribs, leaving a trail of shivers in its wake. He palmed one breast, his thumb rubbing over the nipple until it throbbed.

She arched against him, craving his touch, craving him. Their future was as substantial as the tropical haze that hung in the dense valleys, but she ached to get lost in the sultry mist with him once more.

His head lowered a fraction. She met him halfway, their mouths brushing once, twice, before melding—a teasing glide of lips and tongues that sent a hum of need vibrating through her. She squirmed, desperate to get closer, to rub against the heat of his sex.

He obliged, grinding against her and making the hammock swing erratically. Her stomach did an odd quiver—and not a pleasant one.

She pulled back, gulping. "This might not be a good idea."

He went still, his intense eyes narrowing to convey his patience would not tolerate any of her machinations now. "You no longer wish to make love?"

She shook her head and let her own hands drift around his torso to trace the tense muscles on his back and the deep indentation of his spine. "Not here. This hammock is a rather unstable bed." And her stomach tended to get queasy.

More so since the jaunt to Noir Creux. She was also a bit light-headed, though looking up into André's magnetic eyes chased both symptoms away.

A slow smile curved his sensuous lips, and raw desire flared in his dark eyes, the combination leaving her breathless for what was to come. "But I thought you enjoyed taking risks."

"Never." Though she was taking a monstrous one now. "I'm a very proper Englishwoman. Brisk walks along well-trod paths and the like."

"How boring."

And so very lonely. But she wouldn't admit that. She'd never revealed this awful emptiness that dwelled within her to another soul. She held close the fact that with him she'd felt a connection and purpose she'd never felt before. She knew no matter how good it seemed now, their affair was tenuous at best.

"Kiss me again," she said, tangling her fingers in his hair and pulling him to her.

"With pleasure."

His mouth was sheer heaven, his kiss so deep and drugging that she couldn't think anymore. Just feel. His taste, his power, his passion were more potent than any drug.

His tongue parried with hers while his hands pillaged her body, molding her breasts, teasing the nipples until she was reeling from want. She arched against him, finding small relief as she rubbed against the hard wall of his chest like a cat in heat.

Sensations crashed within her, her heart swelling with love, her body crying for release. She was drunk on him, torturing herself with a need that the world couldn't contain.

She spread her legs wider and he settled fully against her, his engorged sex hot and hard on her belly. A whimper tore from her, for she needed him in her, filling her. She needed the connection of another soul dancing with hers.

Arching against him only intensified her frustrations, so she wrapped her legs around his hips and ground against him. She was done with the torment—done with the waiting.

His mouth left hers with a gasp, the eyes staring into hers near black. He whispered in French, his voice low, pausing to nuzzle her ear, lap at the lobe, then tug it with his teeth, sending liquid heat rushing through her.

I love him. The litany sang in her heart, filling her with wonder, chasing the dark shadows to their corners.

She moaned, grinding against him, running her hands down his back to skim the taut swell of his derrière, holding back the words that ached to break free. For she was afraid that truth would shatter the mood. Make him think. Doubt.

Her fingers dug into his taut arms as she arched against him, gasping as he shifted and his hot sex moved between her legs.

Yes, she thought, squirming, clutching his back, his ribs, his buttocks. The gentle breeze kissed her through the netting, but she burned with a sensual fever that could only be broken with completion. Only with him.

She panted with need, her senses consumed by him, her heart ensnared as well. The hammock rocked and shimmied, the ropes biting into her bare back. If he didn't make love to her soon she'd die.

His hips rocked forward, his sex pushing inside her. She gasped and smiled, clinging to him, welcoming him home, wanting more, wanting all of him.

He shifted again, pulling from her. "*Mon Dieu*, you're tight. Perfect."

She moaned, frustrated by the torture and the insatiable need for him that raged within her. He was large, powerful, and driving her mad with want.

"You are taking too long," she said, clutching at him.

He pushed into her before the last word left her mouth, filling her completely, touching her heart, her soul. The heat of his unsheathed sex sinking into her pulsing core ripped a gasp of wonder from her. She hadn't remembered this feeling from before, coming at the end of a long night of passion.

This time it felt new. A beginning. Giving birth to a hope she harbored in the secret recesses of her heart. Could it be?

The power and carnal promise in each thrust lifted her higher toward the sun, burning her with his desire, with his need. His brand of absolute possession seared her soul.

She was his. Now. Always. She accepted it. Embraced it. For she knew she'd never find this oneness with another man.

His movements came faster, deeper, keener, stealing her ability to think. He'd pushed her past reason to a shimmering aura where she could only feel, into a spray of glorious rainbows that blinded her.

She clung to him, trembling with the force of her climax, welcoming his release. Nothing she'd experienced came close to this wonderful feeling of unity.

He held her so tightly she thought they'd become one, was sure there no longer existed a place where he ended and she began.

"*Mon amour,*" he said, nearly chewing out the words.

She smiled and blinked back tears, for he'd whispered the only French she knew, the only words she'd ached to hear.

My love.

Yes, she was, she admitted, gliding her hands down his

sweat-slicked back and marveling at the steely strength rippling beneath her fingers.

She could've lain there the rest of the day, but she felt him pulling away from her. Knew this ideal had come to an end.

It was too soon. She wanted more. She wanted forever.

The hammock shimmied beneath her. She stilled and grabbed his arms, the muscles taut. He gave a swift jerk, his body bowing and pulling her flush with his.

Her breath caught in her lungs as the hammock shuddered and flipped. She yelped and clung to André.

Her world turned upside down, air whispering over her bare body, the weight of him on her removed. She sprawled on him, breast to broad chest, stomach to corded belly.

She felt his arms tremble with the strain of holding on to the hammock as he became a new cradle for her.

"Relax, *ma chérie*. The best is yet to come."

She stared into his handsome face, his tension gone and his smile positively lascivious. The impeccable island tycoon garbed in tailored French suits had been replaced by a wild-eyed pirate with seduction oozing from his pores.

Naked and free. And hers.

"Show me," she said.

His smile widened as he let go of the ropes. He dropped, taking her with him, his arms cradling her long before he slammed into the sand.

She straddled him, glorying in the shift of position, of power. The admission was shocking, for she'd never dreamed she'd have sex with a man in the middle of the day on a beach and feel no shame. That she'd revel in being on top.

"The appetizer was wonderful." She dropped a quick kiss on his gorgeous mouth. "What's the entrée?"

"Amour sous le beau ciel."

"I hope that's not fried squid or eyeballs boiled in seaweed."

He threw his head back and laughed, the sound rich and sensual. "Not at all. It means love under the beautiful sky."

"I like that." Especially the love part. For without a doubt, despite everything, she'd fallen hard and fast for André.

She glided her palms up his taut belly, her thumbs tracing the line of black hair that widened over his pectorals. He treated her to much the same torment, sliding his palms up her ribs to cup her breasts.

Their gazes locked, their breaths labored. She stared into eyes that had gone nearly black again. Her fingers danced in an erotic melody over his tanned skin, kneading, marveling at the play of muscle.

She grazed his nipples with her thumbs, dragging a moan from him. Before she could savor her feminine power his hands cupped her breasts, then shifted to tug and roll her nipples between his fingers.

Her mouth opened on a soundless sigh of pleasure, her head tossed back, her world reduced to this moment. This man who knew her body better than she knew it herself.

"About that love under the beautiful sky…" she said, dropping a kiss on his chin, his brow, his nose.

"But of course," he said, between plucking kisses, his voice deep and ragged and oh, so sexy. "Whatever the lady wants."

His heart, she thought. To love and be loved. Now. Forever. Was that too much to ask? She knew the answer. Knew that it was impossible with him.

His hands shifted to her back, gliding from her behind to her shoulders, kneading the taut muscles in both with such erotic precision she moaned with pleasure and awakened need. Live for the moment, she thought. That was all she could do—all she wanted to do right now.

"I want you," she said, her mouth lowering to his.

She got a fleeting glimpse of longing in his eyes before he jerked his gaze toward the sea. Before she could register that something was wrong, he pushed her down and lunged across her body.

"*Sacre bleu!* Paparazzi."

André yanked a rope on the shelter's post and a bamboo shade unfurled and rolled to the sand. But not before she'd seen the small speedboat bobbing near the shore on a mocha-tinged wash of gold and copper.

Kira flattened on the sand, angry the world had intruded to catch her and André again. How long had they been out there?

André tossed his shirt at her. "Put this on."

She shrugged into it while he stepped into his denim cutoffs. Even with the media drifting dangerously close he left them unbuttoned, seeming content to let them ride low on his lean hips.

He punched numbers into his mobile phone as he hurried her up the slope and into the concealing forest. "Step up the patrol. Paparazzi are offshore at my private beach."

"Don't they ever give up?" she asked, when they'd emerged from the forest and had started toward the house.

"No," he said, giving her a pointed look. "Interesting that they came when we first made love, then again the night you first arrived here, and now."

All times when they'd made love—or nearly. "It's as if they know when we're intimate."

He released a short bark of laughter that sent a chill down her spine. "The same thought crossed my mind, *ma chérie*."

"Do you believe someone is tipping them off?"

"*Oui*—and who among my trusted employees on this small island would betray me?"

She shook her head, having no idea. Then she caught the accusatory glare in his eyes and wanted to retch.

"My God, you can't think that I've alerted the media?"

"Someone has." He opened the door off the back terrace that led directly upstairs and motioned her to precede him.

"It wasn't me," she said, but he merely stared at her.

After the love they'd shared, after isolating her here on Petit St. Marc, he still believed her capable of the impossible. He continued to believe she'd betrayed him, instead of considering that a disgruntled employee had alerted the media.

"If I'd had any means of getting a call out I wouldn't have risked my life rowing to that island today," she said. "I'd have rung my solicitor straightaway and tried to find out who had betrayed *me*."

He shrugged, as if dismissing that possibility. "You could have stowed a cellphone in your luggage."

She jammed her fists at her sides because she truly wanted to cosh him for being so cynical. So arrogantly pig-headed. "I only had one mobile and you took it from me at the Chateau. My God, if you don't believe me, have my room searched."

"It's already been done."

She stepped back, shocked when she shouldn't be surprised. Throughout her days at boarding school everything she'd done, said, or put on paper had been watched. Edouard's orders. Because of his suspicions, shredding paper documents and eliminating electronic ones had become second nature to her— even destroying something as innocuous as jotting down a luncheon date with a friend.

But André's invasion of her privacy had crushed the fragile emotions she held close to her heart. His ordered search of her belongings reminded her that she was a prisoner here. Like her years at boarding school, she was here because of a billionaire's largesse. He didn't trust her or want her.

"You didn't find a mobile phone," she said, the ice of cold reality stabbing her heart when he gave a curt nod. "Have you kept me under surveillance as well?"

His sensuous lips thinned, but his silence was answer enough.

"I'm tired. I need to rest," she said, pushing past him.

Her only thought was fleeing to her room, putting a wall between them when she longed for a continent to divide them. Even then it wouldn't be enough, for André would always be a part of her. Their child would be a constant reminder of what she'd loved. And lost.

She hurried up the stairs. Her feet felt as leaden as her heart, and tears threatened to cloud her vision.

Halfway down the hall her balance deserted her and she stumbled. She pitched forward and threw out her hands to catch herself. Strong arms caught her and swept her off her feet. She gasped, instantly flinging her arms around his neck.

Their eyes clashed. His unreadable. Hers no doubt windows to her soul, her heart.

André broke eye contact first, and the dismissal was another blow in a long line of them.

"Does it bother you to touch someone you distrust so much?" she asked as he carried her to her room, straining away from the welcoming warmth of his chest. The last thing she wanted was his false comfort.

"*Oui.*" He laid her on the bed, then stalked from the room.

Good! She didn't want to be near him. Didn't wish to be subject to his foul mood any longer. But before she could set aside her inner turmoil and will her tense limbs to relax, he returned with a carafe of cold water.

He poured some in a glass and handed it to her. "Drink. I've sent for a doctor."

"That isn't necessary." She took the glass, careful not to touch the fingers that had given her such pleasure an hour before, refusing to look into his eyes and see cold accusation glinting there instead of passion.

"I say it is," he said.

"And, as everyone knows, Monsieur Gauthier's word is law on his island kingdom."

She saluted him with her glass and stared at the wall, her pulse thrumming in time to his harsh indrawn breaths, his shadow looming over her like a dark specter. But she refused to be intimidated—refused to be cowed by him.

"The doctor will be here within the hour," he said.

"Will you stay to oversee his examination?" she asked. "Or watch it through your surveillance cameras?"

"Neither," he said, not denying that monitoring devices were in place, that at some point he had in fact watched her.

Without another word he crossed to the door and shut it with a demoralizing click.

Silence throbbed around her.

Kira closed her eyes, furious. Hurt. Torn by the conflicting emotions clawing for dominance in her heart. She hated him. She loved him.

And loving André Gauthier could destroy her.

After the doctor had visited Kira spent the day in her room, eating and drinking whatever Otillie brought her and attending to a presentation she'd been working on for the Chateau. Though André owned it all now, she needed to see the project through—if only for herself.

She was just putting the finishing touch on it when her door opened. Assuming it was Otillie again, with more food or water, she continued working.

His spicy scent enveloped her a heartbeat before his shadow fell over her. "Is this your renovation plan for the Chateau?"

"Yes. I've been working on it for a month." Likely wasted hours and energy—more dreams crumbling in her grasp.

"I wish to study it."

"You're the boss," she said, trying for a light tone, trying not to feel excited that he was interested in her plans.

If he noticed, he didn't comment as she saved the file to a portable drive and handed it to him. That was when she looked up at him. His powerful aura always took her breath away.

But tonight his dark hair was windblown, and there was a darkly intense gleam in his eyes. He looked as rugged and wild as if he'd just climbed down from the ratlines of a tall ship. And so sexy she trembled with renewed desire.

"You seem pleased with yourself," she said.

"*Oui*. It's begun."

She took a breath, afraid to ask. "What do you mean?"

"Bellamy Enterprises." He tossed the portable drive in the

air and caught it, over and over. "I launched a hostile takeover bid roughly an hour ago."

The breeze drifting through the windows died to a whisper, as if awed by the power he'd wielded. Or perhaps, like her, simply stunned he showed no more excitement over destroying another man's empire. No, not another man—her father.

"You'll control it all, then?" she asked, when she could trust her voice to remain steady. "Blend the two companies into a massive corporation?"

"No. I'll take the dozen or so properties that interest me and sell the rest."

She shook her head, admiring his cunning in the defeat of an adversary. "Peter will have to start all over to acquire half the wealth his father amassed."

"*Oui*. He'll have to earn it."

Which he'd never done. Peter was the heir, whereas she'd had to prove herself to gain her shares in the Chateau.

"Will I have to earn back my position at the Chateau as well?" she asked. "Or have you already dismissed me?"

"I've not replaced you—yet."

She waited for him to go on, to give her an inkling if he would keep her on or let her go, but he simply stared at her, his expression closed. If he shut her out now—

"Does it upset you that I've ruined Peter?" he asked.

"No."

She was certain now that Peter was responsible for selling Edouard's shares in the Chateau, and her own as well. She knew she'd gotten caught in a battle between Peter and André. She knew there was only one way to stop it.

That was the story of her life. In limbo, with neither parent wanting her. She'd lived in the shadow of Edouard Bellamy and his son. She was tired of being a pawn in rich men's games.

That was what she'd been to Edouard. To Peter. And to André, she realized with a sinking heart.

He'd forced her from the Chateau to break Peter, and he'd

crushed her hopes and dreams when he'd seized control of her hotel. Now it was over—or nearly so.

"If you are not grieving for your lover, then why do you look so sad, *ma chérie*?" he asked.

Her lover? If he only knew—

She shook her head, sighed. "Perhaps you are right. I am grieving over the fact that my lover believes I came here to ruin him, that I conspired with his enemy. I'm sad that he believes lies and discounts everything I say."

"The facts are black and white, *ma chérie*. They don't lie."

She'd never win with him. Never. And that realization broke her heart all over again.

"Let me go, André. There's no reason for you to keep me—"

"You are pregnant with my child." He stood over her, as warm and welcoming as a marble statue. "Or is there something you wish to tell me?"

Yes, I am Edouard Bellamy's daughter! The unwanted, unloved, daughter of André's enemy. Get it out in the open. Swiftly. Brutally. Like ripping the bandage off a wound. Then deal with the consequences. And there would be consequences.

If she thought he loved her— If she believed that he could come to love her—

"Answer me, Kira. What are you afraid of?"

She looked up into his mesmerizing eyes and spoke with her heart. "That you'll toss me aside after I've served my purpose to you, when you grow tired of me."

He stared at her a long, charged moment, his body impossibly stiff and unyielding. Then he drew her to him, his head bent so close to hers she saw an inferno of need blazing in his eyes.

"I can't imagine that day ever coming," he said, and captured her mouth with a kiss that seared her to her soul.

She could imagine it coming when she revealed the secret that was festering in her. He'd despise her. She'd be the enemy.

But for the moment she was still his lover. She wanted him

too much to spoil the moment with painful confessions. Just one more night together.

Talk could come later, for it would signal the end she wasn't prepared to make yet. Never mind André had used her—was using her now. She wanted him. She was using him to fill that void.

And, most importantly, she loved him.

It was that simple, and that complex.

She'd pour everything she had into this moment, willing him to believe her, to look into her heart and see the truth. If only she could win his heart, his trust, then maybe the truth wouldn't be so horrible to bear.

And if she was wrong?

She closed her mind to the crippling fear that his hatred would blind him to reason. Blind him to her.

Nothing was stronger than love. She had to believe that.

His long strong fingers entwined with hers as she drew near, the warmth of his touch melting her chilling fears. He brought her hand to his mouth, his eyes ablaze with passion. The kiss he pressed into her palm fired her with heat and she trembled with guilt and anticipation.

He escorted her into his room and peeled off his shorts. Her body quivered at the sight of him, warmed her skin and her heart, for he was beautifully sculpted, his tanned skin stretched smooth over chiseled muscles gleaming like bronze.

"You are magnificent," she said.

"I am just a man." He took her clothes from her, then dropped kisses on the flesh he'd exposed. "But you are a goddess of pleasure and beauty."

His compliment needled her conscience, for she was a goddess who'd kept something vital from him.

He trailed kisses up her arms, his breath hot against her skin, his body burning her where it touched. Hot, cold. Fiery passion, cold reality.

She opened her mouth, guilt spoiling her pleasure. Her confession was poised on her tongue. But his mouth fused to hers, his kisses an addiction she could never get enough of.

"Only in your arms," she said. But how long could this passion last?

A lifetime wouldn't be long enough, she admitted, as his hands played a lusty symphony on her breasts while his teeth nipped at her collarbone, her neck. She clung to his broad shoulders and let her head fall back, surrendering to him.

He made a rough sound in his throat and tugged her into his *en suite* bathroom. And he proceeded to teach her a whole new appreciation for high-dollar French water jets.

In the small hours of the morning André sprawled in bed with Kira snuggled to his side. He should have fallen asleep shortly after she had, but slumber had eluded him.

Their lovemaking had been intense, passionate, deeper than he'd ever experienced in his life. He'd deliberately avoided talk, for he planned to spend the night making love with lazy abandon—a rich dessert to savor in nibbles and bites after a sumptuous meal. To celebrate. To seduce. To delight in each touch, each kiss, each joining.

But he'd sensed a desperation in Kira that had left him on edge. As if she feared this would be the last time they'd make love. A time or two he'd glimpsed guilt in her eyes.

Oui, she was keeping some secret, one that was causing her anguish. The likely scenario ate at him like acid.

The baby was Bellamy's—not his. Despite the passion they found in each other's arms she would chose Bellamy over him. She'd betray his trust and make a fool out of him again.

André set his jaw, anger tensing muscle and tendon, eroding the exquisite pleasure he'd found in her arms. Pleasure he'd never experienced to this extent with another woman!

Even knowing she'd been Peter's mistress, he wanted her for himself. The admission came hard. He hated to be so captivated by a woman that he'd debate even for a second considering having something more than an affair with her.

But the brutal fact remained that he wanted Kira as his lover, his wife. As the mother of *his* children. He would give her anything she whimpered for to please her. He wanted her child to be his.

But if it wasn't?

The guilt he'd sensed in her burned like acid in him, for it could only mean one thing. She'd already been carrying Bellamy's child when she'd first come here to deceive him. His enemy was the father of her baby.

Mon Dieu, she was the fire that coursed through his blood. The siren who invaded his thoughts. She'd made a soft home in his hardened heart.

He wanted her. Now and forever.

But he couldn't—*wouldn't!*—claim Bellamy's child. Admitting that pained him as nothing else had, and if that was her secret he'd lose Kira forever.

He should be relieved. When he was free of her he'd regain control of his life, his emotions.

He would escape the silken trap that had destroyed his father. He wouldn't become intoxicated by a conniving woman, rendered drunk by her essence.

He would escape this affair with his pride and honor, leaving with only a few scars to his heart. They'd heal. He'd forget her. He would.

Then he'd be rid of this driving need to cover her luscious body with kisses, to sink into her welcoming heat and forget the world. Like he ached to do now.

He lurched from the bed and crossed to the window, refusing to heed her siren's call, offering him the sweetest nectar of the gods. It was a trap, for her kind lured men to their ruin.

André heard the slither of silken sheets on the bed and tensed, willed her to stay there even though his body begged her to come to him. He'd be strong. Unyielding. Resistant to her charms.

"Is something wrong?" she asked, her voice soft and sexy.

"No." He flattened a palm on the windowsill, staring out into the night when every cell in his body ached to return to the bed. To her.

"I don't believe you."

His mouth pulled in a mocking smile, and he applauded her for her insight. "Go back to sleep."

"I'd rather talk."

Talk was the last thing he wanted to do. He didn't wish to hear her confession. Didn't wish to end this idyll.

A sudden gust of wind sent the filmy curtains fluttering over his heated skin like feathers, filling the room with whispers of the dark desires he'd run from all his life.

He was lost and he knew it, because he still wanted her. Standing here wouldn't change that. Perhaps she was right. Perhaps it was time they talked. Then she'd know what he was willing to give her, and what he'd never be able to relinquish.

"Very well. What is it you wish to say?"

He heard her shaky indrawn breath, and took satisfaction at knowing she was as off balance as he felt.

"What did Edouard do to merit your vengeance?" she asked.

Mon Dieu, she dared to bring Bellamy into their bed?

André whirled to face her, his body taut with anger. "I told you—he destroyed my family."

"How?"

"C'est sans importance!"

"Speak English!"

He made a slashing movement with his hand and stalked across the room. "It's not important. Nothing can change the past."

Because if it had been possible he would have done so. He wouldn't have told his father what his headstrong sister had done. He held himself to blame for setting in motion the events that had led to his parents' deaths and his own abandonment.

"Please. I want to know," she said. "I must know."

He looked at her then, and a good deal of his rage cooled. She was huddled against the headboard, the sheet pulled tight around her. Even in the wan moonlight her face looked unnaturally pale.

Looking at her, he had trouble believing this woman with scruples had conspired with Peter to gain control of Edouard's empire—that, like his sister, she'd done whatever a Bellamy wanted on the promise of inheriting the Chateau. Kira had come here to seduce him when his defenses had been at their lowest. Like his sister, she'd chosen a Bellamy over him.

How could he ever forgive her for that? He didn't know if he could, and that realization had him tied in hard knots.

"André?" she asked. "Please?"

"My sister was Edouard's mistress," he began. "Seduced by him when she was fifteen."

She jerked her gaze from his, staring at the wall as if enthralled by watching a drama play out. When she spoke, her voice was a pained hush that vibrated along his raw nerves. "You hate him for stealing her innocence, then?"

"*Oui*, it started then," he said, and then wondered if anyone had given a damn when Bellamy had taken Kira from the schoolroom and become her benefactor.

He had proof of it even if she denied it. Even though she had ended up becoming Peter's mistress.

"What's the rest?"

He shook his head, bitten with guilt that his concern now rested with Kira instead of his family. Even admitting it didn't change anything, for he suspected she'd been an easy target.

She should be the last person he'd wish to share his deepest grief and guilt with. Not the one woman he wanted to talk to about his tragic past.

"It's complicated," he said.

"Most intrigues are. Please go on."

"My parents were outraged and forbade Suzette to see

Edouard," he said, frowning as memories of his parents' heated arguments filtered back to him. "But my sister was charmed by Edouard's wealth, by his promises of showering her with riches."

"And Edouard was relentless in his pursuit of her?" she said, accurately guessing that much.

"*Oui.* One night she ran away." He shook his head, having relived that event a thousand times in his nightmares. "I was twelve, and I took great pleasure rushing to let my father know."

She swallowed, the sound loud in the tense stillness. "Did he go after her?"

He stiffened, his hands fisting. "No, my mother did. My father jumped in the car to stop her, for her driving was atrocious. They never made it down the mountain."

She winced, pinching her eyes shut. "And your sister?"

"I learned later that Edouard was waiting to whisk Suzette away to America." To the Chateau Mystique. He stared at her, letting her see the anguish and torment he'd lived with for years.

"What happened to you after your parents died?"

"I was shipped off to a distant relative."

"Then you were raised by family?"

André laughed—the sound as cold and calculating as his mother's conniving cousin. Only by the grace of God and his own determination had he survived.

"They didn't want me, *ma chérie*, but they gladly accepted the monthly allowance they were given to keep me."

"I know how difficult that kind of life is."

"You can't begin to guess. While you were taking your lessons at an elite boarding school, I was working when the local school wasn't in session."

He glanced out the window at the bloated moon, the pain of being shuffled off to strangers still festering under the service. He'd had a roof over his head, a small closet-like room with a cot to call his own, and food that had been better fitted for the swine raised on the farm.

"Who provided your allowance?" she asked, her voice small.

"Edouard Bellamy. He paid them to keep me out of his and Suzette's way."

André had counted the days until he could escape that hell. Marked time toward the day he would ruin Edouard Bellamy.

"I'm so sorry," she said.

"Don't be." He didn't want her pity. Nor would he admit how deep those scars cut—how much he blamed himself for telling his father what his sister had done. "Suzette made her choice. I made mine."

How ironic that Edouard and Suzette had died after a horrible car wreck. Poetic justice? Perhaps.

"Why can't you give up your vengeance?" Kira asked.

"Pride. *Le code d'honneur*," he said, and when she slid him a questioning look added, "My honor demands I avenge those who have wronged my family."

She shook her head, looking rather appalled. "That's it? You vowed to ruin Edouard because your sister willingly became his mistress?"

Mon Dieu, she made it sound trivial. "There is more to it than that."

He drove his fingers through his hair, loath to talk about his parents. They'd been spoiled and rich, living for the moment in whatever spotlight shone on them. They had been ill suited to raise a family or manage their wealth.

André reasoned it had been only a matter of time before his parents made a powerful enemy. Not surprisingly, it had been his mother who'd played a dangerous game with Edouard Bellamy—all to make her husband jealous enough to cease his wanderings.

He doubted either parent had realized Edouard Bellamy was vindictive to a fault. That when Bellamy realized he'd been played for a fool he'd ruthlessly lured André's father into bankruptcy and André's sister into his bed.

"André?" she asked. "What happened? Tell me."

"My father built the Chateau Mystique for my mother," he

said. "His gift to her. Before it was completed Bellamy set out to acquire it by dubious means. I am merely reclaiming what belonged to my family and restoring our honor."

She stared at him for the longest time, then lifted her hands and clapped, the sound obscene in the tense stillness. "Bravo, André. You have accomplished what you set out to do in the name of honor by employing dubious means—just like Edouard."

He bristled, hating the comparison. Hating that she was right. But at least he wasn't alone.

"Look in the mirror, *ma chérie*. You came here to do Peter Bellamy's bidding. You are the one *enceinte*. Or have you so quickly forgotten the role you played for him three months ago?"

She scooted from the bed, her face ashen. "I'm going to my room to sleep. The ghosts in here make it too crowded."

André took a step forward to stop her, then stilled the urge. The timing was bad. He'd only dig a bigger hole for himself if he pulled her back to him as he longed to do. If he kissed her. Loved her. Sought comfort in her arms.

His emotions were too raw. Tomorrow, he thought, as she left the bedroom without looking back.

Tomorrow he'd have total control of Bellamy Enterprises— and of Kira Montgomery.

CHAPTER EIGHT

KIRA curled in a ball on her bed, too heartbroken to cry. What good would tears do now?

Her father hadn't just crushed André's family. Edouard had ripped André away from everything he'd known. Everyone he'd loved. He'd somehow acquired the Chateau—the hotel André's father had built for his mother—and he'd ensconced André's sister there as his mistress.

She understood André's agony, his rage, for she'd lived with something similar herself. Only it had been her own mother who'd abandoned her to Edouard's care, and his brand of accepting responsibility had been to ship her off to boarding school in England.

From the day she'd first met Edouard he'd referred to her as his "shameful obligation." She'd believed herself inferior to his legitimate family. Insignificant. And always unwanted.

To think she'd tried so hard to win Edouard's favor, his attention, as a child hungry for affection. To think she'd been so desperate for love that she'd agreed to keep her paternity a secret all her life. That she'd never gone against Edouard's wishes and contacted his "real" family.

Yes, she and André had both suffered at Edouard Bellamy's hands, though she feared André would not view her experience the same way. Because she was a Bellamy, and there was nothing she could do about it.

A man like André did not forgive deceit. And she'd deceived him. Was still deceiving him.

Her hands glided over her belly, cradling the life that grew there. She should've told him the truth from the start. Gotten it out in the open before she lost her heart to him. Let her ghosts dance and rattle their chains along with his.

But she hadn't, because postponing the inevitable was easier than facing the truth. Because she was afraid to trust that he'd do the right thing. Because she didn't want anything to throw a pall over their passionate tryst on this island. She wanted to prolong the inevitable.

Now she was too tired to think straight—too exhausted from spent passion and from the tangled dreams she'd spun of her and André and their child. She was simply too heavy of heart to risk seeing the thin thread binding them snap in two.

She'd seek him out in the morning and tell him everything, for the guilt of lying to him was tearing her apart. She had to believe that love was stronger than hate.

André had been hunched over his desk since dawn, gaze fixed on the computer screen. The work he'd hoped to immerse himself in this morning stared back at him. The latest financial report was a jumble of words, none making sense. The spreadsheet might as well be random figures.

All he could think about was Kira and the stricken look on her face when she'd left his bedroom. He'd shocked her by admitting he was Suzette's brother, and shocked himself by revealing so much about his family's connection to Edouard Bellamy. None of his contemporaries knew. Not one. So why had he trusted Kira with the truth?

He caught a subtle whiff of her perfume a heartbeat before his door opened a crack. His gaze flicked from the wealth of auburn hair to her eyes that gleamed with moisture.

"Are you too busy to talk?" she asked.

He was, and talk was the last thing he wanted to do with

her—especially if she was emotional. But he didn't wish to turn her away either.

"Come in," he said, rising and hoping she wouldn't hear his heart slamming against his ribs. "What's on your mind?"

She slipped inside like a shadow and closed the door, her eyes seeming too large for her face. She swallowed, looked away, then met his gaze again.

"Something you said last night…" She waved a hand in a classic gesture of nervousness and eased onto the chair, but sat on its edge as if ready to bolt. "I've never told anyone before."

"A confession, then?"

"A secret, actually."

His gut clenched, but he erased all emotion from his face. This was it. The declaration of guilt he'd dreaded to hear. Their affair would end swiftly and unpleasantly.

She took a deep breath. Expelled it slowly. His gut clenched again. He was dreading what truth would spill from her lush lips.

"My mother was a Las Vegas showgirl and my father—" She frowned. Swallowed. Paled. "My father—"

He took pity on her struggle for a way to tell him. "I've seen your birth certificate and I know you are illegitimate."

A flush kissed her cheeks, but he couldn't tell if it was from embarrassment or anger. "Yes, my mother obviously wasn't sure which was one of her lovers was my father when she gave birth to me."

He stared at her, stunned for a heartbeat. In his mind he'd pictured her mother as a quiet Englishwoman, reserved and withdrawn. He'd imagined Kira had run away from the staid life she'd been born into to the glamour Bellamy promised.

"Your mother sent you to England to be schooled, then?" Away from the lurid nightlife and her liaisons?

A deeper red tinted her delicate cheekbones, and he knew at that moment that no matter what she told him she'd seen more than a young girl should. "She gave me up when I was quite young. Actually, I barely remember her."

"Is she still alive?"

"I wouldn't know."

"You've never tried to find her?"

"No, and I never will."

André wasn't sure what to make of that admission. Kira was compassionate to a fault. She wouldn't cut her mother from her life without just cause—that cause being that the woman had obviously placed her lovers before her child. Yet Kira had followed in the woman's footsteps—unmarried and pregnant.

But where her mother had obviously been derelict in her duty, André believed Kira would make a fine parent. He trusted she'd cherish her child. His soul knew she'd put her child first, even above him. He trusted her with the care of their baby.

He shook his head, keeping the last observation to himself. "I take it you were adopted?"

"No, I was simply a ward." She looked at him then, the lonely ache of her childhood plain to see, touching his heart as nothing else ever had. "As I said before, I know how you felt, being foisted off on people who cared nothing for you."

For a moment he thought she'd expand on her upbringing, but she stopped talking and frowned.

"Then you understand why I must bring down everything Bellamy built," he said.

"No, I don't understand that at all," she said.

She couldn't mean that. "I don't believe you haven't thought of ways to make your mother pay for abandoning you. Or wanted to lash out at the guardian who closeted you away instead of welcoming you into a family."

Kira looked away, but not before he caught a flicker of anger in her expressive eyes. "I locked my ghosts away long ago. I knew to dwell on what I couldn't change would turn me bitter and ultimately destroy me."

He sensed there was more, that she was holding something back, something that she was hesitant to divulge. He understood her reluctance, for he suspected she had never allowed herself to be angry at the cloistered life meted out to her. She'd been conditioned to accept her fate.

"Will it help if you tell me about your ghosts?" he asked. "I assure you I'm not one to fear them."

"André," she said, her face too pale and too drawn.

André waited for her to go on, but she fell silent.

Mon Dieu! He longed to rip open the shroud on her past, to make whoever had hurt her pay for their callous disregard. He wanted to hold her and love her and promise her all would be well—that he'd slay her dragons too.

But he couldn't bring himself to step over that last fence. For, like her, he wasn't accustomed to divulging any of his secrets—especially personal ones.

They had the power to cause heartache. To draw blood.

Oui, he couldn't totally trust her. But he could offer an olive branch.

"I read over your plans for the Chateau and I applaud your foresight," he said.

Her expressive eyes went wide, and her smile brightened the room and his heart. "You did?"

"But of course that's not what I wish to discuss now. I'd like your opinion concerning a resort I plan to redesign in Cap d'Antibes," he said, turning his attention to the spreadsheet on the computer. Her radiant expression had burst inside him like the sun cresting the horizon, flooding him with new hopes, new dreams. It made him forget his quest for vengeance.

"Are you familiar with the area?" he asked, his voice sharper than intended.

"Only what I've read about the French Riviera," she said.

He'd take her there. Give her a tour of the old city from a native's viewpoint. Show her the castle steeped in history and the villas where movie stars and royalty spent their holidays.

He'd escort her to the casinos that never slept. Then do something he'd never done before—take a lover to the old villa where he'd been born.

"Please—tell me more." She shifted in her seat, her eyes still wide with excitement.

Mon Dieu, to think his business enthused her so! To think her excitement was rubbing off on him—in more ways than one.

"I recently bought the hotel. It's a fine property, but the last modernization stripped it of its charm." He leaned forward, captivated by her interest. "I would like to reinstall its original nineteen-forties style."

She sat back, her expression thoughtful. "You want to recapture its heyday?"

"*Oui.*" André rocked back in his chair, then tossed his pen on the desk, as if it didn't matter whether she liked his idea or not. It did matter. He'd seen her credentials and knew she had a head for business.

"It's daring. Unique." She smiled, and his heart nearly stopped beating. "And a cutting-edge business strategy."

"I'll show you the plans—" His mobile phone chirped and he answered it.

"*Bonjour,*" said the manager of La Cachette, his high-class resort on St. Barthélemy. "*Comment allez-vous?*"

"I am well. To what do I owe the pleasure?"

"A small matter, really." The manager explained that there was a continuing problem with an employee—André's distant cousin.

"Philippe is not doing his job?" André asked.

"No, his work is excellent." There was a long, tense pause. "It is the ladies. He romances them, and there are complaints."

André smiled at the mental image that conjured. "So Philippe is working his way through the female employees, *non*?"

"Employees, guests—it makes no difference to him. Complaints have been lodged." His manager's sigh crackled over the line. "Perhaps if you spoke with him?"

"*Oui.* I will arrive this afternoon. Prepare my suite."

André ended the connection, then rocked back in his chair and pinched the bridge of his nose, annoyed he had to speak with Philippe again about his discretion and maintaining high business standards. Irked he had to leave Kira here. Though a night away from her might be just the thing to put his emotions back in perspective.

"Problems?" Kira's voice reached across the desk to stroke over him in a silken caress.

"*Oui*. An ongoing one." But no more. His cousin had been warned what would happen if he continued to play around.

He met her gaze, annoyed her excitement had vanished. Was she sorry to see him go, or was it a ruse?

No, she wasn't deceiving him this time. He'd set out to bind her to him and he'd succeeded. But he'd not anticipated his plan would ensnare him as well.

He should leave her here and attend to business. But he selfishly wanted her to join him.

"We leave for St. Barth within the hour," he said, clearly surprising her again.

Again her smile dazzled him, warming something that had been far too cold in him. "You're taking me?"

"But of course."

Her smile rivaled the sun.

Oui, she was excited to go away with him for the day. He hoped she wanted to see the island and La Cachette—to be alone with him in the romantic city. But she might be seeing this as her chance to contact Peter, perhaps even run away.

His jaw firmed, his heart chilling at those possibilities. He'd provide her with the means to deceive him. He'd charge his investigator to do a deeper investigation of her, turning over every rock in England if need be.

Then he'd have an answer. Then he'd know what the hell to do.

Kira wasn't a neophyte when it came to five-star hotels, but the moment André escorted her into his hotel on St. Barth, there was something about La Cachette that set it apart from anything she'd seen before. Something besides the old-world beauty of the salmon-stucco structure trimmed in pristine white. Something other than what she'd read about the high-end suites that ran into many thousands of dollars a night.

The elegant hotel overlooking the expanse of turquoise sea made Chateau Mystique pale in comparison. It reduced the Chateau to what it really was—a glitzy hotel on the Las Vegas strip, an edifice of glass and steel and opulence meant to dazzle guests, like countless other ones in the neon town that played all night long.

Her nerves zinged and her senses absorbed the grandeur of it all as André tapped in a code to access a private lift. But once she and André stepped inside it, a far different excitement took root in her.

She'd been intimate with him in every way possible, yet she felt like an exposed novice trembling at his side. A good part of it was because of desire, for she wanted him with a hunger that shocked her.

But she was still shaken over taking the coward's way out and holding her secret to her heart even after he'd asked for her opinion regarding his property on the French Riviera. At that moment she'd felt their relationship shift, and she hadn't wanted to ruin it. And it had happened again when he'd offered that bit of praise for her ideas for the Chateau.

Her heart had melted.

After three months they'd gone from captive and captor, to sizzling lovers. Could they find even ground in a partnership in business? As parents?

Could they have even more?

She wanted to believe it was possible—that he'd not hold her paternity against her or their child. That he'd brought her to St. Barth not just because she was his willing mistress now.

She had to trust her heart that love would find a way.

That was so easy to do now, as his dark eyes glittered with blatant desire, caressing her in tantalizing increments. Her lips tingled, aching for his kiss. Her breasts felt heavy, tight, and her blood hummed with a strong sensual pulse.

His powerful presence filled the lift, filled her heart. She'd never met a man who captivated her so, who made her ache for such wicked pleasure in his arms.

Though the lift had whisked them to the penthouse, she was gasping for breath, her hand gripping the cool handrail as his gaze fixed on the juncture of her thighs. A deep throb of want vibrated low in her belly, her muscles contracting in erotic rhythm.

The apex of her thighs was growing hot, the scent of her sex making her cheeks warm more from arousal than embarrassment. She squirmed, as restless as if he'd touched her intimately.

The flames in his gaze blazed hotter. His wickedly sensual lips curved in a knowing smile—a triumphant smile, for he surely knew the power he had over her.

As if to prove it he licked his lips and moaned his pleasure. A tremor rocked through her and she pressed her thighs tight together, nearly coming in the lift, aroused simply by his gaze, by the carnal promise in his dark eyes.

With just one look she was lost. She was his.

He knew it, and so did she.

The lift door whispered open. André wrapped an arm around her shoulders and escorted her into the tower apartment, no doubt aware her legs trembled so badly she feared she'd collapse.

She'd expected him to whisk her to the bedroom, but he seemed in no particular hurry. If only *she* could be that relaxed.

Kira focused on the suite to calm her emotions. She'd not expected the apartment's style to be so starkly elegant.

Open, yet intimate. The ultimate playpen for decadence.

Large windows on three sides welcomed sunlight to flood the open salon, which was sumptuously dressed in translucent swaths of lush green that mirrored the colors of the rainforest.

The curved sectional sofa in a warm butterscotch dominated the salon, affording an optimum view of the ocean and the vista stretching to the horizon. Her mind teased her with images of her and André frolicking on that sofa, having eyes only for each other.

An intimate glass-topped table for two sat by French doors that opened onto a white-railed Juliet balcony. A crystal vase overflowed with white lilies, cream isianthus and eucalyptus foliage to perfume the suite.

Her gaze climbed the curved staircase to the loft above. With André so close, and knowing what was to come, this was almost too much for her senses.

"The bedroom," he said.

"Of course." She studied the open plan again, noting one closed door on this level. "Are there others?"

"No."

Her face flushed. She should be offended he'd brought her here. But all she could think of was making love with him on the plush sofa, and later in the tower bedroom.

"Do you want anything?" he asked.

She wanted him to take her now, to pleasure her—love her. "You," she said simply.

An amorous glint lit his eyes. "Ah, *ma chérie*, you do speak my language. Unfortunately I have pressing business to attend to now."

She crossed to him and laid a hand on his heart, emboldened by the strong rapid beat, unwilling to conform to the mistress's role of waiting patiently for her lover. "When will you return?"

"An hour. Two at the most."

A short time for him, but a boring afternoon for her. "Perhaps I'll take advantage of the solitude and do a bit of shopping."

"No—not with the paparazzi lingering."

Her first impulse was to react with anger, but she didn't want to confront the media. "Very well, I'll stay here."

"I'll make your wait worth it." His mouth closed over hers, hot, hungry, possessive.

She kissed him in kind, willing him to remember the promise awaiting him here. Willing him to hurry back to her.

He pulled back too soon, his eyes black with passion, his face taut. "Make yourself at home." Then he was gone, disappearing into the lift and leaving her alone.

Kira stared at the green light on the lift's keypad. He'd not locked it. Had he forgotten?

No, he wasn't one to make that type of error. He'd left it unlocked for a reason. But what was it?

Kira fetched a bottle of sparkling water from the small refrigerator in the kitchen and paced the lavish salon, wondering if this was a test of her loyalty to him.

Could it be as simple as him knowing she wouldn't go shopping and draw the media's attention? Could he know she wouldn't run away from him? Know that when he returned this evening she'd be here waiting for him?

Either way he trusted her—or at least had begun to.

She set the water aside and wrapped her arms around her middle, sick at heart that her secret would destroy that newfound trust. But even if she could prove she hadn't conspired with Peter to ruin André, there was still the fact she was Edouard Bellamy's daughter.

There was nothing she could do to forestall the inevitable. How much better it would've been to have lost him then rather than now. How much more heartache could she bear?

His avowal as they waited out the storm in the cave on Noir Creux came back to her. *It's too late. I paid your price.*

But he didn't know she'd been deceived, and she had nothing but her word to change his mind.

Kira crossed to the phone and quickly dialed the number of her solicitor. Her frustration hitched up another notch when the hotel operator answered.

"Pardon? I don't understand," Kira said.

The woman replied in French—then hung up on her! So much for placing a call.

She reclaimed her water and climbed the steps to the tower bedroom, her weariness eased marginally by the breathtaking view afforded by the bank of windows. No matter where she looked, her gaze fell on the sea.

A massive bed dressed simply and elegantly in jade and black dominated the space. She gripped her bottled water tighter, her body quivering with need. This was insane.

Her world was on the verge of collapsing and she was fantasizing about making love with him. Was she following in her mother's footsteps?

No! She'd put her child first, even above her own needs.

She'd turned to descend to the main salon when she noticed a small desk set in an alcove near the far side of the room. It held a laptop computer and nothing else. *Make yourself at home.*

Doing just that, she sent a quick missive to her solicitor, demanding to know who'd forged her signature for the sale of her stock.

Time inched by as she waited on pins and needles for his reply. Alert, wary, and plagued with new guilt.

Her hands fisted. My God, how deeply André had woven her into his web if she felt guilty for contacting her solicitor about the takeover of the Chateau.

A soft tone issued from the computer as the "new mail" icon flashed on, seeming unnaturally loud in the stillness. She frowned as she read the reply from her solicitor.

He'd been forthright with her from the beginning, a loyal employee of Edouard's. She'd trusted him without question.

But his cryptic reply worried her. Instead of answering her questions, he asked what game she was playing now?

She'd never played any game—that had been her father's forte. Not hers. She'd been taken to Petit St. Marc against her will. She'd been robbed of her shares!

A ding below stairs alerted her that the lift had come up. She typed a quick response to her solicitor, telling him to explain in detail what he meant. She reiterated again that *she* was the injured party here. She'd never authorized the sale of her stock. Never. She wanted answers, and she wanted them now.

She'd find a way to read his reply later. And if she couldn't…?

Kira logged off just as the tap of shoes on tile echoed up from below. André had returned sooner than she'd expected.

She ran into the bedroom, then hesitated, knowing if she rushed down the steps that she'd either look guilty or eager to see him. She latched on to the latter, but when she got to the top of the stairs she froze.

It wasn't André at all, but a woman. Her uniform was clearly that of a domestic. She set a box held tight with a crimson bow on the table and turned to leave, then stopped and looked up at Kira, as if sensing her there watching.

"Bonjour, mademoiselle," the woman said, and smiled. "A gift for you. *Monsieur* apologizes for being detained."

"André sent me a gift?"

"Oui." The maid walked back toward the lift.

Curiosity carried Kira down the stairs. The maid was gone before she reached the salon. She read the note attached to the box.

Instead of returning to Petit St. Marc this evening they would enjoy a dinner at the celebrated La del'Impératrice Chambre.

The fact her casual clothes were unsuitable for the elite restaurant barely registered. All she could think of was spending the night in that massive bed with André, loving him.

Heat spread across her middle, fanning out in delicious shivers. They'd enjoy dinner out, like a real date, then spend the night here.

Kira's hands shook as she tore open the box and swept ivory tissue aside. Her gaze lit on a silky blue fabric that caught the light and shimmered like sunrays skipping over the Caribbean waters.

She held it up, as excited as a child at Christmas. It was indecent. Seductive. Daring. She'd never worn anything like this—had never even tried on risqué clothes.

But André had chosen this for her. The reason was clear.

She was his mistress. He wanted to show her off—boast to other men that she was his possession, his kept woman. She was his conquest over Peter Bellamy.

Her excitement dimmed as that fact stole away the glow she'd been basking in. It would end soon, for she couldn't go on avoiding the inevitable much longer.

Kira dropped her gaze to the designer gown clutched in her hands. She couldn't wear it and keep her self-respect. But she couldn't resist trying it on either. Just once.

She was about to retreat upstairs when a scrap of color in the box caught her eye. No, he hadn't—

But he had.

She picked up the flesh-hued scrap of silk that was panties. They felt like heaven in her hand but were surely devilish in design, for the cloth was transparent.

She might as well be wearing none at all! No doubt André had thought the same when he'd bought them.

The square box that accompanied the larger one had to be shoes. Curious to see what he'd chosen, she slipped the ribbon free and flung off the lid.

Her hand trembled as she lifted one beautiful mermaid sandal from the box. Shoes were her passion. Her weakness. And these sexy stilettoes called to her.

What would it hurt to try the entire outfit on, as he'd intended her to do? Nothing. André wouldn't return for hours. Nobody would know. Nobody but her.

Flushed and excited at the prospect of being that audacious—even in private!—she rushed upstairs to don the daring dress. The second it slid over her body she felt wicked and sensual. And horribly self-conscious.

The design was pure seduction. Thin strips of fabric covered her breasts and tied behind the neck, leaving her back bare nearly to the swell of her buttocks.

The silk caressed her with each step, each breath, the glide over her nipples teasing them erect, the whisper of cloth over her hips and thighs keeping her senses tuned to a high pitch.

Just like André's hands and mouth would do.

She swallowed hard, near panting with desire. She'd never felt this sexually attractive in her life. Never been so aware of herself as a woman.

Kira allowed herself one last look in the mirror, scarce believing that temptress was her. But her bare feet ruined the effect. Damn, she'd left the sandals downstairs.

She glanced at the clock, sure she had time to try on the shoes. She hurried down the stairs and did just that. The fit was perfect, like a fairy tale.

Another ding rang through the apartment. She froze, her gaze locked on the lift door. Her stomach quivered; her pulse hammered. She knew André had arrived even before the door whispered open and he stepped from the lift.

She had no idea where he'd acquired the elegantly cut black tuxedo, or where he'd shaved, but he looked like a page torn from a designer magazine. He looked like the fantasy in every erotic dream she'd ever had. The essence of *savoir-faire*.

It was one of the few French phrases that had stuck with her. Oddly appropriate as André possessed social grace and aplomb. And a sensuality that seduced her across the room, robbing her of all thoughts save one—making love with him.

He strode into the salon and stopped, freezing in place like a mannequin, with a hand poised to smooth back his dark hair. His gaze locked on hers, hot and hungry.

Her stomach flip-flopped, tightening. Her thighs clenched. Her breasts felt full, the sensation of her nipples peaking against the silk almost too much to bear.

Her heart quivered, overflowing with love. Love?

Yes, I love him.

Forever. Fatalistically.

She smiled with all her heart and strode toward him, hating that she was continuing her deception. But she didn't want to ruin this night either.

Tonight she'd be his willing lover. She'd love him as if there was no tomorrow. Because when the truth came out she feared there would be no future for them. She knew putting off telling the truth didn't change it.

But when she did this affair would be over. Her life, her hopes, her dreams with André would end.

And when they did a part of her would die.

André's chest was so tight he could barely draw air into his lungs. When he did manage it, he drew in the floral scent she wore as well as her womanly essence.

He'd known when he bought the gown that the sapphire silk would complement Kira's wealth of auburn hair, known that the fabric would caress her full breasts, hug her lush hips, and glide down the expanse of strong shapely legs like his hands and mouth longed to do.

She was a vixen. The colors of the sea and the sand and temptation. A lover molded just for him.

And for Bellamy?

His hands fisted, his gut twisting, for he didn't want his enemy to shadow him tonight. Not now, when this strange warmth was spreading over his chest, filling him with a sense of rightness.

For the first time in his life he had found a woman he wanted in all ways—as his lover, the mother of his children. As his wife?

Mon Dieu, he couldn't marry Peter's mistress. But the idea of another man touching Kira enraged him. His hungry gaze swept over her, stripping off the dress that set his blood on fire. His fingers tingled to put action to the thought.

Every man who saw her would feel the same. His gut clenched at the certainty. He'd be damned if he'd share her.

No one would see her luscious curves in that dress but him! Nobody but him would touch her, kiss her, desire her.

He would be the last lover she'd ever take, because it must be so.

It *was* so! He knew that now. Mother and child were his. *His!*

André strode toward her, his hunger for food gone, replaced by a carnal appetite that was stronger. He'd have her now. Hear his name on her lips as she climaxed. See her smile rest on his face before sleep claimed her.

Now and always.

He pulled her to him, his finesse shattering like fine crystal, his patience vanishing like smoke. "Our plans have changed. We will stay here."

"Good," she said, lifting her face to his. "I would just as soon order room service."

"*Oui*, a late dinner," he said, gliding his hands down her bare back, watching her beautiful eyes gleam with the same powerful desire that raged through him. "Much later."

She was a worthy partner for him, capable of bringing him low with one innocent look, causing his blood to race out of control with that bed-me gleam in her eyes. Like they had now, her head bent just so, her tongue caressing her lips and making him crazy with want.

She was his to have. Without doubt. Without reservation.

André claimed her mouth, vowing he'd soon hold her heart and soul in his hands as well. She melded against him, capitulating to his sensual siege, her mouth surrendering.

Each stroke of her tongue fanned the flames of his passion, until he feared he'd spend himself here in the salon. He who always maintained control felt it crack as her greedy hands explored his torso and caressed his hips, her thumbs tracing over the ridge at his flanks, feeling like fire and ice and sweet, sweet heaven.

He swept his palms over her rounded hips, certain the finest satins and silks could not compare to the exquisite smoothness of her skin. The deep valley of her spine invited him to follow it in minute measures down to the soft swell of her bottom.

The gown was no barrier as he dipped his hands beneath the indecently low back and splayed his fingers over her satiny flesh, barely covered with the minuscule triangle of silk.

He smiled, pleased she'd worn his gift. For him. Only him.

She arched against him, her fingers wadding his shirt, the scrape of her nails sending fire licking through him.

He heard the rending of fabric, then sucked in great gulps of air as her palms swept over his bare chest, her thumbs brushing his nipples. "Aggression becomes you, *ma chérie*."

"I want you naked, André. I want to feel you moving on me. In me."

The growl that escaped him was foreign, feral. He swept her into his arms and mounted the stairs, their mouths straining at the other, their lips dueling with fierce intent.

They fell onto the bed, tearing at their clothes, thousands of dollars' worth of silk rendered to rags. He moved over her, his sex tight and hard, poised at her moist cay.

"Yes," she said, grabbing his sides. "Now."

"Not yet."

He palmed her breasts as his mouth moved down her body, tasting, teasing. She cried out his name, arching her back as if desperate to impale herself on him.

But that pleasure would come too soon. Too rushed to be appreciated at this moment in time.

He hooked his thumbs under the lace banding her panties and pulled them off by inches, his heart slamming hard as her scent filled his nostrils, driving him wild.

"André!" The reedy sound of his name on her lips roared through him like flame. "Please."

He would. By God, he would please her. In her pleasure he'd find his own reward.

His breath rasped hard as he tossed aside her panties, his patience with obstacles and leisurely sex gone. She was gasping for air as well, her beautiful body bared to his hungry eyes, her lush breasts thrust forward, the nipples peaked, her sleek legs parted in wanton invitation.

"You are exquisite," he said, his palms sliding up her legs to the dark curls at the apex of her thighs.

She grabbed for him, her fingers gliding off his slick chest, her eyes dark with passion. "Kiss me."

And he did, bending his head to the heat of her, his fingers spreading her as his tongue flicked over her damp swollen flesh, certain nothing on earth was as delicious as she.

Mewling sounds came from her as her fingers twined in his hair and pulled, but he blocked out the slight pain and continued his ruthless oral seduction of her.

He laved her once, twice, his own need close to the edge, his fingers slick with her desire, his senses drunk on her essence. He felt her muscles clench, the spasms rippling through her and into him.

"No—yes," she said, her fingers tightening on his scalp to hold him to her.

He speared her once more as the tremors rocked through her and her back bowed, a keening sound ripping through her. Nothing had ever sounded so sweet as he covered her body with his and plunged into her.

His teeth clenched with the effort to go slow, for he felt her body shudder to adjust to his size, feared he'd hurt her. But she took control, wrapping her legs around him and arching, seating him deeper in her.

Her fingernails raked his back, his flanks, and hung on. He surrendered to her. He who never lost control with a woman did so then.

The pleasure of two bodies joined heart and soul poured through him, raging as a river, cleansing away the strictures he'd abided by all his life.

The pretense was stripped bare. Over. Ended.

Nothing could ever be more right than this moment, André thought as he held her to his side in the aftermath of the most explosive passion he'd ever felt. She was his sun and moon, his addiction.

She shifted closer and sighed. "I love you."

The avowal was a whisper of sound so hushed he nearly didn't hear it. He frowned, considering how this changed things.

This was what he'd hoped to gain—her love. But he no longer wished to crush her.

No, he had better things in store for Miss Montgomery.

He stared at her in sleep, growing more certain of his decision by the moment. It was right. It was time.

He was going to propose marriage.

CHAPTER NINE

ANDRÉ'S mobile phone chirped early the next morning. He took the call on the downstairs balcony, so as not to disturb Kira—she needed sleep, for they'd made love into the wee hours of the morning. He smiled, thinking of the passion, the feeling of rightness that hummed within him.

Hearing his detective on the line tempered his euphoria. He squinted at the horizon and wished he was upstairs with Kira, wished he'd not had to order a more thorough investigation of his lover.

"Any news on the money?" he asked, squinting at the horizon as the sun burst through the windows to gild the room in gold.

"Yes, sir. I checked my resources twice to ensure the information was correct."

The pause crackled with tension, lashing the calm André had harbored since waking with Kira curled against him. "Spit it out," he said, impatient to know the truth.

"The two million you paid to acquire the Chateau was immediately diverted into an account held by Peter Bellamy."

"You're positive?" André asked. "There can be no mistake?"

The detective answered immediately. "There's no error."

André pushed away from the railing and stormed into his suite, his gut erupting with the destructive force of a volcano, his suspicions running as hot as lava. All this time Kira's beautiful mouth had spouted lies.

She'd sworn time and again she didn't know Peter Bellamy, yet moments after receiving a wire for two million dollars the funds had been routed to Bellamy. Her protector.

What had Bellamy given Kira in return?

"There's more," the detective said.

"Concerning Miss Montgomery?"

"Yes, sir."

André laughed, the sound deceptively soft as he stared up the stairs to the bed where she still slept. "Goes from bad to worse, *oui*?"

"Not my place to say."

Of course not. That was his decision to make.

He'd used this detective before. Knew that he was like a dog with a bone, that he wouldn't give up until he'd discovered everything about the person in question. In this case, Kira.

But it had taken a damnably long time to gain the truth. André's patience for intrigue was gone. He wanted all the facts. All the secrets revealed. He wanted to see the whole picture, warts and all.

"Out with it," André said.

"I tracked down Kira Montgomery's mother," the detective said, without inflection or pause. "She swears Miss Montgomery's father is Edouard Bellamy."

The words went into André's mind and exploded, sending something dark and dangerous coursing through him. He gripped the railing as the sharp ache of betrayal speared his chest, stealing his breath. His heart skipped a beat, then started racing as the awful truth sank into his soul.

Of all the scenarios he'd imagined, of all the contrivances he'd suspected, this hadn't been one of them. This news blind-sided him, drove a spike in his heart.

Oui, he'd been blind too often where Kira was concerned. Too ensnared by her beauty, her artful innocence, her passion.

Not anymore.

"There is no question this is so?" André asked.

"Only DNA tests can dispel doubts. But I spoke with the woman myself and followed up tracing the dates and places. It fits that Kira Montgomery is Edouard Bellamy's illegitimate child."

He thanked his detective and ended the communication, his mind a whirlpool of dark, putrid thoughts. Her insistence that she wasn't Peter's mistress tolled in his ears—at least in that she told the truth. *Mon Dieu*—they were brother and sister.

It was all so obvious now—Edouard Bellamy had educated her. Given her a coveted position at his La Cygne Hotel in London and forty-nine percent of Chateau Mystique. Because she was his daughter!

Mon Dieu! With Suzette dead, Edouard must have known that André would launch a takeover. But, according to the proof he had, *Peter* had sent Kira here.

She and Peter had conspired to forestall André. Not by engineering a public and humiliating end to his engagement, as he'd assumed—never mind that he and his fiancée had secretly parted ways the week before, by mutual agreement. And not by destroying a lucrative business deal that he'd worked hard to achieve.

No, she and Peter had trumped André with an innocent baby.

They'd ruthlessly plotted to force André to make a terrible choice, certain he'd choose the one that would damn him in eternal hell. For Edouard's blood coursed in his child's veins through Kira.

Kira had played well the part of corporate whore.

If André held to his vow to destroy the Bellamys he'd see the downfall of his own flesh and blood. An innocent life, caught in the crossfire.

He strode back onto the balcony and stared down at the palace he'd created. Peace eluded him.

The hell he'd been plunged into shrouded the beauty surrounding him. All he saw was Kira—memories of her loving him, challenging him, deceiving him.

His earlier thought that she'd make a good mother taunted him, enraged him. Not for *his* child.

Her conspiracy left him no choice—his only thought rested with the child. *His* child. When the baby was born, when tests had confirmed the child was his, he'd take sole custody.

Kira was a Bellamy. Not his lover, not the mother of his child, but his enemy's daughter. She was his enemy as well.

He swiped a shaky hand over his mouth, shoving compassion and his passion for her from his mind. She'd baited him—now she'd pay the price.

She'd give birth on Petit St. Marc and he'd see she had the best care money could provide. But she'd never know his child. *Never!*

He'd employ every resource available to him as he waged this war against her. When he was done with her she'd regret that she'd agreed to deceive him.

At midday, Kira went in search of André. He'd barely spoken to her on their early-morning return to Petit St. Marc, and she'd been too exhausted from their night of lovemaking to take offense. Back on the island, he'd insisted she take a nap.

She hadn't argued. But her rest had been fitful.

Keeping her secret was twisting her stomach into knots. She had to tell him now.

He was going out the door just as she descended the stairs. She quickened her steps. "Do you have a moment to talk?"

His spine stiffened, his shoulders snapping back as he stopped abruptly in the doorway. He glanced at her, and his fierce expression burned holes in her courage.

"Is it urgent?"

She thought it was vital, but, considering his mood right now, she shook her head. She'd taken the coward's way out this long. A few more hours wouldn't make any difference.

"No," she said, forcing a smile. "It can wait."

"I will see you this evening, then."

And he was gone, without any explanation of where he was taking himself off to. Not that his business was hers. Even the Chateau was his now.

Kira aimlessly strolled through the house, her mind too cluttered with worry to do anything else. She ended up at the door to André's office, surprised Otillie hadn't intercepted her yet. But the house was quiet, as if she was the only one there.

She slipped inside with thoughts of scanning his bookshelf. But the glow on his desk changed her mind. He'd not only left his computer here, but it was on.

In moments she'd accessed her mail. Her solicitor's reply slammed into her so hard she dropped on the chair.

She couldn't believe he suggested she should hire investigators to look into her claim. He insisted he'd seen the document, with her signature, authorizing the sale of her shares of the Chateau, but that he'd couldn't divulge where the money had gone.

In short, because she'd divested herself of the shares, company counsel no longer represented her.

She logged off and returned to her room, so sick at heart she could have retched. Edouard had told her Peter resented her. Told her not to contact him because he would not be receptive to her.

Had her half-brother set out to destroy her the moment their father had drawn his last breath? How could she prove it?

She was so deep into piecing together the irregular sections of this ugly puzzle that she didn't realize Otillie had entered her room until she spoke.

"You have not been drinking water, *mademoiselle*," Otillie said.

Kira glanced at her full pitcher of water and frowned. Her throat did suddenly seem parched. Her head ached from her efforts to make sense of this debacle she'd been thrust into, and she was growing more miserable.

"I forgot," she said, accepting a glass of water and drinking deeply.

"Monsieur Gauthier will not be pleased," the woman said.

That was the least of her worries, considering what she had to tell him when he returned. She sat her empty glass on the table, her spirits low, her worries shooting into the impossibly blue sky. That was when she noticed the large box on her bed.

She motioned to it. "What's that?"

"A gift for you from Monsieur Gauthier," Otillie said.

Her lips parted and her heart began racing. Two gifts in as many days? That was an extravagance she'd never experienced before.

Was this another indulgence for his kept woman? Or an apology for his earlier abruptness? Don't be a fool and look for a deeper meaning, she chided herself.

She read the attached note—*Dinner at seven. Wear this.*

No endearments. No explanations. Still she smiled as she stared at the strokes of his signature, as strong and demanding as the man.

She tore into the package, unable to stay her excitement.

The gift was a sarong, the fabric pure Carib. The soft greens, golds and browns seemed to be plucked straight from the heart of Petit St. Marc.

Kira glanced at the clock. She had less than an hour to get ready. Less than an hour before she divulged the secret that might signal an end to her idyll with André.

Forty minutes later, reality dimmed her enthusiasm. But the sarong was simply gorgeous and sexy, and she absolutely loved it.

A narrow bandeau barely covered her breasts, which were fuller, more sensitive, and flushed a telling shade of pink. Her neck and shoulders were bare, covered only by her hair, which she'd let cascade in thick curls down her back.

Three sharp raps sounded at her door. Her gaze fixed on the louvered panels, noting the tall shadow at her door.

André. He'd come for her.

She tamped down the nervous laugh that threatened to bubble up in her. This was a wretched time to be struck by a case of anxiety.

Taking deep breaths did nothing to calm her. Her hands shook as she smoothed her palms down her skirt, her stomach heaved—muscles clutching. Her legs trembled, as if ready to give way.

She forced herself to walk slowly toward the door, even managed to affect a welcoming smile as she opened the louvers.

The sight of him robbed her of breath. He was dressed entirely in black. The silky shirt lay open at his neck, exposing whirls of thick black hair.

The long sleeves were ruched up, yet full, lending him a rogue's look. The trousers lay flat over his washboard belly and hugged the long muscular lines of his legs.

Casual elegance, she thought.

His face was a study in art itself, the brow strong, the nose straight and not too thin.

His cheekbones were high, the jaw was firm and dusted with a rakish five o'clock shadow, making him look more daring. More resolute. More sexy. Her pirate.

"Bonsoir." His sculpted lips pulled into a smile that melted her heart. "You are beautiful."

"So are you," she said, her heart brimming with love.

She'd never been so terrified in her life, but they'd get past this last obstacle. They had to. Love would find a way.

"Thank you for the sarong. It's fabulous."

"It suits you."

His dark gaze swept over her, much like a predator would watch easy prey. Sudden tension needled up her limbs, and she had the sudden urge to flee. Run while she had the chance.

Then he extended his arm to her, smiled that pirate's grin, and the moment was gone. "Shall we?"

Kira nodded and slipped her arm in the crook of his. The heat and power under her hand left her breathless, even more unsure of herself.

She'd been affected by his potent sensuality from the first time she'd met him, but what she sensed in him now had nothing to do with carnal promises.

The leashed anger in him was palpable, stripping away her

shaky confidence and flooding her with renewed apprehension. She'd felt that same raging tension in him when he'd come to the Chateau, when he'd forced her to leave with him.

"What's wrong, André?"

"Nothing. All is in order."

Yet a litany of doom pulsed in the air as she descended the stairs. He walked indecently close behind her, his hand on the small of her back, one finger resting in a dimple on her derrière.

The heat of him burned her through her dress, branding her skin. But the touch blazed with power rather than affection.

He seated her at a table dressed in stark white, and she finally filled her lungs with air when he strode to his chair. Crystal chandeliers held long white tapers, their golden flames casting a sultry aura over the table.

He poured sparkling water for her, champagne for himself. The romance of it wasn't lost on her. But there was no warmth in his eyes.

She took a sip of water and her stomach pitched, rebelling again. She would not be able to manage food tonight. She'd not be able to tolerate this tension that made her head spin.

A bead of sweat popped out on her temple, slowly streaking down her face. She dabbed at it with what she hoped was an offhand movement, hating that her hand shook, that his dark, expressionless eyes remained on her. Inquisitive. Or inquisitional?

Was this how a mouse felt when cornered by a cat? Her stomach fluttered and her breath came short and shallow.

Sweat gathered beneath her breasts. She licked lips that had gone dry. How could she possibly confess her secret when he was in this dark, dangerous mood?

This moment was more unsettling than when he'd swept into the Chateau and forced her to leave with him. The eloquent hands that had brought her such pleasure held his glass too tightly. His admirable posture was too rigid, the broad shoulders held with military precision, his spine too unbending.

He'd hated her then because he'd believed she was Peter's

mistress. The truth would be worse. She knew it. No matter that they'd shared exquisite passion in each other's arms. No matter that she carried his child. No matter that she had somehow fallen in love with him.

Her heart broke as she met his dark gaze. He was still the most handsome man she'd ever met, and she was painfully aware this could be the last time she shared anything but disdain with him. However could she begin?

"I used your computer today," she said, to break the horrid silence that roared in the room.

He took a sip of champagne and regarded her over the lavish tulip glass with eyes that caught the light and threw its glare back at her. Like an inquisitor. Reserved. Controlling.

"Did you email your brother again?" he asked.

Kira nearly lost her grip on her glass—did lose her breath. He knew. My God, he already knew her secret! No wonder he stared at her so coldly.

"No." She set her glass down with care, her hand shaking so badly it took effort. She drew in a breath, then another, but neither seemed enough for her starving lungs. "I never have."

He snorted and tossed back his drink. When he looked at her this time, his gaze was openly hostile.

A demoralizing dread seeped into her.

His rage threatened to consume her. Burn her alive. The flames different than the passion, more powerful because of the dark emotion fueling the fire. This inferno would not just burn her. It would kill her.

"How long have you known?" she asked, proud her voice remained calm despite the tempest whirling around her.

"Since this morning." He set his flute down and reached for the champagne bottle, his movements slow, precise.

He poured champagne in his glass, his finesse obviously shaken for he spilled some on the table. His scowl conveyed his annoyance at the minuscule lack of control.

She stared at the bubbles in his glass and thought ironically that they mirrored the riot going on in her stomach—a cold boil that popped around her, leaving her on shaky ground.

Kira chanced a look at him and wished she hadn't, for his rage was evident in the hard, unyielding lines of his face. She stared at her hands, the fingers bleached white from gripping the table linen as the awful truth weighed her down.

She'd never been subjected to such cold scrutiny. Never been the recipient of such scathing wrath.

Never wanted to right a wrong more than she did at this moment. "I—I intended to tell you tonight, after dinner."

His laugh was brittle and cold. "But of course you would say that now."

"It's the truth. I've thought of little else today."

Except for those moments when she'd become lost in the memory of lying in André's arms. Of those strong hands playing over her skin, making her senses sing with pleasure.

"Interesting, as your deceit has been on my mind as well," he said, his thumb idly stroking the tulip glass.

She looked at those hands now, watching that slow glide, and flushed hot as her breasts grew heavier. She couldn't still want him to touch her, to pleasure her? Yet she knew if he did she'd be lost in his arms again.

Panic took root in her, for her body was betraying her. Her body wanted him any way she could get him. She was weak—exhausted by his relentless onslaught of her senses.

She hated his power over her. Hated that he was playing the tyrant to perfection.

That would stop now. She wasn't afraid of him. She was his equal—his lover—whether he admitted it or not.

"If you'd just allow me to explain?"

He made a magnanimous gesture with his hand, the shadow of his movement caressing the wall much like that same hand had caressed her last night. "Please do."

Kira took another sip of water, hating that her hand trembled, that her breathing hitched, that her stomach remained queasy. She could barely force the much needed fluid down her throat, even though she was thirsty. It had been like that all day—nerves and tension and the unknown, all battling together in a gigantic knot within her.

"You must understand," she began. "I—I've never told anyone before, you see. Edouard insisted, and I never thought to disobey."

"Then I should feel honored to be the first to hear your story." He saluted her with his glass and drank deeply. "Bravo to you and your father for launching this honeytrap. You planned it well—right down to getting pregnant."

"There was no conspiracy," she said. "I just came here to meet with you about the Chateau. How dare you insinuate that I set out to trap you?"

He smirked, the expression a barbed taunt that angered her more than any insult, any accusation. "How fitting that you should begin with a lie."

She closed her eyes a moment, knowing he'd read it as guilt but no longer caring, knowing he'd not listen to her denials again. He'd believe what he wished.

He'd close his mind to the truth.

The door to the kitchen opened, and a Carib bustled in to serve them. Kira stared at the exquisite meal and knew that she'd never get a morsel down her throat.

She draped her napkin over the plate, hating that she'd offend the cook, and met André's hooded glare. She read hatred in his eyes. All targeted at her.

"It is senseless to continue. You know the truth and you've condemned me without hearing my side. Enjoy your meal." She rose, praying her trembling legs would support her.

"Sit down." His command cracked like a whip.

She hesitated a moment, staring into his dark eyes and silently challenging him. A crazy thing to do, for she knew André could pounce on her with the stealth and power of a jaguar.

He could crush her with a condemning look, rip her heart out with a word—for he'd done both with ease. Was doing so now. And the pain of his hatred was tearing her apart inside.

She grabbed the edge of the table, her fingernails biting into the polished surface. "If you'll listen to me, I'll stay."

He leaned forward in his chair, his gaze never leaving hers, his anger so strong she felt it pulsing in the room, in her veins. "You'll stay whether I choose to listen or not."

"Fine. Rant and pound your chest if you like." She dropped onto the chair, so defeated, so weary. "How did you find out?"

He pushed his own food away without sampling it and lounged back in his chair with an insolent air. "Through a private detective. He tracked down your mother."

Kira stared at him, unblinking, an incredulous laugh escaping her. How ironic that the one person she hadn't seen in over twenty years should return to ruin her life.

"She's still alive, then?" she said, hearing the bitterness ring in her voice and not caring.

She'd given up being concerned about the woman who'd given birth to her long ago.

"You don't like her?" he said.

She shrugged. "I told you before, I barely remember her."

He looked away, frowning, and she wondered what went through his mind. He'd had a mother and father who'd loved him. A family that cared.

"I hope you didn't pay her for the information," she said, angry. Hurt. "She made far too much off me years ago."

"Did she?"

"Yes. She sold me to my father—which was odd, since he didn't want me either."

Something shifted in his eyes, a flicker of something warm. Or was it just a reflection from the candles?

Kira didn't know anymore. Her head pounded and her back ached. She hurt inside. Felt drained, battered. Everything was an effort. Sitting here, talking, breathing, thinking about what had happened. Worrying about what was to come.

"Tell me," he said.

She shook her head, believing there was no point in divulging so much now. All her life she'd held her secrets close, hid them and hid the pain.

"Tell me, *ma chérie*," he said, his voice softer, lower, intimate.

How devastating that the hushed timbre of his voicing the endearment melted the starch holding her up. She dashed away a tear that slipped free, but another quickly formed, then too many to stop.

Silly, really, for she couldn't remember crying for her mother. Not once.

"I was an accident. She never wanted me, but for some reason she kept me for a few years. Until I was hurt in a boating mishap." She frowned, remembering that horrid event so clearly, yet she had trouble remembering her mother's face. "Edouard told me that she offered me to him then. He paid her price and I never saw her again."

"How old were you?"

"Nearly five."

"That's when he placed you in an elite boarding school in England?"

"Yes. I spent the rest of my formative years being shuffled from nannies to boarding school. Not once did my father welcome me to his home for a holiday or a brief visit. Not once."

She looked away, for there was really nothing more to tell. She had studied, read, and had seen Edouard once or twice a year when the mood had struck him.

And all the while she'd dreamed of one day having a family. Of having someone in her life who cared about her. Who would love her and who she could love in return.

Her hand stole to her belly to cradle her baby. She would have that dream become a reality soon.

"What was your reward for seducing me?" André asked.

She shook her head, scowling, angry that he thought she'd seduce him for money, that he equated her with her mother. "There was no reward, because there was no conspiracy."

"The truth, *s'il vous plaît*."

She slapped both palms on the table, her patience and energy spent. "I am telling you the truth."

He swore and jumped to his feet, chest heaving, fists clenched tight. His gaze raked over her, furious, insulting in its curt, deliberate movement.

Then he stalked from the room.

Kira put her head down and sighed, giving in to the tremors that whispered over her. But that only made her dizziness worse and set her stomach churning. If she could just find the strength to return to her room...

She heard heavy footsteps approaching. She'd tarried too long. Her respite was gone.

André stopped beside her chair, currents of anger radiating from his body in hot, scalding waves. He dropped a stack of paper before her.

"Try to deny these."

She stared at the heading, recognizing her corporate email address. Above it was an address she was unfamiliar with.

She skimmed the first note and paled. Then read another. And another.

This couldn't be...

But it was.

This was the electronic proof he'd told her about. The evidence that she and Peter Bellamy had conspired to launch a smear campaign against André. Sickening details of every calculated move, right down to her agreeing to come here on the pretext of a meeting when her intent was to seduce André while Peter alerted the paparazzi.

Except she *hadn't* carried on this dialogue with Peter. She *hadn't* set out to seduce André and humiliate him publicly, so the large corporation he'd been trying to solidify a deal with would pull out because he lacked family values. And she certainly hadn't tried to become pregnant.

She hadn't been aware of Peter's calculating plans until now. Hadn't written one word of this correspondence. But it had been sent from her email address, using her electronic signature. How could she prove she'd had no part in this? She couldn't.

Still, she lifted her chin and said simply, "I didn't write any of these."

CHAPTER TEN

ANDRÉ had expected her denial. But when the lie spilled from her sweet mouth the cynical curl to his lips eased a fraction. His blood slowed, his chest growing warm, his heart hesitating. For he almost believed her. Almost.

His weakness for her disgusted him.

Kira stood up and took a step toward him, stopped, her throat working, her face as white and delicate as the lace tablecloth. Her gaze lifted to his, her expression open, vulnerable.

He fisted his hands at his sides, fighting the impulse to reach for her, pull her close. Kiss her. Caress her. Sweep the servings from the table and take her here. Now.

Tell her all would be fine. Tell her that he forgave her.

That he loved her.

He'd vowed never to say those words. He'd thought it a simple promise to keep, for he believed himself incapable of such a crippling, all-consuming emotion.

"Someone else wrote these emails," she said.

He laughed, thinking that for someone possessing such guile she was quite naïve. "Using *your* email server? *Your* electronic signature?"

"Someone hacked into my account," she said, and frowned, clearly troubled, her clasped hands trembling.

Guilt, pure and simple. He'd trapped her in her own lie, and she was afraid. Terrified of what he'd do.

For once he was uncertain how to proceed. The satisfaction that usually filled him over besting an enemy was absent. Because in hurting her he hurt his child. He couldn't abide that.

Mon Dieu, but he hated this untenable situation, hated the desire for her that wouldn't die. He drove his fingers through his hair, tugging the strands, when he really wanted to weave his fingers in *her* hair, feel the skeins of silk brush his bare chest, his thighs.

Madness. He'd lost his mind. Lost his heart.

Lost *her* since she persisted in lying to him.

"Only one person had access to your account. You." He nodded to the emails lying on the table. "Admit it, *ma chérie*. Be done with the lies."

She shook her head slowly, fat tears spilling from her eyes. His gut tightened as he watched them course down her ashen face, and he jammed his hands in his pockets to keep from reaching out and wiping them from her soft cheeks.

He'd done it. Broken the enemy. Bested her. Won the game. But his victory was hollow.

He hurt more than she possibly could, because she'd forced him to take a resolute stand. He wouldn't forsake honor. He couldn't forget his vow of vengeance.

She drew in a shuddering breath, her slender shoulders squaring, her chin lifting even though it trembled. Proud. Strong. Qualities he admired in her.

"Could you have ever loved me?" she asked, the raw quality in her voice belying her courage.

"The daughter of my enemy? Never," he said.

She flinched, as if he'd bellowed the denial, as if he'd slapped her. As if she believed him that easily. "Then let me go, André. Let *us* go. For if you can't set aside your hatred for me, you won't be able to for our child either."

He stared at her, incredulous. Never mind that the same realization had crossed his mind. He couldn't live with her, and he wasn't sure he could live without her.

"One has nothing to do with the other."

"You're wrong. Can you honestly say it doesn't bother you that your child is part Bellamy?"

Her question was a knife-thrust to his heart. His own nagging doubts the twist that filleted the emotions he'd held in check for so long. He crossed to the French doors that opened onto the rear terrace, staring at his meticulously groomed garden, whose wild fragrance paled in comparison to the subtle scent that was uniquely Kira.

Her fragrance reached out to him with silken arms, commanding all his senses, promising pleasure. Promising hope.

It would be so easy to put pleasure before honor. Go to her. Love her. Forget the world for this night. But their differences would still be there in the morning.

One shallow breath drew her deeper into his blood, into his soul, into his heart. When he'd brought her here he'd foolishly believed he could use her and then cast her aside. Forget her.

He couldn't. Not then. Certainly not after he'd discovered she was with child. And not now, when his own emotions were so raw.

But he couldn't forgive either. Forgiveness wasn't in his blood. And she'd deceived him in the worst possible way.

André loved passionately, and he hated with the same intensity. There were no gray areas. No subtle riffling of the emotions at either extreme.

So he loved Kira and he hated her. The two emotions were ripping him apart.

"Let me go," she said again, more strident this time.

Never, he thought, pressing a palm to the cool dark wood, feeling the grain bite into his flesh. He couldn't bear to let her leave, and he couldn't stand to live with a Bellamy.

"Where would you go?" he asked, turning to face her, hiding his own inner war behind practiced insouciance. "To Peter?"

She looked away, eyes closed, as if the sight of him pained her. Good. She should hurt as much as he hurt. Should feel this awful ache to her soul. For she'd come to him first, seduced him, bound him to her forever through their child.

"To the Chateau. Please, let me return to my job."

"Out of the question." He had to protect his child from the Bellamys, and the only way he could do that was by keeping her here, where he could watch her, or at least have her watched. "Your only job for the next six months is pampering yourself and my baby."

"I don't need to be pampered," she said, her eyes too wide. Too bright. "I'll fight you every day that you keep me on the island against my will."

He smiled grimly, for there'd be no winner in this battle. "I expect no less from a Bellamy."

Kira gripped the table, barely able to breathe through her choking anguish. The headache that had plagued her all day pounded relentlessly, each drubbing in her veins taunting her challenge to André.

He hadn't moved. Hadn't so much as blinked. Just watched her with a lethal intensity that sucked the moisture from her mouth. She licked her lips, but they burned, the skin too dry.

Her throat felt parched. She reached for her glass, but her hand shook so badly she tipped it over.

"Leave it," he said, when she attempted to mop up the mess she'd made.

She ran her tongue over her lips again—so very thirsty, so very tired. The carafe of water was so far from her. The room spun. Her world careened out of control.

Kira had to get out of here—away from him and his heated glare. She couldn't fight him now. Not with her strength depleted, with her heart breaking in two.

She took a shaky breath, steadied herself, and stared at the intricately carved newel posts, hoping if she focused on the staircase the dizziness would be tolerable.

"Where are you going?" he asked, grabbing her arm to stop her from walking past him.

"Let me go."

His grip eased a fraction. "Answer me."

She closed her eyes, disgusted her body ached to lean into him. "To my room."

"You haven't eaten."

She glared at him. "I lost my appetite."

His seductive lips flattened in a disagreeable line. "You need to eat. I'll send Otillie up with a tray."

"Don't bother. I won't be able to keep anything down tonight."

He dropped his hand, only to punish her more by placing both hands on her shoulders. "You need food. The baby—"

"How dare you think of my child's welfare now?" She shoved away from him and headed toward the stairs, each step a challenge.

Odd twinges ribboned across her belly. Her back ached so badly she thought it would break in two.

She reached the stairs and grabbed the newel post, clinging to it for balance and drawing air into her lungs. But each breath only fanned the flames that felt like they were burning out of control within her heart, her soul.

"My child. *Mon enfant, ma chérie*. Don't forget that."

As if she could. She looked back at him, thinking he was still the most handsome man she'd ever met. And dangerous, leaning a hip against the table, a replenished champagne flute held casually in one elegant hand.

"Go to hell, André." She started up the stairs, each step slow, unsteady, her head throbbing, her vision blurring.

"I am already there," he said, his voice sounding oddly distant.

They both were, she thought.

She made it to the third step when cramps sliced through her, far worse than the last time.

The doctor's admonition blared in her mind. Avoid the sun. Drink two liters of water a day.

She hadn't done either. But she would drink her fill as soon as she reached her room. As soon as she was away from André and his dark accusations.

Her next step sent pain knifing across her middle, so sharp and piercing it took her breath away. She gasped and bent double, gripping the railing for dear life and cradling her belly with the other. But her world continued to spin away.

"André!"

She heard glass shatter. Then he was beside her, gathering her in his arms, his face ashen beneath his tan. But it was the stricken look in his eyes that terrified her, for it confirmed her worst fear.

"Our baby," she got out, as black pinpricks danced before her eyes to block out the light.

She fell into the blackness, into his arms. Her last tormenting thought was that she was losing the baby.

André paced the hospital corridor. The last hour had passed in a hellish nightmare, from the time Kira had collapsed in his arms until they'd arrived on Martinique. He'd never felt so helpless, so afraid for anyone in his life. He'd never been gripped with such crushing guilt—even after his parents' deaths.

For all his tough exterior and his vows to keep his heart removed from a woman, André wept silent tears in the velvety night, holding her close to his heart, his chest so tight he could barely breathe.

Seeing Kira so helpless had stripped him of all pretense, all thought but moving heaven and earth to save her and his baby's life. But as they'd raced across a moonlit sea fear had clung to him like the dense sea mist.

She'd been too pale, too cold. She hadn't roused, hadn't done anything but lie in his arms like a rag doll.

He hadn't prayed in ages, but he had then, and he continued to now, in the hospital. Prayed and paced. He relived every tension-riddled moment between him and Kira that had led up to her collapse. He held himself to blame.

Mon Dieu, he should have recognized something was wrong with her at dinner. But he'd been too intent on castigating her for being a Bellamy, for trying to ruin him, staunchly clinging to his pride, his vengeance.

He'd attacked her with the same energy and ruthless bent as he would a corporate adversary. Perhaps worse, because his emotions were tangled in knots when it came to Kira.

For once in his life he couldn't separate his business and personal life. She was too much a part of both. He'd removed her from her job and placed her into the role of his mistress.

But she didn't fit that image well because she was carrying his child.

A child whose life he'd endangered. A child who might die.

Sacre bleu! If anything happened to either of them he'd never forgive himself. Never!

The accusations he'd hurled at her played over and over in his mind. She denied authoring those emails. Still denied she'd conferred with Peter Bellamy.

Yet the small fortune he'd paid for her shares had gone straight to Peter. He'd been sure she'd contact her half-brother when she was offered the chance on St. Barth. But, no, she'd emailed her solicitor, believing that ineffectual man could somehow help her regain her shares. He'd offered no solution. In fact he'd seemed pleased she was no longer a part of the "family" corporation. Had she been disowned? Betrayed?

It seemed that way. Peter had never contacted André after he'd seen him shuffle Kira from the Chateau. It was as if Peter had been glad to see her go. But if that were true, why had her millions gone to Bellamy? And why send the paparazzi to the island again?

The doctor emerged from the emergency room, his white coat fluttering wide. But it was his scowl that captured André's attention.

"Monsieur Gauthier. On your word, you promised that Miss Montgomery would heed my advice, no?"

"*Oui*, I did." But it was obvious he'd failed miserably. He'd been too intent on his quest for vengeance to care for the mother of his child. "How is she—and my baby?"

"Miss Montgomery is seriously dehydrated. We could not rouse her enough to drink fluids." The doctor paused and shook his head, and André's gut clenched. He was fearing the worst, fearing he'd lost them both. "We've forced fluids into her intravenously, and she is improving now."

"The baby?" he asked, afraid to hope they'd avoided a heart-wrenching disaster.

The doctor smiled. "The fetus has a strong heartbeat."

André simply stared at him, for though he'd believed Kira carried a child, he'd never thought a heartbeat could be detected so soon. He'd not thought of anything but vengeance and lust in turn.

"I ordered tests to check her chemical balance. If her electrolytes are normal, we will release her today."

"*No!*" André ran a hand through his hair, damning the way it shook.

The doctor canted his head to the side. "No?"

"She can't be trusted to hydrate herself this soon," André said, hoping the doctor wouldn't see through that flimsy excuse.

In truth, he didn't trust himself around Kira right now, for his emotions were still bouncing between love and hate.

The doctor rubbed his chin and frowned. "She will not like being detained, *monsieur*, for she has told me she wants to go home."

Home. The Chateau Mystique had been her home, and he'd taken that from her. He'd stripped her of everything.

"You will be rewarded for keeping her here for a few days," André said, calculating that would give him enough time to do what he must. "Tell her she must stay, for the baby's welfare."

"Very well, *monsieur*. We appreciate your largesse." The doctor turned to leave, then paused. "You may see her now."

André wanted to, but he didn't dare see her face to face until he found out if she'd been telling him the truth. Because if she was innocent, as she proclaimed, then his honor demanded that he right the wrongs he'd done her.

But even if that wasn't the case he would give her anything and do everything to keep her well, so she would deliver a healthy child. *Their* child.

His chest tightened, his heart heavy and burning. Raw.

He'd been ready to marry her. To make her his forever.

But she was a Bellamy, and no matter how much André desired her, no matter how much his heart ached to make her his, he couldn't marry his enemy's daughter.

Kira sat in bed, staring out the window at the thin white clouds drifting across the azure sky. The scene hadn't changed much in the two days she'd been hospitalized. Clear blue sky broken by occasional clouds, their formation the only variance.

Inside nothing changed either. The same nurse and doctor tended to her every whim, as if she were royalty. The food was above par, though her appetite was nil. But she ate and drank for the baby's sake.

Thank God her child was safe. If she'd lost the baby, or hurt it in any way because of her neglect, she never would have forgiven herself.

But she'd lost André. She was sure of it, for she hadn't heard from him since that confrontational scene at his house.

She'd relived that moment when she had walked away from him a thousand times. The anger blazing in his eyes had burned into her, incinerating her will to win his heart, her determination to carve a niche for herself and their child in his life.

Yet she was tormented by that moment when she'd collapsed, when she'd seen pain and regret and fear in his eyes.

Tears blurred her vision and she angrily swiped them away. He hadn't visited her at the hospital once. How could he abandon her and the baby? How could he just walk away?

Because she was Edouard Bellamy's daughter.

He hated her—he hated their child as well.

A hollow ache expanded in her chest, her heart grieving for what would never be.

She should be thankful the ugly truth was revealed. That he'd left her in peace. That she'd likely never see him again. For if she did it would be a tense, unpleasant meeting.

She should be happy. But she'd never been so heartbroken.

On the morning of the third day something roused her from a restless sleep, snapping her awake and wary. Kira scanned her room, her heart accelerating as her gaze fell on the tall man standing at the window, his back to her.

She stared at those incredibly broad shoulders and blinked. Was she dreaming?

No. This was real. André had come at last, and her foolish heart was rejoicing even as her brain tried to warn her to move with caution around him.

Everything about him pulsed with raw intensity—his potent masculinity, his arrogant bearing, his brooding indifference, all more sharply defined as he stared out the window.

"How long have you been here?" she asked.

"Not long. The doctor says you and the baby are well."

"We were lucky," she said, detecting no rancor in his voice.

But there was no emotion either. Or rather no more than one might bestow on a stranger in the wake of an accident. Simply a comment in the face of a near tragedy—an acknowledgement of survival—something to fill the tense silence.

She sighed, unable to be that detached even now. "Thank you for getting us here so quickly."

One shoulder lifted in a careless shrug. "Don't. I should never have confronted you with such—" He waved a hand, as if trying to snatch a word from thin air, as if annoyed that he couldn't grasp a title for their situation.

"Animosity?" she supplied.

"Venom," he said. "My behavior was inexcusable."

"Yes," she said, unwilling to forgive him so easily for setting her up for a verbal attack from which she couldn't defend herself, unwilling to forgive them both for not putting their child's needs first.

It would not happen again. No matter what he said. No matter what happened in the future. *If* they had a future. At this moment she could not guess what was going through André's mind.

"We have unfinished business between us," he said.

"Business? Are you talking about the Chateau?"

"No, personal business."

Surely he didn't mean—? "We have a child between us."

"I am aware of my obligations, *ma chérie*."

She flinched, angry and hurt that he chose to regard the tiny life they'd created as an obligation. Hurt that he thought so little of their precious child, and angry at herself for deluding herself about André Gauthier.

He didn't want her, and he certainly didn't want their child. He was just like her father—cold, calculating, ruthless.

André had returned for one reason—to bestow a settlement on her. To shuffle her out of his life. He'd likely want her to sign a document agreeing to his denouncing any obligation to her or their child.

"Fine. State your business," she said, her fingers bunching the sheet in a tight knot that rivaled the hard ache in her stomach.

"I have confronted Peter Bellamy."

She released a bitter laugh, more saddened than surprised that André still believed the worst of her. "Did he deny there was a conspiracy? Or did he perhaps swear I'd concocted some devilish scheme alone?"

"Neither. Peter laughed, pleased by the turmoil he'd wrought. He hates you."

She'd known her half-brother resented her. She'd deduced he'd been the one who set out to ruin her. But she'd not considered that he'd be so pleased by her downfall. That he hated her so much.

Her insides felt raw, scraped of emotion, of feeling. She'd been a fool, longing for family, doing as asked by her mother for that brief time she'd known her, and by her father, who had been little more than a name throughout her life. She'd not asked for more, for it had been drummed into her that what she had was all she'd get.

She'd abided by her father's rules, and in the end her family had betrayed her. Family she hadn't even known.

But it crushed her spirit, her heart, that André had shut her out of his life after all they'd shared. Even now he stared out the window, as if unable to tolerate looking at her.

"Yet you still believe the worst of me," she said.

His shoulders snapped a bit straighter. "You were innocent of his machinations."

That admission failed to tell her how he felt about her, only that he believed her claim of innocence long after the fact.

"Is that the business you came here to attend to, then?" she asked.

"Not entirely." André strode toward her, his broad shoulders straight, his jaw resolute, his arrogantly handsome face—

"My God!" She leaned forward, her heart hammering as she took in the bruises, the cut lip, the swollen eye. "What happened to you?"

His fierce scowl made him look more ravaged, more dangerous, despite the custom-tailored suit that screamed sophistication. "Peter and I fought as our ancestors did when pirating ships collided."

Her mouth dropped open. She was shocked that the billionaire who was famed for his rapier-sharp verbal sparring had engaged in a physical fight on her behalf. That he seemed proud of it. What was she to make of that?

"You attacked him?"

"*Oui*. I could have killed him for his underhand dealings involving you, but I didn't," he said, looking away from her as if the admission pained him.

A tiny bud of hope unfurled inside her. He'd stood up for her. But that didn't mean he cared for her.

André was a complicated man. His reasons for fighting Peter

could have nothing to do with her at all. It could all center around defending his honor.

"Why, André? Why did you do it?"

He jammed his hands in his trouser pockets and stared down on her, his bearing so rigid she felt it snap the air with electricity like an approaching thunderstorm. "I have no tolerance for a man who endeavors to ruin his sister."

"Illegitimate half-sister," she said, unable to feel anything but pity for the half-brother who'd attacked her with such hatred.

"The same Bellamy blood flows in you and in him."

She laughed at that, for even her father hadn't welcomed her into his legitimate family. He'd sequestered her from them all her life, and made it clear she was never to admit her paternity to anyone. He'd stressed that if she ever directly contacted his family there'd be severe consequences to bear.

She'd abided by his wishes because she'd learned to be happy on her own. Because she'd had no wish to cause more scandal. Yet Peter obviously hadn't felt the same.

"In this case water is thicker than blood," she said.

He stared at her a long, uncomfortable moment. "*Oui*. You became the target of familial vengeance the day Edouard placed you in a position of power at Le Cygne."

She suspected it had begun the day Peter had learned about her existence, but he'd bided his time until Edouard couldn't defend her. "Peter obviously resented that his father had acknowledged his by-blow so richly."

"*Oui*. But it was your solicitor who took umbrage."

Had she heard him correctly? "Claude? But why?"

"You really don't know?" He faced her, and she shook her head in answer. "Claude Deveaux is Edouard's brother-in-law."

More family. More hatred. She blinked back angry tears, sick of being manipulated by powerful men with hidden agendas.

"I trusted him," she said.

"You made it easy for them both."

She reached for her glass of water and drank, waiting for

him to expound, forcing more than a sip down her emotion-clogged throat. But he simply watched her, his expression unreadable.

"How long have you known all this?" she asked.

He shrugged, a careless gesture she loathed and loved in turn, for she was never sure if he was the uncaring rake or the troubled man she'd lost her heart to. "I suspected something was amiss when your shares went public. But I didn't begin to believe you were a pawn until our jaunt to St. Barthélemy, when you emailed your solicitor demanding answers."

When had he had the time to check his computer? Or had he charged someone else to search it?

The Windward Islands were his domain. His world. She was merely a puppet in it, dancing to the melody he'd arranged.

"You set me up—knowing I was desperate to get word out," she said.

That emotionless mask she detested stared back at her, giving nothing away. "I was certain you'd contact Peter, that I'd catch you devising a new plot to ruin me. But you didn't."

She called herself a fool for not suspecting the trap. For trusting him. *Trust.* As he'd said, she had made it easy for his enemies—and him—to deceive her.

Her chin came up, and she damned its tremor. "You knew that I didn't email Peter, yet you still believed I'd conspired with him?"

He shrugged. "You are a Bellamy."

"And you could never trust a Bellamy. You certainly could never love one." Not her. Not even their child.

His jaw clenched so tight she feared he'd crack the bone, but his eyes gave nothing away. "I will provide for you. Nothing more."

Kira set her glass down carefully, when her anger goaded her to lob the whole thing at him. That night on St. Barth, when he'd held her close to his heart and called her his love, his darling, she'd believed him. She'd thought that they would have a chance for a lifetime of happiness in each other's arms.

She'd hoped they could surmount any obstacle, though she'd known it wouldn't be easy for him to accept her parentage.

She hadn't totally given up hope. She'd foolishly trusted that love would conquer all.

But in the morning he'd treated her with biting indifference, as if he was furious with her again, and she'd feared the wondrous night had been a dream.

She'd never guessed it was because he'd discovered she was Edouard's daughter. That he'd intended to lay a trap for her on Petit St. Marc instead of coming to her and talking it out.

Something in her changed, twisted, died. He'd used her so well—in bed and out. Would continue doing so if she let him.

And, sadly, she wanted him with every breath she took. Her weakness toward him shamed her.

Unabashedly, Kira knew she'd never meet another man she loved with the same intensity as she did André. She'd never even try, for she'd never trust another man that much again.

It wasn't worth the heartache.

She'd found her one great love. And she'd lost him.

"Do you feel *any* guilt for your part in this?" she asked, her voice cracking as she felt the rift between them grow wider.

"I did what I had to."

And so would she. She'd take the only course left to her.

The men in her life had used her. None of them had cared for her, respected her. Not her father, who'd seen her as an obligation. Not her half-brother or his uncle, who viewed her as a usurper they must eliminate at all costs. And certainly not André, who'd used her in the worst way, by capturing her heart completely just to satisfy his quest for vengeance.

"I hope Peter's face looks as battered as yours. I hope you're both in pain." She stared at his beautifully masculine features, her tears unable to put out her fiery heartache. "I hope never to see you again."

His body jolted, so slightly she'd have missed it if she

hadn't been staring at him. Or maybe it was just a mirage caused by her tears.

She'd meant to shock him. But she'd shocked herself as well. For her love for this man was so great that she already grieved over having André in her life.

"Is that your wish?" he asked.

She forced the lie past her dry lips. "Yes. It's the only way. For you have no room in your heart for a Bellamy."

A muscle in his cheek throbbed to the wild beat of her heart as he pulled an envelope from his jacket pocket and dropped it on the foot of the bed. The battering to his pride was evident in his bleak gaze that touched hers briefly, like a fleeting kiss, bittersweet.

"Au revoir, mon amour."

He walked from her room, and she bit her tongue to keep from calling him back. Her breath hitched, her tears fell in a scalding waterfall, but they couldn't wash away the hurt.

This pain was too great to ignore. She needed time to deal with all that had happened—time to heal, time to sort it out in her mind. She had to search her heart for what she should do.

So in the quiet of her room she curled into a ball and cried for her loss. And thanked God that through her child she'd always be tied to André. She'd always have a part of him to love.

Long hours later, Kira opened the envelope with trembling fingers, suspecting André had made provision for her as he would a mistress. She wouldn't take it, of course. For that would sully the love they'd had.

She unfolded the paper and read, the chill that had gripped her fading as she read the document. Once. Twice.

Her gaze fell on the accompanying bank draft and her heart raced. She could scarce draw a decent breath as the enormity of what he'd done sank in.

All the shares of Chateau Mystique had been transferred to her. The hotel was solely hers—as was the bank draft for four million dollars. A fortune. All hers.

She'd gotten more than she'd wanted—would never have to depend on a man's charity or whim again. But without André in her life having it all meant nothing.

CHAPTER ELEVEN

KIRA had been back at the Chateau for an entire month—enough time to reevaluate her staff and replace those untrustworthy sorts. The number was few, and those who had stayed exhibited the loyalty she'd always hoped to inspire.

Work filled her days, and the wonder of going into her second trimester warmed her lonely nights.

But her heart bled for André, for the loss of what they'd held in their grasp and for the crippling pain of letting it go. She'd been too afraid of following in her mother's footsteps to fight harder for their love. For believing that they could surmount any odds.

So she dreamed he'd stride into the Chateau as before, and take her back to his island. As days turned into weeks, she knew that wasn't going to happen.

André wasn't coming back to her—and why should he?

She was a Bellamy. She'd told him she never wanted to see him again.

He'd taken her words to heart—words she'd spoken in anger, words she wished she could call back.

Anger boiled in Kira like a storm-tossed sea. She couldn't accept that he wanted nothing to do with the innocent life they'd created. Wouldn't believe it—not until he told her so.

And if that were the case… Then she'd love her child enough for both of them.

Kira smiled and pressed a hand on the tiny bulge of her belly.

For the first time today she'd felt a fluttering there, the wings of an angelic butterfly making itself known.

Her baby.

Hers and André's.

It pained her to think that his hatred had poisoned him so, that it had killed their love.

But he'd never said he loved her. Never said he wanted her in his life. Even if he had told her in so many words that he would fight for what he wanted.

He didn't want her.

Maybe for him it had just been lust. What else explained how he had cut her and their child from his life?

He'd had his revenge, his say.

But she hadn't. She wanted closure.

And she desperately wanted to see him, touch him, kiss him. She loved him. That would never change.

She pinched her eyes shut, almost feeling his touch, his scent, his potent power sweeping her away.

Yes, she wanted André. Ached for him still.

Countless nights she'd picked up the phone, then talked herself out of ringing him. She wouldn't chase after him. She wouldn't grovel and beg, no matter how much she ached for him. But she had to talk to him once more. Just once.

So that night she put the call through. But Otillie answered, because André wasn't in residence. He was miserable, the older woman claimed, and begged her to come back.

"*Monsieur*—he does not eat. Does not sleep," Otillie said.

Kira gripped the phone tighter, torn over what she wanted to do and what she had vowed not to do. "I don't know—"

"Please, Mademoiselle Montgomery. Come home."

Home. How odd that she'd begun to think of the island as just that. She pinched her eyes shut again, debating whether to listen to her head or her heart.

Her baby made the decision for her, giving her the tiny kick she needed.

"Expect me in a few days," she said.

Kira brimmed with excitement as she dashed to the pharmacy to replenish her prenatal vitamins, worrying about André, eager to see him soon.

The handsome face commanding the cover of one of the tabloids changed her mind.

She picked it up, stared at the image, her blood chilling.

The photographers had captured André at various clubs and functions on the Riviera. Pictured him with a gorgeous woman on his arm. The headlines were disgustingly similar. Which beauty would win the billionaire's heart?

The fact he'd replaced Kira confirmed he'd never really cared about her at all. He'd fallen into the jet-setting lifestyle he'd supposedly despised. That told her she'd really never known him at all.

No wonder he wasn't eating or sleeping. He didn't have time!

She threw the tabloid down and marched from the store.

André Gauthier had cut her out of his life with surgical precision. It was past time she did the same. Time would heal this awful ache that stayed with her day and night, robbing her of sleep, of peace of mind. But she knew that the hole he left in her heart would never be mended, even after she did what she must do. Why did love have to hurt so much?

André stared pensively out the window of his private jet, anxious to set down, annoyed he was arriving in Las Vegas a week later than he'd intended. Exhaustion tormented every fiber of his being, having spent the most miserable month of his life throwing himself into work at his Riviera hotel—work he'd neglected when he'd decided to abduct Kira and take her to Petit St. Marc.

Kira. His heart gave a painful kick. He missed her more than he'd thought possible. Regret, fear and stubborn pride had kept him from calling her as he'd longed to do.

All his life he'd secretly feared he'd fall victim to a consuming passion like his parents had. To the eyes of a young boy, his parents' heated fights and explosive ardor had been something to avoid.

He hadn't realized a man could love that deeply, that intently. That a woman could become so much a part of him that losing her was more painful and traumatic than losing an arm or leg, that she pulsed through his blood and gave him life. That she filled his heart and gave him hope.

He'd believed by walking away from her that he'd done the right thing, for she was Edouard Bellamy's daughter. To admit he had lost his heart to her would mean his enemy had won.

But he'd been wrong.

When he'd walked away from Kira he'd lost the best thing that had ever happened to him. He'd been a fool to believe her mother's claim that Edouard was Kira's father, to let that probability poison him.

The woman had *sold* her daughter to Bellamy. Why? *Was* Bellamy her father? Or the wealthiest former lover that her mother had been able to con?

André had to know the truth, which was why he'd charged his detective with digging deeper into her past. But the answers he sought eluded him still.

What did it matter anyway? If Bellamy was her father, then he would find a way to deal with it. He could not alter the fact any more than he could rearrange the sun and the moon—any more than he could change the past.

The past was just that—the past.

His future was with Kira.

She was his woman. The mother of his child. He'd do anything to gain her favor and forgiveness. To win her heart.

She'd resist him out of hurt pride at the very least. But he'd captured her heart before. He would do it again. Only this time he'd never let her go.

The sun was just starting to graze the expanse of glass and steel stretching down the Las Vegas strip when André walked into the Chateau Mystique. Unlike before, he marched straight to the front desk and announced that he must speak with Kira immediately.

"Your name, sir?" the clerk asked, the image of poised efficiency that he himself demanded in all his own hotels and resorts.

"Gauthier. André Gauthier."

The clerk's eyes widened a fraction, to hint that she recognized his name. "One moment, please," she said, and hurried off into the manager's office, situated at the end of the long cherrywood counter topped with rich pink granite.

Before André could stew about the wait, the door to the office opened and the clerk motioned him in. "This way, sir."

"Thank you."

André's gut tightened, his heart thudding far too fast as he strode to the door. He knew what he must say, what he wanted to tell Kira. But he wasn't poetic, and he had certainly lost his patience.

He'd simply blurt it out, then take her in his arms and kiss her. Everything else would fall into place then.

She'd forgive him for being a high-handed ass. Maybe not today, but soon.

She'd agree that they would get married immediately, for he couldn't bear to wait any longer.

She'd take him in her arms and ease this terrible ache that had filled him since he'd left her in the hospital, for she was the most loving, most genuinely good woman he'd ever met in his life.

André closed the door to afford him and Kira privacy.

Only Kira wasn't in the room. A young, dignified man rose from behind the desk to greet him, his smile polite yet wary.

"How may I help you, Monsieur Gauthier?" the man asked.

André didn't mince words—didn't have the time or the patience to jump through hoops. "I must speak with Kira Montgomery immediately."

The young man let out a nervous laugh. "I'm sorry, sir, but Miss Montgomery isn't here."

André inhaled deeply and blew it out in frustration. Fine. He would wait.

"When will she return?"

"I don't know," the manager said. "She left a week ago and told me not to expect her back anytime soon."

He hadn't anticipated that. The Chateau meant the world to Kira. She wouldn't leave it indefinitely unless something pressing had come up.

Fear lanced through him. *Mon Dieu*, the baby!

"Is she all right? Where did she go?" André asked.

The manager stiffened, his smile replaced by a professional mask. "I can't divulge that."

André gritted his teeth. Loyalty could be an annoying quality in employees. "Then tell me how I can contact her."

The manager gave a wry laugh. "Sir, I was left with strict orders that Miss Montgomery was not to be disturbed, unless there is a pressing problem at the Chateau that I can't handle."

André slammed both palms on the table and leaned forward, crowding the young manager's space, ready to beat the truth out of the cheeky man if he must. "I am André Gauthier, and I demand to speak with Miss Montgomery. Now, where the *hell* is she?"

"She mentioned being homesick," the manager said. "Before you ask, she didn't divulge where her home happened to be."

That couldn't be. The Chateau was her home. "You are sure?"

"Yes, sir."

He stormed from the office, so angry at himself he could have bellowed his rage. She shouldn't be traveling in her condition.

And just where *was* home? England? The boarding school where she'd spent the bulk of her life?

The possibilities were endless. The fear that he could lose her seeped into his bones, rattling his confidence, shaking his world.

His hand shook as he called his investigator. "I need to know where Kira Montgomery has gone on holiday."

"I'll get right on it," his private detective said. "As for the paternity issue—Bellamy was cremated. Blood type can reveal if it was possible for him to have been her father, but it won't prove conclusively if he actually is."

"Forget it, then. Just find Kira."

He stormed from the Chateau and arranged to return to Petit St. Marc. He'd wait there, worry, throw himself into work to keep from losing his mind.

But, no matter how long it took, he'd not give up finding her and making her his.

André stormed into his house, barely acknowledging Otillie waiting at the door, her face wreathed in an effusive smile.

"Bonsoir, Monsieur Gauthier," she said. *"Comment allez-vous?"*

"Exhausted," he said. As well as angry, and worried sick, and in no mood for pleasantries.

He strode to the stairs just before that subtle floral scent snared him, that silken string of remembrance bringing him up short. Just like he'd been tormented in his dreams. Only this was real. Kira!

He whirled, scanning his house, alert, hoping to hell that he hadn't finally gone mad and imagined her. "Where is she?"

Otillie laughed. His opinionated Carib housekeeper, who'd taken a dislike to Kira when she'd barged into his house months ago, who'd been furious with him for going after her and bringing her here, was laughing with great pleasure.

"Mademoiselle is in the salon," she said at last.

Heart beating savagely against his ribs, André crossed the hall in six long strides. He stopped in the doorway and leaned against the jamb, simply because he wasn't sure his legs would carry him the rest of the way.

For a long moment he drank in the sight of Kira curled on his sofa, looking radiant and inviting in his home. Their home.

Mon Dieu, what a fool he'd been. She'd told her staff she

was going home. She considered Petit St. Marc home. Thought his house was hers. That had to be a good sign.

She was here with him at last—had returned to him of her own accord. All would be well.

But, no, she was frowning at him now, looking wary. Unapproachable.

His blood pounded with the need to touch her, kiss her, love her. At this moment he felt every inch the pirate, rugged and ruthless, uncouth and unashamed of grabbing the spoils of war. For this fabulous English rose was his booty.

He'd wanted her the first time she barged into his office. He'd taken her, believing she was involved in the cutthroat war he'd waged with Bellamy. He'd continued to take her even when doubts had encroached.

She'd deserved so much more than the cold life meted out to her by Bellamy. She certainly hadn't deserved André's hostility, his constant doubts over her innocence, his refusal to give her anything but physical love.

Oui, he was unworthy of her. That was why he'd walked away from her that day in the hospital.

But he couldn't let go of her. He, who'd vowed never to let a woman embed herself in his heart and soul, caught himself thinking about her during his days, dreaming about her during the long, lonely nights.

He loved her. The admission came hard for a man who had vowed never to fall victim to that crippling emotion. But refusing to admit it crippled him more, for he was haunted by her smile, her touch, her love.

No, he couldn't let her go. Not now. Not ever.

He pushed away from the doorway and strode to her, stopping when he reached her side. His fingers curled into fists, trembling, for he knew if he touched her he'd tumble her back on the sofa and caress her everywhere. Make love to her, here, now, without a modicum of finesse.

"Marry me," he said.

Her eyes bugged and her inviting lips parted. "What?"

A gruff sound of impatience rumbled in his throat. "You look beautiful. You are pregnant with my child, *mon amour*. Marry me."

She flushed, her body stiffening, putting up a wall he hated, one that would geld him should he attempt jumping it. But he would jump it.

"I was pregnant a month ago, when you rushed me to the hospital, yet you didn't offer marriage then," she said.

Touché—a direct hit. Damn, but he was doing this badly. "I was an ass."

"And now you're not?"

He drove his fingers through his hair, frustrated, trembling like a schoolboy, tasting fear and despising it. For if he said the wrong thing she'd never marry him.

Mon Dieu, was this the tangled emotion that had gripped his father? That had made him act the fool with his mother?

"I am the father of your child," he said. "The man you love."

"True." She stared at him a long, uncomfortable moment. "But you hate all Bellamys. You've spent considerable time and money to destroy Edouard's dynasty and ruin Peter. Need I remind you that I am Edouard Bellamy's daughter?"

"I hate Bellamy, not you. Never you, *mon amour*."

She squirmed, seeming to grow more nervous by the second. "You say that now, but what about a month from now? A year?"

"I've treated you badly. *Us* badly." He knelt at her side and laid a hand over her stomach, trembling as heat shot from her into him, feeling their bond clear to his soul. "What must I do to convince you that I want you as my wife, as the mother of my child? That I wish to grow old with you?"

Her gaze softened, her lips trembling into a smile as she reached out and cupped his jaw in her hands, her touch seeping into his skin, his blood, his heart. "I want to believe you, but blood is telling, André. I have to be sure you will not resent me because I am a Bellamy, because our baby has the same blood."

"Our child is Gauthier," he said, leaning forward to kiss her once, twice. How had he lived without kissing her the past month?

"And part Bellamy," she said, pulling back.

He sighed, hating the caution still banked in her expressive eyes, hating that he was responsible for putting it there, dreading how she'd accept his last confession. "Maybe yes, maybe no. I had my investigator attempt to prove you are Bellamy's daughter, but without Edouard's DNA it's impossible to determine."

"We'll never know, then," she said. "There will always be that doubt."

"Only if you let uncertainty torment you." He cupped her face in his hands and stared into her eyes, his own shining with a warmth and affection that she'd only seen in her dreams. "*Ma chérie*, everything you know and believe about yourself is the same."

"I'm afraid to hope."

"So was I. Which is why I had to look in here for the answer." He thumped a fist on his heart. "I realized that I'd fallen in love with you even when I thought you were Edouard Bellamy's puppet, and I continued to long for you even when I was sure you were Peter's mistress. When I thought you'd conspired to ruin me I still loved you. It nearly drove me mad to admit that despite what I believed of you I wanted you as my lover, my wife."

"Oh, André, you love me?"

"Eternally. You are in my blood, my skin," he said. "My heart pounds for you. Marry me, *mon coeur*. Be mine forever."

"Yes," she said, wrapping her arms around his neck and kissing him back.

André pulled her against him, pouring his heart and soul into the kiss, his hands roaming her back, her slightly thicker waist, her small belly where their child thrived. "We will marry next week."

"Why the rush?"

"Need you ask?"

He caressed her belly, pleased by the mound there now. His throat felt thick, his heart was thudding too loud.

His woman. His child. He'd considered them his before, but the depth of what that meant hadn't hit him until he'd nearly lost her.

"I don't want a big wedding," she said. "Something quiet."

"*Oui*, intimate. We can marry here."

"I'd love that." She kissed his cheek and sighed, a contented sound that rumbled in him as well. "I love you."

"*Mon amour.*" He trailed kisses up her neck, addicted to the taste of her skin, her scent, her love. "*Mon coeur.*"

"I need to learn French," she said.

"We will start now. Repeat after me. *Je t'aime, avec tout mon coeur.*"

She did, saying each word slowly, carefully. "What did I just say to you?"

"I love you," he said, "with all my heart."

She smiled, blinking rapidly, her love for him shining in her eyes. "It's true."

He kissed her, a soft lingering kiss that dragged a sigh from her. "I love you, Kira Montgomery. That's all that matters. You are mine and I am yours and we have created our own family."

She smiled and felt her heart melt, felt a sense of home and harmony envelop her. For he was right. She'd found her family in his arms, her future in his heart.

As long as they had each other, nothing else mattered.

After five months of having a protective husband indulge her with his attention and his passion—until the latter had proved too great a risk—and after enduring a killing backache for the past few days, Kira made a speedy trip back to the hospital on Martinique.

As before, André insisted on holding her as the captain

drove the *Sans Doute* at breakneck speed. This time she was able to see the love and worry in her husband's eyes, and her heart melted all over again.

This time, instead of nearly losing her baby, she gave birth to Antoine Louis Gauthier. The nearly nine-pound boy had his father's piercing dark eyes and beautifully sculpted mouth, but he had inherited her broader nose and auburn hair.

Her heart overflowed with love as she trailed a finger along her son's plump cheek, hardly able to believe that their small family circle had been completed.

Family. She could scarce believe her new life was real.

She had prayed she'd one day have a family all her life, but she'd never dreamed that she'd have a husband who openly adored her. That she'd deliver a healthy child to complete that circle of love.

Family. Never again would she live on the fringe of her relatives, the unwanted child nobody spoke of.

For her husband wanted her. And now she and André had a son. She was certain Antoine would be spoiled rotten by his adoring parents.

He'd never doubt he was loved. Wanted. Cherished.

André sat on the bed, his eyes glittering with adoration. "My son has a healthy appetite," he said, as she nursed Antoine for the first time.

"He's his father's son."

"*Oui*, he is."

A proud smile curved André's sensual mouth. Her husband no longer guarded his emotions around her, a fact that had allowed them to draw closer.

"He's beautiful," André said. "Thank you, *mon coeur*."

She smiled, thankful, and so happy that she couldn't stop tears of joy from spilling from her eyes. This was contentment. This was love.

He shifted closer to her and their son. "It has been too long since I was part of a family."

"Having a family is a whole new world to me, but then so is marriage and being a wife and a mother. It takes getting used to."

"Regrets?" he asked.

"None." She smiled, understanding this complex man who guarded his heart so well, loving him, wanting him. "It's been too long since you kissed me."

"Then I must remedy that, *mon coeur*," he said, his eyes glistening with love as his head dipped to hers.